PROJECT
GENE ASSIST
THE COMPLETE SERIES

ALLIE POTTS

2021

AXIL HAMMER PUBLISHING

PROJECT
GENE ASSIST
THIS VOLUME CONTAINS:

BOOK 1: THE FAIR & FOUL

BOOK 2: THE WATCH & WAND

BOOK 3: LIES & LEGACY

THE FAIR & FOUL
PROJECT GENE ASSIST
BOOK ONE

Vials of various colors and volume filled the medical refrigerator. They shone like jewels on display. Juliane shifted in her chair on the other side of the lab to better follow her colleagues' movements, however, the straps keeping her in place made it difficult to watch everything.

Alan glanced over his shoulder at the man seated in the chair closest to him. A wrinkle crossed his brow for a moment, but turned back to the refrigerator and selected a ruby red vial from the rack. He then fit the tube into a pneumatic apparatus resembling a tattoo artist's needle with a snap.

Freed from its holster, the pneumatic tool emitted a hum. The tip of the device flickered with a bright glow. Alan held it in the light and shook it with an exaggerated flourish.

"Can you try not to look like you are enjoying the idea of sticking us with a needle?" asked Juliane.

"It's not every day you get to be the one to usher in the next evolution of mankind. This is a big moment," responded Alan with a laugh as he leaned in, ready to pierce the occupant of the other chair's skin with the needle. "Now count back from sixty. This may pinch a little."

Alan swapped the needle tip with a fresh one and approached her while his assistant, Betty, disposed of the old one. Juliane watched the needle enter her arm and felt the liquid push against her veins. It created a sensation that somehow was both ice and burn. Then it was replaced by a feeling Juliane couldn't quite describe.

"It will be easier on you if you don't resist," Alan whispered in her ear as he began packing up their supplies.

"What do you mean?" she asked. Her heart raced. Beads of sweat dampened her forehead. Her stomach flopped like she'd descended too quickly in an elevator. Her vision blurred.

"Your immune system is attempting to repel the serum. It is after all, effectively a virus. You know full well it's the best way to deliver the software to your DNA."

"Is that why I'm still strapped to this chair?" She pulled at her restraint.

Alan nodded and tapped her arm. "Right. As I was saying, it's best not to fight. Over the next few hours, you will feel feverish and may experience some other unpleasantness. You need to let whatever happens, happen. No matter what."

Juliane narrowed her eyes in an attempt to see him more clearly. "No matter what? That sounds rather ominous."

"Well, yes. It was meant to be. You see, a person's will has a remarkable influence on their physical well-being. Perhaps, one day we'll better understand the how and why . . . Right now, you need to will your body into accepting the spread of the virus."

"There's a chance my body won't?"

"Correct."

Juliane frowned. "What happens if my body rejects it?"

Alan's words began to sound muffled to her ears as if the air around them had transformed into sludge. "If your body tries to fight it, then, unfortunately, it will fail. This is not the sort of virus it is used to dealing with. Your body will consume itself, trying to halt the inevitable. If that happens . . . "

"We can die from this?" Juliane blinked until her vision was clear. "You should have mentioned that before!" *What have I done?* "You said upstairs the trials were successful!"

"And they were, but the subjects were all animals and animals trust their instincts so much better than we do. They don't have to be told to adapt and survive. They just do. There is bound to be a higher rate of success."

"You said this was safe," she shouted. She pulled at her straps again.

"Did I?" Alan shrugged. "Or did you simply hear what you wanted to hear? We wouldn't be in this room if I didn't have the utmost confidence that, in your case, the risk of rejection is low. However, the downside of being first to do anything is it always involves the chance for failure. I thought you of all people accepted that." The corners of his lips quirked up. "Ah, I know what it is. You're feeling feverish already and not thinking clearly. Would it make you feel better if I told you I injected myself yesterday?"

A bead of sweat rolled down the side of her head as she thought about his question. Alan had given her ample experience to hone her willpower—she might have told him off at least a half-dozen times otherwise, and certainly, he was a genius. If he could make it, so could she. "You did this to yourself, already?" Her mouth felt like a desert.

Alan grinned. "Don't worry, you'll feel like a brand-new person before you know it."

Juliane's gaze darted to the occupant of the other chair, Louis. He was slumped over, a sheen of moisture covering his face. "You told him too, didn't you?" she demanded. Not waiting for an answer, she tore at her restraints. This time they gave way. Freed, she attempted to race to his side, only to be stricken with such intense vertigo that she dropped to the floor.

Alan sounded far away. "Betty, we need some cots in here. I believe Dr. Faris has her assistant on speed dial. Would you mind giving him a call?" The lab alternated between arctic freeze and volcanic heat. Juliane couldn't have given Louis any further assistance if she tried. An image of Louis crumpled in his chair swirled around her vision. Juliane took a deep calming breath, closed her eyes, and willed herself to remain alive.

TWO

SIX MONTHS EARLIER

Juliane gingerly touched Dr. Henderson's inscription on the worn children's book. Its binding had long since faded to illegibility, and the cover was likely to fall off altogether if she jostled it too much. Even with all her care, a yellowed newspaper clipping managed to escape from the pages.

She knelt to retrieve Dr. Henderson's obituary. He left the school system shortly after she did, hoping to achieve publication, but he had succumbed to a rare blood disease only a few years later.

Juliane understood his original motivation for leaving. Why should he limit himself to teaching a small population of students when he could improve the lives of so many?

She smoothed out a crease as she reinserted the clipping into the book's pages. The world lost an amazing teacher. It was too tragic to be tolerated. Dr. Henderson had recognized her potential before anyone else. His legacy would be her legacy.

Juliane sighed as she closed the book and placed it back between a volume on theoretical computer science, which was her graduate focus, and one of several texts with a psychological focus, which had been her postgraduate work. She glanced at her watch. A message flashed, reminding her that her presentation was scheduled to begin in fifteen minutes.

If she arrived too early, she risked appearing unnecessary. But if she waited too long, Alan could start without her, sending the same message to the audience.

Her gaze slid to the right of the bookcase. Off to the side, hidden from casual view, was a small framed photo of a pair of Bullmastiffs laying in the sun. It was the only photograph on display in the entire room. She closed her eyes, blocking the image.

Silencing one sense only served to enhance another. Her heartbeat began to race in anticipation. Juliane inhaled deeply, filling her lungs to their capacity. She savored the air's pressure as she counted to ten before releasing the breath. Repeating the cycle, she felt her heart calm. *Get it together. It's not like this is your first time,* she thought.

She did not need to see the minutes change on her watch to know that it was time to make her move. The only other personalization in the room was a small bronze paperweight shaped like a chameleon, which sat atop a filing cabinet near the door.

Her mother's friend, Daphne, had given it to her after it became clear that Juliane's mother was never coming back. It was the only thing Juliane kept after her brief guardian's heart attack. Juliane reached over and rubbed its forehead as if the physical activity would simultaneously crush the butterflies in her stomach.

Summoning as much swagger as she could muster, she pulled down the door's handle. Anyone watching her as she made her way down the hall would think she was the embodiment of cool confidence.

Her destination was in sight as a young woman with brown hair pulled back into a ponytail sprinted across the courtyard, cutting her off. The woman's toe caught on an uneven paving stone, sending her tumbling to the ground. Her face turned crimson as she attempted to collect a stack of papers that had littered the ground during the fall.

"Are you okay?" asked Juliane. She could feel seconds pass waiting for the woman to answer.

"No. I mean yes. I mean, other than being mortified that you just saw that, I'm okay." As the woman attempted to stand, Juliane noticed the woman's pant leg was torn at the knee. The woman took a step toward her scattered paperwork and winced.

Juliane bent to help collect a few of the scattered pages. "Are you sure?" she asked.

"It's just a scrape. It looks worse than it feels. Dr. Than is going to kill me for getting her paperwork out of order."

"I'm sure she'll understand."

"Have you ever met her?"

Juliane smiled. "I'm sure she is no worse than some of the people I've worked with over the years. I also think she'd probably be even less understanding if you bled all over her office. How about this? I need to go into a meeting, but I'll have someone swing her precious paperwork by her office before the end of the day. In the meantime, you go clean yourself up."

The woman glanced at her torn clothing and the stack of papers. "You wouldn't mind?"

Juliane held out her hand. "Aren't we all here to make life better for others?"

three

The heavy slam of the auditorium's double doors punctuated her entrance as a similar sound echoed on the other side of the room. Even with the delay in the courtyard, she must have arrived at the auditorium at the same time as Alan.

Juliane had been right to be concerned about the timing of her entrance. Alan never wasted an opportunity, not even a minute. He'd launched into basic introductions without preamble as he made his way to the stage.

The audience, of course, was captivated the second Alan entered the room. He could have been reading the ingredients from the back of a cereal box. They would still be eating out of his palm.

Juliane began handing out carefully-bound supplement materials without needing to be cued. Presentations changed, but some tasks were routine as muscle memory.

The words "My lovely assistant" caught Juliane's ears. It was all she could do to keep her face expressionless. *Now's not the time.* She fought the urge to grind her teeth in annoyance.

It will all be worth it, she thought to herself for the hundredth time during these project review board presentations. She and Alan both worked for the ACI. It was a multibillion-dollar entity, part private-enterprise, part university-partnered think tank, whose breadth of technology product offering was only surpassed by the size of its research and development.

Alan was its superstar. Juliane had been aware of his reputation even as a postgraduate student at Berkley. He had received his doctorate in biotechnology before he was fifteen, and had published the same year. His inbox was always stuffed with peer submissions awaiting his review.

"In 2013, a team of researchers was able to find methods to not only store a megabyte's worth of data into a speck of human DNA, but they were also able to retrieve that stored data. This, of course, has allowed us to move away from semiconductor technology over the years for memory storage; however, we still have not been able to find a means of accessing that data without some computer interface to interpret the results. That is until now." The audience stood in rapt attention as Alan continued. Juliane didn't blame them. She too had once been awestruck in Alan's presence, especially when he discussed his work.

When he called, inviting her to join his team, the phone call had sounded like a validation of every sacrifice she had ever made. She'd followed his career. She knew he commanded the best audiences whenever he presented. From what she could see, all the premier journal editors jumped at the chance to take his call, and if the various co-eds that always appeared to fill the background of his interviews were any indication, he possessed more than a few groupies.

Partnering with him, then, seemed like the only logical choice, especially if she was ever going to join the upper echelons of science. She took what she could carry on the first plane to the East Coast within hours of hanging up.

It had been nineteen degrees the day she arrived in Meriden, Connecticut, but the weather soon proved to be the least of her surprises. After only a few weeks of working together, her hopes became her dismay.

Alan could have easily gotten what he wanted out of a teammate by enlisting the help of a coat rack. She was relegated to a mere prop in his presentation, her contributions overly simplified time and time again, rather than relied upon as an expert in her own right.

"And I am sure you will be happy to report to the junior Mr. Evans that initial trials with synthetic tissue have well exceeded our wildest expectations."

Juliane's attention snapped back to the present as Alan's words registered. She was certain that only a nanosecond of surprise had flashed across her face, but equally certain that Alan had noticed it. While the ACI had ties to the university, it was controlled by the Evans family.

The Evans family had been generous in their endowments over the years, not only in their company investments but to the global community as well. The elder Mr. Evans was respected and admired even by the competition.

His son, Louis, however, was rumored to be a completely different matter. From what she knew about him, he'd grown up near the coast of Italy, enjoying hobbies such as windsurfing and extreme sports. She knew he had attended the Swansea University in Wales and that he had led the boating team to victory year after year only because she had witnessed more than a few individuals try to cite similar experiences as a way to earn favor with the board. The efforts had always backfired.

To her knowledge, Louis had nothing to do with the company. At least he hadn't for as long as she had been employed. But Alan's offhand remark implied that Louis's role was now much larger. Juliane cringed at the thought. Putting a jock like Louis in charge of the ACI could have only one outcome. *Epic disaster.* She needed to make a name for herself, do so quickly.

Alan did not appear to share her concerns. *Why should he? It's not like he has to worry about his reputation. He could quit tomorrow and get ten job offers without sending out a single resume.* He was now strutting around the room making broad gestures. He was proud as a peacock displaying his plumage. She mumbled under her breath, "Showtime."

Alan paused for effect. Juliane could see the attendees practically salivating in anticipation. They should. It was a discovery that would indeed drastically impact society. The things they would be able to do once the technology was further proven would cement the ACI's place in history.

Juliane absently patted the back of her hair, which was knotted viciously in a dark and glossy bun at the nape of her neck, as if to reassure herself that each strand was still in its proper place. A weaker-minded individual might be satisfied watching history be made from the wings; however, her mind was the least weak part about her. She was more than just Alan's lovely assistant, and it was time the rest of the world knew it. She had to find a way to inject herself into the conversation.

As the lights dimmed, Alan turned to verify that the projection on the wall matched his talking point. He caught her eye and paused. *This is my chance.* Juliane's heart raced. *Time to show them exactly what I can do.* She fought to control the excitement from showing on her face.

The presentation, which at this point had been filled with standard two-dimensional charts, graphs, and data points. Not trusting that a digital designer would properly understand her vision, Juliane had spent the last several weeks programming the next section herself.

Alan's lips turned up, but the smile he directed her way was anything but sincere. She knew in that split second that Alan understood this was the type of work that reputations were made on, but had no intention of sharing those honors with anyone.

"Ladies and gentlemen," he said before she could get a word in. "Today we can say that we have mastered the ability to access data through the mind alone!"

The audience leaned forward in their seats as the presentation on the screen spun into a breathtaking computer-rendered simulation. The only sound, aside from Alan talking, was a pen being dropped.

She suppressed the urge to interject or cry. Neither would earn her any points with the board.

"And it is all thanks to a simple firefly." An insect crawled across the screen and launched itself into an artificial twilight. "The science behind how these simple creatures illuminate the night, its bioluminescence, is nothing new."

More insects joined the first on the screen. "But what we've been able to do with that enzyme certainly is." Their bodies flashed randomly at first but then settled into a coordinated symphony of light.

"Through a process of genetic imprinting, we believe we can now signal human epidermal cells to release a similar enzyme." The sky surrounding the insects condensed and warped until it was the outline of a human hand.

"You want to make people glow in the dark? Like bugs?" asked a man seated in one of the center rows.

There was a collective intake of breath in the room. No one interrupted Alan during a presentation. No one. Juliane would be surprised to see the man in the auditorium ever again.

Alan's lips tightened, but he continued without addressing the audience member directly. "Note that this technique would also allow for a degree of cellular control unmatched in the animal world. A person's skin would illuminate only just enough to be recognized by a receiving node. Then, through a series of high-frequency flickers—so rapid that they are nearly imperceptible to the human eye—a person's cells would then be able to transmit data packets similar to data transmitted by LEDs."

Alan paused to drink from a water bottle, although Juliane suspected the pause was more for the audience's benefit than to address his thirst.

"So where are the receiving nodes?" the man asked.

The corners of Alan's lips twitched as he turned his attention to his questioner. "The better question is where wouldn't they be? Traditional routers would still work, but they could just as easily be found in the person next to you. After all, a sunflower can track the position of the sun even though it has no eyes. It can do this thanks to yet another specialized cellular protein. The same sequence that can force the production of one enzyme can be used for another."

As irritated as she was with Alan, Juliane couldn't help nodding like a proud parent. While Alan's work centered on getting the data to interact with a person's internal cells, her algorithms were the key ingredient in making the system dynamic and adaptable. Together, what they had accomplished was almost magical.

"Imagine a world where no one has to worry about another ugly wireless tower going into their backyard, a world with ageless infrastructure. Imagine a world with Internet-enabled telepathy. I call it, Project Gene Assist."

As the lights came back up, Juliane readied herself to answer whatever questions would come her way. Her algorithm was designed to automatically calibrate performance regardless of skin tone, age, or gender. It was perfect. She could still salvage this opportunity. All Alan had to do was hesitate long enough to give her the opportunity.

As the minutes passed, her shoulders ached from refusing to slump in defeat. Alan was able to answer every question with ease and confidence, never once looking her way for assistance. She had to acknowledge he had come to this meeting well prepared.

Not for the first time, she wondered how things might have been different had she not taken his call that fateful day. The projects she would have worked on might have been less impressive, but she would have had an easier time distinguishing herself from less capable team leaders.

Juliane frowned and shook her head. She hadn't gotten this far in life by taking the easy route. She just needed to change her tactics. That smile had proven Alan knew exactly what he was doing. Perhaps it was time to take a different approach and confronting the issue directly.

As the last of the board members filed out of the room, Juliane dropped her statuesque calm facade. "We need to talk."

"What about? Do you think something went wrong? I rather thought our presentation went perfectly."

"Oh, now it's our presentation?"

"Your name was on it, was it not?"

"Oh yes, in small print on the opening slide. Very memorable."

"As was mine. I'm afraid I don't understand what the issue is."

"The issue is, as far as the board is concerned, that's the extent of my involvement."

"What is?"

"My name. On a single slide. In small print."

"They knew you were involved more than that. After all, why else would you be on the stage with me?"

"That's a great question. Why was I on the stage? You certainly don't act like you need me here. If my name wasn't on that one slide, no one would have known I had any input on the project whatsoever."

"You could have chimed in at any time during the question-and-answer round."

"No, I couldn't. You answered every question."

"And were any of my answers wrong?"

"No, but it was my area of expertise." She knew she had started to sound like a whiny child, but trying to regain her self-control was like trying to plug a broken dam.

"I see, and had they followed up with a question about how the data is stored in the proteins, or how the brain can access the information, could you have followed up on that?"

"We both know I wouldn't be prepared for that."

"So, you agree that we both knew enough about your *contribution*"—she didn't need to see his fingers make the air quote gesture to hear it in his tone—" to provide expert answers, but only one of us knew enough to provide complete answers on any topic." Alan paused. "If we had done things your way, this entire process would have continued twice as long, and for what? Your ego?" As he paused his eyes bore into her own. "What is that thing you like to say? Our purpose here is to find ways to make life better for others. There is no place for ego in the pursuit of the greater good, only efficiency. We make our presentation, get our funding, and go on to the next project as quickly as possible."

Juliane said nothing as she absorbed her words twisted against her. He was as prepared for her accusations as he had been for the presentation. She was forced to concede that he had won this round. She would leave, lick her wounds, and come back to fight another day.

"I am going to interpret your silence as agreement." He shut down the wall projection and put together the balance of his belongings. Without waiting for a reply, he turned and disappeared. Juliane closed her eyes and clenched her fists, swallowing a scream of frustration before it could consume her. Her time would come. She just had to be patient.

Four

Shadows stretched across the greenway as she exited the building that housed Dr. Than's office. It hadn't taken much effort to organize the woman's paperwork before handing the stack over to an idle runner in the lobby. Her office and lab space was in the Gould Building near the center of the ACI campus. When it was constructed, Louis Evans Sr. had just begun expanding his company's holdings. He had always been quick to invest in technology. As a result, the building was one of many structures built in the 'experimental' style loathed by the town's historical community.

It was a cylindrical structure with a glass dome top that provided spectacular views of campus. While the glass was clear, the dome acted as a solar collector, powering the entire building. At its base, the architects had installed a series of camera and pixel displays, which would then project whatever the view was on the other side, rendering the base invisible to the casual observer. The effect made it appear as if the top of the building was a floating hemisphere. Supposedly, Louis Evans Sr. had thought the town needed modernization to counter other structures such as Castle Craig, a tower made to look like a medieval castle set within nearby Hubbard Park.

To Juliane, the building was a testament to the ACI's willingness to invest in the unproven, but not all experiments are successful. The panels were enough to achieve the effect the designers were looking for, but what the architects hadn't anticipated was the extent of injuries their design would inflict upon those who never looked up as they wandered about the campus.

The entrance to the building was easy to miss. It was only identified by a subtle alteration to the otherwise repeating layout of brickwork that cut through the commons. As she approached, she noticed a man lounging against a walled planter near the base of the building. He looked to be about her age, in his early thirties, dressed more sharply than one might have expected at this time of day.

Juliane would have expected a person dressed like that to stand at attention, careful to avoid contact with anything that could mar its appearance. But based on his relaxed posture, he couldn't care in the least if his clothes were damaged by their proximity to dirt or brickwork.

His skin was gorgeously tanned and unblemished, his hair stylishly tussled. His face was partially covered by a full yet manicured mustache. Juliane decided it suited him.

He spoke as she grew nearer. His voice was velvet smooth with a singsong quality about it. It was not an accent she was familiar with. She was so caught up listening to the sound of the words and not their content that she did not immediately realize he was addressing her.

"I'm terribly sorry, Ms., but would you happen to know where in the blazes the entrance to the Gould Building is? I must have circled this spot nearly a dozen times and all I've gotten for my trouble is a bruise to my leg." Unlike the dozens of times she had heard similar complaints from new visitors, the man seemed more amused than annoyed.

Juliane remembered all too well her first visit to the building and offered him a sympathetic smile. "Sure, you've almost found it. Follow me." Juliane led the way, and within moments, several panels ceased displaying projections from the other side of the building, allowing a door to become visible. "The trick is to look for changes to the pattern of the brickwork. Around here the pattern is everything."

"Why in the world would a building be made with a door so hard to find?" he asked.

"I am sure the designers thought a door would destroy the effect," Juliane answered while sparing a glance upward and toward the dome. "Architecture aside, it also helps provide a higher degree of security. Several projects are being reviewed inside that the competition would give anything to know about."

They entered the building together. The marble of the floor tile shone in near mirror quality with images of the high-end fixtures reflecting on its surface. The interior of the Gould Building was more typical of a *Fortune 500* tower rather than most research and design facilities. Juliane had expected the man to stop to fully take in their surroundings, but his stride never broke. He nearly walked into Juliane's heel.

They continued through the building's lobby, finally reaching the elevators. "The directory is on the wall over there. Do you think you will be able to find your way from here?"

The man laughed. "Not if the interior of this place matches the exterior. I've been sitting out there waiting for someone to either enter or exit for probably the last thirty minutes. I was already late for a presentation before I arrived. I've likely missed it entirely by now, but I suppose there is a chance that I could go directly to the source for a download—assuming my contact is here." He looked around the empty hallway. "There doesn't appear to be a lot of traffic in this building."

"No, I suppose not. We tend to get lost in our projects and forget about the basic human necessities. Some of us even prefer to sleep here."

"We? I thought this building was nearly solely occupied by research and development. Are you one of the academic liaisons then?"

Academic liaisons were part-time employees, full-time students, and basically a step above servants. Within any other organization, they would have been called interns. However, the ACI had chosen the unique title as a way of acknowledging that in addition to being tasked with all sorts of menial work in support of assigned research teams, these individuals were also expected to serve as a bridge between the ACI and their various universities.

They had helped the ACI make millions, yet they were expected to put up with any number of indignities for little more than the hope that their indentured servitude might one day grant them the recognition that they had never been able to achieve on their own, and for what? Recognition that they might one day be invited to join the ACI full time and given the opportunity to repeat the cycle. Juliane wrinkled her nose at the thought.

It was common for new recruits to spend a year or two in such work, but a person still doing that work at her age? Juliane shuddered. *If an AL is my age and hasn't been recognized by now, they never will be.* It was a matter of personal pride that Juliane had never spent a second as an AL.

"I have had the pleasure of maintaining my own office here for the past few years."

He stopped in mid-stride, and Juliane batted her eyelashes, returning his false sincerity with her own. His gaze swooped over her body from head to toe, while his head cocked to the side and his thumb stroked his chin as if appreciating fine art. "What did you do then, graduate high school when you were twelve?"

She found herself wanting to shake her hair free from its bun in slow motion like women in the movies did whenever they were attempting to be seductive. *Where did that come from?* she wondered. Juliane was relatively certain that had she gone through with the move; she would have looked ridiculous. Juliane knew she was attractive, and had even gone on a couple of dates, but had found that most men were a complication she hadn't missed. Instead, she heard herself giggling. "Sixteen." *What has gotten into me?*

"Well, you don't look a day over twenty."

Juliane decided the banter had gone on entirely too long. As much as she enjoyed the moment, she shouldn't allow this smooth-talking stranger to turn her into a person she didn't recognize. She reminded herself that women before her had fought too hard to penetrate her otherwise male-dominated field. She had fought too hard. She would not allow herself to play the role of the vapid female, even if that's exactly the sort of person her mother would have raised her to be— if her mother had bothered to stick around. She rolled her shoulders as if shrugging off a coat while tightening the control on her expression.

"You mentioned that you were here to see someone? I'm not completely surprised that they didn't come down to see you when you missed your appointment; as I mentioned, we tend to lose track of time. Do you know what floor they are on?"

The stranger seemed oblivious to the effect he had had on her and her internal struggle. "Well, if I am being honest with you, even if I had managed to attend the presentation on time, it would have been a surprise visit. I'm here to see Dr. Faris."

Juliane froze, her finger on the elevator call button. She fought the rush of fire that sought to consume her cheeks. "If you were intending to surprise, you certainly did. I'm Dr. Faris, but I don't believe I have a meeting with you on my calendar."

She risked a glance in his direction, only to be disappointed to see that he did not share in her embarrassment over their prior exchange. If anything, he looked as if he enjoyed himself more knowing who she was. His eyes twinkled in amusement, and the corner of his lips turned up in a sly grin. "Okay. So that's not the only thing I need to be honest about. I've known who you were since before we met. I just wanted a chance to break the ice before we got to the formal introductions."

"Oh? And why is that?" The fire in her cheeks was immediately extinguished, replaced by a sick feeling in the pit of her stomach.

"Well, I have reason to believe that you might have made excuses not to meet me otherwise."

Juliane wondered if she might be dealing with some sort of stalker, an attractive, smooth-talking stalker but a stalker nonetheless. She knew it was only a matter of time before her success earned her one.

"And who might you be then?"

"I'm Louis Evans. I believe you might have heard of me?"

Five

Juliane and Louis rode up the elevator together in silence. Mentally, she replayed her words over and over again, analyzing them to see if she had said anything she might be ashamed of, now knowing who her companion was. By the time the doors opened on her level, she was still far from making a ruling.

"My lab is down this way." Juliane gestured toward a door with J. Faris displayed on the nameplate. Not waiting to see if Louis followed along, she picked up her pace. As she pulled open the door, she was greeted by Chad, her academic liaison and research assistant.

While he was an asset most of the time, Chad was hardly what Juliane would describe as dependable, due in large part to his involvement with another AL, Nadia. His girlfriend seemed to demand more of his time and more importantly, his attention than Juliane ever could.

Frustrated one afternoon after yet another missed assignment, Juliane lodged an official complaint, but that hadn't made an impact. She'd learned Chad's family had sway within the ACI—much more than it seemed she did. Juliane had concluded that until she found a way to be taken more seriously, his flighty personality would have to be just another inconvenience she'd learned to live with, much as a rock exists with moss.

"How'd the presentation go, boss?" Chad came to her side with a clipboard and a cup of coffee. His burnished red hair, pale skin, and freckled face combined with his earnest expression made him look like a child playing doctor in his white lab coat.

"As well as could be expected. Brace yourself, we're about to have some company." Juliane took the cup from his outstretched hand, grimacing as she realized the liquid was long out of the pot.

The door opened behind her as Louis entered, sending Chad back to his desk in a scurry. Juliane rolled her eyes. Why Chad had even bothered to apply to the AL program remained a mystery. She would have thought that a person with his level of social anxiety would have looked for a position that required less interaction with other people.

"Chad, I'd like to introduce you to Louis Evans, here to . . ." Juliane trailed off as she realized that Louis had never mentioned the reason for his visit. Louis spoke up before the pause became uncomfortable.

"Please accept my apologies, Dr. Faris. I realize I didn't give you any advance notice, but as I've recently become more active in the company, I decided I'd like to take a more hands-on approach, especially with some of the more promising work." He held up a hand. "But before you start to worry, I want to be clear. I'm just trying to get my finger on the pulse, not decide whether or not to pull the plug. And I've found all the pomp of a planned visit tends to get in the way."

Juliane's forehead knit as he spoke. His vague answer left her wondering what his role in the company truly was. Whatever it was, Alan and their audience earlier had been more familiar with it than she was. However, it didn't explain why Louis was meeting with her and not with Alan. Juliane frowned. She hated unknowns.

"I'd heard about your father. I am sure he'll be back behind his desk in no time."

Juliane nearly jumped when Chad spoke, it was so out of character. Her frown intensified. She had no time for office gossip and used advanced filters to mute sensationalized stories, but in doing so, she must have missed some momentous news. *Whatever it is, it must be really terrible for Chad to speak up. It has to be a scandal.*

Juliane contemplated changing her filter settings. If she relaxed them, she might be better prepared in the future, but then she would also be bombarded by all the garbage news that wasn't worth her notice. The frown deepened into a scowl. *No.* She would leave her settings as-is. What was the chance that she would ever be blindsided again to this extent?

Chad must have seen her frown and misinterpreted its cause because he quickly bowed his head and returned to his work.

Louis shrugged. "In any case, I am here now as acting CEO."

Juliane felt as if the floor dropped out from under her feet. She had prepared herself for Louis to say that he was in some training program, or come up with some bogus title designed to keep him from causing too much trouble, like Assistant Coordinator of Cool Research. She did not expect her career to now be in his inexperienced hands, even if his comment that her work was 'promising' was a point in his favor. Whatever had happened to his father must have been truly awful for the board to favor this decision.

I've run out of time. "So how do you intend to do that?" Juliane asked. She bit her tongue before her doubts about his abilities could spill out. "I mean what do you know about my work?" She once again fought against the rush of blood threatening to color her face. Questioning the big boss's competence wasn't the best strategy for distinguishing herself within the new hierarchy.

"Well, I know that our financial statements show a recently signed purchase of three, large, top-of-the-line three-dimensional scanners to a J. Faris with only the barest description of their intended use. Additionally, I saw requisition paperwork for several holographic projectors. Based on your association with Dr. Dronigh, I might have thought the scanners were being used to grow synthetic body parts, but that can't be it for three reasons." Louis held up his hand, counting off each point on a finger. "His reports are much more complete, there is no tie-in at all with the projectors, and finally because I know of at least three other groups who are decades ahead on that front."

Louis toyed with his mustache. "I would hate to think I paid for a poor copy of someone else's work. So, I am wondering, Dr., just what *did* the requisitions buy?"

Juliane's hands froze by her side. As much as he claimed to only be attempting to get a feel for current projects, he sure sounded like an ax man verifying his target before swinging the blade. *I have nothing to be ashamed about.* She straightened. *I followed standard operating procedures. The request went through the entire approval process. It's not my fault no one realized it wasn't for one of Alan's projects.*

Before she could say anything at all, Chad spoke up again. "Oh no, it's not like that at all. Dr. Faris is brilliant in her own right. She doesn't need to copy anyone else's work."

Juliane beamed in pleasure at her assistant. He might be as unreliable as the rain, but at least he was loyal. She told herself that she would try to be more forgiving the next time Nadia's demands caused him to come in late or leave early. *At least, I'll try. After all, I can't allow that sort of behavior to go on indefinitely; otherwise, nothing would get done.*

Louis's lips turned up. "Brilliant, eh? Well then, feel free to elaborate."

Her eyes narrowed at his grin. He'd known who she was downstairs and yet willfully led her to believe he was just another lost visitor. *Why?* So, he could make her look like a fool? Did that mean he thought she was a joke? Admittedly, she might have implied he wasn't qualified for his job either, but that had been an accident.

His behavior on the other hand, from the moment they'd met, had been deliberate and intentionally deceitful. She grit her teeth before her temper got the better of her senses. "How much do you understand about deep learning and artificial neural network processing?"

Louis's smile broadened. "I'll do my best to keep up."

"Hmm . . ." *How do I explain my work in terms this man will understand?* "Maybe it would be best to start with a demonstration instead?" she suggested. *Could this day get any worse?*

"By all means. Demonstrate away."

"Follow me." Juliane led Louis to the center of the room where a large tower made up of a trio of metallic arches took up most of the floor space. "You enter it here," said Juliane, gesturing at the blackout fabric hanging from the interior of each arch. "But put these on first," she said, handing him a small wireless earpiece and a clip-on microphone.

"Guess it's a good thing I'm in charge here, otherwise, I might ask if I need to sign a release," asked Louis with a twinkle in his eye as he immediately placed the fob in his ear. He affixed the microphone as he entered the tower. Juliane shook her head. He jested, but there were several other projects on the campus that dealt with strange radiations or otherwise unstable force. Only a person lacking a healthy sense of mortality would make a joke like in the campus labs.

Juliane clipped a small microphone onto her collar. "It's perfectly safe. I wouldn't dream of suggesting you do anything that could harm you. You have better lawyers than I do." Sound did not carry well from inside the tower by design, but she heard a hearty chuckle in response even before she attached her own earpiece.

She nodded at Chad to begin the power-up sequence, while she turned on a series of display screens. A series of lights illuminated the center of each column, pulsing up the length of each pillar.

Her screens lit up in an exact match to what was displayed on the inside of each archway wall for Louis. Without having to be told, Chad brought her digital notebook before returning to his post by the desk. He leaned into another small microphone. "Test Beta 152. Subject Louis Evans, male, Caucasian, systems scan complete. Initiating simulation."

Juliane took a brief sip of her coffee. It had somehow defied the laws of physics by becoming colder. "Chad, would you please get me a fresh cup? This is awful."

"No problem." Chad pulled out his phone. "Uh, er . . . it's Nadia." He waved the device. "I need to take a quick break. I'll bring it immediately afterward."

Juliane looked at her display and was met with the sight of the Italian coastline. It was a gorgeous day, fit for the movies, and pulled directly from a scan of Louis's mind. She sighed remembering her promise to be more patient. "I suppose can manage this from here. Just make sure it's still hot this time." Juliane waved, but Chad never looked away from his phone's screen as he hurried off.

Louis's voice spoke up in her ear, bringing her attention back to her demonstration. "This is incredible! It's like I'm there. Wait. I know that beach. I used to come here every summer. My father's cell phone reception couldn't reach this far, so we'd come here to escape for a little bit. It's so off the beaten path, it shouldn't be on anyone else's radar. My dad would be annoyed to see that it made it onto a computer's stock footage."

"It's not stock footage. My system has tapped into your neural processors. The landscape in front of you is what my algorithm has determined you most want to see. Based on a series of readings, it continuously takes on what neurons fire as well as changes in your body's chemistry." It was hard to keep the pride from entering into her voice.

"So, you are basically reading my mind."

"Well, yes, to an extent, if you want to simplify it like that."

"Should I be worried?"

"That is up to you. There are several layers of consciousness, and the system can only display so much before the images would get lost in mental noise. We just see what is in that topmost layer of your thoughts."

Juliane watched as the brilliant blue sky within the seascape display faded to an equally gorgeous sunset. A ring of rocks appeared on the beach surrounding a small fire. A tin filled with ice-cold beers materialized aside the fire.

Juliane had grand visions for her 'side project.' Seeing thoughts on a display was seeing your imagination take life, but there was so much more her algorithm would be capable of doing once she had proven the concept. As a stand-alone system, she saw applications beyond augmented reality. It could be used as a means of easier diagnosis and treatment of those with mental illness or those who otherwise lacked a voice. As a networked system, it had even more potential.

"You are getting the hang of it. But I need to warn you, the system does not differentiate between intended thoughts versus unintended tangents."

Silence. *First rule of effective communication, Juliane, know your audience.*

"Sorry, I'll try to explain it more simply. Right now you are thinking about a gorgeous day at the beach, but maybe while you are looking at that beer cooler, you allow a stray thought to bubble up about an incident in which you, I don't know, cut your hand on a broken piece of glass or step on a broken bottle. Suddenly, you might find yourself surrounded by distinctly less pleasant images and unable to regain control."

Louis made no comment to indicate he understood.

Juliane sighed. "In other words, you could go on a very bad trip."

While Juliane watched the screen, a woman draped in semi-sheer cloth leaving little to the imagination began approaching the fire ring, her black hair dancing in the virtual sea breeze.

"Careful, Louis. I was just telling you about how important it is to control your thoughts while in there." The features of the woman's face, which had been somewhat blurred, sharpened until Juliane realized that she was viewing a scantily-clad version of herself.

She hung her head. It wasn't even out of beta testing and already her work was being perverted for the adult entertainment industry.

Juliane clenched her fists. This entire demonstration had been a mistake. While she hadn't expected him to completely master his thoughts while in the simulation, she hadn't anticipated his tangent thoughts would take the same route as a sixteen-year-old male.

Juliane grimaced as the virtual woman wearing her face on the screen slowly lowered onto her knees, one hand reaching around to clasp her hair in a loose ponytail, while the other stroked the length of her body seductively.

Louis's thoughts would have to be fairly strong too, for the display to show that level of detail. Juliane's shoulders slumped. If she wasn't already apprehensive about the future of the ACI with Louis in charge, the last few minutes would have been enough for anyone to consider updating their resume.

Grateful that her assistant was not present to witness this latest mortification, Juliane began the shutdown sequence. "I believe that's enough."

When Louis did not respond, she continued. "I have to say I am sorely disappointed, and now, my entire official test records are sullied." She waited with arms crossed. Louis did not immediately emerge. "I am sorry, but there is no cold shower. You'll just have to come out as you are."

The curtain lifted and out stepped Louis. Tears of laughter streaked his face. The microphone was no longer attached to his shirt and not even the faintest hint of shame colored his skin. In fact, he looked even more confident and at ease coming out of the emulator than he had going in. He took one look at her stormy expression and laughed harder until his entire body shook.

He'd never lost control of his thoughts, Juliane realized. *Not even for a second.* Righteous indignation was replaced with an indecisive paralysis. She wanted to slap him. She wanted to shake his hand.

Other than herself, no one previously had been able to gain that degree of skill and control in her interface on the first try. Admittedly, the number of subjects who had logged time in the emulator was limited to Chad and the occasional passing AL they managed to flag down in the hall, but those early results couldn't be described as anything other than failures.

Her entire world had just been turned on its head. The taste of disappointment fled her mouth, leaving her lips dry by its sudden absence. She bit them to return their moisture.

Only time would tell if there was more to Louis than the crude exterior he showed the world, but if a person could display mental strength like a bodybuilder displayed muscles, the man standing before her might just be Mr. Universe. *Perhaps the ACI has a chance after all.*

six

"That's a fun toy."

Juliane shook herself back into awareness. Now seated at Chad's desk, he appeared to scan some of their notes from previous recordings. His cheeks were no longer wet from spent tears, although he still maintained a glow.

"I beg your pardon. My Total Immersion Reality Emulator is not a toy," replied Juliane, like the mother of the school's overachieving valedictorian being told that she had a 'good' student.

"Well, that's a pity. Add in a little haptic feedback and you'd be able to print money from red-light districts to the gaming industry."

"Haptic feedback? Oh, no. I will not cheapen my work by putting my software in little video booths with air jets."

Louis looked up. Juliane thought to herself that he must have been born with an amused expression on his face; there was just nothing that could spoil his mood.

"I do so hate to remind you that it's not just 'your' technology or 'your' software." He rested his head on a propped-up arm. "But just for the sake of argument, what would you do with it?" He gestured at the machine. "I will give you that you have probably developed one of the most realistic virtual reality programs I have ever seen, and the fact that you don't have to use of one of those ill-fitting sensor caps is a nice touch, but beyond that, there isn't all that much difference from what has been out there for the last fifty, sixty years." He raised his eyebrows as if challenging her to contradict his last statement.

Juliane straightened her back and shoulders, pushing out her chest. She noted that Louis's head tilted ever so slightly, a gesture she begun to interpret as one of appreciation. "Perhaps, had you arrived earlier and seen the presentation about the other project I've been working on, you might have realized the bigger implications too."

Louis's eyes twinkled. Juliane couldn't decide if she wanted to slap the grin off his face or if she wanted him to do something else with those lips. "Yes, that was rude of me, wasn't it? Please feel free to school me."

Juliane felt her body begin to tingle in a flush fueled by pride in her vision. "Had you been there, you would have heard that Alan and I have found a way to turn the human body into, essentially, an Internet server."

Louis's expression showed no indication he grasped the synergies between that news and the demonstration he had just experienced. But his performance in the emulator proved that his mind was vastly more capable than he let on. *Or maybe he just plays a lot of video games.*

"Just as the Internet is made up of a series of electrical connections, so is the human brain—both are simply processing data. Thanks to my mind-mapping algorithm, information, like the images you saw in the emulator, can not only be read onto a screen but could be potentially transmitted directly to a person's brain by mimicking pulses sent by optic and nerve endings. At least, in theory."

"Like augmented reality contact lenses?" Louis asked.

Juliane's shoulders loosened. Louis wasn't unimpressed due to not understanding the technology. He was just making sure that there wasn't something already on the market.

"Those lenses are limited to what information can be processed by sight. One-dimensional. You can improve the experience with an earpiece, but even then, the experience is limited. However, thanks to my algorithm, we will now be able to transmit things like taste, smell, and even touch—all with a thought. My virtual reality would look and, more importantly, feel real to anyone accessing it at any time. It wouldn't just be a virtual reality; it would, in fact, be a synthetic reality—and the data transmissions—well beyond what we call the Internet today."

Juliane felt more than a surge of satisfaction as she watched the amusement finally leave Louis's face. "So, what if two people logged in to your system at the same time? Might they think they are . . . I don't know . . . sitting by a fire drinking wine together, even though they are physically thousands of miles apart?"

He certainly has a one-track mind. "Yes, to them it would feel as real as if they were in the room together." *Fine. If this is what it takes to keep my project alive.* Juliane stepped closer. "They both would feel the heat of the fire, the taste of wine on their lips." She caressed her throat. "The carpet they were sitting on would feel just as soft or scratchy as they believed it should feel like." *Wait, that came off too naturally. Am I flirting?*

"I can think of a number of ways that could make life interesting."

Juliane felt ridiculous. *Now, who was being unprofessional? Of course, I'm not flirting.* Louis was technically her boss, even if he didn't want to act like it. She had every right to go to human resources and report him, if she wanted to, for his emulator joke. *Not that it would do me any good.*

"It's only a theory for now," said Juliane, hating that she had to include the disclaimer. "It will require people to agree to modify their DNA, which I don't see happening anytime soon. This is why my emulator is so important. It allows people to visualize the benefit—assuming the majority of people have more maturity than a teenager." Juliane looked pointedly at Louis, who still lacked the decency to blush; if anything, his grin came back with a greater vengeance.

"But even so, your system is a long way from being perfect," Louis stated.

"What do you mean?" Juliane's forehead wrinkled. Her program was exquisite.

"Well, as you said, all it takes is for one errant thought and the system can take a user down a path that they didn't want to go down. Therefore, in a shared experience, who would really control the simulated reality?"

Juliane paused, surprised. It was a complication she hadn't considered. "I suppose whoever had the strongest will would take over the entire simulation."

"And what if a shared reality was, I don't know, hacked or hijacked? Espionage isn't limited to the movies. What then?"

Juliane's fingers tapped absently across her equipment as she thought through his question. She realized she had no ready answer. "I suppose there is some potential for abuse. I'll design in a system limiter."

"How much would that cost?" asked Louis, pantomiming the motion of pulling out and opening his wallet.

"It doesn't have to cost *you* anything. It's just a matter of programming time."

Louis raised his eyebrows briefly as he snorted. "And who do you think pays for your programming time, exactly?" He clapped his hands. "How about this—I will be presenting new advances in our technology in Vegas in two months. You need to convince the masses. Yes? That's all the publicity you could hope for."

He extended his hand. "I'd like you to be there with me, with this . . . What did you call it? The Total Immersion Reality Emulator?" Louis twisted his expression as if he had tasted something unpleasant. "I'll need to ask the marketing team to help with that one. TIRE doesn't exactly scream high tech. In the meantime, you'll need to figure out a way to get those limiters in place. Do you think you can do that?"

Two months. It took a minute for Louis's words to register. *That's not enough time to properly reconfigure and test the system. At least, not at that scale. It's . . . it's . . . it's my one and only chance to prove myself.* Juliane plastered a smile on her face and shook his hand. "I'll be ready."

Chad returned as Louis turned to leave. Seeing Louis approach, he jumped to the side. Coffee sloshed over the rim of the cup and onto his hand.

"Did you burn yourself?" Juliane asked, glancing around the room for something to blot the liquid.

Chad shook his head. "It's okay. It wasn't all that hot anymore. Is the demonstration already over?"

Juliane sighed as she took the cup from his hand. She wondered if she could put an on-demand coffee maker on the list of requirements for Louis. "Let's just say I showed him enough."

Louis turned at the room's exit with a grin. "I do believe Vegas will be a memorable experience—for both of us. Looking forward to seeing what you can do. Two months."

seven

Chad was late again. Juliane's earlier promise to be more patient with him had long since expired. The symposium was only a month away and she still hadn't figured out how to demonstrate her technology to a large audience, short of forcing them each to file into the chamber one by one.

Even if that was an option, she wasn't convinced that the average person coming in off the street would be able to grasp its greater potential. The more she had thought of it, the more worried she had become that Louis's use of the chamber would be considered the norm.

She needed to adapt her algorithm to better serve the mental capacity of the average person coming in off the street. To do that, she needed another brain in the room for it to reference in testing. Chad's continued absences were causing delays she couldn't afford.

Juliane was just about to write him off for the day when her assistant burst through her office door. "I'm so, so sorry, Dr. Faris! I know I am late, but Nadia needed to finish telling me what I need to expect this weekend."

Juliane rolled her eyes skyward. "I hesitate to ask, but what is happening this weekend?"

"Nadia believes it is time we took our relationship to the next level. I'm meeting her parents, and I have to make a good impression—"

"Oh, and this announcement delayed you by . . ." Juliane glanced at the clock even though she was already very much aware of what time it was. "Fifty minutes."

"Really? Eh . . . I feel terrible, but you don't understand, she's daddy's angel," Chad stuttered as he was prone to do when he became particularly agitated. Juliane gave him a pointed look; she had previously given him tips on how to center himself, as she couldn't stand listening to his pained attempts to force out words.

Chad took a few calming breaths and continued. "If this conversation doesn't go right, well then, I might as well consider our relationship over. She's written out a list of everything I need to do to prepare for tonight. I hate to ask, but can I leave early today?"

Juliane took a calming breath herself. It was too close to the symposium to find and train a new assistant. If he would only apply himself toward his career with half the energy his relationship consumed, he might just have a chance to get through the academic liaison program. Juliane fought the urge to shake her head in disgust; wasting your talent was worse than having no talent at all.

A familiar voice spoke up from the doorway before Juliane had a chance to reply. "Oh, Jules, you know if you ever wanted to come by my office, I would be more than willing to provide you with some one-on-one mentorship on how to inspire those under you."

Juliane schooled her expression. She would not give Alan the satisfaction of seeing how much his words agitated her. "Alan, please, we've been through this nearly half a dozen times. Please don't call me Jules."

"Yes, we have, and yet, I still don't understand why you insist on getting angry about it? You are a gem, and it makes sense that your name reflects how dazzling you are."

Juliane fought the urge to gag. If the condescension rolling off Alan's tongue was any thicker, it would be visible to the naked eye.

"You know, Jules," continued Alan, dragging out each sound of the word, "if you ever tire of the whole ice princess thing, you might try to learn how to accept a compliment. You aren't that hard on the eyes after all. Who knows? You might even learn how to land yourself a prince. I'd be happy to give you some one-on-one mentoring for that as well."

Alan was good looking, but Juliane was attracted to more than surface appearance. "I assume that you had other reasons for coming down from Mount High to see me?"

"Now, Jules, why do you hurt me when you know I have only ever wanted to look out for you? What other reason might I need?"

When Juliane didn't speak, he continued, "Ah, but you are right. This isn't strictly a friendly call. I know that you landed yourself a direct assignment from Mr. Evans. I also know you'll be with him at the New Tomorrow Tech Symposium."

"I expect most everyone in our building knows that by now."

"Yes, well, I imagine you're probably getting pretty nervous and starting to think you aren't ready, but I just want you to know that the ACI wouldn't have signed off on you going—no matter who backed your invitation—if they thought for a moment that your work was going to reflect negatively on them."

"How unexpected of you, Alan. I appreciate your concern, but no, I'm not nervous at all." Juliane lifted her chin and rolled her shoulders back in an attempt to ooze confidence. *Alan can't possibly know how far I am behind schedule, can he? If Chad said anything to the other ALs . . .*

"Excellent. I am glad to see that you aren't wasting any energy on an emotion like that. It isn't as if you will have that large a crowd anyway." Alan turned to leave, placing his hand on the doorframe. Juliane remained silent. She would not ask for clarification. She would not.

"Our hall fits 200," Chad said.

If Juliane hadn't been working so hard to show only a calm and cool demeanor, she would have slapped her forehead at Chad's remark. This was not the time for him to attempt to defend her honor. She knew how Alan operated and was therefore unsurprised when Alan responded.

Without acknowledging Chad's presence, Alan directed his answer to her. "Well, that's a pity, as the majority of attendees will be in *my* presentation hall, but at least, on the bright side, you won't have to worry about violating any fire codes."

Juliane nearly bit her tongue in two as Alan departed. "Do you never think ahead? How could you set him up like that?" Juliane watched a rather impressive color change sweep through Chad's features. His skin became alabaster before blazing with a red that could put his hair to shame. She slumped down at her desk, rubbing a hand over her eyes as if it might somehow wipe away the sudden exhaustion she felt.

"I'm sorry, Chad. I know you couldn't help yourself. He's very good at reading situations and manipulating people to get the outcome he wants. I've seen him do it over and over again, and you are a particularly easy read. Just—word of advice—don't ever play poker with him." She began to massage her temples.

Chad also returned to his desk and picked up a ball made to look like an eight ball from a billiards table. Juliane watched as Chad looked at it, returned it to its spot on the desk, only to pick it up again and repeat the process a few seconds later.

"Why do you keep doing that?" she asked.

"Oh, this is a Magic 8 Ball."

"Are you asking it to grant you back the last hour?"

"It's not that kind of magic. Did you know my family agrees with you?" Chad's words were barely audible. He continued to look toward the toy.

Somewhat intrigued, she caught herself asking, "As well they should, but about what?"

"That I don't think ahead. But unfortunately, I do, and that's kind of my problem. For example, you might ask me if I want to watch a movie. If I say yes, I'll have to answer a slew of follow-up questions."

He turned the ball over and over. "What movie do you want to see? What theater? Are you going to want popcorn or a drink?" His eyes pleaded for her to understand. "There are any number of choices. But what if, as a result, we go to this one particular theater that has new kids on the staff who don't know how to properly pop the corn. What if they are always leaving too many kernels? What if the restrooms have doors that stick? What if after drinking too much soda, you leave the movie with a handful of popcorn to go to the restroom. You don't want to take food with you into the bathroom, so you try to eat it in one bite, but a kernel mixed in with the handful of popcorn sticks in your throat, blocking your airway, and the door back out is jammed."

He grabbed his throat and made a gagging sound. "Then, no one notices that you choked to death alone in the restroom until it is far too late, and it is my fault because I decided that we should go out to the movies rather than staying in."

Juliane sat in stunned silence. It was probably the longest conversation she had ever had with her assistant outside the topic of their work. "How do you manage to leave the house at all, thinking like that?"

Chad shrugged, returning his focus to the oversized Magic 8 Ball. "There are even more terrible scenarios for those who remain home alone all day. My parents gave me this," Chad waved the plastic ball in Juliane's direction, "as a joke."

She had seen the sphere before on his desk but had assumed it was just some random knick-knack. Now, she could see that the missing piece of the ball was filled in with a dark, flat surface.

"It was my grandfather's."

"What? That plastic thing is an antique?"

Chad shrugged. "Well, they don't make them anymore, so I guess it is a bit of a collectible."

Juliane rolled her eyes. She never could understand people who would pay an arm and a leg for an old toy when the new toys were so much better.

Chad, lost in his thoughts, continued, "I remember it sat on the top shelf at my grandfather's house. I was told I wasn't allowed to touch it until I was tall enough to reach it. He said it was magic."

"And, of course, you believed him."

"He told me it could tell the future."

Juliane snorted.

"Laugh if you want, but I was a kid. For that reason, I couldn't wait. One day, I stacked a footstool on top of the desk and climbed to the top, but it was still just out of reach. I stretched out as far as I could go, but I lost my balance and accidentally kicked the footstool out from under me. I grabbed hold of the shelf in an attempt to right myself and wound up bringing the whole shelf down with me."

"Obviously, you survived." Juliane knew she should be more sympathetic, but she needed Chad's attention to be back on their work.

"I did. But I wound up breaking my grandmother's favorite vase. That was the first lesson on unintended consequences."

It became clear to Juliane that Chad was not going to return his focus on the present until she allowed him to finish this little trip down memory lane. "So, tell me, how does it work?" she asked.

That question caught his attention. Chad eagerly showed her its underside. "It's filled with water, and there is a twenty-sided die inside with things like yes, no, or maybe printed on the sides. You think of a question, turn the ball over, and then, poof! It tells you the answer." Chad put the globe back down on his desk. "I haven't needed it much, though, since meeting Nadia."

Juliane bet he hadn't. As far as she could tell, Nadia made all the decisions for both of them. "Fine. I'll bite. What have you been asking it?"

"Whether or not I will impress Nadia's father later."

Juliane closed her eyes, intending to count to ten, but all she could see was Alan's gloating face in her mind. As a result, she asked, more shortly than she might have a mere minute ago, "And what does it say?"

"Outlook cloudy, try back later."

"I see." Juliane looked straight at their Total Immersive Reality Emulator. Her eyes darted to the side, and her head cocked ever so slightly as she grasped a stray thought. "So, your toy is just a random answer generator."

"I guess so."

"But people still believe it?"

"Well, I don't know if anyone believes it can predict the future, but it's nice to pretend."

"But what if it wasn't? Random, I mean."

"What? Like as in destiny?"

"No. Not destiny. Weighted probability," Juliane chided. She stared at her emulator. "Okay. I'll make a deal with you. I'll let you leave early today to study up on Daddy Dearest, but tomorrow, if I have a way to show you your potential future, do you think you might just be able to return to our work at hand?"

"Absolutely. You won't regret this."

Chad disappeared through the doorway before the sounds reached Juliane's ears.

"I'd better not," Juliane muttered to the empty room.

———— ∞ ————

After an all-night marathon of software tweaks, the Total Immersive Reality Emulator was ready for another round of testing. Chad fidgeted by the side of the fabric entranceway, his earpiece and microphone already fixed in position.

"Whenever you are ready."

Juliane watched as he stepped through the archway, the LEDs on each pillar beginning their familiar scan. She clipped on her microphone while her displays came to life, showing an image of the exterior of one of the local restaurants from the vantage point of a car pulling into a parking space. Nadia was in the passenger seat, and she remained there even after the car came to a complete stop as if waiting for Chad—who had been in the driver's seat in this simulation—to open the door for her. He must have also made this realization as the display showed him acting like a classic gentleman.

Nadia entered the restaurant first, and a man rose from the bar area to greet her. Nadia was an attractive woman, and this man possessed a more than passing resemblance, obviously her father.

Her face lit up as they embraced, and she gestured over in Chad's direction. Juliane's earpiece throbbed with the din of the restaurant bar area. "Dad, I'd like to introduce you to Chad." Her father nodded his head briefly in acknowledgment, but the smile that had been on his face when greeting Nadia was severely diminished. The hostess came up to let them know that their table was now ready.

Juliane watched as the dinner scene played out. As she had expected, Chad allowed himself to forget that he was essentially in a program and began to react more naturally. They spent perhaps five minutes talking about his life as an AL and his most recent work; the rest of the conversation focused on Nadia, but Juliane could tell that Nadia's father hadn't warmed to Chad during this time.

Juliane's fingers flew over her display, toggling a keyed sequence. The simulation jumped ahead. Chad and Nadia were in an apartment, most likely Nadia's from its interior. Nadia explained to Chad why they just weren't going to work out.

Chad made repeated attempts to change her mind, but nothing worked. A glowing light shone under the apartment door. Chad went toward it, and the simulation started over, once again in the car.

The entire process repeated, beginning at the restaurant. Each time, Chad tweaked his response per Juliane's instruction, until dinner ended with Nadia's father shaking his hand and Nadia showing her appreciation back at the apartment. Juliane shut down the simulation.

"So, do you feel more ready now?" she asked Chad as he exited the arches.

"It was nice to have a reset button, but you can't know for certain that he was going to react that way. I mean, I've never even met him. I've only seen his photograph."

"That might be true if I based the simulation on only your brain patterns. But while you were obsessing over the unknown, I was adjusting the program to look up supplemental digital information. Now, the system doesn't just create a simulation based on your brain patterns; it also creates a response profile based on digital history—in this case, Nadia's and her father's social media interactions, browsing history, and spending behaviors. Using that data as a reference point, the system was able to incorporate their probable reactions into its prediction of your future, even though it has never taken their readings."

"Er . . . not that I am not completely impressed, but doesn't that violate their privacy somehow?"

"It might have been more black-and-white fifty years ago or so, but it's more of a gray area today. The data is out there, just waiting to be utilized, as long as you know the right channels to go through—and I do. Now, I believe you made me a promise yesterday."

"Well, you technically can't say you showed me the future."

"I never promised that. I said I would show you your probable future. You have to admit what I've done is far better than your silly Magic 8 Ball. Shall we get back to work?"

"Forget about the presentation. You could make billions with this playing the stock market."

"Please. We've only barely begun to scratch the surface of its potential."

"Well . . . you're the boss. What do you need from me? Should I go and get you some more coffee?"

"You should get a few cups for yourself as well. Neither of us will be sleeping again anytime soon."

Eight

Juliane smiled. Her system's predictive model wasn't perfect. A butterfly had flapped its wings in the Amazon, triggering a breeze that changed the weather pattern, resulting in Nadia wearing a light jacket. There would always be some element of chaos, but it was pretty impressive nonetheless.

Chad reported that the evening as a whole had played out so close to the simulation that it almost felt scripted. He'd also surprised her by making good on his promise as the last few weeks leading up to the symposium passed without further interruption.

Even though Chad was correct in stating the new predictive capabilities could gain the attention of analysts on Wall Street, but they both knew it would be impossible to capture the market's attention if the only exposure to the technology was from one-on-one demonstrations.

They had to make it bigger, much bigger, and make it a shared experience. With that in mind and Louis's signature on the bottom line, Juliane and Chad built up several other scanner pillars. These pillars, once assembled, would transform the entire presentation room into an emulation chamber.

Satisfied that all her equipment had been packaged and shipped to her standards, she made her way to the airport. After the grueling pace, Juliane was grateful that the ACI had taken care of making all of the arrangements.

The gate assignment on her ticket stub had brought her to a portion of JFK she had never known existed. It was a private hangar on the far side of the airfield, and she had reached it only by boarding a small trolley car.

When she entered the hangar, she was met with the sight of a single aircraft, whose image was mirrored in the high-gloss hangar floor. The aircraft itself could be considered a work of art by some circles. It featured a blended wing and body rather than the more traditional tubular fuselage and separate wing design.

Several aircraft builders had talked about migrating over to a similar design for the past several decades. Supposedly, the intent was to make aircraft quieter and more fuel-efficient, but as far as Juliane knew, none to date had been willing to risk their stock valuations on a design with unproven commercial results. And yet, here was a working concept with the ACI logo visible from every angle.

Juliane smirked as she found herself wondering if the Evans men were the type to overcompensate for shortcomings through the acquisition of large, fast, and expensive toys, and she attempted to muffle a chuckle before someone overheard and forced her to explain herself.

A glance around soon proved that she hadn't needed to worry. Louis was nowhere in sight. Juliane realized she was relieved yet disappointed. As she entered the craft, she paused in the entranceway. Louis might not be there, but she wasn't flying alone. Seated in one of the many swiveling, leather-clad chairs, was a man pouring himself a drink who she'd never seen before.

Juliane's eyelashes were longer than the man's hair, which was so blond it was nearly white. He wore a tailored suit similar in style to one of Louis's, which had to cost more than what she paid for rent in a month. As she crossed the threshold, he stood at attention, like a gentleman of old, but had to be close to the same age as Louis.

He stepped toward her while placing the drink to the side in one graceful motion, and he clasped her hand in his own. She was taken aback at how very strong his grip was.

"Ah, you must be Dr. Faris. I'm Durham Ladensham, professional entourage, and part-time legal counsel, at your service." He must have seen Juliane's wince at the strength of his handshake as he immediately softened his hold. "My apologies. I've recently taken up fencing and occasionally forget that my grip is a bit tighter than it used to be."

Juliane attempted to smile back in understanding but wasn't quite sure how to process his statement. She'd never encountered anyone who had taken up fencing as a sport. The people she interacted with tended not to take up any sport unless required to by their doctor; even then, it was typically either jogging or golf.

He continued, misinterpreting the cause of her hesitation. "I'm a longtime friend of Louis's. He asked me to serve as your unofficial tour guide while he wraps up a few other details ahead of the symposium. Don't worry. He'll be joining us in Vegas."

Juliane raised a single eyebrow. Louis thought she needed a traveling companion, did he? What did he think she was going to do? Wander off and miss her chance to stand in the spotlight?

"He's not told me much about what you are getting ready to present," Durham continued, oblivious to her reaction. "I am hoping that you might be a little more loose-lipped." He smiled, daring her with his eyes.

Juliane met his gaze and shrugged. If Louis wanted to play coy with his friend, she could play along, but first, she had to dispense with any suggestion that she was some dainty maiden in need of an escort.

Without breaking eye contact, she moved to the aircraft railing and swept up the drink he had been in the process of pouring. She raised the glass to her lips, halving its contents. She tasted smoke as the rich scotch warmed her belly.

It was the type of drink one might suggest would put hair on your chest. Certainly not one a stranger would have poured for a lady. She savored the flavor before asking, "So, fencing?"

Juliane felt victorious as his eyes left hers, tracking the motion of the glass. His smile deepened in appreciation along with the tone of his voice. *Message received.*

"Well, it's hard to keep up with the old lacrosse circuit when you travel as much as I do. I felt like the ultimate FOGO. I figured that this way, all I have to do is find a club nearby." He shrugged.

"Sorry, I have no idea what you are talking about."

"Oh, well, some of us aren't as lucky as you are, and have to find other ways to maintain our girlish figures." Durham snorted at his joke.

"It's not been that hard. I just don't go out to eat much." Juliane forgot to eat altogether some days. It depended on how engrossed she was with her work and whether or not Chad was around to remind her that Nadia was waiting on him for their next meal. "No, what I meant was I have no idea what FOGO is."

"Oh, I see. Louis and I played on the same team for a while. FOGO: Face Off, Get Off. I felt like I would only show for a game and then wouldn't see the team again until the following season. Louis has this huge banner of the WLA, er . . ., Welsh Lacrosse Association, on one of the walls at his place. I tend to forget that not everyone grew up with the terminology."

The crew must have completed their final safety checks because the aircraft door was closed, and an attendant interrupted the conversation, motioning them to take their seats. Juliane sank into the plush cushion. "I may never be able to fly coach ever again," she sighed, sinking even further with the jet's rapid acceleration.

"Well, if your presentation goes even a fraction as well as Louis anticipates, I suspect you may never have to. Welcome to the good life." He had poured himself another drink right before their ascent and raised his glass from his seat. She returned the gesture, emptying the balance of her glass.

Their ascent was over before Juliane could put her glass down. As soon as cruising altitude was reached, Durham swiveled in his chair toward her. "What is the big hush-hush project anyway?"

"Does Louis normally keep you in the dark?"

"Normally? No, which is why I am now so intrigued. I'm not just a pretty face here. I like to know what is going on so that I can advise him on what he needs to do to come out on top."

Juliane shrugged. "Well, I suppose he has his reasons. I would hate to ruin whatever he has planned." Juliane watched the smile slip from Durham's face for a moment. He bowed his head, and when he raised it again, he did so with a fox's grin.

"Well, we are heading to Vegas with some time to kill. How about I play you for the information?"

"What kind of game do you have in mind?"

"How about the game of kings?"

"What? Chess?"

"The fact that you even caught that reference tells me that it's a great choice. You're a genius, right? Well, then, you've got nothing to fear. What do you say?"

"Chess." It was a question as much as a statement. Lacrosse in Wales, fencing around the globe, and chess as his go-to game of choice. The man sitting before her had quite a different upbringing than she had.

Durham didn't waste time waiting for her to answer. He pulled out a chess set from a small compartment located near his seat. Then he pushed a small button and a table rose from the floor.

"Convenient you have the board ready."

"Isn't it, though?" Durham grinned like a child. The pieces were set up in a matter of minutes. "Ladies first."

Juliane marveled at the board as Durham placed the final piece. It was a beautiful set; each piece appeared hand-carved out of marble and polished to a high shine. She hesitated to mar their surfaces with her fingerprints. She moved her first pawn as if it might shatter on impact.

A few moves later, several of her pieces had been captured. As she suspected, Durham was quite skilled with the game. She watched as he swooped in to take out another, this time a knight. With each move, he had grown bolder and bolder while her available moves dwindled.

"Really, my fine doctor, you ought to pay more attention to the game at hand—a couple more moves like that and your king will be completely exposed." He paused.

She had been hunched forward, studying the board, but looked up when he had begun speaking.

His smile widened to a near leer. "Or are you hoping for an excuse to bare all your secrets?" She glanced down to realize that her neckline had drooped low, providing him with a display of cleavage. She successfully fought back a blush. *Stay confident, Juliane*, she told herself as she acknowledged his comment with a quick tilt of her head and a single raised eyebrow.

She watched as he raised his eyebrows in surprise. She saw his Adam's apple bob in a quick gulp before he regained his composure.

Juliane turned her face back toward the game at hand, although she continued to look up at Durham through her eyelashes. "Oh, I think I might still have a chance. Don't you?" Her voice deepened to a near purr as she reached out to caress one of her chess pieces. "You know, we never did agree what I get if I win."

"In full disclosure, I feel that I do need to tell you that I've beaten some of the best in the world, including Louis. But in the event that happens, you can name your reward."

"Anything I want?"

"Anything at all."

"Day spas, shopping sprees, fine dining?"

"Sure. I'll hand over my card, but you might find yourself needing a big strong assistant to take you to all those places."

"And you'd be willing to do all that if I win?" Juliane drew the piece she held ever so slightly along her face so that its tip rested just beside her lips.

"All that and more. If you win, I'll be your personal slave as long as we are in Vegas," Durham responded eagerly.

Juliane shifted her head so that it rested on her other palm as she placed the piece back on the board, rubbing her thumb along its head. Durham took a quick glance around as if verifying that they were alone in the cabin. "Well then, I believe you should hand over your wallet, as do I believe you have found yourself in a back-rank checkmate."

Durham's eyes darted back to the board. His king was firmly trapped behind his ranks with no available moves, and it was at the mercy of her queen. Juliane smiled, batted her eyelashes, and said, "Oh, and while you are at it, would you please fetch me another drink?"

The look of shock upon Durham's face was too much to resist, and Juliane threw back her head in a burst of unrestrained laughter.

"What just happened?" Durham asked as he moved to refill her beverage.

"You don't play women often, do you?" she asked as she shrugged a shoulder with a look of mock innocence.

"You play dirty. I'll remember that the next time we play," he replied.

"Who says there is going to be a next time?"

"There is always a next time. Just ask Louis."

"Oh, dear. It sounds like I may have bitten off more than I can chew."

Durham launched into tales of he and Louis's various exploits. By the time they landed, Juliane felt much more knowledgeable about her new boss.

However, she now understood why Louis hadn't told him the details about her project. Durham was a voice in need of an ear. Even so, he was entertaining enough, and before long she found herself looking forward to sharing his company in Vegas.

Nine

S he had gone into the first boutique more out of curiosity than need. A sideways glance at an exposed tag showed a price well beyond her average means. As she moved through the rows of clothing, Juliane had selected garments without hesitation, interested to see how far Durham would let her take her victory.

Rather than stopping her, he had given an indulgent grin along with his credit card. However, she didn't swipe it once, much to the chagrin of the sales clerk, who was denied a significant commission. While she might be willing to employ some of her mother's tricks, others left a sourer taste in her mouth.

"You know you really could have gained an entirely new wardrobe," Durham announced as they made their way toward her hotel.

"Thanks, but it wouldn't have been right."

"Why not? You beat me fair and square."

"That was just a game. I'm not going to spend your money on my clothes. Especially not here. Did you see those prices?"

"Chess is so much more than just a game. It's about strategy, and our strategy for the presentation should involve getting you outfitted in something that will take the room's breath away. Please, let's make one more stop. You earned it."

Not waiting to hear her protest, Durham steered Juliane into another boutique. Juliane's eyes widened at the outfits on display. Before she could turn around and leave the shop, Durham flagged the attention of the store's clerk. This clerk was not as willing to abandon a commission, and within short order, she pulled a white suit from the back of the shop.

It was made of some newly-developed material that put standard cashmere to shame. It was the color of Antarctic snow and accented by subtle lines of silver piping. The sales clerk dragged Juliane to one of the fitting rooms. Juliane couldn't help herself. The fabric was so soft, she had to try it on. The outfit fit as if it had been designed for her and her alone. It complimented her every curve.

"Gorgeous. Simply gorgeous," exhaled Durham as she exited the room.

"I still can't accept this," Juliane sighed.

"That's too bad, because I paid for it while you were in the fitting room, and I am sorry to say this shop doesn't have a return policy. However, to complete the look, you really need to do something with your hair. Good thing I've already made you an appointment at the hotel's spa."

"You really shouldn't have," protested Juliane. She ran the numbers in her head. *If I put aside a few dollars each paycheck, I might just be able to write him a check in . . . five years.*

"Yes, I should, and you shouldn't pretend you don't want to go. This could be your regular life soon enough." Durham's expression softened. "The world won't know what hit them."

Durham left her at the spa entrance to go check in with Louis. She had been plucked and trimmed with near surgical precision. Her skin, normally pale, had taken on a rosy hue after their ministrations and shimmered due to a post-treatment moisturizer containing a subtle body glitter. Without a single split end to mar her hair's shine, her dark hair cascaded down her back as if it was a blackened waterfall. Looking into the mirror, she had never felt so stunning. *I'm never going to be able to pay him back if I'm only ever seen as Alan's lovely assistant.*

Before he left, Durham had arranged private transportation for her between the spa and the auditorium. Seeing how the bright white shone, she was relieved not to have to risk her new clothes on the monorail shuttle.

She entered the recently renovated convention center like a queen, basking in the admiring glances turned in her direction as she made her way down the hallway, all the while pretending it was just another day.

Though the common areas were crowded, she recognized Alan's voice. He was seated under bright lights and giving an interview to a reporter. She acknowledged him with a subtle nod of her head as she passed.

The reporter repeated his question. Alan's response had none of its usual polish. Her lips turned up ever so slightly as she continued toward her room.

Finally, she arrived in her auditorium. All the pillars were positioned exactly where she had specified. It was an arrangement four times larger than the original configuration at the ACI campus. Everything was going to plan.

The pillars nearly encircled the room but were placed in such a way that they blended into the room's perimeter. She could see Chad's red hair behind the array of equipment as she strode up to the podium.

As she approached, she had to stifle a laugh. The tan suit he had chosen to wear, combined with the black cords in his hands, made him look like a meerkat. The image was further strengthened when he froze in place at the sound of her approach.

"If that's how you clean up, I have to find an excuse to get you out of that ivory tower you call a lab more often." Juliane spun around to see Louis leaning casually against the auditorium entrance. As if sensing a predator, Chad immediately dropped back down out of sight, continuing his work.

"Durham's probably relieved to be off escort duty," Juliane replied.

"The last I saw him, he was happy enough with the assignment, and I can see why."

Juliane stifled a laugh. Within moments, his long strides had brought him nearly an arm's length from her.

Louis changed the subject. "Durham also tells me you beat him at chess. I should have warned you against that. Now he is going to be gunning for a rematch every time he sees you." Louis rolled his eyes. "He can be a little like a dog playing fetch that way."

He chuckled at his joke before becoming more serious. "I should have warned you about that. Now that you've demonstrated that you have some skill, if you ever do lose to him, you are going to hear about it until the end of time. Trust me, I know from personal experience."

Laughter entered back into Louis's voice. "I swear he is going to make sure that people thousands of years from now know that he once won a game."

A venue representative ran up beside Louis with a clipboard in hand. "Mr. Evans, sir, I believe we have everything set up as requested. Video and sound checks were great. Guests should begin filing in within the next twenty minutes. Do you want to be in here when that starts or be announced?"

"Yes, I think it might be better to make an entrance. I'll stand over there and will come on stage after the introductions."

Juliane looked at Louis and the man, her brows knit in confusion. "What do you mean? I thought I was giving the presentation?"

The man looked nervously from side to side, avoiding eye contact with her. Juliane waited for Louis to respond, while a terrible but oh-too-familiar feeling began to grow in the pit of her stomach.

"I know that this is your project and, therefore, your baby," Louis answered. "Nobody in this world would be able to tell the world about its inner workings better than you, but that's just it, you know too much about its inner workings. You said it yourself. We have to convince the masses that their need for this technology outweighs the risk. We want to sell people on its potential. We want them to dream."

Louis paused as if waiting for Juliane to come around to his way of thinking. She kept her silence.

"If we tell them exactly what it can do, they are going to focus on what it can't." He finished as if it were the most obvious logic in the world.

"But what about the script I submitted?" Juliane asked.

"Yes, thank you for those talking points. They were extremely helpful. Have I mentioned that you look positively amazing? The media is going to have a field day trying to figure out who the gorgeous woman is beside me."

He gestured toward the crowd. "Trust me, by keeping an air of mystery about you beyond the initial introduction, you are going to have journalists practically selling out their own mothers to get your name and your entire backstory out into the news sphere first. Why pay for marketing when they'll do it for you?"

"And why should I trust you?" Juliane exclaimed. "You were planning this for some time, but didn't bother to tell me."

"You should trust me because my family has been doing this sort of thing successfully since before you were born." Gone was his friendly demeanor and in its place was all business. She was reminded that the subject of her anger, was also her boss.

Juliane's shoulders slumped. She had no argument that would change his mind. She was going to have to suffer through being a prop once again. Alan would no doubt make a point to stop by and gloat the minute they were back in the labs.

Juliane glanced over to the coordinator by Louis's side. The man studied his clipboard as if it contained the secret formula for eradicating cancer in all its forms.

She noticed he also had a few programs of the day's events clutched under his arm. She snatched one quickly, adding a glare that dared him to object her rude behavior. She scanned the page until she found her event. Printed on the page in black and white was Louis's name beside her topic.

Louis's tone softened. "I am sorry you misunderstood my expectations for today. The management group or someone from our public relations department always takes the lead on the topics that we feel have the greatest chance of success. Considering how many people fear public speaking, most people we work with thank us for doing this. I just assumed you knew about the standard arrangement."

Juliane's lips had tightened into a fine line. "I guess I missed that fine print. If that is the case, then would it be fair for me to assume that someone has at least briefed you on the latest benefits of the new algorithm? "

Juliane's barb landed as she knew it would. As the deadline had approached, her progress reports had only covered the barest details. She hadn't felt the need to include everything at the expense of her program. Back when she thought she was going to be presenting, she didn't think the lack of complete documentation would matter.

Louis had the decency to allow the fairest hint of blush to pass over his face. "The last report on your progress was a couple of weeks ago. I was planning on just presenting based on that lovely demonstration you provided when we met, just on a larger scale. What should I know?"

"You wanted something that dazzled. Think of this as virtual reality meets one of those ancestry websites meets documentary."

Juliane could tell that he failed to see the connection. "Ah, well, I guess the show has to go on. I'm better winging it on the fly anyway."

The nervous little man coughed. "Well, if everything has been worked out, it's probably time for you both to take your places."

Sparing Louis one more glare, Juliane whirled around and marched toward the stage, each step sharply punctuated by the click of her heel. At least her time with Alan had given her plenty of experience standing around in someone else's spotlight.

As she passed, Chad gave her a quick sympathetic nod. She hoped for his sake that he had merely seen the program at some point while she was away at the spa rather than knowing about it in advance and not informing her.

The lights began to dim as visitors filed into the room. Each was given a pair of slim glasses as they entered. Louis had disappeared into the shadows. Juliane saw Alan pass by the auditorium doors on the way to his room and plastered a killer smile on her face. She tried to at least take some measure of satisfaction in the knowledge that every person who entered was one less person attending his presentation.

Eventually, the room reached its capacity. The nervous little man with the clipboard made a few welcoming remarks as other staff in the back closed the heavy doors. She flicked her wrist ever so slightly, signaling Chad to begin the show.

Remaining lights abruptly switched off, sending the room into absolute darkness. Juliane listened as a few of the guests shifted nervously. The pillars' lights began to pulsate. The ceilings were replaced with the impression of a starry night.

This, in time, was replaced with the dawn of a sunrise as the display panels came on-line.

The walls became a panoramic view of a seashore. On the horizon was a tall wooden ship. A smaller rowboat was slowly coming closer. Then the rowboat hit the shore.

Men and women dressed in garb hundreds of years out of date crawled over the railing, some with joy radiating from their faces, others with trepidation. Juliane heard at least one person in the crowd gasp. The figures were so real, you thought you could reach out and touch flesh. Her skin prickled in response to where it was hit by virtual ocean spray.

The scene changed once again. The ocean transformed into a land worn to dirt and scarred from heavy wagon wheels. A hot dry wind blew, kicking up dust and grit, and filled the nostrils with the smell of horsehair and manure. Juliane could see a few people's brows break out in a sweat as the artificial sun shone down upon them. A group of men rode by, startling several spectators. Once again, Juliane heard gasps, and she let out the breath she didn't know she had been holding.

The sun was replaced by artificial lights. The desert was replaced by the sterile cleanliness of a room very different from the one they were in. Gone was the smell of livestock, replaced with bleach and bad cologne. The room was filled with rows of large CRT monitors, large buttons, and dials. The image on the monitors showed a rocket firing into space. The operators of the monitors were jumping up and down in celebration, showing glimpses of garish plaid polyester pants on some.

Mission control faded away. They were in a city surrounded by traffic-congested streets. A tower of steel and glass blazed like fire as it reflected the orange hue of the sky at sunset. Nearby, a man-made waterfall cascaded down the sides of a square. Even from this distance, several names could be seen etched into its sides.

A crowd of people nearby cheered as a spire was raised on the tower, which happened to be one of the most recognizable structures of all New York. Its existence was both a reminder of the past and a challenge issued to the future. A challenge to always rise and move forward. A challenge to never be beaten by fear of the unknown.

It was a challenge that Juliane accepted long ago. As a man bolted an etched brass plate into position, Juliane heard someone shout, "Where did they get this footage? That's my grandpa!"

She ached to explain that the simulation had been more than just canned footage and approximations. Her system had homed in on a few individuals within the crowd and cross-referenced their identification badges with historical reference information to create figures based on the composition of identifiable genealogy in the room. The gasps from the crowd had been those individuals either recognizing the event itself from their personal histories or a striking family resemblance.

The display panels turned off, and they were all once again in the Las Vegas Convention Center auditorium. Juliane looked into the shadows where Louis stood. He was frozen in place with his jaw hung open.

She had provided a high-level summary of her plans for the introduction along with her script, but it was one thing to read about what would be on display and quite another to experience it. Meeting her eyes, Louis closed his lips and nodded in appreciation.

Louis stepped onto the dais to thunderous applause. The audience was rapt as Louis painted a picture of a bright future utilizing her technology, one where children could attend school from the safety of their own homes and live history lessons; one where international corporations could trim expenses by conducting meetings without travel, but also without sacrificing senses like touch; one where consumers could sample virtual products before buying them, reducing the need for stores to carry excessive inventory.

The crowd ate up his every word as he worked them into a fever pitch. If there were any investors in the room, they had to take satisfaction in watching their wallets expand before their eyes.

Louis paused in mid-stride and smiled at Juliane before turning back to the crowd. "We are now at the dawn of a new age, an age where our history can be brought back to life and one where reality can be what we make of it. I give you . . . the Datasphere. And now, I would like to introduce you to the brains behind this amazing advancement. If you haven't already done so, please take off your glasses and put your hands together for Dr. Juliane Faris."

As the lights gradually returned to full brightness, Juliane noticed a woman near the center of the room wipe away a tear as she removed her glasses. Whether the tear was from joy or sorrow Juliane couldn't tell, but really, it didn't matter. That droplet of moisture proved their system was a success. Anyone could manipulate senses such as sight and sound, but that tear proved the scenes had been real enough to produce an emotional response.

Juliane scanned more faces in the crowd. Toward the back, cloaked in near shadow, was a man with hair nearly as black as hers. He was dressed in a dark, expensive, tailored suit. He met her gaze, inclining his head ever so slightly, before handing his glasses back to the small man with the clipboard and exiting the auditorium.

Ten

Juliane waited while the audience finally filed out of the auditorium. Her high from the presentation's success had already transformed into uncertainty about her next steps.

A trio of individuals, two males, one female, continued to orbit around Louis. They were an odd group. One man was desperately trying to hide a balding hairline in the front but appeared to lack the same concern about his backside. The other man, significantly younger, had coated his hair in enough gel that it could likely stop a bullet. The woman, a young blonde, had a smile fixed on her face that never quite reached her eyes. Juliane had the nagging suspicion that she had seen at least two of these three once before.

She watched Louis gesture toward the pillars with his charismatic grin firmly in place, but the motion was an afterthought. Rather than returning his hands to his side, he twirled a pair of glasses while answering the rest of their questions. As impressive as his speech had been, Louis continued to misunderstand where the power behind the technology was housed.

The trio had closed in around him so tightly that she was unable to hear exactly what their questions were, but they looked like they were lapping up whatever he was dishing. The little man with the clipboard hovered impatiently on the fringe of the room. Most likely he would prefer to move the impromptu question-and-answer session out of the room so that he could begin preparations for its next usage, but he was nervous about interrupting such a powerful personage.

As Juliane watched Chad pack up their computing supplies without waiting for instruction, she realized she almost envied Chad's complete lack of personal ambition. He was content to be a drone. Do as instructed, set up equipment, clean up equipment. Repeat. Her next steps were not as clear, yet whatever she did could impact her reputation.

Should she take charge of the cleanup? It might reinforce that she was the expert, but it might make it look like she couldn't handle delegation. Should she inject herself into Louis's conversation? It might potentially jeopardize his media dynamic. Should she continue to play coy? Chad saw her looking at him, shrugged at her unspoken question, and continued with his task.

Juliane considered leaving the auditorium. She could listen to one of the other presentations, but that might ruin the illusion of mystery she was expected to maintain. *Am I still supposed to be mysterious after Louis's introduction?* she wondered.

She could go back to her room, but that would feel like surrender. She could go in search of something to eat but found she had no appetite. Unsatisfied with any option, Juliane decided to continue to wait in the shadows while Louis basked in the glow of the public's adoration. *I've turned into Chad.*

After agonizing minutes, Louis finally looked her way. She captured his focus and returned his attention with a fierce glare, the type of which frequently caused Chad to remember some errand he had to immediately attend to.

She realized she shouldn't have bothered with the effort. Rather than shivering from its icy point, Louis threw his head back in laughter. She was not able to maintain her ire faced with such genuine humor, and her visage softened. He gestured her quite urgently to come to his side.

"Of course, as I said on the dais, none of what you witnessed today could have been made possible without Dr. Juliane Faris, here. You may want to start lining your interviews up now, as she is destined to go down in the history books as one of the great innovators of our generation."

The trio, who had barely registered her presence, turned toward her like children shown candy. "Unfortunately for you, you aren't going to be able to start with those interviews at this moment." The woman pouted. Juliane recognized her then as Melissa Bryant, a field reporter for the Financial Sector Times Network. *The other two must also be part of the press corps*, thought Juliane, although she was not as familiar with either of them. Louis crooked his elbow expectantly. "M'lady?"

Juliane allowed her lips to turn up while taking his arm like an old-fashioned debutante. Together, they departed the auditorium to the relief of Mr. Clipboard. As she glanced back, Mr. Clipboard put his finger to his ear, likely speaking into a wireless headset, as the convention center's version of a SWAT team descended upon the now-vacant room.

Along the way down the hallway, they passed the room where Alan was giving his presentation. He did still have a fair turnout, but Juliane took a nearly indecent pleasure in the knowledge that his crowd was less than her own. The day might not have gone completely as she would have preferred, but at least she had this small triumph.

As she turned to leave, she noticed the same man with a dark suit and hair she'd seen before. He was near the front of Alan's stage, looking out toward the crowd rather than at Alan, and she could tell he had noticed her watching.

The corners of his mouth pulled back in a wolf's grin. As much as she wanted to continue walking, her legs were rooted to the floor. Louis turned to investigate the cause of the delay, and the moment was shattered.

Louis's expression hardened. The man tipped his head in Juliane's direction before turning his attention back to Alan. Juliane jumped when Louis spoke. "I think today's presentation was a success, don't you?" His tone felt forced. However, as quickly as it came, the cloud over his features passed, and Juliane found herself thinking of an eager puppy dog looking at the expression that took its place.

Her early annoyance melted away too. While she might not have been allowed to shine to her fullest, her algorithm had.

"Durham's probably out there getting himself into some trouble," said Louis. "What say we join him?"

She laughed. She had only spent a few hours with Durham but could guess that Louis's jest wasn't far from the truth. Everything Juliane had done since childhood had been done with precision and had gotten her nowhere.

Durham, on the other hand, struck Juliane as one who lived in the moment. And yet he was able to fly in a private jet and party with the rich and famous. Perhaps Alan had been right. Perhaps she should try letting her hair down too. She always did appreciate an intriguing experiment. She nodded at Louis to lead the way.

Louis's private car met them at the door. Although Juliane couldn't see any of the media represented, Louis continued to play the part of the gentleman, waiting by the door as the driver helped her enter the vehicle first. Once inside, he opened the bar compartment while the car departed toward the Vegas strip. It did not take long before Juliane began to feel the alcohol's effects on her empty stomach.

Traffic was still heavy, resulting in a slow procession down the strip. "Would you care for another?" Louis asked.

Juliane finished hers before they arrived at their destination, Club Dareeque. Rather than entering through the main lobby, Louis escorted her through a nondescript side entrance protected by some very large individuals in the standard uniform of black t-shirt and black pants. They made no effort to block their passage. Once inside, an extremely scantily-clad woman offered them more beverages, which Louis and Juliane both accepted with enthusiasm.

The nightlife was alive inside. As Louis predicted, Durham was its heart. He shook his neck and shoulders, loosening his muscles as he halved the distance between them.

Multicolored lights throbbed in time with the blaring music. Conversation was futile as Durham pulled her onto the dance floor. Beverages continued to flow freely. At some point, she must have removed her jacket, but she couldn't recall where it might be. The silky silver camisole she wore underneath shimmered as she twirled and swayed with Durham.

She stretched her arms briefly back into her hair to cool her neck from its weight. She had never felt so alive. A voice inside her head urged her to slow down, warned her of tomorrow's hangover, but she couldn't force herself to care.

She felt a warm hand on her waist. She spun to identify its owner and was pulled toward Louis's muscled chest. A glance back informed her that Durham had already migrated back into the crowd. She could see he was well occupied by another energetic partner.

Time lost its hold. Juliane lost track of how many drinks she had consumed. Others attempted to cut in, but never with long success. Again, and again, Louis pulled her toward him.

She thought she saw the flash of a cell phone camera, and in her inebriated state, she decided to give them a show. She felt the heat of Louis's leg pressed against her thigh as she grinded her body against his. Her skin glistened as she arched her back suggestively.

Her heartbeat pulsed in time with the music. A man—she assumed it was Durham, but her vision had begun to blur—
appeared by her side. She closed her eyes, giving herself fully to the moment. A hand pulled at her arm. She wasn't surprised that Durham wanted to cut in, but she was surprised by how violently she was pulled to the side.

She opened her eyes at the feeling of pain. The hand didn't belong to either Louis or Durham. Instead, Alan had materialized out of nowhere. He grimaced as he pulled her away from the dance floor and into a quieter alcove before unceremoniously shoving her down onto the leather bench.

A glass of water appeared before her. She hadn't even noticed Alan ordering it. It must have taken longer to stumble over to the alcove than she had originally thought. Away from the music, her head began to throb as she tried to estimate how much time had passed since her presentation. *Who'd invited Alan?* Juliane wondered. "Why, Alan, to what do I owe this unexpected pleasure?" she slurred.

"Were you aware that your antics are being broadcast on every gossip rag as we speak?" Alan scowled.

"I thought that what happens in Vegas stays in Vegas?" Juliane chortled at her own joke.

"Apparently when you throw yourself on one of the world's most powerful playboys, people break that little rule."

"I wasn't throwing myself at him; he's the one who keeps coming back to me. Besides, we're just out having some fun. Something, it appears, you need to do more often as well."

"Jules, stop acting like one of these children." Alan gestured toward a small group of females in tight-fitting clothing hovering near the edge of the dance floor. One of the group wore a tiara and sash but very little else.

None of them looked old enough to be making life-changing decisions like marriage, ruling out a bachelorette party, but they were obviously celebrating a major milestone. Juliane suspected it was the woman's twenty-first birthday.

Alan had no right to compare her behavior to theirs. At least half of that party wouldn't have any recollection of tonight's festivities tomorrow. She would remember this evening until her dying day. At least she thought she would. *Where did that jacket go?* she wondered. The room began to spin.

Juliane was distracted by another group, this one comprised of young but significantly more sober males. They also watched the women but were doing so like hyenas lying in wait to take advantage of a weakened gazelle.

One of the men swaggered over to the women with a drink in hand. Within moments, the woman with the sash followed him onto the dance floor. He wasted no time. Juliane could see his hand descend around her buttocks within the first few beats of the song. After losing sight of the couple in the crowd, Juliane returned her attention to the glass of water in her hand. She stared into its depths.

No, her behavior had been nothing like that at all. She had been dancing with Louis and Durham. It wasn't as if she had been letting random strangers grope her.

Juliane savored the feeling of water coursing down her throat. It was not the tap water she was more used to. The liquid tasted delicious on her tongue after the workout she had given her body.

Alan's tone softened. Juliane wondered if he had interpreted her action as a gesture of shame and not just parched thirst. "You are better than that. We are better than that. You and I, we are cut from the same cloth. I understand that it isn't easy for a person like you to work for someone like me. Always in the other's shadow. Always coming up second. But I've always been impressed with you."

If Alan expected a response, Juliane made sure he was left disappointed. He continued, "I wasn't surprised to hear your presentation was a smashing success. I would have demanded nothing else from you. However, I am disappointed that you didn't stick around long enough to allow me to take you out for a celebration. Had you just asked, I would have been more than willing to show you the town. Hasn't anyone ever told you that great things come to those who wait?"

"The music is pretty loud in here, but did you just really say that you would have taken me out if I was only more patient?"

"I did." Alan smiled, resting his hand on her shoulder. "I still would. You have such great potential. In all ways. You just need to learn how to wait."

"And what makes you think I would want to go out with you?"

"Please, Jules. Consider your available options. Sure, he is rich and powerful . . . now. But that womanizer is only going to hurt you. You would be just another plaything. To be used and discarded after you bore him. And you would bore him, assuming he didn't bore you first." Juliane felt her eyebrow rise at the comment. "He wouldn't be able to understand a fraction of what you say, and men like him can't handle feelings of inadequacy. You would be wasting your time with someone like that."

Juliane plucked Alan's hand off her shoulder. "You don't know half as much as you think you do."

Alan sighed. "But I do. People like you and I are extremely rare. You have barely seen the world, but eventually, you will realize that for yourself. You don't have to accept my company today. But believe me when I tell you that spending a night alone in your room would be a better use of your time than what you are doing here."

"Not that I need to justify who I want to spend time with to you, but Louis is not the vapid, spoiled rich guy you think he is, and I am not a child. We were just dancing, but if I wanted to take it further, I could. And again, stop calling me Jules!"

Her attempt at a dramatic exit was ruined when her foot began to slip out from under her as she rose. She felt a searing pain as her ankle twisted in her attempt to remain upright. Alan caught her before she could fall. She fought to push him away even as she attempted to stabilize herself, but he was relentless. "Let me take you back to your hotel. You've had enough."

"I don't need your help!"

"Please, you wouldn't be able to make it to the door on your own."

"I'm not ready to leave anyway. And even if I was, I certainly am not leaving with you." She attempted to hold him back and was surprised to feel iron muscles hidden behind his shirt.

"You are being ridiculous, Jules." Alan pulled her toward him.

"Jules, is it? I did wonder what your nickname might be." Juliane stopped her struggles at the sound of Louis's voice behind Alan. She attempted to draw herself up straight but found she couldn't quite put all her weight on the injured ankle without wincing.

"Ah, Louis, your timing is perfect. Some people just don't know how to respond to rejection." Juliane smirked. Louis appeared immune to the expression of pure hatred that danced across Alan's face.

"Fine, learn your lesson the hard way. Be my guest. Enjoy your time with the common people. You know where to find me when you realize I was only speaking the truth," Alan spat the words as he threw her at Louis, only then storming off toward the club exit.

"Well, I have to say, that is the first time I've ever been referred to as being part of the common people." Louis shrugged, his smile, as usual, in place. "I thought that when you suddenly stopped dancing that you were just in need of some air, but Durham mentioned seeing you leave with 'some guy.' Might I be correct in guessing that it wasn't entirely by choice?" Juliane nodded. "You want to get back to the party?"

Juliane took a step and sucked in her breath as a sharp pain raced up her leg. "Unfortunately, Alan may be half right. I have to call it a night. I must have hurt my ankle more than I originally thought."

Louis knelt beside her, caressing her leg more than was strictly necessary as he examined her injury. She felt her body shiver. She leaned over to inspect her injury herself, using his broad shoulders as support. The skin had begun to develop a purple sheen.

"That is a nasty mark. You've probably sprained it. You need to stay off your feet and keep that ankle elevated." His touch to the damaged flesh was a feather-light touch, but it still caused her to hiss. Within a moment, Louis had scooped her up as if she were the child she so recently protested not being. Only now, she found herself wrapping her arms around his neck.

Juliane stared into his eyes. Alan's parting words played in her ears. There was nothing common about this man. Suddenly she wanted to do something more in her hotel room than ice her ankle. She found herself murmuring, "On second thought, I'm not ready to call it a night after all. I can think of something that can keep my ankle very, very elevated." She trailed her fingers down the side of his neck, making her intention clear.

Louis raised an eyebrow, but the hunger in his eyes mirrored her own as they exited the club. Her vision went black as her eyes adjusted to the bright lights and colors of the Vegas strip. The loss of sight accentuated the crush of his lips on hers as the door closed and the car pulled away.

Eleven

T he following morning, Juliane stepped out of the bedroom with bleary eyes and a pounding headache. She'd made a mistake. A huge, colossal, career-ending mistake. She'd slept with her boss. *What was I thinking?*

Had she acted the way she did last night only to antagonize Alan, or was it possible that there might be something more between her and Louis? *Our bodies certainly connected*, thought Juliane with a satisfied grin as she exited the bedroom and stumbled over her suitcase.

"Oh, good, you're up," said Louis.

Juliane blushed. "About last night—"

"That was amazing. I asked Durham to take care of your other arrangements," Louis mumbled from behind her. "I'd like you to stay with me for the rest of the weekend." Juliane was troubled that someone had been able to enter the room without notice, but then Louis's hand had begun stroking her thigh and she forgot all about Durham or the thousands of reasons going back into the bedroom was a horrible decision.

After that, she and Louis rarely left his spacious suite; a series of rooms complete with its own bar, kitchenette, and entertainment area. The hours passed in a lust- and endorphin-filled blur.

Feeling adventurous the second afternoon, Juliane decided to try sunbathing in the nude next to the room's private pool. Skin unfamiliar with the effects of sunlight was teased alive by his ministrations. Louis had brought out various exotic fruits and chilled wine which they had sampled together, only to then sample each other once again.

She didn't recognize herself around Louis. It was as if his very proximity silenced rational thought. No one had ever affected her in such a way. She wondered if she could ever go back to the way she was before. Basking in a contented afterglow with Louis sleeping by her side, she allowed herself to wonder, *why would I ever need to?*

Durham arrived on the third morning to take her back to the airport. As she opened the door, Juliane noticed that Durham's eyes were covered by a pair of mirrored sunglasses which he never removed. *He can't still be that hung-over.* She could see Louis approach in their reflection.

Louis's arms encircled her waist as her body melted into his embrace automatically. Louis gently pulled her hair back, caressing her neck with his lips. Juliane wanted nothing more than to spin around and return to their room. She closed her eyes to better enjoy the sensation.

Durham coughed, reminding her that they had an audience. Louis chuckled as he handed a few bills to the bellhop waiting behind Durham. Within the hour, she and Durham were back in the air, and Juliane found herself wondering if the events of the last few days had truly happened.

Shortly after takeoff, Durham had placed a travel pillow around his neck and leaned back in his chair without pressing for a rematch of their chess game. After Louis's warning, Juliane assumed it was probably for the best, but found herself disappointed all the same.

Left to entertain herself, her thoughts returned to the deliciously naughty things she and Louis had done to each other. Could it have been only a few days?

At the airport, Durham lingered only long enough to help load her belongings into her car and sneer at her choice of transport, a fifteen-year-old Tesla purchased for its ability to get from point A to B reliably.

She had barely noticed its dings and rust spots before, but each imperfection must have tripled in size during her stay in Vegas. She thought to herself that its like would never be seen in Louis's collection. Even if he kept a beater vehicle, it surely had to be in better condition.

Though the hour was late, Juliane decided to stop by her office. After spending the past few days with Louis, the idea of going to her empty apartment just felt too isolating. As she walked down the hall, Alan met her at the door. "What? Mr. Wonderful too busy to make sure you got home safely?"

Juliane rolled her eyes. "He has to continue the promotional tour. Surely someone as smart as yourself can comprehend that?"

Alan leaned against the door frame and said, "How convenient for him. Speaking of convenience, did you happen to stop by any of the campus stores on your way here?"

Scattered among the various ACI buildings were several independently owned and operated convenience stores placed to ensure that ACI employees had few reasons to leave the campus. All should have been closed for the evening hours ago. Puzzled, Juliane replied, "No . . ."

"And, I take it, you haven't been home yet either?" Alan asked with a smug smile.

"I came straight here." Alan's smile deepened. "But you probably already knew that. Why don't you go ahead and tell me whatever it is you came here to say? Obviously, you want to."

"Go online. I'm sure you'll find it soon enough."

Hating herself, Juliane pulled out her phone to check the news feed. On the screen were a series of stories, many of which alluded to the presentation. "Looks like my emulator made the front page. Funny, I don't see your presentation anywhere here. That must be terrible for you. I know how hard you must have worked."

"Oh yes, terrible. Why don't you read the article rather than just scan through the headlines?" Alan might as well have screamed 'I told you so.' The words were clearly written across his features.

Juliane clicked on a link at random. It mentioned the presentation in passing, but the heart of the article centered on speculation of Louis's relationship with a mystery woman. There were a series of photos of the two of them engaged in several suggestive positions. The photos had been taken while they were enjoying themselves in the suite, not just in the dance club. Juliane felt the blood drain from her face. "How? Why?" she whispered in horror.

"I suspect they used a drone just like anyone else. I did try to warn you. You should have listened to me."

Juliane opened another article link. More photos appeared, each worse than the one before. Exactly how many drones had been hovering outside? How could she have possibly been so unaware of her surroundings?

Alan reached out and touched her arm, his smile slipping. "You can't possibly be surprised, Jules. I mean, really? How many times have the media done this to other women in your position? I'm only disappointed that you made it so easy for them. Hotels have drapes for a reason."

She had enough of his smug attitude, even if there was truth in his barb. She would no longer allow him to treat her as his subordinate. They were equals, and it was past time he recognized it. Ice crystals began to permeate her bloodstream as her humiliation was replaced by anger.

Alan took an unconscious step backward into the hallway. She had to take a calming breath before she could trust herself to speak again. Even then, her voice was hard as blue steel and sharp as a blade.

"What I do outside of these walls is my own business. I thought I had made that clear to you before." Juliane's voice took on a dangerous edge, an edge so fine it could cut a diamond.

Alan swiped a hand through his hair, and then back down along the length of his face. "I've been going about this all wrong with you. Jul—I mean, Juliane, you don't understand. I don't think less of you for having a little fun. I just think you can do so much better in your choice of company. You have to admit that you and I, on that last project, made a great team. Together, there would be no one to challenge us."

He clasped his hands around hers. "We wouldn't have to resort to such petty tactics to get noticed, forced to bow down to the powers that be for handouts. Always working under the threat that grant funding is going to dry up before a project is realized. You and I don't need people like Louis Evans."

Alan gestured at Juliane's phone, to images of Louis pushing reporters to the side while casually saying no comment. "He might like to think of himself as a dragon, considering that silly crew team flag he displays everywhere, but people like him are worms. Good for helping fertilize a garden but not much else. People whose only contribution to the world is their family name on a building. We are better than that. You are better than that."

The ice in her veins thawed to a trickle at his words, replaced by pity. She had thought the same things about Louis before she had gotten to know him better— before she had seen that eternal smile, listened to his carefree laugh or wrapped her body alongside his finely defined bulk. Her body began to hum at that last thought so completely she wondered if it might be audible.

"Alan, no, it's you who doesn't understand. I didn't spend the rest of the time in Vegas with him just because of his money or his connections. I did it because I respect him and he respects me, something that you have never demonstrated."

Alan pulled his head back as if he had been slapped. "I've always respected you. Why do you think I asked you to join my team? It's because I respected you that I couldn't make it easy for you."

He slammed a fist into an open palm. "I could have gotten half a dozen girls from one of the lesser departments to stand there and look pretty on a stage if that was all I wanted. Someone just bright enough to keep her mouth shut when she didn't know the answer so as not to embarrass me. But I needed someone with the potential to equal me one day. Only a person like that could challenge me."

"Someone with the potential to equal you . . . one day? Alan, I believe I passed that point quite some time ago." The faint lines on Alan's forehead began to knit. "I can see you are confused. Louis acted as my spokesperson. He may have done most of the talking, but it was my invention. I understand why you don't see it. I didn't recognize what he was doing at first either, but I wasn't the prop this time, he was."

She shook her head. "I'm sorry you didn't get the chance to witness him live in action. He was glorious in the role. He has an air about him, a raw energy you just want to connect with. With his talent and my drive, we could reshape the world."

As the words gushed out of Juliane's mouth, she realized that she meant every word. She suddenly couldn't wait to get back to the privacy of her apartment. She would call up Louis and describe in detail all the wonderfully wicked things she would like to do the next time he visited. So lightheaded in her testimonial, she hardly noticed as Alan's face darkened. "Jul—Juliane, I would be surprised if he saw your relationship quite the same way. He is using you."

"We're using each other."

"You aren't thinking with your brain."

The conversation had gone on entirely too long. She didn't want to hurt him, but he wasn't giving her another choice. "If you had just had the past few days I had, you wouldn't be either."

Alan's shoulders dropped—defeated.

The images that came to mind as she thought back on her time with Louis softened her edge. "I'm sorry. That was cruel. But you and I are never going to have anything other than a professional relationship. He loves me, Alan."

Louis hadn't said the words, precisely, but Juliane thought it best to leave no doubt that she was unavailable. It might not be an exaggeration on her part either. While neither had verbalized their feelings outside of passionate pillow-talk, She and Louis had established a connection that was hard to describe as anything else.

"We're just waiting for the right time to let the rest of the world know." This last part, was true, in that they had agreed it would be best for both of their sakes if they kept their relationship under wraps a while longer. Louis was still establishing himself as the new head of the ACI and while Juliane had made a splash at the Vegas conference, neither of them wanted anyone to think she hadn't earned the right to be on that stage based on what she did outside of the lab.

Alan straightened abruptly. "Don't apologize. I know that sometimes it's better to destroy and rebuild rather than try to salvage something. But you misread my intentions. My interest is purely professional. Alan waved his hands in the air, gesturing at the Internet news still streaming in compromising images. "If you want to pursue this distraction then, as you say, that's your business. I just don't want you losing your focus. Especially not now."

Alan pulled out a slip of paper showing an Internet link. "Your little stunt may have made the front pages here, but there is still real news happening in the world."

Juliane typed in the link on her phone. Her eyebrows rose as she started to scroll down the opening paragraphs. Her anger evaporated as quickly as it had arrived. "Is this saying what I think it is saying?"

"Indeed." Alan once again spoke with the calm authority and confidence that she once had so admired. "Obviously, these so-called journalists aren't half the subject matter experts they think they are. They see this as a more efficient means of altering biochemical bonds, but I thought you would see the bigger implication, and you just proved me right.

He nodded to himself. "With your algorithms at our disposal and my subatomic experience, we can create a device that can manipulate particles as tiny as the Higgs Boson on command. The competition wouldn't stand a chance! We could do this. Together. This is why I came here. I need you on my team, and I need you now."

Juliane thought about Alan's offer for a minute. The article had snapped her out of lust-filled thoughts, and she once again was in a position to weigh the pros and cons. Even so, Juliane knew her decision had been made the moment Alan made his offer. She would take it, even if it meant working with him again. "Fine. But only if you admit we're equals now. Oh, and I get to pick members of the support staff."

Alan released a breath. "Done. I've already started soliciting resumes. I will send their files to your office in the morning."

twelve

It had been several weeks since she had accepted Alan's offer, and they were still no closer to identifying a suitable candidate to complete their team. Each day Juliane would find another printed stack of resumes on her desk to review. A matching stack would appear on Alan's desk.

Out of an unspoken agreement, she and Alan interacted at a bare minimum beyond swapping notes. The few times they did speak, Alan seemed humbler and more considerate, but there had been little consensus between the two of them.

A year ago, Alan would not have had the patience to keep his promise and would have hired the candidates from his list regardless of her wishes. In truth, she was a little surprised that he had stayed true to his word for this long. The lack of forward progress had to be chafing on him.

It was chafing her as well. As much as she enjoyed irritating Alan, each day they didn't have their full team gave the competition a chance to reach proof of the concept first.

She and Alan couldn't be the only ones who had seen the report on altering biochemical bonds and realized the scientific advance's greatest potential. Time was running out and they were running out of the option to be choosy.

Louis had been away nearly all of this time. Juliane told herself that was a good thing. She was troubled by how often her intellect left her whenever he was around. However, as much as she knew she shouldn't want distractions right now, she ached for him all the same.

Louis, on the other hand, seemed much more capable of separating business from pleasure. *It's so unfair*, she thought. She fought the urge to dial his number. She reminded herself that he was a newly appointed CEO trying to launch new technology. *Her technology*. If they were going to replace the Internet with the Datasphere one day, he needed to work the media circuit.

His work didn't stop with publicity tours either. He needed to conduct factory audits and negotiate commercial dealings not just for the datasphere access points, but for other technology being developed by the ACI in parallel.

Juliane still hoped that one day she would be able to integrate her algorithm into the biologic network she'd worked on with Alan, which he had dubbed Project Gene Assist. This would eliminate the need for bulkier equipment, but that was still months if not years in the future. The ACI would expect an income stream long before then.

The ACI, on the other hand, didn't mind requiring datasphere users to purchase a headset nearly as much as she did. As a result, approvals for continued investigation into the biologic network had been placed on the ACI's back burner. In its place, several teams focused on developing better, slimmer, and most importantly, more profitable network access gadgets.

Unfortunately. those product development teams needed her insights on a daily, if not hourly basis. The stack of resumes on Juliane's desk were forced to wait as the ACI prioritized its short-term gains.

It also didn't help that Louis had spoken truly regarding the media's reaction to their work and their relationship. She was forced to change her phone number twice before removing it altogether from public records.

Changing her number proved to be the only way to get a minute's work done in between meetings with the product development teams and interview requests. Even the building's hidden entrance was only a moderate obstacle.

She had arrived one morning to find the hallway outside of her office polluted by roving gossip reporters. Juliane had told herself that she would be featured on all the major networks one day; she had just hoped it would be for her work rather than her relationship. Shortly after that morning, she had been moved into a new location offering more privacy.

Determined to prevent a similar occurrence, and to further protect her identity as well as the sensitive nature of her work, she demanded that a fake name be used on the hallway nameplate and directory.

Her day-to-day contacts within the ACI had moaned about accommodating each of these requests, but she didn't hear any complaints about the additional publicity her notoriety had brought to the organization. If anything, she was convinced that they were partially responsible for at least a few tips-offs to the media about where to find her.

Then, just as the frenzy began to die down, Louis would materialize somewhere close to the campus, launching another flurry. The media seemed to know when he was nearby even sooner than she did.

She had told Louis exactly how little she appreciated the interruption these unplanned visits caused to her routine, but if anything, he had made an even greater point of appearing in the most unexpected places. It was almost as if he enjoyed throwing her off balance.

Most unprofessional thoughts about Louis's preferred strategy for working his way back on to her good side filled her thoughts as she arrived at her office. Although she hadn't turned the key, the door swung open without effort. Juliane frowned. She could have sworn that she had secured her office the night before.

She worried for a fleeting moment someone might have stolen sensitive documents. Then she saw him. Louis was comfortably sprawled in her desk chair as if her chair was located in his home rather than her office. His feet rested on top of the stack of applications, and Juliane felt her pulse quicken as she took in the sight.

She tried to maintain an expression of annoyance. This was her place of business. It was her sanctuary. How dare he let himself in like he owned the place? *Okay*, she conceded, *perhaps he did own it, but really?* How hard would it have been to call her first? Louis, as usual, seemed impervious to her displeasure. He stretched even further in the chair as she shut the office door, calling to mind images of other calisthenics they had enjoyed together. Her unruly body tingled with anticipated pleasure.

He wore a well-broken-in pair of jeans as well as a wrinkled button-down shirt. His collar was open at the top, providing a tantalizing hint at the muscular chest beneath.

His chin, darkened with stubble from a missed shave, was a far cry from the tailored man she had first met. Louis must have come directly from his jet to her office.

A sense of smug satisfaction warmed Juliane. "One of these days you should tell me how you manage to sneak in here so easily. Or, let me guess, the company has recently appropriated a teleportation machine." She laughed as she bent over to store her purse in the modest credenza at the back of the room.

"I have access to more technology than you'd ever believe, but appropriate? That hurts. You make it sound like I just go gallivanting around the world stealing other people's ideas," Louis said.

She felt his eyes on her backside as she stood. She was pleased with the knowledge he was also affected by her presence. When she turned, she found Louis standing at full attention behind her.

He placed one hand on her waist and twirled her around the rest of the way until she faced him. His height forced her to stand on her toes to kiss him. However, she kept it chaste. She wouldn't make this too easy on him. He had broken into her office, after all.

Louis growled, "Speaking of travel, I've just crossed the world three times. Is that really how you are going to greet me?" He pulled her closer.

Juliane pushed away from his embrace in mock indignation. "It is if you're going to keep showing up with that stubble. My skin is delicate. Scratches would show on my face for the rest of the day."

"I guess I'll just have to find some spot to kiss you that isn't quite so noticeable." Juliane's senses squealed with excitement as Louis scooped her up and swung her onto the top of the desk. The stack of applications launched into the air like feathers released during a pillow fight.

Juliane gave up any appearance of displeasure. She wrapped her legs around Louis, her skirt hitching up and showing an indecent amount of thigh in the process. She felt like a wanton hussy and didn't care. She dropped her hands back to support herself as she closed her eyes, abandoning all senses but the feel of his lips and his hands on her skin as they laid claim to all of her curves.

"Juliane, I don't believe this is what the ACI signed for when they approved your request for an office space with additional privacy."

Juliane's eyes snapped open. It took a moment for her vision to clear, but when it did, her gaze fixed on Alan standing in the doorway. She had been so lost in the glorious sensation that she hadn't heard the door opening.

Louis returned to an upright position but did so without urgency, making no effort to straighten either of their clothes. There was no hint of blush on his cheeks, and he left his shirt unbuttoned.

Juliane struggled to emulate his cool demeanor while attempting to stand back up, pull her skirt back down into position, and straighten her blouse. She accomplished none of these things with grace. Her legs felt like rubber, and she swayed while regaining her balance.

"Louis was just stopping by for an update on headset designs," she announced, mentally kicking herself. *You are pathetic*, she thought to herself. It didn't take a genius to see that what they were in the process of doing was anything resembling a progress report. She would have been better off owning the situation and daring Alan to judge her.

Louis's proximity had once again resulted in a surge of hormones at the expense of logic. Perhaps men were not the only victims of blood loss within the brain while aroused.

She caught sight of a wall calendar near Alan. As much as her libido was frustrated, it was a good thing that Louis's business schedule would keep him occupied for the next several weeks; otherwise, she might be as much of a contributing member on the team as Chad had been on the last one.

Alan snorted. "Oh, this is a business meeting then?" He gestured at the papers littering the ground. "Remind me some time to check out your minutes. They are bound to be . . . informative."

Juliane glared at Alan but remained speechless, not trusting her ability to respond with a witty comeback in the present circumstances.

Alan continued, "In any event, I need you to disentangle yourself from your present *conference* for a few minutes. We have some urgent business of our own to discuss."

Juliane looked toward Louis. He answered by shrugging before walking back over to her desk chair, rolling it back into the corner and making himself comfortable once again. "Don't mind me. I'll just wait over here."

Alan scowled. "This doesn't concern you, Mr. Evans," he said, emphasizing the mister as if it was the lowest of insults.

"I believe that the only business you and Dr. Faris have together is your work with the ACI, which makes it very much my concern. Or is there something more to your relationship you haven't shared?" Louis's jovial expression had never left his face, but his eyes grew cold and steely.

Juliane met Alan's gaze when it swung back her way with a smug smile. *What woman wouldn't feel appreciated by the occasional flare of jealousy?* she thought to herself, yearning to resume their 'business meeting.' It had been too long since she had last seen him, and it would be too long again before she would enjoy another of his visits. Her body had no interest in sending him away now.

Alan's nostrils flared. The clash of wills in the room was nearly tangible. Outnumbered and outranked, Alan would have no choice but to concede defeat.

"Fine." Alan walked over to her desk, making no effort to avoid the stray papers on the ground. "I had come here this morning to discuss the progress, or lack thereof, that we've made in our team's selection. I shouldn't have to remind you that while you've been otherwise . . . distracted, we've fallen further behind." He glared daggers at Louis. Louis raised an eyebrow but did not contest the statement.

"I know that I promised that you would have a say in the creation of the team, but I can't continue to wait for you to become bored with the little games you are playing. You can bring Chad on if you want. He understands your style, but I've made the remaining selection. She's already been notified." He slapped a folder onto Juliane's desk.

Opening the folder and scanning its contents, Juliane looked for a reason to reject the applicant and found none. She had to admit that had she been given time to research the candidate on her own, she would have recommended her selection as well. It struck her that there were many similarities between the applicant's academic and professional trajectory and her own, albeit via a different course of study.

She glanced down at the paperwork strewn about the room and saw its copy lying among the others. It had partially slipped under the desk. If she hadn't been looking for it, she most likely would not have seen it for days. As much as she hated to admit that Alan was right, she had lost her focus.

She looked back at Louis. His body continued to call to her for attention. He leaned back in the chair, rocking it slightly, the movement causing his hips to thrust ever so slowly. She felt her pulse quicken again and fought her most basic urges.

She closed her eyes, preventing Louis's body from discouraging logical thought. "I look forward to meeting her."

When she opened her eyes, she had halfway expected Alan to gloat over his victory. Instead, he nodded. "Excellent. Now that this matter is settled, allow me to get to the point of my visit this morning. We are going to need an edge to make up for time lost if we are going to remain relevant. I've decided to move forward with trials. Would you like to join me?"

Louis spoke up from the back of the room. His voice, the low rumble of a tiger, equal parts purr and threat, tempted her once again to shove Alan out of the office. "Trials? For what exactly?"

Juliane snapped back to full attention, mentally berating herself from allowing her mind to wander once again.

"The human variety. You might recall the little project that Dr. Faris and I were working on ahead of your . . . eh . . . more active involvement. Well, I haven't been twiddling my thumbs here and can tell you with absolute certainty, the process is no longer theoretical."

Juliane nearly broke the sound barrier as she twisted back toward Alan, his words registering in her brain. "You've achieved live imprinting?"

"I believe that is what I just said. You weren't the only one with a side project. While you've been otherwise occupied, I secured approval to conduct small animal trials. Of course, they were a resounding success."

"Why didn't I hear about this?" asked Louis.

"The study was so far along and the risk so small, I am not surprised your signature wasn't required." His cheek twitched. "However, the study results have been sent to legal for review, if you feel the need to second guess the process."

Alan turned his attention back to Juliane. "Juliane, I am confident the process works and would like you to be a part of proving it once and for all. As one of the first subjects. Think about it. This is our opportunity to evolve!"

Juliane hesitated, not sure how to respond. Alan was suggesting moving to human trials before the ink dried on the patent filings. Without those patents, the ACI would not authorize the publication of the study's results. There would be no chance for peer review. Could Alan have really gotten the necessary approvals to move forward? Even if he had, who would they find willing to participate in the study under those conditions?

"Won't you join me?"

Juliane's eyes widened as she realized what Alan wasn't saying. He was moving forward with Project Gene Assist, with or without her. Alan's smile deepened, but there was nothing soft about his expression. The paperwork in her hand sent another clear message. If she missed this opportunity, it would not come again, nor would future collaborations. Alan wasn't just looking for a person to fill out their immediate team, he was actively searching for her replacement.

If the process worked, she would be forever changed, but all the combined knowledge of the world would be open to her. She would be able to access any server anywhere with just a thought. She had no doubt it would work. To be among the first was the opportunity of a lifetime. The process wouldn't just give their team an edge on this particular project; it would blow rival companies out of the water.

Louis came over to her side, placing a hand possessively on her waist. "Well, I'm game. Lead the way."

Thirteen

When they arrived in Alan's lab, a young woman was already seated at the desk. "Ah, good. I do so appreciate it when people arrive on time," Alan quipped. "Dr. Faris, I would like to introduce you to Dr. Elizabeth Omondt."

The woman rose and extended her hand in greeting. "It is so nice to meet you, at least formally. You saved my behind that day with Dr. Than."

If she hadn't been the only other person in the room, Juliane might never have noticed her. Her features were only striking in their averageness, and it was as if the woman wanted to blend into the crowd.

She wore her brown hair in a braid that stretched down just beneath her shoulders—a hairdo that did nothing to soften her sharp beak-like nose. Her clothes hung over her frame like a bag, and her brown eyes were hidden behind a pair of oversized glasses.

She could not have looked more like the stereotypical researcher had she tried. *Who still wears glasses?* Juliane thought. She fidgeted as if aware of the nature of Juliane's scrutiny.

"Umm, maybe you don't remember me. I was trying out contacts that day, and well, let's just say they aren't for me, but the leg is all healed. Oh, and I have my doctorate now." She bit her lip. "Of course, I have my doctorate. I wouldn't be here if didn't have it."

Juliane took the offered hand and shook it, hoping the other doctor hadn't picked up on her initial reaction to her physical appearance. The woman's shoulders slumped in relief.

"Anyway, I know that you and Dr. Dronigh must have been buried under applications. I can't tell you how excited I am to be able to join this team. Getting to work with you both at the same time is truly an honor. Please, call me Betty."

"And you can call me Alan," he practically purred out the phrase.

Juliane did a double-take; it almost sounded like he was attracted to the woman. Betty's cheeks reddened as she pulled off the glasses. Juliane had to admit, the blush was a charming effect with her complexion. Perhaps she had misjudged Alan's earlier intentions after all.

"I took the liberty of calibrating the equipment. The system is warmed up, and we can proceed whenever you are ready."

"Well, Jul—Juliane, which is it to be? Age before beauty or ladies first?" Alan bowed while gesturing to a nearby gurney.

"I'll go first," Louis spoke up before Juliane had a chance to respond. Betty seemed to jump a foot off the ground.

She wasn't prepared for company, thought Juliane as she watched Betty try to figure out how to react to Louis's unexpected presence. *She and Chad will get along splendidly.* Juliane couldn't blame Betty for being surprised. Louis moved like a panther. Silently. Dangerously.

Juliane shook her head to clear her thoughts. Now was not the time to get lost in daydreams. Aloud, Juliane asked Louis, "You're not considering being a test subject, are you? We don't know for certain that Alan's process is entirely stable."

"Are you planning on participating?"

"Well, yes, of course."

"Then I've no reason to worry, do I?"

Juliane chewed her lip. "Er . . . I don't imagine the board will be all that thrilled with your risk-taking, that's all."

Louis leaned in and whispered conspiratorially, "Well, then I guess I just won't tell them. Besides, you just said there isn't any reason to worry."

A short time later, Betty had him strapped to a chair. Alan looked positively gleeful as he adjusted instruments.

Juliane silenced her misgivings by imagining tying Louis down in a very different manner. Louis leered at her, and she knew he had been thinking along the same lines.

I've made my choice. I just hope, this time, it's the right one. Time to evolve.

⁕ ⁕ ⁕

Juliane woke with no concept of how much time might have passed since she'd been given the injection. She remembered that after freeing herself from the straps, she'd collapsed on the cold laboratory floor.

However, at some point, she must have been moved to one of the temporary cots that were hidden away in various nooks and crannies throughout the building. It was common for staffers to conduct tests and experiments over several days, and the ACI had decided that it was cheaper to purchase the beds than take on the liability of researchers driving home with only a couple hours of sleep.

Louis. Her gaze darted around. Louis had been slumped in the chair the last time she'd seen him. Alan hadn't warned him of the risk. Alan hadn't warned either of them. *I'm such an idiot*, she thought. *I should have demanded to see evidence the process was safe with my own eyes before agreeing to let that man come anywhere close to me with a needle. What was I thinking?*

She groaned. *You weren't thinking at all*, she reminded herself. She'd warned Chad that Alan knew how to manipulate people into doing what he wanted, but hadn't followed her own advice. He'd dangled a chance to be a part of something greater than herself and once again she'd taken the bait.

However, it had been one thing to risk her life for science. It was quite another to risk Louis's. *Had he survived?* Doubt settled into her gut. Would he blame her for putting his life in danger?

Betty sat near the head of the second cot, dabbing the occupant's forehead with a moist cloth. She must have pulled together a full tray of the happy homemakers' basic flu remedies. Juliane could smell the chicken soup from where she lay. Her stomach turned in protest as she struggled to pull herself upright.

"What happened? How long was I out?"

Betty wrinkled her brow in thought. "I guess it's been close to eight hours. Quite impressive really. I looked over Alan's notes after you all started to collapse.

According to his observations, the transition in animals tended to take much longer."

"Out of curiosity, how long was Alan's transition?"

"About thirty minutes less than yours." Alan's muffled voice came from the direction of the cot.

"But I thought you injected yourself yesterday. Why would it only affect you now?" Juliane asked as she scanned the room. There were no other cots in the room. Where was Louis?

"I didn't say that I injected myself yesterday."

"Yes, you did." Juliane distinctly remembered saying as much right after he admitted that the procedure wasn't as safe as he'd implied in her office.

"No, I asked if you would feel better if I said that, and you did. See? I told you that you had nothing to worry about." Alan's voice sounded weaker than it had this morning. He might have known what to expect, but the process had taken some toll on him as well.

Her gaze continued to dart around the room, but Louis was nowhere to be seen. She fought the desire to panic. *Betty wouldn't be acting so nonchalant if something had gone wrong.* "Where is Louis?" she finally allowed herself to ask.

Betty said, "Oh, Mr. Evan's people called probably an hour after you fell. They didn't seem at all surprised to find him out cold, but were fairly annoyed that he wasn't where he said he would be."

The news was good, but not enough to dismiss Juliane's concerns. "Has anyone checked on him since then? Did he make it through the transition?"

Betty shrugged. "I wouldn't worry too much. If he suffered any worse than you did, I am sure we would have heard about it by now. He may not have even woken up yet." She turned toward Alan. "At least you'd better hope he's okay. I'd prefer to have not killed the big boss on my first assignment."

Juliane fumbled around until she located her phone and dialed Louis. The call went straight to voicemail. Panic mixed with disappointment. Louis's impromptu appearance in her office this morning had allowed her to hope they might be able to spend a little more time with each other. As memorable as his last visits had been, they were far too brief.

She pushed the feelings deep down. *Provided we survive this, we'll soon have all the time in the world together.* Until he returned her call, there was little she could do. "All right, Alan, we're upgraded. Now what?"

"Animals operating on raw instinct really are beautifully simple. All I had to do to prime the system was hack into their biologic network, but I believe the process for humans will be a bit more complicated. We build up so many walls, you see. You'll have to figure out a way to open the data exchange yourself."

"And how, pray tell, do you suggest I do that?"

"You just have to focus your intent; the neurons should do the rest. It should be similar to how you control that emulator system you were so proudly showing off at the conference."

"Except my emulator doesn't have the risk of knocking you out cold. You could have warned us about the side effects."

"You should have asked."

"Do I need to prepare for any other unpleasant surprises?"

"Oh no, the only surprises from here should be pleasant, quite pleasant. It's a brave new world, Jules."

Juliane attempted to clear her mind and ignore Alan's use of the nickname for the time being. Nothing happened. "Any other brilliant suggestions?"

"All my suggestions are brilliant. Try relaxing. Think of something pleasant."

Juliane smiled as she thought of how the sunlight played upon Louis's face in the early morning, making him appear more youthful than his business dealings let on.

"Something a little less personal perhaps. Maybe a flower blooming, the warm glow of a fireplace."

Juliane raised an eyebrow. She was going to need to double her effort to school her features. Alan noticed too much. She visualized a stream.

"Now stop. Visualize making a connection."

Juliane's mind went blank. It was as if a dam burst behind her eyes as the stream became torrents of data rushing through her mind. She had access to the full breadth of the Internet. She had always lived for the pursuit of knowledge, and now it surrounded her. She pictured herself dipping an arm into the raging current of bits. The ones and zeros pulsed against her senses. She dipped deeper, wondering just how far she could reach.

Then, she was flying through the air. She could see a forest of trees beneath her and rooftops in the distance. The setting sun behind her created a blurred shadow on the ground below. She could just make out the shape of animal remains beneath her just as her body began a rapid descent back downward. When she landed, she could not tell what the animal used to be, as it had already begun to be picked over.

Another wave of nausea took over and broke her focus. She shook her head and was back in the lab atop the cot.

"What was that?" she exclaimed.

"What was what?"

"I started accessing data, but then I was flying. And not just accessing satellite feeds. I mean, truly flying. Then I saw some roadkill and I was back here."

"A few days ago, some of my early test subjects, a few rats and birds, went missing. It occasionally happens. Animal rights activists." Alan sighed. "They never worry about what they might be unleashing on the public with these 'liberations.' But until now, I haven't been overly concerned. The virus isn't transmittable after all. It wasn't worth reporting."

Alan's eyes shone. "You must have been able to access one of the subject's vision as if they were just another node on the network. Did it act as if it was aware of your presence?"

"I can't be sure, but I don't believe so."

"Do you think you can access mine?"

Juliane opened herself once again to the stream of data. She focused her intent upon Alan, but all she could see was him staring back at her. She shook her head.

"Excellent. I visualized putting up a firewall. It must have been successful. Fascinating. Absolutely fascinating."

Juliane focused her intent on locating Louis. She shifted through the data stream until she found the location of his jet's departure log.

Betty was correct. Louis's people must have been in a panic to reach him. It was a wonder he had taken the time to visit her at all. His jet took off immediately following his transportation from the campus to the airport.

She was able to access some security camera footage which showed him being wheeled to the craft, but nothing that would indicate that he was in serious condition. While the log had given her the basic time of departure, it had not provided any further information such as where he was going or what time he might arrive at his destination.

It was as if there was no formal flight plan filed. *How was he able to get away with that?* she wondered. She was unable to access any of his physical senses as she had with the bird. She couldn't be sure if that was due to distance, his lack of consciousness, or his natural self-preservation instinct. Juliane decided she would try again once she knew for sure that he was safe and well.

She returned her attention to Alan as he attempted to pull himself off the cot using an eager Betty for support. It occurred to Juliane that Alan might be similarly testing his ability. Alan had too much control of her life as it was; allowing him in her head would be disastrous.

She visualized slamming a wall down within her mind. The datastream raged against her interference. She felt her eyes well up as its pressure surged against her insides. She changed the mental image, softening the wall, allowing the current to flow but only as directed. The pressure eased, and she could once again see clearly. She hoped it was enough. Alan did nothing to indicate he noticed her effort.

"Betty, would you mind running down the hall and fetching us a little more coffee? I don't think we will be sleeping again for a long while."

Betty frowned and looked as if she would like to refuse. Juliane hadn't seen Betty leave Alan's side since she woke; however, Alan's gaze hadn't left Juliane since the firewall test.

He finally turned toward Betty when she did not immediately jump at his command. Juliane could not see what look must have passed between them, but it was enough to cause Betty to purse her lips and exit without protest.

Alan came over to Juliane's side, each step surer than the last. He began to speak, but Juliane couldn't understand the words. A thought struck her, and she cocked her head, listening to the frequency of the sounds passing his lips.

Her mind began to match the sounds to a database of language, and within a moment, she could understand Alan as if the language he was speaking was her mother tongue.

"I assume that you've just discovered that there is no such thing as a dead language anymore."

"Possibly, but the database is only as good as the information within it. What we are saying is only based on speculation as to what Sanskrit might sound like. If that database was lost, then it truly would be lost again."

"Always the pessimist, aren't you? There would be nothing to prevent us from replacing it with whatever we wanted. Who would know but us?"

Juliane rolled her eyes at Alan's rationale. "Have you always been this willing to rewrite history?"

Alan smiled in response as if he was a three-year-old who knew he had been up to no good and was determined to try getting out of the situation by being as cute as possible. Juliane chose not to point out that it was the exact expression that Louis so frequently used.

Betty returned to the lab with mugs of steaming coffee and Chad in tow. Chad rushed to Juliane's side. "Are you okay? I am sorry I wasn't here sooner, but Nadia and I were taking a little day trip. I don't think Nadia's going to forgive me for a while, but I made us turn around and come back as soon as I got Betty's call."

"Nadia will forgive you. In fact, I suspect she might just respect you more for putting your foot down." Juliane also realized that if Chad was just arriving, it meant that Betty had been forced to care for both her and Alan all by herself. Juliane wasn't sure how the woman had been able to move them both to the cots. She must be quite a bit stronger than she appeared.

Betty handed her one of the cups, and Juliane sighed in contentment as the warm liquid settled in her belly. At least there was someone else on the team who appreciated the importance of a good cup of coffee. "It would seem that I need to thank you, Betty. I had no idea that the process would have that side effect. I'm sure Alan and I can come up with a gentler method in the future."

"I'd prefer not to wait if it is all the same," Betty stated.

"Alan wasn't upfront with me on the risk. As you saw, the process still has some pretty significant flaws. You need to have a strong will and self-control." *For a few minutes, I lost myself in a bird. A bird,* Juliane thought.

She didn't know this woman at all. *Who knows what could happen to the casual user?* Juliane no longer shared Alan's belief that the process was ready for human use. *Why hadn't Louis reached out to her yet?* Aloud, she continued, "We'd have no way of guessing how you might respond to the procedure."

"I am well aware of the risks. I was here while you were out cold on the floor. Alan mentioned something about having confidence in your success from your experience with some emulator device. If it would help ease your conscience, I would be happy to prove myself using that program first."

Juliane looked toward Chad. "I suppose you would like to be upgraded as well?"

Chad looked like a gazelle spotting a lion. "Absolutely not. We both know how I've done in the emulator. I think I can wait until the process is a little more proven, but I can go fire up the chamber for Betty if you'd like."

Juliane's lips twisted as she engaged in another mental debate. "I think that is a great idea, Betty," interjected Alan. "Juliane, it's not our place to deny evolution, especially not to such a brave volunteer. Take her to your chamber and truly do your worst. I am confident that if she can survive you, she can survive my little procedure."

Fourteen

Not entirely confident on her feet, Juliane leaned on Betty for support as they made their way back to her old lab space which still housed the original emulator. Chad had run ahead to ensure that the system was online before they got there.

"All right, Betty, just enter the chamber and the test will begin. The system will be monitoring your brain pattern and will be creating a whole world for you. You will need to maintain control of the environment at all times." Juliane's fingers danced across the keyboard. "I'm going to put you in three situations. In each case, you will need to find a way out of the simulation; otherwise, I will not allow Alan to administer the serum. Are you ready?"

Rather than answer, Betty attached the earpiece and microphone. She stepped through the glowing arches with her head held high while Juliane continued to fume behind her screen.

If something happened to Louis because of her need to establish herself at any cost . . . *I'm not going to let Betty undergo the procedure as blindly as I did.* Who knew if Louis was ever going to wake up, and if he did, would he wake up as the same person?

Juliane squashed the thought before it could undo her and focused on the newest member of her team. What was done was done. There was no turning back, but she could make sure Betty was more prepared for the risk than she had been. If that meant helping her find her breaking point, so be it.

The simulation appeared on the display. Realizing her upgrade meant she no longer had to watch the test unfold on a monitor, Juliane created a mental connection with her program. Her vision was replaced with the image from the screen. Even before the scene came into focus, Juliane's nose twitched from the smell of heavy application of bleach.

A bedroom appeared. Bits of yellow paint could be seen behind movie posters and photo collages. A mountain of stuffed animals covered a slim white daybed positioned along the length of the far wall.

The bed coverings themselves were wrinkled, tucked in with hospital corners. A desk made out of particle board sat on the other side of the room. The desk was immaculately organized, with paper in a neat stack. Pens and pencils were sorted by type and color filling black plastic containers with the same excess as the room's other decorations.

The bedroom door opened, and a middle-aged woman entered. The floorboards creaked over the sounds of a TV playing down the hall. The house must be decades old to produce such a sound as the woman couldn't have weighed more than a child. "Mom?" Juliane could hear unshed tears in Betty's voice.

"Were you expecting someone else?"

Betty ran over to the woman and crushed her in a hug. "I know you aren't real, but it is so good to see you!" Juliane could feel the woman's graying hair tickle her skin as if she was standing there instead of Betty.

"What do you mean I'm not real?" The woman's hand caressed Betty's cheek, and to Juliane, her touch felt like lace. Betty jumped backward. The woman's hand hung in the air for a moment where Betty's face had been. Then, as gently as an autumn leaf, it fell back to her side. The woman's brow knit in confusion.

"You're just a simulation. You may look like her, sound like her, and even smell like her, but you aren't my mom. She died years ago, and this isn't my room. Dad had to sell the house to pay off the medical bills."

"Oh, Betty dear, have you been up late studying again? You always have those crazy stress dreams whenever you fall asleep at your desk. You know your father and I are so proud of you, but you work too hard. I don't know that I want you to go to that fancy college if this is what it's going to do to you. I know, how about we spend the day together and relax, just you and me? We can go shopping and then end the day with pedicures. Won't that be fun? Why are you crying, Betty?"

"I would give up anything to be able to go back and spend more time with my real mom, but you're just a computer program. I reject you."

Betty's mother looked crestfallen. "Betty, honey, you are starting to worry me. I have been feeling a little under the weather, but I didn't die, and I definitely haven't run up any medical bills." She held her arms out wide. "I'm right here. Your dad and I haven't gone anywhere. Sweetie, you look so pale. Let me feel your forehead." Betty's mother took steps forward, eliminating the distance Betty had put between them. Betty leaned her brow against the back of her mother's outstretched hand—

Betty reeled back again as if struck by a snake. "No. As much as I want this to be real, it is not, and I have to go." Betty walked toward her bedroom door with determined strides, giving her mother a wide berth as if another touch would break her resolve. She didn't risk looking back, but paused in the doorway long enough to whisper, "I love you, Mom."

The scene faded to black as Betty crossed through the bedroom doorway. "I wasn't expecting you to make it easy, but I didn't expect you to be cruel."

Juliane had wanted to challenge Betty but hadn't expected the simulation to take that turn either. She released a breath she hadn't known she held. The scene would have gone much differently had Juliane's past been put on display. While she and Betty might have had a similar career trajectory on paper, it was clear they had vastly different backgrounds.

Juliane's stomach knotted as she buried a surge of resentment. As the next test began, Juliane reduced her connection with the program, limiting its impact on her senses. Betty was the one whose self-control was supposed to be tested. Not hers.

Spray from an ocean wave crashing against the side of a small boat slapped Betty's face as the vessel appeared beneath her feet. Betty collapsed against the side railing as the floor rocked with the motion. Another wave pounded the craft as Betty struggled to regain her balance. After a few more failed attempts, Betty abandoned efforts to remain upright, and instead, leaned against the gunwale while the boat heaved up and down.

A strong wind turned Betty's hair into miniature whips as steel-gray clouds took over the portion of the horizon not consumed by water. Electricity began to pulse through the sky, providing shadowy evidence of shark-shaped creatures hidden beneath the surface.

Betty glanced around, but there was nothing in the boat that could come to her assistance and no sign of land as far as the eye could see. Another wave struck the side of the boat, and its wooden boards groaned in response to the abuse. Betty grabbed the side of the vessel once again, her knuckles white.

The change in the boat's weight combined with the rising waves caused it to lean over precariously. A slick dark body briefly crested near Betty's fingers before dropping back into the surrounding depths.

Betty pulled back into the center of the dinghy, but not before the dinghy began to take on water. As if the water had merely been waiting for the initial invitation, more waves followed suit, soaking through Betty's clothing and filling the base of the hull.

Boards snapped from their fastenings. The little boat would not protect Betty from either storm or ocean inhabitants much longer. The boards near her feet echoed with thunks as something large came into contact. Betty screamed, but the sound was muted beneath the weight of the storm.

Another large wave, at least twice as large as the last, began its approach. It would close in fast and when it hit, the little boat would not be able to withstand its onslaught. Betty curled her body, bracing for impact. Another splash of water briefly sent the boat underwater.

Juliane watched as Betty stood fully erect. The boat continued its plummet toward its inevitable demise, but as it dropped down, Betty remained in place, hovering in the air. Upon impact with the rogue wave, the boat splintered into hundreds of shards.

The destruction of the boat did little to halt the progress of the storm. The debris, now lethal stakes, churned in reckless abandon as a new wave came closer, but Betty's face no longer showed signs of distress. Her lips thinned into a small line as her arms dropped down by her sides and she squared her shoulders.

"This is a computer program. That is not the ocean, and this is not real. I reject it all!" Betty shouted into the wind.

The wave slammed into an invisible surface directly in front of Betty, and her entire vision was consumed by a wall of water. What hadn't hit the wall flowed under her, but her shoes no longer showed signs of being wet. The undulation ceased, and the dark water became the floor beneath her feet. The wind's howls became a mere whimper before ceasing altogether.

Once again, Betty was surrounded by darkness.

"I nearly drowned once when I was just a child and avoided the ocean for years. Your system is good, but no amount of simulation can compare to the real thing." Betty's fists remained white and closed, while her breathing remained labored.

A sliver of light penetrated the darkness of the chamber, and Alan rushed in. "Betty, I could hear you screaming from down the hall. Is everything all right in here? What have you done to her, Juliane?!"

"I'm fine, really. Nothing I couldn't handle," Betty sputtered as if still battling against the onslaught of the wind and waves.

"You are positively shaking. Juliane, I think you've sent her into shock! What is wrong with you?!" Alan shouted.

"No, really. I'll be okay. I just need a couple of minutes to catch my breath. Dr. Faris is just doing what you asked her to do—her worst." Betty glared as if she could see Juliane through the curtain. "I hope that I've now proven that I am just as capable of handling the effects of the procedure as she is."

"You don't have to prove anything to me. I knew from the minute that we met that you were perfect just the way you are." Alan wrapped Betty in his arms, pulling her close.

"You mean I will be perfect once I've had the procedure like you and Dr. Faris."

"That can wait for another day. You don't have to rush into anything. I don't want to risk losing you." He brushed his hand against the side of her cheek.

"But what about the project? Surely you need all of us on the team to be able to contribute at our highest levels?"

"I don't know about you, but I am exhausted from earlier. I doubt that Juliane or I would be able to accomplish all that much in the next few hours anyway. Why don't we call it a day?"

Betty pulled back from Alan, although not so much as to break away from his embrace. "I've read through some of your previous project notes, and I did my own background search on you. I know a little thing like a stomach bug isn't going to hold you back for long. Weren't you the one to go for four nights without sleep just to prove a point?"

Alan smiled, urging Betty's face toward his own with another caress of his hand. "I do so love a woman who does her research. I'm sure Juliane won't mind locking up, will you Juliane? Come with me, Betty. You know I can make waiting worth your while." Alan closed his eyes, leaning his head in toward Betty's lips.

For a moment, Betty looked as if she would meet Alan's advance, but then shoved him away. "No! You aren't real. This is just another one of her tests!"

"No, Betty. This is no test! I heard you scream and made her turn the device off. This is real. You and I are real." Alan reached toward Betty; she took another step back.

"You said you love a woman who does her research, and I did. Everyone knows you call Dr. Faris 'Jules' because it drives her crazy."

"What are you talking about? What does that have to do with anything?"

"You've called her Juliane repeatedly just now."

"So?"

"I've heard the jokes around the building and the two of you talking. I know that even when you do call her Juliane, you still always stretch out the last syllable as if you are making a point to call attention to how considerate you're being."

"Now I am seriously concerned. Dr. Faris's testing has put a strain on you. I wouldn't approve subjecting you to the procedure now, regardless of how well or not well you've done in her test chamber. Betty, I know that we haven't known each other long, but I feel as if I've known you all my life. We have a connection. One that I would like to develop more. You need some rest. Please, I am begging you. Come with me." Alan reached his arm out to Betty once again.

"Alan doesn't beg. This is not real. I reject you." Betty's eyes welled up with tears as she spoke the words. "Dr. Faris, I believe we are done here."

Alan faded away as Juliane drew back the curtain surrounding the pillars. "Yes, Betty, I would agree. I'll call upstairs and have Alan prep for another upgrade."

Fifteen

When Betty and Juliane arrived back at the medical lab housing the Gene Assist serum samples, Alan was not there. Juliane, grateful that her mind was much clearer than before, used the time while they waited for his return to look over Alan's procedure notes, all of which were handwritten in nearly indecipherable scratch.

"I probably would have saved myself a few hours of terror after you all collapsed if he would have stored his work online like most other people," muttered Betty.

Juliane, not looking up from the page, remembered her early struggles with Alan's script. "It took me a while to figure out the trick of it myself. Alan has trust issues."

Betty grumbled something in response that sounded like, "I wonder why." The following silence between them was an oppressive wall. Juliane found herself looking forward to Alan's return if only so that he might help break it down. Betty appeared shaken by the results of the test. *Does Betty think that I would share any of that?* Juliane didn't think any less of her. If anything, she now had greater respect for the woman's drive.

"Betty, I know you think I am an awful person for putting you through those tests, but I had to be sure that you were going to be able to handle the upgrade."

"I understand." Betty's voice was clipped in anger. "I didn't realize that the system could see quite so clearly into my head."

"Those thoughts weren't as hard to find as you might believe. I had the system home in on your greatest fears, wants, and regrets to ensure that you were able to stay focused."

Betty made a harrumphing sound. "Well, what's done is done. You now know everything you need to know about me. I trust I won't have to go in there again." Betty was being childish.

"You were the one that insisted on being tested." Juliane tried to remain calm and composed, but Betty was completely overreacting. Juliane wondered if perhaps it was due to being exposed to all three strong emotions in such short order. It might be something worth incorporating into her algorithm. Her mind immediately began framing the problem in terms of variables.

Three strong emotions. Three-X. Juliane stopped turning the pages of Alan's notes. Could the solution be so simple? "Betty, I believe that Alan's dosing equation is off—however, this is not my area of expertise. Would you care to take a look?" The question was more of an olive branch, as Juliane was confident enough in her assessment. Whether or not Betty chose to accept it would tell Juliane much about her character.

Betty seemed grateful for the distraction and hurried over to look at the page. "Well, I understand why he would have come up with this equation. It is definitely the most expedient method of uploading the data, but you're right. He didn't consider the subject's natural health response. By modifying the frequency and dose rate, we can reduce the risk factor by at least a multiple of three, if not ten."

"And decrease the subject's potential strength as a result." Both women were startled by the comment as Alan returned to the lab. As the door closed behind him, Juliane could see that Alan was accompanied by another man with dark hair; whoever he was, the man did not follow Alan through the doorway. "And yes, I did take the subject's health response into consideration. However, I felt the payoff worth a little extra risk."

There is no possible way that the procedure would have been approved based on this equation. "Alan, you didn't get approved for human trials based on this information, did you? She still hadn't heard from Louis. Juliane fought to keep her anger in check. If something happened to him, Alan might be the only one who would know what to do. They couldn't afford to put him on the defensive; he could leave the room and never come back.

"Especially when the alternative is so obvious!" added Betty.

"Ah, good. The heat must be back on. When I first opened the door, it felt freezing in here. I assume then that your testing went well?"

"I have no further concerns."

"Well then, if you both are so confident your way is better, how about we go ahead and update Betty using your recommendations?"

Juliane knit her eyebrows. As Betty had pointed out, the alternative had been extremely obvious, almost as if he had planned for one of them to stumble across it, but she still had expected more of a fight from Alan.

Before she could ask if Alan had some master plan he wasn't sharing, Betty launched herself onto the procedure bed. "I am ready to begin whenever you are."

"Your wish is my command. It is so nice to see some enthusiasm around here. You'll not regret it. Ready, Juliane?" asked Alan.

He did stretch out the last syllable. Juliane sighed, closing her eyes. Data flowed in her veins, warming her and making her more aware of the world like only a good cup of coffee could. Alan was right. The payoff was proving to be worth the risk. She had survived, and she had to believe that Louis would wake soon. How could she deny anyone else the same opportunity?

"Right, let's begin." Alan made a show of bringing the equipment around. While he might not compare to Louis for showmanship, occasionally Alan did have a flair for the dramatic. "Betty dear, you may feel a little pinch."

sixteen

As they anticipated, Betty's reaction to the treatment was less severe than what Juliane, Louis, or even Alan had experienced. She had still grown pale and feverish, but overall, the difference was like a slight cold compared to an extreme case of pneumonia. More importantly, she never once lost consciousness.

Louis finally made contact while Betty practiced mastering her focus. He had woken up in the air hours ago. Other than the fever and blacking out for a few hours, he hadn't suffered too many ill effects. Juliane had wanted to tell him about her experience with the bird, but before she could bring up the subject, the call was disconnected.

He must have traveled into a cellular dead zone. It has to be why he didn't call sooner. Juliane had returned her attention to Betty. Within hours, Betty too was accessing information across the globe as if she had been born with the ability, albeit not quite as powerfully as Juliane.

As the weeks passed, Chad continued to abstain from the procedure himself, even after seeing how well Betty responded, preferring instead to support the team by running errands. Even with only the three of them online, they were able to compile data with record speed. Juliane reveled in her ability to access massive amounts of computing power by mere thought.

A supercomputer is limited in that it can only respond to the parameters of its programming. It was one of the major challenges in the development of artificial intelligence, but they had no similar limitation.

Seemingly unconnected data points were correlated together for no logic-based reason, yet they fit together perfectly. Soon the team developed a basic working equation that would serve as the backbone for the rest of their next experiment.

The team then set up a collaborative online platform using Juliane's virtual reality software. They could then access the virtual world Louis had named the datasphere and manipulate objects and materials without the need for additional programming as easily as modeling clay in the real world. Except, there was a lot less clean up required.

If it were up to Juliane, they would conduct all their work in the virtual world, but that would limit Chad's involvement, leaving her feeling outnumbered. Except for that first day, Betty didn't act like she still held a grudge against Juliane, but she did tend to side with Alan whenever a topic came up for a vote.

As Juliane left the datasphere for another day of face-to-face meetings and office work, she clenched her teeth. There had been no further negative side effects. Juliane couldn't understand Chad's continued reluctance to upgrade. Chad was only able to enter by donning bulky gear kept on the campus, which meant their meetings were in person. *I could be in the comfort of my home right now.* If it hadn't been for Chad, she wouldn't have to deal with Alan in the flesh.

At least she had Louis. Juliane closed her eyes and accessed her email server. There were no new messages since the last time she checked it ten minutes ago. Her text feeds remained equally empty. It felt like it had been ages since he'd last visited.

Juliane knew she shouldn't complain though. He more than made up for his absence when his schedule did allow for an occasional check-in. She reminded herself he was still trying to strengthen his position in the company as much as she was.

Think of the positives, she told herself. The media frenzy surrounding their relationship had finally died down—and this time stayed down. Without the media's constant interruptions, Juliane had been able to pay more attention to her work.

It also meant they no longer had to be as secretive about their rendezvous. This was unfortunate as Juliane had found she rather enjoyed the added element of stealth. It made their lovemaking seem all the more dangerous and forbidden.

She'd also discovered her body now associated the flash of the camera with the anticipation and afterglow of time spent during those clandestine meetings. As a result, she now experienced a Pavlovian reaction whenever she spotted nearby reporters and reason to reason to avoid the gossip outlets. *Unless Louis was in town*, she amended to her thoughts. Then, it was quite a different experience.

Lost in her delicious thoughts, Juliane did not hear the door to her office open. As if summoned by magic, there stood the object of her daydreams.

"You never call. You never write," Juliane said with a smile on her face as she ran to him.

"You know I can't risk putting anything about what we do in writing, at least not yet, and I'm always in meetings." Louis pulled her close, lifting Juliane in his embrace while using his back to close the door. Returning Juliane to the ground but only unwrapping one-half of his embrace, he reached behind and turned the lock with an audible click.

"I can't stay long." He looked into her eyes. His eyes shone with hunger. Louis pivoted his heel, bringing Juliane with him, pinning her to the wall near the door.

"You never stay long." Juliane pouted.

Louis leaned in, nuzzling her neck.

Juliane tilted her head to the side, giving him more access. Having him here, in person, was always so much better than any of her imaginings.

"Louis?"

"Mmm," he answered, not halting from his ministrations. One of his hands began similar strokes along her thighs.

"I know I said I wanted to keep up the mystery act, but you could take me with you sometimes."

Louis stopped what he was doing. Juliane's body ached in protest. He pulled back and looked at her. "And take you away from your work? When you are so close? You'd never forgive me."

Louis was right. She wouldn't. She needed to see this project through, but it was so difficult to remain focused on the future when her immediate needs were demanding an altogether different form of satisfaction. "I know. It's just that I miss you so much when you aren't around." Juliane bit her lip. She could see his body tense up as if to further pull away. She shifted her hips, where his hand still lay frozen. "There's just so much more I'd like to do to you and never enough time."

Louis smiled and leaned back toward her. "Is that so?" His hand once again began its exploration. "Why don't you tell me more? What would you do?" His voice dropped into the husky baritone that she associated with some of their more enjoyable phone calls. If only the feeling of his lips upon her could be as easily transmitted over distances. She could do such wicked things to him if only she could be two places at once.

The thought brought her up short. "What if we established a private network?"

Louis muttered, "I must not be doing something right. You sound like you just switched into work mode."

"I'm serious. You've been upgraded. I've been upgraded. It's just a matter of manipulating data. We could do it."

"Do what?" Louis asked.

Juliane threaded her fingers through his hair. "We could set up a network between us, and no one would ever know. No risk of public leaks. We would be able to not just tell each other what we'd like to do, but show each other," she murmured. "Explicitly." She felt his hand slip behind her waistband as she once again lost her grip on logical thought.

seventeen

Juliane attempted to straighten a few of the books on her office shelf which had become jostled when Louis had sought better leverage. She smiled and shook her head when her eyes spotted her solitary picture frame. Perhaps she would add a few more photos one of these days. "You never did answer me."

"About what?" Louis asked while straightening his clothes.

"About the idea of establishing a private network between the two of us."

Louis wrinkled his forehead in thought. "Do you think that is necessary?" he asked as he walked over and unlocked the door.

"It could be the perfect solution to our problem." Juliane turned to face Louis. "Your father sure could have used it."

Louis's face darkened. "My father made mistakes. I don't want to discuss him. Ever. Is that clear?"

She took a step toward him. "I'm sorry. I didn't mean to sound judgmental." She took another step and helped adjust his tie. "If you ask me, the girl was asking for trouble, even if she wasn't a princess. I am sorry that your father was sent away and how hard it's become for you to travel in the open without looking over your shoulder. But think of it this way, if they hadn't made those choices, you and I may never have met."

Louis's eyes softened as he lowered his head to kiss her forehead. "That's true. Fine. If you think this will make you happy, let's try it."

Juliane closed her eyes and focused. She could see the datastream flowing through Louis. She visualized reaching out to him, her own data stream branching out to him in a line separated from the flow of the rest of the network. As the connection was made, she was flooded with additional sensations. As a test, she projected her feelings of euphoria resulting from the aftermath of their passion. She opened her eyes in time to see his smile deepen.

"It was good for you then?" Louis asked with a smirk.

The corners of his eyes tightened, and Juliane suddenly felt a warmth travel down her torso, the same path that had so recently been traveled by his hands. Her breath quickened. He didn't move from where he stood, but Juliane found that she could feel his lips press against her nether regions. She fought the urge to moan.

"This may have been your best idea yet," gloated Louis.

Louis's phone rang, shattering their concentration, and the sensation dissipated, leaving Juliane aching for satisfaction.

"It's time, sir," the voice on the other end of the line announced.

"I'll be right there," advised Louis. Hanging up the phone, he said to Juliane, "I have to go, but don't worry. We'll finish this later."

After taking a few minutes to regain her equilibrium, Juliane joined the rest of the team in Alan's lab. She was deep into programming when her vision of the room was replaced with an image of herself in a compromising position. Along with the image, she received a sense of Louis's hunger and arousal. She blinked, clearing the image, and looked about the room. None of her colleagues noticed anything unusual.

Once again, she felt the sensation of his body on hers. Her breath became shallow.

Betty looked up from her workspace. "Is everything all right?"

"I'm fine." Juliane gritted through her teeth, biting off the moan that threatened to escape from her lips.

"Are you sure? You look flushed."

Alan turned around and scanned her face. "Your eyes are glazed," he announced. "You aren't coming down with something?" he asked.

"Coming down?" Juliane advised. Spiraling out of control maybe, dancing the fine line between torture and ecstasy definitely, but sick? "No. I feel wonderful."

Alan frowned. "Good. We can't afford to lose our momentum now."

Juliane visualized smacking Louis on the buttocks and received back a sense of unapologetic mirth. She must have gotten her point across because the rest of the sensations faded away immediately, allowing her to continue work uninterrupted.

Back in the privacy of her apartment, Juliane tried to find Louis. For some reason, she still was not able to pinpoint his exact location even with her advanced abilities. When asked about it, Louis had only shrugged and told her that he had equipped his phone with some additional security since his father had made some enemies.

Why Louis would need the same level of security as his father was a little unclear to Juliane. It was more than a little paranoid in her opinion. She guessed Louis must have his reasons, but he could be so frustrating at times.

She searched until she believed she had identified his whereabouts to within an approximate ten-mile radius. He was on the West Coast and likely in a meeting with some very influential business leaders. Juliane's lips turned up in a coy smile. Perfect. She projected her desire across their network and waited for a response. When none immediately followed, she imagined the feel of his chest beneath her hands and pushed. Still nothing.

Disappointed, she sent a message through their private network. No response. She sent another message through the public network. This time, Louis sent a message back. He was sorry to report he hadn't felt a thing but was looking forward to chatting with her soon.

Juliane contemplated sending Louis an invitation to meet her in the datasphere but thought better of it. She didn't trust that Alan wouldn't be using the virtual world, and the last thing she wanted would be for him to find them there for any reason outside of pure research.

More days passed, and Juliane hadn't found the source of the issue. It was as if Louis was blocking her transmissions for some reason. He, on the other hand, did not seem to have the same problem.

He had also remained uncharacteristically in one place for all of this time, and the time difference had placed her at a distinct disadvantage. There had been a few occasions when she had been forced to excuse herself from the lab before she embarrassed herself due to his preferred manner of wishing her a good morning. The team had begun to take notice.

As enjoyable as those moments were, the private network overall was rapidly losing its appeal. At least in Juliane's opinion. For Louis, well, Juliane didn't quite know what Louis thought about it. His recent calendar allowed for little time to talk. And even less time for the kind of talk that didn't first involve play.

After facing yet another morning of her team's glares and wrinkled foreheads, Juliane decided it was time to disable the network. *So much for being spontaneous. Louis will understand*, she told herself. *He probably won't even notice it is gone.* She really had to put her full attention into the task at hand; otherwise, when he eventually did have time for some well-deserved rest and relaxation, she wouldn't be able to join him. *He is bound to be back soon. I'll explain it to him later.*

Juliane isolated the network link in her mind and severed the connection. Immediately, her body felt cold as if she were physically bleeding out. It was as if, without the link, she was suddenly less whole, less alive. Even her vision was affected. The world looked grayer. *How would someone go about cauterizing a virtual wound?* she wondered.

Juliane slogged toward the lab. She felt a desperate need to be surrounded by other people, yet she wanted to lock herself away in her office until the end of time. Her body felt foreign. Wrong and alien. Something had gone very, very wrong.

Eighteen

Juliane glanced at a clock only to realize that several minutes had passed of which she had no memory and minimal accomplishment. Most of the last several weeks had passed in a similar state of fog. The fact that Juliane was able to focus long enough to complete anything at all had become her daily victory.

"Have you completed the next simulation profile? Juliane? Juliane? Earth to Dr. Faris?" Betty's voice cut through Juliane's thoughts.

"I'm sorry, Betty. Yes, the simulation profile is ready. Would you care to go online with me to view it?"

"Excellent, Alan should already be there waiting for us."

Juliane attempted to glance around the room without Betty noticing. Until Betty had spoken, Juliane hadn't realized that Alan wasn't still in the room. *How long have I been out this time?*

"Is the meeting in the same place as before?"

"It seemed appropriate enough."

Juliane closed her eyes and imagined entering the virtual reality universe they had selected. It was a process that had grown routine. Not that she was complaining. Even if she was only going through the motions, she was at least going forward. Her avatar appeared outside of the CERN reactor laboratory.

As Betty had advised, Alan was already there, rendered in full lab coat complete with safety goggles and clipboard. The corner of Juliane's lip twitched as if she wanted to smirk but just couldn't remember exactly how. "You certainly seem to enjoy looking the part in here."

He smiled as he answered, "As they say, 'When in Rome.' I'd hate to see the dry-cleaning bill on the outfit you are wearing in real life."

Juliane looked down. She hadn't given a thought to how her avatar should dress when she entered the virtual world. As a result, her subconscious had chosen for her. Her outfit was a version of the same iceberg white suit from the symposium; only here it was made with a fabric that could be described as being a modern take on samite. Her loose hair swayed in a breeze that she alone could feel. *I must look like an ice princess*, she thought.

The virtual Betty, on the other hand, appeared exactly as she did in real life. Juliane couldn't be sure if that was by choice. Betty did not seem to be able to perform more than a handful of actions at a time in the datasphere. Alan had speculated that the safer procedure would have such an effect, and Betty's performance would suggest he was right.

"Have you uploaded the latest equations?" Alan asked.

"Chad should be processing Juliane's portion now," answered Betty.

Betty disappeared and then re-appeared by Alan's side. Chad had shared a rumor that the two were dating outside of work. At the time, Juliane wasn't able to muster the energy to scold Chad for spreading gossip.

She told herself it wasn't any of her business. What did it matter if Betty and Alan chose to have a romantic relationship in addition to a professional one? She'd be the last person at the ACI who could pass judgment. But today, seeing them so close together, she couldn't help wondering if there was any truth to the story. It was like trying to ignore a scab that refused to heal.

Alan had mellowed since she'd severed her connection with Louis as if he could sense something different about her. He'd even stopped calling her 'Jules.' The corner of Betty's lips turned up as Alan's virtual hand hovered near hers for a moment.

Juliane realized how badly she wanted what they appeared to share, and she cursed the shadow of her former self she had allowed herself to become. The next time Louis was in town, she would re-establish the link if only to feel whole once again. Then, they would find some way to make it, and their relationship work properly out in the public.

She wondered for the thousandth time how he must be coping with the connection's loss. She hoped for his sake that whatever had been limiting its effectiveness on his side had in some way shielded him from its loss. She was afraid it hadn't. Her calls and messages had thus far gone unanswered.

"Ah, Juliane? You were fading out just then. There isn't anything wrong with the simulation?" Betty asked.

"No, nothing is wrong. I was momentarily distracted, but I am back now."

Juliane forced herself to forget about everything but the simulation. A series of components began to appear before her and gradually assembled themselves into shape. Juliane reached over and pressed a small switch. "Now this is based on available components found today. I would suspect that once we have a workable tool, much smaller, more commercially-available substitutes will be on the market, and we will be able to offer a version greatly refined in size and shape."

The device began to hum. Juliane waved her hand, and the floor around Betty and Alan became a pool of water, which remained even after Juliane switched the device off.

"And you are one hundred percent sure that you did not create that pool purely by thought?" Alan asked. "Accidents can happen here if you aren't careful."

As if she didn't know that. "I am positive. I had keyed in a program restriction just to be sure." Juliane nodded, emphasizing her point. It was one of the few things she was sure about.

"Well then, I will begin the requisition process for the materials in real life."

"Do we have a budget for that? Isn't the board going to need more proof of concept?" Betty asked.

Alan laughed. The sound seemed eerie and wrong in Juliane's ears. "You let me worry about that."

"Alan has had the board eating out of his hand for years," elaborated Juliane. "I don't know exactly what he has over them, but he's always been able to get them to sign off on whatever he needs to be successful." Juliane's jaw ached. She may have spoken more today than she had in days.

Alan did not offer any additional comment other than a smirk.

With childlike glee, Betty clasped her hands, beaming with pride at their accomplishment. "I guess that's all we can do for now. Alan, will you be coming by later? Er . . . you too, Juliane? I feel like celebrating."

Alan turned to her. "Not right away. Juliane makes it sound like all I have to do is snap my fingers. I'm good, it's true, but there is a certain amount of paperwork required first."

"Oh yes, of course, there is. How about you, Juliane? You've been working so hard over the last few weeks. Would you like to go out for a celebratory toast?"

Juliane sighed. "Thank you for the offer, Betty, but I'd prefer not to celebrate, at least not yet. Chad? Would you work up the remaining task list? I'll start work on the costing proposal. Alan can explain it later. If that's all, I am going to sign off."

Before either could respond, Juliane opened her eyes back in the real world. Betty's blank expression was evidence that she lingered in the virtual space. Chad would be still tethered to the machines. Alan was nowhere to be seen in the lab. Juliane found herself wondering where Alan might have disappeared to, but was grateful for his absence.

Had he been there, Betty might have returned promptly as well and then she would have been forced to listen to more of Betty's bubbly happiness. It was more than she could take.

She took a step and was momentarily blinded by a splitting headache. Juliane reached out to stabilize herself as the room spun and her legs buckled. The entire episode lasted less than a minute while Betty continued to sit like a doll in her chair. While vertigo may have left, Juliane still felt weak. The lab walls felt oppressive. She had to get out of the room.

Juliane made it as far as her office before she had to rest once again. Reaching into her desk drawer, she frantically tried to find her phone before remembering that she had stopped carrying it some time ago. While her head no longer felt as if it was being puréed in a blender, she was unable to focus, leaving her with no access to the network and no other means of locating Louis. She didn't have his private line programmed into the desk phone. She had never needed it.

"Dr. Faris! Are you all right?" Chad stood in the office doorway, but she had trouble focusing on him. "When was the last time you slept?"

Juliane wasn't able to form the words of a witty retort, so she settled on a futile attempt of waving Chad away. Chad ignored the gesture. He came to Juliane's side and reached out as if to hold her hand, but froze in mid-movement as if afraid of her reaction.

"Migraine. I need to talk to Louis," Juliane whispered. The sound of her voice created aftershocks of stabbing pain. Blinking rapidly did not help her vision, but she still noted Chad blanch, and he took a step back.

"Er . . . hmm . . . well . . ."

"Chad, I can barely stand my own voice. If you've nothing to say, then don't." Each word was like a miniature ice pick in her brain. "I don't have my phone. Find his number and call him. Now."

"Um . . ."

"Now, Chad."

"Well, I'm not sure that is such a good idea . . ."

"I don't remember asking you for your opinion." Inundated by another wave of pain and nausea, Juliane was forced to rest her head back down on the desk.

The staccato melody of Chad's phone ringing played across her ears like a jackhammer. As she was taken over by blissful darkness, the last sound she heard was something that sounded much like Chad saying, "I don't know if she's heard yet or not."

nineteen

When her eyes fluttered open again, her head was wedged in between the pillows of her bed. The warm pale light on the wall suggested early morning. *How did I get here?* she wondered.

Chad must have moved her after her collapse in the office. But how would he have gotten into her apartment? He must have rooted around in her purse to find the key.

She wouldn't have thought he would possess the nerve. She risked a glance down and was relieved to see she was still in the same attire that she had worn before. It was stiff and wrinkled, but otherwise all there. Juliane's lips inched upward a fraction. At least there had been some limits to Chad's caregiving.

Juliane pinged Louis's location with her next breath. Her fists tightened on their own accord as she realized that not only was he in transit, he was moving in an easterly direction. *Finally.* He had to be coming this way. He must have heard about her collapse and dropped everything for her.

Once he got here, she would explain everything. They would debug the private link issue, and everything would be just as it should be. Juliane closed her eyes, displacing the threatening tears.

Juliane's lips settled back into a fine line. Now she just had to summon the energy to get herself out of bed. It felt like trying to open her car door in the dead of winter. She filled her lungs in anticipation of the effort and nearly gagged. *Is that smell coming from me?* Juliane rubbed her fingers over her temples. Her skin felt cool to the touch, more like it belonged to a porcelain doll than a person.

She pulled herself upright only by a supreme act of will. Stumbling, Juliane made her way to the shower. As the water began to flow, she could feel the impact of each droplet on her body like hailstones. Juliane began to worry that she might shatter under the assault.

Emerging from the shower, she did not recognize the face in the mirror. Her normally alabaster skin was tarnished by dark lines, giving her skin the appearance of veined marble. Her dark hair, still wet, clung to her neck and shoulders. The dryer, a dead weight in her hand. Chad was right. She had been working herself too hard. She would go into the office, finalize the remaining tasks, and then insist on some time off.

She went through the rest of her morning ritual on autopilot. Every step she took was a small victory. Each time she felt like giving up, Juliane reminded herself that everything would be better soon. Following the success in Vegas, Juliane's paychecks had increased. After paying back Durham, she'd splurged on her clothing, making sure everything was tailored. If she was going to be featured in the tabloids, she wanted the picture to look good.

Dress for the job you want, she told herself as she paid for the extra service. Fine suits became her armor, but she noticed that her clothing no longer fit her to perfection. *When did that happen?* Juliane realized she couldn't recall the last real meal she had enjoyed.

As she put on her shoes, the entry door opened. Juliane immediately stopped struggling to line up her foot with an errant shoe. Pulling on its pair had taken several minutes. "Louis," she whispered. She lost her grip on the shoe.

As it clattered on the floor, Juliane's vision once again blurred. A shadow came toward her. She felt a hand on her arm, pulling her upward. Juliane realized she must have fallen along with the footwear.

The figure's face came into focus. She had expected to see Louis's wickedly sexy smile. Instead, she was greeted by Chad's look of concern. There was something else though about his expression. Something she couldn't quite place. It was the same look that had met her at the door of each foster family. *Pity.* She recoiled from the sight.

"What are you doing here, Chad?" she asked, fighting back the tears threatening to consume her. No one pitied her now. She had come too far. Chad must have forgotten who was in charge. She would have to be careful not to show any more weakness in front of him.

"Oh, thank goodness you're moving around! I worried that it might be time to call the emergency room!"

"It was just a migraine, nothing to get that worked up about. Definitely not worth going to the hospital over. I am grateful that you got me back home. It was much nicer to be able to wake up after a day like that in my own bed."

"Umm . . . it's been more than a day."

"What? Two?" Juliane sniffed.

"Er . . . more like a week."

"A week. How could it possibly have been a week?" she demanded.

Chad frowned. "You don't remember." Never letting go of her arm, Chad walked her to a chair. Even after she was seated, he did not completely release his grip as if he was afraid she might fall again.

Juliane pushed him off, straightening her back. "Remember what?" she asked.

"When I brought you back here, you were awake, but in a daze. The following morning you drank some water when I came by to check on you but demanded I leave you alone. We were beginning to worry you might not be willing to come back. Nadia wanted to call the doctors right away, but I . . ." Chad trailed off.

"You what?"

"I couldn't help worrying what could happen when they started treating you without knowing what effect that procedure might have done to your systems. I didn't want to be the reason if you got worse."

Chad's face was flushed brilliant red. Juliane took a deep breath as if the added weight in her lungs would somehow help anchor her back into the land of the living. "Well, I feel fine now," Juliane responded as if the words being spoken out loud would make them true. "At least you were able to get through to Louis. How about the project? Was Betty able to help Alan finish up the requisition process?"

"Oh yes, I've never seen anything like it. I don't know what he did or said, but everything we asked for was in the lab the next day. The final assembly should be taking place today. If you think you are up for it, we could go together for the trial." Chad glanced down at his phone. "But we all understand if you would prefer to stay away one more day."

"Nonsense. I told you I am fine. There is no reason I would miss this." Juliane waved Chad toward the door, determined to rise and make her way on her own.

Arriving at the lab, Chad hovered behind as if she might break into a thousand pieces at any given moment. True to his report, when she opened the lab door, she was met by a large metallic device. It was a near-replica of the simulated one she had created in the virtual world, only missing a side panel. Betty and Alan were crouched over a corner desk examining the remaining electrical components and wire harnesses like puzzle pieces.

"Branching out to new fields of study, are we?"

Although Alan did not glance up as Juliane and Chad entered, Juliane watched as he slowly returned the component he had been holding back to the table.

Juliane had been building circuits almost as long as she had been programming, but Alan had never quite mastered the skill. There was a certain amount of artistry involved by tapping into an innate skill that just couldn't be taught. It was a talent Alan lacked, and they both knew it. Juliane knew it had to gall him that there was something he wasn't the best at.

Betty, on the other hand, immediately jumped up and ran over to them. She reached out to touch Juliane as if she needed reassurance that the real Juliane was in front of her and not just a virtual simulation.

"Thank goodness! We were streaming soldering for dummies, but I think even the dummies have more experience with electronics than I do. I am so relieved you're back on your feet. I am so, so sorry that I wasn't there for you. Why didn't you tell anyone you were feeling ill?"

"You and Alan seemed to have other things on your mind. Besides it was only a little headache, nothing at all to concern yourself about."

"A little headache doesn't keep you from our work for over a week," Alan spoke up. "I'm glad you're feeling well and rested now, but you could not have picked a worse time to have a breakdown."

"I'll try to make sure to schedule the next one at a more convenient time."

"See that you do."

Juliane scanned the workbench and the supplies strewn about it. Random silver blobs appeared in between twisted wires and broken chips. Her nostrils detected the smell of metal and burnt fabric. "Your iron is too hot and the sponge is too dry, but you haven't done too much damage yet. Chad? Can you please bring me my tools? I should be able to get us back on track in no time."

Juliane soon lost herself in the work at hand. She was aware that Betty was speaking, but her voice was like white noise. It wasn't until a distracted Alan suffered a burn from an ill-placed soldering iron that she returned to the present. Alan glared at Betty as he moved to take over the mechanical portion of the assembly. Juliane realized that hours had slipped by, but unlike before, she wasn't troubled by their unnoted passage. She almost felt alive again.

Finally, the last bolt was tightened. The device was just as Juliane had designed it in the simulation, a series of interlocking tubes surrounding a grouping of transformers and power generators.

"Well, I guess that's everything," stated Chad. "Who gets the honors of flipping the switch?"

"Should the rest of us go behind a screen or something?" Betty asked, eye-balling the device. Juliane took a deep breath, calming her racing heart. She told herself she had no doubt about the device's performance. They had logged hundreds of hours in the simulation environment for just this moment. Did Betty think that time spent had been merely for fun?

Juliane spotted Alan as he took a step forward placing him in between Betty and the device. Betty appeared to relax as if his presence was all the reassurance she needed. Betty might interpret the gesture as heroic, but Juliane wasn't convinced his motivation was as selfless as it seemed. *I miss a few days and Alan immediately thinks he has been in charge this whole time*, she thought.

Juliane realized that she was frowning and forced her features back into a neutral expression. If Alan and Betty were in a relationship, it meant she was well and truly outnumbered. Chad would shy away at the first sign of tension. Of course, if Louis were here, there would be no question as to who should take the honors.

Thinking of Louis again, Juliane's eyebrows knit in confusion. Where was he anyway? When she had last tracked him, his trajectory had suggested that he would be in the general area by now. Juliane tried to get another reading on his location and was shocked to discover that she could no longer locate him at all.

It was as if he were no longer on the grid. Her pulse quickened. Had something awful happened to him in transit? His jet was safer than most, but accidents still happened.

Lost in her concern, she did not protest as Chad led her back into an observation room along with Betty. Alan moved to the center of the room, the twinkle in his eyes blurred by the oversized safety goggles he wore.

Alan paced around the perimeter of the device as if this last inspection might find some undetected design defect. Juliane snorted at Alan's attempt at showmanship. Out of the corner of her vision, Betty's chest swelled with pride. *No doubt about it, they are definitely in a relationship.* It was everything she could do not to roll her eyes.

"I feel as if I should have prepared some formal statement," said Alan, "as this moment will go down in the history books for sure."

"What? You didn't prepare for this moment? Here I was hoping to be inspired." Juliane might have spoken with more venom a year ago, but she had to admit that Alan's childlike glee was infectious. It couldn't cut through all of the fog from the loss of the link, but it softened the fog's effect.

"I am sure that Juliane and Chad will agree to sign off on whatever speech you want to claim you made in the final report," said Betty. "The suspense is killing me! Say the magic word or something, and turn it on."

Alan laughed. "What a marvelous suggestion! Chad, make sure you are recording this. Three . . . two . . . one . . . Abracadabra!"

The device lit up as it came online indicating that all systems were functioning normally. Even in the other room, Juliane thought she felt the barest tingle on her skin. A layer of water materialized on the lab floor, just as it had in her simulation.

Chad took a step back. "We've done it," Chad whispered before correcting himself. "You've done it . . ."

"Glad to know you never doubted us, Chad." Alan's voice vibrated as if his teeth were chattering. Juliane broke her gaze away from the growing puddle to really look at him. Alan saw the light of the sun about as often as she did, but could he be paler than he was just moments ago?

"No arguing with me this time, Juliane. It's time to celebrate!" Betty ran over to the small cooler in the back of the lab and pulled out a bottle of champagne. When Juliane looked back at Alan, whatever she thought she had seen in his expression was gone; if anything, Alan's cheeks now looked flushed as he swung Betty up into an embrace with uncharacteristic abandon.

"You did consider the increase on my insurance premiums and made sure to install appropriate drainage in this room before this little experiment, correct?" a voice she hadn't heard in weeks spoke up from the lab doorway.

The bottle crashed to the ground, sending fizzing spray across the room. The sound barely registered in Juliane's ears. She spun toward the doorway, not bothering to watch for broken glass on the ground as she leaped toward Louis. Only then did she notice that there was something off about his expression. Juliane realized then what was missing was his characteristic smile. Without it, he looked older, less forgiving. She pulled up short.

He hadn't made any move toward her. His posture was formal, matching the tailored suit he wore. Juliane detected a figure in the shadows behind him. Louis turned, and the smile she missed bloomed once again on his face, only this time it wasn't directed at her.

"I received a call that the project was nearing finalization and thought it was time to schedule an impromptu inspection. Had I realized that you were already preparing for the trial, I wouldn't have dawdled at the airport." His voice was pure business, only softening with a hint of mirth when he mentioned being delayed at the airport.

Juliane was confused. Why wasn't he rushing to meet her? Why wasn't he pulling her into one of his crushing embraces? Hadn't he worried about her? She looked at her teammates. Chad's eyes immediately dropped to the floor. Had any of them even tried to reach him about her health? If he didn't know she had been out of commission for a week, it would explain why he didn't arrive sooner, but why wasn't he making eye contact?

A female voice spoke up behind him. "Are you going to make me stand here in this hallway all evening?"

"Where are my manners? Dr. Dronigh, Dr. Faris, I would like to introduce you to Elena." A delicate-looking woman stepped into the lab light. She had long blonde hair that flowed down her back in soft curls, blue eyes, and flawless skin. Juliane's eyes darted between Louis and the woman like a hummingbird seeking sustenance. A wave of hot blood hit her ears in a futile attempt to block out Louis's next words. "My wife."

Although Louis had always spoken with a slight accent, it was as if he now spoke a different language. Each syllable leaving his lips blended as if the words fought against the forward movement of time. Though Juliane clearly saw the woman standing next to him, a double vision of her entering the lab and Louis encircling her waist with his arm played over and over again in Juliane's mind's eye.

She looked to Chad in a desperate attempt to find someone who could make sense of the situation. His gaze was at least off the floor, but his expression lacked the sense of shock she felt. Juliane began to question whether she had heard Louis's introduction correctly. None of the others had made any attempt at greeting the new arrival either. *Is this a bad dream?* No, the pain of crawling out of bed was much too real to be a dream. *Am I hallucinating?* Juliane wondered. *Is that woman even there?*

Juliane closed her eyes and took a deep breath in an attempt to calm her nerves. When she opened them, the woman was still there, Louis's hand continued to rest upon the small of her back, and Louis's smile still had an idiotic dreamlike quality to it.

Chad's eyes met hers and softened. *Pity.* A quick glance showed a similar reaction on Betty. This couldn't be happening. The taste of copper filled her mouth as she bit her tongue to keep from screaming.

She felt as shattered on the inside as the broken glass that marred the lab floor, but drew herself up like an empress. She would not shed tears. Not in front of this woman. Not in front of Louis. Not in front of anyone.

Alan's voice cut the awkward pause. "Rest assured, Evans, we are more than equipped to deal with a little water here. As you can see, it is already finding its way to the drainage system."

"I don't understand. What is all the fuss about a little water?" the woman, Elena, asked.

"The fuss, as you so put, is not about the water, but where the water came from." Alan launched into his lecturing tone. "I will try to keep this to the high-level concepts. Nearly half a century ago, researchers were able to finally confirm the existence of a particle, dubbed the Higgs Boson."

Elena glanced up at Louis, who nodded for Alan to continue.

"This particle is important because it is what gives an object mass. Without it, you and everything with mass around you would merely be raw energy instead of what you see today." Alan tapped on a countertop to illustrate his point.

"There have been several attempts to study the power of the Higgs Boson over the years through various experiments, but until today, no one has been successfully able to control its power and modify the particle's bonds at will with such a small and deployable mechanism." Alan splashed the water with the toe of his shoe. "What we have done here today is, well, you could effectively call it magic. In simple terms, the water you see here was created out of thin air."

When Elena did not immediately respond with gushing praise, Alan sighed. "I am sure your husband can explain this all to you while you travel to wherever it is you are going next." He waved toward the door.

When neither of the pair moved, Alan added, "Mr. Evans, as you can see, we've had a rather eventful day, and while I can't speak for the others, I am exhausted. I'll issue our formal report at the end of the week along with a demonstration. You would be welcome to attend, or if you would prefer, you can have your people contact me to schedule a more convenient time."

Without waiting for a response, Alan began collecting his things. Betty fidgeted nervously in the corner of the room as she attempted to pick up the shards of glass from the broken bottle. "Er . . . yes, it has been an extremely busy few days. We can celebrate after the formal report . . . unless any of you would like to come out with me after this mess is cleaned up. Juliane? Chad?"

"I'm supposed to meet Nadia in the next thirty minutes or so . . . so . . ." Chad continued to look at Juliane, his shoulders slumped in apology.

Juliane said, "No, Alan's right. There is still quite a bit of work to do, and I've been away from the office for far too long as it is." The image of Betty's pitying gaze burnt in her memory. She had to get back to her office where things still made sense. "Betty, if you can take care of the rest of the cleanup, I believe I'll head that way to get started on some paperwork."

Juliane began walking toward the door directly into the path of Louis and Elena, frowning when it became clear that neither was moving out of her way. Whether Elena's vacant expression was a result of not understanding Alan's explanation about their work over the last several months, or if she truly had come into the room without any thought to what her reception might be, Juliane saw no point in wasting her breath asking either of them to stand aside.

Juliane glared at Louis. His grin slipped, but Louis appeared more irritated at Alan's borderline insubordination than ashamed of his actions. As she continued her approach, Louis raised the arm not currently attached to Elena's waist briefly. Juliane arched an eyebrow in disbelief. *At least a part of him acknowledged our past connection*, Juliane thought to herself. Immediately, his arm dropped back to his side.

Louis moved first, but only to take a step closer to Elena. Juliane briefly paused on the threshold, taking another deep breath before taking the first step into the hallway. A large part of her wanted Louis to say something to break her professional demeanor, anything that would explain this sudden change in their relationship.

As she walked away, she heard Elena barely whisper to Louis, "Did Dr. Dronigh call her Betty? I thought you said Dr. Faris's name was Juliane?"

"Juliane was the one who just left, but don't worry about keeping the names straight. Alan Dronigh is the only name that really matters."

Juliane stopped and stared at the hallway lighting fixture in an attempt to regain her equilibrium. She envisioned funneling the tempest of her anger and hurling it into the light. She imagined that the LED bulb pulsed in response.

The lab door had not entirely closed, and Juliane heard Betty exclaim, "Alan, did you turn the generator back on? We've got a situation. Everyone get back! I don't know what's happening here!"

⁕

Juliane found herself back in her office, although she didn't remember making the trip. She debated going back to see what the commotion was about, but that would mean coming back into contact with *that* woman again and Betty's pitying eyes. *No.* She wouldn't go back. She couldn't go back. Only forward. Just then, Alan entered the room.

"You missed all the fun, Juliane."

"What fun would that be?"

"Well, just after you left, there was an energy surge, and the generator came online by itself."

"I guess it's possible that some of the capacitance didn't fully discharge." Juliane leaned over the papers on her desk again. They were surrounded by technology, but the ACI had still never fully embraced going paperless. She could access all the documents in the world digitally, yet her inbox remained full. Normally, she hated paperwork, but right now, she was grateful for the distraction caused by the waste. "You can ask Chad to take another look at the groundings."

"Ah, but I haven't told you what happened next."

"I'm on pins and needles." She continued to move papers from one pile on her desk to another, adding the occasional signature.

"Well, it seems that there must be an error in at least one of your equations."

Unable to ignore such a statement, Juliane put her pen down. She folded her arms and gave Alan her full attention. "I didn't make any mistakes. You saw the results of the simulation. Everything went exactly as I had anticipated."

"Well, then, how would you explain the lack of stability in the resulting water?"

"What lack of stability? When I left, the water was draining exactly as it should." Her forehead knit in confusion. Juliane knew she was being led along, and she wondered what grand point Alan was trying to make.

"Yes, when you left, it was, but almost as soon as the door closed, the outer perimeter of the pool ignited. Then boom!" Alan spread his fingers wide like a child describing simple fireworks. "The floor is completely damaged, and poor Mrs. Evans"—Juliane's lips tighten at his casual use of the name—"may have gotten herself a little singed. It's a wonder the entire room didn't explode." He casually examined his fingernails as if the nail beds might still show evidence of ash. "I dare say, neither of the Evans left impressed. We may have just lost our funding."

Juliane felt a flutter of panic. She could not understand why Alan seemed pleased to deliver such devastating news. They both had leveraged much of their reputation on this project. Such a failure could set them back years within the ranks of the ACI. "No, I can't believe Louis would do that to us. This is only a mild setback." The words rang false even to her ears.

"Right. And Louis has proven how loyal he can be. If he could toss you aside so easily, why wouldn't he do the same with our funding? As far as he is concerned, you and our project were merely distractions. Now that he's occupied elsewhere, we will all be forgotten."

Juliane slouched in defeat. "I just don't understand. What did I do wrong?"

"Don't take it personally. I suspect some of the hydrogen and oxygen bonds began to break down. Then, with all that pure oxygen floating about, it wouldn't take much, maybe just the spark from some static cling or some preservative in the champagne to ignite the hydrogen. Fairly basic chemistry." Alan shrugged. The smile plastered to his face told Juliane that he was purposely misinterpreting her question.

Juliane closed her eyes and took a calming breath to center her emotions. Had Chad or Betty been in front of her, she might not have had the strength to continue, but she would not break down and cry in front of Alan. "You know what I mean, Alan. None of you were surprised when Elena," Juliane spat the name, "entered the lab. What did you know? What happened while I was ill?"

The smile dropped from Alan's lips. "You really had no idea at all? After all that moping around the lab over the last few weeks, I thought for sure you were reading those rumor rags Betty so enjoys. You seemed to be paying them a lot of attention when you were featured in them every other day."

"I admit it. I read the occasional article about myself. I'm only human, but the magazines aren't exactly high on my daily reading list." As she had started to fade from being a regular feature in the tabloids, other more farcical stories had taken her place. Stories about athletes rumored to be shooting up with extremely experimental performance-enhancing drugs, giving them competitive edges, but the drugs had monstrous side effects, such as fingernails hardening into claws and gums that receded, making teeth look like tusks. Ridiculous stuff.

"Then, I am sorry you had to find out the way you did. You were so calm in there—I mean, I could tell you were rightfully pissed, but overall calm. I thought you had to have heard the rumors even if you didn't know for sure." Alan ran his hand through his hair, taking a few steps closer to her.

"I still don't know. What are these rumors you keep referring to?" Juliane pushed her seat back, wanting to keep the distance between them constant. Alan recognized the move and stopped his forward progress.

"You may need to talk to Betty. She's the one who told me, but what people are saying is that Louis suffered a nervous breakdown, anxiety attack, or something like that about a month ago, and this Elena person saw him wandering the street. Supposedly, she had no clue who he was and no idea about his fame or wealth or anything. The magazines say she took him back to her home where she nursed him back to health. They got married by the end of the week. Betty tells me it is being portrayed as quite the fairy tale romance."

The timing of his 'attack' would have put it around the time when Juliane first severed the bond. While she was here trying to fill the void with her work and feeling miserable, Louis was off getting played by wannabe Florence Nightingale.

Juliane felt a coldness settle into her heart. "Idiot." Juliane wasn't sure if she was referring to Louis or herself. "He should have called me. I could have explained everything."

"Could you?" Alan asked. "Because I would like to know what the hell has been going on with you lately. If you didn't already know about the rumors, then what is your excuse for the last few weeks? And what really happened today with the generator?"

Juliane ground her teeth together before answering. "The generator surged and the hydrogen ignited. You just finished telling me that."

Alan closed the remaining distance to the desk and leaned on it. "You and I both know you don't make mistakes. Something or someone sent a command to the generator. It wasn't Betty, and even I didn't know it was capable of doing anything like that." Alan leaned over further. Juliane could see her stunned face reflected in the safety glasses he still wore. "I believe it is your turn to do some explaining."

twenty-one

Juliane bowed her head. "I didn't know. I swear. I didn't mean for anything like that to happen. I overheard him tell her that I was nothing. I was so angry, but it couldn't possibly . . . I never would . . ." Juliane chewed her lip as she played the scene back in her memory. Louis's words. Elena's smug smile. Her shoulders slumped. "I haven't been myself ever since I disabled the private network."

"What private network?"

"The one I established with Louis. I thought we would be able to have a deeper connection, only it never worked right. I broke it off thinking we could just fix it later, but I think I did even more damage and now, now . . ."

Alan stepped around the desk and put his hand on her shoulder. Juliane decided to ignore that it was Alan offering comfort. She was tired of fighting. There was no point. She was never strong enough. Never good enough. Nothing had gone according to plan. Juliane admitted to herself that at that moment she needed someone. Anyone. Even Alan. Juliane leaned into the gesture, whispering, "I don't know what's happening to me."

"You are evolving. We are evolving." Juliane looked up from her seat. The way Alan stood above her allowed for the glow from the overhead lights to reflect on the surface of his eyes, giving them a near fiery appearance. He was confidence manifested.

Juliane pulled away as if burned. Alan was too confident. He might not have had his heart torn inside out, but his career was equally affected by the accident. "Tell me you saw this coming and that everything is going according to your grand plan."

Alan snorted. "Juliane, after all this time we've been together, how can you even doubt it? Everything is going according to my grand plan. Everything."

"But what about our project? What should we do?"

"I think it may be time to introduce you to my other benefactor." Alan smiled, but it was a wolf's grin.

———

Alan arranged for all their transportation to his mysterious benefactor. He hadn't elaborated other than to say that the office was a mere ninety minutes away from campus, in Worcester. When the car arrived, Alan opened the door for her as he held a quick exchange with the driver. Juliane was deaf to whatever passed between the two of them.

As they left the campus, Juliane turned off her newsfeed filters. *Gossip news be damned*, she thought. Immediately, she was bombarded with articles featuring Louis. Pictures leaked from the private ceremony adorned several magazine covers, and interviews by the friends of the new Mrs. Evans filled the feed.

Other, more insidious rumors began to weave their way into the conversation. Juliane saw her name appear in the feed summaries. She clicked on a few links. The articles speculated that she had only been a paid cover to divert the media's attention from the real relationship.

Reporters and celebrity profilers alike dissected every detail about Louis and her relationship, looking for the telltale sign that things hadn't been what they had seemed. What did their body language say? Where was she during high profile events? Where was Elena at the same time? The reporters even attempted to estimate how much she might have made in such an arrangement.

Unfortunately, once her filter program was turned off, it was incredibly difficult to turn back on, especially now that her name was involved. As all media continued to stream directly to her brain, there was little she could do to escape its onslaught as the car sped toward their destination.

The car pulled up in front of one of the several towers in the heart of the city. It had been constructed out of sandstone and glass. It was easily the tallest building in the area. A mountainous pillar of beige and blue scraping the sky. And yet it almost appeared natural, as if it had been carved directly out of solid rock by the elements rather than man-made.

The top of the tower consisted of only a moderate slope and lacked many of the gaudier finishing touches so prevalent on the tallest buildings found in other locations. At least Juliane thought it did. It was difficult to tell for sure from the base of the building. A plaque next to the door announced it housed a group called Apex.

The interior was elegant, yet minimal. Juliane's heels clicked on the floor as she and Alan crossed the cavernous lobby toward the elevator doors. A guard looked up as they passed but appeared to recognize Alan and allowed them to continue unchallenged.

Alan walked past the first three elevator doors before stopping in front of a fourth, set slightly out of sight. He held his thumb on the call button for an unusual length of time. Alan noticed her look of curiosity; he leaned over and whispered, "Biometric security."

Within minutes, the elevator doors opened, and they ascended in silence made even more notable by the lack of easy listening music or sound of whirling gears or turning belts.

The lobby at their only stop mirrored the one below, with a few small differences. High-end pieces of artwork hung on the walls, although none of them were by any artist Juliane recognized. Juliane judged that they were most likely originals rather than reproductions.

The woman at the front desk smiled as they approached. "Alan, how nice to see you. I hear that congratulations are in order."

Juliane shot Alan a quick glance. "I thought we were supposed to keep our research under wraps."

The woman tilted her head in Juliane's direction. "Ah, you must be Dr. Faris. Rest assured; he's never shared any of what you do over in Meriden with me. I was congratulating him on his engagement, of course."

"Engagement? You and Betty are engaged?" Juliane couldn't prevent the depth of her disbelief from entering her tone.

"Jealous?" Alan asked with a smile.

"No. I am just surprised, that's all. When did this happen?"

"Oh, a few days before your . . . recent personal days. It isn't relevant to our work, so we didn't think it worth mentioning." Alan paused as if considering to deliver his next words. Juliane readied herself for a biting retort.

"Betty also seemed to think you wouldn't react to the news well under the . . . ah . . . circumstances," Alan murmured.

Juliane felt a blush begin to bloom on her cheeks and fought it back with icy determination.

"I suspect now she was right."

The woman at the front desk continued to stare at Juliane. Her eyes momentarily widened, and Juliane knew she had made the connection between her name and the various news stories. Then, Juliane saw it. The softening of the woman's face. *Pity.* Pity from this stranger. Another blast of ice water hit her veins. She had made a mistake letting her guard down with Alan back at the office. She would not show weakness again.

"Well, let me also extend my congratulations to you both." Turning back, Juliane arched her back and held her head straight. She looked down at the woman without lowering her chin. "Now I don't believe we came all this way to exchange gossip and pleasantries. I believe we have an appointment?"

The woman blushed. "Yes, of course, right this way. Mr. Knightley is expecting you. Can I get you anything? Coffee, tea, water?" She scurried around the desk and toward a large pair of double doors.

"Juliane, was that tone necessary? She was just trying to be friendly."

"I didn't come all this way to make new friends."

"That may be, but that's a quick way to make enemies, and you don't want to be on Sarah's bad side. Besides, Damien has been a good friend to me for some time. He's been quite eager to finally meet you."

The room behind the double doors continued with the minimalist theme except for a large water feature that took up a portion of one wall. The water trickled down a series of slate stones and emptied into a narrow pool at its base. Scattered around the base and throughout the pool were a series of flames. Juliane couldn't tell if the flames were gas-powered or merely simulated. In either case, the effect was captivating.

Juliane didn't realize how mesmerized she was until a voice spoke up from the center of the room. "I see you appreciate my serenity wall."

She broke her gaze from the fountain as she realized that she recognized the voice's owner.

It was the same man she had noticed in the corner of the Vegas auditorium. The same man who she spotted later near Alan's platform. She vaguely remembered that Louis had appeared to recognize him, but did not seem particularly happy to see him.

The man Juliane presumed was Damien Knightley walked over to the serenity wall where Juliane stood. Just like in Vegas, he wore a finely tailored suit and not a hair was out of place.

"It is very peaceful," Juliane said.

"It only looks that way from a distance. If you were smaller and positioned on one of those rocks, I am sure the view would be quite terrifying. Everything comes down to a perspective, don't you think?"

Juliane raised her eyebrows in quick salute of his observation.

"I must say I have looked forward to meeting you for quite some time," Damien Knightley continued. "I can't say most people would describe me as a patient man, but he kept telling me that you weren't ready yet. I was beginning to worry that Alan here intended to keep you to himself until the end of time."

Juliane risked a glance at Alan, whose teeth shone brightly in the room's lighting.

"I'm sorry, ready for what? Alan's not told me anything about why we are here," Juliane said. Her hand tightened into a fist on its own accord. More secrets.

"Really, Alan? You know, one of these days, your little flair for the dramatic is going to backfire on you." Damien attempted to scowl at Alan, but his eyes didn't quite commit to the gesture.

"It's your program. I thought you might prefer to tell her all about it yourself."

The man clicked his tongue, then paused. "I suppose you are right. Now let us start over. I may have heard about you, but obviously, Alan was not polite enough to reciprocate the favor. My name, as you probably have already guessed, is Damien Knightley." He paused as if he was expecting Juliane to recognize it. She didn't. He shrugged after a second and continued, "I happen to head up a fairly discreet group made up of individuals who believe that there needs to be an alternative to the ACI. A group not afraid to take bold initiatives for the greater good, rather than just for profit."

Juliane relaxed, unclenching her fist. She looked again at Alan as another thought took her. "You've been working for the competition. All this time? What does that make you, a corporate spy?"

"Labels," Alan snorted. "I saw an opportunity and I took it."

"But what about your contract? Couldn't you get into serious trouble for violating your non-disclosure agreement?" Juliane asked, alarmed.

"What non-disclosure agreement? I certainly have never signed anything of the sort. At least, not anything legally binding." He smirked.

Juliane's gaze darted about the room. She took a step back.

"Oh, come on, Juliane," Alan sighed. "We both know that you've been willing to bend a rule or two when it helped you get ahead."

"Bending the rules is one thing. You've been doing much worse."

"You've been as much a part of this as I've been," Alan countered, taking a step toward her.

"I most certainly have not." Juliane drew her head up, refusing to be intimidated.

"Think about all those projects we've worked together on. The ones that needed quick funding. You never once wondered where the extra money came from?"

"I just thought you knew ways to fast-track approval."

Alan grinned. "And I did." He swung his arms out, emphasizing the lavish room. "I do."

Juliane turned her attention to Damien. "I don't understand. Isn't the ACI the competition? Why would you be writing checks for its projects?"

Damien shrugged. "Business is rarely black and white. I invest when and where I see potential."

"So why did you bring me here? Alan might think he can get around his contract with the ACI, but I have no interest in participating in corporate espionage."

Damien's eyes softened. "No. Unfortunately, you would have little value for my organization in that capacity. Especially not after recent events."

Juliane felt her shoulders slump. Damien was right. The explosion in the lab would ensure she would never be granted access to sensitive projects ever again. If she was Louis's wife and had been on the receiving end of that explosion, she would have made sure of that. "Then why?" she whispered.

"I told you, I invest when and wherever I see potential. You are that potential. I want to invest in you," Damien said.

Juliane blinked as she tried to make sense of Damien's words.

He laughed. "For being made up of a number of geniuses, the ACI has still not learned how to fully capitalize on its assets. If you don't mind me saying so, you are the complete package: ambition, brains, and beauty. So often we only encounter people with one or two of those traits."

Damien began to stroll around the perimeter of the room. "Sign with me and you would get to pursue whatever you fancy, as long as there's a business case for it." Damien's voice softened into the quiet tone of a concerned parent. "My group may not be as large as the ACI, but we are comprised of the very best in their fields, the most promising individuals of our time. I allow those who sign with me the freedom to pursue their interests as they see fit, provided we all work together toward the group's benefit."

Damien stopped behind his desk. "By accepting my offer, you would, however, need to sever any remaining ties to the ACI." He paused to scan her face for a reaction. "But am I wrong in thinking that this might not be a large request?"

"I didn't know what to expect when Alan invited me out here, and I don't know anything about you or your firm." Reaching the pinnacle of respect and success within the ACI had been her goal for so long, it was difficult to consider anything else. If she stayed with the ACI, she would likely have to grovel before Louis or worse Elena with every proposal. The thought was unbearable.

Starting anywhere new, especially if the lab accident came to light, would mean clawing her way back up from the bottom. Although Juliane was uneasy with the arrangement Alan had with Damien, Damien was at least offering her a chance to start at the top.

Damien smiled. "Of course. It just so happens your timing today is excellent. I have a meeting scheduled in just an hour with several of my other key players in the organization. Why don't you and Alan go and enjoy a cup of coffee and then join us in the large conference room on the sixteenth floor?"

"How much does the rest of the group know about me?" Juliane caught herself asking. She didn't know if she would be able to stand more looks of pity.

"Oh, they are aware of most of the work produced within their fields but are not always as tied into the history of specific individuals. As a group, we tend to be too busy to pay attention to gossip. Alan has only discussed you in detail with me. But I haven't felt the need to pass your information along to the rest of the group. Besides"—Damien directed a pointed glance at Alan—"I wasn't sure if Alan was ever going to arrange a meeting."

"If I do agree to join your team, I would like to have a fresh start. Would you be able to offer that?"

"I can understand the desire to rebuild your reputation in private considering your present, er . . . celebrity," Damien said the word as if it was a delicate piece of china. "As I mentioned, we pride ourselves on our discretion here. If you would like me to introduce you under a different name or gloss over your most recent background, I would be happy to do so, although I can't promise that they won't eventually make the connection. Would that suffice?"

Juliane considered his offer. Shaking her head, she said, "No, I don't think that will fool anyone. They might not recognize me right away, but someone would be bound to connect me with the woman on the news."

"What if they didn't see you in the flesh regularly? Would that satisfy you?"

"What do you mean?"

"Several of our group prefer to maintain their primary offices elsewhere. I would be more than happy to grant you the same privilege. Thanks to that upgrade of yours, you might not even have to physically step through these doors again after today. Would that offer you enough of a fresh start?"

Juliane chewed her lip. Damien's suggestion would give her more freedom than she previously had with the ACI. She could make her avatar look however she wanted. She could blur its features or change its look, and none would be the wiser provided she limited her face-to-face visits. Then, even if someone did make the connection to her name, they might think it was just some unlucky coincidence. His idea could work.

Damien glanced down at his watch. "I don't want you to feel as if I am rushing you into a decision, but I do need to make a call. Why don't you think about my offer over the next hour?"

Juliane nodded. "One hour."

As if by magic, the office doors opened. Either Damien had a secret call button or his assistant had been listening to the entire conversation. Juliane's stomach tightened. Perhaps she had, as Alan suggested, made a tactical mistake by being rude to her.

"Until then."

twenty-two

As the elevator doors opened, Alan took a sharp left, directing her to a coffee shop located just outside the lobby. Gesturing for Juliane to take a seat, he ordered for the both of them, not bothering to ask how she liked hers.

The steaming mug was thrust under her face. The swirling dark liquid smelled and looked perfect. Juliane tipped the cup back in ready anticipation of the first sip. As she did so, it occurred to her that Damien's offer meant it was unlikely she would have to suffer Chad's coffee-turned-sludge ever again. She sputtered, setting the cup down on a table. *Wow, that's bitter*, she thought. They must have over-roasted the beans.

Alan settled into a chair covered in plush purple fabric in prime view of other shop patrons. As he drank from his mug, he looked very much like a medieval lord surveying his court. *He doesn't have a care in the world*, Juliane thought. *And why should he? Everything always works out for him.* Her eyes tightened, and she turned away.

She tried to imagine what life would be like, being equally respected and appreciated through Damien's firm. She realized then that her subconscious had already decided to take him up on his offer.

Lost in her thoughts, she was startled when Alan placed his hand on her shoulder, a finger coming into contact with her skin along her neckline. "Are you ready to meet the others?"

As she stood, the anxiety and remorse of the last hours was replaced with a feeling of confidence and calm. Starting over. She had a lifetime's experience starting over. She would not be weak. She would not be pitied. She had a sudden vision of herself as a newly-crowned queen being escorted to the balcony to greet her subjects for the first time. "Lead the way."

Alan must have sensed some of her state of mind because he bowed slightly at her words.

When they arrived on the designated floor, she followed Alan into a large conference room shaped like a piece of honeycomb. He hadn't needed to stop for any directions, so he must have attended a few meetings in the room. She wondered how long Alan had been working for both sides.

Ten members of the board were in the room already, seated at a large U-shaped mahogany table. Juliane didn't look at any of them. Her gaze was instead caught by the room's interior. The walls were decorated with large canvases of paint splatter. At first glance, each piece looked as if the artist had thrown colors against the surface at random. She was startled then to realize that if you scanned your eyes over all the pieces together, the chaos they individually represented was transformed into a beautiful landscape. It was breathtaking work.

"Your timing is excellent." Damien's voice brought her attention back to the table and the meeting in progress. "Everyone, we have a special guest visiting us today." He nodded to an empty seat. "But perhaps you would prefer to make your own introduction?"

"I'm Juliane Faris." She wouldn't hide. She was done pretending to be anything but who or what she was—a capable woman who deserved to be recognized for her own merits. "My experience to date has been in augmented reality and bioprocessing, and I look forward to joining the team."

Damien grinned. "Short and to the point. Maybe you will rub off on some of the rest of us." He directed a glance at Alan. "Well, then I would like to introduce you to Camille Nadal, who has thus far led all our efforts within the general health and wellness space as well as applications that touch on behavioral science. There are so many advances being made in biotechnology. I expect she is eager to get some of that work off her plate.

"Next to her is Eithan Yuan, our resident expert on genetics and gene therapy. Lillian O'Rail heads up finance. Rhett Mossel leads our political advocacy. Alan, of course, helps us with market intelligence, research, and the occasional talent acquisition." Damien smiled at his joke. Each team member had inclined their head as they were introduced.

The door to the office opened again, and the woman from Damien's front office entered, carrying a stack of papers, which she distributed. "Ah, yes, this is Sarah, my assistant, whom you've already met. Don't let her friendly manner fool you. In addition to keeping me on schedule, she handles most of the day-to-day management of the support staff. I hear she can be quite the taskmaster."

Sarah's lips turned up as if she was well used to her boss' accolades, but the smile never reached her eyes. Juliane suspected Sarah was the type who could hold a grudge. When all the papers had been distributed, Sarah took a seat to his right at the base of the U.

"Finally, last but not least is one of our newest team members, only joining us a couple of months ago. I will admit that I was overjoyed when he reached out to us, as he is quite the steal. Heading our legal department is Durham Ladensham."

Juliane started. A smile crept on her lips. *So that explains where he disappeared to.* She hadn't seen Durham since they'd left Vegas or heard from him since sending him a check. However, a friendly face would make the transition to the Apex team much easier. The smile slipped from her face. *He's Louis's friend. He'll be able to report back everything I do. Is there no escape from that man?*

He turned in his chair. While there was a shine in his eyes, there was no warmth radiating from him in response to Damien's words. *Or maybe he won't.* Juliane was startled to realize there was no sign of recognition at all. *How does he not recognize me? Did Louis ask Durham to entertain so many women that we all blended together?*

Perhaps she should feel grateful for Durham's lack of recognition rather than irritated. But they'd spent hours together. how could Durham not recognize her?

Juliane forced her hands to unclench. If he wanted to act as if they'd never met before, that was fine by her. She had already announced she was joining the team, so there was no going back now.

She focused her thoughts, accessing the datasphere and her simulation software. Several scenarios played out in her mind's eye at a fraction of a second. There was nothing he could say or do now that she wasn't prepared for.

Decision made, she stepped toward the empty chair as Alan took a seat near Sarah with a cocky and amused expression on his face. Shoulders straight, Juliane looked Durham squarely in the eye. She was Juliane Faris, and this time, he would remember her, but for the reasons she wanted. She would make sure they all did.

twenty-three

Less than five years had passed since that first day in the conference room, but already her contributions since joining Damien's group could be seen attached to the ears and around the necks of individuals in every major city and many small towns as well.

She launched a line of slim devices made to look like jewelry but also encapsulated nano-processors and sensor packets in various form factors. Louis and the ACI might have the headset market locked, but overall, she thought her solution was far more elegant.

True to his word, Juliane had been free to launch a company around her technology provided she occasionally reported into the main office. She'd named it Fair Use—a nod to her name as well as the fact her devices ensured the ACI couldn't achieve a monopoly on access to *her* datasphere.

One of her products was an ear clip which sent a signal into the brain, allowing a wearer to interface with the virtual world simply by closing their eyes and opening their mind. It wasn't as fast or as powerful of a solution as genetic imprinting. However, the Gene Assist serum was not something she could replicate without wasting millions in patent litigation. As a result, it was an option available only to those who never had to ask how much something cost and offered exclusively through the ACI.

The pendant version was an entry-level model for those even less risk-averse and budget-conscious. She'd put everything she had into the launch. Framed images of models wearing her products as they walked down the runway hung along one of her office walls.

Even though Betty still worked for the ACI, and certainly didn't need the access point, she had worn one of Juliane's earliest product releases at her wedding to Alan. The device caught the light at just the right moment in one of the photographer's shots and the product had gone viral. Early product reviews and press releases covered the other wall. Her company's more recent news was much less frame-worthy.

"There was another suicide reported last night." Juliane glanced up from her desk as her assistant, Stuart, added another stack of documentation to the top of the increasingly unstable pile.

"You are positive it was a suicide?"

Juliane sighed. It was the fourth reported death at her manufacturing partner's factory. Her only chance to get her product into the hands of enough of the population to revolutionize society was through a low-cost production facility.

That meant long hours in locations not known for high wages. There was always a risk that the demands might eventually take their toll on individual technicians employed at these sites. Eyes wide open to the risks, she had toured numerous locations all boasting programs for their workers designed to maintain, if not increase, worker morale, and she had ultimately selected what she believed, at the time, was a quality partner.

"An investigation is underway, but it appears that way."

"Well, at least we don't have to worry about a murderer being on the loose." Juliane knew as soon as the words were out of her mouth that she was being insensitive, but another investigation would only further delay their next launch.

First, all work would stop while the root cause was investigated. The worker's friends and family would be interviewed. New processes, procedures, and safety nets would be installed. Each of those things took time to implement, as necessary as they were, and it cost money she might have spent elsewhere.

An alert scrolled by her vision. A research center in Southern California speculated that there could be a link to cancer from the overuse of her ear clips. She ran a quick cross-reference. The center's proximity to Elena's hometown should have thrown the validity of the research into question, but the media always seemed to latch on to potential issues with her products, or her partners, with far more glee than they did with Louis's . . . especially after the ACI announced that it had found a way to embed nano-generators into roadways, building materials, and even some fabrics.

Almost overnight, everything was self-powered. All you had to do was pay a royalty to the ACI, and the world was grateful for the privilege.

Politicians and pundits raved about how generous the ACI was with their cheap energy. Juliane grimaced. *If they only knew what technology the ACI held back.*

People in developing nations were still dying of dehydration and illnesses spread through contaminated water. The ACI could have been giving them instant clean water if only they hadn't shelved the matter generator project after the accident.

It's all Elena's fault. If that wasn't irresponsible enough, tens of thousands of people were put out of work as power plants were taken offline, replaced by the ACI's nanos.

Does anyone care? No. Everyone loved the ACI, especially Louis, and why? Because their little electronic toys were powered indefinitely just by standing near the street.

Meanwhile, she and her company were at risk of being made to look like a monster. Juliane crumpled a piece of paper that she hadn't even realized she had picked up from the stack on her desk.

"I'll arrange a conference call with the production facility manager," her assistant said, already backing out of Juliane's office.

"And go ahead and start working up the press release. We may need to get out ahead of this one."

Juliane had ensured that all of her production heads were equipped with functioning ear clips or pendants as part of their manufacturing agreement, so at least she wasn't going to have to squeeze in an international flight. They all wore them constantly per their agreement, which came in handy for meetings like the one she needed now.

Juliane closed her eyes and sent a meeting command. You really could not get a sense that people understood the gravity of the situation on a conference call, but thanks to her virtual world, she could make sure those that worked for her did. All she had to do was create the correct motivation.

twenty-four

Nets, he said. Juliane's lips curled in displeasure. *Nets.* Nets would only prevent tragic landings. They did nothing to address why a person would jump from the facility in the first place.

The conversation with her initial contact had been a waste of her time. As she listened as the man detailed the list of fees and upgrades the facility would need, she wished she had the luxury of shifting the entire production line, but that wasn't an option. At least not now.

Signing off, Juliane decided she needed to discuss strategy with Damien. Surely some of his connections had found reliable manufacturing partners who could provide volume manufacturing at a reasonable cost without devaluing human life.

Her office door burst open to a very pale Betty. Upon first glance, the years had not been kind. Betty's eyes were sunken and her skin shone with a waxy hue. Juliane couldn't quite remember the last time she had seen the woman in the flesh. She had always looked the same as she had the day they first met whenever they corresponded in the virtual world.

"I hope you don't mind that I let myself in. Your assistant wasn't at his desk."

"Yes, we have a situation that I need to attend to."

"Oh." Betty froze, glancing furtively at the door. "Am I keeping you from something?"

"Well, I might not be able to give you a whole lot of time, but I can spare a few minutes. Unfortunately, we have gained some experience dealing with these sorts of things."

Papers positioned next to the chameleon paperweight on Juliane's desk fluttered from the breeze caused by Betty's sigh of relief. Juliane caught sight of the lizard's grin and scowled. It was designed for one job. One.

"I appreciate it." Betty's voice was hardly more than a whisper. "I hate to bother you at the office. I know how busy you always are."

Juliane nodded in acknowledgment as she attempted to gather up a few of the files she would need for the next hours' worth of meetings.

"Betty, you know I would love to be able to spend more time after hours with you if I could . . ."

"That's not why I am here—"

"Don't apologize. What can I do for you?" Until the factory was held accountable, each minute wasted was putting more lives at risk.

Betty moved like a cuckoo bird, only one that had lost its voice. "I don't know where to start."

"Well, trying usually goes a long way." Juliane had meant the comment as a joke, but her present mood made the words terser than she intended. She looked away, only to have her gaze catch on the only framed image on her office wall not featuring a Fair Use product—a pair of dogs. There was no time to consult with Damien. She knew what she had to do to get through to these people.

When she had entered the room, Betty's face had been somewhat yellowed; the subsequent blush made her resemble rotting fruit. "You're right, but of course you are always right, aren't you?" Betty chuckled at her joke, but the laughter was forced. "It's Stevie."

"Your son? He's what, two now?"

"Four, actually."

"Has it been so long?"

"He's seeing things."

"It's perfectly normal for a boy his age to have an overactive imagination."

"I wouldn't be here if it was an imaginary friend. What he is seeing is much worse."

"Could he have stumbled across some of your and Alan's work? Images of the human body dissected can be quite traumatic to a young boy."

"Alan and I . . . we aren't working together anymore . . ." Betty's voice trailed off. Juliane had to strain her ears to make out Betty's last word.

"Oh?" Juliane didn't expect a response but took Betty's silence as confirmation. "That's a shame. You both seemed to be quite the team."

Juliane mentally checked her internal clock. Stuart likely had notified the majority of the remaining production heads by now. If she could wrap this up in the next couple of minutes, she might still have time to pour a cup of coffee before beginning the interrogation. "As nice as it is to see you, I'm the last person you should be coming to with family problems. Perhaps you might want to talk to someone like a—"

Betty interrupted, "I don't know how much more time he has!"

Juliane returned her attention to the woman in her office, taking in the dark circles under her eyes. With a thought, she sent a message to her assistant informing him that she would be delayed for a few more minutes but to start arranging the next call.

"What do you mean? What's going on?"

"It began several months ago. Stevie started telling us fantastic stories about places we'd never been to and about awful people we've never met. At first, we thought what you did, he had just started to create imaginary friends."

Juliane nodded in encouragement.

"But then he described seeing some place that sounded like a torture chamber with people being transformed into monsters. Alan and I had a huge fight about it." Betty twisted her shirt. "I accused him of allowing Stevie to watch inappropriate movies. Then it got worse."

"Stevie would start screaming for no determinable reason, only to go catatonic immediately afterward. I tried everything to snap him out of it, but nothing worked." Betty's eyes shone. "He just wasn't there. The episodes started getting more frequent, and he would be gone longer and longer."

"I've had to stop working—one of us had to be home with him at all times." She grumbled. "Now I'm afraid to even sleep, terrified that one of these days he won't wake up at all."

Tears flowed freely down Betty's cheeks as Juliane took a nervous step before freezing in place. Juliane was completely out of her element and at a loss as to what might be expected from her after such a revelation.

"Where is he now?"

"There's a children's clinic here. He is there for observation, but no one seems to know anything."

Juliane crossed the remaining distance until she was at Betty's side, placing an awkward hand on the woman's shoulder. "Well, I am sure that they will be able to figure out what is the issue. You look exhausted. Did you come here to ask to take a nap on my couch while you wait for the results?"

"I would have slept at the hospital if I just wanted a nap," Betty snapped.

"Sorry—I just don't understand then. What does Alan think is the matter? I would advise you if I could, but I'm not a medical doctor. My studies were purely theoretical. I don't have any experience with what you described."

"Yes, you do." Juliane pulled her hand back as Betty spun with violence to face her. "You and Alan have more experience than anyone." Gone was any appearance of nicety from Betty's expression. "The doctors aren't going to find anything. They don't know yet what they're looking for, but I do. I was there. I saw what it did to you and Alan." Betty's shoulders sagged under the weight of her pronouncement.

"You think Alan performed the procedure on your son? He takes incredible risks, but I can't imagine he would risk a child's well-being." Juliane considered what she knew about Alan. "Well, perhaps he would with other people's kids, but never his own! What did Alan say when you asked him about it?"

Betty's shoulders slumped as the fight left her body as quickly as it had arrived. "He denied everything of course."

Juliane was out of her depth and racked her brain to find a way to defuse the situation. Pressure expanded behind her temple like a thunderhead. Her virtual vision flashed with another headline.

There was no time for distraction. She had to get back to the business at hand. "Alan and I don't see eye to eye very often, but I would be inclined to believe him. There has to be another explanation."

Betty raised an eyebrow at Juliane's statement but did not challenge her further. "Alan may not have strapped him to a chair and stuck him with needles, but he's wrong about not being responsible."

Juliane's forehead knit. "What are you suggesting?"

"If he didn't have the procedure, then there is another fairly basic explanation. He was simply born with the upgrade, but doesn't have the mental maturity to control it."

"But that's not possible. The serum—"

"Required a virus to work. Viruses mutate. You of all people should understand how survival depends on adaptation. Now, unless I can figure out a way to help him control it, I expect the energy drain is killing him."

The room took on a temporary red hue, and Betty's features blurred as a meeting notice flared within Juliane's mind. Stuart must have successfully gotten everyone online.

Betty was under a lot of stress. That much was clear to see. Her marriage was suffering as was her child, but she had to be grasping at straws. There was simply no way Alan would have allowed the virus to escape his control. Juliane knew him too well.

The minute hand on her internal clock shifted again. By now, her first contact would have briefed his colleagues on their earlier conversation. If she was going to be able to bring them around to her way of thinking, she needed to make sure this time they understood exactly how displeased she was, and each second was more time for them to agree on some lip service statement. Her legacy, as well as several lives, were potentially at stake.

As much as she wanted to help her friend, there was nothing she could do better than the care he was already receiving at the clinic. While Juliane had debated her options, Betty had wiped her tears away, but her skin remained smeared with moisture. Clearly, she was looking for some form of comfort, but Juliane was still unsure of what she could offer.

"What did Alan say when you talked to him about this possibility?" Juliane began moving toward the door, hopeful that the motion might encourage Betty to follow.

"At first he tried to convince me it was something like night terrors or epilepsy—like I wouldn't have already ruled those out. When I didn't agree, he practically accused me of hiding a genetic defect in my family history." Betty's lips drew thin. "As if our son's condition couldn't possibly be a result of something from his side of the family tree." Once again, Betty's cheeks flared with pent-up anger.

Juliane could almost see the remaining evidence of tears evaporate when exposed to the fire of Betty's expression. She had never seen her friend look so fierce.

Pulling the door open for Betty, Juliane commented, "I know too well how Alan can be at times, but he is one of the most brilliant minds alive today. I am sure that if he just has time to look at the problem, he'll be able to figure it out."

Betty refused to budge.

Juliane continued as if Betty wasn't like a land mine posed to go off with a single misstep. "Until then, I am sure the doctors are going to take great care of your son."

Betty remained where she stood.

Looking at the open door, Juliane wondered if it might be easier to join the call from a nearby conference room. "You are still more than welcome to stay and get some rest here before heading back to the hospital."

Betty chewed her lip as she took a small step toward the open door. Her voice dropped to a dull monotone when she next spoke. Her shoulders shifted not unlike a lioness readying herself for a strike. "I don't believe you realize how close you came to dying in the labs while you adjusted to the change."

Betty pivoted and began strolling along the side of the room, running her finger along the wall. "If Chad and I hadn't made sure you were cared for, you wouldn't be in this fancy office today."

Stopping near Juliane's desk, she picked up Juliane's paperweight and held it as if studying its living counterpart. "You always thought yourself so much better than the rest of us . . ."

Betty returned the metal lizard to its resting place. "Remember how concerned you had been about my ability to handle the upgrade? You didn't think I could. Now, imagine what it must be like for my son. He's only a child."

Betty wrung her hands. She looked at Juliane. "All I am asking is for you to help me take care of him. There is no one in this world as experienced as you to guide him through the process." Betty's eyes shone with unshed tears. "Please, Jules. I am begging you."

Juliane winced. She recognized that the woman was a desperate mother, but if Alan suspected the child's condition was caused by epilepsy, then it probably was, and no amount of mentoring would change that. Juliane shook her head. There was nothing she could do.

Betty's nostrils flared. "I see. I came here looking for a friend. But I see now, I never had one here. The next time you need help, and you will don't look to me to bail you out," she spat.

The room flared red again. Juliane drew herself up. She had never asked for Betty's help. She had managed for years without anyone. She didn't need anyone. Relationships just got in the way. Juliane sighed as her headache began to ease. Perhaps it was better this way. She'd keep it professional, but perhaps it was time for them all to focus on the bigger picture.

Juliane mentally summoned Stuart back to the office. He must have returned to his desk as he was instantly inside the room. "Dr. Dronigh has had a tiring past few weeks. Can you please make sure that she has something cool to drink while I attend this meeting and arrange for a car to take her back to St. James Hospital?"

Her assistant's eyes closed as he began to make the requested arrangements, but Betty interrupted them, "There is no need. I am perfectly capable of finding my own way back."

Before either of them could say a word, Betty made her way out of the office door, her every step like that of a death row prisoner resigned to her fate.

twenty-five

"Dr. Dronigh's just under a great deal of stress," Juliane explained to Stuart as Betty exited the office. "Even if she won't accept our help, can you please make sure that someone follows her back to the hospital to ensure she makes it there safely?"

Juliane paused in thought. Betty wouldn't appreciate the gesture, not after Juliane's refusal. "But have them hang back a few feet. I am not sure that she would recognize it as kindness in her present state."

"Right away." Stuart turned, following Betty's path. Juliane forced Betty out of her thoughts; she could not allow herself to be distracted, especially not in the virtual world.

She closed her eyes and focused on accessing her domain. The virtual image resolved into a well-furnished conference room, mirroring an office space located on the other side of the planet. A trio of individuals sat around the table.

Her first point of contact was seated on the end and lacked the degree of command over his virtual appearance displayed by the others. His clothes alternated between power suit and armor. A woman appeared on the other end of the table. While her appearance remained constant, her body was as translucent as a ghost. The third, another man, appeared solid from the waist up but had neglected to visualize his feet.

Juliane frowned. Their lack of competency in the virtual world should have been an indicator of their competency in the real world.

"Let's get started. I've called you here today because I just received word that there has been another incident reported. I trust that you have already initiated the required counseling for his roommates? Who would like to tell me more about the unfortunate worker and what is being done to prevent a recurrence?"

The man in the center of the trio began to answer, but Juliane couldn't understand the words. She bit down on a curse. While caught up with Betty's dramatic visit, she had neglected to turn on her translation program. It really did not take up that much processing power; she decided that once she finished this meeting, she would just keep it running in the background continuously.

The words began to flow into English as the translation tool took effect.

". . . not been able to identify any family or next of kin. We acted very efficiently in response. The body has already been sent to the furnace for incineration." Juliane pursed her lips. The translation program's only failing was it occasionally substituted an incorrect word, especially with languages that contained multiple dialects. *It couldn't have translated that last bit right.*

Juliane felt a tug on her senses. *What now?* she thought. Turning back to the trio across from her, she said, "It would seem that I need to cut this meeting short."

It was time to make a lasting impression. "These sorts of incidents cannot continue." The conference room transformed into a wilderness. "I shouldn't even have to use the plural of that word." She willed her avatar to grow in size until she could easily grind them under her shoe like bugs.

"I need you to make significant changes, and I need you to do so now. We may not have to worry about a family coming around, making demands, or talking to the media this time, but we cannot afford for there to be a next time."

Storm clouds rolled in, filling the artificial sky. Creatures with disjointed limbs, razor teeth, and gray-scaled skin slithered toward her audience. The translucent woman tried to stand and run away. Juliane exerted her will, rendering her incapable of movement.

"Consider this your number one priority. I don't want you to sleep or eat unless you first bring me a more permanent corrective action. If you do not, you can believe I will reprogram your brains so that all food tastes of ash and only nightmares find you when you close your eyes."

She shifted her focus to the man in the suit of armor. The metal plates became red hot under her gaze. His lack of experience with the virtual world was apparent as he struggled to physically remove the suit rather than just wishing it away. She stopped only when he stood naked before her.

The third paled when she turned her attention his way but did not attempt to fight or flee. There might be hope for at least one of the sorry group after all. "I believe I've made my point. Now go. I expect a full report, and I expected it yesterday." All three disappeared like soap bubbles popping the instant she released them.

⌇⌇

"And you tease me about my flair for the dramatic." Alan strode into view on the virtual landscape as she shrank herself back to her regular size. Alan gestured in the direction where the trio had been. "At least one of them is now trying to explain the loss of bladder control without losing face."

Two Dronighs in one day? Juliane shook her head. Her meeting was supposed to have been set up in the datasphere with private access controls. "Eavesdropping again?"

Alan shrugged. "It's not my fault you don't take better precautions."

Juliane ground her teeth. Stuart must have been lax in setting the meeting up. She'd have to have a word with him later.

"But now I am curious," said Alan. "Would you go through with it?"

"Through with what?"

"Reprogramming their minds?"

Juliane sniffed. "Of course not. That would be cruel as well as against every law on the books."

Alan cocked his head the way he did whenever he wanted to engage in a conversation that seemed to have no point other than cause her blood to boil. Juliane took a breath and reminded herself that the Dronighs were in a bad place. "I'm sorry to hear about Stevie."

Alan sighed and glanced at the framed photograph on her wall. "You know, it's always seemed odd to me that you'd have a picture of dogs framed. Childhood pets

I assume based on the image quality." He scanned the contents of her office. "You don't have any other family photos."

"My mother wasn't exactly the family portrait type." Juliane pressed her lips together. "And the dogs weren't pets. They belonged to one of my mom's boyfriends. Troy."

"Why then do you have their picture?"

"It's a reminder." Juliane bit her lip, debating whether to tell him more. She didn't owe him an explanation. She didn't owe anyone. However, Betty's parting words still stung. Betty and Alan might be going through issues, but he was her husband. Perhaps if she made more of an effort to be nice, Betty might eventually cool off and forgive her.

"I used to be so envious of those dogs. I wasn't allowed to make a sound. My mom told me that after working all day my voice gave Troy a headache, but the dogs could jump and bark, and no one seemed to mind." Juliane's eyes tightened as the memory came back.

"My mom doted on those animals." She nodded at the photograph. I think she thought Troy would love her more for it. I would be starving, and she would make sure they had a piece of steak from the table."

Juliane's eyes tightened. Explaining the why behind the photograph was harder than she anticipated. "Then they would laugh about the dogs having a job while I didn't."

She pressed her lips together. "I didn't know what that meant until I saw a few bills drop to the floor as Troy came inside stinking of cigars and wet dog. I realized then that Troy was betting on the animals.

"I could have turned him into the police. I could have turned them both in. But I didn't. No, I thought if I could prove I was just as tough as those dogs, maybe then I wouldn't be treated as just some kid who got in the way." Juliane sighed at the memory of her misguided self. Not having witnessed a dog fight firsthand, she didn't then realize what a horrible practice it was. Troy's dogs never showed a hint of injury.

"And I regret to say my plan worked," she continued, "Once Troy figured out I knew what was going on, he stopped trying to hide it. He started to tell me about how well his dogs did, more specifically, what they had done to the losers." Juliane grimaced.

"I suspect the idea was to make me cry, but I found that if I focused on the statistics of the fights instead of the gorier details, I could forget we were talking about living things. That's when I started to notice patterns." She waved at the picture. "Those became my first theorem, and I used it one night, to tell Troy how to place his next bet."

"It didn't take him long to recognize I wasn't just some airhead." Juliane's mouth twitched. "Suddenly, I was served steak, and Mom, the leftovers."

Juliane took a breath and turned her back to the wall. "Unfortunately, my mom couldn't handle not being the center of attention, so we left but not before Troy taught me one last lesson. When it comes to gaining respect, love is a nice concept, but sometimes a good healthy dose of fear works even better."

The smug look, normally plastered to Alan's face, had softened as she told her story. He shook his head as if he realized he'd let his empathy show.

"I've no doubt you managed to be permanently etched in all three of those workers' memories," Alan said, once again himself. "I just wonder how many of them are going to change their ways because it is the right thing to do, versus how many of them are going to do as instructed just because they are terrified of you."

Juliane tilt her head. "Does it really matter what their motivation is? I'm saving lives."

Alan's eyebrows rose with the corner of his lips. "I'm sure you know how to deal with your people best."

Juliane smiled at Alan's acknowledgment. "Indeed. So, what can I help you with? I assume you didn't come here just to discuss my lack of a childhood."

Alan placed his hand against his heart. "You wound me. I always look forward to our little get-togethers."

"So much so that I haven't seen you for nearly a year, yet you show up uninvited on the same day that Betty visits. I am sorry, but I can't believe it is entirely coincidental."

The smile left Alan's face, and his avatar instantly aged several years. "Ah, Betty has already been here then?"

"She's the one who told me about Stevie."

It was the first time that Juliane could recall Alan appearing to be anything but in control of the situation. "Well . . . that is"—his tongue flicked out as the words escaped like a serpent sampling the air—"regrettable. I am afraid that the last few months have not been exactly kind to my wife. The combination of stress and parenthood may be getting to her."

"She needs sleep. Maybe you two should take some time off."

"She needs more than just a weekend getaway."

Juliane fought the blush from showing on her cheeks. "I didn't mean to suggest . . ."

Alan waved the words away with a flick of his hand. "No need to apologize. She and I will work through this time just like any other problem we've faced. I am only sorry that she chose to share our personal life with you."

"For what it is worth, I am sorry that he is going through this—that you all are going through this."

Alan shrugged again. "The boy will survive or he won't."

Juliane fought the urge to rub her arms to fight the coldness of Alan's words. It was no wonder that Betty was seeking help if that was the support she was getting at home. "How can you say that? He's your son."

"That came out harsher than I intended. What I meant is you shouldn't be concerned about Stephen."

"I shouldn't? Betty said—does that mean you think he is going to be okay?"

Alan pressed his lips together. "I'm a number of things, but a pediatric specialist is not one of them. I'm letting *qualified* doctors make that analysis. Something I wish Betty would do too. No one enjoys being second-guessed when they're trying to do their job—as I am sure you know." He shook his head.

Juliane exhaled her relief. His son's condition couldn't be as dire as Betty had led on if he was acting that calm about it. "If you aren't here about Betty or Stevie, what brings you today to my world?"

The smile was immediately back on Alan's face as his avatar transformed back into the confident individual she remembered back from their time together.

"Damien offered me a pair of box tickets to see the Sharks play this weekend. Betty can't make it, for obvious reasons, so I wondered if you might like to go with me instead?"

Juliane's brow wrinkled. "You're as much a sporting type as I am a dog person."

"It's not about the game. It's about the experience. Or so I've been told. Frankly, I don't exactly see what the appeal is, but they are perfectly good tickets and I would hate to see them go to waste. Come with me. We can laugh together at the ridiculous commentary."

"I'm not sure . . ." *Now that the conference call is over, I really should go to the hospital if only for moral support.* She pressed her lips together. Then again, if Alan was right and Betty was simply being paranoid, she might interpret a visit as validation. "I don't follow any of the teams."

Alan dropped down onto his knees. Juliane scrunched her face further. "Nor do I. I'm begging you. Please don't make me make small talk with some random wannabe jock that Damien might find. I'd much rather go with a friend."

Friend. She would never have used that word to describe their relationship, but he hadn't attempted to insert himself into her business dealings over the years, nor had he ridiculed her for her upbringing just now. Perhaps Betty there was hope for him yet. Juliane looked back out to the field, which so recently played host to her little drama with the production heads as her head began to ache again. *It might be nice to spend some time out of the office,* she thought.

When she did not immediately respond, Alan stood. While the corners of his lips remained turned upright, the line of his mouth had thinned. "I wasn't supposed to say anything, but Damien specifically requested I bring you."

She lifted an eyebrow. So much for thinking this was his way of extending an olive branch. The invitation became far less interesting—and yet, if it was Damien's idea, the tickets were also harder to refuse. "Why in the world would he make that suggestion? He knows too well what pressure I've been under."

"I think that is the point. From all reports, you've been locked away up here for months."

"Don't be ridiculous. Of course, I leave the office. I travel to any number of places."

"I don't mean leaving here just to go to another meeting. When was the last time you saw the inside of your home?"

"I took my lunch there just this afternoon."

"I am not one of your employees, Juliane. Seeing the inside of your home via a virtual interface is not the same as physically being among your own things."

"But I am among my own things. Don't you see? Everything you see in this office is mine. Every scrap of paper, every piece of furniture, every detail on the wall is mine. This"—she spun around with her arms outstretched—"is my domain. I am more at home here than I could be anyplace else."

"It's not healthy for you personally or for your company. What you are doing within the virtual world is truly impressive, but things are happening in the real world that you need to be a part of. Life is moving on without you."

"Are you getting philosophical on me?"

"Perhaps, but I've had a lot of time to think recently, without you or Betty around to interrupt me in the lab," said Alan with a laugh that sounded forced.

He is worried. He just doesn't want anyone to know, thought Juliane. "Why don't you install a mirror in there? Then you'd have the assistant you've always wanted," she joked. If the way he needed to cope with his family's situation was to pretend everything was fine, she'd let him.

Alan threw his head back as he laughed. "Oh, how I've missed our talks. Don't think I haven't already considered that option."

Juliane snorted. "Fine." She would call Betty after the game and apologize. Then, after everything with the factory was resolved, she'd even offer to watch Stevie so Betty and Alan might then take a night off. It was a perfect plan. "You can report back to Damien, like a good little errand boy, that I'll go with you. I imagine there are team colors or the like that I should find to wear."

"I've already taken care of that for you. I have a whole outfit here for you made up of licensed apparel. Damien is a part-owner of the team, after all. It wouldn't do for you to be seen wearing anything else."

Juliane shook her head. "Saying no was never an option, was it?"

"You always have a choice; I was just tasked with helping you to make the right one."

"Send the bag over. Stuart will ensure that it gets to me in time."

"It's already here, Juliane."

Juliane glanced about. There was nothing on the field remotely resembling a bag of clothing, and she was puzzled how he intended to transfer the bag from the virtual world to the physical world.

"Juliane," he sighed. "That's exactly my point. The bag is here in your office because I am here in your office. I've been standing just a few feet from you this entire time. We've practically been touching."

Juliane blinked, and the field was instantly replaced by her solid office walls. Just as he said, Alan stood on the other side of the room, a plastic bag with the Sharks' emblem on its side resting next to his foot. She had seen about as little of Alan in the flesh as she had seen Betty over the years.

Unlike Betty, Alan didn't appear to have aged more than a day. In fact, he almost looked younger than he had when they first began working together. Obviously, he hadn't been losing the same amount of sleep over his son's condition than his wife had.

It was further evidence that Alan had to whole-heartedly believe his son's condition was treatable, unless he was a monster of a parent. She felt the last of the guilt from turning Betty away melt from her shoulders.

"What is that expression on your face, Juliane? If a person didn't know you better, it would almost look like you were happy to see me."

Immediately, she forced the grin from her lips. "We can't have that sort of rumor start, now can we? I'm just shocked to see how great you look, that's all."

"You say that as if you expected anything else." Alan swiped his hair back as he struck a pose normally found on a fashion runway.

"Betty just looked so . . . um . . ." Juliane bit her tongue, hoping Alan would not hear her unspoken words.

"She looks drained. I'm well aware of it. If you listen to her, you might think that being a mother and spouse is sucking the life right out of her body."

"Er . . . I didn't mean to suggest . . ."

Alan interrupted her by holding up his hand. "No need to apologize for speaking the truth. It is hard on me, seeing her like that, but she's fully embraced the idea of being a martyr. She's much like you in that regard. Once she has decided on a course of action, there is little that anyone can do to change her mind."

He bent down at the waist, blocking his face from her view. He paused with his hand on the bag's plastic handle, and Juliane saw the rise of his back as he took a deep breath before returning upright.

A message scrolled across her vision. "We briefly lost visual on Dr. Dronigh, but the visitor's log confirmed she did make it to the hospital without incident. Our associate is heading back to the office now."

Juliane blinked the message away. Alan locked his eyes onto hers while handing over the bag. His gaze was so intent that she briefly wondered if he could somehow see the text over her vision, but then she shook her head. It wasn't as if there was a lens over her eye physically displaying the information.

"You, though, haven't changed a bit over the years either. Frankly, I prefer the real you. Your avatar doesn't do you justice."

Gesturing to the bag, he added, "I took a chance on your size and am confident I got it right." Alan started to turn to the door. "Before I forget, Damien mentioned that while he wasn't going to be able to stay through the entire game, he and a few others might stop by. I trust that won't scare you off. It will be nice to have a chance to swap some war stories, don't you think?"

twenty-six

The football stadium referred to by the fans as the Reef, and its surrounding parking lot was already packed by the time they arrived. By the sounds blaring from inside, it was close to kick-off time. Juliane was thankful they had a professional driver as the car maneuvered around stumbling fans on their way to the gates.

"That one over there sure has started early. I wonder if he will remember any of the game," observed Juliane as she watched one man regain his footing. The man would have been flattened by the passing traffic had he not been pulled to safety by his more sober companions at the last second.

Alan glanced in the direction Juliane gestured and shrugged. "Sometimes the tailgating experience is the best part of the game. The Sharks aren't the division favorite at the moment." Alan looked just as ridiculous in the oversized team jersey as she felt; however, he didn't seem to be nearly as aware of his appearance as she was. It was probably the first article of clothing she had worn in years that wasn't designed for either the boardroom or bedroom.

"No? Well, I can't imagine Damien is happy with that."

Alan chuckled before answering. "You don't know the half of it. Why do you think he has to force the likes of you and me to fill the seats? He keeps saying that his team is on the brink of greatness, but just like any other fan would say, it is always next year."

"How many seasons has it been?"

"The team isn't all that old. It was one of the more recent expansion teams, but they've not exactly exceeded expectations since the day he signed the check. You should bring it up sometime. I am sure he'd love to go over his team's record with you. Maybe you could help him draft more winners." Alan eased himself back into the comfort of the leather interior.

"Well, if it's that sore of a subject with him, what is he doing about it?"

"What he has to, I'm sure."

The car finally pulled up to a VIP entrance tunnel. Alan sprang out of his side without waiting for the driver to open the door.

"It doesn't look like you were forced to be here."

"When Damien first offered the tickets, I was just as hesitant to accept as you were. I know this might shock you, but I was never really the athletic type growing up. Frankly, I didn't see what the big deal was, but then I started studying up on the subject." Alan raised a finger as if an idea had just struck him. "Much like you did with the dogs."

He beamed and pointed at the entrance. "You'll see what I mean. When the game starts, don't bother watching the individual plays. Instead, try to see if you can decipher the strategy behind the coach's game plan. It's almost like watching generals test out battle plans but without the ammunition. Absolutely fascinating."

Juliane raised one manicured eyebrow.

"Doubt me if you want to, but it's good to develop an appreciation of well-executed tactics whenever you see them. You never know when you might need to apply them."

"I'll keep that in mind the next time I find myself deep in enemy territory trying to execute a counter run play."

Alan roared with laughter. "And here I thought you weren't interested."

"I looked up one or two things on the way here." She nodded. "I'll admit, you might have a point."

"I knew you'd come around to my thinking . . . eventually."

Juliane attempted to twist her lips into a scowl, but Alan's laughter was contagious.

They arrived at a set of elevator doors guarded by a pair of men in ill-fitting ticket handler's smocks who examined their credentials without speaking a word. The movement from one floor to the next was seamless. Juliane had just begun wondering if the elevator was broken, as she could feel no movement when the doors opened on the mid-level deck.

Several other people were mingling in the lobby, but Juliane could tell by the way they held themselves that these individuals were an entirely different sort of fan than the ones they had passed on their way into the parking lot.

A pale light in the corner of her vision caught her attention. When she turned, the light seemed to encapsulate a nearby woman like the glow from an aura. Within a second, the glow faded out, and Juliane was left wondering if there had been anything there in the first place.

"Everything okay, Juliane?" Alan touched her arm. "Supposedly someone will come by once we are in the box to take our order, but we can grab something now if you'd like."

Juliane shook her head. Out of the corner of her eye, she thought she spotted an additional glow from other people in the room, but those faded out just as quickly. *It must be the way the lighting of the room is designed*, thought Juliane. Audibly she said, "No, sorry, just taking it all in. It's not quite what I imagined. I guess I expected a little more . . ." Juliane frowned. What had she expected?

"A little more grunge, a little less sophistication?" Alan suggested.

"Perhaps."

"I am sure we'll see more than enough of the less desirable before the day is through."

"Our seats are this way?" She pointed and walked with purpose toward one of the doorways. She needed to get out of the room before the effect gave her a headache.

Their box was just one of several nestled within the end zone of the stadium. While the majority of each unit was walled off, providing occupants with a degree of privacy, the outside wall and the adjacent quarter of each side was a sheet of glass, including a portion of the floor. Juliane was rather glad that she had chosen not to wear a skirt as she toured the room from end to end.

"You don't have to worry. It's one-way glass."

Juliane looked at Alan in curiosity.

"Admit it. You were worried that someone might be sneaking a peek at you just then."

"I was simply pitying the people below us who must feel like a crowd of people are going to come crashing down on their heads if this so much as cracks."

"If that glass cracks, then they have larger issues to worry about."

"Speaking of worries. Have you heard anything more from your son's doctors? Are they made any progress?"

"He is still under observation. How is your factory's investigation coming along?"

Juliane sucked in her breath.

"Listen, I know you mean well, but I'd rather not discuss it more than we already have. Can we at least pretend to have a carefree life, if only for a few hours?"

At a loss for a response, Juliane looked out toward the sea of humanity below her, placing her hand on the glass. She was surprised to feel it vibrate. "Is it supposed to buzz like that?"

"Well, it's slightly more advanced than your standard window. I am given to understand there is a control panel around here." Alan scanned the back of the room. "It's more force field than glass. Supposedly, by just adjusting a few settings, we can make it so that the fresh air and noise from outside can pass through, or keep it in its current privacy mode."

Locating the control panel, Alan adjusted a dial, and Juliane was surrounded by the roar of the crowd and the metallic smell of smoke from used fireworks as the players took the field.

Juliane was struck by how enormous the players were. Even knowing that some of their bulk was made up of pads and other protective gear, they appeared unnatural in proportion. One could almost describe them as ogres. The opposing team looked like fragile dolls in comparison.

Without taking her eyes off the advancing players, Juliane asked, "And you say the Sharks aren't winning this season?"

"Damien pushed for some organizational changes. They must have gone along with his suggestions. I heard the news that they are heavily favored to win this one."

"I would think so. The other team doesn't even look like it is in the same league."

"Well, that might have something to do with their ownership philosophy."

"How so?"

"Let's just say that some teams are blinder than others to their players' efforts to improve their competitive edge through the wonders of modern science."

"Damien lets the Sharks cheat?"

"Damien doesn't have time to be involved in every detail managing the team. That's why he hires other people. Besides, the Sharks are hardly the only ones looking for an edge. It's a violent sport; muscles tear and bones break. A person who depends on their physical performance for their livelihood can hardly be blamed for wanting to go under the knife if the surgery minimizes the potential for career-ending injuries."

Alan shrugged. "They found out that artificial muscle made up of spider silk was over fifty times stronger than natural muscle. It was only a matter of time before athletes found a way to trade up. Heck, even I am considering that one."

The monitor showed a close-up of a player attaching his helmet before running from the sideline to the field. His nose was broad but flattened, and as he ran, his nostrils flared, making him appear goat-like.

"Now that is a face only a mother could love."

"The man makes several million dollars per season. I know for a fact he's not suffering in that department. He's dated five supermodels in the last year alone. Rumors have it that he intentionally altered his nose so that he has increased airflow. Supposedly, it makes him faster and able to make quicker decisions on the field."

Juliane grimaced. "What some people will do to get ahead." The camera panned to another man who could have passed for a werewolf in a horror film.

Alan raised his eyebrows with a quick laugh. "Indeed."

The snap of the football sent the crowd into a frenzy, preventing further conversation through the first half. Alan had been right when he suggested that she focus on the coaches' strategies rather than the individual plays. Even though the Sharks had a significant size advantage, the other team was nimble and their trick plays proved remarkably successful. When the clock ran out, the Sharks were down by fourteen, and the majority of the crowd had been silenced.

Alan stood up and rolled his shoulders. "I don't know about you, but I think my legs could use a stretch. Would you like to come with me?"

"Why not? I could use some refreshments."

As they returned to the central lobby, a man's voice came from the direction of one of the other boxes. His words were slurred, but that didn't prevent him from doing his best to ensure they carried throughout the area.

"What incompetence! I think I am going to have to have a word with the management."

Juliane froze and scanned the crowd for the source. An opening broke through the sea of people. At first, Juliane only saw a slim woman with blonde hair laughing in response, but then the woman stepped back. Standing with his arm wrapped around the woman's waist, his face flushed, was Louis.

Juliane sucked in her breath as Louis looked her way. He looked as if he had gained a little weight around his waist over the years but was mostly unchanged. Juliane screamed to herself, *No, no, no!* as he began walking toward them with the woman, who had to be Elena, in tow.

Juliane looked to Alan as she tried to come up with a way to avoid the situation, but Alan appeared oblivious to Juliane's distress. If anything, he looked pleased to see the pair.

Louis, dressed in the opposing team's colors swayed from side to side as he walked. "Juliane! I never expected to see you here. Visiting old friends? We should catch up. How long are you in town?"

Juliane felt a pressure build behind her eyes at Louis's easy manner. He smiled boldly as he approached as if greeting a long-absent friend. His body showed little of the discomfort she felt at seeing him so unexpectedly. Juliane ground her teeth. *He still doesn't regret how he treated me at all,* she thought.

Louis leaned into his wife and whispered something in her ear. Elena looked at Juliane and let out a quiet, musical laugh. Juliane's muscles tensed as she steeled her nerves. She reminded herself that she had grown in multiple ways since he had so casually tossed her aside. Factories filled with enough people to populate small cities cowered in fear of her displeasure. She was a force into herself and needn't shy away from anyone. *Even Louis.* She drew up her back like a queen.

"I never left, as I am sure you know."

Louis stumbled, and the grin momentarily dropped from his face. His eyebrows wrinkled together as if he had trouble deciphering her words.

"Actually, I didn't. I am sorry to admit that I haven't exactly been following your status updates since you left the ACI. For some reason, Elena tends to look down upon that sort of thing. Don't you, my dear?" He attempted to nuzzle Elena's neck, but in his state, he slightly missed the mark, leaving a mark of saliva on her shirt collar. Elena didn't seem to mind, giggling at his gesture.

"If you aren't aware of what Jules here has been up to, it's no wonder we are losing our competitive edge," said Alan without humor in his voice.

Louis glanced at a passerby rubbing a delicate ear clip. "Ah. Yes. That's your work then?"

"Yes, and has been for some time now."

"Alan, I'd hardly call her little trinkets a serious threat, but you are right. I should know the faces behind the competition."

"Honey, the game is going to start up again, and I am still thirsty. Why don't we let these two get back to enjoying their date?" Elena patted her husband's arm, breaking the tension.

Louis rubbed his free hand over his face. Juliane watched as his eyes widened as his gaze darted between their faces. A sly grin crept back onto his face. "Tsk, tsk, Alan. Sneaking behind your wife's back? Surely, Betty deserves better."

Juliane did not need to look in Alan's direction to feel the heat generated by Louis's words. *You're one to talk.*

Louis, on the other hand, was either blind or too drunk to care about how his words were interpreted. He continued, "Well, I can't say I am entirely surprised. I always thought there was something between you two. Ah look, Elena, Jules is blushing!"

"It's Juliane," she said through clenched teeth.

Louis swayed, falling onto Juliane while pulling on his wife's waist. Elena had been holding a cup; the sudden movement sent a portion of the contents spraying onto Juliane's shoe.

Juliane struggled to maintain her composure as the liquid spread its stain. It took every ounce of her will not to run back to their seats.

Louis smiled at his wife. "It can't be that great of a date. Those two are much too serious." Alan pushed him upright as Louis continued, "Aren't these games supposed to be the great American pastime? You should be relaxing and having some fun." At least that was what Juliane thought she heard him say. His accent combined with his inebriated state made the words swim together.

"You are thinking about baseball." Alan using a clipped tone that reminded Juliane of her old professors.

"Well, aren't you a fountain of information? I bet you are a blast at parties." Louis suddenly leaned in, nearly bringing his wife down with him. "Speaking of party tricks, you two should appreciate this." Louis removed his arm from Elena's waist to block the room's light from one hand with the other. He cupped the hand in the shadows while Elena leaned back to sip her drink.

Just as Juliane began to wonder if Louis had forgotten what he was going to say, his shadowed palm began to glow. "I sometimes forget which house I am in and couldn't find a light switch anywhere. After I stubbed my toe for the hundredth time, all I could do was think of how badly I wanted a light, and then, the next thing I know, poof! I'm glowing. If Edison could only see me now . . ."

Louis glanced back at Elena, who grinned as she enjoyed another sip. As he straightened and returned his arm around her waist, she handed him the cup. He finished its contents with one large swig before crumpling the plastic and tossing it into a nearby garbage bin. "Well, my dear, it looks as if I may have stumbled across yet another unanticipated discovery. Alan, isn't that what am I paying you to do?"

The pair lurched back toward the concession stand, but before they had taken more than a few steps, Louis turned back. "On that note, I think, Alan, seeing you fraternizing with the competition, makes me think you may not have the ACI's best interests in mind. Consider yourself a free agent."

"I always have," whispered Alan as Louis and Elena walked away. He sniffed. He turned his head toward Juliane. "Now, how about I get you that drink."

Juliane watched Louis order and consume another round of drinks. Instead of stopping him or urging him to cut back, Elena just stood there, enabling him. Juliane was disgusted. "I'm suddenly not thirsty anymore." Spinning on her heel, Juliane walked back to their seats.

The box was no longer vacant when they returned. Damien stood near the back of the room deep in conversation with Eithan Yuan. Apparently, she wasn't the only Apex board member to be invited to tonight's game. Juliane glanced around to see if Durham was around, but if he had a ticket, he hadn't arrived yet.

At their entrance, Eithan cocked his head, acknowledging their presence. He then bowed to Damien and departed.

"Damien, did you know that Louis would be here when you asked Alan to bring me today?" asked Juliane.

Damien's eyebrows rose as he answered. "I assumed he likely would be. He does own the Suns, after all, but I wouldn't have expected him on this side of the stadium. Perhaps, they cut him off at the concessions closer to his box." Damien shrugged. "In any event, I hope he didn't cause too much of a problem for you."

Juliane drew herself up straight. "Nothing I couldn't handle."

"I never doubted it. You are the mother of enhanced reality. The ACI should never have let you go. He should never have let you go. You are singlehandedly going to bring his company to its knees."

Juliane smiled at the pep talk.

Alan produced a sound that was a cross between a laugh and a gag. "Well, Damien, as long as we are talking about bringing down the competition and launching a whole new world order, I should mention that I will no longer be able to serve in my current capacity."

"No?"

"It seems that our dear friend Louis has decided to make a few organizational changes of his own."

"That is a pity, but that can only mean that he is feeling scared, which means we must be doing something right. I think it may be time to start upping the ante."

"Exactly what I was thinking."

Juliane waited for Damien to elaborate on his plans, but there was no further explanation.

The stadium began rocking as speakers blasted music and the crowd regained its roar. Walking up to the edge of the glass, Juliane stared at the players as they returned to the field. They seemed different from the first half. She gazed at the monitor. "The team looks even larger than they did before halftime."

When Damien spoke up, he was directly behind her ear. "I decided to stop by the locker room to give them a little pep talk before heading up this way."

The enormous scoreboard flashed to the interior of the visiting owner's box. Louis and Elena waved to fans as the players lined up below. As they represented the opposing team, Juliane expected to hear some boos but instead heard some applause.

Just before the camera panned away, Juliane saw Louis's hand creep up the side of Elena's blouse. "I would never have anticipated that they would still be together after all these years, especially after such a short courtship period." Damien must also have noticed their display of affection. "It is enough to make you wonder if there might be some truth to those rumors."

"Down in front!" Alan shouted, bringing Juliane's attention to the movement on the field.

"Do you think we have a chance in beating the Suns?"

"His team may have speed and agility, but just like their namesake, they will eventually burn out. My team, on the other hand, has strength and stamina. They won't just beat the Suns—
they will rip them to shreds."

"Juliane?" Damien asked.

Juliane realized that she had allowed her eyes to drift back toward the opposing owner's box.

"I think you've hidden in that office of yours long enough."

"I haven't been hiding. I've just been busy."

"I know you have, but I have plans, and I'd like to know you can be counted on to play a big part in them. Don't you think it's past the time the world recognized you? I mean the real you."

The second half began with a kick-off return for a touchdown, and the Suns never regained the momentum. As Juliane and the others left the stadium, the car's newsfeeds were alight with stories about broken records and interviews with several of the most outstanding players of the game.

The interviews blended together—many of the players were products of multi-generational dynasties and thanked their parents as well as their coaches—and Juliane tuned the noise out. It had begun to sound more like an animal breeder announcing their fine pedigrees than news.

The following morning, Juliane awoke completely disoriented. It took a few seconds before she realized that she had fallen asleep in her own bed rather than the couch in her office. As she regained her bearings, she stretched her fingers out against the surrounding fabric. Her sheets were still nearly as crisp as they were upon initial purchase, even though she hadn't updated her furnishings in close to a year.

Her feet screamed in protest as she stood. She must have walked more yesterday than she had originally thought. After being sheathed so long in heels, her arches ached as she padded flat-footed across the room.

Doing her best to ignore the pain, she entered into the kitchen and its promise of coffee on demand. Juliane allowed herself a smile as she placed a coffee pod into the machine.

One of the first things she had done after leaving the ACI was to buy a French press. However, she never was able to get it right and mug after mug contained floating grounds. She'd thought of Chad after each failed attempt. Perhaps she'd been too hard on him. Coffee from the machine might not be as good, but it was the proper temperature.

The various gears whirled as the machine came online and the liquid began to drip into her cup. A message indicator flashed in her vision, signifying that her inbox had been working overtime while she slept. Alan was right; it had been too long since she enjoyed the convenience of her home. She ignored the alert. It could wait until after she had eaten some breakfast.

The message indicator flashed again. Juliane disabled the alert with a thought. Another indicator flashed informing her that someone was trying to place a call. Juliane disabled that alert as well.

Once her stomach had been satisfied by a quick breakfast, she returned to the living room. As much as she had enjoyed her morning's peace, Juliane knew that she could not afford to be off the grid for much longer. With a sigh, she re-engaged her messaging protocols as she scanned the newsfeed.

Juliane sank into her couch. Her breakfast felt like an anchor as her feed was filled with hundreds of variations of the same headline. Louis had been involved in an accident after the game. Images of his automobile accompanied many of the stories. It was hard to imagine that crumpled ball of bent metal and shattered glass could have carried anyone from one place to another.

No one seemed to have firm details as to the cause of the crash or the conditions of the victims, but all the reporters were free with their individual speculation. There was no mention of who drove the car when it happened—nor did alcohol appear to be a factor.

Louis must have arranged for a driver, especially after consuming as much as he had, thought Juliane. *Or Elena had.* Juliane read further.

The reports morphed into nothing more than gossip. Reporters were reaching out to anyone, regardless as to how tenuous the connection to Louis might be, for their comments and initial reaction.

By mid-morning, additional details had been gathered, although there was still some doubt as to the authenticity of the sources. According to an individual who wished to remain anonymous, there hadn't been a driver. Instead, Louis had been at the wheel at the time of the accident. He had been driving at excessive speeds when he lost control of the vehicle. The reporter commented that Louis had been lucky. He had been thrown from the car just before it ignited into a fiery inferno. His condition was listed as extremely serious. His wife, however, was not as fortunate.

Lacking any further comments from hospitals, friends, or family, many of the outlets chose to cobble together featurettes on the charitable contributions of the late Mrs. Evans. Previously submitted press photography showed her caressing children's faces in their hospital beds, feeding children in developing nations, or otherwise looking angelic.

One might think Elena was on her way to canonization by the way the stories were positioned. Juliane pressed her lips together as she read more interviews. Everyone, it seemed, bemoaned how the world was made a little bit darker by Elena's loss.

Then, the stories began to rehash the details of Elena and Louis's whirlwind romance. They described Elena as Louis's true partner and love of his life. Juliane felt her eyes tighten as reporters reminded their audience of the rumors regarding those days and how early their relationship truly started. Juliane even saw her own image and old name referenced in a couple of stories.

Juliane's phone alert flashed once again. She glanced at the identification code in the corner of the screen and accepted the call.

"Durham. I'm surprised you are up this early."

"Good morning to you too, Juliane. We need to talk," said Durham.

"About what?" Juliane frowned. He wouldn't be calling her about Louis, would he? Durham hadn't mentioned Vegas once over the last five years. As far as she could tell, he'd never recognized her from the time when she and Louis were together at all.

She suppressed a groan as the other reason Apex's legal consultant might be calling. *The factory.* If he was calling about her factory, that could only mean that the news had leaked to the media, and she still didn't have a satisfactory report from the production heads.

"About last night."

"Last night? Was there another . . . look, my people at the factory are still conducting their investigation. I'll forward the report to you as soon as I get it." She frowned.

"You were at the game last night."

"Yes, with Alan."

"Not just with Alan."

"No, you're right. Damien and several other thousand people were there too."

"Like Louis and Elena."

Juliane rolled her shoulders. He was calling about Louis after all. She couldn't decide if that was a good thing or not. "Yes . . . they were there too."

"There are witnesses who saw you together, claiming that there was a somewhat heated exchange."

"Louis made a fool of himself and terminated Alan, but it was hardly a heated exchange. If anything, Alan acted happy about it. We walked away and watched the Sharks beat the Suns in the second half. That's all. What are you implying?"

"I'm not implying anything. I am merely trying to understand the facts so that I can get out ahead of any rumors that might come out of this."

"Rumors? What kind of rumors could there be? If you ask me, the real story I'd like to see investigated further is how the ACI managed to keep alcohol out of the press. Louis was practically a bottle of antiseptic; he had so much in him."

"Unfortunately, you just confirmed the stories I've been hearing that Alan was fired. Not only that, but fired very publicly. And what about you?"

"What about me?"

"You haven't been seen in public in years, and then, the first time you are, you just happened to run into your ex-boyfriend? Some people might question anyone's mental stability in the situation."

Juliane bit back a quick retort as Durham's words registered. "You recognized me after all?"

"Juliane, I am not an idiot. Of course, I recognized you. All of us did. Well, at least most of us," Durham amended.

"Why didn't you say anything?"

"Damien told us before the meeting began that you wanted a fresh start, and after what Louis did to you, I chose to respect your wishes." Durham paused. More softly he said, "I'd hoped . . . After all . . ." His voice trailed off.

"After all what?"

Juliane could hear him inhale over the phone. "Didn't you ever wonder why I left the ACI?"

Juliane looked out her window. "I assumed because Damien paid you better." The day had started with brilliant clear skies, but clouds were beginning to roll in. She realized she had been pacing around the room's perimeter.

It was one of the rare times she wished she still maintained a separate phone device. She had read some classic novels over the years and finally believed she understood why the characters would waste time twirling cords.

The silence stretched. Then Durham's voice all business again. "So, back to last night. Is there anything, anything that I should know about what happened at the Reef?"

"I went to the game. We saw Louis and his wife during halftime. The Sharks came back in the second half to win. I was dropped off here. Nothing else."

"And you stayed in your condo all night?"

"That is what I said."

"I meant that once home, you didn't log into your virtual reality program?"

Juliane frowned. Durham had undergone a version of the upgrade procedure too, the same as all of Damien's high-level officials. If he hadn't recognized her program's benefits yet, he likely never would. Some people were just blind.

"No, I had promised Alan that I would take a night off. But it is beginning to sound like I shouldn't have. Are you satisfied yet?"

"It is better I ask these sorts of questions than the police."

"I still don't understand why in the world the police would be involved in the first place. Louis was obviously under the influence. I don't see why any investigation would need to look any further."

"Well, that's an interesting thing. There's not a single report which would suggest Louis was intoxicated at the time of the accident."

Juliane found herself shaking her head before remembering that Durham wouldn't be able to see the gesture. "That's exactly what I find odd about the news too. I assume that's because his publicist is trying to keep that aspect quiet. The company's value would plummet if Louis ever lost the cult of personality thing he has going for him."

"Well, the interesting thing is, according to my sources, the reason why alcohol isn't mentioned as a possible cause is because he had none of it in his bloodstream at the time. In fact, he had nothing in his system that would have impaired his judgment or his reflexes at all."

Juliane's eyebrow shot up. "Someone has to be altering the records then because he clearly was having a good time yesterday."

"I have been assured that the records are accurate. My source was there as the blood work was analyzed. She saw the results firsthand."

"How did you manage that? Doesn't that sort of information violate some confidentiality?"

Juliane didn't need to hear Durham's answer. She could picture him shrugging with a smug smile.

Durham sighed into his phone. "Juliane, I know all too well how it feels to be tossed aside, and I do apologize if you thought I had done the same to you."

His words forced Juliane to remember the day she was first introduced to Damien's team. Those terrible minutes when he had made her feel like a discarded plaything. Now, while he obviously had a relationship with this woman in the hospital, he was casually throwing around information that could cost the woman her career as if they were talking about the weather.

"We were on our way to being friends once. Now that everything is out in the open, I'd like to . . . um . . . do you think we could try to be friends again?"

Another friend. Aren't I just Ms. Popular all of a sudden? "Sure, but not right now. I've told you all there is to say about last night." Another headline crossed her newsfeed. "I need to go." She terminated the connection.

The headline said Louis's condition had stabilized. While he had suffered some severe trauma, he was expected to recover. The stock market was already responding with record purchasing on any company associated with one of Louis's business ventures.

The market action reminded Juliane that the weekend was over and it was time to return to the office. She had already wasted too much time lounging around the condo and had yet to receive an updated report regarding the factory's internal investigation. Once that was in, she would make her way to the hospital to visit Betty. Louis's news was terrible, but Juliane couldn't honestly say she was going to miss Elena. If that made her a terrible person, so be it.

As she reached her destination, Juliane's vision began blinking with another incoming communication request. She rolled her eyes. The call had to be from a reporter. Durham must not have been the only one to make the connection between Louis and the woman seen at the game.

"This is Juliane Faris." She braced herself for the onslaught of questions.

She was expecting a brash tabloid journalist to be on the other side of the line. Instead, the voice was weak and broken up as if every word was a struggle. It took Juliane several seconds to realize that the voice belonged to Betty.

"Betty? Is that you? I was just about to call you. We must have a terrible connection. I can barely make out what you're saying. Can you repeat that?" Juliane heard a large crash in the background, followed by a tear-fueled scream.

"Betty! Are you there? Are you all right? Betty? Betty!"

A male voice answered—one that Juliane was not familiar with. "Are you a friend of Dr. Dronigh's?"

"I was. Yes, I mean I am. I don't know. It's complicated. But yes, I know her. Is she okay?"

The person on the other end sighed. "Would it be possible for you to come this way?"

"Have you called her husband?"

"She refuses to see him. She's refused to allow us to call anyone."

"Is everything okay?"

The man on the other end cleared his throat. "I think it might be best if we spoke face to face. Can you come over? Please."

"I'm on my way."

twenty-eight

Juliane hadn't bothered to ask the caller for additional information that might help her locate him when she reached the hospital. She had just assumed that she would be able to trace the call and locate the source.

However, when she entered the hospital's main entrance, her Internet connection was severed. Signs posted along the walls periodically suggested that wireless signals had been intentionally disrupted due to concerns about interference with medical equipment. As a result, Juliane had to rely on a series of signposts and building maps that took her down several hallways, across walkways, and in and out of no less than three elevators.

As she arrived at the suite of rooms, she couldn't be sure what floor she was on or even if she was still in the main hospital complex or some satellite building. She hadn't felt so lost in years. "How can people work like this?" she muttered under her breath.

The medical staff must have access to some limited network, thought Juliane. Her skin tingled as if she could sense wireless activity just outside of reach. After living with constant connection for so long, the lack of data made her itch.

Juliane had heard of the rise of technology retreat centers. They were spas designed to help clients relax by embracing similarly disruptive materials. She cringed at the thought. She would never be able to relax feeling this incomplete.

A tall, older man met her as she entered through the suite door. His eyes were nearly hidden under thick furry eyebrows. His skin around his neckline was loose as if he had recently lost significant weight, but his belly still extended. He reminded Juliane of one of the troll dolls she had seen in Chad's collection of old toys. All he lacked was a smile. Juliane pushed the comparison out her mind. She was here for Betty.

"Thanks for coming over so quickly. I am Dr. Thomas," said the man as he reached to shake her hand. "I am sorry you had to come down this way, but I just didn't feel like we could discuss this over the phone."

Juliane hesitated to meet the gesture. "Where's Betty?"

"We have her resting in a private room."

"What happened? What is wrong with her?"

"Frankly, that's why I asked you to come here. Would you happen to know if your friend has been under psychiatric care or on medication that could alter her mental state?"

"I don't know. We used to work together years ago, but haven't kept in touch as well as we should recently."

Dr. Thomas ran his hand through his hair as his shoulders sank. "You were listed on her information as her emergency contact." He sighed. "I was afraid that it might be a long shot, but I hoped that you might be able to provide us with a little more information than what the records show."

"I still don't understand why you aren't contacting her husband. I know that you said she doesn't want to allow it, but surely, he has to be able to provide better insight than I can."

"We've tried but have yet to reach him, and we are running out of time to react."

"What exactly are you trying to react to?"

"Well, at first we thought her behavior was merely a result of the strain caused by coping with her son's condition, but over the last twenty-four hours, she began to display symptoms of extreme paranoia. We attempted to sedate her, but it would seem our efforts may have made the condition worse."

He pressed his lips together. "Please understand I am only telling you this because of the severity of the situation and because she'd previously added you, specifically, to her disclosure forms."

"Which I still don't understand."

"That's between you and her. In any event, she suffered cardiac arrest, and her levels indicate some internal hemorrhaging, except we cannot seem to determine the source. There is a chance that the sedative triggered the attack if she was already being treated with other medication." He glanced at the contents of a manilla folder and frowned. "We may have successfully stabilized her heart, but unless we identify the source of the bleeding, we cannot be sure that other treatment options might not cause additional issues, and we don't have much more time to waste."

The doctor kept talking, but Juliane couldn't process the words. She sent a ping to Alan, only to receive a message delivery error. She cursed the hospital's signal suppression under her breath. He should be here, not her. "I am truly sorry. I wish I could help, I do, but I really don't know why she put me down as a contact."

He sighed. "I'd like you to try talking to her. She trusted you. Maybe hearing from a friend will rally her enough to respond to some basic questions."

The doctor ushered Juliane into a room the size of a closet. Her one-time colleague lay on the bed, connected to a multitude of machines and tubing, her skin washed out under the harsh ceiling lights. She looked much smaller than the woman who had entered Juliane's office just a few days prior, fragile and weak. As Juliane approached the bed, a machine whirred and a plastic cuff located around Betty's arm inflated.

Another machine sounded an alarm, and a nurse pushed Juliane to the side so that she could replace a depleted IV drip bag. After adding a quick notation to the chart located at the foot of the bed, the nurse disappeared as quickly as she had arrived.

Juliane tentatively reached out to touch Betty's skin. She felt like a plastic doll that had been left out under the sun for too long, soft and waxy. "Betty, it's me, Juliane. Can you wake up?"

Juliane and Dr. Thomas glanced up at the monitors to see if her words had resulted in any activity, only to see that there was no reaction. "Betty, you need to wake up. The doctors can't help you if they don't know what is wrong."

The machine attached to the arm cuff whirred again, punctuating her words.

Juliane walked over to Betty's chart, more out of a lack of better ideas rather than any expectation that it could offer any clues to the cause of Betty's condition. The numbers and readouts shown on the chart could have been written in a foreign language for as much help as they offered.

Another nurse entered the room and whispered into Dr. Thomas's ear. Dr. Thomas's lips tightened. "Keep trying," he encouraged Juliane as he spun and followed the second nurse back out into the hall.

Once again Juliane cursed the hospital's lack of network connectivity. If she only had access to her full capabilities, she would be able to access a whole slew of data. She could compare Betty's condition instantly with any number of case studies. She could run a simulation program and help rule out treatment options. She could do any number of things, but she was helpless. To do anything, she would either have to find a way to hack into the hospital's network or somehow get Betty's chart and all of her vital sign readings outside.

Juliane looked at the monitors again, weighing her choices. Either option would drain vital minutes. Minutes that Betty didn't have to spare.

"Betty, wake up!" Juliane tossed the chart back into its holder in frustration. She began to pace. "Why in the world wouldn't you call Alan?"

Juliane slapped the bed's railing, sending the chart clattering to the floor. "And you thought calling me instead was a good idea? What could be going on in your head? I may have made the occasional bad decision, but that one has to be worse."

She looked at the monitors again. Betty's readings showed no response to Juliane's diatribe. One of the other machines beeped, and the first nurse appeared to make an adjustment before returning the chart to its place at the foot of the bed. She vanished once again. The sound couldn't have been loud enough to have been heard at the nurses' station. Juliane realized she was looking for communication ports along the walls as if her eyes wanted to look at anything other than Betty lying still on the bed. All she saw were a handful of silver electrical outlets dotting the otherwise white walls.

Somehow the equipment must be communicating with the staff. Juliane became even more convinced that there was a form of private network managing the data inside the hospital walls. "Where one private network exists, so could others."

"This is for your own good," announced Juliane as she reached out to Betty's prone form. As her open palm connected to Betty's exposed skin, Juliane exerted her will. With Louis, she had established the connection in a heartbeat, but this time, it was like her mind was pressing up against a brick wall. She issued commands, breaking up the data packets. She visualized her commands as tendrils of ivy upon a wall and pulled. Betty's defenses were no match for her. The wall crumbled. She could feel Betty's mind open before her as she established the private connection. She could feel all of Betty's hurt and could sense Betty's life draining away as if it were her own.

Choking back a sob, Juliane closed her eyes and imagined their old lab, focusing on happier times. A few more seconds passed. Juliane wondered whether or not the effort had been enough. She glanced around the room. She hadn't seen the interior of the lab in years and expected some of her memory to be blurred, but everything showed as clearly as if she were physically standing in the room.

Movement along the length of one wall caught her eye, and Juliane watched as shadows converged into a solid dark mass. The shape seemed to pull itself from the wall's surface; some tendrils reached out farther than others, causing the mass to lighten as it stretched into a fine mist resembling the Betty that Juliane used to know.

"How did I get here?"

"You aren't really here, Betty. It is just the datasphere. I just had to come up with a location that we both knew."

"Where is my son?"

"I'm not sure, but I believe he is still in the hospital."

"I can't stay here. I need to go back to him." Betty began to run toward the lab door. The thought must have occurred to her that she didn't need to physically leave the room as she stopped moving in mid-stride. She frowned as she spun back on Juliane. "Why can't I wake up?"

"I wish I knew. It's been what I've been telling you to do for some time now."

Betty's forehead knit in confusion. "What do you mean?"

"Apparently, your doctors misjudged your dosage when they sedated you."

"Why have I been sedated?"

"Your doctor told me that you were suffering from an episode of paranoia. Unfortunately, something in your body decided to fight the medication. I am not going to sugarcoat this. Your condition is now quite serious. Have you been taking anything recently that could have triggered a reaction?"

"I'm not taking anything. I never have been. They think I'm crazy, but it's not paranoia when it is the truth." Betty's form began to pulse.

"We didn't just undergo some cosmetic procedure," she continued. "We completely altered our DNA. The changes made by the Gene Assist serum. They'll pass to the next generation, and might well kill us unless we find an alternative power source."

"Alternative power source? What are you talking about? The technology doesn't need one."

Betty's lips pursed as she scolded. "Of course, it needs a power source, and right now, it is pulling from our natural energy reserves. The greater the processing need, the greater the drain. It's the same concept as your body burning calories during any other exercise. I started thinking about those times you passed out when you were still getting used to everything, and it was the only explanation that makes sense!"

"But I still don't see how that would destroy the human race."

Betty sighed. "All the mysteries of the world are open to you, yet you don't have a clue sometimes. It's kids, Juliane. We all start out as kids."

"I know that. I was one once too."

"Were you? Then you should remember that kids aren't as strong as adults. They can be insanely energetic at times, but only in bursts, and my son is proof that they are being born with the same amount of processing speed as I have. My son, your kid—assuming you ever get around to having one—or any child of an upgraded person is going to have the same issue. They will simply burn themselves out, a whole generation gone unless we can find a way to teach them control at an early age."

"Or redirect the energy pull," suggested Juliane. Betty's paranoia had a certain degree of logic to it.

"I've tried that, but so far, the fix is only temporary and won't last much longer." Betty's appearance had grown fainter as they were talking, reminding Juliane that she did not have time to waste on idle theories.

"Betty, I'd be happy to discuss all of this with you, but first, you need to wake up so that the doctors can help you."

Betty laughed, but there was no humor in the sound. When their eyes met again, Juliane saw pity reflected. "One day, with any luck, you'll understand." Betty faded further. "The doctors aren't going to be able to save me because I won't let them. My son is still alive only because he is pulling energy from me, but I am afraid he isn't going to last long after I'm gone. I am going to need you to pick up on my work, not just for my son, but for the thousands of other children who are going to be born with this same condition."

Suddenly, Juliane's vision of the landscape shifted. She was no longer in control. The lab morphed into a hospital complex, infinitely long, with children wasting away in their beds surrounded by helpless parents. Thriving cities emptied after a few short generations. Floating a short distance away, Betty was nearly transparent, having lost the majority of her form's definition.

"And Alan isn't able to help with any of this?"

The beds, children, and empty cities faded to black. Betty's semi-transparent form was all that remained, her head the only feature that still maintained some slight definition. Betty's voice hissed, "You can't trust Alan! Save my son. Chad knows where to find my research. Contact him. Do it quickly, while there's still time!"

Betty's face faded further into the darkness. Juliane watched her lips move, but no sound escaped. It was almost as if she had said, "I'm sorry."

Juliane's mind felt as if it was hit with a sledgehammer as she was pulled violently from Betty's bedside. It began to throb, quickly outpacing the pulsing sound of the machines as the doctor and nurse rushed the bed out toward an operating room. Betty hadn't been out of view long when Juliane felt her private network connection sever as sharply as if she had been physically cut in two. Juliane knew then that Betty would never wake again.

Juliane felt another pain crest, but this one was more distant, and her shoulder made contact with the tile floor. Her body screamed as the pain spread and intensified. Just like when she had broken the connection to Louis, it felt as if she had a gaping wound in her brain, except, this time, it felt even rawer around the edges. Juliane's vision began to blacken. *No!* she thought. *Not again! Never again!* She did not know if she was fighting against the impending unconsciousness or the lack of the network. She no longer cared.

Twenty-nine

Juliane blinked to clear her blurred vision as she pulled herself back upright. A handful of personnel in scrubs rushed past, barely noting her presence. As she made her way down the hall, Juliane was hit by waves of vertigo. She was in a hospital, but she couldn't quite remember the reason she was here. Her shoulder throbbed as she crashed into the hallway railing. She wondered if it might be better to take a day to recover before returning to work.

Juliane took more confident steps as her sight cleared. She would have Stuart begin rounding up the task force. The room spun again.

A patient, a young boy, was wheeled past her, strapped in a bed. A dull drone emitted from machines as they passed. Her vision blurred again as another wave of nausea hit. She hadn't felt this lethargic since she first severed the connection with Louis. A man in a white coat, looking much like a troll doll, rushed by. "Stay with me, buddy," he pleaded with the child.

"Are you all right, Ms.?" another male voice asked.

Juliane couldn't answer. It was as if the act of moving her lips required too much energy. The droning sound of the machine ceased, only to be replaced with a ping that reverberated in her ears. If she didn't get out of here soon, Juliane was certain she would go mad.

"I need you here stat," shouted the troll doll from down the hall. "We've got a reading." The person hovering near Juliane turned and sprinted toward the patient.

The sense of disorientation ebbed Juliane as the trio passed beyond a large pair of swinging doors. Why did the boy make her think of Betty? *Wasn't her son two years old?* It had been ages since she last saw them, or was it? Juliane turned and took a hesitant step forward, keeping the thought of her own office out of her mind. A thought danced in the back of her mind just out of reach. There was something she was supposed to do. Something she needed to remember. But it was like the information was on another side of a wall. Getting around that wall would require a significant effort, and all she wanted to do was go home and sleep until next week.

As drained as she felt, suddenly Juliane had the strangest compulsion to seek out Chad. It had to have been even longer since she had last seen him. She fought through exhaustion. *Did the hallway lights flicker?* With each step further away from the double doors, her vision cleared. By the time she made it to the exit, the ground was once again stable beneath her feet.

thirty

Juliane realized that she hadn't bothered to confirm Chad was still with the ACI before making the drive from the hospital. She accessed the online directory and released a breath as she spotted Chad's name in its listing. A specific office was not listed, but at least he should still be on the campus. Somewhere. Their old building would serve as a good starting point for her search.

As she made her way to the Gould building, she was struck by how every brick, every flower, along the ACI campus looked just as it had the day she left, as if the campus itself was impervious to the passage of time. A crow pecked at something on the ground as she reached the building's entrance, flying away only when she was close enough, she could have picked it up had she wanted to.

Entering the building, she felt hollow. She had spent so many years here, but it felt as if her memories of the place could fit into the span of a handful of days. Lost in her thoughts, she was startled when she heard someone approach from behind her.

"Dr. Faris? Is that you?" Chad stood inside the hall. His disheveled hair surrounded his head like a fiery halo, making him appear even more like the stereotypical mad scientist than she remembered. His arms were filled with stacks of folders covered in streaks of coffee stains. A pair of coffee cups balanced precariously on top.

"Chad! Just the person I was looking for!" Juliane smiled as Chad shifted his burden, jostling one of the cups and sending beads of coffee flying. *At least some things never changed*, she thought. She should have visited ages ago. Her smile faded. Why hadn't she looked him up over the last few years? She had always meant to, but it was as if every time she scheduled a moment to reach out, something would come up that required her immediate attention and the urge would evaporate.

"What happened to you? You just vanished. People here thought you might have died."

"Really? What were they saying?"

"Well, some people thought you must have had another episode while at home and got eaten by random dogs; other people thought you must have perished in one of your crazy experiments."

"That's one of the reasons I don't like to listen to gossip." Juliane laughed. "Ridiculous," she snorted. "What about you? What did you think happened?"

Chad paused before answering, and when he did, it was without humor or recrimination. "I just assumed that when opportunity knocked, whatever it was, you didn't hesitate to answer."

Juliane blinked. She must have been staring. She felt a heat rise in her cheeks and fought to control it. *Stop it, Juliane,* she thought. It was only Chad. There was no reason to react like this. After all the time they had spent together, of course, he knew her. It was a good thing Betty wasn't with them. She no doubt would tease her relentlessly.

Juliane felt her throat tighten as if there were bags of sand in her lungs, holding her down, preventing her from drawing a full breath. A piece of the mental wall chipped away as an image of Betty on a hospital bed flooded her mind. Her ears rang with the distinctive sound of a monitor's flat-line alarm. Pieces of the last few days and Betty's final words came rushing back.

Chad caught Juliane as she staggered, causing the coffee cup to spill onto the floor.

"Are you okay?" he asked.

Juliane's head pounded as she struggled to stand up again, but as quickly as the headache's onset began, it faded away to something like the pins-and-needles tingle of a limb allowed to fall asleep.

Chad's arm shifted under hers. Juliane pushed herself away. The vision of Betty in the bed remained behind her mind's eye, but it was muted. Like a dream. Colors were grayer. Details blurred. It was almost as if she hadn't even been in the room with her at all.

"Sorry about that. I must have slipped," she answered.

Chad scanned her face. "Are you sure?"

"Betty told me that you might have some of her research material." Juliane changed the subject.

Chad's face tightened. "She isn't going to be asking for it herself, is she?"

Juliane shook her head, unable to voice the words.

Chad's shoulders crumpled, sending a few papers to the floor where they landed dangerously close to the coffee spill. As they both bent down to pick them up, Chad whispered, "Come to my apartment later tonight."

When they were both standing once again, Chad spoke at regular volume, "Nadia is going to be so upset that she didn't get to see you."

"You two are still together?" Juliane tried to smile, but her lips refused to turn up. "I'm happy to hear that. Have you made it official yet?"

Chad shook his head. "Nothing formal yet, but that's her choice. She knows I will be ready to take that step whenever she is."

Juliane suppressed the urge to sigh. She wasn't surprised at all that Chad was content to wait for the lady to do the proposing. As much as she used to think Nadia treated her assistant like a doormat, she now could see he had always needed someone strong and opinionated. Chad smiled, and for a moment, Juliane wondered what it might have been like if their relationship had ever taken a romantic turn.

Chad glanced down at his wrist. "You wear a watch now?" she asked, stunned. Not only was it a watch, but it was an antiquated analog version.

"Well, you were always the one reminding me about how late I always was. Nadia, apparently, thought the same. She gave me her grandfather's watch a few Christmases ago. I find there is something nice about knowing that its sole function is to tell time and only requires a few spinning gears."

"But it's just so . . . so . . . unnecessary."

"Perhaps, but now and then, I've found it to be nice to do things the old-fashioned way." Chad glanced down at his wrist again and blanched.

"Unfortunately, bad habits are hard to break. I really have to run these papers over to the team I am working with now. They have me running simulations on extreme climate change. Did you know that the Sahara went from green to a desert in a flash?"

"How thrilling for you. Do you think anyone will mind if I stick around the building a little longer?"

Chad hesitated in mid-stride. "I don't know if that's the best idea. If the wrong person saw you, who knows how they might react."

As Juliane made her way back to her car, she tried to call Stuart to see if the factory had sent in any further report. However, each time she attempted to instigate the call, she would be hit with another wave of vertigo. She decided that she would find a place to rest while she waited for the business day to end and Chad to return home. *There has to still be a few cafes nearby.* She could not remember the last time she ate.

Rose light from the setting sun blanketed the parking lot as Juliane arrived at Chad's address. The apartment was located in a complex about twenty minutes away from the campus. It was a nice enough space, a definite step up from traditional student housing, with well-manicured common areas and clean lines.

Juliane spotted movement from one of the upper balconies. A short minute later, Nadia emerged, gesturing her inside while holding a finger to her lips.

"Why the whole cloak-and-dagger routine?" asked Juliane as the door closed behind her.

"Chad should be here in the next few minutes. I'll let him explain."

Nadia fidgeted under Juliane's glare. "He shouldn't be too much longer. Would you like me to make up some tea while we wait?"

Chad let himself into the apartment just as the kettle began its whistle. Nadia poured the steaming liquid into a pair of cups. To Chad, she said, "It's a beautiful night. I think I will go out for a bit while you two have a chance to get reacquainted." Without waiting for a response, she leaned over to kiss Chad briefly before grabbing her purse off the counter and departing.

"What's with all the secrecy?" Juliane asked.

"Betty did tell you what she was working on, right?"

"She explained her theory to me."

Chad paused before taking a quick sip of his tea. "And you think she was paranoid?"

Juliane left her cup on the end table and sat down on the couch across from Chad. "I am not as convinced that the situation is that dire. Alan would never design something he couldn't control." There was something else she needed to remember. Something else Betty wanted her to do. *What was it?*

Chad placed his teacup back on the countertop with care. "Betty seemed to think that was exactly what he did."

Pressure began to build behind Juliane's temples. *Not another headache,* she thought. It was harder to think straight when all she wanted to do was lie down.

She needed something tangible to focus on. *The teacup.* "Maybe she allowed their marital problems to influence her opinion."

Chad shook his head. "That was my initial thought as well when she first discussed her theory with me, but think about it this way. What if what might appear to the rest of the world as a careless mistake wasn't so careless?"

"You mean, what if he purposely designed the virus to mutate so that he could intentionally put the entire population at risk?"

"Exactly."

thirty-one

Chad had handed Juliane a small metallic keychain fob. "Betty asked me to give you this."

It didn't look like much. It was just a small tube of plastic connected to an empty keyring with some unknown company's name printed on it. She turned the fob over and noticed a break in the material.

She pulled at the plastic. A portion of the device broke away, exposing a contact plate. It was an old throwaway flash drive—the type no one used anymore. Juliane closed her fist around the exposed metal surface. Immediately, a command prompt appeared behind her mind's eye, followed by a series of ones and zeroes. She issued a quick command, and the data packets were transformed into large high-definition photos of Betty's son in various poses.

Chad looked at her expectantly. Juliane shrugged and opened the next file.

File after file had been more of the same. Juliane began to uncurl her fist; Betty must have given Chad the wrong storage drive by mistake. Another wave of vertigo hit and Juliane ground her teeth in frustration as she sank further into Chad's couch.

When the room finally stopped spinning, Juliane noticed a framed picture placed on a nearby end table. Alan was behind a podium presenting something unclear while Chad and Betty looked on from the sidelines.

The shot must have been taken shortly after Juliane had left the team to join Damien's group. Chad looked embarrassed to be in the spotlight while Betty looked positively aglow; her eyes were locked on Alan with rapt attention.

Juliane's headache made it feel as if her brain were being torn in two. She felt a pain that was almost electric run down her spine, breaking her connection with the device. Juliane ground her teeth. *There has to be something on this drive worth all this trouble*, she thought. She clenched her fist again, and the files immediately reloaded. Once again, Juliane saw image after image of a young boy. His pale gray-blue eyes shone in the sunlight, carefree and happy. His eyes mirrored Betty's in shape, although his were a different color, but Betty's son was two. This boy was clearly a few years older.

There was something about the eyes. They just seemed wrong. On a whim, Juliane sent a command to change his iris color so that they would truly match Betty's. A few pixels in the image shifted. She adjusted the hue by a few points. Suddenly, the photo in her mind dissolved and was replaced by documents detailing out research notes and equations. Juliane sucked in her breath as the balance of files were decrypted. Another piece of the mental wall chipped away.

She glanced at Chad, and her brow wrinkled as she attempted to make sense of the scrolling data.

"Well?"

"I'm not sure, but I think I am looking at radiant energy transformation equations. But if that's what it is, why go to all the trouble of encrypting the formula?" The pictures dissolved, and Juliane felt lightheaded as the pressure of her headache eased. She blinked several times as Chad's face came back into focus.

"She stopped by here a few nights ago in a panic. I tried to get her to tell me what the matter was, but all she would say was that I was to give that to you and only you. You know how Betty used to always want us to go out to celebrate this, that, or another thing?"

Juliane nodded, the corner of her lip turning up at the mention of the memory.

"She was like that. Except not like that at all." Chad shook his hands. "Ugh. How to explain it . . . It was as if she had all the same intensity, but all the life had been drained away."

Juliane thought back to Betty's fierce reaction at the office when she had told her that she wouldn't be able to help. Betty had seemed like an animal backed into a corner.

"She looked awful, though," continued Chad. "I asked her if she wanted me to call Alan to come and get her, but all she would say was that she had already been away too long and had to get back." Chad picked his cup up and took another sip. "She looked terrified." He stared into his mug as if reading tea leaves. "I hate to say anything, but you look a little like that too."

Juliane traced her finger around the rim of her teacup, the file drive still clutched firmly in her other hand. "I've been under a bit of stress recently, but I was there, Chad. I was at the hospital when she died." Juliane sighed. "Alan wasn't. She had a bad reaction to the drugs the doctors gave her. It was a tragedy, not a conspiracy."

Chad jumped up. "I'm sorry, but I think you are wrong."

"Why?" Juliane allowed herself a half-smile. "Because you think Alan is an egotistical maniac?"

"Well, you have to agree he does have more than the average ego." Chad began to pace around the room.

"True, but that doesn't automatically mean that he is planning genocide." Chad spun to face her.

The door burst open, and Nadia came running in. Whatever Chad was going to say was lost in her entrance. "I know I promised you that I would let you have your meeting in private, but you have to see what is on the news," she pleaded.

Chad pressed a small button located on the wall, and a piece of artwork hanging nearby transitioned into a video display. Juliane toggled on her newsfeeds in her mind to run as a supplement to the images on the screen.

"Any particular channel?" Chad asked Nadia.

"He's on all of them."

The screen showed the exterior of the same hospital where Juliane had been not long ago. Louis sat in a wheelchair near a makeshift podium, supported on one side by a team of doctors dressed in the traditional white lab coats. Each stood straight, unafraid of the camera. Another man dressed in a sharply tailored business suit stood by Louis's other side. Juliane assumed this man must have replaced Durham in the role of go-to lackey.

The cameras zoomed in onto the man's face in anticipation of an official statement. The man said a few words, explaining that Louis was in recovery and would not be taking any questions.

The cameras panned over to Louis as he struggled to rise from his seat. He looked terrible in both senses of the word. He was bandaged and braced, with gray skin and several bruises, but his eyes shone with fierce determination.

His knuckles turned white as they clutched the podium, and his lips twisted in pain. Had the caption not identified the man as Louis, Juliane might not have recognized him. It appeared as if the man Juliane knew as Louis might have perished in the accident after all.

"As many of you have undoubtedly heard by now, I was involved in an accident that so tragically took the life of my beautiful wife, Elena. We as a society have become too trusting in our acceptance of technology. I was too trusting. We have ignored the fact that our devices are only as smart as the person who writes the code. We have allowed programs which we do not fully understand to run in the background alongside critical systems."

Juliane's brow wrinkled. Where was he going with this?

"Fifty years ago, society was afraid that the machines would rise one day to enslave humanity. That day came about years ago. There was no war, we went willingly, and I, I have been their biggest recruiter. No longer. From today on, I am redirecting my company and all of its available resources into reclaiming our independence. Elena, in life, was my sun."

Juliane's lip curled before she caught herself.

"She made every day brighter with her presence. In death, may she serve as a beacon of hope for others."

"He's lost his mind," mumbled Nadia. "Poor man."

Louis let go of the podium. One of the doctors moved as if to reposition the wheelchair closer. Louis waved him away, and after an initial tentative step, he left the conference. Several reporters shouted questions, but the man in the tailored suit waved them away before following Louis. Not having much else to focus on, the camera stayed fixed on the empty wheelchair Louis left behind.

The newsfeeds returned to stunned anchormen and women who offered their own opinions on what had and hadn't been said. One group speculated that Louis was only suggesting that there needed to be more emphasis on consumer education; another group believed that Louis had just declared war on the very products that had built his family's fortune.

Business feeds focused on the valuation of large public technology companies. If the overseas market activity was an indicator, the following day was going to be a busy one on the trading floor.

Juliane's vision flashed with incoming communication requests, the majority coming from Stuart. Fortunately, the alert did not trigger another wave of vertigo or pain.

Her assistant appeared in the corner of her vision. "Juliane, you need to come into the office."

"What is it? Is it the factory? Have we gotten their final report?"

"You aren't going to be happy."

"Let me guess, they determined that the worker was a troubled individual. They weren't able to find any evidence of poor working conditions or ways to improve the facility, all of his dorm mates have been transferred to a better place, and we won't be hearing from any disgruntled family members. Meanwhile, nothing has changed."

"You would be right except—"

"Except for what?" Juliane rubbed her hand over her forehead. The small burst of energy from the caffeine in the tea had already drained away. She glanced at Chad and Nadia who were still riveted to the video screen, their hands now clutched together.

"I think this will be better discussed face to face," answered Stuart.

Juliane stifled a groan. Aloud to Chad and Nadia, she said, "As entertaining as watching Louis commit career suicide is, I have some work to do." She left the apartment without waiting for them to respond.

Stuart's avatar remained in the corner of her vision. "I'm on my way to the office now."

She unclenched the fist which still carried the hard drive. She was somewhat surprised to have found she hadn't crushed it. She would take a more thorough look at the files after she finished the debriefing. *What am I missing?*

When she arrived at her office, Stuart stood at full attention. "I hope that this means you are ready to give me a full report."

He nodded. "You may want to take a seat though."

She made no move to sit. Her assistant shifted his weight from one foot to the next. "Perhaps you have forgotten where we left off. You were going to tell me how this incident was somehow different from the last three."

Stuart coughed once before speaking. "There won't be any further incidents from the factory, and we won't have to worry about disgruntled former employees or their families leaking information to the press, because there is no one left to report anything."

Juliane's forehead wrinkled. "And why did I have to come back to the office for this news?"

"They can't, because they are all dead. Someone executed everyone there and then torched the whole complex. Not just the factory, but the worker's village too."

Juliane gasped. "What? How is that even possible?"

Stuart shifted nervously from side to side. "The rumor is that whoever committed the act did it based on your orders."

Juliane realized her mouth was hanging open and quickly shut it. She took a step forward. Stuart jumped back.

Juliane cocked her head as she took in Stuart's panicked expression. "And do you believe them?" Juliane took another step forward. *It just wasn't possible.* Her assistant's matching step backward told her more than any verbal response he could have offered.

"I see." Her shoulder's slumped. Juliane felt that tightening pressure behind her eyes again. An icy rage filled her heart. *They can't all be dead. He had to be wrong.*

A story that sick had to be a lie. Why couldn't he see that? She glared at Stuart. He thought she was a monster. She would show him a monster. "Under the circumstances, you must understand that your services are no longer required. I can't trust my sensitive information with someone who doesn't trust me, but I thank you for your professionalism."

Stuart stood motionless for a few awkward moments. "Was there anything else?" Juliane asked. *I'll get to the bottom of this myself.* She knew she hadn't ordered anyone's death, but if even a fraction of the story were true, someone would have contacted her much sooner. *Wouldn't they?*

She had failed Betty. If only she had gone to the hospital the day before, she might have been there before the doctors gave her those sedatives. *Why had they given her sedatives?* Now she may have failed hundreds of others.

"I believe it would be best if you took your leave now, otherwise I might have to notify the security team." She crossed the room toward the desk and pulled out her chair as her office began to spin. Out of the corner of her vision, she noted her former assistant back out of the room, but then he was out of her thoughts altogether before the door finished closing.

Left alone once again, her nails dug into her palm as she clasped her fist around the hard drive. The pain distracted her from the tears that threatened to consume her. Some dams could never be rebuilt. Opening her palm only long enough to expose the drive's connector, she accessed Betty's research files. She would not focus on anything except the drive in her hand.

thirty-two

Juliane awoke on her office's couch. The light from the rising sun filtered across the room. She had become so engrossed by trying to solve Betty's puzzle that she hadn't realized how exhausted she was until it was well beyond the point of safe travel. As she had delved deeper into Betty's theorem, she realized that the energy equation was only simple on the surface.

There were a few missing elements, but Betty's file appeared to be a bridge system that could wireless transfer power at a previously unheard-of rate. However, as far as she could tell, it had nothing to do with the upgrade or her son.

Betty's work had begun with a grand postulation; a deeply buried thermal energy matrix storage system could be paired with an orbital solar power plant. It was the sort of thing that the world could benefit from. *So why keep it a secret? Was she afraid Alan would steal her idea and take the credit?*

Juliane rubbed her temples. She had stayed up way too late reading over Betty's math. The few hours of sleep she had gained on the couch weren't nearly enough. She needed coffee to fully recharge her batteries.

She stretched her neck and rolled her shoulders to work out their stiffness before walking over to her office's "kitchen cabinet"—a coffee maker and food-based 3D printer built into part of the wall. She inserted a coffee pod into one orifice and a puree cartridge in the other. As brown liquid poured into her cup, a tan paste was extruded onto a heating tray. Within moments, the smell of a fresh-baked scone and Arabica blend filled the room.

The smell in both cases was more impressive than the taste. Neither appliance would win culinary awards, but they allowed her to fill her nutritional requirements and came in handy for days such as these. *Like eating at a hospital.* Betty was given sedatives because her son was in the hospital and she wasn't sleeping. *I wonder if he has been told yet about his mother.*

Together, the files represented a method of generating additional power. Power was already cheap, but Betty's proposal would make it nearly limitless. A single deployment of the system could potentially produce enough power to fuel half the planet. If Betty was right, it was the type of system that should be implemented immediately—not hidden away. There had to be something else on the drive she was missing.

Juliane frowned as an indicator light on the machine informed her that the device had initiated recharging mode. An idea struck her. *What if instead of powering small appliances, a building's power cells could help supplement people too?* She tapped a finger on the machine and shook her head. *The embedded power cells might be able to handle one-off jobs, but if everyone was upgraded that would create too much strain on the grid. Unless . . .* Unless Betty's generator came online.

The texture of her food felt like cardboard. Betty asked her to help her son. Her four-year-old son.

She considered calling Alan. *His wife just died. He isn't going to take calls.* She issued another communication command. "Durham, it's Juliane."

"Yes?"

"Listen, do you know if Alan's son is still in the hospital?"

"I don't know. Don't you want to ask Alan?"

"His wife . . . Betty passed away, and if their kid is still sick too, I . . . er . . . think it best not to intrude on his privacy. Unless I have to."

"Ah. I didn't know. Yeah, I'll need to offer my condolences to him, but why ask me? Or Damien? You're both closer to him than I am."

"I was hoping you might ask your friend."

Silence. "What friend?"

"The one that works at the hospital."

"I'm not sure that's a good—"

"On behalf of another friend," Juliane offered. "Please."

Durham sighed. "I'll ask, but you might wish I hadn't."

"I understand"—Juliane chewed her lip—"and Durham? Thank you."

After quick use of her office's shower, she pulled a spare set of clothing from another hidden cabinet and dressed quickly. She arranged for her clothing from the previous night to be sent out for dry-cleaning and returned to her condo.

She picked up Betty's drive and accessed the data once again. Now that her head no longer felt split in two and she could tell which way was up, Juliane identified the basic building blocks in Betty's proposal.

She closed her eyes, opening up her virtual senses to the building's infrastructure, searching for inductive modules. She attuned herself to a few of their signals. The light on her coffee maker turned off as she adjusted her body to the inductive power flow's signal. It did not take long before she felt a rush much like a triple espresso.

Her vision showed an incoming call from Durham. His voice told her the news was good. "Well, you'll be happy to hear that the boy was released yesterday evening. I was told he made a miraculous recovery. My friend is simply beside herself."

"That's a relief! Thank you so much for checking on that."

"No problem. You can pay me back with a rematch sometime."

"Mmhm." Juliane's mind raced as she ran through the implications of what she'd just done.

Durham paused. "It's nice to be able to talk to you again, Juliane."

"You too," said Juliane. She disconnected the call. An alarm sounded from the food printer as it went into battery mode. Juliane laughed to herself; the printer could go offline permanently for all she cared. Based on the way she felt now, she wouldn't need it again anytime soon.

Betty's equation would work. Juliane was sure of it. However, Betty hadn't been right about everything—not if her son was out of the hospital. Her son's condition couldn't have anything to do with Project Gene Assist.

Juliane's smile fell. *It was just in your head, Betty.* Juliane sighed. Betty might have succumbed to paranoia, but Juliane could still make sure her legacy was continued.

Juliane sat down to access the various newsfeeds before the workday officially began. Now to fix her own. She let the newsfeeds run in the background while she attempted to connect to someone at the factory.

She checked her contacts' online statuses. Everyone was marked away. She sent messages and frowned as they all came back with delivery failure notifications.

The building's lower floors housed the last remaining phone bank, installed as a courtesy for visitors who might need backup communication. Juliane wasn't even sure the devices were still operable. She'd never had reason to use them before.

Juliane rushed out of her office and into a waiting elevator. She punched a lower floor number with almost enough force to break through the keypad's plastic overlay.

A young man in a business suit scurried through the lobby as Juliane crossed the room. The man nervously adjusted his collar before running out of her line of sight. Juliane took a few calming breaths while she attempted to access the personnel directory for landline numbers or mobile numbers. Each time she dialed a number, a recorded voice answered that all lines were currently out of service.

Spinning on her heels so fast they threatened to crack the tile floor, she ran back toward the elevator. *Perhaps*, she thought, *I will have more success visiting the factory's site in the virtual world.* She didn't have to have an established meeting connection to go there.

She could just appear and then see who else might be using the location as a meeting site, just like the Internet chat rooms of old. *Alan did it all the time. Why can't I?* Her contacts might not be answering her pings, but there had to be someone goofing off in that environment who knew something.

Before she could reach the elevator, a bright light flashed outside the main doors. Turning her head, Juliane saw that several people were stationed just beyond the entrance. Another light flashed. At least a few of the people had cameras. "Reporters." Juliane's lips curled.

The various headlines that had been quietly scrolling in the corner of her vision became more insistent. She brought them up to her primary field of view. The stock market wasn't yet open, but analysts were already preparing for a tailspin of massive sell-offs in anything related to the world of technology. Reminders of similar events that happened nearly seventy years ago were only adding to the pre-open hysteria.

Then another headline, much further down in the world news report, caught her eye. Two American journalists had disappeared abroad. The pair had submitted their last report from a town close to the scene of a large factory explosion. Before their disappearance, the news source had asked the pair to investigate rumors of inhumane work conditions at the plant and now believed the pair were likely victims along with potentially hundreds if not thousands of other workers.

Juliane's face paled. She knew the part of the world referenced in the article all too well. The factory she used served as the chief employer for the entire region. It was extremely unlikely that the story could be about any other factory than the one she used.

A cold feeling settled deep in her stomach. She realized that Stuart may not have exaggerated as much as she had previously wanted to believe.

There wasn't much else to the story. The local government was acting tight-lipped and was not releasing much more as to the exact size of the explosion or its cause. Rumors as to the explosion's source ranged from the improper use of equipment to a raid by a rival company.

Juliane glanced at the lobby entrance. She could hear the sound of a growing crowd.

Her newsfeed flashed back to market commentators discussing the tech segment. Juliane felt her saliva consolidate into a wad when one commenter brought up her company only to suggest that Juliane might have intentionally caused the fire to collect on insurance claims based on the company's sinking value.

Juliane waited for someone to correct the commentator. The timeline of the explosion couldn't possibly support his theory. *Or did it?* The memory of Stuart's expression as he made his report came crashing to the top of her consciousness. Stuart seemed to think so, and he seemed to think it was somehow her fault.

But why would anyone think a catastrophic loss of life was what she wanted? She needed that factory to produce the pendants and earpieces which enabled people without genetic upgrades to access the virtual world she had created.

Everything she had done over the last five years had been to grant access to that world. There would be no grand insurance payout. She had no ownership stake in the factory. All her money had been tied up in producing product, and that inventory was now up in smoke, and she certainly had no motive to hurt anyone there.

Juliane spared the reporters another glance. *First, they made me out to be a whore, now they are making me a monster.* She toggled a setting on her communication program to automatically hide all but the most critical incoming call notifications.

She had to get away from the cameras. Punching elevator buttons, she quickly returned to her office. Stuart's report was laid open across her mind's eye before she had even closed the door.

One of the attachments in the file was an audio clip. Juliane's translation tool automatically adjusted the speech. On it, a woman could be barely heard, her voice trembling as she whispered. In the background, Juliane heard screams and a repeating metallic popping sound.

"Oh please God! Help me! There are bodies everywhere. Help me! Please!" The popping sound resumed, cutting off some of the whispers. " . . . to find me. You've got to do something. I can hear"—more pops and screams—"getting closer! Do something! Do something! Oh God! No!" There was a muffled sound like something being dragged away, and the audio ended.

Juliane's body shook as she took in the recording. If the popping sound was the explosion, then there had not been just one but instead, a fairly lengthy series of chain reactions. *It had to have been an accident.* Every fail-safe in the entire facility would have needed to be manipulated to achieve such an effect.

Juliane pounded her fist on the desk. Without being able to connect to a witness, she would have no means of determining exactly what happened, but she could no longer deny that something truly horrible had occurred.

Juliane flipped through more documents. The section related to the original investigation had shown much of what she had known from the beginning. The victim was described as a loner who had increasingly been the source of troubles on the line and who was facing disciplinary actions.

His superiors had performed all intervention activities per approved practices. They had even scheduled an all-hands assembly to discuss the matter and present support options, which was why there were so many people present in a single location when the explosion occurred.

A local team of first responders had made a handful of reports before they too seemed to disappear off the grid. Satellites provided WiFi around the world, but unless a person in the area was equipped with a pendant or ear clip, they had no access to it. It could be the reason why there were no further reports from the first responders, but it was becoming hard for Juliane to convince herself that there were any survivors.

A note showed that Stuart had tried reaching out to some of the locals. Only, his notes showed that people living in villages somewhat farther out had become superstitious and refused to assist in any further investigation. Juliane clenched her teeth. She didn't know if she should feel relieved. There was nothing in the report that suggested she or her company played any role in the disaster, but that didn't make the explosion any less tragic.

Juliane considered replaying the audio recording to determine if she might be able to pull out additional details but knew deep down it was unlikely that she would ever need to hear it again to remember the sounds of panic. *There is nothing else you can do, Juliane,* she told herself as she rocked back and forth, her arms wrapped around her chest. *Make the world better for those they left behind. Focus on the mysteries you can solve.*

Juliane may not be able to do anything to help those poor victims, but she still could make a difference. Reminded of Betty's equation, Juliane felt a stirring hope. She looked at the clippings adorning her office walls, and her shoulders slumped. Without production, she had no assets. She had no way to implement any of Betty's legacy on her own. Juliane considered her options. Her position within Damien's group granted her access to several potential investors, but her years of self-induced isolation limited her personal Rolodex.

She could beg Louis for funds. He already had a vested interest in the project, but that idea was repugnant, and he would be unlikely to accept her proposal based on his new position on technology anyway.

She could go to Damien, but to secure the level of funding she would need would require her to submit her proposal in front of the entire board, which meant that it would be impossible to honor Betty's wish to keep it a secret from Alan.

Juliane chewed her lip as she made her choice.

Juliane spent the next few days refining her needs and perfecting her proposal. The reporters had dispersed when she hadn't made an immediate appearance. Juliane, remembering her tabloid fame, did not trust the quiet. She assumed that while the whole press corps was no longer outside her door, at least one or two reporters or paparazzi were still camped out in more clandestine locations, either around her office or by her condo.

She sent a query to a real estate agent. Selling her condo wouldn't be enough to fund her next steps, but it would at least help her maintain a little more independence. She'd been homeless before. It didn't scare her, and Alan was right; she didn't live there anyway.

Juliane considered calling Durham to see if he might know a way to access some additional money but couldn't bring herself to ask for more help. She would have to follow through with her original plan.

As prepared as she could be, she made her way across town toward Damien's building. The building looked much as it had the first day she had seen it. The sandstone exterior was just as clean and bright as the day it had first been constructed. *Damien must spend a fortune in upkeep*, Juliane thought. The material was beautiful but prone to blacken as it absorbed everyday urban gases.

When she reached Damien's floor, his executive assistant met her at the door. Sarah had grown in confidence over the years. Gone was the people pleaser. She had always been an extremely capable administrator, but there was now an edge about her. She seemed harder, less forgiving. She and Juliane hadn't gotten along any better since the day of their first meeting.

"Juliane. You finally decided to come out of hiding?"

"I need to talk to Damien about some recent developments."

"I'm sure you do, but you should know that he is well aware of the recent . . . unpleasantness."

Juliane fought the urge to bite her lip or otherwise signal to Sarah that her words meant anything to her. The other woman would only use them against her. Sarah's wounded pride from their first encounter was something that time would never heal.

"Then I am sure he would be willing to fit me into his schedule."

Sarah broke eye contact first, looking up and to the right, and yet at nothing in particular. Juliane watched as Sarah's body took on a slight glow. If Juliane hadn't been looking for it, she might not have noticed it.

"You're accessing the network," Juliane stated.

Sarah blinked, and the glow disappeared. Sarah allowed for one side of her mouth to twist in a half-smile. "How could you tell?"

"You glowed. I saw your skin interacting with the network."

Sarah's smiled melted into a frown. "I was told that the light fluctuations wouldn't be noticeable."

"And they probably aren't to the average eye, but I've had a few years of experience. I assume that you were checking Damien's calendar just then?"

Sarah's frown deepened. "You may go in. It seems he has been expecting you after all."

Juliane inclined her head in acknowledgment before turning and entering Damien's suite.

Damien was already walking toward the door as she crossed the threshold. "Ah, Juliane, you are looking lovely today. The fresh air from the other night seems to have done you some good."

"Thank you again for the tickets. It was . . . um . . . a new experience."

"One that I hope that you'll want to repeat again soon."

"We'll just have to see what time allows."

"Always so non-committal when it involves anything other than your work. How is everything going by the way? I heard that there may have been an explosion involving one of our manufacturing sites."

Juliane felt her eyes tighten at his choice in words. She had been operating Fair Use Jewelry independently for so long that she had forgotten that he also had an interest in the news story too. "That's what I've been able to ascertain as well, although communication seems to have been completely cut off."

"So why are you here telling me this?"

Juliane's forehead wrinkled. "I came here to discuss next steps. I've recently come into possession of some research that could—"

Damien's laughter interrupted Juliane's pitch.

"I meant why, Juliane, are you in my office when you could be at the site confirming the extent of the damage firsthand? Are you not at all curious as to what happened?"

"Of course, I am!" She couldn't eat. She couldn't sleep. Juliane could hear the screams of the woman on the audio file in her memory as if on constant playback. After the first two nights ruined by nightmares, Juliane had taken to pulling energy constantly from available inductive sources. "But that's not what I am here about."

"Oh?"

"I have recently inherited a big discovery. Potentially life-changing. I've already proved that a portion of the theory works, and now I just need a little help in deploying it on a much larger scale."

"Damien." Sarah did not even attempt to offer an apology for interrupting their meeting. "I just received word that there is a credible threat against several of our retail distribution sites."

"Threat?" he repeated. "What kind of threat?"

"Messages were intercepted between members of a radical anti-technology group, which detailed plans to blow up several major distribution hubs, ours included."

"Was anyone able to determine when this attack is expected to occur?"

"Unfortunately, no."

"And do they know how the bombs are expected to enter the buildings?"

Sarah shook her head. Damien continued as if he never anticipated that she might offer another answer. "Then we really have no choice but to increase our level of diligence internally, but we need to externally appear as if everything is business as normal. We don't want to incite a panic."

Sarah bowed her head and began backing out of the room. "Yes, sir. I'll notify the appropriate parties."

Damien turned back to Juliane. "It would seem that you might not be the only one with problems that need addressing. Perhaps it is for the best that you stay in the country after all. Now, why don't you tell me more about this theory you've come across?"

Juliane felt her shoulders relax. "Well, on the surface, it is quite simple," she began.

thirty-four

For the hundredth time, Juliane squashed the urge to fling her arms towards the sky in celebration. Everything was working out better than she had originally anticipated. She couldn't remember why she had ever hesitated to confide in Damien.

She gazed up at the monument she and Damien had worked to erect and was momentarily blinded by its brilliant white surface. She grinned. The statue with its intricate whirls and detailed carvings was just a simple shell. The true marvel was the power transformation system inspired by Betty's equation.

Hidden underneath the stone was a series of converters, relays, and transformers. Once the complete system was online, it would also act as a receiver in addition to distributing power along the grid. Another monument located on the other side of the globe would perform a similar function. Juliane caressed the marble. This was a legacy to be proud of. *This is for you, Betty.*

To maximize the system's potential, the placement sites were critical. Unfortunately, as Juliane had realized in the months following her original discussion with Damien, alternative energy projects weren't always as well received in practice as they were on paper. No one wanted them in their backyard.

Damien had immediately thought of a way to get around the problem. He had suggested that they disguise the necessary antenna pairs as beautifully sculptured works of art. The land where they would be placed would be manicured like a park.

It added extra expense to the project, but as long as the monument didn't look like a power plant, the neighbors likely wouldn't attempt to delay the project. Once the plan was set, his speed to execution was dizzying.

Damien had commissioned a master artist to design both monuments in honor of his favorite scientists. The marble construction towering above her was dedicated to Marie Curie and showed the woman reaching toward the stars, a globe representing an atom perched on her extended fingertip.

The second statue had been dedicated to Charles Darwin. It too had a matching globe on top of a walking stick. The hand not resting on the walking stick was stretched out toward the sky, while a series of marble animals lay draped down the statue's steps.

Both statues had been beautiful on paper but were breathtaking in reality, especially if one ignored the real animal droppings that marked their surfaces within minutes of their unveiling.

Betty would have been bringing the champagne out around now, thought Juliane. Her grin slipped, thinking of her friend and former colleague. *You always did want to celebrate too soon.* Breaking ground on the park had been the easy part.

To complete the project, Juliane still had to deploy solar sheets into orbit and bury the thermal energy matrix storage system deep underground. Damien had been willing to sign off on the park's construction, but she was going to have to approach the board to request the rest of what was needed.

Juliane was confident the board presentation was a minor rubber stamp in the process, otherwise, Damien would not have already invested so much. However, she hadn't yet figured out how to continue to keep Alan from learning who originally came up with the system's equation. While she had figured out its potential, the idea's basis was far from her area of expertise.

Juliane's lips twisted. Thus far, honoring Betty's last wish to keep her work from Alan was proving to be less difficult than she first imagined it might be. As much as she wanted to verify that he was managing her loss and that Stevie was okay, she hadn't seen or heard from Alan since the day of the football game. *The poor man must be devastated. We'll talk when he's ready.*

Her vision flashed with an incoming call notification; it was Damien. She accepted the call without hesitation.

"Hi, Juliane, I just wanted to check in to see how the construction is going."

"You are an absolute magician. I don't know how you were able to pull it all together so fast! I thought we would still be knee-deep in the permit process."

"I take that to mean that you are pleased with the process."

"More than pleased. I almost wish that my proposal had required more than two towers."

"Well, I am glad to hear that. Any trouble with the locals?"

"A handful of people were opposed, but, for the most part, the majority of the locals are excited about what this park will do to their land values."

"Excellent."

"One of these days, Damien, I want you to share how you are able to accomplish so much so fast. Alan is good too, but you, sir, are a master."

"Perhaps now you will be more willing to visit my office on a regular basis. I have a few secrets I'd love to share with you."

Juliane's jaw began to ache from smiling so much. After so little use over the years, the expression felt unnatural.

"The board will meet in two weeks," Damien continued. "I'd like to add phase two to the agenda. Would you be ready by then?"

Juliane looked up toward the globe. The stone surface was so highly polished that Juliane thought she could just make out her reflection in its surface.

"I can manage that."

"Good. It will be worth your time. There are a number of other projects that have been developing that I believe you will be interested in learning more about."

"I look forward to it." Juliane disconnected the call and leaped from the stone stairs.

An early model Porsche 918 Spyder pulled up at the park's entrance just as Juliane reached the street. While the muscle car was aged, it had been well-maintained. The glossy exterior shone like black enamel. While the majority of vehicles on the roads were silent, this one still possessed the quiet roar of a tsunami. Even with the top down, it took a few moments for Juliane to break her attention away from the car to recognize its driver.

"Sarah? Is that you?"

Sarah smiled, although the expression never reached her eyes. "Who else would it be?"

"I just would have guessed you drove something more . . . er . . . practical."

Sarah tilted her head. "You aren't the only one who appreciates the benefits of being associated with the rich and powerful." She frowned. "But, in this case, you'd be correct. This is Camille's car. I'm to take you to her."

"Camille?" Her hand had risen as if it wanted to scratch her head on its own accord. She pulled it back to her side through conscious effort. "What does Camille need me for?"

Juliane had little reason to interact with the group's medical technologist over the years professionally and even less interest in forming any personal connection. Especially after noticing that she and Sarah seemed to be friends.

"Camille doesn't need you for anything . . . You need her."

Juliane's forehead wrinkled.

Sarah rubbed her temple. "Do you remember asking me about being upgraded?"

Juliane nodded.

"Well, accessing the Internet is just a fraction of our potential. Camille's been able to do so much more. Damien thought you would appreciate a little demonstration."

Sarah sent the car racing within seconds of Juliane strapping herself into the seat. The wind of their passage transformed Juliane's hair into a whip. She reached up to secure it into an informal ponytail as they drove. If she had a car like this, she would have to cut her hair short like Sarah's.

"Why weren't you at Betty's funeral? Weren't you two friends?"

"I'm honoring her memory in my own way." The truth was, Juliane hadn't learned there had been a memorial until after the fact. It would seem she hadn't been invited. *So much for being Betty's primary contact.*

It was just as well. Thinking of Betty lying lifeless in a box blackened her vision and caused her legs to lock into place. She remembered the feeling of their connection as it severed and shuddered. *Cursed private network,* Juliane thought once again. She would never, ever, establish one of those again.

"Such a tragic business. To lose one's spouse, well, that is a terrible thing, but at least he still has his son . . ." Sarah trailed off. Juliane wasn't sure if she was hearing Sarah correctly over the roar of the engine, but her tone seemed as if she were discussing a spring shower upsetting picnic plans.

Sarah continued. "I was told that I will likely never have children of my own, so I have always had to live vicariously through others." Sarah glanced in Juliane's direction. "You did know Alan had a son before this?"

"Of course."

Sarah mouthed "of course." More subdued, she said, "Well, *I* might never have known if Damien hadn't said something. I asked Alan once if I could see a picture, and do you know what he told me? He didn't carry a single photograph. He said Betty was the family photographer. He's regretting that now. He told me he can't find any of her files now. Can you imagine how awful that must be?"

"Oh, so you've talked to him?" Juliane asked

"Only for a moment," said Sarah.

Juliane kept her gaze locked on the road in front of them. "Alan was never much for clutter, hard copies or electronic. Betty was always the less organized one. I am sure she has a few scattered about."

"I heard you were with her when she died. Is that true?"

"I visited her at the hospital."

"Did she ever share photos with you? I only ask because I am worried about how Alan is holding up in this situation."

"She was unresponsive when I got there." If Juliane told Sarah about the private network, she had little doubt that Sarah would try to establish one just to prove she could. *No one deserves that*, thought Juliane. *Not even Sarah.*

They pulled into the parking lot. "You're late." Camille met them at the door of her facility and escorted them back to her office.

"I thought you would appreciate it if I didn't damage your car," Sarah retorted with a warm-hearted laugh.

"What have you told her?"

"Very little. You know me. I just do the filing."

Camille's eyes twinkled at what had to be an inside joke and turned toward Juliane. "Are you at all aware of the works of Jonathan Hutchinson or a condition known as progeria syndrome?"

"I can't say that either has come up in my field of study."

Camille closed her eyes and took a breath. "It is an extreme genetic condition which manifests as premature aging in afflicted individuals. Those with the condition typically age at a rate eight to ten times faster than normal, all because of a mutation in a simple protein."

"That sounds terrible. I assume you have been working on a cure?"

Camille tilted her head, stretching the muscles in her neck before answering. "A cure would only help a small portion of the population. No, Juliane, we are thinking bigger. Once we were able to isolate the cause of the mutation, it took little imagination to see the benefit in applying the same technique to normal human cells."

"Are you telling me that you are working on creating a technique that could potentially cause people to appear to age only one year when, in fact, ten years have passed?"

Camille turned her nose up, allowing the hallway light to shine fully upon her face. "We aren't working on a technique. We've perfected it."

Only then did Juliane see that neither Camille nor Sarah possessed the fine lines around their eyes that would have normally given away their ages. "You've undergone the procedure."

"Yes. Everyone on the board has. By the way, I imagine your visit here today will cause at least one person to lose their wager. Most of us thought that after spending so much time with avatars, you might never notice un-aging people in real life long enough to question why we always looked so young."

"We're effectively immortal now," interjected Sarah.

"No, Sarah," corrected Camille. "We are still very much mortal. The process only slows down aging and even appears to reverse its effects to a point, but the process doesn't stop aging altogether."

"I'm surprised this technique of yours hasn't already been blasted on the news," Juliane said.

Camille smiled and shook her head. "The fountain of youth doesn't exactly need help with advertising."

"I suppose you're right. But don't you want to share this accomplishment with the world?"

"The idea of being a public figure has never appealed to me."

"But you could have the world eating out of your hand," Juliane sputtered. *How can he be so nonchalant?*

"Why do you think I can't have that while remaining private?"

"But if you don't release what you have done, how would anyone realize your service is any different from the dozens of other cosmetic procedures?"

"The difference would be that my clients could potentially reach their seven-hundredth birthday. However, I would imagine that the word would have gotten out long before then."

"But you could have it all tomorrow. Don't you want that?"

"Juliane, I've already undergone the procedure. Time is no longer my enemy. I can afford to be patient. Until then, rest assured that those who have the means and the motivation will find me. Now that you understand the full implication of what we have achieved here, would you be interested in giving the procedure a try for yourself?"

If what Camille said was true, she would have several lifetimes to continue her work. Juliane caught her reflection on a mirror hung in Camille's office. By accepting, she would not only remain mentally in her prime but physically as well.

"Absolutely."

Sarah and Camille exchanged a glance, and Sarah exited the room, returning later with a small rod.

"For this procedure to work, a candidate must have first gone through the original upgrade. So not just anyone will be eligible for treatment, which is another reason I've held back from releasing this news to the press. At least, they're not eligible today. We're working on a way to apply both sequences at the same time."

Camille pressed a button and the rod hummed to life. "Next, this rod will upload a command sequence to the code already running in your DNA. Once that is done, the specific protein in your DNA will be isolated and modified by your own natural chemistry."

"So, in theory, I might have been able to modify the protein without its assistance?"

Camille shrugged. "And enough monkeys typing at random could replicate Shakespeare. You might have stumbled upon it one day if you tried hard enough. This just speeds the process along. Think of it as a cheat code in a game."

"I was never much one for video games." Juliane felt a pinching along the length of her body as if she had been bitten by hundreds of mosquitoes. She hissed.

"That uncomfortable feeling is your cells responding to the treatment as your skin begins to firm and tighten. Don't worry; it's only a temporary effect. You won't even notice the sensation an hour from now."

Juliane glanced back at the mirror. She did not realize how many lines had begun to etch her face around the corners of her eyes until they blurred away. She still held herself with the confidence of someone experienced with the world but had the smooth skin of a twenty-year-old.

"I'll admit, I am impressed."

"I'm so glad my work meets your approval," Camille said, putting the rod down on a nearby table. She looked at Sarah. "I believe I have done what I said I would. Now may I return to my real work?"

Sarah nodded. Camille turned and exited the room without saying good-bye.

As the sound of her footsteps faded, Juliane asked Sarah, "I take it that bringing me here wasn't her idea."

"Damien made it clear that he wanted all board members to have the opportunity to improve themselves."

Juliane thought of the football game. "I understand. It's hard to say no to him."

Sarah's lips tightened. "You have no idea." She appeared to chew on her response. "Not all of us are treated like the prodigal daughter. Some of us have to earn our place."

Juliane gazed into the mirror, patting her hair smooth. It would take a while to get used to her new reflection. "I earned my place, just the same as you. I may have just done so a little differently than the others."

Sarah slammed her fists down upon the table with such force that Juliane had to return her attention to the enraged woman.

"What—"

"You cannot begin to comprehend what I have done, what I have sacrificed, to have a place by Damien's side."

Juliane's forehead wrinkled. "I'm sorry, I—"

Sarah picked up the rod from where Camille had left it and examined it for obvious damage before pocketing the device away. "Why don't I take you home?"

Juliane, stunned by the venom in Sarah's voice, took a step back. "Okay."

Juliane and Sarah did not speak again until they were both secured in Camille's vehicle and the medical complex was a mere speck in the rearview mirror. "Look, about today . . ."

"I know I shouldn't be mad, but I am. You like to think you're smart, but there are so many things you don't seem to comprehend at all. For example, you have no clue how easy you've had it being Damien's favorite, how much freedom he has allowed you over the years. Even now, when he is bringing you back into the fold after your epic failure, he is doing so with gifts."

Juliane sat in silence for a few moments. "What epic failure are you referring to?" The sound of the woman suffering in the factory audio played in her mind. *It was an accident. A terrible, terrible accident.*

Sarah rolled her eyes. "This is what I mean about you being treated differently from the rest of us. I bet you never once asked yourself why the press let that disaster at your factory go so quickly. Two of the victims were reporters," said Sarah. "*American* reporters. The disaster at *your* facility should be the *only* thing people are talking about."

Juliane steeled her jaw. Was what Sarah implying true? Damien had the means, but she'd never asked him to do anything on her behalf. Was she now involved in a cover-up? Her reputation had taken enough hits. Her career, and more importantly her credibility would never recover if rumors were to get out. "It might not be the news story you think it is. Everyone knows that there is always a risk of corners being cut when dealing with low-cost manufacturing regions."

"So that's it? You admit that corners were cut."

"I am not admitting anything to you or anyone else. I am only saying that I recognize that there was a risk. Funds for a formal investigation went up in flames with the factory, and the local government isn't talking. If they don't want to pursue justice for the victims, then I have to respect their sovereignty."

Sarah snorted. "That's rather convenient for you."

Juliane shrugged.

"So instead of doing the right thing and funding an inquiry, you are playing gardener and building statues."

Sarah doesn't know the real purpose for the statues, realized Juliane. That meant that Damien didn't trust his own assistant with the information. Juliane replayed her conversations with Sarah in her head. *What if Sarah hadn't been making simple conversation when she asked about Alan's missing photos? Was paranoia a side effect of Camille's procedure?*

But what if she wasn't being paranoid? What would Sarah or Alan stand to gain from the files now, that they weren't eventually going to have access to in a few months when the project was completed?

It just didn't make sense. The statues would provide billions with clean, renewable energy. *Why hide that from the board?* Juliane felt her temples begin to throb. *Was this how Betty felt during her final days?*

thirty-five

The car pulled to an abrupt stop, startling Juliane out of her thoughts. Traffic was at a standstill in all directions. Sarah's knuckles were white where they gripped the steering wheel.

Chunks of concrete and piles of glass lay scattered across the street. A number of people stood on the sidewalk. A handful, however, had their faces concealed behind red and white masks that looked like lizard heads.

One of the masked individuals stood out ahead of the others. The figure lifted his or her fist into the air and let a scrap of cloth fall. This must have been some cue for the others as they seemed to melt into the cityscape.

Within seconds, all that remained was the red and white cloth as it came to rest upon the broken glass remains of a burnt-out storefront's windows. Those on the sidewalk who hadn't worn a mask took this as their signal to run as well.

The gaping holes where a pair of destroyed shops' front windows once stood called to her. Juliane was out of the car before she even realized what she was doing.

From the car, Sarah said something, but Juliane couldn't make out her words. Screams of panic, the stampede of feet, and squealing tires filled the air. Juliane shook her head in confusion. Sarah shifted the car into gear and sped off.

A large chunk of a shop's sign lay among the rubble. Based on the few words that remained legible, as well as the pieces of inventory scattered about that were not destroyed, the store had provided basic, run-of-the-mill electronics.

She ran a mental search query. The neighboring shop had been a high-end pet boutique. *The masked figures had definitely targeted one of the two shops, if not both, but why?*

Juliane accessed the newsfeeds. Traffic cameras clocked the event within seconds of Sarah and Juliane's arrival. Had they arrived a moment sooner, they too might have been hit by flying debris.

The masked figures appeared on her newsfeed. At least one person nearby had been live-streaming at the time and had captured footage of them leaving. However, they hadn't recorded the explosion itself. Headlines scrolled across announcing it was a developing story.

The masked figures looked even more serpentine on the amateur video as they had when Juliane spotted them outside the car. As a group, they even moved with the undulating motions of a reptile. The red cloth floating on the breeze appeared on the feed like a tongue tasting the air.

The lizard people melted into the alleyways as quickly on the feed as it had appeared live. The reporters weren't able to provide any concrete evidence as to who the group was or what their purpose might be. They ended the report by asking for anyone with more information to give the news desk a call.

An eerie silence fell over the street and Juliane became aware of how very much alone she was. *Sarah ditched me.* The people responsible for the attack could be anywhere. She needed to get out of sight and quickly.

Without thinking, she darted through the closest shop's doorway. *What am I doing?* wondered Juliane. *There was just a major explosion, there are crazy people out there, and what do I do? I jump into a building that has just been destabilized.* Juliane spun. She needed to get out of the building before more of it came down.

Blue-white lights flashed near the entranceway. Juliane could see exposed wires arc overhead. She heard a pop as a sprinkler head was engaged. *A little late*, she thought. A black liquid began to pool near the entranceway.

Juliane glanced toward the shop's back. Perhaps there was an alternate exit.

Racks of twisted metal blocked her path. The air was thick with smoke and melted silicon. "I can't see a thing in here," Juliane said to herself.

Juliane looked down at her hands. She imagined making them glow as Louis had done during the football game. At first, there was light only at the center of her palm where the skin was thinnest, but it gradually spread out to her fingertips. *Much better than a party trick.*

She curled her digits, encasing and consolidating the light until it was transformed into a directionless orb. *It would have to be enough*, thought Juliane. *At least I might not break my ankle getting out of here.*

Two doors stood at the shop's back. The remains of an exit sign hung from a broken ceiling tile near the larger of the two. Juliane began to reach for the larger door's handle, then paused. There was something odd about the smaller door. *Probably just a storage closet*, she told herself and took another step toward the larger door.

A pink-blue light arched from the door's handle to Juliane's outstretched hand. A shock of pain broke her concentration, causing what light she was able to generate to go out.

Juliane reached toward the wall with her other hand. She was blind in the darkness. She inched her way toward the smaller door. Maybe there was something in the closet she could use to ground the exit door so that she could open it safely.

It took a few tries to jostle open the second door, but finally, it gave way. Juliane concentrated. Once again, she was able to create a soft glowing light from her palm.

This was no storage closet. The space had been spared from much of the damage that ruined the rest of the store. Empty animal crates lay open, scattered across the room. The floor was heavily scarred as large equipment had been moved without regard for surface damage.

The backroom must be a shared space with the pet shop, thought Juliane. *If the wiring next door is a little safer, I might just be able to get out of here.*

"Where is everyone?" whispered Juliane. She wasn't exactly looking forward to seeing a dead body but based on the level of damage surrounding her, Juliane was a little surprised she hadn't yet seen any evidence of human casualty.

As she gingerly made her way across the room, Juliane thought she could hear voices coming from the other side of the wall. Juliane let out a relieved breath. *Thank goodness. The first responders are here.* She swiped her hand along the wall, hopeful that its light would soon illuminate the second doorway she knew had to be there.

The voices grew louder. Juliane could just make out their words. *Where was that door?* she wondered. *Oh, forget about the door. I'll just make a new one.* Juliane raised a fist. She would break through the wall herself or at least get her would-be rescuer's attention.

"The news is making the attack out to be the work of an animal rights group," laughed a male voice.

"Animal rights? Why would they think that?" asked another.

"It seems the owner of the pet shop was engaged in some illegal side business. Trading exotic animals or something like that."

The voices grew louder. Juliane pounded on the wall.

"We're looking for a lady, right?" asked the second voice.

Juliane shouted, "Hello? Hello? I'm back here!" She hit the wall again.

"What does she look like again?" continued the second voice.

"Tall, brunette, mid-thirties," answered the first. "You'll recognize her when you see her."

Juliane's blood ran cold. They weren't looking for just some lady. *They're looking for me.* Were they members of the group responsible for the explosion? Had they seen her duck into the building?

She jumped back from the wall, scanning the room for a place to hide. As she did, the light from her hand reflected her image off a sheet of metal near the pile of crates. She lifted a hand to her face.

Camille had stated that a person might learn how to take command of their cellular structure without the need for her program. If that was true, what else might a person be able to do?

"I'll get an ax out of the truck," she heard the second voice say.

Juliane bit back a scream. *This has to work,* she thought as she knelt closer to the metal sheet making her reflection almost as clear as if she was looking in a mirror. Her dark eyes stared back unblinking. She fired off mental commands as if she were changing the parameters of a computer program. Did the rim of her irises lighten?

"Stay put, ma'am. Help is on the way," shouted the first voice. More softly he said, "Call the boss."

Yes. Her irises lightened. Juliane let out a sigh of relief. Within moments, the eyes in the reflection were a silver hazel. The overall effect looked alien on her face, and she blinked, breaking her concentration. When she looked back, her eyes had resumed their natural color.

The wall shook from the impact of the ax on the wall.

"Focus, Juliane." She starred at her reflection again. Three large freckles appeared over the top of a natural blush. The ax struck again, and her visage was once again flawless alabaster.

"There has got to be another way," she muttered, standing upright once more. "If only I had something like an invisibility cloak." The thought reminded Juliane of her old office at the ACI campus with the setup of cameras that fooled the eye into thinking that the lower levels weren't there. The ax struck again, this time breaking through. She was nearly out of time.

She reached out with her mind as if she was interfacing with her emulator program. Suddenly, it was as if she could see and feel the man's neurons firing as if she was setting up a private network but with far less intimacy. She visualized herself twisting and pulling at their endings.

"It's not her. Just some kid," yelled the man at the wall to his partner as the ax broke through the rest of the way. "Blonde girl, probably seventeen . . . nineteen tops."

The man was dressed in a thick dark jacket of heavy material. *A firefighter* realized Juliane. She shivered. Her first thought that they were first responders must have been correct, but that didn't mean that was all they were.

"She must have gotten away."

The words served to confirm her fears. *They're not here to rescue me.* Her heartbeat raced. The wail of sirens could be heard in the distance. *There is no way I am going to be able to keep this disguise up with that many people,* thought Juliane.

"Keep your eyes out. She can't have gotten far."

To Juliane, the firefighter said, "Don't worry, Miss. We'll have you out of here in no time."

The hole in the wall widened.

"Now how did you get stuck back there?"

Juliane shook her head, afraid to speak.

"Wrong place, wrong time?"

Juliane nodded eagerly.

"Did you see anything—notice anything strange before the explosion?"

Juliane vigorously shook her head.

"Anyone else back there with you?"

Juliane shook her head again, this time more slowly.

"Maybe this is your lucky day after all." To his partner, he-yelled, "All clear."

Turning back to Juliane, he continued, "Miss, if I were you, I'd be a bit more careful where I go alone. There may be some dangerous people in the area. Do you have someplace else you can go?"

Juliane nodded.

As he pulled the last bit of wall separating them away, the firefighter glanced in the direction of his partner. The other man was turned away, still talking on his phone. "Then you'd better get out of here, kid."

Juliane ran out of the pet shop and down the street as fast as her feet would carry her as the sound of additional fire trucks and police cars could be heard arriving on the scene.

thirty-six

Juliane stared at her reflection in the bathroom mirror as she fought back another wave of panic. A breaking news alert flashed across her vision. It was a report of yet another bombing attributed to the lizard-masked individuals, but in another city, states away.

What was happening out there? She closed her eyes, filling her lungs with slow breaths as she reminded herself that it had been several days since she had found herself in the shop's backroom. No one had come to her door making threats. Maybe the lizard people didn't know who she was after all. She had no reason to keep looking over her shoulder, but they could be anyone.

The Apex advisory board waited for her upstairs. As far as Damien was concerned, business was expected to operate as usual. He'd called for a meeting with the board immediately following the explosion down the street and explained it was their responsibility to show strength in times of uncertainty. They needed to set an example for the masses.

She opened her eyes to examine her outfit for the tenth time. It was pure white, tailored and pressed to perfection. It screamed power. Now all she had to do was master her features so that her expression matched. Today was not the day to appear to be anything but completely in control. Damien had made it clear that she had his backing, but she still needed to convince the rest of the group. Her stomach turned over.

Juliane frowned as she fought the urge to vomit; Sarah and likely Camille would be looking for a reason to reject her proposal out of personal dislike. For the first time, she regretted not attending more of these meetings in person. Then maybe she would have a better sense of who her true allies might be.

She arrived at Damien's tower and proceeded to the sixth floor, where she was the first to enter the hexagonal conference room. Her gaze took in the artwork on the walls. The piece was really quite lovely, whether it was viewed up close or afar. One of these days, she needed to ask Damien who the artist was.

Juliane heard voices in the hallway. Her pulse quickened as she imagined the voices belonged to masked men. She clenched her fists. Her nails bit into her palms as she fought the urge to flee from the room.

Her legs threatened to lock as she pulled out the chair opposite from Damien's usual spot. Once seated, she crossed her ankles, locking her feet behind the chair's rollers as she waited for the rest of the board to file in. The door opened, allowing Durham and Sarah to enter. So distracted by their conversation, neither acknowledged her presence.

"Eithan is exasperated," Sarah pronounced.

"Well, I would think that's an understandable response, all considering," replied Durham.

"It's making him reckless."

Durham shrugged. He stopped in his tracks when he noticed Juliane in the room.

"Miss, I believe you are in the wrong room."

Juliane felt her body begin to relax. As she leaned back into the chair, Durham stuttered. His mouth flapped open and close, yet no sound escaped.

Sarah's eyes narrowed to slits. She stared at Juliane until Juliane thought the glare could bore a hole through her skull. "Juliane?"

Juliane forced a smile. "In the flesh."

"Well that was a neat trick," said Sarah.

Juliane willed her features to remain serene. *What trick? What had they seen? Oh no,* she thought, *the near panic attack.* She must have involuntarily modified her features. How could she explain what she had done without letting Sarah know how easily she had been affected by what was going on miles away? Sarah would make sure someone so jumpy couldn't be trusted with making sound decisions related to Apex resources.

"I thought it would be nice to share what I've learned," Juliane replied. *Nicely done,* she thought.

"Juliane? Here and sharing? The world truly has gone mad." Camille entered the room, standing close to Sarah.

"After you were kind enough to share your youth program with me, I thought it would be rude not to return the favor."

Durham's face also showed an ageless quality, except no one would mistake a person possessing a chin that strong to be anything other than a full-grown adult. He had shaved his head recently, and only pale white stubble broke up the gleam of his scalp. The effect did nothing to help hide a small, round red-gray bruise from the center of his forehead.

She forced her gaze to return to Sarah and Camille. Juliane could not decide if it was only the room's lighting, but it appeared that they too had a similar mark.

"Juliane." Alan had arrived. Juliane had been expecting to see a broken man, or if nothing else, a grieving one. She did not expect the carefree individual who strode into the room. Out of curiosity, Juliane glanced at his forehead but found no shadow mark.

"I truly am sorry for your loss."

"Are you?" Alan purred. "Well, that's small comfort." His stride remained unbroken until he stood directly across from Juliane, his hand caressing the leather of the seatback. "I am glad to see that you were able to join us today. I know I am not alone when I say that the board has missed your presence."

The room was silent. Alan tapped the chair where he stood three times before taking a step back and sitting down one position over. Sarah glanced at Alan with her eyebrows raised as she took the chair immediately to his right. Durham said nothing as he sat at the table a few chairs down from everyone.

Damien had continued recruiting additional team members throughout the years. Their group was now thirteen, in addition to Damien, and the others began filing in, filling seats where there was room. Eventually, the only ones missing were Eithan and Damien himself.

Sarah rose from her seat and placed a finger on a small pad mounted on the wall. A portion of the artwork moved to become a video monitor. It was definitely different to see the room from this side of the screen. Juliane took a deep breath. She could get through this.

"Good afternoon to you all. I am so glad that you were all able to make it today. Eithan and I are not able to join you in person for reasons which will be made evident soon enough." He paused, and several of the others exchanged questioning looks. *It seems that I am not the only one who has secrets for Damien to keep,* she thought.

"As all of you know, many of our firm's efforts have centered on technology to improve the human experience. Juliane is here today to pitch a new energy collection, storage, and disbursement strategy."

Juliane saw several eyebrows rise. She wasn't surprised. The way Damien described it made the project seem a world away from her area of expertise. Only a few years ago, they would have been right.

She could feel the throb of energy coming from the walls as if the room were alive. It felt like the building itself was encouraging her to continue. As Alan leaned forward in her seat, she told herself she had no reason to be afraid—not of the board, or a bunch of psychos running around outside in masks.

Damien's words brought her attention back to the meeting at hand. "Following her presentation, I will be turning the discussion over to Eithan, who has been hard at work cracking the next big advancement in nanorobotics and bioengineering. Juliane, you have the floor."

Juliane rose and began her presentation. Alan watched her every move like a raptor but remained silent throughout the entire proceeding as if he had been given an advance copy of the script. The vote passed without a single voice of dissent. She hadn't needed to worry at all.

Before she regained her seat, memos were sent instructing various outlets to move forward with the balance of land and material acquisition. They had authorized the construction of orbital solar sheets, which would harness the energy and then convert the power into a signal that could be received by the statues' antennas.

Juliane slumped in her chair. Now that it was over, the entire experience felt rather anticlimactic. Even so, she couldn't stop feeling like she should be far away from the room and everyone in it.

The video screen focused on Eithan. The geneticist appeared frazzled and altogether out of sorts, yet triumphant. "As many of you know, my workspace over the last few weeks has been rather . . . fluid." Several of the others in the room chuckled. Juliane frowned in confusion. *Must be an inside joke,* she thought.

Eithan continued after the laughter died down. "However, my primary research location has remained secure, and I am pleased to state that I am ready to begin phase two. I would like to thank those who have already volunteered to act as test subjects; I am honored by your trust."

Eithan paused again to collect his thoughts. Juliane glanced around the room. Sarah seemed to be struggling to keep a smug smile from her face. Durham rubbed the mark on his forehead.

Juliane scanned the rest of the room. At least two of the others shared a pale bruise in the center of their forehead, though she would not have seen it had she not been looking for it. *Was Eithan's work related to the mark?* thought Juliane to herself.

Her attention was drawn back to the video monitor as the camera zoomed out. Damien could be seen in the background leaning against a white and chrome cylinder that had to be at least seven feet long.

Eithan joined Damien. He caressed the metallic surface before turning back to address the board. "We were told by our elders from the time we were children that there are only two certainties in life, death, and taxes. I am here to say that we were lied to. While there is still no easy way to get around taxes, death should consider itself officially on notice."

Juliane realized she had been holding her breath. As she released it, she heard at least one person in the room snort in derision.

"The road ahead will not be painless. Some of us already have firsthand experience." Juliane heard more chuckles. "But there will always be some pain in any worthwhile change."

Juliane looked around for the source of the laughter in time to see Sarah nod her head at Eithan's words.

"Fifty years ago, technology such as cryogenics was relegated to the science fiction bin, and those of us who pursued it were ridiculed out of the scientific community. That is until we discovered nanorobotics."

Juliane took another look at the cylinder on the screen and raised an eyebrow. To her knowledge, those that were researching pseudo-sciences such as cryogenics were still laughed out of any worthwhile positions. Just what was Eithan suggesting?

"Thanks to Camille's research, we have unlocked the ability to rebuild cellular structures. However, that technique is limited by its very nature. She has admitted that all she can do is slow down the natural aging process."

Juliane glanced at Camille, who looked as if she had just tasted something sour. Juliane found herself feeling sorry for the woman. If what Eithan implied was true, Camille's work would wind up being only a footnote in the annals of history rather than the headline it deserved to be.

"I would like to introduce you all to my hard-working assistants."

The video feed switched over to a super magnified image. The nanobots looked similar to cartoon renditions of bombs. Tendrils extended out from their base and could be seen interacting with cellular platelets.

"Nanobots have been around for several decades. Studies in the early twenty-tens found that nanobots could be used to repair muscle damage and made the repaired muscle more resistant to future damage. Researchers took it a step further and began using nanobots to aid in cardiac surgery, effectively dropping the mortality rate for heart disease by a quarter."

Eithan paused again. Juliane suspected that he must be scanning his audience to ensure that everyone followed his presentation. While the science was not her specialty, Juliane was aware of the technology. Likely the rest of the room was too.

Shortly before Louis's press conference, the ACI had announced they were going to be using similar bots instead of a virus for the Gene Assist upgrade procedure.

"Now, thanks to Camille's work, we have identified the root of aging within the human body, but her technique is indiscriminate. Cancerous cells will receive the same rejuvenating treatment as healthy cells. My projections show that brain tumors, particularly in men, would become especially difficult to treat if left alone."

If Camille looked any more displeased by the direction of the conversation, laser bolts would begin shooting out of her eyes. Eithan blanched. He must have also noted the expression on Camille's face.

"I am sure you were fully aware of the risk." Camille's lack of interest in promoting her work made a great deal more sense now. She wouldn't want to be known for increasing cancer's strength.

"Why is the risk more pronounced in men than women?" asked John, one of the newer board members.

Eithan smiled, and his shoulders relaxed. "That's due to the shortened Y chromosome in male DNA." Eithan's skin returned to its more natural coloring. "An injection combined with a deployment of nanobots delivered directly into the prefrontal cortex will become critical. This injection will improve a subject's internal ability to differentiate between healthy and unhealthy cells. The nanobots would then be deployed to damaged areas and commanded to either repair good tissue or destroy cancerous cells."

"So, you've cured cancer?" asked Lillian, another board member. Juliane noted that no one was laughing now.

"No, not cure. We may never fully understand the reasons why one cell turns, versus another. What I am saying is that we now have a treatment that does not require chemotherapy, does not place a person's immune system at risk, and is completely effective."

Eithan grinned from ear to ear. Damien stepped up to pat him on the shoulder.

"But what happens when your nanobots run out of power?" asked Lillian. "As you said, the cancer risk will still be there. What happens when your treatment stops working? Will we all be expected to be jabbed in the forehead every couple of years with a large needle? It looks like some of you are okay with that, but I—for one—am not a fan of needles."

Damien spoke up, "The tube you see behind me should alleviate your concern." Damien gestured for Eithan to continue.

"Yes, of course. Before I learned of Camille's technique, I had been working with the nanobots as a means of inducing a hibernation-like state designed to prevent muscle dystrophy for deep space missions. The tube you see behind me is one of a dozen prototypes. It is designed not only to perform routine body scans, but it also administers replacements as needed. Sarah, Durham, both of you received your injections this way. Would you like to describe the experience?"

Durham spoke up, "I honestly can't. It was nothing like I've ever experienced before. You could feel the pain, but at the same time, there was almost a dreamlike quality to it. Sarah?"

Sarah's eyebrow arched. "I think that it will become an extremely individual experience, just like any other form of treatment. What could be agony for you, could feel like nothing more than a bee sting to me." She continued, "So are you proposing that we advertise this as something like a spa or rejuvenation center?"

Damien laid a finger aside his lips. "That is an interesting proposition, Sarah."

Sarah looked like a child who had just been given the last cookie in front of her siblings.

Camille tilted her head. "I suppose, that would allow us to move forward much more quickly." Sarah's smile deepened. "What do you think Durham? What are the legal risks?"

For a brief moment Durham's eyes tightened, but then he said, "We'd have to be very careful how we market it, but in theory, it could work. But—"

Another board member, Lillian joined in. "If we pull from Juliane's power supply and control this specific nanobot's production, there would be little cost of operation. If we included Camille's treatment as part of the rejuvenating package, we really would control the fountain of youth." She clapped her hands.

"You might not want to start counting those dollars quite so soon," stated Alan. "What if people found out a way to keep the nanobots charged without visiting your so-called fountain? There goes the monopoly."

"It's not like you can just plug yourself into the wall," countered Eithan. "There has to be an active power source."

Alan inched his chair around so that his back was toward the screen. "Oh, I believe Juliane has a workaround for that. Don't you, Juliane? We've shared all our tricks with you. I believe it is now time for you to return the favor."

Juliane pushed back from the desk. Alan knew about Betty's equation. A cold shiver ran up her spine. If that was the case. Why then had Betty gone to such lengths to keep her notes hidden from him? "I am not sure I understand what you are asking."

"Oh, I believe you do." Alan stood and crossed the room over to her. "But you've always been the coy one, haven't you?"

Juliane stood. "I have nothing else to share."

"Oh, Juliane, you wound me. After everything we've meant to each other, everything I've given you freely, you say something like that."

Juliane glanced about the room again. "Perhaps we should take this conversation elsewhere?" she suggested.

"No, Juliane. I am done playing our games. All of our games. Let's be honest with one another. You've always been mine, and I think it is time you paid me my due."

Juliane took a step back. "Yours? Due?" Alan halved the distance. "What are you even talking about?"

"You know very well what I'm talking about."

"No. Frankly, I don't." She raised a hand in defense.

"And now what are you trying to do? Set me on fire like you did that poor Elena woman?"

Juliane gasped before gritting her teeth and hissing out the words. "That was an accident, and you know it."

Alan laughed. "Do I? You once told me quite emphatically that I didn't know your precious boy-toy. You thought then that you knew him better than I did. I hope you've since realized who was right. You keep trying to start over, but you always forget that I know the real you. I've always known you."

Juliane's back touched the wall. Until that moment, she hadn't realized that she had taken additional steps backward. She raised her other hand in an attempt to slow Alan's forward progress. Without a thought, she began to pull on the building's power grid. An electric blue web danced between her fingertips and her thumb.

Alan's eyes flashed like fire. Juliane scanned the room for potential allies. Dull eyes stared back as if they were obvious to the exchange. Except for Sarah. Sarah smiled like a shark. No, there were allies in the room, just not hers.

Alan paused in his approach, although his grin became even more menacing. His brow wrinkled. He raised his hand, mirroring her gesture. The room lights faded as a matching web materialized against his outstretched palm. "And here I was, beginning to worry you weren't going to share after all. Now let me share what I can do."

A series of banging noises followed by the sound of shattered glass from outside the building broke the tension. An office worker ran into the conference room, her arm punctured with a series of small cuts. "Crows! Dozens of them just crashed into the building."

thirty-seven

The other board members looked as if they were waking from a dream as they exited the room to view the extent of the damage. Then, only Juliane and Alan remained. The blue glow from the monitor's interrupted signal sharpened the angles of his face.

The light flashed like lightning as the monitor attempted to regain its signal. Juliane glanced behind her as Alan took another step closer. Against the wall, his shadow appeared to have grown wings.

"Crows!" Juliane exclaimed as the memory of her first experience following the Gene Assist upgrade struck her. She covered her mouth. "They aren't just crashing into the building on their own out there. Are they? They're a distraction. They're you. You're controlling them."

Alan shrugged. "Do you realize how crazy you sound?"

"Absolutely," said Juliane. "But it doesn't make it any less true."

Alan threw back his head in laughter. "No, I guess it doesn't. Fine, I'll admit it. Yes, they're mine. Think of them as another side project. Helped me stay up to date better than any news source. I've been using them to keep an eye on you for years, ever since the first upgrade."

"You've been spying on me? Why? We're on the same team." Juliane's forehead knit in confusion as her eyes glanced toward the exit.

"You have to know that I care about you. In the past, you've suffered from poor judgment. I wanted to make sure that you didn't relapse."

"But Betty . . . Stevie . . . You have a family!" Juliane wanted to dismiss Alan's confession as being nothing more than his grief talking. She wanted to, but couldn't.

Alan's grin grew wider. "In any experiment, you never jump straight into trials with subjects who matter. You first start with animal trials to prove your theory and then build up from there. I know that you've been away from academia for a while, but surely you remember that much about the scientific process."

Bile rose in the back of Juliane's throat as Alan took a step closer. "Oh my . . . Betty was right. You did want the virus to mutate. But that means—" She gasped. "You . . . you wanted them dead. Your own family."

"We were never a family," Alan sneered. "We were barely even the same species. Betty was only a means to an end and Stephen proof of concept. However, I will admit, I was pleasantly surprised the boy pulled through. Then again, he does have half of my genes. Maybe there's a use for him after all."

His eyes shone as the monitor flashed again. "I've told you we evolved. Soon, we will be like Gods to people like them, but my son will still need a mother. A mother who I can consider my equal."

The building shook, dropping Juliane and Alan to the floor. "Oof," said Alan. His grin slipped.

Sarah appeared in the doorway. "There was another explosion, this time just down the street." She walked over and helped Alan rise. "All the roads around here are blocked."

"Damnit," muttered Alan. "Their timing—"

"Changes nothing," said Sarah.

Durham ran into the room. His face looked twisted in pain as if he were running with a broken bone. "Juliane, you have to come with me. We have to get out of here. Now!"

Sarah blocked his way. He attempted to push her to the side to get to Juliane, but she remained locked in place. He might as well have attempted to topple the statue in the park. Juliane recalled what Alan had said about some of the Sharks having undergone muscle enhancement surgery. Alan had mentioned he was considering having the surgery as well. It dawned on Juliane that Alan might not have been the only one.

Sarah and Alan exchanged a glance. She placed her hand on Durham's back. A glow surrounded her arm while the lights dimmed again. Durham crumpled to the floor at her feet. "Durham, when you wake up, we will need to have to have a serious discussion about where your loyalties lie," said Alan.

Juliane crawled toward the conference room door. Sarah walked over to Juliane, stepping on her hand while blocking the exit. Juliane couldn't have dislodged Sarah's foot if she tried. To Alan, Sarah said, "I've always said she was beneath you. What more proof do you need?"

Sarah placed her finger to her ear as if receiving a call. The corners of her lips curled up. "He's here." She nudged Juliane with her toe. "Stay down if you know what is good for you."

An icon in the video monitor showed that a connection had been made. The screen then flickered back to an image from the front desk lobby's security camera.

A solitary figure stood in the center of the room. He was tall and muscular, his face covered with a crimson lizard mask. The doors to the building were barred, and the security guards lay slumped in their seats.

The figure tapped his neck three times. The video monitor's speakers protested as the connection was made. "Come out, come out wherever you are . . ." The figure pulled the mask off his face.

"Louis," whispered Juliane.

"How he was ever considered to have leadership potential is beyond me," scoffed Alan. Not looking away from the monitor Alan commanded, "Figure out a way to connect me to downstairs." Sarah nodded. Removing her foot from Juliane's hand she walked over to the wall console and pulled out a small microphone from a hidden cabinet.

"Louis. I had a feeling we hadn't seen the last of you. I've just been informed that there has been some nearby unpleasantness. You wouldn't happen to know anything about that, would you?"

"Just as I am sure you wouldn't know anything about the death of my wife, Alan."

"I'm afraid I don't, but as a recent widower myself, I sympathize with the pain you must be going through."

Juliane knew she should run while Alan was distracted, but at the same time, she wanted to slap the condescending look off his face. The hand that had been damaged under Sarah's foot throbbed. Juliane pulled herself upright, tightening her muscles in advance. An electric blue light flickered in her vision.

"Tsk, tsk, Juliane. You don't want to give me a reason," gloated Sarah. The electricity danced across the length of her arm as static played across the video monitor.

"Trouble in the ranks?" asked Louis.

"Nothing I can't handle," replied Alan.

"Louis, call for help. Alan has gone insane," Juliane shouted.

"I'm afraid that's not an option, my dear," chuckled Alan. "Haven't you realized? Louis is one of the terrorists. Possession of that mask alone would put him away for a very, very long time."

"I've joined the liberators. It is people like you who are the real threat."

Alan's eyes rolled. "Please don't pretend that you are any better than the rest of us. Your company funded most of everything you are now so intent on destroying."

"Which is why I am taking responsibility for cleaning up my mess now."

"Just like you are taking responsibility by blaming me for your wife's death," Alan sneered. "You are just like your father. It's never your family's fault."

"You did something to me that night. I felt you in my head."

"You were roaring drunk. You carelessly got behind the wheel and overcorrected into oncoming traffic."

Juliane felt a chill move up her spine at Louis's accusation. Alan wasn't denying he did something to Louis. She felt pressure build behind her eyes. Her peripheral vision began to darken. *No*, she thought, *I can't pass out now*. She suddenly had the urge to focus on anything other than the scene unfolding before her. She stared at the artwork on the walls as if she could anchor her awareness.

Her thoughts floated to the first time she had seen the artwork and Damien's serenity fountain. What had he said that day? Something about taking a step back. She really did need to ask Damien about the artist one day. The pressure eased as Juliane's breath calmed. Her eyes traced one of the patterns on the wall. It looked so different from this vantage point. Sleep would be nice. Juliane frowned. *Why am I on the floor?* she wondered.

Sarah snorted at something Alan said. Juliane blinked, and the memory of the last several minutes came back. *I am on the floor because everyone around me has lost their minds.* Her stomach tightened. How could she have forgotten any second of the last few minutes?

She felt the pressure increase once again. It was sharp and cutting. Juliane tasted blood. She's bitten her tongue. She closed her eyes and focused on the pain, willing it back. It felt as if hooks were latching onto her psyche, each attached to alien tendrils of thought that crept and probed her mind like ivy exploiting the cracks of a wall.

Betty must have felt something similar at the hospital when she forced the private connection. Something . . . no, *someone* was trying to manipulate her, just like he had with the crows outside. Juliane's eyes narrowed at Alan. His skin looked paler than it had a moment before.

She wouldn't make it easy for him. Juliane closed her eyes. She issued commands to her processors, isolating each unwelcome data strand. She issued another command, and the data strands were corrupted like ivy taking fire. All except one. The last strand felt different than the others. It pulsated with sorrow and confusion, yet there was wonder in it too.

As she focused on the strand, it widened, filling in the cracks and strengthening her psyche's wall. Suddenly, Juliane understood the reason Stevie survived. The pressure behind her eyes shattered as tears cascaded down her cheeks.

Juliane looked at Alan and saw that he had turned from the screen and now watched her. He deepened his smile as if he could read her thoughts and found them amusing.

Not taking his eyes off her, he responded to Louis. "I believe you've made the mistake of believing we are lacking defenses here."

Nothing happened at first. Then, Juliane saw Louis drop to the floor on his knees.

"What did you do to him?" she demanded.

"I've just exposed him to a blast of high-frequency noise, used effectively in crowd control for years. Don't worry. It will daze him for a bit, but I haven't done anything permanent. Yet."

Sarah chuckled as she and Alan shared a smile. As soon as they returned their attention to Louis and the monitor, Juliane mentally isolated Alan's and Sarah's bio-electric auras. She twisted the signals so that light would appear to pass around her as if she wasn't present in the room like she had done in the wrecked shop.

She had to move quickly but silently to get past them. She sprinted toward the door on tiptoes and down the hall. Juliane caught a sigh of relief from giving away her position as she spotted an open elevator door. She raced inside and commanded the vessel down toward the lobby floor.

thirty-eight

Louis was still kneeling on the marble floor when the elevator doors opened. He held his head in his hands as his body shuddered.

Juliane knew at once than Alan had brought Louis to his knees with more than a blast of noise. She could feel his anguish as clearly as if she had never cut the connection between them. Waves of hurt and want crashed against her with each step overpowering her senses.

Juliane slowed her approach, worried that she might startle him like a wild animal. "Louis?" she whispered.

Louis bolted upright. He shouted something unintelligible, causing Juliane to halt in mid-stride. "Elena?" he asked, taking a step toward her.

Juliane looked behind her but saw no one.

"My golden goddess, I've missed you so much." He reached out, eyes shining.

Juliane took a step backward. "I have to get you out of here."

"No, don't go!" Louis rushed toward her, closing the remaining distance. His next words were indecipherable as he crushed her body against his in a fierce embrace and began to nuzzle her neck. Juliane briefly wondered if his mind had shattered, but as his arms tightened around her, she found she didn't care.

Her body relaxed, accepting his caresses. Louis immediately responded, his hands becoming much more demanding. He forced her face upward, meeting her lips with his own with a possessive fury. He pushed aside a lock of blonde hair for better access.

Blonde? She twisted in his arms. Louis pulled her closer. The heat from his lips on hers could have caused the sun to blister.

Alan's voice over the speaker was a slap to reality. "And here I thought that you were mourning."

Right. Get it together, thought Juliane. They had to get away.

"I was almost feeling sorry for you, but I see now that I shouldn't have wasted the energy. You seem all too eager to move on."

Juliane felt her cheeks burn as Louis snapped back to full attention.

"I wish I could say I was surprised," Alan continued, "but I'm disappointed all the same. While you still have good taste"—Alan paused—"I must regretfully inform you that Juliane is no longer on the market."

Louis looked into her eyes and pulled away as if scalded. He didn't need to say anything for her to know her hair was once again black as night.

"You bitch. What did you make me do?" he said. "Oh, Elena, I am so sorry," he cried.

"Nothing. I did nothing." Her eyes widened. "I didn't . . . that wasn't . . . I was only trying to get us out of here. I didn't mean for that to happen." Juliane willed Louis to understand.

"You always hated her. Everyone knew it." His nostrils flared. "You wanted her dead, and now you think you can just take her place. You disgust me."

"It's not like that. I mean I never meant . . . I would never—"

"Enough. It's not like I would believe a single word out of your mouth," Louis interrupted.

Juliane's skin, flushed by the combination of adrenaline and desire, pimpled as if his words caused a physical drop in the temperature of the room. Her eyes widened in confusion.

"I know all about what you've done. After killing hundreds, do you honestly think I would believe you incapable of killing one more just because you know how to bat your eyelashes?" His lips, still roughened from their encounter, curled back and showed his teeth. "I've seen you turn on the charm when it helps you get what you want."

"No! It's not that!" Juliane glanced toward the barred door and back toward the elevator. Louis locked his hand around her wrist.

"I heard the rumors before, but I never wanted to believe them. I was so blind then, but I see everything perfectly now."

"Let me go! You're hurting me!" Juliane twisted in his grip.

"At least you aren't trying to deny it anymore."

"Deny what?" she exclaimed.

"I am talking about the night you and Dr. Dronigh murdered my wife. I'm talking about that factory and all those people you had executed. Or have you killed so often the events all blend together?"

She finally escaped his grasp and darted backward, massaging the blood back into her hand.

"I had nothing to do with either of those things."

"Ah, that may not be an entirely accurate statement, my dear," interrupted Alan over the speaker. "I'll make a deal with both of you," Alan's voice echoed in the lobby. "Join me on the basement level, and I'll do my best to clear this whole business up in person. I'd come up there, but I don't exactly trust the company either of you've been keeping lately.

Juliane looked longingly at the exits. A storm crossed Louis's features.

"Afterward, I'll even turn myself in to the authorities for whatever transgressions I may be responsible for," Alan continued, "but you'll need to bring Juliane along to pass the elevator's biometric security."

Juliane looked into Louis's eyes as her vision blurred behind a well of tears.

"Louis, don't listen to him. We can still walk away. We just go out those doors and pretend none of this ever happened."

Louis glanced toward the entrance. It could have been made of stone for all the light that was able to pass through its doors. Faint sirens could be heard in the distance.

Juliane's wrist throbbed as Louis relaxed his grip. If she could only get him away from the immediate danger, she would explain the severed network and how it must have affected him. It might take him a while to forgive her for the accidental impersonation, but at least they would be safe. "I have so much to tell you. You want to make the world a better place? We can do it"—she reached toward him—"together."

"You have a deal, Alan." Louis's iron grip shackled her wrist again, and he dragged Juliane back toward the elevator shaft.

thirty-nine

The elevator closed behind them. Louis released her wrist with such force that Juliane's back slammed into the wall. At her grunt, Louis shot her a look of such disdain, further words died on her tongue.

Juliane had never had reason to visit the lowest levels of the Apex building before. The space was filled with a raised platform and a series of thick cables and insulated piping.

Damien and Eithan stood on the platform in front of the white and chrome tube. The video feed upstairs had only captured the single tube, but in this larger space, Juliane saw that there were several identical components scattered around the dais.

Conference chairs had been positioned on the ground level and were filled with the various board members, who must have made their way down during her unsuccessful escape attempt. Durham was among them. He was seated upright, his eyes glazed and unseeing, and flanked by Alan and Sarah. Juliane overheard Sarah tell Camille, "It was lucky we found him when we did. Something must have hit him during the initial panic."

Juliane rushed over to the stage's edge in front of Damien. She tried to keep panic from flavoring her voice as she gestured for him to come closer. "Alan's gone mad," she whispered. Her eyes darted to Sarah and then to Louis. "The whole world has. You have to get everyone out of here before something happens."

Damien leaned down and whispered back, "Louis might have disrupted the video, but Eithan and I were able to hear everything upstairs. The situation will be under control in no time. Just don't make any more sudden moves, and let this next part play itself out. We'll be okay."

Alan gestured to the other board members. "Why don't you share with the group? You've got yourself a captive audience."

"We had a deal, Alan," Louis said with the monotone voice of a man defeated.

"That we did, and I am more than happy to complete my part, but why don't we first allow Eithan to finish the presentation you so rudely interrupted?"

Juliane glanced back toward the elevator door. Sarah sneered at her; blue-white light danced along her arm as she brought a single finger up to her lips.

Eithan turned toward Damien, who shrugged and nodded toward the seated board.

"Er . . . Ah, well, yes, um, where was I?"

"You were in the process of telling us all about how you've found a way for us all to live forever," Sarah said as she examined the nails on one hand.

"Right. Well, yes, I mean in theory. I still have some work to do, but it is promising."

"And you need more volunteers for the next round of testing," suggested Sarah.

"Precisely." Eithan seemed much more at ease. Juliane glanced about. Everyone did. *How could they possibly think this was business as usual?* It was like watching drones.

"Assuming you are released for additional human testing," supplied Camille.

"Of course," Eithan responded.

"Isn't that going to be somewhat of a more difficult problem for you now?" Sarah asked.

Snippets of forgotten conversation flashed in Juliane's memory like puzzle pieces. Juliane suddenly recalled the scratches on the floor in the room behind the wrecked electronics and pet boutique. "That was your lab. The one that was bombed," stated Juliane.

"You and Damien keep saying how smart that woman is, yet she is always the last to figure anything out," laughed Sarah to a scowling Alan.

The smile slipped from Eithan's face. "Yes, yes it was. It was one of a few sites. Luckily, I caught wind of a rumor that activists were targeting my work. I was able to get most of the critical projects out of harm's way, but even so, I have had to deal with significant setbacks." Eithan glared at Louis. "All thanks to you I presume."

Louis shrugged. "You were trying to play God. There were bound to be consequences." Eithan's eyes bulged, and he scurried toward the steps, only to be held back by Damien.

"You aren't above the law, Evans," said Eithan.

"Nor are you." Louis scanned the room, resting his gaze on Alan. "Nor is anyone in this room. I've had enough. Tell me why I came down here."

"Whatever you say." Alan laughed. "Where to begin, where to begin?" Alan said in a singsong voice. "You may want to have a seat." Alan gestured toward an available chair. Sarah rolled it over, forcing her down into the cushion.

"I guess we should start back on the day of our first upgrade. You probably remember it as the day you and Juliane first . . . blacked out.

"I remember that day somewhat differently. Shortly after the procedure, Juliane here started mumbling about connecting with a bird, and the next thing we knew she was running out of the office talking about flying."

Juliane's cheeks heated. She couldn't help remembering that initial disorientation combined with an exhilarating sense of freedom.

"Luckily, I was able to catch her and bring her back to the lab just before she was about to attack a random passerby."

Alan began to pace around the room, before stopping to address Juliane directly. "I'll admit it. I began to worry. I grabbed you in a last-ditch effort to capture your attention, and you were back, only you didn't seem to have any awareness of what you had just done. I realized later that when I reached for you, I did so with more than just my hands. I could sense your mind working. I could feel what you felt. I tried to pull back but was afraid I would only do more damage. Until that moment, I had no idea how fragile you were back then. You were desperate to connect with anything or anyone. But I also understood that I had seen only a fraction of your potential. You just needed a gentle hand to guide you."

Juliane didn't know what to make of Alan's words. He had to be lying. She would never have lost control like that. She certainly wouldn't have forgotten about it. It just wasn't possible. *Or was it?*

"I worried that you might break if you knew what I had done. All that potential might be wasted, so I figured out how to wipe the memory away." He swiped his hand in the air.

"Actually, it was surprisingly easy to do. Your subconscious must have wanted the memories gone as much as I did." He shook his head. "I knew then what I had previously only suspected. We were destined to be together." Alan grinned, reaching out his hand.

"I could have claimed you then," he said, dropping his arm back to his side. "Perhaps I should have, but other experiments needed my attention."

"And the fact that I was with Louis at the time wasn't at all an issue," said Juliane.

"Of course, it wasn't." Alan gestured toward Louis. "He never saw you as anything more than a casual distraction. Everyone could see that." He sniffed.

"Louis loved me," Juliane responded.

"You keep saying that, but did you ever hear those words from Louis? Even once? Did you ever ask his friends what he said to them about you?" Alan swung his arm toward Durham. "Because I did." Durham seemed to be frozen in place, oblivious to the exchange. A bead of drool began to descend from the corner of his mouth.

Juliane glanced at Louis. *Alan's a liar,* she wanted to scream. *It hadn't been like that.*

Louis remained silent. Sarah threw back her head and cackled. Juliane wished she could blast them all away. A machine hummed over in the corner of the room, and she felt a surge of energy.

"You've still not been able to get a hold of that temper of yours, have you Juliane. Sarah? Would you mind?"

Sarah walked over to the machine, which had to be a generator of some sort, and punched a button. The humming ceased, and Juliane felt her energy drain from her body as if her body were a sieve.

Juliane felt sickened to her stomach. The person prancing about the room was some twisted caricature of her former colleague. It had to be the madness Camille warned them about. She attempted to meet Damien's gaze; whatever Damien was planning, she wished he would get on with it.

"Where were we?" Alan glanced at Sarah, who rolled her eyes. "Ah, yes. The factory." Alan strolled over to Juliane.

Juliane felt her blood crystallize. Her brain ached trying to follow the conversation. All she wanted was to leave this room and continue the work that had been so promising an hour ago. She looked longingly toward the elevator door.

The humor left Alan's voice. "For this next part, Juliane, I am sorry. Truly I am. I preferred you never knew."

He left her side, returning to the center of the room. "As many of you know, Juliane here chose to set up her center of operations in a region of the world that had less than ideal working conditions." He paused, and several of the other board members bobbed their heads like marionettes.

"Recently, she was notified of the tragic ending of a simple line worker. A day after this tragic event, she came to me looking for a confidant. A shoulder to cry on." Alan paused.

Juliane imagined that she possessed a quiver of poisoned darts. *That wasn't how it happened. Wasn't what I did. How could anyone believe any of this?* The panic she felt earlier paled against her desire to find a way to remove that smug expression from his face.

"There had been other messes, but this one felt different."

Juliane fantasized about tying Alan to a post and burying him in the ground up to his neck only after dribbling honey all over his body.

"It didn't take much convincing on her part before we were booked on the next flight out." Juliane glanced toward the door. Death by ants was not nearly enough for a liar like him. Perhaps she would need to slice him up with a million paper cuts and then dose him with a spray of lemon juice.

"I arrived at dawn and met with the inspection committee. I originally had signed on for the trip, only in the role of a concerned friend, but within the first few minutes, it became clear that Juliane was not going to be satisfied with a few signatures on a report. She had made it clear that heads should roll."

Juliane decided that being eaten alive by ants was too easy. No, Alan needed to truly wish for death before she was done with him. Perhaps it would be better to tie him to a post and remove each lung individually like the Vikings had done centuries before.

"As I was in discussions with the welcoming committee, I caught sight of a man scribbling on a notepad. I knew what would happen if the story got out, but I must not have been the only one to notice. Another team showed up. I assumed they were third-party inspectors. They told me to wait outside while they took care of the matter per Juliane's wishes."

Even though Alan was twisting events, his words cut close to her darkest fear. Could the threats she made in the virtual world actually be the cause behind the massacre at the factory? The audio from the recording came tumbling back in her mind.

"Oh, please God! Help me! There are bodies everywhere. Help me! Please!" She listened again to the popping sound in between the whispers. " . . . to find me. You've got to do something. I can hear"—more pops and screams—"getting closer! Do something! Do something! Oh God! No!"

When she had listened to it the first time, she had thought the sounds of the screams would be permanently lodged in her brain. Could it be possible that she was in some way responsible for pulling the trigger?

No, Alan had to still be lying about everything. The Viking death would be too quick. The Persians had it right. She would lock him in a box and cover him with a combination of milk and honey. Flies would then visit, depositing their eggs. The larvae would then begin to devour him days later.

"An hour later, they brought me down to the factory floor. Her entire staff was there, and the people with me opened fire on them. It only took a few seconds to decimate the first rows. What could I do?" Alan shrugged.

"It was one of those moments where you have to decide whether you want to do the wrong thing and live or the right thing and die. I'll have to live with my decision for the remainder of life, but up until today, thanks to my kindness, Juliane wasn't going to have to."

"Enough," shouted Juliane. "Tell me you're lying. You've got to be lying. I wasn't there. I never left the office. You're making it all up. The fire at the factory was an accident. It had to be just a terrible accident."

"An accident. Just like when the generator exploded and just happened to burn Louis's wife and only Louis's wife." Alan shrugged. "I am not surprised that you don't want to accept these events, but it doesn't make them any less true. Look up your travel records. You'll see a ticket."

Juliane glanced around the room for support and once again found none. Those in chairs nervously fidgeted as if afraid to make eye contact. Hating herself for listening, she pulled up her calendar. There, mixed in with other meeting notes and attachments was a printed flight confirmation with her name on it. "That doesn't prove I was there with you."

Juliane turned toward Louis. He recoiled. She pulled her hand back instantly. "You can't possibly believe him." Juliane reduced her voice to a whisper. "You know me. You know I'm not capable of something like that. Anything like that."

Louis met her gaze. "When we first met, nothing was going to stand in your way. Why should I think that you would be any different now?"

"But he's describing a brutal massacre of hundreds," she shouted.

"Hundreds that you probably considered beneath your notice, or worse, a threat to the idea of your legacy." Louis's eyes tightened. "I've seen firsthand how you respond to those who threaten you."

Juliane stared into his eyes, urging him to take back his words. Instead, Louis turned toward Alan, showing her his back.

Alan laughed. "So, Juliane, still convinced you two were meant to be together?"

"It doesn't matter what she thinks," Louis said. "None of this does." A small beeping sound emitted from Louis's pocket. He smiled as he unfastened the buttons of his shirt. A large belt fitted with wires was exposed as he pulled back one side of the garment. Louis pulled another device from his pocket and held it out for everyone to see.

"It seems your time is up, Alan," Louis said with a smile. "That sound tells me that my associates have now placed devices similar to the one I am wearing near key structural positions throughout the building. I will only have to press this button to bring this entire building down."

Louis nodded toward the other members of the board who were looking around as if wondering how they had gotten into the room. "I wasn't originally going to target all of you, at least not at the same time, but when Alan invited me down here, it was just too tempting of an offer. However, I am not the monster some of your associates are. I'm willing to make a deal. If Alan tells me what happened the night of Elena's death to my satisfaction, I'll give the rest of you a sporting chance at survival."

"Tell him what he wants to know!" screeched Camille. She ran up to Alan, pulling him by his sleeve.

As if Camille can force Alan to do anything he doesn't already want to do, Juliane thought. Camille would have had more luck convincing a shark that tofu was the better option for dinner.

Others in the room began pressing their backs against their chairs as if a few inches of distance could help save them. Juliane's stomach twisted. Damien, however, remained on the dais, looking as confident as he had from the time she entered the room. "Anytime you want to take charge, Damien," she muttered.

Juliane glanced at Alan. Alan appeared to be leaning toward Louis and the device. The smile plastered on his face was one of satisfaction, not madness. Alan wasn't acting surprised. He met her gaze, and his smile deepened. No, if anything, Alan had anticipated this development. For all she knew, he had orchestrated all the events leading up to this moment. But why? Why would he want to put them all in a position to be blown to bits?

Sarah equally looked nonplussed, although paler than usual. She must have had some inclination of what could potentially occur today.

"Now, Alan, I've been more than patient with you. Tell me what I want to know . . . now."

"First, send Juliane over. She's proven to have more than a few tricks up her sleeves, and I would hate for her to miss the rest of the show."

"You two really were made for each other." The disgust rolling off Louis's tongue was palpable. "You want her so badly even after all you say she's done? Fine. She's yours." Louis shoved Juliane painfully toward Alan's outstretched arms.

Alan whispered into her ear as he claimed her abused wrist, "You have always been mine."

Forty

"Now that is settled, where were we? Oh yes, you want to know about the night of your unfortunate accident." He nodded to Sarah, who proceeded to adjust the controls on the video monitor. "You've already been told what happened, but as they say, a picture is worth a thousand words."

Still pulling painfully on Juliane's wrist, he dragged them both over to an open chair and forced her down into its seat.

"You should know that Damien is very invested in the Sharks organization and takes the security and safety of his players extremely seriously. And, like any responsible owner, he had positioned several security cameras throughout the facility. Some of these cameras are fairly obvious, and that public footage he freely shared with the police. However, other cameras are more innocuous."

Alan paused as the image on the screen transitioned to a playback. The time and date stamp were visible to all. Louis and Elena could be seen sashaying down the corridor, their arms interlocked. Louis stumbled and Elena pulled him back upright. Louis could be seen throwing his head back in laughter as the two stumbled out of the camera's field of vision.

"Just what are you trying to prove with these? I freely admit that I was at the game and that I had enjoyed myself, but I know how to pace myself otherwise everyone would have heard a different story when the toxicology report was published."

The video flashed, and the time stamp showed the image to be only a few minutes from the first scene. This time, Louis and Elena were one of the several couples loitering in the concession lobby. It had to be halftime and the moment of their confrontation. Juliane had no sooner placed the scene when the crowds parted and she could see Alan and herself.

There was no sound, but their body language spoke volumes. A security guard entered the shot several feet away. Juliane hadn't realized that their conversation had been noticed, but it must have raised at least one person's concern.

Juliane watched as Louis fell on her with Alan pushing him back toward Elena. It was just a moment, but in that moment, Alan's body flickered and the video feed was temporarily disrupted by static. Louis and Elena were already on their way when the static cleared.

There was something different about Louis though. His steps, as they moved back toward the concession line, were straight and sure. Elena, on the other hand, appeared even more intoxicated. It was Louis's turn to provide additional support.

"Are you going to tell me that you didn't do something to me just then?" demanded Louis.

"Absolutely not," scoffed Alan.

"I fired you and you wanted revenge. But it didn't go as planned, did it? I survived your little trick."

Alan roared with laughter. "Oh, Louis, you have such an inflated sense of self-importance."

Louis growled, "I don't see the humor."

"No?" Alan rubbed his hand over his mouth. "Of course, you don't." The smile was replaced with bored indifference.

"Then let me explain this in a way you would understand. For me to worry about outdoing a rival, I would first have to recognize that an equal is in some way threatening my position. I have never been threatened by you. If I was, would I have ever agreed to upgrade you on that first day?"

"You expected the process would kill me."

"I accepted that outcome and I did reassess my opinion of you that day. Even so, I still didn't view you as an equal or a true rival. You are as much of a rival to me as a sparrow hawk is to an eagle. Sure, they might both be at times interested in the same meat, but only the eagle has the strength and stamina to bring the larger game home."

Louis's skin erupted into a sea of red. "So, you were targeting my wife. What did Juliane do? Beg you to finish what she started in the lab? I can guess what she promised you in return." Louis leered at Juliane.

Juliane reminded herself how terrible the loss of the private connection could be. Louis was only lashing out because he didn't know how to control its loss. She wasn't his enemy, and if he would just calm down enough to see that, they could still walk out of this room. No one had to get hurt.

"Between you and me, you aren't getting the better end of the bargain," continued Louis. "I've had better."

Durham made a choking sound. A valve located behind Sarah blew, hurtling a piece of plastic into the room. Sarah called out as she was struck in the side.

A hiss of steam escaped while backup controls on the equipment powered into their fail-safe mode. Juliane wished she could similarly lash out. Juliane felt her skin tingle and realized that she had called forth another electric web across her palms.

"I don't think that is a good idea, my dear," noted Alan. "The man is outfitted in an explosive belt. As much as I've always loved that brain of yours, I have no wish to see it on the outside."

Juliane flicked her fingers and the web was dispelled.

"That's better." Returning his attention to Louis, Alan continued.

"You still have it wrong. Neither Juliane nor I ever plotted against your precious wife. Elena had already ensured herself a lifetime of suffering when she married you. Why should I harbor her any further ill will?"

"Then what exactly did you do? Answer me honestly, and I will leave this room, taking my vest and the detonator with me."

"I know you would like to believe otherwise, but I'm really not a terrible person. You had too much to drink that day. All I did was introduce a program that would redirect the existing alcohol in your bloodstream so that you didn't make a complete fool of yourself. It is that simple."

"You didn't want me to be drunk?" Louis sounded incredulous. Juliane had to agree with his assessment.

"Seeing you in the news, happy, sad, or otherwise distracts Juliane, and I want her focused. The way you were acting was going to get you noticed by the gossip channels, which could then undo weeks of progress. That could be all the reason I needed, or maybe I did it just to prove I could. You should know now that I enjoy experimenting. In either case, there was nothing nefarious behind my motivation.

"But you interpreted my gift as a challenge. Rather than slowing down, you eventually outpaced my program. You passed out while driving, and we all know where you were when you woke up. Only by then, my program had caught up and the alcohol was out of your bloodstream. There. Mystery solved."

"You, Louis, you are the sole cause of your wife's death. Shake your fist at technology all you want, but technology could have actually saved her. She's gone because of your irresponsibility, and no amount of exploding labs or war against technology will bring her back."

The red sheen of Louis's face had faded and only the color of gray ash remained. He looked down toward his belt and scanned the room. With meticulous care, he casually covered the belt with his shirt and returned the detonator to his pocket.

Louis's shoulders dropped, and he suddenly looked as if he had aged twenty years as he turned toward the board members. "I made a deal. Truth for a sporting chance. If I am not in the room with you when the explosives detonate, then you will still have a chance to make your way back to the surface."

Louis turned and made his way back toward the elevator shaft. Juliane struggled to run after him, but her wrist was still held in a manacle-like grip.

"Louis! Please! You don't have to do this," Juliane called out.

Louis turned as he reached the doors. His eyes met hers, and in that brief moment, she saw all that might have been drown under an infinite sea of regret and sadness.

Forty-one

"So now what?" asked Sarah.

"We wait," replied Alan.

"What? Down here? Did you not hear Louis say that several bombs are going to go off any minute?"

"There's no safer spot to be. Why do you think I worked so hard to get us all down here?"

"I understand why you and I are here, but why did you invite *him* down here too? I thought the plan was to drive Louis to those anti-tech serpentine nut jobs and make a few billion as the ACI tanks. Personally, I—for one—would prefer not to be blown to bits before I can spend my fortune."

"Juliane needed to hear the truth. And you heard Louis; we won't be blown to bits down here. We have a sporting chance."

"Being buried alive isn't high on my to-do list either. Why put us at risk?" Sarah asked.

"Were you not paying attention?"

"To what, you professing your undying love for Juliane? Oh yes, that was made perfectly clear."

Alan snorted. "To the presentations today."

"What about them?"

"We are in a room filled with several personal cryogenic chambers suitable for space missions. There are enough for all of us. All we have to do now is take a nap. It's that simple."

"We don't know that Eithan's little toys work."

"They work," stated Eithan.

"You see. Nothing to worry about. Now, how about you pick out which one would suit you first? I don't imagine our friends upstairs will allow us too much more time to argue."

Sarah glanced toward the elevator doors with longing in her eyes.

"An elevator is probably not where you want to be when the explosion begins."

Her forehead creased while she considered his words. She rubbed the darkened spot in its center before shrugging and ascending the dais. She traced her fingers along the length of the canister before stepping in. Others began following her cue. Alan stepped into a cylinder as the lights flickered. A sound like thunder could be heard above. Alan blew her a kiss as his lid closed and the LED showed the device activating. Soon, only Damien—who had assisted placing a still vegetative Durham into a tube—and Juliane were left.

The ground began to shake as additional devices were detonated above. Bits of ceiling tile began to drop like autumn leaves. Damien placed his hand on the side panel of one of the last cylinders. "There isn't much time, Juliane."

"You said you had everything under control," she said.

"And it is," said Damien, extending his hand.

Juliane took one last look at the elevator door before accepting his hand and climbing into the tube. Damien's hands flew across the control panel. Within seconds, her toes and fingertips were numb. Damien glanced down at her and smiled, like a father easing his child into bed. "It's just a short nap. Everything will be exactly as it should when you wake up."

"But what about you?" she asked.

"You don't need to worry about me. I've taken care of everything."

Juliane could no longer feel her legs beyond her knees. Her arms were reduced to icy weights pulling her body down, but at the same time, she felt as if she were floating. Everything seemed to slow down around her. More debris came tumbling down, but to Juliane, it moved like a bubble in the breeze.

She found herself thinking of Alan's explanation for the events at the factory. The pieces simply did not fit. She accepted that her memory might have been manipulated, but she hadn't been there. She knew it to her bones.

She couldn't care what the others thought of her, but couldn't bear that Damien might view her as being less than she knew she was. "Damien, you don't believe that I ordered all those people dead, do you?"

Damien smiled and stroked her cheek with a finger like a father would a daughter as the dais swayed. "I know you didn't."

Juliane sighed. She felt an icy chill up her spine as more of her body was put to sleep. A thought entered into her mind like a pebble in a shoe. "But how?" she asked.

"How?"

"How do you know?"

Damien smiled. "I know because I was the one who gave that order."

Juliane felt tendrils of fog enter her thoughts. Something Damien had just said was wrong. Very wrong. She felt she should be shocked right now. She felt she should be pulling away from his touch, but she could no longer move her head.

"Why?" she whispered.

"The factory had served its purpose. Loose ends had to be eliminated."

She mumbled a sound, her mouth no longer functioning.

"Shh. Remember it's always easiest if you don't fight these things. I am truly sorry that you had to go through all that, but Louis showed up too early. I told Alan I needed him to cause a delay."

He sighed. "It made it so much easier to convince you all to enter the tubes willingly. However, I am surprised you accepted Alan's story so readily. I had thought that you, compared to all the others, would be least likely to doubt yourself. But it is for the best. As it was once said, 'It's okay for people to respect you, but when they fear you, you know you have the power.' And you, my dear, wear power so beautifully."

The tiny grain of Juliane still awake wanted to scream and run away, but neither option was available. Damien returned his attention to the side panel. The sound of gas escaping could be heard as a glass screen began to inch over her face. Even covered, she could still make out Damien's words thundering in between crashes of destruction.

"Sometimes the only way to save something is to break it down to its foundation and rebuild; give it a fresh start. I believe that's a concept you are familiar with. It has become clear to me for some time that humanity was on a collision course with self-destruction."

Damien's tapped the edge of the tank. "Alan's a purest. He believes that the future of the world should be decided purely by the survival of the fittest. His belief might be a tad extreme, but that doesn't mean he is entirely wrong. We accelerated the process while there was still hope for our future. I chose each of you for a very special reason. You each represent the best minds in your respective fields. When you wake up, you will be like Gods to the children left behind."

His hand brushed errant hair away from her forehead. "And there will be children left behind, thanks to you. We will be able to make real the vision of the future we all share. And I will be there to guide you all along the way."

The lights in the room flashed as fixtures fell from the ceiling. The dais shook as if the earth was readying itself to swallow them whole. Damien could no longer be seen. Juliane was now completely sealed within the cryogenic unit. The lights flashed one more time before only a few emergency lights remained.

Juliane hung onto consciousness by a fingernail. Everyone around her had gone mad. Louis, Alan, and now Damien. Betty hadn't been paranoid. Rather, she had been the only sane person in Juliane's life. Damien was wrong. He hadn't recruited all the best minds. He hadn't recruited Betty.

She heard another sound whirling within her tube and saw a mechanical arm extend out over her forehead. The motion of a mechanical finger descending brought her consciousness back to the forefront. Juliane suddenly remembered Eithan's nanobots. They were supposed to be beneficial, but could she trust anything produced by Damien's group? Alan had done enough damage from hacking her mind. Could she risk her body being hacked as well? She willed her body to move. This time, her will wasn't enough. Her body betrayed her, remaining stationary in the cylinder's cradle.

The pain as the needle penetrated her skin was like nothing she had ever imagined. Her eyes burned, but tears would not form and no sounds escaped her throat.

She had to find the strength to reject the nanobots just as she had once instructed Betty to do during the test in the emulator. By now, thousands of the tiny machines must be navigating her bloodstream. Her thoughts grew cloudy and more difficult to form. She was powerless to fight their onslaught.

Then, there was nothing. No pain, no worries, and no heartache. Each of her senses departed, and Juliane's consciousness was left floating like a disembodied presence expanding into the vacuum of space.

"I'm so sorry," Betty's voice whispered. A photograph of a smiling child briefly came into focus. Powerless. An equation. Out of time.

"Coffee?" asked Chad. Energy. Fountain of Youth. Hope.

Light. A web of light shone through the darkness. Her mind instinctively floated closer. Feelings of warmth, innocence, and stubborn determination—the emotions of a child—wrapped around her consciousness like a net, preventing her mind from drifting further into the nothing. *Thank you, Betty. I'll try to be worthy.* She clung to the net's webbing and pulled from its strength just enough to solidify her thoughts. She was not powerless, but she could ensure the nanobots were.

Juliane summoned the will for one last command, pulling energy from the machines. It wouldn't be enough to halt the cryogenic process, but she hoped her mind would be her own when she woke. Because if it was, this time, she wouldn't start over; she'd finish what she started.

THE WATCH & WAND
PROJECT GENE ASSIST
BOOK TWO

"Now entering the arena," a female voice announced in Stephen's earpiece. He toggled the command to open up his inventory menu, selecting the missile launcher. A pixelated rendering of a dark cylinder appeared on his avatar's shoulder. Stephen smiled. The graphics in the program were terrible, but his chosen weapon was as unmistakable as it was deadly.

"Nice of you to show up," said another voice belonging to player Wes51d3 or, as Stephen called him, Wes.

"You could have gotten started without me. As slow as you read through the objectives, I would have caught up in no time."

Wes snorted. "What? And miss out watching you blow yourself to bits, again?" His friend's laughter relayed all too clearly through his earpiece. "Or did you forget we decided to play one of the close quarters and hostage themes today?"

Stephen scowled, returning to the inventory menu. *Killjoy.* Replacing the missile launcher with a handgun with good range and killer accuracy, he replied, "You're jealous because all you know how to use are knives." *Besides*, he told himself, *my character hadn't self-destructed that much.*

Stephen lost track of how many missions they'd gone on together. In all that time, he had never once seen Wes's avatar brandish anything resembling a gun. He muttered into the microphone, "You know what they say about bringing a knife to a gunfight."

"That even with a knife, I am still a hell of a lot more effective than you." Wes's avatar, clad in an identical uniform featuring three-dimensional geometric shapes, supposed to represent camouflage, dropped into view. There had once been better games out there, with graphics and sound effects so realistic, players forgot where the game began and reality ended, but this one had what all the others hadn't. Staying power. The game, *Colony Defenders II*, had somehow found a way to survive even after the breakdown of civilization, as they knew it.

The simple interface started with all players in a neutral zone upon login, a feature designed to give noobs a safe area to practice the game's commands and work out a basic strategy while the computer issued mission goals. Enemies weren't programmed to appear until players crossed through a flashing starting gate. Thus, it came as a surprise when the screen flashed red and Stephen's health meter dropped a point. "What the—?" Stephen shouted. Considering Wes was the only other person left in the world besides himself who still knew about the game, the hit could have only come from one source. *With friends like mine . . .*

"Demonstrating a point."

Stephen flipped a finger at the screen even though his machine lacked a camera. His friend's laughter played in his ear as if he saw the gesture anyway. Stephen's frown deepened as he scratched at his thin raisin-brown hair tickling his jawline. He should shave, but other priorities had a way of taking precedence. *Not that how you look matters.*

"Oh, don't be a baby." Wes's avatar threw him a virtual medic pack, restoring Stephen's health meter to full value. "Are you ready to do this thing or not?" Wes's character vanished through the start gate.

"Let's go." Stephen followed. The background dissolved into a gray corridor as soon as they passed under the gate. Large brown blocks representing crates lay scattered along its length. *Whoever designed the game must love crates,* Stephen thought for the millionth time. Fifty more than were necessary were always strewn about in every mission. A green-skinned, four-armed creature popped up, and Stephen fired. The scoreboard showed a direct hit. Then the screen flashed red again as Stephen's health meter took another dip. He turned; another creature must have snuck up on him from behind. He fired another shot. "What in the. . . Wes, you are supposed to cover my rear."

"It's not my fault your rear is so big," Wes replied. His avatar jumped up on a crate, slashing at another would-be assailant.

The creatures froze while alien hisses continued to play in stereo over his earpiece. Stephen didn't need to see the action to know his avatar was under attack, even if the screen didn't show it.

"Dude. Are you waiting for an engraved invitation? According to the map, the hostages are supposed to be in the room to your right."

A map icon flashed in the upper right-hand portion of the screen. Then the entire display became awash with purple, yellow, and blue pixels. "Damn it." Stephen slapped his monitor, even though it wouldn't do any good. "My system's going down again."

"Why do you bother with that old machine anyway?" Wes asked. The screen flashed an icon recommending immediate plugging in of his machine. Stephen scowled. His eyes followed the length of cord from the inlet connection to the electrical outlet on the wall. He jiggled the plug, and the icon vanished, but the game's action remained frozen.

"You're right." He slapped his forehead. "I'll just walk over to the store and get a new one." Stephen snorted at the thought. The system was a relic—technology considered ancient fifteen years ago. The only reason Stephen could communicate with Wes at all was because someone must have decided it would cost more to recycle for parts than chuck into the back of a forgotten storage closet.

Without the benefit of store-bought components, it had taken Stephen more than two years, and a bit of luck, to get the system up and running again. He should have been praised. Instead, his grand accomplishment, the testament to his engineering genius, had to be hidden away. Stephen's scowl deepened at the difference fifteen years could make. At least, he'd been told life wasn't always this way. *Repeatedly.* Stephen wouldn't know. He'd been four when the world went mad. *Must have been nice.* Stephen ran a hand over his face in frustration. The plug-in icon reappeared.

He kicked the wall and winced when he heard the wood crack. The glorified shed they used as a barn didn't need his help to accelerate its declining condition. "One of these days you are going to have to tell me why you never have any of these problems."

"I keep telling you, you need to come see me."

"You know why I can't." Something rustling in the corner caught his attention. *Please don't be another rat*, he thought. He shouldn't care, but the beasts had a way of popping up at the worst possible times. If he didn't know better, he might think they were showing up on purpose. All he had to do was sneak away to work on his computer or play games. Even worse, once spotted, they never ran away back into the shadows as Stephen thought a rat should. Instead, they would sit there, watching him with their beady eyes, until Stephen worked up the courage to chase them off with a broom or shovel. Just thinking about another rat in the room gave him the creeps.

"About that. They. . . you. . ." Wes's voice broke up.

"What about me?" Stephen scanned the room. The rustling could have come from something else, like a draft. It didn't have to be a rat. *Right. Keep telling yourself that.*

Wes sighed, the connection clear again. "Never mind. Lost my train of thought. But hey, you know the invitation is always open. So. . . the usual, but on time for once?"

"I wasn't that late."

Wes asked the same question week after week to the point that Stephen wondered if his friend suffered from some sort of short-term memory loss. He might have teased him about it, but with his computer acting up again, there wasn't time to give his friend a hard time. *Don't forget, you might not be alone in here.* He shuddered.

"Don't make me track you down."

"Quit complaining. I'll have the old girl working by then." *That's it. Time to find a cat.* Maybe if he started leaving scraps out, one would show up. His stomach grumbled at the thought of going without even a sliver less food. *Probably would wind up attracting more rats.* Nothing was ever easy, at least not in Stephen's memory.

"All right. If you want to talk before then, I'm a keystroke away. Later, man."

"Wes51d3 has left the arena," announced the female voice, more garbled than before. The screen flashed again. An empty battery symbol replaced the plug-in icon.

"I get it. I get it." He toggled the keys to initiate the shutdown sequence. Nothing happened.

Stephen removed his headset and held the power button until the whirl of the computer's fan confirmed complete system shutdown. Why he bothered escaped him. The machine would have powered itself down in another two minutes. It was just one of those things he had gotten into the habit of doing. Once off, he closed the screen and hid the device beneath a loose board in the barn floor.

He rustled the crease in his hair from the headset before stepping out of the barn. The windmill a few yards away caught his gaze. Its propellers remained stationary, even though a gust of a fall wind caused Stephen to shiver. He zipped up his cotton jacket. *Well, that explains the power.*

"Generator's out again, Ed," Stephen announced, entering the farmhouse on the other side of a dirt and gravel path connecting the two buildings. A slew of screws, nuts, and metal plates littered the kitchen table. "But it looks like you already knew that."

Ed Thomas appeared from the other room. A cream and brown cloth wrapped around his left hand highlighted the swath of dark freckles running up the rest of his arm.

"What happened?" Stephen asked.

"I think squirrels must have gotten into it. Again."

"No. I meant to your hand." Stephen said, pointing.

"Oh. That. Driver slipped." Ed gestured at the offending tool on the table. As he did so, Stephen noticed a red circular stain on the cloth. Stephen didn't need to see the wound underneath to know that it would be ugly. They always were. No doubt in the coming weeks he would have yet another pale line to add to the collection of scars along his hands, arms, and legs—assuming, of course, he'd manage to sew himself up without infection. They'd been lucky so far, but Ed had always been more than a little clumsy and seemed to be growing even more accident-prone every year. A serious injury was no longer an *if*, but a *when*.

"How bad?"

"Needs a new solenoid."

"Once again, not what I meant," Stephen asked, nodding in the direction of the bandage.

"I should live. But I may need you to pick up a little more around here for the next few days."

Stephen glanced back toward the kitchen door and the barn across the way. Sneaking in thirty minutes between his chores already created a stiff challenge. If he had to pick up Ed's too, it was going to be difficult if not impossible to get the machine rebuilt in time for the next virtual meet-up with Wes.

"Yeah. Not how I intended to spend my golden years either." Ed grinned at his joke, but Stephen failed to see the humor in his comment. It wasn't right. Ed was far from what should have been considered old. He wouldn't have even been called middle-aged, but now. . . Stephen glanced again out the window to avoid looking at the white-laced hair where fiery red should be or at the spots of age that now dotted his skin in between the freckles.

"You see something?" Ed asked, on guard.

Stephen sighed, rubbing his face as he pulled his gaze from the barn. It didn't take much to spook the man. Edward's paranoia made Stephen's feelings about rats seem downright sensible. "Just checking to see how much sunlight we have left. If I leave now, I can get to Earthaven by nightfall."

"You aren't going to Earthaven." Ed arranged the tools and fasteners on the table using an indecipherable, system-bucking sort of logic.

"Someone has to." Stephen pointed at the components scattered on the table.

"And where would you go then? You know it's too dangerous to be out at night."

"It's only Earthaven." Stephen imagined walking over to the table and switching out one bolt for another just to see how long it would take the older man to notice.

"Yes, and there are reasons we're here and not there." Components clinked together as Ed moved the piles around.

"But. . . Earthaven. . ." Stephen turned his face before Ed could see him roll his eyes.

"Just because nothing has ever happened in the town doesn't mean nothing ever will." Ed gestured with his bandaged hand as he spoke, scattering the contents of one of the piles.

"And we're still talking about Earthaven," repeated Stephen as he bent down, picked up a screw from the ground, and placed it back on the table with the others. Ed picked it up and placed it in another pile.

"Not this again." Helen Thomas entered the farmhouse holding a bowl of vegetables. Dirt smeared her otherwise reddened cheeks. Strands of her hair, also more white and gray than the brown it should be, rebelled against the plaited braid.

"Let me help you with that" Ed reached for the vegetables, sending more metal parts to the floor.

"Oh no, you don't. I harvested them. I can wash them." As she batted his arm away, Edward winced. "Operating on yourself again, I see? I swear, Stephen, I turn my back on him for one second. . ."

Stephen grinned. "Sorry. Didn't realize it was my turn to watch him."

"So what were you two arguing about?" Helen asked as she turned the dial on the faucet, allowing water from the rain barrel to flow for a few seconds into the sink basin. The contents of the barrel could fill the basin with more to spare, but the summer had been dry, and a little conservation now could make a huge difference in the days or weeks ahead unless the weather turned.

Then again, Stephen thought, *it could rain for a month and Helen would still act as if they were in a drought.* "My ability to walk five miles." Stephen reached down and handed her a small potato that had rolled away from the others.

"After dark," grumbled Ed as he rearranged the contents of the piles, making their composition even less consistent.

"I'm nineteen now. Weren't you both considered adults at this point?"

Helen's shoulders slumped. "Honey, we know you aren't a kid anymore, but the world is nothing like it was when we were your age. There were millions of more people, for starters." She looked at Ed's piles of components. "Not to mention reliable power." She paused. Her lips twisted. "And if we got into trouble, we had phones."

"Yeah, and yet you somehow have managed to live all this time without those things. All I am asking is the chance to do the same. To actually live."

Helen scrubbed the potato with a stiff brush before transferring it to a cardboard box near the sink.

Ed broke the silence first. "This isn't the life either of us wanted for you, but—"

"No, he's right." Helen put the brush down. "Good or bad. It's time we give him the opportunity to make the occasional decision." Helen moved to the table and picked up the component that had thus far eluded Ed's notice. She placed it in his good hand. "Goodness knows you could have used a little more practice back then." The two shared a grin over some secret joke before Helen turned back to the basket of vegetables. She turned the root over in her hand as she cleaned it, inspecting its skin and eyes before placing it to the side of the basin rather than in the box with the others. "Besides, as he said, it is only Earthaven. Jim will keep an eye on him."

"My point exactly." Stephen raced over to kiss Helen on the cheek, grabbing a washed sweet pepper harvested along with the potatoes.

"But what if. . .?" Ed gestured again. A piece of fabric from the bandage caught on one of the components, sending the piles tumbling once again to the floor.

Helen came over to Ed's side and helped him gather his supplies. "Who's left to remember, let alone care about—?" Helen started. She glanced in Stephen's direction and dropped the sentence. Returning to the sink, she continued as if the words had never been spoken. "Besides, you clearly aren't fit to go."

Stephen didn't want to risk Helen changing her mind by asking either of the two to go into more details about whatever it was. *More of Ed's paranoia, I bet.* Stephen bit into the pepper, tasting dirt as much as vegetable as he raced to the door. He wiped the pepper's skin on the side of his jacket as he threw open the door and jumped down the stairs. "I'll be back in the morning," he shouted without looking back.

"Keep your eyes open," Ed called out as Stephen ran into the woodlands hiding the farm from casual view. Stephen's ears barely caught Ed's last words. "And don't trust anyone."

TWO

The sky was a deep purple, the color of one of Helen's favorite eggplants, when Stephen reached the edge of Earthaven. A handful of stars freckled the horizon. *What would it be like if you just kept going?* he wondered, looking out to where the land met sky before returning his attention to the buildings up ahead making up Main Street. Earthaven was little more than a village, designed as an experimental community more than seventy years ago. In the years leading up to the economic crash to end all crashes, it had become almost a theme park, providing visitors with a glimpse of the distant pre-industrialized past. The fact that the residents were already used to off-grid and self-sufficient living was the main reason it survived when so many much larger communities failed.

As he walked down Main Street toward Piper's Tavern, the lamplighters were already hard at work, illuminating towers filled with chopped wood rather than electric bulbs. According to Ed, Piper's Tavern used to be a restaurant and still was if anyone asked, but it had since morphed into a place where goods and services of all kinds were exchanged. It was also one of the few places in town Ed and Helen ever went, though they never stayed long. The rest of the town might as well have been on the other side of the world.

The door squealed on its hinges as Stephen opened it, alerting its proprietor, a lean individual, more bone than man, to his presence. "Stephen," Jim called out. "Is that you? Gosh, it must be a year since your folks stopped by. People were beginning to think you all had moved on." He placed a rag on the back of a chair and grabbed Stephen's hand, giving it a quick shake. "I'm afraid that it's close to closing," said Jim, gesturing to the room behind him. A single table remained occupied by a trio, all wearing bands of tied red cloth on their left arms.

Jim frowned, lowering his voice to a near whisper. "I know your folks don't like to travel much at night, but it's best they turn back. The folks around today haven't been the kind they'd be interested in trading with." Glancing over Stephen's head at the torches and the evening sky, he added, "Where are your folks? Are they taking the scenic route?"

Stephen buried his disappointment. He'd hoped to make it in time to track down the part tonight so that he would have more time to be on his own in the morning before heading back to the farm. "Don't worry. They aren't coming. Do you know where I can stay for the night?"

"Jim, the way you've chased patrons out this afternoon it is amazing you are still in business. The kid looks like he's exhausted. Why don't you offer the boy a drink?" a woman at the table asked, leaning in her chair.

Jim pursed his lips. "Can I get you some water before you go?"

"Thanks, but a room would be even better." Stephen glanced at the woman whose attention had turned back to the pair of men beside her.

Jim shook his head at Stephen's quick response. "I still can't believe the old man finally let you off the leash." Jim let go of the door and walked toward the bar area to pour Stephen a drink. "That's something I never thought would happen."

Stephen's smile faded as he took the offered glass. "I'm not on anyone's leash."

He held up his hands in surrender. "I didn't mean anything by it." Jim began wiping down the bar with a second rag. "Would it be too much to hope that your folks gave you something for a room?" As Jim continued his work, Stephen grimaced. He hadn't thought that far ahead, so eager to get away from the farm before Ed changed his mind. Perhaps he shouldn't have been so quick to eat the pepper. Food in hand always went a long way at the bargaining table.

Jim sighed, having read Stephen's expression. "Yeah, it's just as well. I don't think most places would be willing to take in a stranger nowadays, even a paying stranger. At least not any of the places I'd be comfortable recommending."

"Please. I can't go back tonight, and I don't know any place else to go."

Jim rubbed his hand over his forehead. "Hmm. I guess I could put you in the back office, but you'd have to work for it."

"The back room would be fine." Stephen eyeballed the rest of the room's empty chairs, calculating that three or four of them put together might prevent him from having to sleep on the floor. "What do you need me to do?"

As if Jim read his mind, he added, "I keep a cot back there—for emergencies." He walked over to a small closet and pulled out a broom. Handing the broom to Stephen, he said, "And you can start by finishing the sweeping up."

"So, what brings you into Earthaven?" the woman asked, rising from her chair along with the pair of men who flanked her sides.

"He's passing through, Dr. Lambda," Jim answered from the other side of the bar.

"Is he?" Dr. Lambda's eyebrow arched. "From what I overheard, it sounded like you were old family friends." The woman's eyes narrowed. "Your face looks familiar. You're what? Somewhere between eighteen and twenty-one?" Her companions nodded with her assessment. "Have you ever visited the Watchtower?"

"Nineteen, and no. I've been lucky. Never had worse than a cold."

"Well, that is lucky, indeed. I've seen plenty of patients who would love to know your secret."

"Good genes, I guess."

The corner of Dr. Lambda's lips crept up. "I guess."

The slap of the rag on the counter behind him startled Stephen. "Well, I hate to break up the conversation, but if I don't close up now, I will have one angry missus to deal with. She likes being walked home." Jim stretched his unburdened hands above his head with a yawn and then rolled his shoulders as his joints made an audible popping sound.

"There you go kicking out customers again." Dr. Lambda chuckled, dropping a handful of coins on the bar.

"I'd rather take my chances with the Watch than an angry wife," Jim answered. Dr. Lambda's smile slipped as Jim's face flushed bright red. "Oh, that didn't come out right. I mean. . . I mean. . . Have you met my wife? No, of course you wouldn't have. Why would you?" Jim winced.

Dr. Lambda's smile returned, but it seemed different to Stephen's eyes than the one flashed before. More knowing than welcoming. "That's all right, Jim. I'm sure no one on the Watch would find being compared to your wife offensive."

Jim whispered to Stephen, "If you need anything, I'll be across the street, but don't tell anyone. Most people think I live here."

Gripping the broom, Stephen got to work as the doctor and her escorts made their way outside and didn't stop even after he heard Jim turn the latch on the tavern door. The entire exchange had been the most excitement Stephen had seen in months, and all it would cost him was a few extra hours of hard labor. Maybe after tonight, he'd convince Ed and Helen to allow him to make more solo runs in the future.

⸙

The air smelled of smoke from all but one of the extinguished candles as Stephen made his final sweep across the room. As Stephen placed the broom in its closet, he heard a *scratch-tap-tap* at the glass window nearest the door.

"Psst," a female voice whispered. "Psst," the voice said again, this time more insistent. "They'll be here any second."

Stephen picked up the remaining candle and began walking toward the back office.

"I know you are in there." While still a whisper, the voice now took on tones of panic. "I can see light under the door. Let me in."

Stephen hesitated.

"Fine. Be like that. Just know that when I get questioned, I will be sure to tell them what is also on the Piper's menu."

Stephen had no idea what Jim was involved in, but without Jim and Piper's, he'd never have an excuse to leave the farm again. The bolt was a hair's width out of the locked position when the door opened and the girl entered the room.

The girl might have come up to his shoulder if they were to stand next to each other and was as slight in frame as Jim. She wore a thin charcoal sweater that had seen better days and a brimmed dark knit hat, which covered all but a few stray ends of white blonde hair. He tried to get a better look at her in the dim candlelight, but before he could make out more of her features, she kicked the door with her heel and spun to refasten its bolt. Grabbing Stephen by the arm, she pulled him down the hall toward the back office.

"Hey!" Stephen shouted as she closed the office door. "Just who do you think—?"

The girl placed a hand on his mouth, muffling his words. Satisfied that he would not utter another word, she dropped to the ground and placing her ear next to the floor.

"I don't think. . ." Stephen started. He'd made a huge mistake letting the girl in. Ed's parting words not to trust anyone mocked him in his mind. *Jim is never going to trust me again.*

The girl twisted, glaring up at him, cutting off the rest of his statement with an expression that said, *no, you don't,* as clearly as if the words had been spoken aloud.

The silence broke with the sound of glass shattering. Several voices shouted out from the street, although their words were indistinct. Stephen made a move back toward the door to investigate. The girl placed her hand on his leg. She crouched in a ready-to-run stance, as if waiting for the door to the back office to burst at any moment.

Minutes passed as the voices faded into the night.

Stephen offered his hand to the girl. She batted it away and rose unassisted. The shadows danced across her face, making her scowl even fiercer. *What got into her breakfast?*

"Where's Jim?" she demanded, crossing her arms over her chest as if he was the inconvenience rather the other way around.

"Gone." If she wanted to hand out attitude, he was happy enough to return the favor.

She tapped her toe. "You are sure?"

Stephen rolled his eyes. The girl was cute under that hat, he'd give her that, but her appearance did not make up for her lack of people skills. He shrugged. "Do you see him here?" He glanced in the direction of the main entrance. "Look. I was told to sweep and keep the door locked. That's it. A job I now realize I should have done better." He pointed at the door. "If finding Jim is such an emergency, I suggest you head back out there."

The girl's scowl deepened. Crossing her arms over her chest, her fingers tapped on her arms just as her toes had a moment before. Glaring at Stephen as if he had the power to re-materialize Jim and was holding out on her, she asked, "Is he coming back?"

"I'm not his keeper, but my guess? Not until morning." *You just had to go and try to do the nice thing. That'll teach you.*

The girl rubbed her hand across her face, shielding him from what Stephen was sure had to be a dagger-like expression. "Then I guess we are roommates tonight."

The room was the size of a glorified closet, with a folded cot wedged in one corner. Though small, it would have served Stephen's needs for the night considering what he had available to trade for the privilege, but there was no way it could sleep two, especially if one of those two prickled more than a cactus. He glanced at the girl again. She glared back. *Nope, her staying here with me was not a good option.*

He cleared his throat. "I think you'd better find someplace else."

Stephen heard the girl mutter to herself, "So much for that plan."

He'd taken a step back when the back of his foot met a bucket by the wall. *What are you doing, man? You gotta step it up.* He puffed out his chest and returned to his original stance. "I don't know you." His claim to be able to take care of himself replayed in his mind. He couldn't even make it a day without finding trouble. "And I don't want to."

"Do you not understand what is happening out there right now? Who I just protected you from?" She threw her hands up in the air.

Stephen paused, wondering at her words for a split second. *Nothing to do with you,* he told himself. *Don't back down now. She's the one with the problem. Not you. You were just fine until she started banging on the door.* "I let you in, remember? From where I am standing, I protected you," said Stephen as he gestured at the door, "from whatever or whoever has gotten you so worried."

Her body seemed to deflate as she absorbed his words. Stephen heard her mutter to herself, "New plan."

The way she talked to herself made him wonder if she had spent much time around other people. *Perhaps she doesn't realize other people can hear her.* He started to comment, but decided he was safer not saying anything.

She looked up at him, her face once again hard and resolved. "The Watch is conducting a raid." The candle flickered, causing their shadows to dance upon the walls. "If you were smart, you'd be worried, too."

"A raid? The Watch?" Helen called them thugs. Ed seemed to make it a point not to mention them at all, but they were all that stood between civilization and complete anarchy in this part of the world. *Weren't they?* The doctor lady from earlier was one of them, and she didn't seem so bad.

"Yes. Them."

Stephen shrugged. "I've got nothing to fear from that group." He thought of the barn with his hidden stash of electronics and fought any guilt from showing on his face.

"Oh really? What about your family? I assume you have one. Can they say the same?"

Ed and Helen weren't technically his parents, but they were the closest thing to family he had. While it was true, the couple hadn't adopted him through the traditional legal channels, he was sure what they'd done would no longer be considered a crime. Stephen doubted an official process existed anymore. Why would there be? So many people had fallen victim to either the riots after the initial crash or the plague that followed. Who would care about who anyone lived with? *No, they'd done nothing wrong.* If anything, by opening their home to some random kid, his guardians had done something right. He nodded to himself. Besides, that was years ago. If pressed now, he wasn't sure he could even tell anyone what his old last name started with. At least not with any certainty.

Doubt gnawed at him. Whether it was the fall of civilization or their natural-born inclination, Stephen's guardians had always seemed cautious to a fault, at least in Stephen's opinion. The three of them kept to themselves unless they had no other choice than to make a trade for other supplies, and those they traded within the tavern had already been grayed around their edges with skin marked with age spots as early as he could remember. There were never any new faces. *Were they hiding bigger secrets?*

No, they couldn't be. Not from him. They might be holed up in the middle of nowhere, but Ed couldn't keep a secret from the family if he tried. Stephen remembered the time Ed caught him sneaking a treat one evening. Rather than scolding him, Ed had joined in, telling him it would be their little secret only to turn around and confess everything to Helen the next morning. All Helen had done was frown at the tray. Well, he almost confessed everything. Ed had taken the majority of the blame, making Stephen out to be his accomplice and him the mastermind. No, the thought of Ed keeping a secret was ridiculous.

Still. . .

"Fine. You can stay. But I get the cot." He looked at the folded piece of fabric on its wooden frame. *It is too tight in here,* he thought. Stephen opened the door to better maneuver around his roommate, but swung it too far, knocking into a bookcase in the process. Pots and other goods staged for trade the following morning came tumbling down.

From the front of the tavern, Stephen heard a pounding on the door. "Guess the jig is up." He reached for the knob.

The girl clenched her teeth, but it didn't prevent her from saying, "Idiot."

"As I said. I have nothing to hide. What's the worst that can happen?"

The sound of an explosion answered him. Stephen fell to the floor as the ground shook and a flaming piece of roofing broke through the tavern's front window. He watched in disbelief as the fire spread onto a pair of thick curtains. The smell of smoke filled his nostrils. "What should we do?"

"Now," the girl grimaced, "we run."

three

The girl latched onto Stephen's arm, pulling him back through the tavern's kitchen as the flames from the great room continued to spread up the wall. "Jim would have had an escape plan. There should be another door," she said, feeling the wall. The fire in the other room caused shadows to stretch and dance. Edges became difficult to judge as the red-orange glow of the destructive light reflected on the metallic appliances in the room.

Stephen took a breath and regretted it as the smoke filled his lungs. "There's nothing there." He pulled her back before succumbing to a coughing fit.

"It's got to be here." Her voice rose in pitch as she continued to scratch at the wall. "Look for a panel. A secret knot. Something."

Her refusal to accept the obvious would get them both killed. He pulled her again toward the main room door. They could still make it through the front door, but that would mean facing the Watch. Still, it was better than getting burned alive. "All I see is a wall. Come on, we have to go."

"No!" A combination of confusion and terror reflected in the girl's eyes. He pulled again, but the girl refused to budge. It was as if she thought being consumed by the growing fire was the better option. "You don't understand. I can't."

Leave her. A voice whispered in his mind. *You don't owe her anything. Save yourself.* The light from the other room was now bright enough for Stephen to see scratches along the wall where the girl had dug in. *She'll die if you leave her. Could you really live with yourself after that?* Desperate for another option, Stephen's eye caught on a grid-like shadow a few feet away. "There." He ran over to what he had assumed was another shelving unit in the kitchen. "It's a ladder! Maybe it leads to a roof access."

Stephen began to ascend. His head came into contact with a metal plate, causing his grip to slip. "Shit," he exclaimed as his vision blurred.

"What?" asked the girl from the base of the ladder.

"The panel, it's stuck."

"Fix it." Gone was the panic from her voice and in its place was the bully from the other room.

Oh, did I miss that this is my fault? Large beads of sweat had begun to drip down his face. Visibility at the top of the ladder was already nonexistent with more smoke filling the room. This was it. If he couldn't get the access panel open, they'd go back out the front whether she liked it or not. Stephen traced his fingers across the plate's edge until he discovered a square box hanging from one end. "It's locked," he shouted down to the girl.

"Maybe there's a key," she answered. He heard her open cabinets and pull drawers out, sending their contents to the ground.

Stephen's thumb passed along the base of the box and each of its sides. He couldn't detect a keyhole anywhere on it. Only a ridge made of narrow buttons and concave surface. "Not that kind. It's electronic." He could hear the crackle of fire now. He didn't have to look to know the main room no longer contained it. *Too late.*

Going out the front wasn't an option now even if he knocked the girl out and dragged her by the hair.

The heat from the fire warmed the metal ladder where he gripped it. The image of Ed and his injured hand sprang into Stephen's mind. *I guess I don't have to worry about picking up Ed's chores.* He wanted to laugh. He coughed instead. He was going to die in this room. And for what? All because he took pity on some paranoid girl.

"I found a crowbar," announced the girl. "Can we break it open?"

"Cracking the case is the last thing we want to do. Whole thing will permanently fuse together."

Metal clattered to the ground. "I'm open to ideas."

Stephen guessed they had maybe five to ten minutes before the whole building became nothing more than a smoldering heap and even less time to breathe. "Grab me a knife."

"I thought you said we don't want to break it."

"Just do it."

She climbed up and handed him a steak knife. Stephen located a tiny hole at the base of the lock and jammed the knifepoint into it. A red LED flashed while Stephen pressed and held the buttons in a particular combination. The heat from below tempted him to use more speed, but the timing was just as important as the sequence. The LED flashed again and turned yellow. Stephen placed his thumb on the pad.

The box twisted in Stephen's hand causing him to drop the knife. "Look out below," he said. Stephen pulled himself as high as he could go without choking on smoke or hitting the metal plate with his head again. He pressed the pad one more time. A gap between the box and the plate opened. "Got it," he shouted downward as he yanked the lock free from the latch.

Stephen pushed on the metal plate and his vision cleared, showing the star-filled night sky. He gasped for breath as he pulled himself through the square opening.

The surface of the rooftop was cool against his cheek as he crawled further away from the opening. In the dark night, he heard the girl as she followed suit. Once Stephen regained his breath, he rose to a crouch, scanning the rooftop. The fire's light, escaping through the access hatch, illuminated a slight wall running along the perimeter. The building shuddered as the flames consumed more of the building's interior. "Great. Now what?" he wondered aloud.

The girl jumped up and ran in the other direction, hurling her body over the side of the wall. Stephen raced over to that edge and saw a large dark shape several feet below. The girl stood on the ground next to it, unharmed. She glanced in the direction of the tavern's entrance and then back at him. Gesturing to the dark shape, she waved her hand, for him to jump.

She's crazy, Stephen thought as he scanned the wall for a ladder or other exit point. Looking down, he saw the girl raise her hand again, making the okay sign. He shook his head.

The building groaned as the sounds of glass shattering punctuated the night. The girl glanced in the direction of the tavern's entrance and back at Stephen. She gestured for him to follow again with more urgency. Stephen hesitated. The girl took a step backward as the building shuddered again followed by a crashing sound below. It wouldn't be much longer before the tavern's roof collapsed.

"If she can do it," he grumbled to himself, "I can do it." Taking a few steps backward to allow him to gain some extra speed, but also to keep him from chickening out, Stephen ran and jumped over the wall. Then he was falling.

Idiot, he thought to himself, echoing the girl's words from before as his body made contact with an unyielding metal surface. *Dumpster.* Stephen tasted blood in his mouth. He must have bitten his tongue upon impact. It had been everything he could do not to scream while he descended.

A pale white hand touched his leg. Uncertain about the condition of his body after his fall, Stephen rolled to the dumpster's edge. The feeling of solid ground beneath his feet almost sent tears to his eyes. Stephen spit the blood out of his mouth as if it was the physical manifestation of the terror he had experienced.

"You should go," the girl whispered in his ear. "Run as far as you can."

"But why?" Stephen leaned against the wall while he regained his sense of equilibrium. The brick was as warm as if it were noon during the peak of summer. "I mean, I get you're involved in something, but why should I have to run away like some sort of criminal when I'm not? And what about Jim?"

Stephen didn't need to see the whites of her eyes to know she'd rolled them. "What about him?"

"You were desperate to find him before. Why aren't you worried about him now?"

"I didn't find him in time."

"What do you mean?" The wall was even hotter now than seconds before.

"Do you think the building across the street blew up by accident? Jim's dead."

More glass shattered. She cocked her head and pushed Stephen behind the dumpster.

"Hey—"

She covered his mouth.

Voices echoed from the front of the alleyway. "Boss isn't going to be happy."

"No shit. There goes our lead."

Another voice joined the mix. "Neighbors say they saw a girl sneaking around. Description fit. Kid let her in right before."

"You think he's part of it?"

"You'd have thought he'd come out by now if he wasn't."

"Well, guess they're toast then."

"I don't believe that for a second. No, they are still here somewhere. I can feel it."

"So, what do we do?"

"We find them." A groan like a threatened beast filled the night and brickwork toppled to the ground. Stephen heard shouts and more footfalls as the men scattered.

"Well, that's that. How far is your place from here?" she whispered as she pulled him back up.

"My place?" Stephen's throat begged him to cough and for cleaner air. "Don't you know another place we can go, like another safe house or something?"

"Do you think I would still be standing here with you if I did?"

The plot of land that made up their farm was only a few miles away, but it would be near impossible to find now that evening had fallen. Ash filled the air, choking out what remaining light the moon and stars offered.

Stephen suppressed a wince as he stepped away from the burning building and into the dark night. He must have damaged his leg in the fall. Gritting his teeth, Stephen increased his pace to a run as they made their way through the town's network of back alleys. No matter what twists or turns they took, the girl matched his pace stride for stride, never pulling ahead of him nor slowing unless he did, too. "So, are you going to tell me now why they are after you?"

"Are you going to tell me how you knew how to hack that lock? I'm pretty sure that's on someone's no-no list."

How could he explain it was one of those things he'd just known, like rebuilding the computer or connecting it online? Once he'd stopped thinking about the fire, the locks had become another puzzle demanding a solution. Electronics spoke to him. He hardened his jaw and looked straight ahead. It was not a skill that was healthy to admit.

"How about telling me your name then," said Stephen as the town receded in the distance. His lungs burned from the effort and his right ankle now throbbed in time with the beating of his heart. *It's going to be purple in the morning. Ed's never going to let me leave home again.*

The girl answered him as if they were taking a casual stroll in a park. "You can call me Bean."

"Bean? Like the vegetable?" Stephen asked in a winded voice, slowing their pace to a walk. He looked back. The road behind them lay empty and there was no sound of sound of pursuit. Maybe the Watch had given up.

"You have a problem with that?" Her shoulders tensed, and one hand balled up into a fist.

I'm guessing I'm not the first to ask that question. "No. It's just. . .unique."

Bean laughed. Her fist relaxed and her fingers wiggled. "Well, so am I."

Stephen turned from the road without warning and walked down a grassy slope and into the woods off to the side.

"Wait?" Bean asked, pausing in mid-step. "We're not going through there."

Maybe she's not as tough as she lets on. "You said you want to go to my place. This is the way." *I wonder how Helen will react to me bringing a girl home.* Stephen's smile slipped. Not well, considering the strict anti-visitor policy in place as long as he could remember. Ed's reaction would be even worse. *Maybe it would be for the best if she stays in the barn.*

"Aren't there roads where you live?" she replied. She touched the ground off the side of the road with a toe in the same way Stephen might test the water in the nearby creek in springtime.

Stephen snorted. "Scared of the big bad woods?" he asked. It was hard not to be nervous, seeing the dark mass of trees in front of them, and for good reason. The ferocious way his guardians had hammered into him how easy it was to get lost in the woods in the dark had always come across like a lesson they'd learned through hard experience. A stick cracked under his feet and an owl hooted.

"Woods, no." Bean frowned. "Things that live in the woods, yes."

There used to be a road connecting the farm to Earthaven, but even if they could find it, it wound around the woods for miles more than necessary. It would take days to get there by foot, which is why they never used it. Going through the woods was a more direct option. "We'll be fine." He took another step off the road.

The forest encircled them as they ventured further away from the main road. Doubts began to eat at his mind. *This is a terrible idea.* While smoke no longer filled the air, the trees blocked much of the light from the moon to the point that Stephen lost his confidence they were still moving in the right direction. *Go back to town. They aren't looking for you.* Bean remained close based on the sound of crunching leaves. Maybe going by the road wasn't such a bad idea, even if it would take all night. *But what if they are?* Bean froze, and he strained his ear for sounds of pursuit. He had to acknowledge that Bean knew more about the Watch than he did, and that was enough to send her diving over the side of a building without a second thought. If the Watch was still looking for them, the road was the last place they wanted to be.

Another owl hooted. *Or was that the same one? Have we gone in a circle?* Stephen heard a large thwack to his left as a large piece of wood broke in two. "What was that?" he asked. He'd grown up surrounded by these woods, which never stopped looking menacing at night. He could only imagine the terror that must've been going through his companion's mind by now.

"You scared? Big stick," answered Bean. "I figured I could use it as a club."

Or not, Stephen thought. *Yeah, Ed's not going to like this one bit. She's definitely sleeping in the barn tonight,* thought Stephen as they continued into the forest. *Assuming we ever find it.*

Four

Stephen cursed the night as they stumbled through the woods. In the darkness, familiar landmarks such as a large rock or fallen tree looked much like any other shadow. His nostrils flared as they took in an unmistakable odor. Stephen held out an arm to stop Bean in her tracks.

"Why are we stopping?" she asked.

He heard a whoosh as she brought the club-like branch up, ready to swing.

Stephen reached over until he touched the limb and pushed it down. "Do you smell that?" he asked, cringing at the thought of how loud their voices must sound compared to the forest's usual nocturnal inhabitants.

Stephen heard Bean's intake of breath followed by a coughing fit. "Ugh. What is that? Smells like something rotten."

Who'd made it this long without ever smelling a skunk before? he thought. "Skunk." He shook his head. *She must be from a bigger city, but what city is still around and bigger than Earthaven?*

"Is it nearby?" He sensed her inch closer.

"Near enough." He took a breath to calm his racing heart, regretting it almost at once. "But that's not what I'm worried about."

"No? Getting sprayed seems pretty bad to me."

Stephen fought the urge to laugh at her remark, although to be fair he wasn't thrilled with the idea of smelling like a skunk for the next week either. *Yeah, that would go over swell at home.* "I'm more worried about whatever threatened the skunk. Think about it."

"Oh." He heard a twig snap as she took a step closer, but couldn't tell if the step had been intentional or not. "We're not alone."

"Smells that way." *Could be a bear*, he thought without saying aloud. Humanity's population was a fraction of what it once was. The local wildlife had been more than happy to make up the difference.

She huffed. His hand brushed hers. It was shaking. *She is afraid. Jim probably told her about that time he thought he saw a werewolf in the woods.* The story shared over a trade had given him a nightmare for a week. Helen hadn't been amused. "I know it's scary out here, but it's too late and too dark to go back. It's hard for me to tell if we are going in the right direction as it is. I hate to say it, but we might be better off stopping and staying here until I can see landmarks in the morning."

"What about our company?" She shrugged off his hold.

Stephen was clueless, but she didn't need to know that he'd never spent a night away from the farmhouse, at least he hadn't as long as he could remember. Stephen made a mental note to look up wilderness survival techniques the next time he got online. He'd need them if supply runs became his regular thing. "I can take care of it. Give me the club."

"I don't think so," Bean replied. "I'm the one who found it."

Animals can sense fear. They'll smell it on her. "Will you just give it to me? I've got this."

A fiery pain flared across his arm. A jagged wooden edge dragged across his skin. "What the . . . "

"You asked for it," she answered. "I was just trying to hand it to you. Not my fault you weren't paying attention."

I was better off taking my chances with the Watch. Once in hand, he hit trees next to him and stomped his feet while growling.

"Are you sure you know what you are doing?" Bean asked. "Won't that attract more attention?"

So asks the girl who up until now had been treating the forest like her own personal piñata. "With any luck, whatever it is will think we are a bigger than them and will move along." Stephen plastered a smile on his face, injecting his voice with a confidence he didn't feel.

"But what we if aren't bigger than whatever it is?"

"Then we can either run, which, by the way, is a terrible idea when you can't see anything, or we climb," he said while slapping a nearby tree trunk. "Now try to be as still as possible and listen." A chattering sound caught his attention. "Wait, are you cold?" The woods were always several degrees cooler during the day thanks to the shade of the canopy, and the temperature had started to fluctuate wildly at night, but even so, it was far from what Stephen would consider cold. Then again, she was wearing a knit hat in September. Maybe she hadn't been afraid, after all, but was more sensitive to the cold than he was.

"I'm okay." The chattering continued.

Stephen reached out and found her hand in the dim light. It was like touching an icicle. "You're freezing," he announced.

"I'll be fine." Her words were clipped. Her teeth sounded more like a woodpecker with each passing second.

"No, you aren't." He unzipped his jacket. "Here, you can borrow this."

She took a step back. "Really, don't worry about me."

"You need it more than I do." He closed the distance between them with the intent of spinning her around and forcing the jacket on her whether she wanted it or not but stopped when his hand found wetness near her shoulder. *What is that?* He pulled his hand back and examined his fingers. Something dark and smelling of metal covered them. "Are you bleeding?" He touched her sweater again. The fabric was torn and half of the back was soaked. "Why didn't you say something?"

"I might have gotten a little scrape at the tavern when you dropped the knife. No big deal." It took Stephen a heartbeat to make sense of her words.

"No big deal? A little scrape wouldn't do something like this." Spending the night outdoors in the woods was no longer an option. Not if she was bleeding. The smell would be irresistible for a predator. They might as well turn on an 'Open for Dinner' sign. As if summoned by the thought, Stephen heard rustling leaves. He swung around at the sound, grasping the makeshift club in both hands.

"Bean," he whispered. "We need to go."

"I thought you said that was a terrible idea."

"Well, now I am saying it's a great idea. Best I've had all night."

"Can't we stay here? I'm so tired."

Her teeth were no longer chattering. *That's not good.* "Yeah. Well, get over it."

Bean yawned, sinking to the ground. "Just a quick nap."

Not good. Not good. Not good. "No nap. We gotta go, Bean. Now."

Stephen let go of the club. He reached out and around in the darkness until he found her forehead. Her skin was still icy cold but damp with sweat. The leaves rustled again. This time closer, and whatever it was, it was large. Stephen braced himself for an attack, placing his body between the girl and the sound. The girl had survived a blind jump from a burning building. She was tough, he'd give her that, but she would be no match for something like a bear. *Neither are you,* the voice in his mind whispered.

The urge to flee whatever threatened in the woods grew stronger. The voice grew more demanding. *And why haven't you yet?* She'd made it clear she wasn't a friend, and he'd already helped her more than enough. Hell, he might not even be in this situation if it wasn't for her. *Leave her and save yourself.* More leaves crunched. Louder this time. A branch scraped his forehead, startling him out of his thoughts. The source of the sound was his own footsteps. He hadn't even realized he'd stood up. *Don't be an idiot.*

Stephen returned and pulled Bean up from the forest floor. The sweater was a weight they didn't need and its scent would attract more danger. She whimpered as he removed it, letting the garment drop to the ground while replacing it with his own. He left the jacket unzipped so that her skin might be warmed by contact with his own as he held her close. She wavered and her body sagged further onto his until only his chest was keeping her upright. She wouldn't be walking further tonight. A wave of exhaustion threatened to undo him, too, but he scooped her up into his arms. His injured leg protested as he carried her away in what remained of the pale mottled light. Bean made no sign to suggest she was aware they were moving.

"For the record, I'm the one protecting you," he whispered.

⁓⁓⁓

Bean's body became like an anchor as the last of the adrenaline left Stephen's system. He wanted nothing more than to shake her awake and force her to carry her own weight, but that would require stopping. *If I stop now and she doesn't wake, I'll never be able to pick her up again.* Stephen once again fought the temptation to drop her under a tree and come back in the morning. *Your problem would be solved,* the voice in his head whispered, *one way or another.*

Stephen grimaced, focused on placing one foot in front of the other until each step became a victory. *We have to be almost there by now. Just another mile or so.* His toe found a root, and he adjusted his stride in time to avoid a fall. *I am so fucking lost.* Stephen looked around. The trees had begun to thin, allowing more of the moon's light to pass, but he didn't recognize any of his surroundings. The farmhouse could be around the corner or ten miles away for all he could tell.

Stephen's back began to spasm as his knees trembled. Deep down he knew that leaving Bean to fend for herself while he sought help wouldn't be a choice he could delay much longer. *That's assuming you don't collapse beside her*, nagged the voice in his head.

He closed his eyes as if he could deafen his doubts as easily as his vision. *Just another puzzle. Focus*, he told himself. No solution came. The light appeared dimmer than it had before when he opened his eyes. He couldn't be sure, as the tree cover did prevent a clear view of the sky, but Stephen guessed that clouds had begun to roll in. Rain. *Yeah, because tonight couldn't get any more perfect.*

Bean groaned as he shifted her weight. Her skin remained cool to the touch and clammy. He didn't need formal medical training to know she was running out of time. Stephen picked up his foot. His ankle throbbed. He took a step. His side complained. Then the ground before him seemed to lighten as if it glowed. He glanced backward, but there was only more darkness. *Stay ahead of the rain.* His thoughts took on the beat of a guiding mantra as he pushed them forward. Without any noticeable landmarks to guide him home, Stephen chased the light and hoped that they both might just survive the storm.

Five

The first blush of dawn bloomed across the sky when Stephen broke through the tree line. Hours must have passed, but as far as Stephen was concerned, it could have been years. His entire body was covered in a sheen of moisture from sweat, not rain. He had no idea how they'd managed to avoid the downpour, but they'd done it. The threat of rain was the only thing that had kept him from giving up. There had been so many times he'd wanted to rest, to catch his breath, if for a minute, but the sound of the drops of rain hitting the leaves behind him as the storm broke had become like a whip, urging him forward.

Well, maybe the rain hadn't been the only thing. He shifted Bean. During all that time, she hadn't stirred. *You better not have died on me.* He hadn't wanted to risk stopping to check. *We're here. We made it.* He wanted to laugh but was too exhausted to even lift his lips into a smile. Somehow, against all the odds, and against all his guardian's warnings, he had found his home even in the darkness. *That's me. Stephen Thomas, friendly neighborhood homing pigeon.* He shook his head at the thought of comparing himself to a comic book superhero. If he had superpowers, he'd have been home hours ago. He gritted his teeth as he entered a field of tall grass. At least he was almost there now. The sea of grass was all that stood between him and the barn. *Only a few more yards to go.*

Midway through the field, he saw the windmill. Its fins were still as frozen in place as when he'd left. Stephen groaned. *The parts.* He'd forgotten all about them. He'd have to go back into town, sooner rather than later. That was assuming anyone was still willing to trade after last night. *And where would they go?* Bean shivered in his arms, reminding him of the immediate issue. *First things first.* Ed wasn't a doctor, but considering how often he'd operated on himself, he had to know what to do. Stephen just hoped he wasn't already too late.

"Ed," he shouted. "Ed. Helen. Anyone. Help."

He staggered through the grass no longer able to feel his arms. Bean tumbled to the ground in front of him as he attempted to correct his balance. Released of her weight, his body seemed to spring forward of its own volition. In one second, his vision changed from a view of the farmhouse to the view of an approaching rock. He twisted his body by instinct, avoiding the imminent collision by an inch. Then everything went black.

<hr>

Stephen woke at the touch of a rough wet cloth as it dabbed his forehead. A sapphire blue sky arched over him, indicating it was now well past morning. All trace of rain from the night before was gone. The sky was the only clear thing in his vision. His other surroundings were blurred shapes and colors. He blinked to clear his vision. A blotch of tan and brown overhead sharpened, and the edges refined until he saw Helen staring down at him, her concern all too clear.

"Don't sit up too fast, honey," Helen said while placing a hand on his shoulder. "You're okay. I'm here." She leaned down to kiss his forehead.

"I got lost," he replied while groaning at how weak he sounded. *So much for finally being treated like an adult.* His head throbbed.

Helen shook her finger as she pulled back. "Which is exactly why you were supposed to stay in town for the night. I thought we'd taught you better."

Stephen's vision blurred as he attempted to follow the movement. "It kind of wasn't an option." An insect landed on his nose.

Helen waved the bug away. "I'm listening."

"The Piper is gone."

"Gone? What do you mean *gone*? What about Jim? He couldn't have given up on the place. Not after all this time. Did he get sick? Is he okay?"

"I don't know. I didn't see him after the explosion. But I don't think so."

"Explosion?" Helen covered her mouth. Her nostrils flared. "I knew I smelled smoke in the air last night." Stephen coughed. Her fingers were cool on his skin as they stroked his forehead. "Did you see it?" she asked, clearing a few loose strands of hair away from his eyes.

"See it? I was there when it happened." Her eyes grew wide as he spoke and glistened with unshed tears. "One minute I was helping Jim tidy up and then, boom." Stephen's voice rose in a disbelief. "A piece of debris came crashing into the tavern, and the next thing I know, the whole place on fire. I barely got out in time." His fingers curled in the grass. "The Watch was there. They must have done it."

Her mouth tightened, blinking away the moisture before tears could fall. "Well, it's over now. You are here and they are not. But if you ever frighten me like that again—"

"Where is she?" Stephen asked, remembering Bean. He swiveled his head from side to side but didn't see her. "There was a girl with me."

Helen's frown deepened. "With Ed, in the house. What were you thinking? Bringing a stranger here?"

"Is she. . . Will she be okay?"

"Honey, I am more worried about you right now."

"But she's okay?" Stephen's stomach turned. "I didn't carry her across half the forest last night for her to die on me the minute we got here."

Helen pursed her lips. "Whatever did you do that for? Her legs seemed to work well enough. Has she never been outside a city before?" Helen snorted at the thought, expressing without words what she thought of a person who would ask to be carried through the woods, let alone at night.

"She was hurt."

Helen frowned. "From what I could see, there's not more than a scratch on her. You, on the other hand." She tapped at his shirt, though her fingers were gentle. "You want to tell more about this stain?"

Stephen sat up, resting the bulk of his weight on his elbows. As he did so, he touched the dark spot on his shirt. It had dried hard, and the fabric clumped together. *No amount of scrubbing is going to get that out*, he thought. Stephen sighed. It had been his favorite shirt, one of the few that wasn't a shade of brown. *Doesn't matter*, he told himself. *It's not like I am out to impress anyone.*

"That's what I was telling you. The blood's hers."

"But that doesn't make any sense." Helen's forehead knit in confusion. She reached out to touch Stephen's clothing again as if the color might fall off in clumps like his usual covering of dirt did. "Are you sure you aren't hurt? Maybe you hit a tree branch or something?" She pulled at his collar, examining the skin underneath as her brow wrinkled further. Her eyes widened. She held up three fingers. "There was a rock next to your head. Did you hit it when you fell? How many fingers am I holding up?" She stopped and looked into his eyes.

"I would remember. And three." Stephen closed his eyes for a moment and lost himself in the memory of the fire as it claimed the walls all around. His heart raced as he recalled their frantic escape from the rooftop.

He opened them again at the touch of Helen's hand upon his cheek. There was a weariness in her eyes, though her jaw was clenched. "It's Jim's, isn't it?"

"No, I told you. I didn't see him again. I didn't see anything." Stephen thought about the voices in the alley. *Technically, that's not a lie.* Helen was already worried enough. *I got away.* He didn't need to add more to her troubles than he had to. "I'm telling you, it's hers," said Stephen. "She was hurt. Bad. I know." He grimaced. "I may have stabbed her with a knife."

"You did *what?*"

"It was an accident. See, there was this lock blocking the roof access and a ladder, and yeah, I might have, sort of dropped it on her." Helen sat back on her heels as Stephen continued, "I couldn't see how bad it was in the dark, but I think it sliced her back on the way down. Then there was the skunk and maybe a bear and she got all cold and clammy." *So much for not adding to her worries.* The words continued to spill out. "It's why we couldn't wait to travel in the daylight. And why I carried her. She would have died out there if it hadn't been for me. I'm actually a little surprised she didn't."

Helen's lips twisted as if there was something she wanted to say, but was interrupted by the rusty metal pull and thwacking sound of the farmhouse door spring as it opened and shut.

"He's awake," Helen shouted over her shoulder to what Stephen assumed had to be Ed. Stephen closed his eyes. *Nope, Ed's never going to let me leave the farm again.* He took a breath as he reminded himself that after last night, never leaving might not be the worst thing that could happen to him.

"Why is he upright?" Ed asked. "Did you find the source of the blood?"

"It isn't his. Claims it is the girl's."

"But there's so much," said Ed. "Did you see his jacket?"

Helen didn't answer as she stood. Ed arrived by Stephen's side. He bent down and lifted Stephen's shirt with his good hand. Stephen batted Ed's hand away. "I'm fine. Tired, but I'll live." Stephen looked to the farmhouse. There was no sign of anyone other than Ed or Helen. "Where's Bean? Is she inside? Is she really okay?"

"Bean?" Ed asked as he helped Stephen stand. "The girl's name is Bean? What kind of name is that? Bean, like in the garden?"

"Be careful saying that to her. I think she is sensitive about it." Stephen started to chuckle. His laughter turned into a fit of coughing.

Ed and Helen's eyes narrowed in sync. "A bit banged up here and there, but she's fit enough to continue on her way as soon as she finishes eating," said Ed. He lowered his voice. "I shouldn't have to tell you I think it would be better if you make your goodbyes quick."

"But she was hurt. I know she was. Shouldn't she stick around," Stephen asked. "I mean, at least for today, just to be sure she will be able to make it on her own?"

"No," said Ed. Helen placed a hand on his shoulder and nodded her head in the direction of the farmhouse as the sound of the door opening and closing echoed through the yard. Ed muttered under his breath, "I don't trust her."

"You don't trust anyone," Stephen muttered back.

Ed arched a single eyebrow.

"Well, it's true," grumbled Stephen. Ed took a deep breath. He opened his mouth, only to cover it with his hand. Stephen's stomach took that opportunity to growl, reminding him that Ed mentioned Bean eating. Suddenly, all he wanted was to go inside and eat a pig or ten.

Helen and Ed turned and began making their way to the farmhouse where Bean waited by the stairs. Stephen started to follow. His leg responded like a wet noodle. *So maybe you aren't as fine you think you are.* He took another step. His leg was steadier now. *That's better. Now walk it off.* He continued, trying to look as unaffected as possible. Working windmill or not, if Helen saw a limp, he might as well forget about going on another supply run any time soon. He'd be lucky if she let him leave his room.

Bean leaned against the building just outside the door as they approached, holding his jacket. As he grew closer, she looked down at his ankle for a moment, before her eyes met his. At the tavern, he'd thought they were the color of slate before, but by the light of day, they appeared more like jade. The corners of her lips inched up in a soft smile. The expression made her look like a different person. The candlelight had made her features sharp and as dangerous as a raptor's, but now, she looked like. . . his mind trailed off as he tried to come up with a word to describe her. *Girl,* his mind grunted. She looked like a girl, and his mind didn't mean the child kind. Thoughts of food evaporated as he found himself very reluctant to see the last of her.

"Glad to see you decided to wake up," said Bean as he reached the farmhouse. "Here," she said, handing him his jacket back. "Though I don't know how useful it will still be." The jacket was covered in mud and grass and smelled like a bonfire. "What a night," she commented, as if the near-death girl he had carried the night before never existed.

"I've had better," answered Stephen. Helen and Ed were no longer by his side. A quick glance around told him they must have gone back inside, though he hadn't heard the door close. Then again, knowing how paranoid Ed could be, he guessed they hadn't gone too far out of earshot. "How are you acting like you are perfectly normal?"

She glared at him. "I am perfectly normal."

"I don't mean it like that. I mean, how are you not dead?"

"And how is that better?"

"Gah." He pinched the fabric at the jacket's shoulder. The bits of fabric not covered in dirt were pockmarked with burn marks, rips, and charred edges, but he didn't see a bloodstain where he thought one should be. *Weird.* "The knife. Me carrying you all night? Any of that ring a bell?" He dropped the ruined garment. Helen might be able to salvage a rag or something similar out of it later.

"Not really. I mean, I remember you saying we should stay in the woods last night. Then I fell asleep, and when I woke up, we were here and I was wearing that." She shrugged. "I'm not even going to ask what you did with my sweater. You're just lucky I had something on underneath." Her expression softened. "Your parents were pretty worried about you, especially when you didn't wake up right away. Your mom wanted to move you inside, but your dad was afraid you'd hit your head or something. I told them your skull was too thick to be damaged, but maybe he was right."

Had he fallen asleep in the woods, too? Was the entire race ahead of the storm the result of a bad dream?

"They aren't my parents," Stephen replied without thinking. *Why did you have to go and say that?* He scanned her face for a reaction. She chewed the bottom of her lip but didn't ask for clarification. *Great. Now it's awkward. Don't be a freak. Say something. Get back on topic.* "You look tanner today." *You look tan? What the heck? You sound like an idiot. Maybe she's right about that thick skull, after all.* Stephen grimaced, thinking of how much time had continued to pass. *Ugh. She hasn't answered. Say something. Do something.* His stomach took that moment to rumble loud enough he was sure the sound could be heard by the barn. *Way to go. She thinks you are an idiot and a freak.*

Bean's smile returned in force. "Hungry much?"

Great. Now she's laughing at me, Stephen thought. His cheeks began to burn.

"I know the feeling. You should eat." She gestured at the farmhouse door as the smell of food emanating from inside tempted his nose. "It is amazing what a little food will do."

Stephen remained frozen in place.

"Well, I guess it's time for me to head out then." Bean glanced out to the forest. He saw her swallow.

"You don't need to go yet," he heard himself say. *Wasn't this the same girl you couldn't wait to get rid of the night before?* He waited to hear Ed object from the inside of the house, but the objection never came. *Maybe they aren't eavesdropping after all.* "You should rest. Besides, you'll need a guide to get back to the main road."

The corner of her lip turned up. "I've survived worse. Really, I'll be fine. Now, go and grab something to eat before whatever was in the woods with us last night misinterprets that growl as a mating call."

"I'm not that hungry." His stomach grumbled. *Liar.* Unwilling to make eye contact after, he followed her gaze to the forest. "And what if the Watch is still looking for us?" *When did 'us' happen?* Stephen found himself wondering.

Bean's lips tightened. "All the more reason for me to go. You've done enough."

"What about the Watch?" Helen asked from the doorway. Stephen jumped. His guardians had been listening, after all. She made a *tsking* sound. "When you didn't come inside, I started to worry you collapsed again." She crossed her arms over her chest once more and looked at him like he was ten years old again. "I also came back to tell you that your food is ready, but that can wait."

"Wait for what?"

"Don't even try to pretend you don't know what I am talking about. Why would the Watch be looking for you? They shouldn't even know you exist."

"I told you. There was an explosion." Stephen caught himself looking over Helen's shoulder for Ed.

"So, you did, but you didn't tell me why the Watch—who you said may have been responsible for it—would be interested in you." Her fingers began tapping her arm, signaling the countdown before the end of her patience. The same gesture would send Ed scurrying to make amends in seconds. Faced with all its implications, Stephen now understood why Ed ran.

Helen's face transformed as he related the events from the night before. By the time he finished the story, her face was pale but as hard as granite. Helen turned to Bean. The icy chill of her gaze sent a shiver down Stephen's spine. Gone was the face of the kind woman who had kissed his injuries growing up; in her place stood a woman capable of gutting Bean like a lion might a gazelle.

"Your turn." Helen's tone commanded an answer.

"My turn for what?"

"To tell why they were really chasing you."

"He told you what happened. The Watch came. They'd found out about the illegal trading going on in the tavern. I knew that they were on their way and was there to warn Jim."

"Right. And it so happens that they picked last night of all nights to stop turning a blind eye to what has been going on there for years." Helen clucked her tongue. "I don't buy it. Everyone knows about Piper's. And no one, not even those in charge, wants to see it shut down. What goes on in there may be against the rules, but it is all that keeps the people from rioting out of hunger some months.

If they were there, it meant that there was something—or more likely *someone*—worth their attention." Bean's lips twisted as Helen continued, "And I know that someone wasn't Stephen, not until you dragged him into whatever mess you're in. I hate repeating myself, but I'll ask again. Why is the Watch interested in *you*?"

Bean's hand reached back and touched the farmhouse wall. Her lips tightened. She pushed away from the wall. Spinning on her heel with the forest to her back, she met Helen's gaze full on. "You're better off not knowing."

Helen's frown deepened as Stephen winced. He had seen her mad enough over the years to be able to anticipate how she would respond to such a blatant challenge, and it didn't bode well for Bean. His body tensed in anticipation of the imminent fireworks. Instead, Helen turned to him. "When the Watch comes, I expect you to turn her in."

"Oh, you don't have to worry about that. I'll be long gone before they arrive."

"Is that so?" Helen replied, placing her body between Bean and the forest beyond.

"Trust me. If you would move to the side, I'd leave now."

Helen's arm shot out, grabbing Bean before she could take another step.

"Hey. What's the big deal?" She twisted in Helen's grip to no avail. "Let me go."

Muscle developed from years of farm labor had given Helen an unbreakable grip. Stephen winced. She'd used it on him a time or two as a kid when he'd tried to skip out on chores.

"Seriously? What's your problem?" Bean continued to struggle against Helen's hold. "I'll leave now, and you'll never have to worry about me ever again. All you have to do is let me go."

"Unfortunately, I can't do that. Now that the Watch knows about us, we need to give them a reason to believe we aren't a threat." She turned to Stephen. "I'm sorry, but this is the only way."

The ground below his feet seemed to shake as a sound like thunder rumbled in the distance. The field of grass parted as the tops of heavy-duty vehicles came into view.

"Let her go." Stephen pulled at Helen's arm. "I didn't carry her all this way just to hand her over to people who might kill her."

Helen shot him a pointed glance. "You made a mistake."

Stephen blinked as Helen's words registered. The question echoed his guilty thoughts from the night before. *Had it really been a mistake? Should I have left her in the woods? At the tavern?* He remembered the voices in the alley and the rustling in the woods. He might have dreamed the knife wound, but there had still been a real danger. *No,* he told himself. *You made the right call.* "I was just trying to do the right thing—to protect her."

"And now I'm trying to protect you. To protect us." Helen's shoulders slumped as the fight left her. "We've always known you were a good boy." Her body sagged as if it had aged another decade. "It's just unfortunate you couldn't prove us wrong this once."

Taking advantage of the distraction, Bean slipped from her grip and bolted behind the farmhouse. Helen looked in the direction where she had run, but the girl had vanished into the countryside. Helen's lips tightened, but she made no move to pursue. "There goes our bargaining chip."

"It's better this way."

Helen patted his arm. "Oh, sweetie, if only that were true." She leaned away from Stephen and shouted toward the door. "Ed, we are about to have more company."

The spring screamed in protest as Ed flung the door open and joined them outside. "Go to the barn, Stephen," he ordered, throwing a backpack at Stephen. "And take this with you. In case you need to run."

"But what about you?" Stephen struggled to pull the pack on. It was strange. He'd never seen it before. Where had Ed had gotten it from?

"We can handle this. Now go before they see you."

"Ed. . ." began Helen.

"I said go."

A car door squealed on rusted hinges, but Stephen did as instructed. He raced toward the barn. *This is a big misunderstanding,* he thought as he came to a stop across from the windmill. *I did nothing wrong. I should just go back there and explain myself.*

From behind him, Stephen heard the sound of a second door opening and the same woman's voice from the night before carried over the worn path between house and barn. Though he'd convinced himself he didn't have any reason to fear, he stayed in the shadows as he continued his approach.

"I apologize for bothering you folks, but you didn't happen to see a pair of young people pass by, did you? A boy and a girl, between eighteen and twenty years old?" she asked. "I'm Dr. Lambda, with the Watch."

Ed answered, "We don't see very many people out here. Prefer it that way."

"We don't want any trouble," Helen spoke up.

"Nor do we, but you should know there was an incident in town last night, and we have reason to believe they witnessed it. People died. Property was destroyed. We're looking for answers."

"I saw a girl, but I sent her on her way. That way," Helen added.

Stephen scowled at the speed in which Helen had given Bean up until he realized that she gestured in the opposite direction from where he'd seen her flee.

Dr. Lambda nodded to someone in one of the other trucks who fired their engine back up and began backing out of the field. "Thank you. I can't tell you how refreshing it is to know there are still honest people in this world."

"We're good people. We just want to stay here and grow our crops in peace."

"And no wonder. It is such a lovely place. Now that I know about it, I'd love to visit more often."

"Ah, well . . . please don't take this the wrong way, but we'd prefer to be left alone."

"I understand your position, but I'm a doctor. Perhaps one of the only ones left in fifty miles. I would feel it is my duty to check in on you from time to time. You might think I am exaggerating, but I've seen whole families wiped out by a sneeze. Families who might have been saved if they'd been less quick to turn me away. You wouldn't want that to happen to you or your husband." She craned her head to the side. "Or your son."

Stephen stepped out of the shadows.

"It's nice to see you again."

"He's a good boy," Helen interrupted, throwing her arm out as if to stop Stephen's approach. "He's never even been to town on his own before last night."

"I'm sure he is, which is why you should have nothing to worry about. We just need him to come with us so we might get to know him a little better. He'll be back with you in no time." She paused and tapped her temple. "In fact, now that I think about it, perhaps it would be best for your nerves if you came with us, too. Both of you."

The truck's doors opened again as several men exited.

"I don't suppose we have any choice," Ed commented.

"You always have a choice," the woman replied. "I just am hoping you make the right one."

seven

A medicinal scent picked at Stephen's senses. It was like the rubbing alcohol Ed used to treat his constant wounds but several times stronger. The smell grew more intense as Dr. Lambda gestured for Stephen to climb into the closest vehicle while she followed inches behind. *She must bathe in the stuff*, thought Stephen as he watched the other pair of men similarly escorted Ed and Helen into the other truck.

"I didn't catch your name before," said Dr. Lambda while closing the door. She followed Stephen's gaze. "I'm sorry I had to separate you from them, but it would have been a little too cramped on the way back to the Watchtower." When Stephen didn't reply, she added, "We were expecting to bring back two."

"Stephen," he grunted as he swung the backpack around and positioned it on his waist.

"Stephen?" she repeated.

"Yeah, you asked me my name. That's it. See, I'm willing to answer your questions. Why can't you ask them here?"

The corner of Dr. Lambda's lip curled up as her gaze met that of the truck's driver. "Ah. Well, you see, as I mentioned before, we're not used to people being honest with us, and find it best when we ask our questions in a more . . . controlled environment. You know. Where we can be sure to check everything off all at once? For example, I noticed you haven't given me your full name."

"So what?" replied Stephen, ignoring her implied question. "Are you going to torture me for it?"

"Torture you?" Dr. Lambda laughed. "Why ever would you think we'd do something like that?"

"Oh, I don't know. Maybe it has something to do with the fact that everyone in town is terrified of you."

Dr. Lambda's smile slipped. "Earthaven is full of bored individuals who would do well to spend less time making up stories and more time contributing to the greater good." She sighed. "I recognize our methods might seem intrusive to some, but it is for the best. How else can you be sure that the neighbor who keeps to themselves down the road isn't stockpiling weapons that could be used against you when food grows short, or carrying the next strain of virus that can take out the rest of us?" Her voice softened as she looked at him. "You are too young to under-stand."

Stephen snorted and rolled his eyes.

Dr. Lambda shook her head. "You think you do, but you don't. You have no idea what it was like. When the economy collapsed, and the children began dying." She closed her eyes. "And for what? So people had an excuse to wait in line for the next big gadget?" Her chest rose with a deep breath, and when her eyes opened, they were clear and bright. "Well, we sure aren't waiting in line now." Her back straightened. "I vowed we'd never be so irresponsible again. Not if I could help it. Not on my watch."

The driver slapped his palms on the steering wheel in his support.

The gravel drive that once served to connect the house with the main road hadn't been maintained in years and was now more ditch and grass than drive. The vehicle carrying Ed and Helen dipped and stopped. Its driver exited and gestured for their driver to roll down his window. "Sorry. I must have hit a pothole or something. I think we blew a tire," said the first driver to the second. "Damn post-apocalyptic infrastructure. Can't anyone bother to fix a road?" Their driver grunted in agreement. "Can I get some help changing a tire?"

Dr. Lambda motioned for their driver to assist the other vehicle. He switched the engine off and rolled the window back up. Dr. Lambda reached over and locked the door before Stephen could react. "Now that we are alone, there is another reason I wanted to talk to you. My men found blood in an alley next to the tavern."

"I don't know anything about that."

"But I think you do because I think it's yours."

Stephen remembered landing in the dumpster and spitting blood from his bruised tongue. "So? Is that a crime? You try jumping from a burning building and not getting a little banged up."

"You could have gone out the front door. That's what a normal person would have done."

"Oh yeah? A piece of the building across the street just came flying through the front window. Forgive me if it didn't seem like the safest place to be."

Dr. Lambda's lips narrowed. "I can see I've upset you."

"Oh, I'm not upset. I just don't know anything and would prefer to be able to eat some breakfast and maybe sleep in my own bed right now." His stomach growled as his faked yawn became a real one.

She reached into a cooler by their feet and pulled out a small apple. Handing it to him, she said, "I'm sorry, but you won't be sleeping in your bed for quite some time."

"Because you are taking me to your headquarters to torture me." Unable to resist, he bit into its side. It was more delicious than any of the shrunken fruit they were able to grow and harvest. *It must be nice to be allowed to use machines.* It was gone all too soon.

"Again, with the torture. No, because you are going to do a job for me."

"Yeah, thanks for the offer, but you see, I'm all booked up with the harvest coming up." He handed her the core and eyeballed the contents of the cooler.

"Agree to do this job for me and, not only will I take care of your parents, but I'll also make sure it is clear your family is under the Watch's protection. We could locate a working tractor for you or help you rebuild that windmill of yours. We have the best mechanics. Moreover, you wouldn't have to worry about trading in secret anymore either. Being a friend of the Watch has a number of advantages."

Stephen thought of Ed's wounded hand. He thought of the chores that could go so much faster with equipment that worked. He channeled his best Helen impersonation. "I'm listening."

"There is a tower east from here. I want access to it."

"Why don't you go there and do it yourself?"

Dr. Lambda's lips tightened before answering. "If it was that simple, I would. But I am afraid the residents have been less than accommodating."

"So why do you think they'll put out the welcome mat for me?"

"Because I believe you share a version of the same affliction they do."

"Affliction?" Stephen blinked. "As in, you think I am sick?"

She placed a hand on his knee. "Not sick; at least not yet. There is something wrong with your DNA. Think of it as a genetic disorder. One if not both of your parents were seduced into thinking they could somehow alter their DNA without consequences. They were wrong. Delusions. Insanity. Homicidal tendencies. Those are just the start. You've been fortunate to have managed to hold it back for this long, but it is only a matter of time before the negative side effects come out of their dormancy."

Had Bean's knife wound and the glowing forest floor been early symptoms?

"What kind of delusions?"

"The people who live in that tower have come to believe they have magical powers." Dr. Lambda leaned back and sighed. "That they can do things with their bodies. Shapeshift. Become invisible. Some probably think they can fly. Those are the claims we've heard about." She shook her head. "Unfortunately, few are seen outside. We don't know how many there are or what goes on inside, but we do know it's a cult, and like any cult, each day it goes unchecked will make it more dangerous. Not just for its members, but for the rest of us as well. I need access to the building and its residents so I can study the cause and determine a treatment before people like them cause further harm."

"And you think these crazy people will let me in?"

"Not crazy. Deluded, but yes."

"And if they don't?"

"You have to make sure they do."

"And what if I say no?"

"Then I'm afraid your parents might be staying with me for quite some time."

Stephen looked into the rearview mirror. The top of the motionless windmill poked out over the top of the tall grass. The rest of the farmstead was out of view.

"I'm sorry, but I do need to hear you say yes."

The doctor's words came back to him. You always have a choice. *Yeah, easy for her to say.* "Okay. I'll do it."

"Excellent." She handed him a slip of paper. "Here are directions. You'll know you are almost there when you get to the bridge."

Stephen stared at the directions. He wouldn't need them. He took a breath. He'd seen them before.

"Now don't tell anyone you are working for me, even those you meet on the street. The people who live in the tower don't leave, but they might still have friends. I'll make sure my people are following you. Run from them. Hide. Tell the people at the tower we are after you. That you are being persecuted. It will make your story seem more believable and make them less likely to kill you on the spot."

"Wait, what?"

The vehicle in front of them lurched forward as the man who had been driving their truck turned and began walking back. The first vehicle was well underway when a rock streaked across their view, hitting the returning driver who crumpled to the ground.

"Where did that come from?" Stephen asked. Dr. Lambda remained in her seat. "Aren't you going to go help him?"

Dr. Lambda smiled. "No. This simplifies matters."

"Simplifies? How? What?"

"You have two weeks to find me a way in, or we will be forced to find another way. You should know, not everyone's methods in the Watch are as peaceful as mine. Lives are now in your hands."

Another large rock flew into the windshield, producing a hairline fracture in the glass.

"Roy?" Dr. Lambda opened her door and leaned out, her face a mask of concern. "Everything okay out there?" Her body went limp as she tumbled out the vehicle, taking the antiseptic smell with her. Stephen clenched his fists, preparing himself to fight this latest threat.

"You coming?" Bean asked, grinning from the tall grass by the driver's side as she waved for him to follow her outside. "Or do I need to send you an invitation by carrier pigeon?"

"What the. . .? That was you? How? Why? Are they dead?"

Her eyes twinkled in the light. "A, I'm a fast runner. B, I'm rescuing you; feel free to thank me later, by the way. And C, not even close. Not that I didn't consider it. Now I'd suggest you come with me, because I really don't think you want to be around when they wake back up. Trust me."

Stephen's hopes lifted. "What about my folks?"

Bean's smile slipped. "What about them?"

"The Watch put them in the other truck."

Bean chewed her lip as she glanced down the road. "Yeah, they are long gone by now," she replied with a small shake of her head.

"Right, but if the doctor is here"—Stephen gestured toward the unconscious figure laying on the ground—"wouldn't they come back when they noticed she's not behind them? We can rescue them, too." It was perfect. All they needed was to hide and wait for the truck to come back. Then they'd free Ed and Helen and then disappear together. There was no need to go to some tower to the east and risk his life over some crazies. *Except you heard the doctor. Without a treatment, you might be going crazy, too.* Running away would also mean abandoning the people in the tower to the mercy of the Watch—everyone in the tower, including the one person in this world he considered a friend.

She frowned. "Yeah, that's not a good idea. Their guard was down and I got in a lucky hit, but they will be on alert now, especially if they see either sleeping beauty. Don't forget there's still more of them than there are of us. We only saw three trucks, but there could be more waiting at the end of the road. No, we need be far away from here before anyone thinks to come back. You know these woods. Any ideas where we can hide?"

The doctor's comment about things simplifying now made sense. Bean's rescue provided the cover he would need, but she would have to come with him if it were to work. "Well, we can't hide in the barn."

She groaned in exasperation. "Then we go someplace else. There's got to be another place you can think of. Somewhere no one else would think to look. Not even your parents-but-not-parents."

Stephen grimaced at the way she threw the words he'd used to describe Ed and Helen back at him but did not argue. "There's a guy I know. But I should warn you, it's a bit of a hike."

Bean's grin returned. "I don't mind walking. Which way?"

"Northeast." *Wes, that invitation better still be open.*

⸺ ⳾ ⸺

"You haven't had many dealings with the Watch, have you?" Bean said.

"Never had any reason to." He strained his ears to hear any sound of pursuit. Dr. Lambda had said her people would chase after them, but seeing how she'd slumped when hit, there was a good chance their pursuers wouldn't know it was supposed to be for show.

"Must be nice." Bean looked straight ahead. "I've had more than enough for the both of us."

"You never did tell me why they were after you in the first place."

"No, I never did."

Stephen swatted at a group of gnats. "Well, will you?"

"Knowing doesn't make it any better." Bean started walking away again. "Trust me."

Between the buzzing of the gnats, the headache that refused to go away, and his growling stomach, he lost his hold on his patience. "And what's that gotten me? If I hadn't trusted you enough to let you inside, I might not be in this mess."

Bean spun on her heel and marched back to him until their chests were a hand span apart. "Right. It's all my fault. The Watch treating people like animals. The explosion. Almost getting burned alive. All of it. It's my fault. Yeah, I totally wanted the one person who was more of a dad to me than my own father to—" She clenched her fists. "So yeah, go on thinking that." She turned. "Jerk." She walked ahead, leaving Stephen with his mouth agape. "I could have left you with them, but I didn't."

She could have. Stephen paused. *She still could. Idiot. You need her. Remember?* Stephen glanced back in the direction of the farmhouse. He could hear the sound of shouting in the distance. The Watch must have found their fallen comrades. Thunder rolled in the distance, and the light dimmed as gray clouds began to fill the sky. *Great. Guess the drought is over.* Somehow, it seemed appropriate. He picked up his pace until he was once again beside her. When she didn't pull away, he said,

"Look, I'm sorry. I know none of that is your fault. I'm just worried about my folks, so I said something stupid. I'm afraid something is going to happen to them, and I can't do anything about it. You know?"

A squirrel darted in front of them in search of shelter from the coming deluge. Bean muttered something under her breath. Louder, she said, "Look. I know the Watch is capable of doing any number of terrible things, but your parents—or whoever they are—made it this long without catching the Watch's attention. I'm sure they can manage a few nights on their own while you figure something out."

She's right. Stephen told himself. *Even if Dr. Lambda doesn't wake up right away, there is still no reason to think either of them is in immediate danger. They haven't done anything.* He thought of Ed's bandaged hands and scars on his arms. *It might even do Ed some good, forced to get some rest. There are worse places he could be than with a medical doctor.* Wes, however, remained in danger. "Does that mean you can forget I said what I said?"

"I guess." She shrugged. "I mean your parents, or whatever you want to call them, love you, so you can't be all bad. I mean, I personally don't get it, but there must be a reason." Raindrops began to fall. "Now are you going to stand there getting soaked, or are you planning to lead the way?"

Eight

Towers, rising up in the horizon like pillars holding up the sky, caught Stephen's eye as he shook the canteen. He'd found it in Ed's backpack along with other survival gear. A sheet of thin silver material folded into a square the size of Stephen's palm had provided a surprising amount of warmth. There were also a handful of freeze-dried meals and a water filtration system, but if Ed had saved an extra supply of water for an emergency, he must have stored it in another bag. Stephen shook the metal canteen again as if that might change their remaining level of water. They had gotten lucky on the second day, discovering a creek thanks to the reflected light of the rising sun. Their luck, so early on, had made them careless. Now, even after rationing their remaining supply, they were going to have to find another source for fresh water, and they needed to find it soon.

Stephen glanced toward the horizon again. The sun, unhindered by any cloud, cast a golden hue on their surroundings as it dipped lower in the sky. *Because of course it doesn't rain when you actually need water.* As long as they kept their pace up, they might even still make it to the towers before dark. A breeze tickled his hair with icy fingers. It hit him then, exactly what the towers in the distance were. Stephen doubled his stride.

They had already passed by a number of buildings where civilization once thrived. Several windows were boarded up. More were blackened. Those that had once been stocked with goods such as food or bottled water were long since raided, but what was just as troubling to Stephen's senses was the complete lack of other souls on the roadway. Even members of the Watch had yet to make their appearance. Had the recent storms kept all the people indoors, or were the streets that abandoned? The emptiness made Earthaven feel like a metropolis by comparison.

"And you're sure you know where we are going?" Bean asked.

Stephen had gotten so used to hearing the question asked at least three times a day, he had stopped answering, but as he looked into the blacked windows of yet another warehouse that might as well serve as a tomb now, he found his confidence wavering.

"You see those towers?" He pointed ahead. "They hold up this huge bridge." He didn't know if he'd answered her again for her benefit or his own. Bean didn't appear as wide-eyed as he felt. He also didn't know if he envied her worldliness or pitied her for it either. "That's where we're going."

"Oh?" Bean asked with a smile. "Have you come this way often?"

"I've looked at maps, okay?" he grumbled, thinking about the images online he'd poured over the first time he'd received Wes's invitation. "But considering we're going to an island, it's a pretty good guess." As if in confirmation, the scent of brackish water filled his nostrils. *Water.* His thirst grew at the thought. *Would it be drinkable though, this close the ocean?* he wondered. His bad mood evaporated as it occurred to him that he was going to see the ocean. Seeing it for the first time with his own eyes would almost be worth putting up with Bean's never-ending quips. *Almost.* He shook his head. If they spent much more time together, he'd be in danger of enjoying them.

". . . we're coming." Her voice cut through the clutter that was his thoughts.

"What?"

Bean sighed. "I asked you a question. You said you know someone there. Do you have any way of letting him know we are coming?"

Stephen shook his head as he focused on the road ahead—anything other than looking in her direction. He heard her mutter, "Well, this is going to be interesting." Her foot connected with a rusted can littering the roadway. The noise sent a nearby gull back into the air in fright.

He looked at the sky again. They could make it to the bridge before sunset, but they would need to press on at full speed. Another breeze sent a shiver down Stephen's spine. He took several steps before realizing that Bean had fallen back. "Come on, we're almost there." He saw her wobble and noticed then that while her cheeks still showed dots of color, the rest of her skin had taken on a pale waxy sheen. *Way to hog the water; now she's dehydrated.* "Here," he said, walking back. He handed her the canteen.

Their fingers touched, and a spark passed between them. "Must have built up some static," she said, shifting and breaking contact. Her fingers lingered on the canteen's surface instead, but she didn't take the vessel from his hands.

"Go on, you need this more than I do."

Her lips twisted as she pushed the canteen back at him without taking a sip. "Save it until we get to the other side."

She was maddening. *Maybe there is a faster way to the bridge than the main road.* Stephen glanced up at a rusted street sign. The words meant nothing to him, but Bean wouldn't know that. *Would it have killed the people who'd once lived here to post better signage?* Tall grass grew out of a broken window across the street. Hundreds of thousands, if not millions once lived here. The majority died here, too. Living in isolation, it had been easy to think of those deaths in terms of numbers rather than people. He wouldn't be able to do that any longer.

Bean turned and her face broke out into a smile so brilliant it seemed to banish any evidence of her earlier exhaustion. "We can go by boat," she announced.

He forced a smile on his face. She didn't need to know the depressing nature of his thoughts. "Which would be a great, except for the fact that we don't have a boat."

"It's worth a look." Bean pointed to a sign alongside the roadway. "Don't you think?" Most of the text had long since been weathered away, but a mold- and dirt-covered outline of the word 'marina' could still be seen.

The rest of the signage hadn't fared much better, and Stephen's hope that they might yet reach the island before the last of the sunlight departed diminished with each step they took further away from the highway. The red sheen of twilight replaced the golden hour. Stephen found himself tiring, though Bean now walked with a bounce in her step. It was Stephen's turn to struggle to keep up. His side had begun to develop a cramp as they reached land's edge. *Yep, maddening.*

A sign painted on a faded arch announced that they had arrived, but a rusty metal gate, dotted with the remains of chipped white paint, blocked the pier itself. The long empty pier stretched out behind it. The closest thing to a sign of life was a small reddish-brown bird picking at the ground. For some reason, the shade of its feathers reminded Stephen of Ed, even though his hair hadn't been that color for years.

Marina. It might as well be a graveyard, Stephen thought, growing angry.

Cities weren't supposed to be like this. He looked at the towers across the water. The windows on the island appeared just as empty as the ones on this side of the river. Dr. Lambda said there were people there, but all he could see were broken buildings and more failed dreams. *What was the point of coming here?* There was no one left to save. He thought of Ed and Helen boarding the truck to the Watch's headquarters. *I should never have agreed to this.* Stephen's knees began to buckle under the weight of the mental refrain as he fought the urge to collapse. *I've made a huge mistake.*

Bean turned just as he reached for the back of one of the benches encircling the place. "Are you okay?"

The earth seemed to move under his feet. Stephen clenched his teeth, preventing the words that had taken over his thoughts from passing through his lips; however, it didn't prevent him from calling out in his mind. To whom, he wasn't certain, but he found he didn't care at the moment who answered.

"Stephen?"

He glanced at his hand. His knuckles were white. So white, in fact, that they didn't look like his. *When had that happened?* They looked like they would have better fit on a mannequin. Stephen's body shook as humorless laughter from the pit of his stomach began to bubble to the surface.

"Steve? Steve-O? Hey, it's going to be okay. We'll take the bridge."

His vision blurred as wet droplets streaked across his face. Last he checked; the sky was still clear. *Where is the rain coming from?* His lungs burned as he struggled to fit a breath in between the mix of sobs and laughter. A hand touched his back. *Bean. Her fault,* the small voice whispered, repeating his accusation from before. The intensity of the thought almost undid what little control remained. He gripped the bench tighter to keep from lashing out.

Her other hand covered one of his and began prying his fingers away from the metal.

"You don't want to do that," Stephen growled as his body continued to shudder.

Her hand froze for a moment overtop his. "Yes, I do," Stephen heard her whisper, and it was as if her voice was a key in a lock. His grip loosened, and then his hand was in hers once more, and her body became the only thing holding his up.

She reached up, cupping his cheek with her hand after wiping a tear off his face. He closed his eyes before she could search them. He feared what she might find. Behind closed eyes, he saw the girl on the road bathed in moonlight and the woman fierce enough to face down an approaching doom. She had ruined his life, part of him remained sure of it, and yet, and yet? Did she even feel half as conflicted about him? He realized he didn't want to know as a warmth spread from where they touched as blood began circulating in his hands once more.

Stephen lost track of how long they stood frozen by the beach near the entrance of the marina. Then, Bean pulled her hand away, causing Stephen's body to sag where Bean's palm once lay. "We're not alone," she whispered.

His eyes, dry and clear once again, snapped open at her words. Stephen turned. The water was dark like ink under the now violet evening sky. The towers on the island across the way were nothing more than black outlines.

"There," whispered Bean as she pointed to where land and water met.

Stephen followed her line of sight. "I don't see anything."

"Look again."

A light flickered midway across the water; a small, round, and white light.

"I think that's just the moon's reflection."

"Too full."

Stephen looked up into the sky. Bean was right. The moon in the sky looked like a bite had been taken out of it, but the light on the water's surface appeared to be a full circle. If it wasn't the moon's reflection, what could it be? The light's color proved it wasn't an insect. Could it be a reflection from a torch or nearby campsite? Stephen glanced around, on edge. The light from a fire would be warm and dancing, and the air lacked a hint of smoke.

Then the light blinked off, as if it knew it had been spotted. Had the Watch caught up with them again?

Stephen dropped to the ground, pulling Bean with him. In the silence, Stephen noticed now what he hadn't a few minutes earlier. A slapping sound came from the direction where the light once shone. Bean lifted her body into a crouch.

"Get back down here." He grabbed at her shirt in an attempt to pull her back down.

"It's a rowboat." Bean stood the rest of the way.

"What are you trying to do? Get their attention?" Dr. Lambda's warning that they might be killed on sight popped into Stephen's mind. *Make it look like you are being pursued.* "What if it's the Watch?"

Bean walked over to what remained of the rusted gate protecting the pier. "I think the Watch would send more than a single person in a rowboat, don't you?" Stephen, still prone on the ground, watched as Bean examined the metal bars before grasping the railing. "Besides, I thought the whole reason we are here was because you were friends with these people." She vaulted over the top of the gate as Stephen scrambled to pull himself off the ground and follow suit.

"A guy. Emphasis on *a.* Not people. That could be anyone." A jagged piece of the metal rail caught on his shirt as he attempted to mimic the jump, causing him to stumble on landing. By the time he'd caught up, Bean sat at the end of the pier with her feet dangling over the side. He grabbed her shoulder. "We have no idea whether or not whoever that is, is friendly."

"Maybe they are, maybe they're not. But I, for one, want that boat."

Stephen's hand dropped from her shoulder as he noticed the short length of metal she had pulled from the gate as she made her way over the side. It was positioned within arm's reach of her body, but still out of view from the waterfront.

The slap sound of oars on water grew louder. Whoever it was would be arriving in short order. Realizing what Bean was suggesting, Stephen grabbed the piece of the bar from her hands. If it was a member of the Watch, they might hurt Ed or Helen in retaliation. If it was one of the tower cultists, they might not let him inside and Wes might die when the Watch arrived. He looked at the bridge in the distance. Going back wasn't an option either. The bridge was too far. Bean might act invincible, but she needed water. They needed more water. He turned the metal fragment over in his fingers. *You always have a choice.*

He looked at Bean. She stuck with him this far and he'd no idea why. He had been afraid to ask for fear that she might realize he needed her more than she needed him. She was just as much a victim of the last few days as he was. He had to stop blaming her for everything that had happened. *Time to make another decision— good or bad.* Stephen nodded to himself. He'd brought them this far. He'd take them the rest of the way. "Go hide. I've got this."

Nine

Stephen clutched at the metal spike as he readied himself to do whatever it took to capture the vessel. *You got this. You got this.* The pier creaked as Bean moved around behind him, though her footsteps were silent. The metal pressed into his hand. If he gripped it any tighter, it might break through the skin. He took a deep breath. *Here we go.*

"Yo, can you help me tie up?" shouted a voice from the boat as a figure rose to a half stand.

At first, all Stephen noticed was the length of rope in the figure's arms. Another idea crossed Stephen's mind. Perhaps it wouldn't come to extreme violence. All they had to do was scare him, then tie him up and go on their way. No one had to get hurt. Given another option, Stephen's heart began to slow its pounding refrain.

"Yeah, you. On the pier. Little help, man?" The figure came closer. The person holding the rope had to be similar to Stephen's age, if not a year or two younger.

Without the sound of his pulse rushing around his eardrums, Stephen caught the figure's voice. Its tone and cadence cut through his consciousness like a bullet. *Or a knife.* Stephen jumped up, releasing the metal spike into the water where his feet dangled a moment before.

"No way."

"Mont?"

"Wes?"

"Dude!"

"I take it it's safe to come out now?" Bean returned to Stephen's side from wherever she had hidden.

Stephen pointed to the boat and gestured that he was ready to catch the rope as soon as it was tossed. "It's him. I can't believe it." Stephen pointed again. "The guy. Seriously, what are the chances?" His eyes threatened to fill once more with tears. At the same time, Stephen wanted to laugh but feared that if he started, he might never stop. It was perfect. Wes would take him inside. He'd leave the door open. The Watch would come, do their inspection, create a treatment, and then Wes could come back to the farm with him if he wanted. He squashed the urge just as he had done with the tears. *Get a hold of yourself,* he thought, while tying the rope to a worn bracket on the end of the pier. "Wes, this is Bean. Bean, Wes."

Satisfied that the boat was secured, he grasped Wes's extended hand. "Nice to finally meet you." Wes tripped as Stephen pulled him onto the pier, sending a pair of glasses tumbling to the ground.

"It's nice to meet you, too," Bean replied, although her tone had an edge to it.

"Meet?" Wes's brow knit. An awkward silence passed. Then his eyes widened. Wes slapped his forehead and then extended his hand out to Bean. "Sorry. I meant that for Mont, but, er, I mean, yeah, it is nice to meet you, too. What did he say your name was? Bean? Like the—"

Stephen coughed and shook his head.

"I'm confused. If you and *Mont. . .*" She raised her eyebrow at the name but didn't correct him. "If you have never met, how do you two know each other?"

Stephen answered, "Through a gaming site."

"A gaming site," Bean repeated. "Right."

"I know what you must be thinking," said Stephen with a grin. "The network's been down for years."

The corner of Wes's lip turned up. "Not everywhere."

Stephen laughed. "Right. Not everywhere. As I . . . As *we* found out."

Bean turned to Stephen. "Are you telling me that all this time that house in the middle of nowhere has had network access?"

Stephen's cheeks burned, glad that the crimson blush he knew coloring them would be hidden in the darkness. "Just because we lived away from town, doesn't mean we're hicks."

"I didn't mean it in a bad way." Bean's shoulders slumped as she shook her head. A grin spread wide across her face, which she covered with her palm. "It's just I figured being so close to Earthaven it was one of those off-grid places, too. How did you keep it from the Watch for so long?"

"Yeah, well, don't tell my folks, okay? They didn't know about it either," muttered Stephen.

Wes took a step backward. "Right. Well, we should get going if we want to make it back to my place before midnight."

The amazement left Bean's voice. "Not that we're not grateful for the ride and all, but why are you here?"

This time it was Wes's turn to point at Stephen. "For him. Er. Um. Yeah."

"And you just happened to show up here. Now." She gestured at the rest of the marina behind them. "Doesn't that seem a little odd to you?" She looked at Stephen. "I thought you said you had no way to contact him."

Stephen glanced at Bean and then at Wes. His smile slipped. Bean was right. It was an impossible coincidence. Something was off about the situation. He took a step closer to Bean, regretting dropping the metal bar in the water.

Wes pursed his lips as he resettled his glasses on his nose. "Lucky. Not odd. Mont's never missed a week. When he didn't show up for game time, I thought either something was wrong, or he was finally on his way here. Either way, I thought I would go and find out. As this is the one and only marina left with a functional pier, it was either come here or go by the bridge. This way's easier, as you must have also realized." He turned to Stephen. "I told you not to make me track you down."

Bean caught Stephen's eye. He shrugged with relief. As impossible as it might be, Wes's story made a certain amount of sense. Bean raised her eyebrows in response, but didn't argue beyond saying, "Whatever."

Wes's held up his hands. "I get it. It's hard to know who you can trust. If I didn't know it to be true, I might not believe it either."

She looked over Wes's shoulder at the towers on the other side of the river. "So now that you've found him, do you think you can manage to get us to the other side?"

"Do you have any water?" Stephen took another look at his friend. His arms and legs were thin. By the look of him, his muscles had gotten more of a workout in the last hour than they had in the last month. Growing up on the farm had given Stephen a much stronger build. "You just need to tell me where to go and I can row, but we need a drink first if you have one."

Wes threw him a plastic bottle, which Stephen handed to Bean. Only after he'd seen her drink did he take a gulp of his own. Then they grabbed oars and were underway, but the difference in their upper body strength caused the boat to turn, and after the fourth course correction, Stephen took Bean's oar as well as his own. Soon, she was slumped on the seat and her breathing had slowed to a rhythm matching the slap of the wooden oar upon the water. Stephen wanted nothing more than to sleep as well, but there was still another half of the waterway to cross.

"I haven't been entirely honest with you. Who I am," Wes said. "I know why you didn't feel like you could leave home, but you've never asked me why I've not offered to come see you before."

Stephen clenched his teeth together to keep from responding right away. *You can't tell him you know about the cult.* "It's cool. You used a screen name. I get it. I did, too, and my folks aren't exactly the welcoming type."

"What do you know about your parents?"

Wes's question caught Stephen off guard. "Ed and Helen? Well, I know they aren't my birth parents, but they might as well be. I've been with them since I was four. But I've told you that before."

Wes's lips tightened into a fine line. "But why you?"

"Why me what?"

"It was the end of the world as they knew it. People were going mad, kids were dying, and the power grid collapsed. Why would anyone take on some stranger's kid back then?"

"They are just caring people." His eyes tightened at the thought that the people who had sacrificed so much for him his entire life could be suffering now all because of him.

"So caring that they hid you away all your life?"

Stephen frowned. "It wasn't like that at all."

"Tell me then. What was it like?"

"Ed and Helen knew my mom before she died. When the world first went crazy, Helen had gone to check on me and my dad." He shrugged as he rowed, sending the boat off course. He took another rapid stroke against a current, eager to return them to the mainland.

"So, she just decided to walk into your house and take you from your dad because the news reported a few buildings came down?"

"Rioting broke out just down the street. When no one answered the door, she found a way into my house. The streets were too dangerous. She needed a place to wait it out. She didn't expect to find anyone inside. Instead, she found me there. Alone. She didn't have a choice."

"And you're sure about that?"

"Yes."

For a while, the silence was broken by the sound of the oars as they hit the water. Then Wes spoke again. "I know I must sound like a dick, but I wouldn't be if I were you. Sure, I mean. If Helen was telling you the truth, then your dad left you, a four-year-old, home alone." The oar slapped the water. "Who does that?"

"Apparently, my biological father." Water sprayed into Stephen's face as the boat cut through the river.

"And have you ever wondered why?"

Stephen tightened his grip on the oar, as he slammed the wood into the water once more. "Of course, I have, but he never came back, and Helen gave up waiting. So, yeah, I guess you can say she took me, but I'm glad she did."

"Steady there. It took me weeks to get this rig seaworthy again. I'd rather you didn't ram it into the pier."

Stephen stabbed the water with the oars in an effort to break the forward momentum. He would have to take Wes's word that they had reached their destination. To his eyes, all that lay ahead of them were more shadows. He cringed as he heard a thud coming from the direction where Wes sat.

"Whoops. Just me getting the flashlight out. Hit the seat."

"You still have a working flashlight?" *That would explain the bright light on the water from before.* Stephen remembered goofing off with one when he was a kid. He had found it in a drawer and had spent several minutes flicking it on and off, but he had gotten a little too noisy with his play, drawing the attention of Helen. She took it away, declaring that it was for emergencies only. Then one day, years later, as he was helping pull together supplies for Ed's upcoming trading run, he found it hidden in the back of a cabinet. He pulled it out with the intention of giving it to Ed, but it hadn't functioned. The batteries inside had corroded the electrical contacts, and he had never seen another. He'd just figured there were none left. Now, seeing Wes's, he suspected it was a device people weren't willing to part with.

Wes pointed the light forward and, in its beam, Stephen could now see the pier. He adjusted their trajectory and speed until they were alongside the platform. Wes handed him the flashlight as if it was just another tool and not a family heirloom. "Hold it steady while I tie us up."

Bean sat up, turning her face with a pained squint away from Stephen and over to Wes. "Ugh. Too bright."

"Have a nice nap?" Stephen's shoulders protested as he continued to hold the flashlight up so Wes could see. *The morning is going to be rough. At least I won't have to carry anyone the rest of the way.* He noticed Bean's lips curl into a smile as if she was aware of his thoughts.

"Any nicer and I might think I was sleeping in a bed again."

"All ashore who's coming ashore," called Wes.

Stephen attempted to stand as his hindquarters protested. "How far do we still have to go tonight?"

"A few blocks, but don't worry, we won't have to go much past the barricade."

"Barricade?" Stephen strained his eyes as if he could somehow increase the projection of the flashlight's beam through sheer will alone, but he saw nothing. Dr. Lambda hadn't said anything about a barricade.

"Don't worry, it's not far from here."

"It's not the distance. I am curious as to why there is one."

Stephen heard Bean snort and suspected that wasn't because her nostrils were stopped up, although the air did smell like a combination of mildew and refuse. His own nose wrinkled in disgust.

"You'll find out soon enough," was all Wes offered as an answer.

Ten

A gust of wind took Stephen's breath away as they began their way down the darkened city street. Every step seemed to echo, and Stephen's shoulders tensed.

"What are your views on magic?" asked Wes.

Stephen had almost forgotten about the mass delusions. *Should I be honest, or should I play along?* How should a person respond to a question like that in a situation like this? He chose honesty. "That it doesn't exist."

Wes chuckled. "I'm not surprised you'd say that, but I like to think of it another way. Take technology for example," said Wes as he adjusted his grip on the cylinder in his hand so that his fingerprints fell into series of well-worn grooves. The bulb flared to life. "Imagine if you didn't know what a flashlight was." He swung the beam around until it came to a stop on a wall made of rusted car doors, cracked glass, and broken chairs at least twenty feet high. "I could call myself a wizard right now and, as far as you'd know, I'd be telling the truth." Wes opened his grip, and the barricade of debris was illuminated by the light of the night sky. Crickets resumed their chirping. "I would also be telling the truth when I say you should be careful with things you don't understand." He placed his empty hand on Stephen's shoulder. "And there is a lot here you don't understand. At least not yet anyway."

He gestured for Stephen and Bean to follow as he turned and walked toward the wall, coming to a stop where the collection of garbage appeared darker than the rest. The starlight cast shadows across his face, but not enough to hide his knowing smile. "I'd ask you if you were ready, but I suppose it's already too late for that to matter now. Here we are."

Stephen shut his mouth, which had fallen open at the sight of the barricade. In his mind, he'd expected maybe some boarded-up doors or a car or two in the way. Nothing like the monstrous wall in front of them. It was no wonder the Watch hadn't gotten through yet. He glanced around. Bean stood next to Wes. The light from the flashlight allowed him to see her lips curl in a grin. He couldn't blame her. She didn't know about the affliction or the people inside. As far as she knew, that wall represented safety, but it sent him a different message. *You are so screwed.*

"I kept saying you needed to visit sooner." Wes slapped him on his back.

Stephen sucked in his breath. *Now what?*

Wes led them one by one through a narrow path cutting through the wall. Stephen couldn't get a good sense of the wall's depth due to the labyrinth of twists and turns. He'd never find his way back to the entrance unguided. When they first entered the barricade, the stars overhead could still be seen in the clear night sky, but little by little, their light was obstructed as they continued deeper inside.

The path stopped. Wes leaned against the wall and turned off the flashlight, making the darkness around them absolute. "Home sweet home." A series of six mechanical pops broke the silence. Then a green glow blossomed, illuminating

Wes's hand on a wall-mounted keypad. Wes reached out and twisted a doorknob Stephen hadn't noticed before. A yellow light shining through the crack was Stephen's only warning before Wes pushed open the door. Stephen squinted as his eyes adjusted.

"Wow, that's bright," whispered Stephen, as if his subconscious was afraid he might scare the light away. "Where is it all coming from? How?"

"See? Magic. It exists." Wes's grin came close to splitting his face in two as he stretched his arms out as if he could touch all the fixtures. "It's amazing what you can power when all the windows in a building are made of solar panels."

"But it's so dark on the outside." Stephen frowned.

"Another trick also known as privacy glass. We found that leaving the lights on for the entire world to see attracted the wrong sort of people. When the lights come on, the glass goes dark," Wes answered. His arms dropped to his side, and the smile left his face. Wes nodded at the door. "It's also why the doors are locked and alarmed at all times."

Seeing him under the steady glow of artificial light, it occurred to Stephen that Wes looked nothing like the person he'd imagined playing the video game. He hadn't thought about it when they first met on the pier. Then again, it was dark out. *And you were getting ready to kill him; don't forget that part.* Stephen crushed that last thought. Even if it hadn't been Wes, he still would have figured out another way to take the boat. *Of course, you would have,* the small voice whispered.

"Unfortunately," continued Wes, oblivious to the darkness of Stephen's thoughts, "the panels power the lights, water filtration, and circulation systems, but little else, meaning no elevators." Wes turned down another hallway on the right where another door stood marked with a figure descending a flight of stairs and away from an icon shaped like a flame. "Just be glad I live on the third floor and not the thirteenth like some people."

Bean arched an eyebrow. "I suspect the people who live up there would say the view is better."

"You have water? As in running water?"

Wes laughed as he gestured for them to follow. "Mont, my friend. Prepare to have your mind blown."

Stephen's lower back and sides ached as they made their way through the lobby, mirroring the pain across his shoulders. He might have more muscle mass than Wes, but it was clear his build wasn't that of a regular rower. "So, how many people live here?" he asked as he massaged his side.

"Eh." Wes shrugged as he pulled open a door marked as a stairwell entrance. "Most everyone keeps to themselves. I think the only ones who might know everyone are Finn and maybe my dad."

"Who's Finn?" asked Bean before Stephen could say anything.

It was almost as if Bean could read his mind. He wanted to smile or joke about how they were now finishing each other's sentences, but even the muscles in his cheeks were exhausted. At this point, he wasn't quite sure he would have the energy to make it up the stairs.

"You'll get the grand tour tomorrow. For now, follow me."

The muscles in Stephen's side and calves burned as they climbed the last flight. When Wes stopped at the first door in the adjacent hallway, Stephen's vision blurred in relief. Wes touched the handle. There was a series of clicking sounds and another green light blazed. Inside, more lights dawned in a warm yellow glow, illuminating a large couch along one wall framed by a number of thriving houseplants. A large pane of black glass filled another wall.

Wes continued through the apartment to an open-style kitchenette where he placed the flashlight onto a stone counter. He then pulled out a pair of drinking glasses from one of the cabinets. Stephen's eyes nearly bulged out of their sockets as Wes filled each with clear water from a polished steel faucet. When Wes handed a Stephen one of the glasses, he stared at it, as if it might disappear if he blinked. Then he took a sip. He almost spit it out in surprise. Not only did it not have a mineral taste, the clear water was also cold.

Wes gave the other glass to Bean, who drank as eagerly as Stephen had. If she was as surprised, she covered it well. *Oh, come on, even you have to be a little impressed.*

"Scott? Is that you?" a voice called out from down the hall.

"Right." Wes blushed. "I got sidetracked before. About my real name—"

"You were supposed to be back at sunset." A man emerged from one of the back rooms. White tufts of hair ringed his otherwise bald head. A matching white mustache covered his top lip. "You know better. If you were missing after curfew—"

"I know, Dad. I meant to leave a note."

"What have I told you about lying, son?"

"That practice makes perfect?" Wes laughed.

The man patted his pocket and took out a pair of glasses as thick as the ones Wes wore. Placing them on his nose, he directed his attention to Stephen. "Now, who is this?"

Wes slapped Stephen on his back again, almost causing Stephen to drop his glass. "This is the friend I told you about. Mont. Mont, this is my dad." Wes paused as if debating whether to say more.

His father filled in the rest, "Dr. Edward Thomas." He extended his hand in greeting.

Stephen stood in shock at hearing the man's name. His hand stayed by his side. *First, Wes shows up on the riverbank as if summoned out of thin air, and then his dad is also named Ed Thomas?* The coincidences were getting more unbelievable by the second.

The corner of Bean's mouth quirked up as she offered her hand in his place. "I'm Bean. Thanks for the water. If I didn't come across as grateful to meet your son on the road earlier tonight, I want to correct that impression now."

The pain between Stephen's shoulders and back refused to be ignored any longer. He gave into a yawn and grimaced. Even his jaw hurt.

A wave of scarlet cascaded under Wes's skin from the top of his head down into the collar of his shirt. "Oh, man, I am so sorry. I completely forgot you'd be exhausted." He glanced at Bean, then at the couch, then at a room through another doorway that likely contained a bed. His lips compressed into a thin line. "Like I said before though, I didn't expect you to bring company." Wes's words trailed off.

"Don't worry about me," said Bean. "I can sleep on the floor."

"No," both Wes and Stephen replied in unison, causing Wes to throw his head back in laughter before muttering something that sounded like "great minds." Wes's attention snapped back on Stephen. "There's a thought." Wes's forehead knit as his eyes took on a vacant appearance.

"What is?" Stephen asked while looking longingly at the couch.

Then the dazed look was gone and Wes was once again smiling. "Finn will let me stay in his spare room. I'll need to go there and tell him about you two anyway." Wes sheepishly looked at his father. "I mean, that is, if you don't mind letting them stay here without me?"

"I suppose." His father looked at Stephen and Bean. His lips twisted, sending his mustache up like a furry cloud. "Unless you two would prefer to share a room."

Bean laughed. "We're not like that."

Stephen's cheeks burned, but that was due more to Bean's quick denial than Wes's father's implication. Wes also looked stricken. "I didn't even think of that," he said. He flared crimson from neck to forehead. "I mean, sure. That would work, too. If that's what you both want."

Bean caught Stephen's eye. "I'd settle for sleeping any place where I don't have to listen to anyone's snoring."

"I don't snore."

"Well, I guess that is settled then." Wes's father turned to his son. "We'll discuss this more in the morning." Then he disappeared back down the hall the way he came.

Stephen closed his eyes and gulped down the rest of his water, enjoying the cool sensation that followed as the liquid flowed down his throat while he regained equilibrium. When he opened them, Wes was gone, leaving only he and Bean in the kitchenette.

"I hope you know I meant it," said Bean.

"Meant what?" His thoughts went to her quick dismissal of their relationship.

"Meant you can take the bed."

"Don't be ridiculous. Of course, you can have it." He tried to laugh, but it became another yawn.

"Why is offering you the bedroom ridiculous when even a blind person could see you need the sleep more than I do?"

Stephen sputtered. "Because . . . because you're a—"

"A *what?*" Bean scowled. "A girl?" She closed the distance between them until she was so close, he thought he could almost hear her heartbeat. "You think I can't handle a night on a couch after a week in the woods? What do you think I am? Some delicate flower? Well, I am sorry if your whole sense of masculinity is feeling a little threatened right now, but it just needs to get over itself. I am just as strong as you, if not stronger, especially when you are this tired. If I say I can get by sleeping on the couch, then I damn well mean it."

The heat of her eyes locked on his and pulled at him like gravity. He was struck by how beautiful she looked when angry, yet at the same time, he wanted nothing more than to replace that scowl on her face with a smile. *Not a girl*, he thought. *A woman.* He closed his eyes as his body leaned in toward hers. And then he was falling backward.

"Hey. You shoved me" he shouted, incredulous.

She reached out a hand and helped pull him back upright. "You fell asleep on your feet."

"I wasn't asleep."

"Could have fooled me. You were practically snoring. And yes, you do." Without releasing his hand, she led him through the open doorway into Wes's bedroom. Then the warmth of her hand vanished as she disappeared back the way they'd come.

As Stephen collapsed onto the mattress, he thought he heard the apartment door open and shut again, but couldn't summon the energy to open his eyes or care. Instead, his last thought before sleep claimed him was, *what just happened?*

Eleven

Dozens of travel posters covering gray walls filled Stephen's vision. Disoriented, he sat up on the bed and placed his feet on the floor. As he attempted to banish the last of sleep from his head, memories of events that had led him to this place trickled in. While it came as some relief to know where he was, Stephen had no idea how much time had passed while he slept. Aside from the posters, there were no windows or clocks on the wall.

He stretched against the protests of his muscles. However long he'd slept, it hadn't been long enough. A sound of doors closing and water running caught his ear. At least one other person was awake and moving around in the apartment. He padded over to the bedroom door, opening it a crack.

"Good morning, sunshine," Wes called out from the direction of the kitchenette. Stephen heard the faucet turn off as he returned to the main room. "We were beginning to wonder if we were going to need to go to more extreme methods to wake you." Wes jiggled a raised glass and pretended to toss its contents at Stephen.

"If you'd spent much time off this island, you might not find wasting water quite so funny," said Bean taking the water from Wes and draining it in a single movement. "Ah." Her face radiated pure pleasure. "Then again, why would you ever want to leave?" The knit hat she'd worn even while she slept over the past few days no longer covered her head. Her hair was short, falling an inch or so below her ears, with a streak of pure white cutting through the balance of pale yellow. She touched her hair as if embarrassed by its condition. Stephen's gaze followed Bean's finger as it pushed a strand of hair away. "Running water also means showers." She took her cap out of a back pocket and pulled it over her head, hiding her hair from view once more. "You should try one."

The hat brought his attention back to her face. Her green eyes twinkled. Wes poured another glass, handing it to Stephen when full. "Here. Saw your supplies— or should I say, I didn't see them. You were lucky to make it to the pier when you did."

That's an understatement. Stephen winced at the thought of how empty the pack had become. *If Wes hadn't found them when he had. . .* He let the thought trail off unanswered.

"My dad would not approve. He's always going on about how everyone needs to stay hydrated," said Wes as he moved about in the kitchenette. Stephen's stomach growled in appreciation as a large slice of bread and a piece of fruit appeared on a plate in front of him. It was all Stephen could do not to dig into it like a beast. "Food is well and good," Wes mimicked his father's tone from the night before, "but water can make the difference between life and death." The door to the other bedroom opened as Stephen licked the last crumbs off his fingers, revealing Wes's father. "Speaking of which"—Wes didn't look up—"Finn says Gavin needs you."

Wes's father frowned. "Gavin can wait his turn, the same as everyone else."

Wes glanced at his father. "Do you want to be the one to tell him that?"

Wes's father's arm fell back to his side. "Fine," he muttered as he shuffled back to the door. He picked up a black bag and removed a ball cap from where it hung on the wall. "I tell them not to overextend, but what do I know? I'm only a licensed doctor. *The* licensed doctor, I should add."

Wes rolled his eyes in the direction of the apartment door where his father had exited. The gesture should have put Stephen at ease. Instead, Stephen's shoulders tightened. A sensation much like an itch danced across his skin. He had forgotten that other people lived in the building. Last evening, he had been too tired to care, but now that he was more awake, he found the idea of so many strangers in close proximity unnerving. "Why does he want to meet with us again?"

Wes shrugged. "He likes to talk to newcomers. You know, to make sure they will fit in, but it's no big deal."

Yeah, no big deal. It's not as if I have the lives of my parents and an entire tower resting on my first impression or anything. "And what happens if I don't make the cut?" Stephen joked.

Wes sent a pointed glance at Bean. *Had they talked while I was asleep? And if so, about what?* The hairs along Stephen's arms prickled, as if a winter wind had stirred them. Wes wasn't telling him something. He caught Bean's eye, and she turned away. *And Bean knows it.* Stephen's stomach turned. *You are overreacting. Your stomach's probably just not used to having real food in it again.* Another troubling thought occurred to him. *Did Dr. Lambda say paranoia was another symptom?*

"You don't look so good. I can ask for more time."

He'd lost too much time already. "Nah, I'll be fine. Lead the way."

⁓

Finn lived on the sixth floor of the building, but unlike the other floors they'd passed, a black panel fit into the wall beside the stairwell's exit door. As they approached, the panel transitioned from black to a glowing pale blue.

Wes paused. "We don't have to go in. We can go back to my apartment if you want to rest more."

"Now is fine."

"Are sure? You still have bags under your eyes."

"I don't think this Finn person will care how I look."

"What about you, Bean?"

"Do you not want us to meet Finn?" She tucked a stray hair back under her cap.

Wes blanched. "No, no, that's not what I am getting at. It's just—"

"It's just *what?*" Bean teased out. "Oh, I get it. Are you afraid we'll embarrass you? After seeing how this guy makes a first impression, I can't say I blame you."

The color returned to his face. "That's not it. Forget about it. I was trying to be considerate." Wes squared his shoulders and stood in front. The panel's glow pulsed and returned to black. Another green light illuminated on the door handle.

As Wes swung the door open, he commented, "Finn can be a little old school. You'll get used to it."

They passed several doors before coming to a stop behind one that looked identical to all the others. Wes glanced back but did not reach out to open the door. "Aren't you going to knock?" Stephen asked.

Wes shook his head. "No need." The door opened. "We wouldn't have gotten this far unless he knew we were here."

A dark-haired man stood waiting on the other side in the center of a near-featureless room. He looked to be in his early thirties, although Stephen hadn't been around enough other people to gauge a person's age with confidence, especially younger people. The plague had been hard on their generation. There was something about his eyes, however, that made him seem much older. *Being a teenager during the end of the world would do that to you.*

His hair, which was neither short nor long, swept back behind his earlobes, but the most striking part about him was the clothes he wore. His shirt was brilliant white and moved with him like a second skin as he crossed the room. Stephen stared in envy. White was impractical, and even if you found something in that color, it almost never fit and it didn't stay that way long.

"Mont, is it?" The man reached out with a hand that lacked dirt under the nails, sun-hardened skin, or other scars.

Stephen glanced down at it, unsure whether to take it. *Were delusions contagious?* The man seemed sane enough to him. *Sane enough to live the easy life.* "And I take it you are Finn," Stephen replied, grasping the man's hand in his own.

Finn released Stephen's hand with a quick nod and turned, extending it to Bean. "And you are? Bean, is it? That's a unique name."

Bean looked at Finn's hand but didn't take it. "So I've been told." She glanced Stephen's way. Her lips twitched as if daring him to laugh at a shared secret. It was a look that gave him hope that in spite of her protest the night before, she wasn't as opposed to the idea there might be more between them than she'd let on.

Finn's eyebrows rose for a moment before he dropped his hand back to his side. "Now why don't you both come in the rest of the way and make yourselves comfortable." Finn gestured for the others to follow him into his suite of rooms. "Can I get you anything to drink?"

"I don't suppose you have anything to eat?" Stephen asked as his stomach rumbled loud enough for the others in the room to notice.

Finn pointed to Wes. "Of course. Scott here will take care of getting us all some food while I get to know you both a little better; won't you, Scott?" Wes hesitated before nodding and disappearing out the way they had come.

"Normally, I prefer to meet one-on-one with our new arrivals unless they're. . ." Finn's words trailed off suggestively. Stephen's shoulders tightened. Together or not, he had no intention of leaving Bean alone with a stranger, let alone a potential deranged cult leader. Bean made no motion to suggest she was willing to go to another room either. Finn sighed. "So, not a couple, but you don't keep secrets from each other?"

Stephen fought the urge to laugh. *All we have is secrets.* "We've been through a lot."

Finn lowered himself into a velvet couch and motioned for the two of them to take a seat on the opposite sofa. "You know my name. What else do you know about our group?"

"To be honest, not much," said Stephen. *You need to earn his trust.* "You have a nice setup. I've never seen any place like it."

Finn leaned back in his chair and grinned. "Life here has its advantages. Are you interested in staying?"

Careful now. Don't seem too eager. If he so much as suspects you have another motive for being here, it will be game over.

"It seems nice enough, but I don't know."

"Let me guess. You've heard rumors."

"Maybe." Stephen glanced toward the door. How much should he say? He suspected most people wouldn't appreciate being told they were considered delusional cult leaders. *Don't forget the part about the affliction causing homicidal tendencies,* the small voice whispered.

"I assure you the truth about us is even more unbelievable. At least it can be for the average person, but you're not average, are you?"

Stephen's brow knit. *It's a trick question. Abort. Abort.* "I wouldn't know. I didn't grow up around a lot of people to compare, to." *Well done.*

Finn nodded his head. "Would you like to find out?"

Bean's pinkie grazed his.

"I suppose." *What's the worst that could happen?*

twelve

"Close your eyes and think of a wall." Finn paused. "Both of you."

Stephen cocked his head to the side at Finn's instruction.

"It will make sense soon."

Stephen glanced at Bean, who shrugged and closed her eyes. *Anything you can do. . .* A soft noise like waves crashing filled the room. Stephen had no idea where the sound came from. He squeezed his eyes shut tighter in an attempt to isolate and ignore the noise. The noise became more distracting. A sound like someone striking a metal plate joined the mix. Stephen grit his teeth. He couldn't afford to mess this up.

All he could imagine was a large black rectangle. "Try to relax," said Finn. Stephen took a breath and let the muscles around his eyelids go limp. "Good. Now try again. This time, relax your whole body." The waves continued to crash. "Focus on the wall. Only the wall." The noise grew muffled. The couch's softness was far too welcoming. He felt himself drifting off.

"Now imagine there is a door in the wall. Visualize it down to the grain." Finn's voice brought Stephen out of his half-dream state.

He kept his eyes closed as he imagined a brick wall and a small blue door. As he concentrated, the door became clearer. In his mind's eye, he visualized it made of the type of wood he'd seen in the barn, with streaks of chipped paint. Oil rubbed bronze hinges and handles decorated its surface.

"Now open it."

The door opened with ease, but there was nothing but blackness on the other side.

"You find a river." Stephen heard Finn's muffled voice command.

The blackness surged at him like a torrent of water. Stephen's eyelids remained shut, though not by his choice now. He was frozen, as if the deluge assaulted his mind. He tried to call out, but no words would come.

"Let yourself bathe in it."

Bathe? I'll be lucky not to drown, Stephen thought as he fought against the surge of darkness. His imagination was trying to kill him. *Right. It's your imagination.* Stephen focused his thoughts and imagined his arms. He visualized picking them up and moving them, forcing the darkness to part.

Still, for every inch he swam, the unseen force pulled him back. It seemed as if he would never break the dark water's surface. Without a frame of reference, Stephen couldn't tell if he was swimming up or making his problem worse. His heart raced as pressure continued to build around him. *Help!* He wanted to cry out, though that would be pointless. *If only there was some light in here.*

A faint mote of light, like the furthermost star, bloomed into existence, as if summoned by his command. As mysterious as the light's source was, it was as familiar as a mother's touch.

"Take control of the flow," commanded a new voice. It was deeper than Bean's and cooler, almost robotic, and yet feminine. It reminded him of the announcer from his video game.

Is this what it's like to lose your mind? Stephen's lungs screamed in need as he fought to take a breath. He was drowning in the inky water. *Wake up. Wake up. Wake up.* He wanted to scream. He locked his focus on the pinprick of light. The sense of direction it offered kept him from losing himself to panic. *If only it was brighter.*

A second light bloomed into existence. "You have to take control, Stephen. Now!" Bean's voice joined the other woman's, echoing her command. *Was she experiencing something like this, too?* The second light was closer, but still out of reach. Stephen's imagined arms ached as he swam to reach it.

The body that he'd visualized began to shake, and he could feel his temperature drop. Muscles that should have been a figment of his imagination cramped. Still, the light remained always a fingertip away. *You aren't going to make it.* His focus fractured as the lights had begun to fade. *Let there be light,* he wanted to shout, but no new lights appeared. *Please. Don't go.*

Thoughts became harder to form until he was left with one thought as much instinct as a word. *Help.* The lights pulsated once as he reached toward them one last time. Then both were gone, and darkness surrounded him again. Only this time, a warmth wove its way around and through the nothingness where he'd once imagined his hand. His consciousness clung to the sensation like a lifeline. Focusing on the warmth, he willed himself to rise out of the depths.

After so much darkness, the color of the painted door threatened to blind him as he emerged from the dark waters. Hovering above its torrent, he imagined a valve in the wall until he could see it as detailed as he had seen the door. He twisted it, and the flow below him slowed from a river to a more manageable flow.

Curious, he dipped one re-imagined finger into the stream. The water this time was warm to the touch. Like the door and the valve, the stream became more detailed as he focused his attention on it. As the image sharpened, he began to notice subtle differences in its makeup. The stream wasn't black at all, but instead, made up of thousands of colors and layers upon layers of images.

This time when Stephen attempted to open his eyes, his lids complied. Bean's face filled his vision. He glanced down and saw her hand grasping his own. The warmth must have been from her. *She saved me.* Her lips curved up into a sly smile. Stephen's eyes widened as blood rushed to his face. *She did not just read your mind.* He thought in a panic. *Because that would be impossible.* He blinked several times. *Yeah, because everything that's happened today is just so possible.*

"I was beginning to worry," Finn said.

Stephen snapped out of his thoughts. He had almost forgotten he and Bean weren't alone. He looked to the source of his irritation. "You could have warned me," he stated in accusation.

"I'm sorry, Stephen. I thought based on what you'd accomplished on your own, I expected it to be easier for you."

Even though he no longer saw the stream, Stephen was still aware of its presence, like smelling seawater or hearing gulls miles from the shore. Only, he detected this stream with a sense he'd never known before. He corrected himself. "What did you do to me?"

"I helped you remove a block, opening your mind to the data stream." Finn waved his hand as if almost dying from a very real case of information overload was a non-event. "It is a funny thing, the mind. It erects barriers, protecting itself from what it isn't able to process unassisted. You aren't the first to have such a barrier, though I will admit yours was more difficult to get around than most, almost as if someone else had erected it. Now I'm curious. Many of my people report experiencing something like dipping their toes into a stream or babbling brook the first time they accessed the data stream with intention. What was it like for you? A river?"

"River?" Stephen's jaw gaped. "More like I was under the bloody ocean."

Finn's eyebrows rose even further. More to himself he said, "I knew you'd be strong, but I'd never suspected. . ." He sniffed. "Well done." Louder, he added, "Look around the room, what do you see?"

He *hypnotized you. That's all*, Stephen repeated over and over in his head. *The river. The voices. None of it was real. It could also be the affliction*, the small voice added. *Next stop, crazy town; population: you.* He rubbed his face. *You aren't helping.* He blinked. Subtle colors twisted and flowed like clouds passing through the sky over the walls Stephen would have sworn were only gray when they'd arrived. *You are the one arguing with yourself.*

"Yes." Finn stood. "It was real, but at the same time, no it wasn't."

"I don't understand." Stephen looked to Bean, only realizing after a heartbeat that Finn's answer was to an unspoken question. Her brow wrinkled.

"Let's start with your parents. What do you know about them?"

"Only that they are gone, and I was raised by friends of theirs."

"Their names are Ed and Helen Thomas."

It was a statement, not a question. Was the man reading his mind? Stephen tensed. What if Finn was reading it now? What if he knew of the deal with Dr. Lambda? He wet his upper lip and tasted a bead of sweat. The tower's defenses were no joke. The Watch might not succeed, but Ed and Helen would be as good as dead. *I've failed.*

"Before you ask, I'm not reading your mind."

Stephen's shoulders sagged. *Because that's impossible. Isn't it?*

"I don't have to. Your expression gives you away." He pointed at Stephen's face and made a circling gesture. "About your name, Scott told me. In fact, he's told me a lot about you."

"I see." Stephen's lips tightened. He buried his thoughts of Dr. Lambda and the Watch, in case Finn was lying. "He's never mentioned anything about you."

"Well, I like to consider myself a bit of an enigma, but we were talking about your story. Scott calls you Mont."

Pull yourself together. Stephen bit his lip. *Pretend you aren't losing your mind and this is a normal conversation.* "Yeah."

"But that's not your real name. Is it?"

Stephen shook his head.

"Don't be embarrassed. We're all survivors here. Many of us have used aliases at one point in time or another. Take Scott, for example. Has he told you his real name is Prescott yet?" Finn's gaze bore into his own, daring him to look away. "No, I'm not surprised he hasn't. After all, everything you two have been doing could have gotten you both into a bit of trouble out there, were the wrong sort of people to find out first." Finn looked toward the wall as if it contained a window. "Lucky for you, the Watch is no friend of ours, as you no doubt have already guessed, or you wouldn't have come." His attention returned to Stephen. "But back to names and why I've been looking forward this meeting for a while now. Your real name is Stephen Dronigh."

Stephen froze. He might have mentioned Ed and Helen's name to Wes, but he was sure he'd never told him his real name and he knew he hadn't told him his birth last name. "How?"

"How do I know your name?" Finn leaned back. "Well, that took a little more detective work. I've known your friend, Scott—or Wes if you prefer—for years, from almost birth really. When Wes told me about your little game, at first I didn't believe him. I dismissed it as a joke. It wouldn't be the first. When your world consists of twenty floors and a handful of miles, boredom can be your worst enemy. There is always some prank going on."

Finn smiled, as if savoring some memory. "But then he kept talking about you and that there were people living away from our island who were able to not only access but maintain a network. With all the challenges on the outside, I found it strange that someone would set one up for something as silly as a game."

"It's not that silly," grumbled Stephen.

"Oh, I am sure it has taught you all valuable sorts of things, like trash-talking. Scott shows off those particular skills daily."

"It teaches things like tactics—and weaponry, too."

Finn smiled. "And have you had to put these skills of yours to regular use outside the game?"

Stephen didn't need to see a mirror to know that his cheeks were now as red as Wes's hair. "I live in the middle of nowhere. I thought it would be good to be prepared."

Finn's smile faded. "My apologies, I forgot what it is like out there." He stood up and walked behind his couch. "So then one day, months later, Scott—I mean, Wes—mentioned something even more remarkable than an online friend." Finn glanced at Bean. "Are you still sure you want her to hear the next part?"

Stephen nodded. *It's not like she wouldn't simply ask me about it the minute we left the room.*

"He and his friend shared more than the enjoyment of a video game." Finn's fingers tapped the back of the couch twice before stepping away. "Your guardians and his parents just happened to have the same name. You see, his mother's name was Helen, too."

"Their names aren't that unique." Stephen shrugged, though if he wasn't trying to school his features, his eyebrows might have launched into the ceiling at Finn's revelation. *Yeah, it's totally normal. Helen, Ed, Thomas. All common names. I wouldn't be surprised if there once were tens of thousands of them. There is no reason to freak out. No reason at all.*

Finn began strolling around the room until he came to a stop by the color-shifting wall where the undulating lines blended together until Stephen could almost make out a shape. "You might not see it as anything more than a simple coincidence, but I have always prided myself in my ability to recognize a bigger picture, and that was one coincidence too many." The colors shifted, and the phantom image was no more. "It made me start to wonder about your story. And you."

It was one too many coincidences for Stephen as well, though he tried to hide it from showing on his face. "Me? Sorry to break it to you, but there isn't all that much there. I live in the middle of nowhere and like to go online and play a game from time to time. End of story."

Finn stepped away from the wall and turned to Stephen. The corner of his lips quirked up. "But that's just it. How has a person in the middle of nowhere, as you put it, managed to get a game back up and running well enough to be able to connect with the systems we have in place here?"

"It wasn't hard," Stephen muttered. He groaned inward. *Once again, way to win friends and influence people.*

Finn's half-smile evaporated once more. His jawline hardened. "Yes, it is. I designed it that way." Stephen sensed more, then saw Bean tense by his side. "So, when I found out some random unknown person from hundreds of miles away had somehow managed to hack his way past our defenses, I had to learn all about him. After a little digging, I learned who and, even more importantly, *what* you are." Finn eyes locked on Stephen's and burned with excitement.

"I'm not a hacker." The argument sounded weak, even to his own ears.

"You are. But you are so much more than that, too." Finn shrugged as the humor returned once more to his expression. "As you should be, considering who your parents are."

"I told you. I don't know them."

Finn shook his head. "But that's my point." Finn returned to his couch, but did not sit down. "I do." Meeting his eyes, he said, "Wes isn't the only one here I've known almost since birth. I knew your father. His name was Alan, and you should know his original discovery is what made all of this possible. Which reminds me, you didn't answer my earlier question. When I stood over there, against the wall, what did you see?"

Fourteen

The colors continued to flow across the wall; some grew while others shrunk, creating more shapes. *The test isn't over.* "It was a raven."

"A raven? How interesting. Why a raven?"

Was that the wrong answer? "I thought I saw wings and a beak."

Finn shook his head. "I meant why did you call it a raven and not an eagle or crow?"

"I don't know. Because that's what popped into my head?"

"How about you, Bean? I've been going on and on about Stephen here, but that was rude, and I apologize. What did you see?"

The room fell silent. Stephen swallowed his guilt as he waited for Bean to answer. He'd forgotten Finn was testing both of them. *What if she saw something else?* Another thought occurred to Stephen. *What if she hadn't seen anything at all? Did she now think he was crazy?*

Bean's face was that of a statue, hard and as pale as marble. Her eyes tightened, and she glared at Finn. "A doll. I saw my sister's doll."

Did that mean she had the genetic marker, too? Stephen didn't know whether to sigh in relief or in concern.

Finn's eyes softened. "For what it is worth, you both—" Finn's eyes took on a vacant expression similar to how Wes's looked earlier. "Ah, your food has arrived."

The door opened, and a man carrying a pair of small loaves entered. He threw the loaves Stephen's way as he crossed the room, stopping next to Finn. "Sorry, I know you hate interruptions, but we've got company."

"How many this time?" Gone was his cordial tone, replaced by that of a military commander.

"Two that we've spotted," the newcomer replied.

"So there could be at least one or two more," Finn muttered. "Let everyone know to meet in the lobby. I'm on my way down."

The newcomer nodded and returned the way he came.

"What's going on?" asked Stephen, passing one loaf to Bean as he tore into his. He'd always had an appetite and never enough food, but his constant hunger was beginning to be ridiculous. *Man, is this bread good.*

"Some uninvited guests," answered Finn. He smiled. "We'll send them on their way. Nothing to worry about." Finn flung the door open and marched out into the hallway. He glanced over his shoulder at Stephen. "However, you will want to see this."

Bean shrugged her shoulders. "Why not?"

Finn smiled, but the expression showed no joy. He stormed down the stairs without turning to verify that they'd done as instructed.

They met a group of the tower's residents in the lobby at the base of the stairwell, including the man who'd brought the loaves. Stephen searched for Wes and was struck by how young they all looked, but his friend was not among them.

The others parted as Finn made his way into the center of the group. Stephen's heart began to race. It took him more than a few beats to realize that the lack of wrinkles was putting him on edge. *Nothing weird about that. This used to be a big city,* he reminded himself. *There are bound to be more young people than Earthaven.* Stephen remembered that Wes's father was working somewhere in the building. *He's not your age.* Which meant, there had to be other adults around. *Just not in this room.*

"Report," Finn barked.

A girl with a face smeared with dirt stepped forward. Some of her hair had slipped out of a tie at the back of her neck, but she didn't seem to notice. Her clothes were more in line with Bean and Stephen's own, making the cleanliness of Finn's white shirt even more striking. "It's the Watch again. Spotted the gaudy armband a mile away."

Finn's lips turned down, but the frown did not reach his eyes. "I'd hoped they'd learned their lesson the last time."

"He appears to be armed."

Finn waved the comment away. "I suppose that's to be expected."

Another voice spoke up. "I spotted a second one coming in from the North, fifteen to thirty minutes behind. Stephen did a double take as he located the voice's owner. Somehow, Stephen hadn't noticed him in the small group. The others shifted, providing Stephen with a better view. It didn't help. It was as if the speaker, another twenty-something, was a floating talking head. It took a second or two before Stephen realized that it was an optical illusion. The guy's shirt had some sort of patterning on it that made it seem as if the design was blending into the background all on its own. It wasn't the sort of camouflage featured in Stephen's video game, but that was exactly what it was.

"I thought that route was closed."

"It was last time I patrolled," said the floating head, "but it's wide open now. A train could pass through it."

"What do you think they want?" asked another girl, even younger in appearance than the first. She held the fabric in her hands, which she handed to Finn as she spoke. Finn's hands moved at a near inhuman speed, covering his brilliant white shirt with her offering. He touched a spot near his neck, and his torso also seemed to blend into the background no matter how he moved. He touched his waist, and the color of his trousers shifted, mixing with the shadows. The effect made Stephen sick to his stomach.

They could be here to help with your story like Dr. Lambda said. This is your chance to win their trust. "Um, they might have followed us," answered Stephen. More of the group swapped out their regular garb for the pattern-shifting garments. It was an act of supreme will not to turn away. "I had some trouble a few days ago, and well. . ."

The girl laughed. "I guess that's unlucky for them." A couple of the others in the group also joined in.

"I thought Wes reported finding you by the river," said the man who had brought them the bread.

"Gavin," said Finn "there will be time for our guest to tell us the rest of his story later." Finn placed his hand on the pad by the door. The green light blinked twice. "Gavin, Baron, you take point. The rest of you, you know what to do." The group nodded before they disappeared into several directions. "Stick to the shadows," cautioned Finn as he held the door open so that Stephen and Bean could pass. A narrow cord appeared in Stephen's hand. "Make sure you don't drop that. You don't want to be stuck out here." The door shut on silent hinges as Finn pulled a hood over his head and climbed a ladder that had gone unnoticed the day before.

Then, they were in the maze of the barricade but several levels higher than the one they'd taken before. Stephen couldn't afford to focus on anything other than each step as they made their way through a path of twists and turns. A single misstep off the narrow ledge would send him tumbling to the ground. Higher they climbed until they reached the barricade's top edge. Bean poked his shoulder and then gestured out to the street below. Stephen didn't see anything moving, but Bean dropped into a crouch. Finn glanced down and grinned as he followed suit.

Stephen noticed the movement that must have caught Bean's eye. A figure crept along the base of the building across the street wearing the armband of the Watch as reported. The figure stood, frozen for a moment, like an animal testing the wind. Then it raced across the final feet to the base of the barricade's wall.

"I thought we made it clear your people weren't welcome here the last time," a voice boomed from below. Stephen thought it was Gavin's, but it sounded deeper and more intimidating than it had before, so he couldn't be sure.

"You are harboring a fugitive," the man with the armband replied. "Perhaps more than one." Broken glass scattered around the base of the wall, reflecting the yellow rays of the late morning sun. It blinded Stephen as he sought a better view of the figure below.

"Fugitive from the Watch?" Gavin called out. "And why should we care? You have no authority here."

"I am within my legal rights." A cloud passed across the sun dimming the glare from below. It was enough for Stephen to see the newcomer pull open the side of his jacket. Stephen made out an emblem of some kind on his chest, but then the cloud passed, blinding him again.

"Legal? Under what law?" Gavin's voice echoed across the otherwise empty street. "Not any laws we recognize." Stephen was struck by how old and formal he sounded and wondered if this particular speech was coached.

"If you do not willingly turn over the fugitives, you will give me no choice but to take them and you by force."

Disembodied laughter echoed through the square in all directions. Stephen thought he saw the Watchman pat his pocket. "You won't be so cocky once that tower of yours comes down."

The Watchman is taking things too far, thought Stephen. With or without magical powers, the people in the tower were not messing around. *You've made my case. Now walk away and let me do my job*, he urged. *No one has to get hurt.*

"Is that a fact?" said the voice Stephen recognized as belonging to the floating head, who he assumed must be Baron.

The man puffed out his chest as he scanned the barricade, searching for the source of the other voice. Another cloud, larger than before, floated across the sun's light. Stephen took advantage of the temporary extra shadow it offered. He shifted his body for a better look.

"We know about your plan."

Do they? Stephen looked around the barricade wall in a panic. There was no place for him to go but down if he needed to get away, and no chance either Ed or Helen would be freed from the Watch.

The contempt in Baron's voice was palpable and sounded much closer to the man on the street than it had a minute before. Stephen wondered if the newcomer also sensed it. "That's right. We know about your friend up the road. You think you brought reinforcements." Baron's voice now sounded like it originated directly in front of the Watchman, but still, no one else could be seen on the street. The teen might as well be a ghost. "You didn't bring enough."

No camouflage is that good, thought Stephen. *Or is it?* He looked again for a shadow or motion. Anything that might give away the teen's location to a careful eye, but the teen remained undetectable.

"Good. Then you know there are even more behind that one." The Watchman stepped back and looked around the empty city street. "This is your last chance. This goes for your other creepy friends, too. Don't think I don't know they are watching." Louder, he shouted, "You are all guilty of obstructing justice. Give up now or else."

The Watchman opened his jacket the rest of the way and pulled out a gun, but the movement also exposed a belt lined with explosives. He turned so that everyone bearing witness to the scene might see the implicit threat, and then he took another step back so that there was no part of him hidden in shadow.

Out in the open, Stephen could see the Watchman had to be in his sixties if not seventies. His thin gray hair lay in strings upon his head, and his face had a pasty yellow pallor. Deep grooves like drooping whiskers ran the length of his face from eye to chin, making him look like a man who had seen too much, and yet a fire remained in his eyes. The Watchman's gaze panned the barricade. He smiled. Stephen should have been concerned. If not for the gun or explosives, then because of the face wielding them. Instead, Stephen was relieved seeing the man's face. It could have been the face of anyone Stephen had ever seen or met in Earth-aven. Then Stephen squinted as he got a better look. It *was* a face he'd seen in Earthaven.

Fifteen

Bean's body tensed beside Stephen like a cat readying to pounce. She recognized the man, too, but based on her body language, Stephen suspected there was no love between them.

Finn's voice whispered in Stephen's ear. "You have a choice to make."

Stephen's eyes widened. "What do you mean?" he heard himself asking, though his gut told him he knew the answer.

"Choose to go with him and nothing more will happen, to him anyway. What your fate will be once off this island, however, would not be mine to say. Or join us and become the person I know your father would have wanted you to be."

Your father left a four-year-old home alone during a riot. Who cares what he wants?

"It is up to you, but I hope you understand there will be a price to pay either way you decide. Consider your friend as well, as either you both agree to stay or neither of you does. I'm treating you as a matched set."

Stephen looked at Bean who hadn't stopped scowling at the man below.

"I believe I know what she would decide."

Finn removed his hood as he stood and touched his collar, halting the camouflage effect. He removed the garment, dropping it on Stephen while revealing his brilliant white shirt. Stephen and Bean pulled back, but there was no way the man on the street below could miss Finn's figure on the top of the wall. "So you're the man in charge here then?" the man below shouted. "The doctor will be glad to finally put a face to the stories."

"I am sorry for what must happen next, but I just can't allow my children to be threatened." Finn's voice sounded as if it carried the weight of decades. "You were warned." He raised a fist.

Stephen looked back at Bean. She looked eager. His heart sank. She would never agree to sacrifice a chance for food or water for someone from the Watch. *Don't blame her. She doesn't know about the side effects of the genetic disorder or Ed or Helen.*

When he looked back, the Watchman was no longer alone. Several of the teens and twenty-somethings he'd seen in the tower lobby now surrounded the older man as he spun, brandishing his gun.

"Stay back. I'll shoot."

"Is that one of those smart guns?" One of the girls, whose neon pink hair shone so bright it was hard to believe she could ever stay hidden, laughed as she closed the distance and placed a finger on the weapon. "That's a little hypocritical, don't you think? Considering the whole technology is evil incarnate thingy."

The Watchman flicked his wrist holding the gun, knocking her hand away before aiming the weapon at the girl's forehead. Stephen pulled back as he watched the man's finger tighten on the trigger. The gun produced a clicking sound, but nothing more.

The girl smiled. "Not what you were expecting, was it?"

The gun clicked again as the man pulled the trigger again; however, nothing fired. The weapon was as effective as the sticks Stephen used to pretend with as an eight-year-old in the woods around the farm.

The time to speak up and diffuse the situation had come and gone. Stephen's shoulders sagged. His silence through the exchange had spoken volumes. Now he could only hope that Dr. Lambda would not risk sending someone else before he learned the tower's access code.

Finn looked at him. Stephen nodded, and Finn lowered his fist.

"My turn," said the pink-haired girl as she raised her hand once more and placed it on the man's extended arm. A light flashed where their skin touched, and the man dropped to the ground. The perimeter made up of others closed their ranks, surrounding the fallen trespasser until he was no longer in view.

"Is he dead?" Stephen whispered to himself.

"Laura stunned him. It's kinder than what he deserved."

Stephen shuddered at Finn's cold matter-of-fact tone. *Weren't you working yourself up to be a killer just yesterday? And that was over a boat.* Finn had a point. The man brought a gun and explosives. *He'd even pointed it at a girl's head and pulled the trigger. More than once.* He lowered his gaze from the scene. *Just because you understand, doesn't mean you have to agree with it.* "So now what?" Seeing the old man helpless on the ground, he couldn't help but picture Ed lying in a similar position, surrounded by the Watch. The Watch didn't strike him as a group who would be content to stop at 'kind.'

"As I said, I can't allow my children to be threatened." Finn stood on the wall with his chest out and his shoulders proud. The only thing missing from his profile as he looked out over his domain was a crown.

"What about the other one?" asked Bean. "His friend." She gestured at the group below. Stephen suspected his companion wasn't suffering any of the same pangs of guilt as he was. "Aren't you going to stick around and welcome him or her, too?"

Stephen turned and blinked. The group at the base of the wall was gone, including the Watchman. "Where did they go?"

"I've made my point, and they've taken him to a place where he and I might have a more private, conversation."

Stephen's eyebrow raised at the comment. "So you are going to torture him."

"Torture?" Finn chuckled. "Aren't you the imaginative one?" He sighed. "No, we aren't monsters, despite what the rumors say. I only want a chat with him. One on one. Then he'll be free to go. Although, if I were him, I might not want to leave. I would expect the reception he receives back at home after failing his mission will be quite painful." The corner of Finn's eye twitched. "But that chat can wait. I'd like to finish ours, and I don't know about you, but I could use lunch first. What do you say?"

⚓

"She wore a stunner, didn't she?" Stephen asked. The events of the past few minutes played over in his mind. He hadn't recalled anyone in the lobby taking weapons with them, but that wasn't to say there wasn't a cache nearby. He'd need to know where such a supply was just in case he needed to make a quick getaway after the Watch came back.

"A stunner?" Finn's eyebrows shot up.

"An electronic personal protection device," said Bean.

Finn's brows returned to their resting position. "Oh, I am well aware of what a stunner is, but I can't remember the last time I saw a functioning one." He cocked his head to the side. "I'm rather surprised a young person like yourself even knows what one is."

Bean snorted. "They still exist. You just have to have the right connections."

"And I'd love to meet some of your friends someday, if you'd be willing make the introductions." Finn dropped from the ladder and waited for Stephen and Bean to join him on the landing before blocking their view of the access panel with his body.

"Funny you should mention that." Stephen pursed his lips, unsure whether to ask the other question that had plagued him earlier.

"Mention what, Ms. Bean's connections?"

"No, your age. You said that like you are so much older than us, but you are, what, maybe ten years older? Fifteen tops."

Finn grinned. "I was wondering when you'd notice. Would you believe I am old enough to be your father? Older actually."

Stephen did a double take on Finn's face. Where were the wrinkles and the silver hair? If he was that much older, why didn't he look more like Ed? Was life in the tower that much easier? His jaw tightened. "So if it wasn't a stunner, what did she do? Some sort of martial art?" asked Stephen when the silence continued. He hadn't seen the girl do more than touch the man, but maybe she knew of some secret pressure point on the human body.

"Laura does have a number of skills, but how would that explain the gun not firing?"

"It jammed, and she got lucky?" Stephen suggested. "I've seen it a million times." He hadn't, outside of games and old videos he'd dug up online, but Finn didn't need to know that.

Stephen's comment, however, must have caught Finn off guard. Creases appeared his brow. "The gun was functional."

"But you can't know that. We were way up there. It could have been a dummy." Stephen pointed up.

"They always have been both real and in good working order in the past." Finn waved toward the lobby door. "Why else do you think we built a wall?"

Because you guys have been stuck on this island too long and have run out of other things to do other than drag out answers to questions for an hour, Stephen thought. Aloud, he said, "Fine then, I give up. If it wasn't a stunner, martial arts, or a misfire, how did she do it?"

"Follow me, you'll want to sit down for this." He walked over to a couch lining the far side of the lobby wall where the lighting wasn't quite as bright. The cushions were worn, and the fabric faded, but after traveling through the woods by foot for so many days and resting on the ground or the occasional fallen tree, it was like sinking into a cloud.

"Comfortable? Good. Now to answer your question, we call ourselves Sorcerers."

Just when you were starting to believe they weren't as nuts as Dr. Lambda said. Stephen snorted before he remembered that he wanted them to trust him enough to give him their access code. "Sorcerers? As in wizards?" *They would have to expect some disbelief at hearing a claim like that for the first time, wouldn't they?* He stood and tapped Bean on the shoulder. "Maybe the rumors were right, after all."

Finn raised his hand, and Stephen halted. "It's only a play on words. As in those who manipulate source code. One of my people mentioned it one night, and the name stuck."

Stephen caught Bean rolling her eyes.

"Ahem," Finn coughed, and Stephen noticed that Finn's palm began to glow as the lights dimmed further. "Have I gotten your attention?" Finn asked. The remaining light reflected off Finn's gleaming white teeth as he grinned. "It may not be magic, in the traditional sense, but what we can do is pretty close. A few years before you were born, your father was one of a small team who found a way to merge the human mind with the Internet. But what the team didn't then realize was they had gifted humanity with so much more than a new way to access data." Finn cocked his head as if enjoying some secret joke. "At least, the rest of the team didn't immediately grasp the larger magnitude of what they'd unlocked: instant knowledge, communication at a thought, total control of one's body at a cellular level, and more. Your father. . ." Finn's eyes twinkled as he shook his head. "Well, I'm reasonably sure the results of that first experiment surprised even him."

"This . . . Alan Dronigh. He's not my father. If anyone has that title, it is Ed." An image of Ed lying in a makeshift cell filtered across Stephen's mind's eye. Stephen immediately banished the thought. *They are going to be okay,* he told himself. "And while that's a neat trick, it doesn't explain what happened outside or whatever the heck you did to us upstairs." Bean tensed beside him. *You went too far.*

"But it does." Finn sighed as if he could see the thoughts torturing Stephen playing out on the other side of the room. "I thought you were one of us. Now I see I misjudged you and wasted all of our time. Your mind will never be open enough."

Idiot. Now what?

"He's worried about his parents. His Ed and Helen," said Bean. "It makes him say things without thinking." She aimed a pointed glance at Stephen. "Doesn't it?"

Stephen closed his eyes and let out a breath. *Thank you, Bean.* But would Finn be as forgiving as she was?

"It's true. The Watch took them days ago. It's why we came here. We were hoping to hide out and figure out a plan to rescue them." Another thought dawned on him. He didn't need to worry about the Watch's deadline or an access code. "I know it sounded bad the way I said it, but that's only because I was still trying to get my head around it. What your people did out there was amazing." He stood up and paced around the room "With your help, we could go to the Watch using your super-stealth mode, then zap"—he placed his hand on Bean's shoulder—"we knock them out, rescue my parents, and come back here to live happily ever after. Mission accomplished. End of story." Stephen meant every word that spilled out of his mouth. If the only way to save his parents was to join a cult who believed they were magicians, then so be it. At least they could be crazy be together. "You can help me, right?"

Sadness clouded Finn's features. "No."

The single word snapped Stephen's excitement like so many twigs he'd crunched underfoot on his way to this place. "No?" he repeated back. "I see." Stephen glowered at Finn before turning back to Bean. "Then I guess we will be on our way." *So much for that plan.* He rubbed his fingers. The trip to the tower wasn't a complete waste. If what Finn said they could do was true, maybe they could rescue Ed and Helen without the help of the so-called Sorcerers. But what if all of this had been a delusion? The Watchman didn't look healthy. What if he dropped on his own and it is all another big coincidence? *Don't be a fool, you know what you saw. That's too many coincidences.* The small voice sounded different from he was used to, startling him out of his thoughts.

The corner of Finn's mouth twitched. "I didn't say no, as in we aren't willing. We would like nothing more than to put an end to the Watch, but it isn't so simple. We can't."

"Seems pretty simple to me," Stephen grumbled.

Finn raised his palm. "My people don't leave the city. At least, not the majority. A few of the more gifted ones—like the ones you saw outside—can spend two, maybe three, days off the island, but most can only last a few hours."

Stephen cocked his head. "What?"

"That's why I was so eager to find you. There is something we need. Something only you can get for us." Finn's grin bloomed once more across his face. "It's a wand. Maybe as thick as your finger and as long as Ms. Bean's hand."

"A wand." Stephen blinked. *Right. Of course it is. Sorcerers have to have their wands.* "So, what's this wand supposed to do? We wave it around and presto! Problem solved?"

Finn's eyes glinted. "I understand what you must be thinking, but I am deadly serious about this. I call it a wand for simplicity's sake, as that is what it looks like, but in reality, it is a piece of advanced technology created by a former associate years ago."

"Well, if it is so advanced, why don't you have it already?"

"It is protected."

Let me guess, by a magic spell. The conversation was getting him nowhere.

Finn shook his head. He muttered, "I told them we would never be taken seriously with that name." Louder, he added, "By biometrics. Which, I might add, is another reason I was so interested in finding you."

"Me? I've never seen your magic wand, and I don't know the first thing about hacking some biometric security system. I'm not even sure I know what biometrics are."

Biometrics: a form of computer authentication designed around individualized human characteristics such as fingerprint or iris profile.

Stephen shot a look at Bean. *Where did that come from?*

Finn leaned forward once more. "But that's just it. If my theory is correct, you wouldn't have to hack anything, as I believe you, Stephen, are the key." Finn's jaw clenched before he spoke again. "The wand would be here already if the access metrics hadn't been tampered with."

"I had nothing to do with it." Stephen took a step back with his hands raised.

Finn blinked twice, and the scowl disappeared. "That wasn't an accusation. I know you didn't. It was someone who I once quite admired. I believe she changed the access metrics so that you are the only person with permission to open the cabinet where it is stored."

"Why would she do that? Ignoring for a second the fact I don't know who you are talking about, why me?"

"Who knows what was going through her head at that time. Bombs were going off in the street set by people dressed as serpents. Everyone acted a little nutty. Maybe she wanted to take revenge on people like us by keeping us on this island, or maybe she wanted to make sure no one else could claim it until you were ready."

"If you know who this hacker is, why aren't you asking her to fix it and retrieve your wand?"

Finn clicked his tongue. "Well, that's complicated."

"Oh, I get it. She's dead." Stephen crossed his arms. "Not all that complicated."

"Perhaps. Perhaps not. But in either case, she's not around to ask, while you, Stephen, were gracious enough to show up on my doorstep. So, will you try to find the wand?"

"And if I find this wand and bring it back, you'll help me rescue Ed and Helen."

Finn nodded. "Once the wand is in my hands, rescuing your guardians will be one of the first things we do." He cocked his head and scratched his chin. "I will even forget your initial outburst and allow all of you to live here afterward."

Bean placed her hand on Stephen's shoulder. "Seems like a rather generous offer for a retrieval mission."

"Well, the locals in the area can be a tad territorial," said Finn. "But as long as you stay out of the center of town, you shouldn't have any problem."

"And once his parents are free? What do you intend to do about the Watch?"

"Then we'll follow Stephen's wishes, whatever they might be."

Stephen grit his teeth as he weighed Finn's request. *If the wand was as valuable as Finn said, then it was likely long gone regardless of whatever security system had been put in place.* Finn's request was a wild goose chase waiting to happen. Even worse, it would cost him even more time. What if the Watch came back before he returned? *But what other choice do I have?*

Finn smiled. "There's one more thing."

Stephen's eyes narrowed.

"Don't worry, it's not another condition." Finn paused and looked at Bean. "I want to teach both of you how to do what you saw us do out there. It will be useful out there." Finn gestured toward the tower door. "But also, because it is your birthright." Finn extended his hand to Stephen before looking back at Bean.

Stephen couldn't help but feel a little disquiet. There was something about the offer. Something he couldn't place his finger on. *You are being paranoid again*, thought Stephen. Still, he hesitated. Time spent training meant more time away from home.

"Don't worry. It will be quick." Stephen's lips twisted at Finn's remark. It was too close to his thoughts for comfort. "And it is in your best interest. You saw the gun. You heard his threats. Imagine meeting someone like that on the road. Now imagine what you could do with abilities like ours. You would be crazy not to take me up on my offer."

Finn had a point. He and Bean made it to the island because they'd been lucky not to have met anyone on the road. There was nothing to say their next journey would be the same. As much as he thought there had to be a catch, Stephen couldn't think of what it might be. He uncrossed his arms and let them fall limp by his sides. "Fine. A quick lesson first. But, to be clear, if I find this wand, I'm not handing it over until my folks are safe."

Finn's teeth sparkled white as he gestured for them to lean back into the couch as he took his own seat. "I'll begin with the basics." Information flooded Stephen's mind.

seventeen

Bean's eyes became glassy and unfocused. She raised her hand with her palm facing the ceiling. Stephen watched in wonder as her palm began to emit a pale blue glow like he'd seen Finn do. She blinked as her clear gaze returned to meet Stephen's. The light on her palm grew brighter. She cupped her hand. White-purple sparks jumped between her fingertips.

Stephen opened his palms and turned them toward the ceiling, much as he had seen Bean do. His fingers, however, remained skin toned. No glow or sparks of light danced across their surface.

A corner of Bean's lips turned up in a smile at his effort as she rose from the couch with her hand still aglow. Biting her lip, she took several steps out of the alcove, without turning her back on their host.

Finn's eyebrows and a corner of his lips rose as his gaze locked on the movement. "Before you go too far, I should warn you. . ."

I knew it, thought Stephen. "Let me guess. There's a catch."

"Not a catch, per se." Finn's lips twisted. "The data stream and what we can do is easier here. We still have the infrastructure. But out there. . . Well, it's like old phone technology."

Bean waved her hand, dismissing the ball of lightning. Stephen cocked his head as he attempted to follow Finn's warning.

"You see, when the signal is strong, the battery lasts longer because it isn't trying to find a better connection, but once a phone starts roaming. . ." Finn shrugged.

"I don't understand," Stephen admitted.

"I forget you kids wouldn't have the first idea what I am talking about. That lightning, it doesn't come out of thin air. It takes energy. Energy you won't have access to, at least not to the extent we have here thanks to this tower's self-sufficient power supply. It will exhaust you."

Stephen blinked, still not following Finn's explanation.

"Think about it this way. Imagine all you have to eat is a single apple. Eat it and stay inside all day reading a book, you might not realize how hungry you are until around dinnertime. Eat that same apple and work outside all day, I bet you are feeling weak in the knees before noon. The same principle applies here, except when you are away from a sufficient alternative energy source, the drain might very well kill you."

Dread filled Stephen's stomach. "Wait. Are you saying we are stuck here now?" Finn's warning didn't make sense. If Finn needed them to go and get the wand, shouldn't he have waited until they returned to remove the block?

Finn shook his head. "No, I don't believe so."

"You don't *believe* so? You mean you don't know?" Stephen bit his tongue in fury.

"Well, it affects everyone in different ways."

"Oh, that makes me feel so much better." Finn's fingers twitched, and his expression hardened. Stephen thought of the other so-called Sorcerers and what they'd demonstrated on the barricade. An icy knot built in Stephen's stomach. *Nice work. You have no idea what this man is capable of,* he thought. *You took him at his word because you wanted to believe, but his people could have killed that man the moment you walked away.* Ed's advice not to trust anyone once again echoed in Stephen's mind. *But yeah, go on and irritate him. Genius.* He tempered his tone. "I mean to say, what makes you so sure?"

"Isn't it obvious?" Finn gestured at the two of them. "Because you are both still alive."

"But isn't that because we didn't know how to do any of this before today?" said Bean.

Finn tilted his head and glanced at Bean before answering. "Just because you were unaware of what you were doing, doesn't mean you weren't doing it. The difference is now you know, and the reason I'm confident you can complete this task is the fact you wouldn't be standing here if you hadn't already figured out how to protect yourself at an instinctive level. Not everyone is so lucky."

"The plague." Stephen's eyes widened as he connected the dots.

Finn nodded. "Yes. The plague."

Stephen frowned. He'd always assumed the plague was something common, like a new strain of the flu. The worldwide economic collapse and fall of much of the power grid hadn't helped either. "If people knew its cause, why couldn't they find a cure?"

Finn held a finger up. "The first thing you need to understand about who we are and what we can do is that it's not a disease but a gift."

Bean snorted. "Some gift."

"So back to this whole mission, or quest, or whatever you want to call it. Are you going to tell me where I am supposed to go to find this wand thing?" Stephen asked.

"It's not far," replied Finn, removing the finger from his lips to inspect its nail. "In fact, I'll even give you a map."

Stephen's head throbbed and his skin itched as a map unfurled across his vision as if suspended in the air. His eyes might have bulged out of their sockets at the display if his stomach hadn't taken that moment to growl loud enough to be heard by everyone in the room.

"You should have spoken up." Finn wagged his finger. "As I mentioned before, never let yourself go hungry." An unfocused look flashed across Finn's expression. Within moments, the stairwell door opened. A girl Stephen hadn't seen before appeared carrying a bag of brown rectangular packets of varying sizes wrapped in plastic. Dropping the sack by Finn's feet, she disappeared with as little fanfare as she had arrived. Finn pulled out one of the packets. "Fortunately, I knew about a large cache of these well before the panic set in." He returned the packet to the sack. "We haven't needed them thanks to the gardens we keep on the upper floors. Take these with you."

"I still don't. . . Will I be able to. . . How did you?" Stephen couldn't help asking.

"It's the same as in the game you like to play. One computer connects to another. Except for the computer in this instance is your mind." Finn gestured to the bag, which appeared stuffed to its breaking point. "Now eat. Never forget what I said. Once you leave this tower, you will need to make sure to always keep your energy levels up."

"But what if I can't?" Stephen asked as he ripped into one of the smaller packets near the top containing a bar the color and flavor of mud. "I mean, I've never accessed the data stream or whatever you want to call that . . . that . . ." Stephen gestured in the air, unable to come up with another term to describe the flood of information that had assaulted his senses earlier.

"It will come to you," Finn answered in a flash, "if you let it." He took a deep breath. "I know what it must be like, for this to all be strange and new." He shook his head. "The more time that passes before you master control will make it that much more difficult. Even now, I suspect your mind is trying to create another barrier. It's afraid. It's coming up with reasons why none of what you've seen or heard is true. It doesn't have to be that way. Retrieve the wand for me, and I'll make sure you and your guardians never live in fear of the Watch again."

Eighteen

A bead of sweat crawled down the length of Stephen's spine under the weight of a backpack loaded to its seams. The street in front of him was empty of people but littered with abandoned cars, making the way somewhat more challenging. "Should we take the bridge or tunnel?" he asked Bean, seeking to fill the unnatural quiet. *Who would have thought that life in the middle of nowhere would be noisier than the big city?*

Bean paused in mid-stride as her gaze glazed over. Bean had been all too eager to take advantage of their new abilities. She surprised him by how ready she was to access the data stream, especially after Finn's warning about the energy drain it could cause, but when questioned, she shrugged him off. "All the more reason to master it before we leave the island."

Stephen remained less. . . He struggled to think of the word that would describe the feeling. *Enthusiastic.* Stephen nodded to himself. Enthusiastic was a good word. Finn was right. He didn't want to believe him, but not for the reason Finn suggested.

"Neither."

Stephen almost jumped out of his skin as Wes stepped out from one of the abandoned buildings. "You could have given me a heart attack."

"Not my fault you don't pay attention," Wes said as he joined them in the middle of the street. "I thought you could use a guide." He glanced up to the sky, tracking the position of the sun. "By the looks of it, I was right."

Stephen's lips twisted. Something about their mission gnawed at him and had since the second they left the barricade behind. It solved too many problems. *If a deal is too good to be true. . .* What he couldn't figure out was what Finn stood to gain other than a piece of tech. Why take the risk with relative strangers when there was a good chance it didn't even work anymore?

He took a closer look at Wes. His eyes narrowed. Had Finn sent him to keep an eye on them? If so, then why? Did Finn not think they'd hand the wand over? He ground his jaw. Handing over the wand was the best chance he had of defeating the Watch and rescuing Ed and Helen. *Or maybe Wes is your friend and wants to help because that's what friends do.* He remembered how pale and tired Wes had looked as they had gotten into the boat. Stephen had assumed at the time that his appearance was a result of city living, but if Finn had been telling the truth, the energy drain might have already begun taking its toll, and yet he'd still risked it to find him when he'd missed their game. "Are you sure you can make it?"

"Finn doesn't have a monopoly on ideas around here. I believe you just need the right sort of antenna." Wes smiled and reached into his jacket. He pulled out a narrow metal rod affixed to a wooden handle and brandished it about. Its tip was covered in a small sphere of crunched-together aluminum foil. "I call it, Insurance."

"Another wand." Bean laughed, her gaze sharp and focused. "Don't you think you are taking the whole Sorcerer thing a bit far?"

Stephen looked at the rod again and had to agree it did resemble a magic wand. That is, a magic wand made out of garbage. "I'm not sure electricity works that way."

"Laugh all you want"—he waved the rod in the air—"but I'm the difference between you sleeping outside for the next day or two, or getting us where you are going in a matter of hours."

"What are you going to do?" Bean wiggled her fingers. "Say alakazam and get us there in a puff of smoke?"

"You'll see," Wes answered with a smile.

The straps of the pack pulled at Stephen's shoulders. While it seemed there were more than enough supplies now to go around, Stephen wasn't confident there would be enough for three on the road unless Wes did have a way of reducing their travel time. He looked at Wes, at his pale skin, which couldn't have spent more than mere minutes in the sun up until now, and at his narrow frame. Stephen would bet a ration of water that Wes had even less experience in the wilderness than he had. *Didn't stop you.* He pushed out his chest at the thought while redistributing the weight of the bag across his shoulders. "Okay, oh great guide, which route should we be taking then?"

"Easy. The rail."

"Okay, so we walk it?"

A coy smile inched up Wes's face.

Stephen's forehead puckered. "You mean, the trains are still running? But I thought the tower couldn't power more than just the lights and the water."

"Not the tower and not all of them. But lucky for us, we only need one to get where we are going."

Stephen and Bean followed Wes as he navigated city streets further cluttered with the rusty shells of abandoned cars and broken glass the further they went. "We cleared the roadways while we were building up the barricade," offered Wes. "Seemed like a good idea. Two birds with one stone and all." Wes threw out his arms as if they could somehow stretch from street corner to street corner. "The thought was allowing the rest of the place to go natural, so it would act as its own sort of obstacle course. Most of us don't even bother coming up this way anymore. I wouldn't be surprised if the others forgot about the rail altogether."

Wes turned and entered a squat building made of a tan stone; it was streaked black. Large panes of glass in the building's windows were either missing or broken, making the entire structure seem all the more ominous. Stephen's misgivings grew stronger. He shook his head again. Life had been so much simpler before he'd allowed Ed's paranoia to enter his mind.

Bean followed Wes, showing none of the same doubts that were plaguing Stephen. *And when did you start trusting her?* he wondered. *The marina,* his heart answered. He remembered how she'd looked at him like she could see into his soul and him, hers. Stephen buried that last thought deep down. *Don't confuse the whole shared survival thing for more than it is,* his brain reminded him. *She's going with you because she has no other place to go.* Stephen muttered a curse as he raced to catch up before the pair were too far out of sight.

"So, Bean?" Wes asked as they maneuvered around a pile-up of onetime luxury cars, now rendered into garbage. "Interesting name. Let me guess, your father's name was Frank. As in, Frank and Beans. You get it, right?"

Bean shot Wes a look. "I can think of a few worse names to call a person."

Wes snorted as he scouted ahead, disappearing behind the remains of a bus.

"You know, your friend can be a bit of a jerk," whispered Bean.

"He's not so bad once you get to know him," replied Stephen. *Do you know him though? Do you really?*

Bean added, still soft enough that the words wouldn't carry, "My real name is Beatrice, but my sister couldn't say it when we were kids. Called me Bean instead. It stuck."

"That's cute." Stephen attempted a wry smile. It must have been nice to have other kids to grow up with. "Where is your sister now?"

Bean's jaw tightened. "Not here."

Way to step in it again. Wes reappeared in that moment, gesturing for them to turn right and follow him into a building that looked as if it wouldn't be standing much longer. Once in the building, each footfall echoed like a gunshot causing the hairs on the back of Stephen's neck to stand on end. What few panes of glass remained in the windows were long since darkened with grime, making the light that did pass through seem diseased. Movement low to the ground and fast caught his eye. Stephen suspected it was a rodent and shuddered.

"This way," Wes's voice boomed, startling some other creatures that had made the building their home. Stephen looked around, trying to locate the voice's source. The play of acoustics made it difficult, but he managed to catch sight of Wes's shirt as he began descending a flight of stairs. Bean, however, was nowhere to be seen.

"Bean?"

"Over here," she answered, materializing out of the shadows like a ghost. While Finn had been generous with the food and water, his generosity had not extended to giving either of them the color-shifting shirts, but it would seem Bean didn't need it. His skin prickled at the thought of what sort of damage she might inflict on those that threatened her. *Good thing she is on your side,* Stephen thought.

"How did you do that?"

"Do what?"

"Are you two waiting for an invitation?" Wes called from the base of the stairwell. Light shone from his palm stretched above his head, cutting the otherwise perfect darkness and illuminating the surrounding ground. "Please mind the gap," he laughed. Stephen raised an eyebrow. "What? I had to look up a bunch of videos about subways to get her up and running. It's funny."

Stephen shook his head.

A screech of metal covered any other words they might have spoken as a train car pulled to a stop across from Wes. Wes patted the metallic cylinder as one might an animal. "It took me two years. Switching the power supply over was brutal. I almost electrocuted myself, but I didn't want to connect it to the tower's grid. She wouldn't be my little secret anymore. Then one day, just as I thought I'd run out of options, it sort of clicked. She's my secret awesome machine. I call her SAM."

"So if not the tower, then what is powering it?" asked Bean, running her hand over the metal surface.

"My guess? It has something to do with those things." Stephen pointed to several large rings wrapped in coiled wires mounted along the base of the car. "What are they, some kind of battery?"

"Sorry." Wes shook one finger before tapping his forehead. "I'm not sure I want that secret getting out." He nodded his head toward the vehicle where Bean was examining one of the rings.

Stephen rolled his eyes. "Who would we tell?" The light emanating from Wes's outstretched fist blinked out of existence as the train car's door slid open. Warm light welcomed them into its interior. Wes took a seat, gesturing for Stephen to take the one across from him while holding onto one of the car's metal railings. The doors closed with a soft whishing sound. Bean stood in the center with her hand wrapped around a support rail.

"How does the Watch not know about this?" Stephen wondered aloud.

"They aren't the only ones." Wes's grin threatened to break his face in two.

"But it's a train. A functioning train," Bean stated the obvious. "Isn't that a little hard to miss?"

Wes's smile evaporated. "Well, yeah, they might have noticed if I'd ever tested it further than the service tunnel."

"So you don't know that it will get us there." Bean tensed and made a move as if to exit the train before it started. She frowned once more at Wes when the door didn't re-open. "Forgive me if I'm not a super fan of the idea of being buried alive down here when this bucket of bolts fails."

"Oh, she'll get us there." Wes patted the metal bar as he had the car's exterior. He muttered more under his breath, but Stephen couldn't catch the rest. The car lurched forward, and Stephen decided to let the comment go. Even if the furthest the train could manage was one or two miles, it was better than walking.

Stephen blinked as the train exited the service tunnel. His eyes, blinded by the light, did not adjust to the brightness of daylight right away. The car continued its acceleration until the streets were passing like a blur. Then darkness blanketed them again. Stephen's ears popped as they burrowed deep under the waterway through another tunnel. Stephen looked over at Wes. Were the cabin lights bleaching out what little color Wes's skin possessed? Or was the drain already taking its toll? He looked over at Bean. *We're supposed to have some built-in resistance, right?* Her skin looked grayer, too, although not to the same extent. *It must be the lighting then.* Forcing himself to look away before she noticed, he shook his concern away.

"Did you ever watch a game?" Wes gestured at a faded poster hung above one of the windows featuring a helmeted man clad in heavy pads.

"Nah," replied Stephen. "At least not any that I can remember. Did you?"

"I've watched the replays." Wes sighed. "Dad was a major Sharks fan before all hell broke loose, with season tickets and everything. You would have thought he was an owner of the team. Or you might have, before. . ." Wes's expression dulled. A muscle in his jaw twitched. "I forget the point I was trying to make."

"That's okay. I wouldn't have gotten it anyway. My Ed wasn't big on sports."

Wes leaned back into his seat. "Yeah, I guess I can't blame him. Even my dad had to admit the players on the teams weren't exactly playing fair. Especially not during those last couple seasons." He shook his head. "I don't care how much money was on the line, you couldn't pay me to turn myself into a monster like that."

Bean yawned and shifted her stance.

I bet Bean knows what he means. Might as well turn in your guy card now. He waited for information, which could offer a hint at what Wes meant to pop into his brain like the definition of biometrics had, but all he could think of was Ed and Helen being held against their will, and all he was doing about it was sitting on a train discussing a profession that no longer held any relevance. "Yeah, roid-rage," he offered. *Lame.*

Wes nodded in the direction of the poster. "If only. I'm not talking about steroids. I am talking about people turning themselves into real live monsters. Like tusks and stuff. Anything they could do to intimidate or get ahead, and all of it was legal. Man, it used to scare the crap out of me watching the players take the field, but Dad ate that stuff up. I mention it because that's where we are going. Shark-fan central."

The sunlight bathed the world outside the car with a rose golden light as the train began its deceleration. Its hue made Wes appear jaundiced. "You're not looking so good," said Stephen, giving voice to his growing concern.

Wes's lips narrowed. "Bit of motion sickness," he answered. He pulled out the narrow metal rod from his jacket, clutching it in one hand so tight his knuckles were white.

Bean turned and took in Wes's appearance beginning at his feet and resting on his face. "You should go back home. After all, Finn sent us, not you."

Wes waved the comment away with a flick of his wrist. "We're almost there." The car continued speeding its way along the track. More sunlight flooded the cabin but did little to improve Wes's skin tone. "Besides, you're going to need me unless you feel like walking back. SAM is mine, remember?"

"Keep her," said Bean. "I'm still shocked that this can on wheels made it this far."

"I'd prefer to walk back than bury you," said Stephen in a low voice. The skin of Wes's hand was taunt and bone white where his fingers and the metal met.

He shivered. "I knew I should have worked on the climate control before taking her out. A cold front must have come through. You can't trust the weather out here. One minute it's summer and the next we're buried under three feet of snow." Wes's lips had taken on a blue sheen, emphasizing his point.

"Dude. Seriously. I think you should go back while you still can."

Wes's deteriorating condition was all the proof Stephen needed that Finn had been telling the truth, at least about the limitations of the Sorcerers abilities. *Your abilities now, too*, he reminded himself. Seeing that it had been an hour or two, Stephen hated to imagine how Wes would have fared had he not found them at the riverfront as soon as he had. The road might have killed him. *How* had *Wes found them on the waterfront?* A thought occurred to Stephen as he pulled the pack back onto his shoulders.

"You knew where we were before you even left the island?"

"What?" Wes replied through chattering teeth.

"It wasn't by luck when you found us the other day at the pier. You knew we were there and not crossing by either the roadway or the tunnel. How?"

A slight pink blush blinked into existence across Wes's cheeks before disappearing beneath his now waxy condition. "You called."

"The bench." Stephen's eyes widened as he recalled that moment of complete despair. Bean looked taken aback and almost lost her footing as the train swayed. *She must think I've lost my mind,* he thought. *Perhaps you have.* Looking at her, he explained. "According to Finn, I've been accessing these abilities for years without knowing what I was doing. I was thinking about giving up. I must have somehow sent out a call for help."

Bean's eyes softened and her body relaxed, if only for a moment. Her free hand stretched toward his. He held his breath as he waited to accept her hand in his, but then her arm stiffened and her back arched as she brought her hand up to cover another yawn. Then she shook her head. Her eyes were once again as hard as the iron rails. The train came to a stop, and the doors slid open.

Stephen's cheeks burned. "So that's what we'll do." Stephen stood and faced the door. The weight of the pack dug into his shoulders.

"Do what?" Wes's words were clipped. Stephen turned back. He didn't need to be a doctor to see that Wes's continued denial about his condition would kill him if he didn't start heading back to the island and the protection of the tower soon.

"I'll send you a message when we have the wand and are on the way back." *Assuming you figure out how you did it the first time that is.*

Wes started to rise in protest, but crumpled back into his seat, releasing his homemade antenna. His shoulders slumped, and his head bowed in defeat. "I'm sorry." His fingers twitched. "Take Insurance. You'll need it."

"It doesn't work, Wes. You have to know that."

"The faster we get off this train, the faster he can go back," said Bean, squeezing by Stephen and jumping onto the platform.

"Please."

⸺⟨ৎ১৲⟩⸺

Stephen's gaze remained fixed on the car as it pulled away from the station, as if Wes might attempt to return the moment it was out of sight. "If you chuck that thing over there, I doubt anyone will notice." Bean's words brought Stephen's attention back to the present. Large cracks in the concrete slab of the unwelcoming platform had given birth to weeds, and insect trails lined beams that once must have supported a shelter roof. A building no bigger than Stephen's farmhouse stood behind them, its windows long since boarded up. Brick buildings lining the other side of the road appeared equally abandoned.

Stephen turned the antenna over in his hands. The handle was narrow, only the size of his thumb and about a third as thick, and the metal rod was no longer attached. The two pieces had broken apart when Wes dropped it. Bean was right; he should throw the whole thing away. The pack was heavy enough, but he'd promised. *Wes named it, after all.* He shoved the handle piece into his back pocket. Figuring out what to do with the metal piece was more problematic due to its size, but he managed to squeeze it into the pack. Fixing things other people viewed as junk was one of the things he could do best. Maybe when all this was done, he could give Wes a new and improved model.

"You coming?" Bean shouted from the edge of the platform.

Stephen grunted as he adjusted the pack's straps and began walking down the center of the roadway. They'd arrived at their destination with a full pack and in a fraction of the time they'd planned. Now all he had to do was find the wand, return home, and take down the Watch, but with each step closer to his goal, he couldn't help feeling like somewhere along the line, he'd made a colossal mistake.

Nineteen

Stephen crumpled the leftover wrapper from a larger packet marked 'MRE: Meal Ready to Eat' and scanned to see if there was a fire-can or something similar where he might dispose of the rubbish. The food, if you could call it that, contained inside was about as satisfying for dinner as a cardboard box, but eating it or any of the other foodstuffs in the pack was a whole lot easier than foraging. *Safer, too.* Giving up on finding a place for the trash, Stephen shoved the garbage into a pocket.

Bean laughed. "What are you going to do when you run out of pocket room?" she asked. "Why don't you drop it? It's what everyone else here seems to want to do with their garbage." She gestured to a pile of water-rotted wood and moldy fabric laying nearby, which once served as a piece of furniture. "I'd bet you a steak dinner that no one would even notice."

The area between the island and their destination once supported one of the most populated parts of the country. Now the roads were lined with buildings long abandoned. It was a good thing they had their supplies. If any grocery stores still operated, they weren't exactly advertising operating hours. Even though he'd just eaten, the thought of food made his mouth water. There might not be grocery stores anymore, but that didn't mean there wasn't a hidden market like Jim's tavern nearby. A couple of the meal bars would be worth a good trade. Stephen shifted the pack's weight, easing his shoulders where the straps had cut into his skin. "Maybe it's time to take the main road?"

Bean raised a brow. "We'd risk getting spotted."

"Would meeting other people be such a bad thing? They could at least point us to where we could trade for that steak dinner or something. Doesn't that sound awesome right now?"

"I'm not so sure. What if those people don't trust strangers?" Bean argued. "They might alert the Watch the second they see our shadows." She stood straight as she flexed a glowing fist.

It wasn't the first time since leaving the train he'd caught her experimenting with their newfound ability. So far, she hadn't acted any more tired than usual. If anything, she seemed more vibrant now, as if not accessing their abilities before had been the more exhausting activity. He wished he felt the same. He shifted the pack again. Thanks to the train ride, it was still heavy with their supplies, but he had no way of knowing how long they'd last if Finn's energy drain did start having an impact. "Are you sure you should be doing that?"

"I'm practicing. I don't know about you, but I'm not in the mood to run anymore." Stephen didn't need Bean to voice the words to understand that she wouldn't hesitate to attack if threatened. He thought back to the decision he'd made at the pier before he'd recognized Wes. He'd convinced himself that he could do what had to be done, but could he if it came down to it? Could he really? He was no longer as sure. Up ahead, a worn sign read 'cester' as if the 'Wor' in Worcester had taken off in a panic with everyone else. One way or another, he suspected he'd soon find out.

Bean looked at him sideways, her lips hinting at a smile. "Welcome home?"

"This was never my home," Stephen grumbled. "Even if Finn says I was born here." He chewed on his lip as he scanned the empty street ahead of them. Nothing about it looked familiar. "Do you honestly think the townspeople are going to turn us in to the Watch the minute they see us?"

"You know as well as I do this is where it all started. If anyone isn't to be trusted, it is people from around here."

Stephen's lips tightened, but he chose not to argue with her as he scanned the streets ahead of them. Even if the people of this town weren't allied with the Watch, if he'd seen all the chaos they had, he wouldn't trust a stranger either. "Fine. You win. We take the scenic route."

Stephen blinked as the virtual map Finn sent him unfurled across his vision. Summoning it was the only thing he had been able to do related to their abilities with any confidence. He blinked again, and the map zoomed in and transformed into a three-dimensional overlay. A large red arrow filled the street. Street names and other details like business ratings and phone numbers floated over the top of the surrounding buildings. Stephen shook his head. As nice as it was to have a map of the area to help guide them, the overlay was proof the map was at least fifteen years old. Who knew what changes might have been made to the city since then? Stephen thought of the elaborate barricade that protected Finn's tower. Those remaining in this city might have attempted something similar if they felt threatened. There could be traps for uninvited visitors or mazes made of salvaged materials.

Once again, Stephen couldn't help thinking the object of their quest had to be long gone as they followed the red arrow, terminating at a checkered flag in front of a gray building. Unlike the buildings to either side, no additional information popped up across his augmented vision. "I guess this is it," suggested Stephen, waving toward the virtual entranceway.

"What is?" Bean asked.

"Our destination."

"A parking lot?"

Stephen took a step back to see if additional information about the building might appear. He wrinkled his nose. Something about the place nagged him. While the building's windows were blacked with grime, they were still intact. There were no signs of graffiti or other signs of structural abuse either. The hair on his neck prickled.

He waved his hand, and the overlay dissolved. The gray building disappeared, replaced with an empty lot. *I knew this was a wild goose chase.* Frustrated they'd come so far to reach a dead end, Stephen picked up a rock at threw it at the lot. The rock bounced in midair, dropping to the ground in front of Stephen. "Did you see that?" he asked.

Beans eyebrows shot up. "Do it again."

Stephen picked up the stone and threw it again. Again, it fell after connecting with something Stephen couldn't see. He closed his eyes and reached out. Stephen's fingers connected with a warm flat surface. He brought the map overlay back up over his vision. The gray building reappeared. Stephen walked toward the entranceway and noticed a panel to its side illuminated as they approached.

"What are you doing?"

"The whole place must be camouflaged. Like those crazy clothes Finn's group uses. Use the map he gave us."

"Finn didn't *give* me anything," Bean grumbled. "Why else do you think I let you lead the way all this time?"

He placed his hand on it. A tiny portal in the building's wall opened, exposing a lens. "What is this place?" Stephen asked as the lens blinked and an indicator light blazed green.

He pulled his hand back as if burned. "I don't know what I just did, but I did something." Just as he was about to drop his hand, he heard the sound of a latch release. He caught Bean's eye.

She shrugged. "So, the lights are still on. Maybe it's like the tower and the people inside know where we can get fresh water around here," she said, gesturing for Stephen to continue inside. As they entered the building's hallway, a warm glow filled the space as they crossed a tiled floor clean enough to eat off its surface. The door behind them clicked shut.

An arrow reappeared in front of Stephen's vision. This time it was black and narrow. *There is no way a building like this is abandoned.* Stephen's neck hairs rose further with each echoing tap their footfalls produced. *Stay alert*, he focused the thought at Bean as if she could read his thoughts. *Be ready.* Bean raised one answering eyebrow, making Stephen once again feel like an idiot. Of course she's alert.

"Go on. Open it." Bean's voice nearly caused Stephen to jump out of his skin as they stopped in front of a rather nondescript office door.

"I'm not sure that's a good idea. We don't have any way of knowing what is on the other side. What if it's been booby-trapped?"

"Chicken." She picked up his wrist and placed his palm on another pad to the door's right. There was a hissing noise along with the sound of escaping air as the door swung on its own accord. The interior of the room looked as if its primary occupant had gone out for a few morning errands, expecting to return later that day. A coffee mug sat in the center of a rich mahogany desk in front of a black leather chair. Several university degrees, including a medical degree showing the name Camille Nadal, hung from the wall. A potted plant filled another office corner. The plant's emerald green foliage put Stephen on guard as the surest sign yet that they weren't alone in the building—until he touched one of its leaves. They were artificial. He let out a breath.

Bean walked around the desk and rummaged through its drawers until she pulled out a rectangular piece of plastic.

It contained a copper chip on one end. "What's that?"

"A key card. Might come in handy."

"Any sign of a wand?"

"Not even close. Maybe it's down the hall." Bean shoved the card into her pocket and exited the office, not waiting to see if Stephen followed. Her pace increased as if she too experienced the same ill ease about the place. She led them further into the building's interior.

Few of the doors were marked by a sign or nameplate, and Stephen soon lost track of which they had or hadn't opened. A few of the rooms closest to the entrance contained bed-shaped contraptions lined with yellowed paper. Others contained plastic chairs whose arms were fitted with paddles and thick straps. Those rooms tended to also contain rows of empty vials fitted with multi-colored plastic caps. None contained anything remotely wand shaped.

"What do you suppose they did here?" Stephen asked.

Bean snorted, shutting the door closest to her. "Isn't it obvious?" The smile left her lips. "Oh, that's right. You wouldn't know."

Stephen peeked into another room. "Check this out." The size alone separated it from the others. Three rows of large work centers broke up the space, each with its own sink and storage areas. Strangely shaped glassware rested on top of the shelves, and large machines whose purpose Stephen couldn't guess lined the walls.

"Looks promising." Bean pointed at another door, this one made of glass, located in the back of the room. A line of metal cabinets, visible through the glass, lined the back wall of varying sizes. Bean pulled on the handle, but it refused to open. She pulled the card out of her pocket. "Maybe this is what the card is for." She waved it in front of the door. An indicator light flashed red. "Too fast?" Bean waved the card again. The red light blinked once more, followed by a bright white flash up above coming from a camera mounted from the ceiling. "I think this thing just took a picture." She handed the card to him. "This place is supposed to be keyed to you. Why don't you give it a try?"

Stephen scanned the door. With the exception of the hole for the indicator light, there wasn't much else to it. "What do you think I should do?"

"Try putting your hand on it or something. That seems to have worked so far."

Stephen pursed his lips. Holding the card in one hand, he reached out toward the handle. His fingers twitched as they came in contact with the cool metal. He scrunched his eyes shut, bracing himself for an alarm or another flash as he waved the keycard with his other hand. *Click.* Stephen opened his eyes. The red light in the upper corner now shone green.

"Who'da thought? Finn was right. You were the key." Bean grinned.

"It still doesn't make any sense. I mean, why me?"

"Does it matter?" Bean countered. "Now, oh mighty keymaster, why don't you go grab the magic wand thingy so we can get the heck out of this place before whoever might be monitoring that camera decides to come and investigate?"

Stephen crossed the room and opened the various cabinets. Some contained vials, while others contained small round trays. Most were empty. His hopes of finding the wand in this strange place were all but dashed as he opened up the smallest cabinet and pulled out a rod that was as long as his hand and as thick as his thumb.

"That's it?" Bean asked. "Doesn't look all that high tech to me."

"If it's not the wand, then we are in major trouble." Stephen swung his pack around to his front and tucked the rod into one of the pockets.

Bean had moved over to the larger cabinets and was peering into them. "What do you think the rest of this stuff was for?"

Stephen shrugged. "Don't know and don't care. Let's get out of here."

"But aren't you at least a little curious?" She started to reach out to touch one of the vials.

"I wouldn't do that if I were you."

She pulled her hand back and turned to look at him with a quizzical expression.

"You said it yourself, we're at ground zero. Do you really want to poke around and let loose another plague?"

She frowned but shoved her hands into her jacket pockets.

"Ready?"

Bean turned to look at the row of cabinets one last time. Her shoulders slumped.

Stephen's senses were on edge as they navigated through the maze of hallways within the facility. With every footstep, every turn, he expected to find some sort of guard or obstacle, but none appeared, and before long, they were at the building's main entrance.

Stephen summoned the map once more to remind himself how to get back to the train station. His vision flashed red. "Now what. . .?" he began as the exterior wall seemed to disappear, giving him an unhindered view of a truck parked outside. *Well, that's a nice trick. I wish I knew how I'd done it.*

"What's wrong?" Bean asked as he struck out his arm, urging her not to open the main door.

"We've got company," he replied. "They're outside."

"Who are they? Can you tell? How many?"

Stephen scanned the area outside of the lab. "Does it matter?" Movement caught his eye. A figure approaching the building from the side. "I only see one." He looked for the telltale sign of a member of the Watch. What would happen to his folks if Dr. Lambda caught him out here? Would she realize he'd reneged on their deal?

"We can take him." She balled her fist.

"No wait, I can't see that far out. There could be more of them."

"We take them out, too." Stephen didn't need to look in her direction to know that lightning once again danced between her knuckles. He thought about the cameras and indicator lights and wondered if the same network that protected Finn's people from the energy drain was in place here. Maybe the whole town was still powered somehow. That might explain why he hadn't tired by utilizing the map as they navigated through the streets or why Bean hadn't demanded more than her share of rations. The man turned to the side and raised a fist. There was no mistaking the cloth that wrapped around the man's arm below the shoulder. *You can't let them find you here.* Stephen pushed her wrist down. "Too risky."

"Maybe for you, but not for me."

"This place screams mad scientist. Who knows what other chemicals or gases are floating around in the air by now. That lightning of yours could cause an explosion."

The light winked out. "What do you suggest we do then?"

"We don't have a choice. We're going to have to find another way out."

twenty

The crash of breaking glass pierced the silence as they made their retreat down the corridors of the lab. "They're in."

"You think?" Bean replied, then winced. "Sorry."

Stephen had grown to expect Bean's sarcastic outbursts. If anything, her attempt at an apology was more out of character. He looked at her and remembered her face the night they met, bathed in moonlight as he explained why they would have to leave the road. *She's scared,* he realized. *She doesn't want to fight them any more than you do.* Stephen remembered the emotions that had swirled around him when he readied himself to take another life. Once the deed was done, there would be no going back. "It's okay."

"No, it isn't." She paused. "Stephen, I'm not. . . I mean to say, there is something I think you should know."

The halls echoed with the sound of more glass shattering. A loud curse echoed followed by several other muffled voices entering the mix. The hallway took on a purple glow. Lightning danced across Bean's balled up fist. Stephen's gaze locked into hers and saw steel resolve reflected back. The look terrified him more than the voices down the hall. He reached out and touched her shoulder. "Whatever it is, it can wait. We just have to find a back way out of here like we did at the tavern."

"It sounds like one of them was hurt coming in. We should take them out now. Maybe not with lightning, but we can still do some damage while they are distracted."

"And what if it doesn't work?" Stephen whispered, nodding his head at Bean's clenched hand. "What then?" He saw her knuckles were white. The more he thought about it, the more convinced Stephen became that the Watch wasn't here for them, which could mean they were after a different target. *The wand. They must know it is here. But how?* He recalled the camera's flash in front of the glass door. What if the security camera did more than take a single picture? What if it kept recording after that initial flash? Anyone monitoring its feed would know the wand was now in play. *And who took it.* "And what about the wand? I don't have a clue what it does, but I'm pretty sure the Watch shouldn't get their hands on it."

Bean stumbled and over-corrected. Her movements became sluggish and she no longer kept up with his pace.

Not the drain. Not now. A fourth voice entered the mix. While he could not make out the voice's exact words, it was clear this individual was in charge, as the other voices went silent. *He knows we are here,* Stephen thought as his gaze darted around the room in search of another exit. "Just a little further. Okay?" He placed his hand on her shoulder. "Don't make me carry you again." The sheer thought exhausted him, but he knew he would do it again if he had to.

Bean glanced at his hand and then down the hallway in the direction of the lobby. Her shoulders rose and sagged. "I didn't make you the last time."

They continued toward the end of the hall, making as little noise as possible. With the exception of the glass room, most of the doors they passed looked much the same as the office where they'd found the keycard. However, soon the hallway ended with nothing to indicate another way out existed.

"Guess it's a showdown, after all," Bean whispered, clenching her fists.

"Not necessarily," replied Stephen, pulling up Finn's map overlay. A sign with lettering as clear as the day it was first printed showed the word 'EXIT.' An arrow printed under the letters pointed to their right. "This way," he said, pulling her toward an even less descript door than the rest.

"The janitor's closet?" Bean asked. "Isn't that a bit cliché?" Her eyes tightened as she looked in the direction they'd come. "If we are going to hide, why don't we go into one of the other offices? That way if they do come this way we at least have some fighting room."

Voices murmured from the down the hall, followed by heavy footsteps. They were running out of time. "It's not a closet." He opened the door.

"Sure looks like one to me," Bean replied, stepping around Stephen. She raised her fist, glowing like a firefly rather than lit by sparks of electrical discharge. The light caused shadows to dance across the row of shelves stocked with bleach and various spray bottles as she moved. "I suppose we can hide behind this?" she added, pushing a yellow pushcart to the side. She turned, causing the shadows to shift once more, and Stephen noticed a line in between the shelves and the back wall.

"It's another door."

"What is?"

"The shelves." Stephen grinned as he reached toward the back wall. "More camouflage." He stifled a laugh as his fingers found a pull hidden behind one of the spray bottles. "Who builds a place like this?" Stephen asked more for himself. The janitorial shelves swung out with ease, revealing a spiral staircase leading down into nothing but darkness.

"Where do you think it goes?"

The map overlaid across Stephen's vision didn't reveal any additional information, and the effort of maintaining it was beginning to give Stephen a headache. "I have no idea," he answered, banishing the map once more.

"Well, I suppose I should lead the way then," offered Bean, raising her fist up high.

They'd found another door at the base of the stairs, which opened to an empty railway platform. A tunnel lined with brick arched above either side. "Where do you think it goes?" Stephen let his hand drop from where it held the door ajar to gesture at the open tunnels. Realizing his error, he spun to catch the door, but he was too late. The sound of the latch engaging was all too clear. "Just great," he muttered to himself.

"Guess we're going to find out. Come on." Bean offered and took the first steps. "Maybe it leads to another way up."

Stephen shifted the pack's straps once more. *She's right*, he told himself. At least they shouldn't have to worry about the Watch finding them any time soon.

The thought that the rail could still be electrified didn't hit Stephen until they were well on their way. They'd been walking for what felt like an hour on top of the rail without spotting a ladder or other way out when they came to another arch. Stephen and Bean shared a glance but passed through it without comment. The air seemed to shift. Before, the air had resembled that of the lab above. Sterile. However, the air smelled of dirt and mold. It was as if the archway had acted as a sort of airlock. They found another concrete platform on the other side. Stephen suppressed a grunt as he removed the pack from his shoulders and hoisted it onto the edge of the platform. After pulling himself up, he reached out to help Bean. The pale glow emanating from Bean's palm dimmed as she grasped his outstretched hand.

It occurred to Stephen that Bean had been maintaining that glow for the entire time they had been in the tunnels. He tried to think of the last time he'd seen her eat. "I think we can take a break," he offered.

"I can keep going," she replied.

"What about upstairs? You were exhausted."

"I caught my second wind, okay?" The light from her hands increased in intensity.

Stephen tried to hide his disappointment as he looked around. When he'd seen the platform, he'd hoped they might find stairs to the surface, but It appeared the platform led to another tunnel. They'd have to navigate the darkness a while longer. He caught sight of Bean's face. It was difficult to determine if she had grown any paler than usual, but he'd known her long enough to recognize she'd be the last person to admit weakness. "You might be all set," he countered, "but I'm starving." He rummaged through the pack by his side until he found a meal bar he imagined tasted much like the combination of clay and ash might. It was one of the better recipes. "Here, I got you some dinner."

Bean smiled as she took the bar from him. "Aw, honey, you cooked." The light from her hand diminished as she tore into the wrapper. They sat there in shared silence as Stephen tried to pretend the bar he was eating didn't smell like asparagus pee.

"You ready?" Bean asked.

Stephen sighed and pocketed the wrapper with the others. "I guess so."

Once again, the purple light bloomed into view as Bean launched forward into the platform's tunnel while Stephen returned the remaining meals to the pack and repositioned it on his shoulders. Bean had gone a few feet ahead when the light came to a stop. When Stephen followed, he saw why. A mountain of black and gray rubble mixed with twisted steel beams filled their view and blocked their path.

"You have reached your destination. Now ending route guidance." Bean's voice sounded robotic, and her eyes appeared glazed over. Bean shook her head. "Did you say something?"

"Not me." Something tickled Stephen's nose, distracting him from her comment. He swat at it and noticed a dark smear on his hand. *Spider,* he thought. *Fantastic. You got away from the Watch just to get taken out by poisonous spiders.* Stephen turned to go back the way they came. They'd have to follow the rail tunnel to its next stop.

"I think I found something."

Stephen looked where Bean pointed. Down near the base of the debris was a hole, large enough for a mouse to pass but not much more. Its edges appeared jagged, and dark shards lay on the ground beneath it. Stephen reached down and touched one of the shards. It broke apart in his hand.

"Wood?" It didn't make any sense that wood would be among the debris . . . unless? Stephen looked at the slabs of concrete and twisted beams again. *What if this wall is only supposed to 'look' like a cave-in?*

Stephen clenched his jaw and gestured for Bean to raise her hand, better illuminating the surface. A rusted metal pole protruded from the middle, confirming his theory.

Stephen reached down to the hole in the door and pulled. A large piece came loose in his hand with a snap. The smell of rotten wood assaulted his nostrils. Whoever built the series of secret doors and passages had forgotten to factor in the environment's effect on their design. His nose tickled again. Stephen's eyes watered with the effort to hold a sneeze in, but it was to no avail. The sound echoed in the tunnel. So not camouflage, but it still might be a way out.

Stephen yanked apart another piece of the door, barely registering splinters as they entered his flesh. The light from Bean's hand dimmed as she joined in the destruction. Together, they pulled until Stephen estimated the hole had to have increased in size large enough to allow their bodies to pass if they crawled.

It wasn't quite enough. The backpack caught on a portion of the opening as he attempted to follow Bean through. He heard its fabric tear as he forced it through the remainder of the way and hoped their supplies within hadn't been damaged, too.

Together, they inched forward in the darkness on their hands and knees. Only when Stephen stopped hearing the pack scraping the debris above did he risk standing up again. He took another step and hit a solid wall.

"Watch your head," said Bean as she stood beside him.

Stephen's hand explored the wall until it touched something cool and angular. He could feel bubbled ridges, which had to be the result of rust. This had to be another door. He pulled. There was no movement. Bean must have noticed his muscles tense in the poor light as her hand joined his. Together, they pulled on the handle until it gave way. The door opened an inch, and as it did, a corner scraped at the ground below. Stephen closed his eyes, wishing he could do the same for his ears as he tugged more until the door opened further. Bean squeezed by him.

The door's closing was smoother, and the light from Bean's hand blazed at the sound of the latch making contact once more. They found themselves at one end of a massive room. The ground beneath them was covered in stone tiles, which sparkled in the reflection of Bean's light as they inched forward. Then her light was joined by another. Stephen turned to identify its source. A large rectangular panel dangled from the ceiling just a few feet away.

As they walked further into the room, another panel began to glow. Bean shook her palm, and the panels became the room's only light source. "How are they still working?" she wondered aloud.

Stephen shrugged, thinking that Bean didn't expect an explanation.

A third panel started to glow overhead. Then there was a popping sound, and the panel went black. Stephen pushed Bean to the side.

"Hey," Bean exclaimed before covering her mouth with one hand.

"I don't know about you, but I'd prefer not to be under one of those things if the wiring is bad." Stephen kept his voice just above a whisper.

Stephen watched as Bean glanced back to the first panel. A narrow cord was all that connected the thing to the ceiling. It swayed in the breeze created by their passage. By the look of it, it wouldn't take much to send it crashing down. He fought his lips from curling into a smile as she scurried further to the side of the room and away from the additional lighting fixtures, even though those remained dark.

Even still, there was now enough light in the room to see a large dais on the other side. Chairs were strewn about in front of the dais, as if a performance had been interrupted at the time of the explosion. On the stage, were several white and coffin-sized chrome cylinders lined against the wall. They beckoned him.

He climbed the stairs of the dais, two at a time.

"What do you think they were supposed to do?" Bean asked as she followed behind him.

Stephen shook his head, but couldn't turn away. One of the cylinders caught his attention, begging him to inspect it first. His feet had their own ideas, taking him over to one of the others located more in the middle.

His feet stopped by its side before his brain processed the walk. His hand ran across the cylinder's surface while pressing down. A door in the cylinder's side opened, exposing a keypad, display, and green indicator lights.

"I don't think you should be. . ." Bean began.

Stephen's eyes widened. "I didn't. I don't." His fingers began dancing across the keypad on their own volition. "I'm not," Stephen realized, in growing terror, that he no longer controlled his own body.

Bean raced to his side and grabbed his wrist. Stephen's other hand shoved at her as his fingers continued to type in commands. "Sorry. I didn't mean to do that. I don't know what is happening," he said, pleading with his eyes for her to understand.

He willed his fingers to stop moving, and as he did so, his peripheral vision caught sight of the cylinder closest to the edge of the dais. Unable to continue to meet Bean's eye after he shoved her or watch as his hand move on its own, he focused on the tube while urging his fingers to stop.

Bean approached him again, touching his sleeve. He didn't know how, and he didn't know why, but she understood the panic going through his mind at that moment all too well. She touched his wrist again, and he focused on the warmth of her touch on his skin until his fingers finally stopped moving.

A beep brought his attention back to the cylinder in front of him. The display flashed 'DEACTIVATE.' Bean drew Stephen back toward the edge of the dais as the cylinder creaked. A gap opened in its side, releasing a gas from within. A large portion of the tube lifted up and slid out. More gas exited. Stephen released the breath he was holding as the mist dissipated into the air.

Then nothing.

Stephen's curiosity got the better of him, and he took a step forward to better see the contents of the tube. Bean's hand encircled his as she followed. Together, they peered over the edge.

"Is he dead?" Bean asked.

Contained within the tube lay a dark-haired man.

twenty-one

"He looks awfully well-preserved for a dead guy," Bean said as she backed away from the cylinder.

From what they could see above the man's clothing, his skin tone was an unnatural alabaster white, but Stephen had to agree with Bean. There were no signs of decay and no smell of death. "But he can't be alive either. Can he?"

"If he's alive, he really doesn't like the sun."

Stephen glanced back at the door from where they'd come. It didn't appear as if anyone had traveled this way in a very long time. He spotted the outline of another door centered in a recessed portion of the back wall. With only two of the ceiling lighting fixtures working he hadn't noticed it before. Was there another way out? He clung to the hope.

"Water," a man's voice muttered.

Stephen almost mistook the sound for crumbling paper, but Bean screeched as she jumped back, stopping herself inches away from falling off the dais. Purple lightning danced across her fingertips and up her lower arm. Stephen tensed into a flight or fight pose, ready for either.

"Water . . ." the man spoke again. This time there was no mistaking that the words were coming from the man within the cylinder. As Stephen stared in shock, a single white finger lifted out of the tube and curled around the edge, followed by another. "Please," he added.

Though the voice was weak, it possessed a tone of command. Stephen was digging through his backpack in search of the canteen before he knew what he was doing. *At least he isn't calling out for blood*, thought Stephen as he twisted open the top. With his white-blue skin and sunken eyes, the man's vibe was too vampire-like for Stephen's comfort.

Stephen poured a bit of their water into a cup and approached the cylinder. The eyes of the man inside were open but darted around as if in search of focus. Unthinking, Stephen reached into the tube and pulled the man upright with one hand while holding the cup to the man's lips with the other. Wires and plastic tubes hung from his torso and his limbs like tendrils.

"Ah . . ." The man closed his eyes after taking a sip. "Much better." The cylinder vibrated as the tendrils released the man and retracted back into its hull.

Color returned to the man's complexion. Though his skin remained pale, it no longer appeared as white as the cylinder surrounding it. His appearance suggested he was somewhere between his twenties and thirties, although it was hard to tell for sure. When his eyes opened once more, they made him seem decades older. *Like Finn*, thought Stephen.

"How?" Bean whispered behind Stephen.

The man blinked twice more, and his gaze became steadier, focusing in on Bean.

"Well, this is a nice surprise." He smiled. "And you are?" His voice became livelier along with the rest of him with every passing second.

Stephen knew without looking that Bean would be frowning at the compliment and forced himself not to smile.

"Someone who doesn't trust reanimated corpses," she replied.

The man shook in Stephen's arms. At first, Stephen thought that he must be having a seizure, only to realize after a few moments that the man was laughing. "Delightful. Please accept my humblest apologies," the man offered. "I suppose my appearance must indeed come as quite a shock."

"Who are you?" asked Stephen.

The man frowned at the question. "You don't recognize me?"

Stephen's eyes narrowed. "Should I?"

The man sighed. Lifting his other hand out of the cylinder, the man grabbed onto the tube's side and pulled himself up until he was in an upright position without the need of Stephen's support. Stephen took a step back to give the man more room to maneuver as the man wiggled one leg then another. "Based on your age, I suppose not. Still, one always hopes." The man grimaced. "Do you know that pins and needles feeling you get whenever you allow your limbs to fall asleep?"

Stephen nodded.

"Well, what I am currently going through feels like that." He wiggled his leg again as his frown deepened. "Except a thousand times worse." The man twisted at the waist as he lifted one leg over the edge followed by the other. He looked at his legs as if they were the worst kind of scum for not behaving. "Would you mind helping me a bit longer?"

Stephen stepped forward and helped pull the man out of the cylinder, supporting his weight with his shoulders while the man touched the floor with each foot a toe at a time. He didn't speak again until he was satisfied that his legs weren't in danger of collapsing out from under his body.

"I'm Dr. Alan Dronigh." A cocky smile returned to his face.

Stephen fought from glancing at Bean as she sucked in her breath. The man could be any number of people, but Stephen was convinced his biological father couldn't be one of them. *Unless he's been here this whole time.* Stephen silenced the voice in his head. The man had an air of charisma about him, that much was true, but he was either delusional or a liar.

"This is the part when you tell me your name."

There was no way he could be the same person. "I'm no one," Stephen finally replied. *But how common is a name like Dronigh?*

"Well No One and Ms. Someone Who Doesn't Trust Reanimated Corpses, would either of you be so kind as to tell me where we are?"

Stephen summoned the map overlay again. Stephen blinked. "That can't be right," he muttered to himself. To the others, he replied, "If the map is correct, we're under what used to be DK Ventures, also known as the Apex Tower. At least what is left of it."

The person claiming to be Alan looked around the room. "Ah, I hoped for something different. I thought I smelled peanut butter."

"Peanut butter?" asked Bean. "All I smell is dust."

"Where do you think you should be?" Stephen asked.

"It doesn't matter. We are here now."

"Would have helped if the front door was more accessible." Bean gestured with her thumb up at the ceiling. "It's more mountain up there than building. I doubt anyone bothered to look for survivors."

"I told Damien he wouldn't regret the expense of reinforcing the structural supports in that area. The foreman bragged it could survive a bomb." Alan chuckled at the comment before looking at their faces and then scanning the contents of the room. "I guess Damien should have paid him more. I'll tell him myself as soon as you take me to him."

Stephen's lips tightened into a fine line. "We don't know any Damien, and we definitely aren't taking you to him."

Alan's smile slipped. "But of course you are." He frowned, and his eyebrows knit in confusion. "Didn't he send you?"

"No one sent us here. We found it by accident."

Alan's frown deepened. "No." He shook his head again. "No, that can't be right. Damien sent you. That was all part of the plan."

"What plan?" asked Bean.

"What plan? The plan, of course." Alan started to shake. This time wasn't caused by laughter. Alan's head began to roll from side to side as spittle began to form at the side of his mouth.

"What's happening?" asked Stephen.

"Like I have any idea," replied Bean. "Maybe it's a side effect from being in whatever that thing is." She took another look at Alan, and her eyes widened. "Lay him on the ground," she ordered.

Stephen lowered Alan to the floor and took a step back to give him air.

"Quick," demanded Bean. "Giving me something I can put in his mouth so that he doesn't bite off his tongue."

Stephen glanced around the room in a panic. A narrow piece of debris caught his eye. Picking it up, he rushed back over to Alan and stuck it in Alan's mouth.

"If he's the real Alan Dronigh, then he's like us, right?" asked Bean, tucking errant strands of hair behind her ear as she looked down at the man on the ground. "So?"

She touched Alan's arm and closed her eyes. Alan continued to shake on the ground. She frowned. "I can't. You try."

"Try what?" asked Stephen, perplexed.

"You're supposed to be the network expert. Pretend his brain is just another computer and connect with it. See if you can settle him down. Like I had to do for you when you first accessed the data stream."

Stephen's brows knit. "But I don't have a clue how you did that either."

Bean reached up and touched Stephen's cheek. "You have to stop fighting so hard. Open your mind like Finn told you to." She pointed at the man convulsing on the floor. "At least try. He is your father."

Stephen crouched to the floor next to Alan's convulsing body and placed his hand on the man's forehead. "He's not my father," he grumbled, but closed his eyes and imagined reaching out with his mind as if it were his arm. As he did so, a pressure built up behind his eyes, as if there was another presence in there with him, fighting him not to do this thing, breaking his focus, and blocking his effort. It was as if the other presence was encouraging him to let the body before him die. "This is pointless." He opened his eyes.

"He's not breathing. Try again."

"I told you I don't know how."

"I don't care. Now focus."

He placed his fingers on either side of the man's temples. The skin beneath his fingers was damp with sweat and twitched in a racing pulse. The pressure returned tenfold. Like that first experience with the data stream, a wave of thoughts that weren't his own rushed across his consciousness. Stephen closed his eyes, tightening the lids as moisture threatened to escape. A comforting warmth spread on his arm where Bean's hand rested. *Pretend it's another node on a network.* He imagined he was back in his hidden nook in the barn staring at his rebuilt console. His fingers flew across the man's forehead with light taps as he visualized entering commands on a keyboard.

The pressure eased as if startled. He pushed through, forcing himself through it much as he had forced the bag through the opening at the top of the stairs. However, just like he'd experienced with the bag, he felt something in his mind tear. Then the pressure fell away, and Stephen pushed his mind and his will forward.

His vision shifted. When he opened his eyes, Stephen was lying on the floor looking up at Bean and his own face. His eyes appeared dull and unseeing. It was as if someone had positioned a wax figurine above him. "What's happening?" he attempted to yell, but there was something in his mouth, blocking the words. He spit it out. The piece of debris. "Bean?" he whispered. "Something's wrong."

"How do you know my name?"

"You told me. Short for Beatrice."

She met his gaze, her lips parting as her eyes widened. "It will be okay." She placed her hand on his forehead. The sheer size of the whites in her eyes betrayed her lie. She looked at Stephen's body. "You're not breathing," she murmured. It was true. His chest was just as still as his face. Turning back to face him, she said, "You were supposed to find his mind. Not take it over."

His panic rose. "What do I do now?" His vision started going black.

"Focus on me. Just me." Darkness framed his vision of her, but at the same time, that growing darkness allowed him to ignore everything but her. Strands of her blonde hair had escaped from behind her ear. He wanted to reach out and sweep it back where it belonged, but the hand that moved was not his own. As he watched, her eyes filled with unshed tears. "Good. Now try to find your way back," he heard her whisper.

He closed his eyes and imagined Bean. She became a flame on a candle in his mind, full of light and warmth, but flickering as it danced to an imagined breeze. He should be fighting to calm himself, but all he could think of was protecting her from the wind. The panic in his chest subsided as the flame straightened. Then he felt a hard shove as if someone had snuck up and pushed him from behind. His stomach lurched as if he fell.

When he opened his eyes, he was looking down on Bean's hunched over form. He attempted to reach out to touch her back and was pleased to see his arm obeyed his command. Bean looked at him at his touch. Narrow lines of moisture streaked her face. His lips turned up. "You do care."

She jumped up and walked away. "Don't you ever try that again."

Stephen looked at Alan lying prone on the floor. The convulsions had stopped, but his eyes were still closed.

Alan groaned. "Don't worry, I'll make sure there will never be a second time. Excuse me." He twisted his body so that he was propped up on one elbow facing away from the others. His torso shook as bile created a puddle on the floor.

Bean wrinkled her nose and took a step back. Alan frowned. "Unfortunately, it would seem that I still require a little more recovery time. If you aren't going to take me to Damien, would you at least move me somewhere a little more comfortable? My head feels as if it might split in two."

Stephen nodded and pulled Alan upright, bracing Alan's body with his shoulder. Bean looked at them and then at the other cylinders on the dais. "Are there any others like you down here?"

Alan turned his head following Bean's gaze. His eyes twinkled under the swaying light. "No." His lips curled. "Rest assured, I am quite unique." He turned back toward them and met Stephen's eyes. "As I am beginning to suspect, you are as well."

TWENTY-TWO

Stephen attempted to shift Alan's weight while checking out the pair of recessed doors on the other side of the room. "Do you think it's a way out?" They had to find a way out. They'd spent too long down here already.

Bean glanced at him, cocking her head in unvoiced question.

"Over there. I think it used to be an elevator," replied Stephen, pointing in its direction. Considering how well-preserved this room was, he had to wonder if the elevator shaft might have also survived intact. He had no idea how they would be able to scale such a thing but figured there had to be a service ladder or something similar inside. Each minute they stayed down here was another minute he risked the Watch returning to the tower. *Assuming they haven't already figured out you aren't there.*

Alan followed their gazes. "I'm afraid that's not an option."

"It could be," Stephen argued. "I mean look around this room. Look at the lights. They survived. Maybe the elevator did, too."

"Ah, I see why you might think that, but no." The corner of Alan's lip turned up. "I'm quite certain we'd find the way blocked."

"You don't know that."

"Yes, I do. The initial explosion took place in there. I'm not sure of the exact location of explosions that followed, but there were more than a few." Alan shrugged. "That's why I went into the pod to wait it out rather than trying to go up."

Stephen took another look at the elevator. He imagined the pile of rubble that in all likelihood still lay above them. "Do you know if anyone was in it? When the building came down? The elevator, I mean." Stephen asked as he repressed a shudder. Anyone trapped inside would have spent their last moments in terror as they ran out of food or water. It would have been awful.

Bean looked at the pair of doors, and Stephen noticed she hesitated just a step. "Do you think it was quick?"

"It was quicker than he deserved," Alan's voice cut through Stephen's thoughts. He gestured at the debris and hanging wires. "You recognized the building's name. What do you know about what happened here?" Alan shifted again.

The change in weight distribution caught Stephen off guard, and it was all he could do not to stumble. *How did I get stuck with this job?* "Not much. I do know this building is pretty much the center of where it all started. As in, ground zero." He scanned the map's information. "Oh, and it once housed some sort of think tank."

Alan snorted. "Some sort of think tank," he repeated. "Oh, we did so much more than that here." Alan swept his free arm, as if to encompass the room. "We didn't just come up with ideas. We took them further, pushing the limits of the human experience. We found ways to eradicate diseases. Make people better, faster, and stronger than they were before. We were maximizing life's every potential."

"So says the man who can't walk on his own," said Bean.

Alan's lips tightened, and his arm returned to his side. His eyes took on a distant look. "There will always be those who fear or can't handle change, and even more who value their profits over the greater good. Unfortunately, those people joined forces." Alan shook his head as he motioned for Stephen to stop. He took a hesitant step on his own. "Ground zero." Alan seemed to chew on the word. "We can discuss that term later, but first, do you happen to know if there were any other survivors? From my so-called think tank, I mean."

Stephen frowned and tried to think of anything Ed or Helen may have mentioned over the years, but his memory drew a blank. The beginning of the end of life as they knew it just didn't come up in their regular conversation. He imagined tapping into the data stream. It offered even less help. Its information stopped at the beginning of the panic.

"If any did, they kept their stories to themselves," replied Bean before Stephen could answer.

"Pity." Alan smiled. "But that doesn't necessarily mean there weren't. Discretion was everything in our business, and we tended to bring on those who knew how to keep sensitive information a secret." Alan took a couple more steps, each more confident than the last. Stephen stayed back and crossed his arms. "So, if there weren't any other survivors, and you didn't come here to rescue me, I must ask, why are you here?"

Stephen glanced at Bean and then at the roof above them. It was well past evening by now.

Alan wobbled. "Ah, I understand you want to keep your secrets. As I said, we are"—he paused to look at one of the hanging light fixtures—"or *were* a discreet group." Alan patted Stephen's hand, before shaking it away. "How about we talk about something else while we get to know one another better? Like why you call this place ground zero."

Bean spoke first. "My parents lost their jobs. So did everyone else. Some company that everyone thought was too big to fail, did. My parents waited around. They thought it was only a matter of time until things got better, but things didn't get better. Kids started dying instead." Her lips twisted. "My parents were stupid."

Stephen realized how lucky he had been to reach the farm with Helen and Ed so early in the initial crisis. If his guardians hadn't connected the dots between events, weeks if not months before the rest of the population, they might never have reached the farm before the real global panic set in.

"Then things really got bad. When people realized that no government was coming to help them, they took matters into their own hands."

"So who is in charge now?" asked Alan.

Bean shrugged. "Big picture? Who knows? But a group called the Watch sure thinks they are around here." Alan's lips twisted. Stephen found himself yawning. Bean, noticing, yawned, too. She asked, "How long do you think we've been down here?"

"Three, maybe four hours," he guessed. *Three or four hours they could have spent on the road back to the tower.* He yawned again. That would mean the time was long past midnight by now. Stephen's back ached from their walk through the tunnels. He looked back into the open room.

"Maybe we should camp here for the night before setting out again."

Stephen's shoulders tensed at Bean's suggestion, but he yawned again anyway. As much as he wanted to be on their way, she was right. *But where?* Stephen frowned. His eyebrow rose as an idea sprouted in his mind. "I guess we could sleep in the pods." *Worst case, we can leave Alan in one.*

"What? The pods?" Alan pulled back. "That's a terrible idea. We can't. Why would you even suggest something like that?"

"Of course we can." Stephen plastered a smile on his face. "They protected you for, what, fifteen years? What's one more night?" They'd reactivate Alan's pod and be on their way first thing in the morning without him. It was a great plan. Then, after delivering the wand and freeing his folks, he'd come back for him or send someone else to do the job. *Maybe.* "They are perfect."

Bean glanced back at the cylinders. She pulled Stephen to the side. "Are you nuts? What if you lose control again?"

"I won't." Stephen scowled in an effort to mask the feeling of helplessness her words brought back.

"Why don't I believe that?"

Alan arched an eyebrow. "They *were* perfect." He nodded his head in the direction of one of the more damaged pods. "Not so much anymore. What if you got in and it sealed itself? We might never get it to re-open."

Stephen turned his attention to Bean. "We need to be out of sight. What about the people back at the lab? What if they found the door? They could be almost here by now." The excuse wasn't even a lie. Stephen glanced at the door. If the Watch knew someone had taken the wand, they could still be out there tracking them.

"You poor things," said Alan. "I can't begin to imagine what an ordeal you must have gone through." He also focused his attention on Bean. "The world ends and you are on the run. No wonder you are both terrified." Alan's voice had smoothed into a near purr.

Stephen smirked as he waited to see how Bean might respond. *This guy*—he still refused to accept that Alan was his biological father—*might think he knows how to talk to women, but he doesn't know Bean.*

Bean bristled like a cat. "I. Am. Not. Terrified."

Alan laughed, "I stand corrected. You remind me of a colleague of mine named Sarah. She was a tough one, too."

"Do you think she was tough enough to survive that?" Bean pointed at the light fixture still hanging by a cord, which looked lower to the ground than it had upon their initial arrival.

The smile fell away from Alan's face, but the laughter never left his eyes. "It wouldn't surprise me in the least."

"So, back to tonight," Stephen interrupted. "I still think our best bet is to spend it in the pods. We just leave them open."

"No." Alan's pronouncement boomed across the space. "No. And that's the end of the discussion."

Stephen raised an eyebrow. He'd use the same tone of voice as Ed had used on him whenever he'd been particularly stubborn. "Fine, we'll sleep somewhere else, but we take turns," he said to Bean. He thought of the screech the access door had made as it scraped across the floor when they'd entered. *At least no one is going to be able to sneak up on us through that thing,* Stephen thought.

Alan's lips curled up. "Something I am more than happy to do. I'll even take the first watch."

Stephen clenched his jaw. He hadn't intended to include Alan in the rotation.

"You both look dead on your feet." Alan pointed at the pods with his thumb. "I've been asleep for . . . what was it?"

Stephen turned away and scanned the room for another location. "Fifteen years." A large section of ductwork lay on the ground nearby. It could shield them from view.

"Well, then I think I can manage to stay awake for a few hours. If it makes you feel better, I'll even keep watch here while you two get some rest over there."

Once they were behind the ductwork, Stephen unzipped the backpack and pulled out the tight roll that served as their sleeping mat, and he whispered to Bean, "I'm sorry."

Bean paused. "For what?"

"For, you know"—he nodded his head in the direction of the fallen ductwork—"all of this. What your family had to go through afterward. I had no idea it was like that."

Bean snorted. "That's hardly your fault."

Stephen stood, and as he shook the mat out, he caught a glance of Alan at the wall. Alan's eyes were focused on the dais. Shadows cut across his face, so his expression was hard to read, but it appeared his lips were pulled in a smug smile as if amused at a joke only he understood.

Alan turned his head, matching Stephen's gaze. *That's not creepy at all,* Stephen told himself. He broke eye contact first, crouching behind the metal as he smoothed the mat across the floor. As he did so, he noticed his shadow against the tubing's surface. It was almost identical in height and form to Alan, and he found himself for the first time beginning to accept that Alan might just be his biological father.

Twenty-Three

Stephen opened his eyes to darkness. He hadn't intended to fall asleep, not wanting to trust their safety to some guy they'd pulled out of a metal tube, even if that guy was his birth father, but it would seem his body had other ideas. As he listened to Bean's rhythmic breathing by his side, he was tempted to turn over and slip back into unconsciousness. Then he heard a scratching noise from the direction of the subway access door. Stephen shot up, banishing thoughts of sleep from his brain. As he did so, one of the lighting fixtures came back online. *They must work with some sort of motion sensor*, he thought. As the light expanded and intensified, he looked around the room, but Alan was nowhere to be seen.

I knew we shouldn't trust him. Stephen reached over and tapped Bean's arm. Her eyes opened in an instant. She rolled into a defensive crouch with one hand clenched into a fist, as if readying to do battle with the other flat on the ground.

A blinking green spot the size of a gnat appeared in his lower vision. Stephen swat at it. *Weird bug.*

"What is it?" Bean's lips hadn't moved, and yet the words in his mind were spoken in her voice.

Stephen frowned and tried to formulate a response in his mind. He imagined a 'send' key and pressed it. "Alan's gone."

"Gone? What do you mean gone?" This time, there was no doubt that her words were in his mind. A grin spread across his face in light of this newest skill, his irritation forgotten for the moment.

"He couldn't walk more than three steps on his own last night. How could he be gone? Where *could* he go?" he heard her say.

Stephen shrugged as his annoyance with Alan returned in full force. *Maybe he really is dear old dad, after all. He sure does have the disappearing part down.* "I don't know. Maybe he knew about another way out of here." This time the words were much easier to send out. As annoyed as he was, Stephen was more than a little relieved that they didn't have to worry about the man anymore. It also meant an exit could be somewhere nearby.

He heard a muffled scratching, scraping sound again, and Alan's whereabouts became the least of his concerns. *The Watch*, Stephen thought. *They must have found the entrance, after all.* If so, they had minutes before the Watch found the door to this room. *Or it's rats.* Stephen shuddered as adrenaline flooded his system. Stephen turned his hand so that his palm was face up and brought his fingers together until they were just shy of touching, as he'd seen Bean do so many times before, and he concentrated. *Think of it as another program*, he thought, focusing in on the ridges of his fingerprints. *Run electric eel 2.0.* A flash of purple light jumped from his thumb to his middle finger. *Yes.* The light winked out. He'd let the joy of his accomplishment break his concentration. He focused on his hand. The purple light flashed again, this time from thumb to pinkie and then from the ring to the index finger. His fingertips tingled as the light continued to jump across his skin, faster and faster, until it appeared to consolidate into a ball hovering just above his palm. *I am Zeus, God of Thunder.*

"It's about time you figured that out," Bean's voice in his mind broke his concentration once more, and the orb blinked out.

He now understood why Bean was so quick to accept the lessons Finn had taught her while not worrying about the risk of the energy drain. The knowledge that he would never again be without defense was intoxicating. He flexed his fingers again, and the light returned on command. He opened his fingers, and the light went away in an instant. Why had it been so hard to believe in what he could do?

"Did you know that the man who first discovered how to do that particular skill thought it little more than an amusing party trick?" Alan's voice echoed in the room. Stephen spun, searching for the source of the voice. "Did I startle you?" continued Alan as he stepped out of one of the room's remaining shadows. "My apologies. After the feeling came back to my legs, I found I could no longer sit in one place, so moved where I hoped I wouldn't disturb you. I also turned off the lights."

How had I missed seeing him? Stephen wondered. The shadow had wrapped itself around him like a blanket. Stephen also noticed Alan's stride no longer showed any semblance of weakness. "How . . .?" Stephen started.

"I reprogrammed the control to ignore my movement so that you could get some sleep. I thought it was the least I could do."

Alan spoke of accessing a nearly ruined control panel and wirelessly updating the code with a mere thought, as if it was the sort of thing a regular person could do any day. Stephen blinked as it dawned on him that as far as Alan knew, everyone still could.

"No, I was going to ask how long were we asleep?"

Alan smiled. "Oh. I'd say about nine hours."

"Nine hours?" Stephen exclaimed. "Nine?" he repeated. He cursed. If they had found an access ladder, they could already be at the train station on their way back to the island by now. "Why did you let us sleep that long?"

"Because you needed it."

Stephen clenched his teeth. "Don't you get it?" He pointed at the door. "There are people after us. People we might have gotten away from in that amount of time who we are now going to have to fight our way past, all thanks to you."

Alan raised an eyebrow. "Must you? Fight them, I mean."

"Listen, I know this must be hard for you to accept. The world was a different place when you got into that pod. But now, we do what we have to do to survive."

An ear-piercing scrape silenced further debate as the door started to open. *Not rats then.* Alan took a step toward it. Stephen stifled a curse. An incautious man was a dead man, and as much as he wanted to be rid of Alan, he didn't want that on his conscience. He grabbed Alan and pulled him down behind some fallen ductwork while Bean followed suit. They might not have any option other than to fight, but at least they might still be able to take whoever it was on the other side of that door by surprise.

Alan started to say something. Stephen covered Alan's mouth with his hand and shook his head. Alan arched an eyebrow, then shrugged. Interpreting the gesture to mean that Alan would follow their lead, Stephen risked a glance around the ductwork.

A man stepped out of a doorway's shadows. His skin appeared paper thin with age spots dotting his balding scalp. He wore a jersey, which hung from his frame as if purchased once for someone twice his size. Most of the paint that once proclaimed the team's name and player's number had flaked off to illegibility. A thin chain with an egg-shaped pendant hung around his neck. Stephen did a double take as the lamplight hit the man's face in full. His nose was broad and flat with nostrils that flared like a beast's. Gaps where teeth should have been made him appear to possess fangs. *Then again . . .* Stephen took another hard look at the man's mouth. *They might very well be actual fangs, or were they more like tusks?*

The man took another step into the room, and Stephen noticed he walked with a limp. *Don't freak out. He's just an old man with a bad leg in serious need for a trip to the dentist.* The old man's nostrils flared once again as his lips curled up. *Tusks,* thought Stephen. *Definitely tusks.* "What are you playing at? Hide-and-go-seek?"

The old man laughed or at least produced a sound that Stephen interpreted as a laugh. It was low, and rough, and could have passed for the bark of a dog. "Not much of a game. You stink, you know." Stephen watched as the man grabbed his less favored leg and twisted. The act made a sickening snapping sound as the leg seemed to rotate into an unnatural position. The man dropped down onto all fours, looking like a bull readying for a charge. "Ready or not, here I come." He scraped the floor with the unnatural leg, now appearing anything but lame. The ground shook with each step.

Seconds that seemed like years compared to the beating of his heart passed. Not wanting to give their position away until they had to, Stephen's hand remained flesh-colored, but his fingers were curled, ready to summon the lightning in an instant. What had Alan called it? A party trick? Dr. Lambda's word for what they could do came back unbidden. *Delusion.* What if that's all it was? Was he really willing to trust his life to something the original creator described as a trick? The man at the barricade had been weak already. Even if the lightning wasn't a figment of his imagination, it wouldn't have taken much to knock him down. This man, this monster, was different.

As the old man's steps grew closer, Stephen became more convinced trusting in their abilities was a mistake. He turned to warn Bean, but she had disappeared. His heart caught in his throat. He wanted to call out but worried the old man might sense projected thoughts as well as audible calls. There was no telling what a person who'd been physically modified like that could do.

Then the footsteps stopped. Stephen risked another glance around the ductwork. The beastman lay in a crumpled pile on the floor, his unnatural legs twitching. Bean stood above him, her fist clenching purple lightning like an avenging goddess. A beautiful, magnificent, all-powerful avenging goddess. *The lightning trick had been enough.* Or maybe Bean was just that good. *Be glad she's on your side.*

Stephen's heart skipped a beat as Bean nudged the man with her toe. The man's leg spasmed, but there was no other evidence of consciousness. Satisfied he was no longer a threat, she left him there and returned to where Stephen still crouched. "I believe this puts me ahead again."

"Ahead of what?"

"Oh, don't pretend you haven't been keeping score."

"I don't know what you are talking about," Stephen murmured with a smile. Bean's eyes seemed more slate than jade and her skin grayer than it had before, but that didn't stop Stephen from wanting to touch her if only to assure himself she was safe.

"Yes, you do. You've been keeping track of how often you've swooped in and saved me." Stephen started to protest but stopped when Bean held up one hand. "Don't even try to say you haven't. You're a terrible liar." Bean's eyes softened as she placed her hand on his chin. "I like that about you," she whispered as she traced her fingers across his jawline while coaxing his gaze to meet hers once more.

Then her lips met his, and all thoughts of their mission, the events of the last few days and even the recent danger, fled his mind. Lost in sensation and focusing on the heat of her skin where it touched his, Stephen forgot they weren't alone until he heard a cough. Bean pulled away, and a shy smile played across her lips. Her cheeks were rosy and her eyes sparkled. Gone was any trace of the shadow he thought he had once seen, and he weakened in the knees to look at her.

Her smile vanished. She took another step back, touching her lips with her fingers. "I—"

Worry took root in Stephen's stomach.

"If you two are quite done," Alan started, jolting Stephen back to the present. "I'd appreciate some help, here." Alan knelt on the ground next to the man.

"Good idea. We should move him before any more of his friends get here." Stephen came over to Alan's side and bent over to pull the old man up.

"And why should we do that?"

"So we can surprise them, too. It's our only advantage."

Alan rolled his eyes. "I told you before we didn't have to fight anyone."

"And I told *you*, we don't have a choice. Look at him." Stephen nodded in the direction of the old man's face. The old man's limp jaw opened as Stephen pulled him upright, allowing ample view of his long canine teeth. "Do you think a guy who looks like this is interested in talking? I mean, do you think he was born that way? Because I sure don't. Who does that to themselves anyway?"

"Any number of the Sharks. They thought it made them look more intimidating to the other team. Based on your reaction, I suppose they are right."

"Sharks."

"Yes, Sharks. As in, the football team. You should see some of the others. Rotledge might have spent more time on the bench than on the field, but you could never fault his enthusiasm."

"You know him?"

"I should hope so. After all, I asked him to come here."

twenty-four

The beastman didn't so much as make a woof as Alan opened the door to the subway access tunnel. Stephen blinked as his eyes took in the beam of natural sunlight shining down from above. His chest ached as he filled his lungs with a deep breath, savoring the scent of fresh air, even if that air was mixed with dirt and a hint of rust. A hatch in the ceiling made invisible in the dark now lay open, exposing a ladder to the surface and freedom from the tunnels.

Bean cocked her head as she watched Alan reach up and pull the bottom rungs down to their level. "I don't get it."

"Get what?" replied Alan as he shook the ladder as if testing its strength.

"Why go in the pod? I mean, if you knew there was another way out, why didn't you take it?" Stephen grinned as Bean asked the question that gnawed on his mind since they'd settled down for the night. It was as if he and she had been connected long before ever accessing the data stream.

Alan stopped his inspection and turned to face them both while keeping one hand on the rung. "I would think that would be obvious." He nodded toward the rock and twisted metal that lay around them. "A group of anti-technological nut jobs had the building surrounded. I thought it best not to give them an easy target."

Alan returned his attention to the ladder and took a step. "And before you ask, I also couldn't possibly know if this access point remained open all the way to the surface, which is why I called for Rotledge to come and clear it for us."

"What should we do about him?" asked Stephen.

"Do?"

"About Rotledge? Should we wait for him to wake up?"

The corner of Alan's lips turned up. "After the thanks you gave him, I very much doubt you want to be anywhere near him when he wakes up."

"But we can't just leave him down here," Stephen protested.

Alan shook his head. "Of course we can."

"But he's your friend."

Alan paused and looked at Stephen. "In addition to our business projects, my company is . . . er . . . *was* invested in the success of the Sharks. He's a former business associate. Never confuse the two. Now, are you ready to return to the surface, or do you want to take your chances with whoever you think is following you down here?"

Seeing no other choice, Stephen followed Alan up to the surface, hoping he hadn't just traded one monster for another.

As they made their way outside and back down the rubble mountain, which had one time served as an office building, Alan picked up a clump of dirt and small pebbles at the base of the pile and began rubbing it across his clothing.

"You don't need to do that," said Stephen as he gestured to the empty open road below. "I mean, if you want your clothes to get dirty, they'll get there on their own."

Alan scraped harder. "Exactly, but that will take time. Until then, if everything is as you say it is, then I'm going to stand out, which is never a strategy for success if survival depends on blending in."

Bean picked up a wad of earth and threw it at Alan. "Here, let me help."

You don't have any reason to be jealous, Stephen told himself. *She likes you*. He paused as he watched the exchange in front of him. *Doesn't she?* Stephen frowned. There hadn't been a repeat of their kiss. In fact, she hadn't even touched him since then. Had it only been a response to her victory over Rotledge? A knot formed in his stomach that had nothing to do with the last meal bar he'd eaten. "Something else has been bothering me," interrupted Stephen.

"Oh?" asked Alan as he continued to rub dirt into his previously pristine clothing.

"You." Stephen glanced in Bean's direction for support but was unable to make eye contact as she scooped up another bit of dirt and handed it to Alan. "This is going to come out the wrong way, but you don't look anywhere old enough to be who you say you are, even if you've been asleep all this time." Stephen glanced Bean's way. "Er . . . I mean, you look my age, which would make you like twelve when you . . . you know"—Stephen chewed his lip to keep from saying the words *had me*, which rattled around in his head—"discovered stuff," he finished with instead.

A dazzling smile returned to Alan's face. "What can I say? I have good genes." Alan chuckled. "You kids might not yet appreciate the humor in that phrase, but one day you will realize it is one of the world's biggest understatements."

Bean shrugged and stepped back to admire her handiwork. "Satisfied?"

Alan looked down at his attire now stained brown with streaks of yellow-green where weeds had mixed in with the dirt clump. He sighed. "I suppose it will have to do." He walked down the street without waiting to see if they would follow.

Alan's connection and command of their abilities had gotten them out of the tunnels. Who knew how long they might have continued without seeing the light of day within him? *Don't give him too much credit. It was the guy he summoned who opened the door.* Stephen thought of his call to Wes across the water. *I wonder what sort of range we have.* Stephen wrinkled his forehead, focused his thoughts, and mentally pushed them until he thought he might give himself a headache.

Alan chuckled. "What exactly are you trying to do?"

Stephen's shoulders drooped. "I was trying to send a message to a friend letting him know that we were on our way back. Like how you called Rotledge."

"Was that what you were doing? From where I stood, it looked like those meal bars you've been inhaling weren't agreeing with you. I was feeling rather glad not to have tried them." Bean laughed at Alan's comment.

Stephen looked at anything but their faces as he sought to come up with a response. *You are such an idiot. Listen to her laugh. She's not interested in you. You were just in the right place at the right time. End of story.* His eyes landed on a pair of boarded-up windows belonging to what once had been a service station. Large swathes of faded red paint swirled across their surfaces, but the graffiti had long since fallen into a state of neglect.

"I give up." He threw his hands up. *Might as well ask. They can't think any less of you.* "How does this telepathy thing work over distances even when so much else doesn't?" Stephen gestured at the building to illustrate his point.

Alan glanced at the service station and then back to Stephen. He cocked his head. "Ignoring the simplistic use of the term 'telepathy,' I fail to see why you might think a failed business has any impact on our ability to transmit and receive information."

"A few weeks ago, I was living in the middle of nowhere, and my only contact with the outside world was done by computer. If our windmill stopped working, it was radio silence."

"How inconvenient for you."

Ignoring Alan's commentary, Stephen picked up a broken piece of asphalt. "Take this rock." He threw it up and caught it with hand. "Here, Bean, catch." Stephen threw to Bean's outstretched hand. "Now throw it back." Bean compiled. "I totally get that she and I might be able to communicate. Well, maybe I don't get *how* we're doing it exactly, but at least I'm guessing it is because I'm near enough for her to pick up whatever sort of signal it is I'm generating." Stephen tossed the rock again, this time further down the street, not caring where it landed. "But there's got to be some limit to my range, and without connecting to another computer, or node, or whatever to power the signal, how does the information get where it is going? It's not like the grid still works."

Alan stepped closer and placed a hand on Stephen's shoulder. "Is that a fact?" Alan walked over to the service station. After studying the window for a few moments, he reached forward and pulled at the boards. "The first thing you need to know is you were lied to. There is no grid, at least not like you think there is." They came away easy, falling to the ground with a clatter. Alan placed his hand on the glass and closed his eyes. Stephen watched as Alan's chest rose and fell twice while the rest of his body remained motionless. A glow began to expand from inside the shop. A sign near the door blinked on, showing the words 'open all night' in blue and red LEDs.

Bean gasped. "How is that even possible?"

"There are embedded power cells in the glass and nanoelectronics in the brickwork full of all sorts of sensors and processors, grouped under the generic term nanobots. The bots are in everything. Walls, streets, everywhere, even a person's blood. They are what gave people who could afford it access to the data stream with a thought. It was one of the very few things that the Evans family and their company ever got right. Now, all you have to know is how to take command and redirect the current."

"The who?" asked Stephen.

"The Evans family." Bean's lip curled. "As in, Louis Evans. The owner of ACI. The idiot who decided technology was bad and let his business go under."

"It seems I'm not the only one less than impressed with his leadership."

"But why not let people know there was still power?" Stephen asked. "People panicked when they were told the grid wasn't coming back online. Cities fell. Tons of people died. Why would anyone lie about something like that?"

"But that means . . ." She took a step back from the building. "All this time . . ." A violent swirl of rage and sorrow tore through Stephen's brain like a tornado. His knees threatened to buckle under its weight. He blinked as he regained equilibrium. It was a feeling so raw, Stephen wondered if Bean was aware she'd projected it and decided it was better not to ask. Her eyes were hard, and her cheeks showed no signs of shed tears. She might have shared her true emotion with him, but intentional or not, it was not something she was willing to share with anyone else. Then another of her sensations blossomed in his mind. It was hatred so fierce, Stephen shivered in response.

Alan shrugged. "Ignorance? A play for power? Greed? I can think of any number of reasons. The question you should be asking is why has the lie continued?" Alan examined his fingernails as if inspecting them for dirt picked up from his demonstration. "The answer that comes to my mind is because the wrong people are still in charge. Which is unfortunate, but in my experience, not unexpected. Now, shall we continue on?" He gestured at the road ahead. "Or do you have more questions?"

Alan stepped away from the storefront. As he did so, the lights from the open sign went dark. Stephen noticed Alan hesitated for a fraction of a second before continuing but did not look back. *He didn't turn the sign off,* thought Stephen. *Maybe it isn't quite as black and white as he wants us to believe it is.*

twenty-five

"And just where do you think you're going?"

Stephen spun at the sound of an unknown voice. A man stepped out from what remained of a coffee shop, based on the sign that hung above the door. The man smiled, showing teeth that were far longer than any naturally born human's ought to be. He took additional steps forward in a lopsided sort of gait that reminded Stephen of a fox or a coyote making its way through the forest. *Or a werewolf.* Stephen's forehead puckered, reminded of Jim's story. *Maybe Jim had seen something or someone in the woods that night.* The beastman's smile deepened as if sensing easy prey.

Alan spared Stephen a sideways glance. "One of these days, you will realize you can't judge people by their appearance alone. You'll find you are often wrong." Alan raised a hand in greeting and called out "Shaw." The man froze in mid-stride and cocked his head. His nostrils flared, as if picking up a scent.

"Dr. Dronigh?" The beastman's threatening smile was replaced with one of delighted wonder. "When Rotledge said it was you, well, we . . . You look great." He grabbed Alan's hand and shook it with gusto. "Especially for a dead guy."

"The reports of my death have been greatly exaggerated," chuckled Alan.

Alan's words were met with silence. He turned to look at Stephen with an eyebrow raised. "That was a reference to Twain." He looked at Bean when Stephen failed to react. "You, too? Mark Twain? No?" Bean shrugged. Alan sighed again. "Well, I guess when society as you know it is brought to its knees, the first thing that goes is a proper education. I suggest you look him up some time on the data stream." While still clutching the man's hand, Alan turned to face them fully. "Bean, Stephen, I would like to introduce you to Shaw McMillan, onetime All-American All-Star Quarterback to the Sharks."

"It's two-time, All-American." Shaw grinned, dropping his hand.

Alan waved the comment away. "Well, to be fair, you only achieved that once as a Shark, and really, that's the only team that matters. How is, what's her name? Amber?"

Shaw guffawed a sound that was both distinctive and displeasing to Stephen's ears. A quick glance in Bean's direction told him she was equally unsettled. "Nah, Amber and I split before the last playoffs. She cramped my style. You're thinking about Ginger."

"Ah, yes, Ginger." Alan tapped his forehead. "Gorgeous woman. How's she?"

"Long gone and good riddance. I caught her trying to palm off some of my old trophies. Dumb bitch. She didn't realize the only currency that still has any value is muscle." Shaw flexed his biceps. "And that's something she'll never lay her claws into again."

"No doubt. What about the rest of the team? What are they up to nowadays?" Alan asked.

"Ah, a little this, a little that. Most of us stuck around the town when all hell broke loose. We couldn't let our fans down by leaving them unprotected."

The smile slipped from Shaw's face as his gaze slipped behind them. "Where is Rotledge anyway? He ran off saying he got a message asking to rescue you from some sort of pit of doom."

Alan's smile turned sheepish. "He's fine. Sleeping off what will no doubt be a monster of a headache. These two tazed him before I told them he was there for us." Alan clicked his tongue. "Rotledge has slowed down since his retirement. I would have expected better."

Shaw's face changed from threatening coyote to wounded pup. Stephen thought he even heard the man whimper. "Yeah. We all have. You don't know what it has been like. Had we known that last season would be the last . . ."

Alan's expression softened. "The years have been tough on all of us." Stephen's eyebrows rose at Alan's comment. Clearly, Alan wasn't going to share with Shaw that he'd effectively slept through all of them. "But you've always struck me as someone who knew how to make the most of whatever was thrown at him. I'm assuming you and Rotledge didn't take up a new career in the protection industry for free."

Shaw slapped Alan on the back. "As I said, muscle is the only currency left in town. You interested in signing up? The boss might appreciate an extra brain on the team."

"I was expecting to meet up with an old friend, but since he hasn't shown up, I would be up for a chance to say hello and catch up with anyone else who remains from the team. It's been far too long."

"That, I'd be happy to arrange." Shaw leaped into motion, the wounded pup now like an eager dog.

Stephen smiled when Bean didn't follow Alan and Shaw as they continued down the road. *Good riddance,* he thought. Now all he had to do was get the wand back to Finn, save Ed and Helen, and maybe—if he was lucky—win the girl. His cheeks blushed at that last thought, but he couldn't help asking, "Do you want to go with him?"

"Why would I do that? We got what we came out here for."

Stephen's relief was interrupted by a loud growl.

"I think that was just your stomach. Again," said Bean with a laugh. "Seriously, how did you not starve before?" She came over to his side. "I'll get you something to eat."

She pulled on the backpack. Its straps cut into his shoulders as she stood on her toes and rummaged around.

"That's okay. I can get something myself." He swung the pack around and opened its pocket. Stephen paused as his eyes saw a handful of empty wrappers and the larger half of Wes's antenna. "Where is it?" He dropped the bag to the ground and emptied its entire contents onto the street.

"Where's what?"

"The wand." Stephen managed to bark out as his hand touched the pack's bottom without coming into contact with the metal rod. "It's gone."

"What do you mean *it's gone?*"

"I think he took the wand," Stephen whispered. "Alan." The smile fell from Bean's face. "He must have gotten into the bag while we slept." He rubbed his temples. He *knew* he shouldn't have trusted Alan. He *knew* it. Their entire mission was a failure. Stephen kicked the empty bag, wishing it was the Watch. "What's so important about it? Dumb stick. Probably doesn't even work anymore."

"I'm guessing Alan knows."

"Knows what?"

"What the wand does. Or at least he knows why it's valuable." She pulled Stephen back from the pack before he could damage their remaining foodstuffs. "Why else would he take it?"

Because he's a selfish jerk who doesn't care about anyone. That's why. "So now what?"

"We get it back."

"Right. We just run up to Alan and demand it back. Yeah, I can imagine how that works for us." If Alan wasn't feeling cooperative, he might use it against them. *No,* Stephen shook his head, correcting himself. Alan didn't need to use the wand on them. All he had to do was call them liars and turn one of his beast friends on them. Stephen looked down the empty road leading back to the train station and the city beyond. His folks would spend the rest of their lives wondering why he'd abandoned them to their fate.

"So we don't ask."

"He knows he stole it. He's gonna be ready for us to try to take it back."

"Not if we act like everything's fine." Stephen's brow wrinkled as he tried to follow her logic. "Like he's welcome to it. You said it yourself. We have no clue what it does. Why should it be any more valuable to us than any other piece of garbage picked up from the side of the road?" Bean pointed the remainder of Wes's antenna mixed in with the pile of bars surrounding the pack. "We don't have to act right away. We can wait until his guard is down. It could totally work."

"So what's our story then?" asked Stephen. "He knows we are on the run. Why would he want us to go wherever it is he is going?"

"Tell him you recognized him after all and that you are his son. Tell him you want to get to know him better."

Stephen pursed his lips. "That's not happening."

Bean rolled her eyes. "If you have a better idea, feel free to share it."

Stephen bent down and grabbed a rock. He flung it at the closest building. The sound of glass shattered echoed down the street. Dogs barked in the distance. "He knows someone is after us. It would make sense for us to look for safety in numbers."

Her eyes twinkled as she began stuffing the bars into their bag. "And here I was beginning to wonder if the only suggestions you listened to were your stomach's."

He bent over to help her, and his hand touched hers. She straightened, leaving him to finish cleaning up the mess on his own. "You heard Shaw. This is his neighborhood. They can't be going far, but we're going to have to sprint if we want to catch up.

Once their supplies were returned to the pack and its straps lay across his shoulders, they took off in a run after Alan and Shaw, finding them a few blocks away. While Alan looked like he didn't have a care in the world, his gait remained slow and tentative. Shaw walked several paces ahead. "Shaw," Stephen called out as they reached Alan. His side cramped. "Wait up." Shaw cocked his head at the sound of his name but didn't stop, like a dog listening for a command.

"Shaw." Alan's tone, infused with command, stopped Shaw in his tracks. "I believe the kids are asking us to stop. I could use the rest, too. Not all of us were born into athletic dynasties like you were."

Shaw shrugged and wandered over to a brick staircase that no longer led to anything habitable. Shaw turned in a circle three times before sitting down. Stephen's eyes met Bean's as she raised one eyebrow before joining Shaw on the step. Stephen removed a canteen from the backpack's supplies and offered her a sip.

"You first," she said. "You're the one lugging all that."

"Well, if you aren't thirsty, I wouldn't mind a sip." Alan sauntered by grabbing the canteen from Stephen's hand as he passed before joining Bean and Shaw on the brick steps. Water splashed on the ground with Alan's enthusiastic swig. Stephen watched as the liquid pooled for a moment before seeping in between the brickwork. Alan's lack of regard regarding the availability of clean water was yet another indication of how much the world had changed since he'd gone into the pod. "I am surprised. When you stayed behind, I thought you had some place you needed to go."

I do, so why don't you give me back what you stole? "We thought you could use some more protection. I mean, it's a lot different out here than when you. . ."

The corner of Alan's lips turned up. "How considerate." He took another drink before handing the canteen back to Stephen. "It has a bit of an aftertaste, doesn't it?"

"That would be the iodine," muttered Stephen.

Alan snorted. "I suppose that would explain it."

Shaw's leg started to twitch. He hopped back upright. "That's about as much of a break as I can take. You ready yet?"

Bean placed a hand on one knee and began to rise. Alan stopped her. "Why don't you run ahead and let your boss know we are coming? I can get us there from here."

Shaw paused. "Um, I'm not so sure that's a good idea."

"And why not?" Alan gestured. "We're old friends, right?"

"Hmm. You were . . . once," Shaw glanced at Bean and then at Stephen. His eyes tightened as his forehead wrinkled. "But who knows what kind of friends you've been keeping since then? Lots of people have changed."

Alan's face took on the look of exaggerated innocence. "Ah. I can appreciate your concern, but you have nothing to worry about. This is my son."

Stephen fought the shock from showing on his face. Had he heard Bean call him his father during the seizure, or was Alan making up a story for Shaw's benefit, and if so, why?

Shaw took a step toward Stephen. His nostrils flared as if taking in Stephen's scent. *Exactly how far had he taken the genetic modifications?* Stephen found himself wondering. Shaw grinned before slapping himself in the face. "I can't believe I didn't pick up on the resemblance before." He spun on his heel. "Right then. I'll see you at the Reef." Launching himself into a run, Shaw disappeared from view within a matter of moments.

"I hope that means something to you," Stephen commented. "Last I checked, the ocean was in the other direction." *Which is exactly the direction I should be going.*

Alan smiled. "It's been awhile, but some places have a way of sticking in your memory."

twenty-six

The road narrowed as they approached what once served as the center of the city, a brick sidewalk lining one side and a rusted chain fence on the other. Trees growing up and out made it seem more forest than a town; however, a stench worse than a field of livestock overpowered the clean smell of the woods. Bean's nose wrinkled in disgust, too. At least they knew they were almost at their destination. As there didn't appear to be any farmland nearby, the smell could only mean they were near a group of people living together.

They turned another corner, and the road they'd traveled most of the afternoon opened up. A gray building with a blue roof appeared in between the overgrown grass, more trees, and the remnants of crumbled buildings. A metal fence surrounded the building, but unlike the other fences they'd passed, this one was well tended with shouts coming from nearby.

Figures emerged from the building's entrance. Their outlines appeared human, at least from a distance, and Stephen released a breath of relief. As they neared and their features came more in focus, Alan extended a hand in greeting. Stephen noticed both had skin like tanned leather, lined with deep grooved wrinkles, though one's skin was dark while the other was light. One wore a faded blue ball cap that only seemed to enhance the crookedness of his nose. The other's hair was streaked with white but cropped close to his skull.

The ball cap man laughed. "Well, what do you know? It *is* the one and only Alan Dronigh. I guess I owe Ahman here a drink." He gestured at the hatless man by his side. The man, who Stephen assumed was Ahman, said nothing, but instead placed his hands on his hips and nodded once. Ball cap tilted his head, "You haven't changed a bit." He scratched his chin. "What I wouldn't give to have genes like yours. One of these days, you need to tell me your secret."

Alan chuckled as he caught Stephen's eye before turning his attention back to the pair. "What about you, Ahman? Aren't you happy to see me?"

Ahman grunted.

"Oh don't mind him. He hasn't been the world's best conversationalist since . . ." Ball cap looked at Ahman with an unspoken question in his eyes. Ahman's jaw clenched as he closed his eyes and sighed. Ball cap continued, interpreting Ahman's response as consent. "Well, not since Cara—"

Alan tapped his chin. "Ah, Cara. How old was she when I last saw you? Six? And already planning to follow her father's footsteps?"

"She *was* five." Ball cap's use of the past tense was unmistakable.

"Oh. I'm sorry to hear that. Did she get sick?"

Ahman's eyes went flat as he shook his head. Ball cap filled in the unspoken question. "No. Not the plague." Ahman's expression darkened. "Well, it wasn't." Ball cap shot an apologetic glance Ahman's way. "At least, not technically speaking." Ball cap brightened. "The team actually was barely hit by the plague at all. Probably due to all that extra conditioning Mr. D had us do." Ball cap winked, but the smile withered on his face the minute he caught Ahman's expression. "We thought we were lucky." He chewed his lip. "Turns out others considered us a little too lucky." Ahman's fists clenched by his sides. "We didn't know . . . didn't realize how bad it'd gotten until a handful of folk decided that the playing field needed to be"—Ball cap looked back at the stadium behind him—"leveled."

Stephen blinked as the man's implication sank in. A kid had been murdered, and for what? The crime of surviving? It occurred to him then that the same might have happened to him if Ed and Helen hadn't gotten him out of town when they did.

"Well, we made sure those responsible aren't around to do it again. Didn't we, my friend?" Ball cap put a hand on Ahman's shoulder as the man looked away. When Ahman faced them again, his expression was like granite, as if daring them to criticize their version of justice.

"I would have done the same," said Alan, and the tension that had crept into the conversation like humidity before a summer storm dissipated. "Had it been a child of mine." He rested his hand on Stephen's shoulder.

Stephen fought the urge to shrug off Alan's hand as the corner of Ball cap's lip turned up. "Shaw mentioned when he got back that you were traveling with your boy." Stephen bit his tongue to help keep his expression from giving away any of his feelings on the subject. "He looks like his mother."

Do I? Stephen filled his lungs and counted to five before releasing the pent-up air. He tried to picture her face, but all he could think of was Helen. He glanced at Alan's hand. *He's distracted. Tackle him, grab the wand, and run.*

Alan squeezed his shoulder. His grip was tighter than Stephen expected. "Don't I know it? Sometimes I used to wonder if he was even mine."

Stephen tried to meet Bean's eyes and failed. The moment passed.

Ball cap laughed. "Well enough of this small talk for now. Let's get you all inside. Jeremy is anxious to meet you." Ahman followed him like a silent shadow as he turned, passing what appeared to be one of the stadium's entrance gates. Instead, they descended a ramp to the side of the building where another, less noticeable door awaited.

Alan leaned into Stephen and said in a low voice, "We got off easy. Darnell was one of the trainers back in the Sharks' heydays. A great assistant, but always a little chatty. A few years ago, the sun would set before he wrapped up the greetings."

As they passed under the arches, a numbing sensation spread throughout Stephen's body like a fog. He attempted to call up Finn's map for more information about their location, but nothing appeared.

"While physical modifications were acceptable, use of nanotechnology during games was deemed unsportsmanlike." Alan sniffed. "There are signal dampeners buried under the field, which are or were powered by the simple act of walking. They have a limited range and don't block everything, but the effect does take some getting used to." He rubbed his arms. "I'd say they are still operational."

Darnell chattered away as they walked. "It used to be the only people who could use this entrance were the field service crew. We sealed off the rest. Too exposed. We didn't like people coming in having the aerial advantage." The hall opened up to what once must have served as a football field. In its place was a shantytown filled with reclaimed metal structures, which appeared scattered across the ground with little sign of any true organization. Ball cap/Darnell looked over his shoulder at them. "I know what you are thinking. Why not the skyboxes? We tried that. Gets hot up there surrounded by all that glass. Only the boss or whoever draws lookout duty goes up there now. Nope, it may be very different from some of the mansions the other guys were living in before the shit hit the fan, but trust me, this is a much better option. Easier to defend, too." He turned the rest of the way so that he walked backward while gesturing toward the structures behind him. "Who needs a mansion when you are living in a fortress? Welcome to the new Reef."

Darnell led them through the structures until the group had reached a point resembling the center and stopped in front of a hut as nondescript as any of the others. He knocked on the structure's side, and a man stepped out into the sunlight.

"So, this is the person responsible for all the recent excitement," the man said as he outstretched his hand. Alan glanced at the man's hand but made no effort to accept it. The man's lips tightened into a line as he swept the hair out of his face in a smooth motion as if he had never intended to extend the arm in greeting in the first place.

Alan frowned. "I know you." It was more accusation than statement, and Stephen could sense Darnell and Ahman tense without looking at them. "You worked for Evans."

Bean tensed. The man, who Stephen assumed was Jeremy, smiled, unaffected by Alan's tone. "Well, isn't that a pleasant surprise?" He chuckled at a joke, which might as well have sprouted wings for how it flew over Stephen's head. "I guess I must have done something right then to have gained *your* notice."

"Just because I left the ACI, doesn't mean I stopped paying attention." Alan rubbed the tip of his middle finger against the pad of his thumb on one hand as he spoke.

"*Left*, is it?" One of Jeremy's eyebrows rose. "I guess I heard a different version of the story."

"I suppose you would have. Your former employer was always good at telling himself what he wanted to hear."

Jeremy threw his head back with a laugh straight from his gut. "Isn't that the truth? If I could have gotten a dollar for every time I had to bite my tongue as he took credit for something." He wiped an unseen tear from his eye. "Still, I never would have guessed he'd—"

"Who would? You'd have to be some sort of psychopath to anticipate a person would do something like that."

Jeremy nodded solemnly. "Well, that's over and done with now. All we can do is move forward." He turned to address Darnell and Ahman. "Why don't you two go and take the children on the grand tour? I believe Dr. Dronigh and I have a few more things to discuss." Darnell gripped Stephen's arm as Jeremy reached under his collar and pulled out a pendant similar to the one Rotledge wore. "Such as how you intend to thank us for answering your rescue call."

Stun him. Stun them all. You might not get another chance. He made a fist. His skin remained flesh colored. Then the man, Alan, and the wand were gone, disappearing into the hut.

"Where should we start?" asked Darnell. Ahman shrugged. "Yeah, that's what I was thinking, too." Darnell led the group along a winding path through the series of huts until Stephen was no longer sure he'd be able to locate the one Alan entered.

Fan-freaking-tastic. His fingernails dug into the meat of his all-too-normal-looking palms. Sweat dripped from his forehead, though the sun was past its peak heat. *There goes another chance.* A vision of Ed's bloodstained bandage came uninvited. The stain grew, spreading until all Stephen could see was red. He was running out of time. Alan said the damper didn't block everything. If he could only get a message to Wes, maybe Wes could explain the situation to Finn in a way he'd understand. *You are supposed to be super strong.* He imagined the computer terminal. He opened his fist. Pink half circles marred his skin where his nails had been. He pushed the message with all his might.

Darnell paused and cocked his head. "You need a bathroom, kid? You don't look so good."

The fog-like sensation intensified. The logo on Darnell's ball cap blurred, and Stephen's stomach churned.

"He's hungry," said Bean. "But what else is new? He's always hungry." She pursed her lips. "We heard shouting before. Where is everyone?"

"I'm glad you asked. Let's finish the introductions," Darnell answered.

twenty-seven

The huts backed to a great green wall of foliage. Ahman parted its leaves and entered it as one would a door. With Darnell still gripping his arm to the point that Stephen wouldn't be surprised if he lost feeling in it, Stephen followed the two through the opening.

Stephen estimated there were roughly thirty men on the other side engaged in a series of coordinated drills, like a small army, while an additional handful lingered to the side of the worn field. Darnell raised his fingers to his lips and whistled. Heads turned in unison in their direction. Stephen suppressed a shudder. Darnell and Ahman's human-looking appearance put them in the minority. Some had noses that were flattened to the point of non-existence save for a pair of nostrils in the center of their faces. It was a look, which reminded Stephen of a snake. Others had more snout-like noses. Some wore shirts highlighting wins and champion seasons long past. Most didn't bother to cover their torsos. While many chests were covered in thick hair, Stephen noticed two of the shirtless men had a gray cast to their skin ridged like a rhino's. *Probably as strong, too,* Stephen thought as he attempted to control the growing unease in the pit of his stomach. *Let's hope they have better tempers.* Stephen scanned the field to see if there was another way out of this nightmare. Instead, all he could see were more misshapen limbs, which would have looked less out of place on a jungle cat. Coming here was a mistake. They should have taken their chances with Finn, with or without the wand.

One stepped away from the rest of the group. *Rotledge. He must have run back here the second he woke up.* Bean stepped forward and raised her chin as if daring the man to come closer. *What are you doing?* Stephen wondered. *There're only two of us, and what?* He looked out at the row upon row, unkind smiles filled with fanglike teeth. *They aren't a team. They're a pack.* A dry hacking sound from behind him caught Stephen by surprise. Darnell's eyes widened. "Your girl's got some spunk. I can't think of the last time I heard Ahman laugh."

"That's laughing? He sounds more like he is dying," Bean replied. Her body remained tense, though many of the men on the field now appeared more relaxed than they had a second ago.

"I suppose you could say that about all of us." Darnell frowned. "But then again, if I were you, I might be a little more concerned about my own health right now."

Rotledge tilted his head at Darnell, who nodded ever so slightly while the others on the field turned their backs and resumed their drills.

"I believe you've met." Darnell's tone was all business.

"We may have gotten off on the wrong foot," replied Bean. If she felt at all intimidated by the situation, there was nothing in either her voice or body language to give it away. "No hard feelings?" When Rotledge didn't react right away, Bean commented to their guides, "He's not much of a people person. Is he?"

Ahman let loose another round of his hacking laugh while Rotledge's eyes burned with an unspoken fire.

"Rotledge," a voice sounded from behind them. Alan and the man from the hut stepped through the foliage wall and out onto the field. "I believe the girl was trying to apologize."

As the other man took in the scene, Rotledge's head dropped. "No hard feelings," repeated Rotledge though his eyes never left the ground.

Jeremy smiled, but the expression didn't quite reach his eyes. "Excellent." He clapped his hands. "Now we can all be friends."

"I feel so much safer now," muttered Bean to Stephen. "Don't you?"

"Now about that little matter of payment," said Jeremy, turning to Alan.

Alan patted his coat pocket. "Not here."

"Why not? Too public?" Jeremy frowned.

"It won't work."

"What about our agreement? Does it not work anymore?" Jeremy's eyes narrowed. "Is that it? Is the device so fragile it broke on the walk over here?" he sneered. "I thought your tech was supposed to be better than that."

"It will work exactly as I promised. Just not here, as in on the field. It needs a signal."

Stephen perked up. A signal meant another chance.

Jeremy raked his fingers through his hair. "Oh. Right. My apologies. We can go to the locker rooms under the stadium. The walls should block the jammers enough. There's also only one way out if we find out you're lying."

Alan's mouth tightened into a fine line. "I don't lie."

"Well then, what are we waiting for?" He looked back at the field. "Rotledge," he shouted. "Come along. This involves you."

⸻⧼⧽⸻

The sounds of the beastmen grew muffled as they reached the entrance to the interior of the stadium. Stopping at the top of an incline, Jeremy picked up a pair of solar-powered lanterns, which grew in brightness as the natural light dimmed. More lanterns hung at the base of the incline on either side of a doorway opening to a room lined with cabinets. He took a seat on a bench in the center of the room. "Now about that payment."

"Right. Rotledge first?" Alan suggested. "After all, he did find us." Jeremy nodded as Alan reached his hand into his pocket and pulled out the wand with a flourish.

"You can't give that to him." Stephen's hands tightened into fists. "It's ours." He visualized lightning bolts, but instead of illuminating the room with purple light, his legs buckled, and a chill danced down his spine. *The drain.*

Way to follow the plan, Bean's voice played in his head. He didn't have to look at her to know her eyes were rolling in their sockets.

"Is that so?" Alan made a *tsking* sound. He addressed Jeremy. "As I said above, I don't lie. I don't have to steal either. Unlike some people." He closed his eyes and took a breath.

He pivoted back to Stephen. "You are mistaken. I know it is mine because not only did I help make it, I also made sure its design included an anti-theft element. Oh, the others thought I was being paranoid, but I knew someone might try to take it without appropriate authorization one day. I might not have been able to receive it right away, but an alert was sent to me the second you left the facility. The so-called *secure* facility." He opened his eyes and his expression was the definition of serenity. "At some point, I would like to hear how you were able to perform that little trick, but I believe now is not the time."

Alan addressed Rotledge, "What can I say? Kids. So dramatic." He shrugged. "Then again, Jules always did like to say that I had a flair for drama. Must run in the family."

"Jules?" Rotledge wrinkled his forehead. "I thought your wife's name was Betty."

"Ah, I was referring to my former partner, my *development* partner." Alan's smiled. "You don't remember her?" He made a tutting sound with his tongue. "She wouldn't like that at all. No, not at all." Alan glanced down at the wand in his hand and his smile deepened. "Well, I guess that means it is up to me to make sure at least a portion of her work lives on." He extended his hand so that the wand lay exposed on his open palm. Rotledge leaned in and sniffed the rod, only to pull away. Alan waved it in front of him. "Go on, take it," he urged.

Rotledge took the wand from Alan's hand as if it might still rear up and bite. He inspected it from end to end. "What's this supposed to do?"

"Oh, you'll see." Alan touched the rod with one finger. Rotledge's knuckles turned white where they touched the metal. The rod appeared to blur in Rotledge's hand as it began to vibrate. He whimpered as his eyes rolled back. Then, as quickly as it started, the rod came into crisp focus once more.

He dropped the wand as if burned, and he fell to his knees.

Then there was laughter as the beastman regained his footing and stepped more fully into the artificial light. Rotledge was different. For one, the limp was gone, and he seemed to stand straighter. His misshapen leg no longer looked quite as out of place, as if his entire body was growing inches in front of their eyes. Then Stephen noticed the age spots, which marred Rotledge's exposed skin, began to shrink. His hair darkened and appeared to thicken. Even the skin on his face seemed to tighten as wrinkles faded from view. Jeremy sat dumbly on the bench as Rotledge's laughter continued.

twenty-eight

Stephen stumbled toward the wand. The laughter stopped. "Don't even think about it." Rotledge snarled as he scooped the wand up. "My senses haven't been this sharp in years." He smirked. "One of the mods I had done was to help me sniff out the opposing team's trick plays and you don't have half their skill." Rotledge tucked the wand into his waistband. "Go if you want, but you're not leaving with this thingy. It's ours now."

"You don't understand," said Stephen. "I need it. Lives depend on me bringing it back."

"You know? I smell something else." Rotledge took an exaggerated whiff of the air. "Something that smells a lot like bullshit."

"He's telling you the truth," Bean spoke up.

"I don't recall asking you." Rotledge barred his teeth. "Which reminds me, we never did get to finish our introductions."

"I thought we were past that." Bean squared her shoulders. "Fine. I'm sorry I tasered you."

"Tasered?" Rotledge straightened his back even further until he towered at least a foot and a half above Bean. "That was no taser, and we both know it." He took a step toward her. "I know what you are." He took another step. "I know all about where you come from." Step. "A couple of us went there, looking for help." Step. "You people—you aren't human."

"Says the dog man." Bean's eyes narrowed. "You know *nothing* about me, old man. Nothing." She crossed her arms over her chest. "But I know *all* about you. You think you were abandoned out here? Well, guess what? So was everybody else. The difference is the rest of us didn't get paid millions to sit on a bench before. We were used to not getting everything we wanted exactly when we wanted it." She dropped clenched fists back to her side. "And guess what? I'm glad whatever happened to your friends happened. Welcome to the real world."

"Bitch."

"Has-been."

What are you doing? Stephen wanted to shout. *We're not far enough away from the signal damper.*

She met Stephen's shocked gaze with a small smile. *What I have to,* he heard her voice say in his head. Aloud she said, "or should I say, never was."

The beastman's eyes glazed over in a fiery rage.

"No," shouted Stephen, summoning what little remained of energy reserves, as he threw himself between the two as Rotledge charged.

The impact of his body colliding with Rotledge's shoulder felt much like Stephen imagined getting hit by a train might. He sagged. Rotledge grabbed Stephen by the cowl of his shirt before he could drop to the floor and pulled him back upright. Stephen's eyes watered as he sucked in air to replace what the blow had taken from his lungs only to get a whiff of Rotledge's breath. The wand hadn't been able to return all of Rotledge to a fresh state. Stephen continued to gasp as he braced his body in anticipation of what Rotledge might do next.

Stephen didn't have to wait long. Stars burst across his vision as his entire body flew back across the room, hitting a wall. The force of his impact was great enough to send one of the lanterns swaying, which caused shadows on the walls to dance like a horde of demons come to collect their souls before the device toppled to the floor. "That the best you can do? I thought you guys were supposed to know how to tackle."

Rotledge roared as he stomped over to where Stephen lay, hoisting him back up. Rotledge's fist pounded into his ribs, forcing out what little breath remained in his lungs after the initial impact. Stephen's body wanted to double over, but Rotledge's fists were relentless. Over and over they pummeled him. Stephen tried to put up a defense, but Rotledge's fists were too fast to dodge. The man was a machine of violence.

Stephen lost sight of Bean, his attention locked onto a dribble of spit, which had formed at the corner of Rotledge's mouth. It made him appear even more like a rabid dog. His reaction time slowed by the previous hits and, unable to look away, all Stephen could do was watch as Rotledge wiped the spit off his knuckle before driving that same fist into Stephen's face. He decided then there was little reason to even attempt to open his battered eye as the blows continued.

Then pain no longer registered. *I must have lost consciousness,* he thought, as he considered the shapeless darkness. The idea that he might be conscious of his non-consciousness amused Stephen. He wanted to laugh at the situation, but he no longer had any sense of the rest of his body either. It was as if he was simply a floating mind out in the emptiness of space. It occurred to him it wasn't that much different from how accessing the data stream that first time had been. *It's better,* he thought. At least this time it didn't feel like he was going to drown any minute. No, after thinking about it, Stephen concluded that getting beat up by a berserk beastman and blacking out wasn't the worst thing to have happened to him since leaving home. Not even by a little.

He tried to imagine what he must look like on the outside in the real-life world. *Probably don't want to think about that too hard.* It occurred to him that his current state might be worse than unconsciousness. He could very well be dying. Rotledge didn't strike him as the type of person who would hold back just because his opponent had tapped out. *Would that really be so bad?* Stephen couldn't decide. *What if you are already dead and this is the afterlife?* He had never been religious. None of them had. Ed was too afraid of picking the wrong one. Helen preferred to restrict her worries to the things she could control. Even so, he found himself reaching out, probing at the edges of the darkness. If there was a God out there, Stephen would like to know why he, she, or it had abandoned so many lives to their suffering.

He detected a presence nearby and directed his floating consciousness toward it, moving much like he imagined a hot-air balloon would. As he approached, the presence seemed to expand like a flower blooming, with data unfurled like the flower's petals. He stretched a tendril of thought toward the petal, and the blackness surrounding him dissolved into a new setting. He was in an office, seated in a high-backed leather chair. A nearby open window let in a warm breeze scented with the smell of lilies.

A strange voice caught his attention coming from a mahogany desk. A figure leaned over. "It was a good thing you came to us when you did," a woman's voice purred.

Another female voice spoke, a voice much like Bean's, but older and with a helpless desperate quality to it. "You can help," the voice demanded. "We were told you could help."

"Please?" another voice spoke up from behind. This voice was a male one and also the voice of a person filled with fear. "We'll do anything."

"It was an accident," a third voice entered the mix. Unlike the others, which sounded somewhat distant, this voice seemed to be directly on top of him. It had the high pitch of a child, but Stephen recognized it as a younger version of Bean's. It was the same as the out-of-body experience he'd experienced during the body switch incident with Alan on the basement floor, with the same disorientation. The only thing Stephen could think of which might explain what he was experiencing was if his consciousness had somehow found its way into Bean's thoughts, too. He tried to pull away as the scene took on a sepia hue. Stephen was stuck in the memory as if he was living the moment in real time.

The speaker's face came into focus. She appeared a few years older than Helen but not by much. A few lines of age creased the corners of her lips as well as her eyes, but the majority of her skin was unmarked. Her stormy gray eyes locked on his, and he recognized the woman as Dr. Lambda. "Your name is Beatrice, right? Why don't you tell me what happened to your sister?"

The vision shifted down, and all Stephen could see were Bean's hands as they fidgeted in her lap.

Stephen's/Bean's arm felt as if it were being ripped out of its socket at the force of his/her arm being pulled to the side. The man's voice practically spat in her ear. "Tell her what she wants to know, Beatrice."

"Bean." The man's grip tightened on Stephen's/Bean's arm. Pressure formed behind his/her eyes, but the tears refused to flow.

"That stopped being cute a long time ago."

"Mr. Kunegunda, I believe you are scaring her," suggested Dr. Lambda.

"Scare? Her?" The man shoved Stephen/Bean back into the chair. "Don't you believe it for a second. The girl is a psychopath. The fire was bad enough. I mean it's chaos out there. Kids make mistakes. But when we found out she'd first put her sister in a coma . . . before the flames." The man's voice broke. "It was no accident."

"I know this has been hard for your entire family, but I do need to hear the story from her perspective. It might be better if you and your wife stepped outside."

"With all due respect, you don't want to do that. You saw what happened to our girl when we left them alone."

"There is a man waiting in the hall. Ask him to come in as you step outside. Don't worry," Dr. Lambda added when no one immediately reacted. "He's the one who told me about your case in the first place. Nothing is going to surprise him."

Stephen could hear the sound of the couple's footsteps as they turned and hit the tiled floor behind him; however, his/Bean's gaze remained fixed on the doctor's hands as her fingers continued their restless dance on her lap.

She looked up only at the sound of the door opening and turned around long enough to see the man and the woman leaving the room without looking back once. When the door opened wide once more, another man stood in their place.

Stephen recognized this man, too. The same man had threatened them at the base of the barricade at Finn's tower. He'd been but a tiny figure before, ragged and half-defeated, but now he loomed before Bean like a terrible child-eating giant. Bean must have thought so, too. He could feel Bean press her body further into the chair as he approached the desk, seeking whatever extra protection it could offer.

"Now, shall we begin again?"

Bean's focus shifted back to Dr. Lambda. "We were just playing," Bean whimpered. "It was a game. That's all."

The woman straightened, pulling her palms together almost as if in a prayer as she rounded the desk and came over to Bean's side. "Well, we can all agree the time for games is over." The woman's voice was honey-covered steel. "Instead, it's time you told what really happened."

"We were just pretending to have magic," said Bean in the same panicked tone he'd heard during their escape from the blaze in the tavern. "Like in the stories. It was just supposed to be a game. It wasn't supposed to work."

"What wasn't supposed to work?" Stephen could feel Dr. Lambda's fingers stroke Bean's hair as if they were passing through his own locks. He could feel Bean's heart beginning to settle in her chest. As she calmed, his/her eyes caught on a picture on the desk. In the center of the photo was a man with a dark mustache giving a speech. Beside him was a stunning blonde woman whose eyes, filled with pride, were fixated on the speaker as if there was no one else in the world. Slightly behind the couple, seated to the right of the podium, was an even younger Dr. Lambda, wearing an equally crisp business suit as the one she was wearing now. A man's hand rested on her knee, but the younger Dr. Lambda's attention was as riveted onto the mustached man giving the speech. Stephen wondered if the man seated next to her had noticed and was trying to stake his claim. Feeling sorry for the man, Stephen focused on his face only to realize he recognized him, too. The man next to Dr. Lambda in the photo was the same person the beastmen referred to as boss. Jeremy.

twenty-nine

The photograph, desk, and even the smell of lilies faded. Then Stephen's world exploded into pain once more. He had to be back in his own body. Stephen risked opening his eye but gave up when he couldn't manage to open it by more than a crack. Alan peered down at him. "Oh good, you're still alive. For a while there, I wasn't sure."

"Rotledge," Stephen attempted to say through a bruised if not broken jaw, though the sound that came out of his mouth was unrecognizable.

Alan raised an eyebrow and looked to his side. "Hmm, perhaps it would be better if you didn't try to speak for a while." He extended his hand. When Stephen didn't take it right away, Alan harrumphed. "Would you prefer I leave you on the floor?"

This time, Stephen took his hand and tried to sit up. Every inch of his body seemed to be on fire as he looked around the room for his attacker. He found him lying on the ground by his feet. Startled, Stephen attempted to scoot away, sending another burst of pain throughout his body.

"He's dead," Alan commented drily. "A fact, I feel, I must mention is going to be somewhat awkward to explain." Stephen took another look at the man's form, only now noticing its motionlessness. The memory of Rotledge's iron fists as they pummeled him over and over again returned in full force. Each hit had been so rapid; he hadn't had time to defend himself. Had he managed to get a lucky hit in any way? Stephen stood, bracing his back against the wall as his brain sought to make sense of the situation.

Leaving him at the wall, Alan knelt over Rotledge's body and turned the body over, bringing Stephen's attention back to the dead old man. And it was clear he *was* old again. If anything, he was even older now than he had been before. Rotledge's hair was white, and large clumps lay beside him. The strands must have fallen out of his scalp as Alan turned him over. The skin of his face was sunken, and the smell of rot and decay overpowered the scent of sweat, blood, and dirt in the room. *What happened to him?*

"Hmm," Alan muttered as he inspected the body. "This reminds me of a movie I saw once. What was the name?" He tapped his finger on his chin. "Something about a crusade." Alan looked back at Stephen and shrugged. "Ah, I suppose that wouldn't mean anything to you. The movie was already considered a classic when I saw it, but it ended with the villain getting the life sucked out of him."

Between the smell and the man's appearance, Stephen was unable to ignore the sourness of his stomach any longer. He turned and vomited, sending painful spasms through his abdomen and causing his eyes to water. "How?" Stephen managed to say once the contents of his stomach emptied. Stephen blinked the tears away as he remembered he hadn't been alone in the room during the attack. "Bean," he whispered. Stephen tried looking around the room, but couldn't find her in his limited range of vision.

Alan gestured at the pile of dirt that was all that remained of Rotledge. "She sucked the life right out of him. Drained him dry." Stephen's legs went out from under him, and if Alan hadn't returned at that moment, ready to catch him, he would have fallen back to the floor. "Careful now." Alan wrapped Stephen's arm across his shoulder. "You're lucky she's gone. She might have done the same to you."

"What do you mean *she's gone?*"

"I mean, while I was over here making sure you weren't dead, too, she bolted." Alan sighed as he shifted Stephen's weight. "I must say, I think you can do better, but your love life is the least of our concerns at the moment." Alan gestured to the corner of the room where Jeremy sat propped up next to the wall with a slack-jawed grin and a vacant stare.

"What happened to him?"

"I found his happy place."

"His *what?* Why?"

"Do you see that chain around his neck? I assume they've been using those for communication." He shifted Stephen again. "Those trinkets were developed to give people who didn't have the stomach to be upgraded a means of accessing the data stream. It's a poor substitute for the real thing with one serious design flaw. Namely, it makes it possible for another person to alter the device's effect and can trap an individual in an alternative reality of their creation." Alan readjusted Stephen's arm. "How much do you weigh anyway?" He shook his head. "To answer your other question, I was forced to take advantage of the flaw when your loyal girlfriend decided to pick a fight with one of our host's favorite lackeys." Alan leaned and braced them both against a wall. "I can only imagine what would have happened if I wasn't here to take care of Jeremy after she pulled that stunt. Don't you know anything about pack behavior? Only the alpha is allowed to put a rogue one down. Anything else would be seen as a challenge." Alan scanned the room. "Do you think you can stand?"

Stephen took a nervous step forward on his own. When the floor didn't immediately rise up to meet him, he nodded.

"Good. Stay right there." Leaving Stephen where he stood, Alan returned to Rotledge's body. Grabbing him by his armpits, Alan started to pull the man toward the row of empty lockers. Stephen heard a snapping sound like a branch breaking and watched as Alan stumbled backward with a single arm still in his hands. The urge to throw up overpowered Stephen once more.

When the dry heaves stopped, Rotledge's body was gone. Alan stood, wiping off his trousers. A mound of a substance that looked like ash lay at his feet. "Well, that solves one problem," said Alan to himself as he dusted off his palms.

"Hey, boss?" a voice called from the direction of the ramp.

Alan whispered, "Don't say anything." He rubbed his throat and shouted in Jeremy's voice, "What is it?"

"We've got company."

"Well, take care of it."

"It's Wendy, boss."

Alan glanced back at Jeremy. A long trail of drool hung from his lips and chin. "We're going to have to risk it," Alan muttered. "Tell her I'll be right outside."

"What about the others? Dr. Dronigh and the kids?"

"Nothing that Rotledge can't handle. Isn't that right?" Alan's face twisted. He rubbed his throat again and, in Rotledge's voice, added, "You know it."

"Okay, boss." Footsteps raced away.

Alan held a finger to his lips and cupped his ear. He nodded. "I believe it would be best if we put as much distance between us and the Reef as possible before anyone thinks to check on their leader, don't you?"

Stephen's shoulders sagged. Only then did he notice the lack of the straps' weight on them. "Where's my pack?"

Alan scanned the room. "Your friend must have taken it with her when she ran." He shrugged. Alan patted the pocket where he'd stored the wand before. His eyebrow shot up. He cocked his head as he nudged the pile of dust on the floor with his toe. He turned and looked at Stephen up and down before his lips tightened. His eyes took on a glazed over look. Seconds passed without him saying a word, then Alan blinked, and his gaze was bright and clear and furious. "Your pack isn't the only thing unaccounted for."

Stephen's stomach threatened to roll once more. *The wand.* She'd taken the wand and left him here. Would Finn still honor his promise to stand up to the Watch and rescue Ed and Helen if he wasn't the one to hand it over? Stephen feared he soon would find out.

thirty

Clouds the color of ash filled the sky as Stephen limped his way outside. "I can't believe she left without me."

"Who knows why women do what they do sometimes?" Alan's scowled deepened. "You do realize we wouldn't be worried about a pack of jocks with reason to kill us now if you'd told me why you had the wand in the first place."

"Right. As if you would have given it back."

Alan shrugged. "I suppose we'll never know now, will we?"

"I needed it to rescue Helen and Ed. There is a guy, Finn, who lives in a tower with an army more than capable of taking out the Watch, but first needed me to bring them the wand so the energy drain from using their abilities didn't kill them."

"Seems unnecessarily complicated. Who are Helen and Ed again?"

"The people who raised me."

"You mean the people I entrusted with your care who failed at the task so miserably. Those people? What about them?"

"Entrusted?" Stephen sputtered. "You didn't *entrust* me with anyone. You left me. A four-year-old. By myself." He stared at Alan in disbelief. "Who does that?"

"You want to have this conversation now?" Alan asked, waving his hands back toward the exit. "This is our chance to get out of here while we still can. You want to blow it by talking, be my guest, but I'd prefer to remain in one piece." He glanced at Stephen who had fallen behind. "However, I recommend you do the same. I don't think you can afford to be torn into much more."

They passed under the arches, and a tingling sensation flooded Stephen's limbs. He summoned the map and was relieved to see its information projected over his vision once more. He focused his thoughts and composed the same message to Wes as he had earlier. He visualized pressing a 'send' button. Stephen squinted at the horizon as he dragged his injured leg. It was going to be a long walk back to the train station.

"You need the wand back. So do I. Now, all I have to do is locate it." A vein in Alan's forehead throbbed. "She's done something to it. Hidden its signal from me.

"She learned about our abilities the same time I did. She wouldn't have the first idea how to do something like that. Not to mention, why would she?"

Alan stopped short. "The simplest explanation is often the correct one." The scowl vanished from his face.

"What does that even mean?" asked Stephen, shielding his eyes from the brightness of the setting sun.

Alan laughed and shook his head. "It means, she lied."

"About what?"

"About when she learned about her abilities."

"No." Stephen's brow knit. He thought about the memory of Bean's interrogation with Dr. Lambda. "Okay, maybe she'd used them in the past by accident, but it's not like she knew what she was doing back then. She couldn't. I mean, I saw her when Finn told us about everything. She had even more questions than I did."

"Did she?" Alan laughed again. "Here's a tip they used to teach young lawyers—never ask a question you don't already know the answer to. It is a way to lead a witness's testimony without being accused of actually leading the witness. If she asked a lot of questions, it could be she was attempting to keep you from asking any of your own." He slapped his leg. "Clever girl. My guess? She's been working for this Finn person for a while as a recruiter of sorts. It was all a ruse to gain your trust and get you to lower your guard. Then once you'd gotten them what they want, all there would be left to do is dispose of the loose ends."

Stephen remembered the taste of her lips during their kiss and that moment in the moonlight by the waterfront. *You can't fake a connection like that.* "No. That's not possible. She wouldn't do that to me."

"Oh, don't be upset with her. It's a technique that has been used since the dawn of time," Alan replied. The corner of his lip turned up. "I may have even performed a similar job in the past." He tapped his lip. "I wonder . . . But that would mean . . . Of course, that does explain . . ." His eyes twinkled with mirth at a line of thought that Stephen couldn't follow. He waved whatever it was away, returning his attention back to Stephen. "Before you ask, I didn't read your mind. The look on your face is clear enough. Well, the look on that swollen mess that currently is your face." Alan arched his neck to look out across the parking lot, where a figure stood waiting by a truck. "I suppose that must be Wendy."

Stephen's eye watered. Between the blurred vision and the fading light, he couldn't make out the woman's features, but he recognized the red armband at once. "Dr. Lambda. We need to get away." A chill settled into his bones, causing his teeth to chatter.

Alan patted him on the shoulder. "And what good would that do? She's already seen us and you can barely walk, let alone run." He muttered to himself, "Lambda. How many can there be?" His gaze took on the vacant look Stephen now associated with a person accessing the data stream. "Ah, she's a medical doctor."

"She's also in charge of the Watch."

"Is she? Isn't that convenient?"

"Maybe for you."

"It would seem our host had no intention of letting us join his little community." Alan made a *tsking* sound. "I'll need to have a talk with him about that later, but for now . . ." He raked his hand through his hair, and the color changed as his features shifted. Stephen's stomach turned, but there was nothing more in it to expunge. When the effect subsided, Alan wore Jeremy's face. He pushed Stephen forward.

"This is a terrible idea," whispered Stephen.

"Play along," he whispered back. Louder, he said, "Wendy, how nice to see you again."

"Cut the crap, Jeremy. You and I both know this is the last place I want to be." She looked at Stephen. "I see you caught the boy. I suppose I should thank you for not dragging this out like you normally do, but did you have to rough him up like that?"

"What can I say? He picked the wrong person to mess with."

Her lips narrowed. "I am beginning to suspect he does that a lot. What about the other one?"

"What another one?"

Dr. Lambda rolled her eyes. "I'm not in the mood for games. The girl he was traveling with. Where is she? Your associates said you'd found them both."

"She got away."

"Of course she did." Dr. Lambda closed her eyes and took a calming breath. "Well, don't just stand there. Put him in the back."

"So what's the plan now?" Stephen whispered as Alan opened the double doors in the back of the vehicle while Dr. Lambda went around to the driver's side. "We zap her and take the truck?"

Alan raised an eyebrow. "Always so quick to violence." He shook his head. "Now you are going to lay back and let the good doctor take you where she will." He pushed Stephen onto a gurney.

"Like hell, I will." Stephen tried to struggle, but his arms and legs didn't respond to his commands. "I can't move." His eyes widened as Alan tightened the straps. "What did you do to me?"

"I'm not doing anything. Your body, on the other hand, is shutting down. You need medical attention. Now you have it." Alan stepped back and slapped the truck door. "He's all yours."

Dr. Lambda glanced into the rear mirror. "You've changed. If you'd been half this cooperative before, maybe we wouldn't have gotten divorced."

"Good chat. Try not to lose him this time. I'd hate to have to clean up your mess. Again."

"Ah, and there's the Jeremy I know."

Alan slammed the truck door as Dr. Lambda cranked the engine and put it into gear. All Stephen could do is look out the window at the sky that the storms that threatened. He closed his eyes. *At least I might find out whether Ed and Helen are still okay.* Then he gave into sleep as the truck raced away.

thirty-one

He was in a lab like the one where the wand had been stored, but different. A woman with black hair stood in one corner. Terminals and equipment, the purpose of which Stephen couldn't hazard a guess, were arranged in tidy rows.

"How did I get here?" a feminine voice asked.

The black-haired woman's lips narrowed as she moved around the equipment and positioned herself in the center of the room with her hands on her hips. "You aren't really here, Betty. It is just the virtual world. I just had to come up with a location that we both knew."

"Where is my son?" the disembodied voice asked.

"I'm not sure, but I believe he is still in the hospital."

"I can't stay here. I need to go back to him." The view of the room spun. A door blocked his path. His hand reached out to the door, then dropped to his side. The view of the room changed again, but this time the movement was slower. Then he was face to face with the black-haired woman. "Why can't I wake up?"

The other woman's pinkie tapped on her side. "I wish I knew. It's what I've been telling you to do for some time now."

The scene and the woman faded away. Stephen grumbled to himself as he attempted to fall back to sleep. It was as if a pitchfork was being driven into his skull. He shifted, seeking a more comfortable position. The pain across his temple intensified followed by another spike of pain.

He opened his eyes and was surrounded by darkness. *What a bizarre dream.* He must have fallen asleep in the barn and forgotten to bring a lantern. Helen was going to kill him if she caught him sneaking back inside. An intense desire to run took him by surprise. He sat up. He clutched the fabric under his hands as another wave crested. *Fabric.* He tightened and loosed his grip. There was fabric under his hands, not wood and straw. *Where am I?* A strong whiff of antiseptic chased the last of the disorientation of sleep away. Memories of the last few days came flooding back.

"What should we tell his parents?" a man's voice said in the hall. "They saw the truck arrive."

A wedge of light cut the darkness as a door swung open. "Tell them there is too great a risk of infection to let them see him now," said a voice Stephen recognized as Dr. Lambda's. He lay back down and pretended to be unconscious as she entered the room.

"I don't think his mother is going to like that," said the man.

"And I think I'm in charge of this facility." Dr. Lambda sighed. "More lives are at stake than just this one. They should just be grateful I need him to be stabilized first."

There was a pinch on his arm and his headache eased, while the rest of his muscles felt as if they'd been transformed into pudding. "Can't go," Stephen muttered as the drug injected into his system took hold.

"Was he awake?"

"A fever dream," said Dr. Lambda. "Nothing more. Now, I've given him something to help him rest more peacefully. Here, cover him with this blanket. He should be out until morning."

Then Stephen could fight sleep no longer.

⁘

Sunlight filled the room when Stephen risked opening his eyes. He was relieved that this time there was only about a third as much pain as the evening before. His head flopped to its side. He had as much control over its movement as he might a wet noodle. Dr. Lambda stood by a counter on the other side of the room, writing notes.

She tilted her head, catching his movement. Closing the folder, she walked to his side and pulled out a wheeled stool. "How are we feeling today?" she asked as she sat down.

"Like I was hit by a truck." He tapped his thumb with his index finger. It was as if the digit belonged to someone else.

She pursed her lips as she folded her hands in her lap. "Well, I suppose after the state we found you in that is to be expected. The good news is, as dinged up as you may feel, you managed to avoid any serious injuries which is no small feat all things considering."

"I hear I have good genes."

She arched an eyebrow. Standing up once more, she reached over and checked a bag hanging from a metal shaft beside him. She tapped the bag and frowned before examining the cord that ran from the bag to his arm. "So we are feeling funny this morning. That's an encouraging sign, I suppose."

"Oh yeah, I'm feeling much better. In fact, I think I feel well enough that if you want to go ahead and, you know, unplug me—"

She tapped the bag a second time. Its contents gleamed in the morning light. "I believe it would be best if you rested a while longer."

"Thanks for all your help, but really, I feel fine. Well, fine enough." He touched the pin entering the veins at his wrist, relieved at the rushing sensation of blood returning to his limbs, even if it felt like a thousand needles stabbing him.

"In layman's terms, I've given you a neurologic chemical inhibitor. The same sort of drug that once was used to treat Alzheimer's disease. Unfortunately, I've found its effects to be temporary at best, but better than nothing. You may feel groggy. You may also experience loss of appetite and increased bowel movements." Her lips twisted as she caught sight of what he was doing. "Please don't do that. It is for your own safety. Do you have any idea what you looked like when I arrived?"

"Probably like I'd been through a meat grinder, but I can handle it. I'm sure you have patients who need you more."

She smiled and placed her hand on top of his. "You don't trust me much, do you?"

Stephen fought the urge to move his hand out from under hers. To pull the needle out of his arm himself. To stun her and not look back, but then he thought of Ed and Helen. The man mentioned they had seen his arrival, which not only meant they were alive but also near. He couldn't risk anything until he knew where they were.

"That's okay. I'm not quick to trust anyone nowadays either. Your parents would approve."

"They're not my parents. Not really." He cringed. What exactly was the drug she'd given him inhibiting? *Was it something like a truth serum?*

The corners of Dr. Lambda's mouth turned up, making her appear years younger. "If you mean biologically, I know. They told me. They told me quite a bit about you actually. Anything they could think of in an attempt to protect you after that getaway stunt you pulled." She winked. "Of course, they didn't know about our deal." She folded her hands in her lap. "Families are made up of so much more than biology, don't you think? Take me, for example. I've never given birth, but I've cared for a whole ward of children as if they were my own."

"Right. So now that I am medicated, and all patched up, are you going to send me back to the tower? I still had a few days left. I can get you through the barricade. I know it now."

The smile left Dr. Lambda's face. "That deal is off. I wasn't aware of who you were then. I am now." She stood. "The IV should have been empty by now," she said, pointing at the clear bag that looked half-full. "Either that or you shouldn't be talking about how fine you feel." She paused. "Unless, that is, of course, you were dead." She walked over and pulled the needle out of his wrist in a single-handed motion, causing Stephen to suck in his breath at the pain. A single bead of blood welled up where the needle had been. "Your blood stopped it. You are healing yourself faster than I could with any medicine."

"That's impossible."

"Yet here we are and I have the proof." She waved the bag in front of his face. "Do you know how many people have died because of the so-called upgrade?" Her nose wrinkled at the word. "How many children? And yet, instead of doing the decent thing and going to the public about your identity, you've been hiding all this time." She began pacing around the room. "You should have told me your real name from the start. Your real last name, that is."

Stephen stared at the drop of blood. When he wiped it away, he noticed the skin beneath it appeared bruised, but there was no trace of a puncture wound. "If I can heal myself, it's news to me." He touched his face. Had the swelling gone down?

"Did you know you don't exist? That you are officially dead? Stephen Dronigh, only son of Alan and Elizabeth Dronigh. Died at age four like so many other unfortunates. At least that's what the official records say."

"I don't understand."

"I took the certificate to be a dead end, but I wasn't willing to give up," she continued. "The original virus was man-made, after all. I was certain it would have been designed with a kill-switch. I thought if I could find the right carrier, I could develop a cure for the disease and save all those children. Because that's what the upgrade is. A disease." Her knuckles turned white where they clenched the bag. "That's why it was so important I gain access to the tower." She paused her pacing and let the bag go, letting it fall to the floor with a slapping sound. "I should have tested you more completely before making that deal with you, but I thought the opportunity was too perfect to waste. I know now I made a mistake."

"So now what? We make a different deal?" He held out his wrist, exposing his arteries. "If I agree to donate some blood to test your theory, you'll let my family go?"

"If I am correct, I may need a bit more than that."

"Oh," replied Stephen, turning his wrist back over. "Well, I guess if I can heal myself, I can spare a pint or two, right? How much blood do you need?"

She approached the cot, pulling out a cloth. "I'm afraid I'm going to need all of it." She reached out with the cloth until it hovered above Stephen's face.

"I can't let you do that." A man-shaped shadow blocked the sunlight entering the room through the open door.

She dropped the cloth. Her eyes narrowed. "You aren't authorized to be here," said Dr. Lambda.

"So arrest me." Ed closed the distance between them with a single step. Grabbing the cloth from where she'd dropped it, Ed used it to cover her mouth. Dr. Lambda's eyes went wide before they rolled back in her head and her body went limp.

Ed lowered Dr. Lambda to the floor before stepping over her form, coming to a stop by Stephen's cot. He held out his hand.

"There's something about Helen and me I think you should know."

"If you are about to say something nuts like you've also been lying to me all this time about who you are and have only been taking care of me all this time because you suspected I was some sort of chosen one born with some mystic abilities or something, I really don't want to know."

Stephen watched as Ed's mouth formed a small O.

Thirty-Two

His legs were like sacks of grain—heavy and awkward to maneuver—as Stephen swung his feet off the cot and onto the floor. He wondered if he was as ready to travel as he'd claimed a second before.

"You may want to put these back on," said Ed, grabbing a pile of clothing from where they lay on the opposite side of the counter from Dr. Lambda's paperwork.

Stephen's cheeks burned when he realized he was only clothed in a sheet. "Did you kill her?"

Ed set his jaw as he threw a glance over his shoulder at the woman on the ground. "I would guess that contained some sort of knockout agent like chloroform. I expect she'll be on her feet and back to her charming self before you know it." He kicked the bag of fluid away. "I was sneaking down here to check on you. It's been two days since they brought you in. Then I was to circle back to Helen. We knew you were hurt, but were told you were being taken care of. We had no idea . . ." He knelt and touched Stephen's damaged face. "If she's responsible for this . . ." His eyes glistened.

"She wasn't." Stephen grasped Ed's arm and pulled himself upright. Together, they stepped over the unconscious Dr. Lambda. "But she was going to kill me. Said my blood contained some sort of kill-switch." His body felt surer by the second.

Ed paused in mid-stride.

"Does it? Does my blood contain a cure?" He stuck his head out the door and looked around. The hallway lay empty.

"A cure? You say that like you think you have some sort of disease."

"She thought so," replied Stephen, gesturing behind him with his thumb.

Ed's lips curved, but there was a worry in his eyes. "You see, years ago—"

"Finn told me all about it. I'm a freak."

"You're not a freak. You're my son."

"Yeah, yeah I know. And really, being found by you guys was the best, but now's not the time." Shadows appeared on the other side of double doors with frosted glass windows. Stephen moved to the side and stumbled into a vacant room on their left, pulling Ed along with him.

"No, you don't understand. You don't know the whole story." Ed chewed on his bottom lip again. "We didn't just *find* you. I might have had a part in creating you."

"What? So Alan isn't my father?" Stephen looked into the hallway. It was still empty, but the shadows remained, moving in animated discussion. He ducked back into the room.

Ed blanched. "No. He is." His eyes widened. "I would never cheat on Helen. Never."

"Then are you saying I was some sort of test-tube baby?" Stephen risked another glance in the hallway. The double doors remained closed, and the shadows were gone. He turned to Ed, signaling all was clear.

"No, nothing like that. You were created the usual way." Ed grimaced, and his face flushed red. "I mean, er . . .I was on the team that originally came up with the upgrade in the first place." His expression bunched. "It wasn't my discovery, but I was there. If it wasn't for me, your mother would never have been injected, and I'm pretty sure no one else outside of the original test group would have either." He looked away as if seeing the distant memory play out once more. "It's one of the reasons we went on the run. Well, at first, we were just trying to get someplace away from the city to wait for things to settle down, but they didn't. Instead, they got worse." He rubbed his temple. "I started thinking about what would happen when people found out. It was bad enough thinking about what would happen if people found out my part in all this, but if they found out whose son you *really* were . . . So, we hid and kept it a secret. Even from you. My name in that previous life was Chad." Red streaked his cheeks. "I'm sorry I was afraid. I should have trusted you."

Stephen looked at the man whose paranoia he had always dismissed as endearing but unnecessary. He tried to imagine what it must have been like to have left their old lives to protect him.

"No. Ever since I left home, everyone I've met has been one doctor's note away from being certifiably insane. First, it was the guy who thinks he is a wizard making me go on some quest to retrieve a magic wand. Then, I met my long-lost father, who guess what? Hasn't been dead all this time, but has instead been sleeping in some underground tomb for the past fifteen years. I've spent almost a day with people who think fangs and claws are a good look, and I just found out the leader of the closest thing we have to a civilized government wants to bleed me out. Oh, and I almost forgot. The girl I thought liked me was only using me, and may or may not have killed a guy. So yeah, you were right to tell me not to trust anyone."

Ed's hand froze. "You saw your father." He dropped his arm to his side. "Is he here, too?"

Stephen's lips twisted. "Would you believe it? He's the one who tricked me into going with Dr. Lambda and then he ditched me. Again."

Ed sighed. "I'm sure he had his reasons."

"It doesn't matter." Stephen threw up his hands. "We've wasted enough time. Where's Helen?"

"She was on the sixth floor when I left her." Ed bit his lip. "It's how we knew they'd found you. It has the best views."

"And what floor are we on?"

Ed bit his lip. "The second."

Stephen stretched. While the muscles still ached, at least the pain was nothing compared to what he had experienced the evening before, and it was getting better by the minute. Even so, getting to her would not only require avoiding detection by the Watch. It required stairs. Lots of stairs.

"Do you think you will be able to make it?" asked Ed. "You could hide out in one of these rooms. I could find Helen and bring her to you."

The corridor intersected with another hallway lined with doors on either side. A sign mounted on the ceiling indicated stairs straight ahead. "I'm done hiding." Stephen crossed the tiled floor with a stride that was both straight and strong. "He's not my dad, you know. You are. Now let's go get Mom and then get out of here."

Thirty-Three

Stephen and Ed wove in and out of the building's corridors and stairwells, ducking behind thick doors or into empty rooms whenever they heard footsteps or voices. The layout of the hallways played tricks on them as much of the time the sounds proved to come from elsewhere. *If only there was a way to see ahead*, he thought. He considered risking another round of dash-and-duck when he remembered Alan's talk about the nanobots in materials and how he'd been able to see through the walls in the lab where they'd found the wand.

Stopping at another pair of double doors, Stephen cleared his thoughts and touched the metal plate affixed to their side labeled 'Press to Open.' His vision blurred for a moment; when it cleared, Stephen could visualize the nanobots embedded in the electric panel as if they were a thousand times their size. He projected a command, taking control of sensor clusters found in the tiny electronics, and redirected their readings into his brain. An image of the hallway on the other side materialized in his brain.

X-ray vision, ta-da. A week ago, he would have laughed at such an idea. *Two days ago you would have laughed.* He corrected himself. *Now stop distracting yourself and focus.* His vision jumped ahead. A quick scan proved that the final flight of stairs was open; however, now that he was accessing their network, the signals emitting from the surrounding nanobots were like a symphony. Each producing its own music and yet complementing those around it. He didn't want to turn them off. Stephen's consciousness jumped from one to another. With each jump, his awareness expanded further out until it was no longer restricted to the walls of the building.

A group of furry shapes bounded in and out of view at the edges of town. *The beastmen. Why are they here?* More motion caught Stephen's eye, closer to the Watch's headquarters. Another group was making their way down the main road, but coming from the opposite direction on horseback. He narrowed his focus to process additional detail. A man who looked vaguely familiar rode in the center of the group. Neither Wes nor Finn was there, but the man was surrounded by more than a dozen of the people wrapped in the color-shifting clothing from the tower, though the garb had not yet been activated. Stephen spotted Gavin, Baron, and Laura's pink hair. His focus slid off their faces as it registered another. Her expression was as much determination as it was agony. He almost hadn't recognized her without her cap. *Bean.* Her hair, no longer hidden, floated on the morning's breeze. Gone was all the dirt from her face. She was breathtaking. So breathtaking, Stephen almost forgot about why his feelings were conflicted about her.

"I'm sorry, Stephen." The sensors picked up the vibrations of her whisper.

He pulled his consciousness back to his physical body. *What was she sorry for?* He tried to grin, but his cheeks were still too swollen to allow for more than the corner of his lips to rise. She hadn't abandoned him, after all. She was making Finn keep to the terms of his original promise. She'd given them the wand, and now they were mounting a full-on assault on the hospital and everyone in it. The joy fled his face as Dr. Lambda's words came back and her reason for needing his blood. The Watch weren't the only people wandering around the halls. There were innocents and children here, too.

Helen saw them first as they flung open the doors to the dining level. "Stephen," she gasped. "Ed, he has no business being out of bed. Why in the world are you letting him walk around?" Armband clad men and women turned, locking their attention on the trio.

Ed hadn't kidded about the view. From shoulder-high to the ceiling above, the walls were made of glass, providing a panoramic view of the town below. *I get why it's called the Watchtower.* Stephen's stomach growled as he caught the scent of food wafting from a back room. "We don't have time." Stephen took a deep breath. He covered his ears as the cackle became pops, which became a high-pitched squeal as the remnants of a speaker system came online.

"Members of the Watch." Gavin's voice seemed to come from every angle. "We have someone with us who wants to say hello."

"Many of you knew my mission," a new voice boomed. "Many of you knew what I intended to do. I am here today to say that everything we are—everything we've stood for—doesn't have to be this way. We can be so much more."

Stephen's brows knit. He'd heard the voice before, but couldn't place it. The speaker nearest them sputtered and popped before going silent. *It doesn't matter. Stay focused.* Stephen scratched his head as he ran through what options they might still have. If only there wasn't so much noise, he might be able to think.

Another boom sounded. This time it came from gathering clouds outside rather than the aging speaker system. *Just great,* thought Stephen. *Another storm.*

Large drops of water began to fall from the sky, creating pings like mini-missiles as they ricocheted off the windows. A bolt of lightning streaked across the clouds. Stephen ducked out of instinct. Trying to move a bunch of sick people in an electrical storm wasn't the smartest plan. *But what other options do you have?*

A blonde man with a red armband spoke up, "You should return to your rooms. We've got this covered." The man turned his attention to another. "Go find Dr. Lambda. Tell her we have a situation."

It dawned on Stephen that the man must think of him as just another patient. The others began turning tables on their sides and taking defensive positions. Clicks and slaps rang out as guns were pulled from holsters and cartridges loaded. One of the men instructed another.

You know what they say about taking a knife to a gunfight. Stephen thought about how the Sorcerer woman, Laura, had disabled the gun with a touch at the base of the barricade. The members of the Watch were too confident. They were outclassed in the weapons department and didn't even know it. It was going to be a slaughter.

Small red text appeared over top his vision. 'Message failed to deliver.' *What message?* Stephen remembered the message he'd sent to Wes. *Idiot. Why didn't I think of it before? I'll send a message to Bean and tell her to call it off.* He sighed as he composed the message. He visualized pressing the 'send' key. He imagined a whooshing sound. *There. One problem down, which just leaves how to get home before Dr. Lambda raises the alarm.* It was somewhat surprising she hadn't already done so. He thought of the pendants Jeremy and Rotledge used to communicate over distances. *I guess she's wishing she kept a bit more technology around now.*

Rotledge. He remembered the vacant look in Jeremy's eyes after the flaw in the device had been used against him. He shuddered. *Maybe it's not such a good thing.* The beastmen would be reaching the hospital's entrance in a matter of minutes. *Why are they here?* Stephen's eyes widened. *They know you left with Dr. Lambda. They are here for revenge.* Going outside was not an option.

'Message failed to deliver.' Red blocked text filled his vision. *Was there something else blocking the outgoing signal?* He tried again. 'Message failed to deliver.' Stephen cursed. "What's the point of having superpowers if you can't use them?"

"Superpowers?" Helen asked.

"Never mind."

The Watchman shouted at them. "Once again, I strongly encourage all three of you to return to your rooms. We'll notify you when the threat has passed."

Sure you will. "I want to help out. Does anyone know where the children's ward might be?"

The Watchman crouched into their positions.

"Anyone?" He looked around. "Good talk." He closed his eyes, knelt down, and touched the floor. Connecting with the nanobots, he summoned their sensor readings once more. As he did so, he imagined he heard a woman's voice announce, *Now entering the arena.*

thirty-four

Based on the heat signatures, Stephen suspected the majority of the Watch lived on the lower floors; however, none of the rooms contained more than one or two people, and all of them were adults.

If you were a ward for children, where would you be? He called up a map from the data stream. A block labeled Pediatric A&E caught his eye. Stephen tapped into the nanobots once more. His consciousness jumped to the area marked on the map. He hit a wall. *That's weird.* He tried again. The nanobots didn't respond to his command. It was as if there weren't any. A loud boom rang out. *Was that thunder or a gunshot?*

"What is it, honey?" asked Helen.

He made his choice. "We need to get to room 3124," said Stephen.

"What's in 3124?" asked Ed.

"I might be wrong, but it's better than standing around doing nothing up here."

The way back through the labyrinth that was the hospital complex was easier with the members of the Watch distracted and the map overlay to guide them. Sounds of shouting spurred them on their way.

They rounded the final corner. The hairs on the back of Stephen's neck rose. The nanobots still weren't responding, but the closer he got, the more convinced he was that it wasn't because they were broken, but because someone else had already taken command and was shielding themselves from view. He could well be leading his parents into disaster. "Maybe it would be better for you two to wait out here."

"We can handle whatever is on the other side of that door."

No, you can't. Not if they think you are with the Watch.

The hard line of Helen's face informed him the matter was not open for discussion.

The hinges swung without a sound, revealing a large room. Between the storm outside and the painted glass windows, the natural sunlight was dim but enough to see inside. Rows of empty beds lined either side of the room, divided by worn cloth curtains painted with balloons. Paper cutouts of animals hung from the ceiling.

He summoned the map again.

An orb of pale purple light formed behind one of the curtains.

Stephen banished the map and created his own version of the light albeit dimmer. His light flickered. "I'm one of you."

"No. You're not." The curtain slid to the side, revealing white blonde hair. "You shouldn't be here."

"Yeah, I know, but I am. You need to call the attack off. There are kids. A ward full of them, maybe not in this room, but they are around here somewhere. If things get out of control, they could die. When I couldn't get a message through to you, I thought I would find them and, I don't know, protect them somehow."

Bean's features hardened. "There is no ward."

"Yes, there is. The doctor told me so."

"And you believed her." Bean pulled the curtain closed as she crossed the room until they were separated by less than a yard.

"Well, she was planning on killing me right after telling me about it, so I'm pretty sure she was being honest." He took a step toward her. She held up a hand. Lightning danced across her palm.

"I bet she told you we were the ones with the delusions, too." Gavin's voice startled Stephen from behind. "Are you done in here? The others are waiting." He passed Stephen on his way to meet Bean, dismissing him as Bean lowered her hand and banished the spark. He squeezed her shoulders. "It was even easier than we expected. She was just lying there."

She met Stephen's stricken gaze with one of stone as Gavin pulled her toward the door. "What should we do about them?"

"Who, him? The guy you called an idiot before? You said all he wants to do is go home. After our victory today, I'm feeling generous. I say we give him what he wants."

"And his parents?"

Gavin snorted. "They can go, too. What do I care? They can't do anything."

⁂

Stephen stood outside the Watchtower under a concrete overhang. A wall of water poured on the other side, limiting his sight.

"I know you are hurting right now, honey, but you're better off. Life can get back to normal this way," said Helen.

"Normal. What is that anyway? I mean specifically, what part of my life up until now would you describe as normal?" He sighed. "You don't need to answer that." A dark shape cut through the rain. An odor of wet dog tickled Stephen's nose. *How could I forget?* "Ed, remember asking me who did this to me? You might be about to find out."

Dark shadows resolved themselves into monstrous silhouettes as the beastmen approached the entrance to the Watchtower. Stephen raised his fists. Bolts of lightning matching those that crossed the sky encircled each. His legs gave out from under him, and he fell to the ground.

"Stephen, what's wrong?" Helen dropped to his side.

His teeth chattered as a frost settled into his limbs. "Too much." Stephen's body shook. "Need energy."

The beastman closest snorted and pushed Ed aside. "Looks like your boy could use a longer stay."

"If you touch him, I'll kill you."

"The boss says we're not here for him," another voice said as more legs came into Stephen's view. *Darnell.* "Consider this your lucky day."

"We're here for what's ours," said Jeremy as the other beastman parted. "Any idea where we might find your girlfriend? No? That's okay. I'm sure we can sniff her out." Stepping over Stephen, Jeremy opened the glass doors to the Watchtower.

"Must warn Bean," said Stephen. He tried to compose a message. His body's convulsions grew stronger.

"Ed, help him." Helen covered his body with her own. "He's freezing."

"I don't know what to do," said Ed.

"Do something."

"What?"

"Maybe there is a drug or something inside that can help."

"I wouldn't have the first idea. What if I choose wrong?"

"Find a doctor, then. I don't care. Just do something."

Ed raced back inside, leaving Helen and Stephen under the overhang. Stephen's eyes rolled back in their sockets.

"There, there, sweetheart. It will be okay. I'm here with you." She touched his cheek.

Adrenaline and euphoria flooded his system. Although his vision faded and thoughts became hard to piece together, his remaining other heightened senses detected an additional source of glorious energy. It was just out of reach, on another side of a wall. It called to him, offering him a power beyond anything he'd ever experienced. All he had to do was break through the wall.

He pushed with his mind. The wall bent, but didn't break. He narrowed his focus, visualizing his intent. He honed his will until it resembled a spear and threw it, piercing the wall. The pain vanished, replaced by exhilaration. He flexed his muscles. Were it not for a weight on his chest, Stephen might float away. Nothing could stand in his way. His vision cleared. The concrete slab above him came into sharp focus. Each individual nook and pore in the material magnified. Grain-shaped packets of electronics pulsed in a net made up of millions if not billions of strings. *The nanobots.* He smiled as their vibrations took on a new frequency. They sang to him, waiting for his command.

He shoved the weight from his chest in a single movement. He was invincible, power made incarnate. He could change the world. He would bring them out of the darkness.

"What have you done?" Ed's voice broke his concentration, and the real world came crashing back.

thirty-five

Helen lay in a crumpled pile at Stephen's feet with her hand outstretched from touching his cheek.

Ed rushed to her side and cradled her in his arms. Helen's head flopped backward. Dead eyes looked out of gaunt gray flesh, which had been aged before its time. She'd been drained of life like Rotledge, only this time there was no one else to blame. "What have you done?" Ed whispered again as he pushed a strand of hair out of her face.

"I didn't know." Stephen took a step back. The power he'd sensed on the other side of the wall. It had been Helen's life force, and in his half-dead state, her touch was all the invitation he'd needed to claim it as his own. "I never intended. . . I didn't mean—"

"You didn't *intend?*" Ed's shoulders slumped. "You say that like our intentions matter." Ed turned away. "You are your father's son, after all. He never stopped to worry about the consequences before acting either."

"Ed?" He reached out with arms that no longer showed evidence of cuts or bruising. "Dad?"

Ed pulled Helen's lifeless body closer to his chest. "I used to think I wanted you to call me that."

"What should I do?" The euphoria that had consumed him only moments before became bile. All this time, he'd been so afraid of what the Watch would do to his parents, he never considered himself to be the greater threat. The beating he'd taken from Rotledge was a mere scrape compared to the hurt which now consumed his soul. *And yet,* the small voice inside him whispered, *to be in command of that much power, can you really trust yourself not to try it again?* Stephen let his arm drop. He now understood why those who lived in the tower, stayed there.

"Do whatever you want. I'm done deciding for you, just don't follow me." Ed stood, gathering Helen into his arms. "I found this with your clothes." A small piece of wood fell to the ground—the handle from Wes's antenna. Then Ed turned away and walked into the rain, still carrying Helen.

Stephen picked the handle up and turned it over in his hands. Wetness that had nothing to do with the storm that raged beyond the overhang streaked down his face. *You should have thrown it away already. A piece of junk.* He cocked his hand back, ready to chuck the scrap like Bean suggested back at the train platform. *Bean.* He clung to her name like a life raft floating in the middle of a hurricane-tossed sea. The beastmen were hunting her down as they spoke. He clutched the device in his fist before shoving it back in his pocket. He couldn't protect his parents, but she still had a chance to get out of this alive, if only he could make it there in time. *No one else I care about dies today.*

Stephen summoned the map of the hospital. Gavin said the others were waiting in the operating theater so that was where he would go. He flung the doors open and re-entered the Watchtower lobby in a run, locking his hurt behind a wall in his mind before the pain could overwhelm him.

The operating theater was on the second floor, no doubt where Dr. Lambda intended to wheel his bed had she been successful with the knockout agent. Stephen climbed the stairs two at a time. The smell of wet animal was heavy in the air. The beastmen had already been this way. *Was he already too late?*

He turned at the top of the stairs and raced into the hall. One of the beastman with rhino-like skin blocked a door. Seeing Stephen approaching the man, the beastman lowered his head and charged. The impact sent Stephen flying back into the hall; however, he had anticipated the attack and had been ready. The beastman dropped to the ground as they crashed together into the wall. What Stephen hadn't anticipated was the man's crushing weight on top of him.

He twisted his hips as he wiggled his way out from under the dead weight. *So much for being Mr. Invincible.* His powers had limits, after all. It was a lesson worth remembering.

He approached the doors to the operating theater with more caution the second time. Opening them a crack, he slipped inside. The theater was constructed in a half circle with several levels of metal risers extending up the sides of the room. Orbs of purple light and barred teeth surrounded him.

Members of the Watch were positioned at the lowest levels. Dr. Lambda lay on a wheeled stretcher, restrained as Stephen had been in the back of the truck. Gavin stood in front of her alongside the familiar-looking man from earlier, while other members of the Watch knelt at the Sorcerer's feet. A beastman growled.

"Uh-uh," said Gavin, leaning over Dr. Lambda. "Jeremy, remind your people why they don't want to come any closer. I would hate to have to hurt someone you care about." Lightning danced across his fist and up his sleeve.

Jeremy held his hands out. "Stay back, boys."

"You made the right decision."

Gavin smiled. His gaze slid, meeting Stephen's. "Ah, it looks like someone else made a wise decision as well. Good to see you decided to join us, after all. Have a seat. The show is just about to begin."

Stephen's forehead wrinkled as he tried to make sense of the scene playing out before him. He scanned the crowd. Bean wasn't among those in the front rows. *Where could she be?* He looked up into the higher levels, spotting her near the topmost row. Her lips narrowed, and she gave an almost imperceptible shake of her head. He climbed the steps to her side anyway.

"You don't belong here." she whispered. "Why did you come back?"

"To save you," he whispered back. "From them. They know what you did."

"Of course you did." She snorted. "Because I've given you so many reasons to make you believe I can't take care of myself." Her face contorted into a humorless grin. "Haven't you figured it out yet?" She stared straight ahead. "How else do you think I was able to beat the drain this long? I'm a monster."

"I don't think you are a monster." He grit his teeth. "I . . ." The words rebelled, dying on his tongue. He didn't deserve to say them. "You are—"

She turned away. "Why did you come back, really? You did it. You rescued your parents. Why didn't you leave with them?"

"My mom is dead."

Bean's shoulders slumped. "I know."

"No, I mean my other mom died. Helen. I . . ." He tightened his jaw as the reality of his statement came crashing back to the forefront of his thoughts from where he'd locked it away during his ascent. "It was my fault." The image of Helen's still form as Ed carried her away threatened to undo his control. "I thought I had to come back. I-I . . ." He bit off his words. His heart was able to handle only so much truth. "I have no place else to go," he said instead, sealing the emotional whirlwind away once more. He couldn't afford to lose his focus now, if only for her sake.

Bean looked up with wide eyes, meeting his gaze. Her lips tightened, and her balled hand twitched where it rested in her lap. She turned her attention to the center of the room.

Gavin gestured to the man next to him. "As you were saying."

The man walked around Gavin and squatted down near one of the members of the Watch. "I know this might sound hard to believe, but it's me."

Stephen started. He remembered now where he'd seen the man before. It was the man from Bean's childhood. The same man who'd been defeated at the base of the barricade, but he was young again. The Sorcerers had used the wand on him. No band of red covered his arm. He'd joined them. *But didn't that mean he had to have abilities too, or didn't that matter?*

Movement caught Stephen's eyes as the man explained to the others about the illness Dr. Lambda diagnosed as terminal and his mission to the tower as a final act of sacrifice and service to the cause. Bean's hands were shaking where they clenched the fabric of her trousers. "He did something to you. Back when you were a kid. Did he hit you?"

"Doesn't matter now."

"It matters." He reached out to cover her hand with his.

She pulled away and turned to him with a fire in her eyes. "No. If you would start paying attention, you'd see it doesn't." She released the fabric and smoothed the creases. "We're all monsters now. What's one more in the club?"

Baron stepped forward and dropped a bag by the man's feet. Opening it, the man pulled out a gun-shaped device and a needle. He attached the needle to the device and pulled out a vial, similar to the ones Stephen had seen in the camouflaged lab. "Now, who else wants to make the right choice?"

A member of the Watch in the middle of the group wobbled as he rose. He pulled the band off his arm and raised his hand.

"So what? Everyone gets upgraded and becomes friends now?" asked Stephen. "What about the energy drain? If all the wand does is make a person young again, couldn't the upgrade still kill them?"

Bean bit her lip. "Something like that.

"But why do all of this then? I mean if Gavin wants everyone dead, why draw it out?"

"Gavin is a fan of natural selection. It's why Finn likes him."

The Watchman rubbed his arm at the site of the injection. Baron gestured for him to take a seat. The beastmen grew restless.

"You'll have your turn, too," said Gavin.

"This has gone on long enough. We aren't interested in any injections," said Jeremy. "All we want is what was stolen from us. Give us the wand, and we'll leave you to your"—he sneered—"upgrades."

"I'm sorry, but I'm afraid the only way you can have the wand back is if you join our side."

"No deal."

"Then I guess we have nothing to talk about."

"And I guess it's time we go on the offense."

Gavin's hand hovered over Dr. Lambda. "I'll do it."

Jeremy laughed. "Do whatever you want to her. She's been dead to me for years."

Chaos broke out as the beastmen launched into action. Stephen glanced to his side at an empty chair. Blonde white hair joined the melee. Bodies flew across the room. The Sorcerers had stealth, but the Sharks had strength as well as stamina.

Stephen watched as a jersey-clad giant cornered Bean. He closed the distance. She ducked under his thick crushing arms. He spun on his heel. She reached out and placed her hand on the beastman's sleeve. Light pulsed. The beastman, Shaw, laughed, pulling back the cloth. Stephen leaped down the stairs, but couldn't reach her in time as the man said, "Good thing I listened when Jeremy said we should add some shock protection to our uniforms today." His arm under his sleeve had an unnatural flatness to it like rubber. The outline of narrow cords twisted around its length. "My turn." He slammed a fist into her jaw.

Bean's head flew back at an awkward angle, and her body fell to the floor.

Stephen ran down the steps until he was by her side as the fighting continued all around. He touched her neck. A weak pulse flickered under his fingertips.

A bench crashed beside him. The cart restraining Dr. Lambda toppled over. A shot rang out. He shielded her body with his. Her pulse grew fainter. A booted foot connected to his side. Stephen grunted, but remained where he was. He thought of the knife wound in the forest and how it had disappeared by morning. Whatever was in his blood that allowed him to heal faster than a normal person, it was in her blood, too. All she needed was enough energy to speed the process along. Stephen looked at the ceiling as he tried to think. The nanobots sang to him. *Redirect the current.* Alan's off-hand remark in front of the convenience store came back to him. *That's how the Sorcerers hold the drain back. It's not just food. They feed off energy from the tower, too.*

"Move it, kid," Shaw said, kicking him again.

He focused on the tiled surface above. He closed his eyes and pictured the nanobots as he'd seen them under the concrete overhang in the front of the Watchtower. When he opened his eyes, the tiny grains of electronics responded to his command again. His consciousness expanded with every connection. The fighting surrounding them took on a surreal quality as the sensors sent readings from every angle into his brain.

The sky above the Watchtower pulsed with a violence of its own as a billion joules of energy arched from cloud to cloud. *A single bolt of lightning contains enough energy to power a sixty-watt light bulb for six months*, the data stream informed him. *That's helpful,* thought Stephen.

He returned his attention to Bean. The hair on his arm rose. Stephen pushed an errant hair out of Bean's face. The nanobots song changed. He leaned in. Time slowed as the data stream took the readings from the nanobots' sensors, such as the man's weight and the angle of anticipated impact and executed calculations on the probability of an average person's survival. The results weren't good. His instincts screamed for him to move. His heart demanded he stay. He closed his eyes and leaned forward. Redemption was never going to be an option—not for him—but she still had a chance. *You always have a choice.* Stephen pressed his lips to Bean's as lightning struck the Watchtower.

thirty-six

Jade green eyes looked up at Stephen. Bean's lips curved into a sly smile. "You better be careful, or I might start expecting fireworks on every date."

Stephen kissed her again.

"Ahem."

Stephen looked up to see Jeremy standing over them. He twirled the wand. Bean jumped into a defensive position. Stephen reached out with his mind to the nanobots, ready to channel their energy into another strike, but their signals were fried by the energy of the storm. The nanobots of the Watchtower were as dead as several of the bodies strewn about the theater floor, including Shaw whose skin was blistered and black.

"Now there's no reason to get worked up. This round is over." He gestured to the overturned bed where Gavin lay slumped. "My team won."

"What are you going to do now? Kill us, too?" asked Stephen.

The corner of Jeremy's lips inched up. "Now that wouldn't be very sportsmanlike, would it?" Bean raised her fists. Jeremy raised an eyebrow.

Stephen cocked his head. He hadn't known him long, but there was something off about Jeremy.

Jeremy's smile deepened. "When you get back, tell your leader I'm looking forward to our next match. He'll understand. He and I have a score to settle." Jeremy bent over and picked up something from the floor. He turned it over in his hands. "I believe this might be yours." He shrugged and handed it to Stephen. "I wouldn't want you to say I never did anything for you."

Then he whistled and turned away. The surviving beastmen filed out behind him, leaving Bean and Stephen surrounded by the dead.

"Don't tell me you still have that thing," said Bean. "Have you been carrying it with you this entire time?"

Stephen held the handle from Wes's antenna up. "I forgot about it." He examined the area where it had been attached to the metal rod and turned it over. A whirl a quarter of the way down its length caught his eye.

"Well, you might as well toss it now."

"Wes made me promise to keep it. I figure I'll give it back to him the next time I see him."

The smile left Bean's lips.

The urge to pinch wood at the whirl took over him. Stephen pulled on one end, and a piece broke away, exposing a tiny plate covered in copper traces. "Huh. It's not a piece of wood, after all."

"There is something you should know."

Stephen focused on the component in his hand. The copper traces were cool to the touch. He narrowed the focus of his gaze as if zooming in on his computer screen until the place where his skin touched metal was nothing more than a pixelated blur. Then he shifted his consciousness into the device.

Wes appeared dressed in an outfit similar to what their avatars wore in the game. "Mont," he began. "I've got some good news and some bad news." He waved his hand, and the rectangular window opened up. A brown-haired woman with pale waxy skin and sunken eyes looked out. "The good news is I found this memory stick in your biological mom's files. Turns out, she was a patient of Dad's. I thought you'd like to see her, even if she was unwell when she recorded her message to you."

Stephen stared at the woman in the window. He touched his face. Darnell mentioned seeing a resemblance.

"The bad news is . . . Well, there's really no easy way to say this. The bad news is I'm gone. As in, game over."

Stephen ripped his gaze from the woman. The drain. Wes had known he wasn't going to be making the trip back to the tower.

Wes took a step back. "Before you get weird, like blaming yourself or something idiotic like that, know that I made a choice. A choice I hope one day you never have to understand. Now sit back and listen to your mother."

Wes faded away as the window expanded, leaving only the image of his biological mother's face from the shoulders up.

His mother glanced up and to the side, as if listening to someone else before returning her attention to the camera. "Stevie, first, know that I wish I could still be there with you. If there was a way, trust that I would be. I love you so much." Her eyes welled up. "Second"—she looked back again—"there's no time." She held up a picture of a black-haired woman wearing a white-and-silver dress. Stephen recognized it as the same woman from his fever dream. "I know you must have questions. About us. About yourself. Find her." His mother reached up, tapped something unseen, and the window went black.

Wes reappeared. "My dad's notes said your mother was being treated in the end for depression and a personality disorder with acute paranoia. She claimed that her husband was into some pretty dark stuff, like mind control. She also claimed he had intentionally released a virus which he and only a select few would be immune to." Wes sighed. "The more I looked into her claims, the more I've come to the conclusion that your mom might have been onto something. Which, I'm sorry to say, would make your dad a complete psycho. It's a good thing you don't know where he is."

But you do know where he is, his mind whispered. *He's now going by the name Jeremy.*

A circle with a cartoonish image of Wes holding his thumb up appeared. "I've uploaded as much as I can of my memories into a program only you should be able to access. If you ever need a friend to talk to, I'm a keystroke away."

Stephen shook his head. "Of course you are."

"If you happen to see my dad, tell him I'm sorry, but it was the only way." He paused. "Oh, but if you see your dad, I suggest running."

The image dissolved. Stephen blinked as the real world came back into focus. Bean looked at him with concern. "What was that? Did you see something?"

Bean already thought of herself as a monster. What would she think after she learned they might have released something even worse? *No*, the small voice corrected, *what you released.*

"I need to find a woman."

Bean frowned. "Come again?" She crossed her arms over her chest.

Stephen wanted to pull her into his arms and kiss her again. Then he remembered where they were and who might still lurk nearby. "Not like that. She's got to be like fifty years old by now. Nothing for you to worry about. This file." He shook the drive. "There was a message from my mom. She said this woman would have answers. I just have to find her."

"Well, are you going to stand there, or are you going to lead the way?"

The first sound to register in her mind was the hissing sound of air escaping. Her eyelids fluttered as her mind attempted to identify its source. At first, all she could see was a black nothingness, but then as she became more aware, she noticed the otherwise complete darkness surrounding her was broken by a growing, pulsing hint of light. Her nostrils were overwhelmed by the smell of rust, dirt, and decay. The sound of metal scraping metal assaulted her ears, followed by the whirl of a dying motor.

Gradually, her consciousness woke up enough for her to more accurately process her surroundings. She was lying prone in a cylinder, the majority of her body still sealed within its frame. She had the most disconcerting feeling that her head was somehow detached from the majority of her bulk, floating separately in the darkness. Her consciousness began to expand into her body like a spider's web tying together the space between mind and limb. It was shocking and unnatural. Almost as if she was being anchored back to earth.

She attempted to shift within the capsule, biting back a scream as the muscles in her back and limbs protested the movement. She did not attempt to rise again until the sensation of pins and needles receded, indicating blood had returned to its regular circulation pattern.

After a few tender experiments beginning with a wiggle of her fingers and toes, she risked raising her arms to the rim of the capsule. Satisfied with the results, she tried pulling herself into an upright position. The effort nearly sent her reeling with exhaustion. Several more minutes elapsed before she was willing to attempt other sudden moves. She felt as if she was waking up from death and perhaps she was, depending on what a person classified as life.

As she looked out into the darkened room, the only sources of light proved to be coming from the occasional pulse of red light blinking on either side of her. It reflected off what could be shattered glass on the floor beside her tube.

She made a quick gesture. Though it was minuscule, the gesture was enough to send her swaying. The room's lights brightened, as if in response to her movement, and she was momentarily blinded. After her eyes adjusted, the increased light allowed her to better process her surroundings.

Fragments of memory began to bubble up to the surface; however, there were still gaping holes. While she could not be completely certain, she believed when she had entered this room last, it was the definition of medical cleanliness. It was for a meeting or a demonstration of some kind. Memories of the scent of lemon rind and industrial fluid danced in her mind alongside an image of several pristine white tanks. The tanks had been accented by glass, arrays of organic bioluminescent panels, and highlighted with chrome trim. Everything she thought she remembered was in stark contrast to what was currently assaulting her senses.

At least a few years must have passed since she last saw the contents of this room based on the condition of the cylinders. *But how did I get here?* she wondered.

She further scanned the room. The walls had collapsed inward in piles of rubble, along with bits and pieces of ceiling. Broken beakers and other tubes were strewn about with other crushed industrial equipment. As she better focused her vision, she noticed several of the tanks showed lines of wear along with their edges, the chrome trim non-existent. Some were also heavily damaged with large dings pocketing along their lengths. A few of the tanks' lids were open, their contents were vacant, but the majority, however, were still sealed. The occupants of these were obscured behind glass blackened by dust and dirt.

The periodic red light had come from a few of the tanks' status panels, indicating that they had nearly exhausted their power supplies. A nagging voice in the back of her mind told her this should be troubling, but could not remember why. The feeling was like waking up knowing that you had just been dreaming and not being able to recall any of the details.

She called out for help. Her voice sounded more like a frog's croak than words. She waved a hand on the chance that someone might be nearby monitoring the area. After several minutes of waiting with no response, she had to accept that no help was coming.

A piece of her wasn't entirely surprised due to the sorry state of neglect surrounding her in the room and shook her head in disgust. At her core, she knew that she had once been someone of significant value. Had she been in her center of power, wherever that might be, no one would have ever dared to abandon her like this. That feeling alone told her that she was far from home.

As her sense of self-importance began to circulate within her consciousness, so did more substantial memories. Memories she was still unsure she could trust. Large gaps remained in her life story, especially those revolving around the most recent events, but she knew one thing to be true.

There was something she had to remember above all else, something critically important, a promise or a face. She groaned, fighting a wave of nauseousness. Whatever it was, it remained stubbornly out of reach. She frowned as she battled to regain control of her body. It had something to do with her legacy, but the same could be said about many of the few decisions and events of her life she could recall. The thought didn't help trigger the memory. So what could it be? She struggled to piece together her thoughts into any sensible order. *My legacy*, she thought with a tinge of pain. She had been so close to securing her place in history. She'd been so close she could practically taste it. So why couldn't she remember what it was?

She screamed in frustration. Even that sounded weak to her ears. She wanted to scream more. She had to get herself out of this room, if for no other reason than to get the blood flowing enough to remind her just what might have been. With that final thought to bluster her energy, she pulled herself the rest of the way out of her capsule. Her muscles screamed in protest, nearly sending her to the floor. She squared her shoulders and took a determined step forward, her shoes grinding the glass on the floor into sand without breaking stride.

Focused on her goal, she wasted not a second thought on the other tanks completing their power-down sequence or if there were other occupants contained within. The darkness of the adjacent ruined hallway was as vacuous as space, the silence as still as a tomb. At least for now, she would be alone with her growing memories.

Beginning with my name, she realized with a start. Her name was Juliane.

LIES & LEGACY
PROJECT GENE ASSIST
BOOK THREE

one

JULIANE

Every push and pull of muscle, every articulation of bone, burnt like wildfire. Juliane had no idea how long it had taken her climb out of the metal tube or cross the raised platform housing the cryogenic cylinders—remembering her name had been difficult enough. Had it been mere minutes? It felt more like days or hours.

Her arms and chest ached where tubes once connected her to the inside of the tank. The smell of stale air, which met her upon waking, took on the scent of dirt, decay, and a hint of animal as the moments passed.

A pair of lighting fixtures dangled askew, giving her pause as she scanned her surroundings. The shadows they cast around the room made her disorientation even worse. The cavernous space should have been a familiar room. However, the image of what the area should look like in her brain directly contrasted with the reality before her.

Large blocks of stone and ceiling fragments littered the room. Pillars of steel support beams stood twisted or lay broken altogether on the ground. The floor should have been marble tile, polished to a high shine. Instead, the area could be better described as dirt-covered rubble than as a room. *A cave is a more apt description. Except a cave wouldn't have a pair of elevator doors on its far side.* That exit was blocked now.

Her heart began to race. *How do I know that?* The memory remained locked away in her brain, and the more she tried to force herself to remember, the more a sharp pain erupted from the center of her forehead.

"Get it together, Juliane," she muttered. The pain receded as quickly as it had materialized. "It's just a broken elevator shaft." Wet drops fell from her face onto the floor below. She wiped the offending moisture away. Crying would do nothing except make it more difficult to navigate her way through the room.

She inspected the ground in front of her more closely. *At least there doesn't appear to be any glass.* She gingerly took another step. She didn't yet trust her legs to keep her from falling.

She looked over her shoulder at the row of cylinders. Two lay open—the one she'd crawled from and one other. Her eyes narrowed at the second cylinder. It had to have once contained another subject like herself. *Or does it?* The throbbing in her head resumed. Though her fingers itched to pry the nearest one open to confirm her suspicion, she stopped herself. If people were contained in the other cylinders and were lying in stasis like she'd been, she might inadvertently cause irreparable harm by powering them down without the proper sequence. Her current situation was enough proof of that.

She tore her gaze from the other metal tubes and turned toward the elevator doors once more as she tried to recall why she'd agreed to go into cold sleep in the first place. There had to have been some reason. However, Juliane didn't recall being sick or having a life-threatening condition. Try as she might, her reasoning— along with the memory of the moments leading up to entering the tank—eluded her. *It doesn't matter*, she decided.

A breeze caressed her cheek. Turning toward its source, she spied another door, one she hadn't noticed before. It led to a small auxiliary room, partially blocked by a pile of boulders. Natural light shone from above, revealing a narrow tube and a dark iron emergency access ladder. The ladder's rungs were covered in clumps of dirt rather than the fine dust that covered everything else. *Had someone recently come through here?* she wondered. Whoever it was, they had left her behind.

Juliane grimaced. The walk from the dais to the ancillary room had been painful enough. Climbing a ladder would be murder on her deteriorated muscles. *What other choice do I have?*

She glanced back in the direction she'd come from. The dangling light fixtures, no longer sensing movement in the room, shut themselves off, leaving a gaping maw of infinite darkness in place of the room. It was as good as a tomb. *That settles it.* Unless she wanted to be buried down there for eternity, it was up to her to pull herself out.

Hair tucked behind her ears, she braced herself against the pain and grabbed onto the first rung, then the next. Pieces of the ladder had eroded with rust, creating pockmarks of rough patches. As much as she tried to avoid them, the narrow passage left little wiggle room. The fabric of her clothing ripped as it was caught on a ragged edge.

She cursed. She'd loved the outfit after discovering the designer years ago. Her brow wrinkled as a few memories began to return. She'd gone into the Apex building dressed to impress. There was a presentation. A door opened. *Then what?* She bit her lip in frustration. Why could she remember that much, but not the following minutes? It was like waiting for the blood to return in a leg after sitting too long.

She made a note to conduct a long follow-up discussion with the person responsible for the cryogenic tank's design. And she'd conduct an even *longer* one with the person who crafted its safety and operating procedures when she was more fully recovered.

A pain shot down her side as her muscles cramped. The sound of fabric tearing returned her attention to the present. She grimaced both from the pain and what the sound meant. *It's only a suit*, she reminded herself as she climbed higher and higher. *You can always get another.*

Emerging at the top of the ladder, Juliane stood and turned around. She should be at the base of a building. Instead, she found herself alone on the side of a mountain of debris. Even more disconcerting, the rest of the landscape was alien in appearance. High-rises, testaments to the highest achievements of civil engineering and modern architecture, should have surrounded her. Instead, all she saw were puddles of mud, empty shells of brick and concrete, and streets devoid of humanity. Perhaps her memories were even faultier than she'd first suspected. *I can't still be in Worcester. Can I? What happened?*

A strong wind picked up, striking her face. Grit found its way into her eyes, causing them to water. *It's the wind.* She told herself. *I am not crying again.*

She scanned the ground, noting a slight path cutting into the rock. She took it as confirmation of her suspicions about the clumps of earth she'd found at the base of the ladder. Someone had come this way not too long ago.

She shielded her eyes from the sun and looked around, searching for more evidence she wasn't the only survivor of whatever cataclysm had befallen here, but found no further clues. The path proved to go no further than around the parameter of the destruction. Soon, she was back at the ladder access. She chewed her lip, debating her next step. *I guess I will have to find my own way out of this mess.*

"Wait." A muffled voice came from the access door. Juliane froze in her tracks. A pale hand reached out through the gap.

The urge to flee sent her heart racing as she looked around for a place to hide. *What are you doing?* She forced herself to remain straight and tall. *You are Juliane Faris. You don't hide.*

The hand was attached to an arm streaked with a mix of red and brown, the color of blood. "A little help here," the voice called again.

She blinked. Thoughts of panicked flight left her as memories of the voice's owner trickled into her consciousness. Her eyes widened. She rushed over to the access door and flung it open. Bending over, she pulled her onetime shopping partner and the Apex group's legal expert from the narrow opening, dragging him out until his stomach rested on the ground. "Durham! Are you okay?"

"I've been better," he answered in between panted breaths. "For a second there, I wasn't sure I was going to be able to pull myself out the rest of the way. What the hell happened?" he asked.

"I was hoping you'd tell me."

"The last thing I remember was being in the big conference room when someone ran in screaming about birds attacking the building."

"You're doing better than I am, then. I'm having difficulties remembering even that much."

"Lucky me." Durham pulled himself the rest of the way up. His forehead was streaked with sweat and dirt, making his normally short white hair appear gray. What was left of his shredded shirt was equally drenched. His arm must not have been the only part of him to have been injured. More dark streaks of dried blood lined his face like war paint.

She saw his eyes take in her appearance from head to toe. He whistled.

"I take it I won't be winning any beauty pageants any time soon, either," she said.

"Speak for yourself. Everyone knows chicks dig scars." He grinned. "I'm going to be fighting them off with a stick after this."

Juliane raised an eyebrow, wanting to laugh, but at the same time not wanting to encourage him. She'd kept her distance from Durham upon leaving the ACI and once again after learning he too had signed with Damien Knightley and the advisory board at Apex—he'd reminded her too much of . . . of . . .

"Right," he said with a chuckle. "I mean more than usual." His smile slipped looking into her eyes. "Hey," he said, reaching out. "It's going to be okay."

Juliane stiffened and pulled back. She'd let her guard down once before. She wouldn't do it again. A winged shadow danced across the remains of the sandstone office tower, reminding Juliane just how isolated they were. "We need to find you some help."

"I've had worse injuries on the field," he said as he tore a scrap of cloth off his shirt and wrapped it around his arm. "See, nothing to worry about. Though, if you are so worried about it, I'm happy to go back to your place." He winked.

"Which might have been an option if my place didn't currently look like a death trap." She nodded toward the remains of a building up ahead. "You need a doctor." Juliane held up a hand. "In fact, follow my finger." She waved a finger from side to side without breaking eye contact.

Durham laughed again. His gaze remained locked on hers. "I think I would know if I have a concussion."

"Oh, really?" she drawled. "And here I was under the impression you went to law school, not medical."

"And here *I* thought *your* title came from a Ph.D."

Juliane pressed her lips together. While he might have a point regarding her degrees, she had spent several years studying the human brain as part of her research work. She might not have a medical degree, but she was far from unqualified to diagnosis an obvious head trauma.

"Fine. I'll call up a ride." Durham's expression went vacant while he accessed the datastream. He blinked. "Um, maybe you should try. I can't seem to reach anybody."

Juliane smirked. "Are you surprised? Look around."

"I've seen worse."

"Hmm," Juliane tilted her head. She supposed whatever had turned the place into a ghost town could be limited to the immediate area. However, she doubted it. Still, to be sure she focused her thoughts and issued a command to access the datastream for herself and opened her utility apps.

A series of icons floated across her vision. Like being able to access the datastream with a thought, the augmented reality was another of Project Gene Assist's benefits. She scrolled through the list with simple eye movement, selecting the rideshare program she installed years ago, but never used. The app icon showed the program's central host was offline.

She re-routed her signal, so it appeared she was looking for a ride in Seattle and then again in Dallas. Those city's local hosts were offline too.

She toggled open her phone app, however, there were few people she could think of to call, even on a normal day, and one of them was standing next to her.

"You got nothing, too?" Durham frowned. "That can't be good. I thought the whole point of the upgrade was to ensure we never lost connection."

"I'm not sure the network is the issue."

The scream of a large bird of prey echoed from above. She glanced up at the violet-tinged sky, but the source of the sound was no longer anywhere to be seen.

"What was that?" asked Durham, who'd also looked up at the sound.

"A bird, I assume," she said, turning her attention back to the empty road ahead. "Can you walk?"

"Not a problem," said Durham. "As I said, I've played through worse injuries." His eyes twinkled. "There was this one time, back when—"

"Is this story going to end with you spraining your ankle after jumping out of a sorority girl's bedroom window the morning of the big match?"

"No," said Durham placing his hand over his heart. "It was my knee."

Juliane rolled her eyes.

Durham continued on as if he hadn't noticed. "If that bush hadn't broken my fall at just the right moment, it would have ended my season."

"That would have been an absolute shame." Juliane scanned ahead. They couldn't possibly be the only people left in the world. *Where is everyone?*

He grinned. The dirt on his face created dark wrinkles that did nothing to make him seem any less boyish. "I'm glad you agree."

The sun shone on them as they made their way down the mountain of debris and into what used to be downtown. The first sign of life, other than the bird, proved to be a wooden building, the sort that could pass for a set piece in an old-fashioned western movie. It stood where there had been empty lots before, complete with horses tied to a railing outside.

The horses shifted nervously as they approached, but appeared well-fed and otherwise used to humans. Other survivors had to be inside.

The breeze whipped grit into her eyes. A hint of coming autumn tickled her nose. *Which would mean we've been in that basement room for at least . . .* She frowned. She'd been so busy with her work, she'd barely noticed the seasons change before. However, she recalled a sea of green around the statue of Marie Curie in the park she'd gone to before making her presentation. *So at least three months.*

She rubbed her forehead. Rage bubbled up inside of her. They'd been left to die down there. *Why?* A male's voice whispered at the edge of her memories. The answer lay inside her mind, she was convinced of it, but his identity and exact words were lost like a half-forgotten nightmare. Her chest tightened. A wave of dizziness struck her, causing her to stumble.

"Whoa," said Durham, catching her arm.

She grimaced. "Sorry about that."

"What's to be sorry for? It's not your fault there's a pothole every couple of feet." His hand lingered on her arm.

"I'm fine," she said, straightening. She tested her ankle, relieved to find she hadn't damaged it like she had that night in Vegas. She noticed he was still looking at her. Her stomach fluttered. If she wasn't more careful, he was going to start mistaking her for some clumsy damsel in distress. *When did you start caring what he thinks about you?* she asked herself. He opened his mouth as if to say something. Her gaze darted elsewhere. "I don't," she muttered.

"You don't what?"

"Nothing. Just thinking out loud. Forget I said anything."

"Whatever you say, boss."

She smiled in spite of herself and turned to use his words against him, when he said, "Huh, no glass."

Following his gaze, she saw the building's only protection from the elements seemed to be a pair of worn shutters. As they got closer, she heard the distinctive clang of tableware being slapped down. The front door was cracked open. By the sound, Juliane suspected it had to be a restaurant or pub of some kind.

"What's wrong?" asked Durham, when Juliane hesitated.

"There is something about this place." She shook her head as if the physical action would counteract her body's instinct to remain out of sight. She pressed her lips together when that didn't work and issued a command to her nervous system, demanding it cease production of adrenaline or any other chemical that might get in the way of logic.

The Gene Assist serum had been developed to give people the ability to access the datastream directly from their minds instead of requiring a device like a phone or tablet. However, the team had learned it had also given them the ability to control so much more. She took a calming breath as the command took effect.

"What? Not a fan of missing windows?" asked Durham. "I wouldn't worry about it. They probably have the kind that swings open from the inside."

She tapped her lip. "It's not the lack of glass," she said, lowering her voice. "There's something else, only I can't put my finger on it." She closed her eyes and took another breath. She opened her eyes as another wave of artificial calm swept through her system and sighed. "You're probably right. I suppose it's the result of waking up the way we did more than anything else." She turned to the door, pulling it slightly more open.

Through the crack, she spotted candles mounted to the walls which illuminated areas the sun couldn't reach. There were a few patrons, but none were seated near each other, and all were clothed in garments that hadn't received a proper cleaning in ages.

"So, are we going to just stand here?" whispered Durham.

Juliane frowned but pulled the door open the rest of the way. She expected all the eyes in the room to turn to them, but instead, everyone remained fixated on the mugs in front of them. "I'll go and talk to the bartender. Maybe he can tell us about what happened while we were asleep."

Durham nodded. "I'll find us a seat while we wait." He looked around the room. "Not that it'll be hard."

As she crossed the room, one of the other patrons rose and beat her to the bar and held his mug out for a refill. The bartender took the mug from his hand and turned to fill it. "Interesting times, Joel," said the patron in a low voice. "People are saying we're on our own again. Watch is gone. Beginning to wonder about who or what might come next."

"I did not set up shop so I could worry about a bunch of stories about things that go bump in the night. I suggest you consider doing the same."

"You've got to be the only innkeeper I've ever met who didn't trade in news on the side."

So, not just a restaurant, then. Juliane glanced back toward where Durham sat waiting. *Good to know there is a place to sleep, considering how long it is taking to get anyone's attention.* However, the last thing she wanted to do was spend the night in this place. "Excuse me," she said, turning back to the bartender. "This may sound odd, but—"

"Perhaps, but I've been in this town since the day it happened—fifteen years. I'd like to survive the next fifteen as well," replied the man behind the bar. "The way you are flapping your gums around makes me think I'd be better off collecting that credit you've run up."

"Could either of you—" said Juliane.

"Now, now, let's not say anything hasty. It's almost winter. I'll need money for salt. In fact, I was hoping you'd be willing to extend my credit based on work or some other barter . . ." The patron's voice, which had already been low, dropped significantly as he continued. "My Elyse . . ." He gestured toward the window. "She's a decent cook."

"Ahem."

He traced a finger along the surface of the bar, checking his finger for dust. "And having a woman around here . . . you'd do well by offering a few more options on the menu." The way the man said the word *options* suggested something altogether different from food.

Questions about the state of their surroundings and how they'd gotten that way fled her mind. The man at the bar couldn't possibly be trying to pay off a bar tab by selling a woman or suggesting the innkeeper do the same. She blinked as his other, earlier, comment struck her. He'd said he'd been here for fifteen years, but Juliane had never seen this place before.

"No doubt it would, but I've no interest in that sort of business," said the innkeeper. "You may, however, want to have a talk with Wally down the street. He always did have a thing for your girl. I suspect he'd be grateful enough to help you pay down some of your tab." The bartender glanced Juliane's way for the first time. "That goes for you, too."

Juliane's brow knit together. "I beg your pardon."

"We don't need any beggars here, either." He made a point of eyeing her up and down. "Or strangers who clearly aren't carrying anything to trade with other than trouble and a pretty face. Best you continue on your way."

Juliane turned on her heel and marched back to Durham. Grabbing him by the shoulder so tightly she nearly ripped his shirt, she said. "We're going."

"Did you get any answers?" He stood and followed her to the door.

"No, and I wouldn't accept help from any of these people now, even if they offered." She let the door slam behind her, startling the horses tied out front.

Durham glanced their way. "Where do you want to try next? I checked my email. Got a couple of messages from my building manager. Stuff about how he couldn't guarantee anyone's safety and how the building isn't liable for any damage. Doesn't sound like going to my place is going to be an option."

"Weren't you seeing someone who worked at the hospital? A nurse or something? Does she live nearby? What about calling her?"

He grimaced. "I doubt she'll want to hear from me . . . hold on." His eyes glazed over for a moment. "No luck. The call won't go through. Timing out. I can't even leave a voicemail. Face it. Nobody's home, at least not in Worcester."

"Hmm . . . where else should we go?" wondered Juliane, aloud.

"Well, while I was waiting for you, I did, overheard one of the guys at one of the other tables say he was heading to New York. Could be that's where most people went."

"I suppose," said Juliane, tapping her chin. "Though . . . in most post-disaster scenarios I've read about people tend to flee from the big cities, not the other way around."

"Well, interesting you say that too, because, his buddy didn't take it well. Tried to talk him out of it. Said some group runs the city now, calling themselves Sorcerers."

"Sorcerers?" The corner of Juliane's mouth turned up. "What? Do they run around in robes? Wave wands around?"

Durham grinned and shook his head. "He didn't say, but what he did say was 'Those that go there never leave Manhattan again.'"

"If Manhattan is still remotely more civilized than this place, I wouldn't want to, either."

"So, you want to head there, too?"

Juliane chewed her lip. "I'm not sure that's a good idea. I'd still like to find out what happened here."

"So, we go to where the people are and ask. You were big on me getting checked out by a doctor a while ago. Bound to be one or two."

Her eyes traced his injuries. "And just how do you suggest we get there? It's at least forty miles from Worcester, if not more."

"I might have an idea," he said with a sly grin.

"Oh? Were you able to reach a working taxi service while I stood at the bar like the invisible woman? It will take us more than a day to get to the closest one on foot."

"I didn't mean walking," he said, nudging his head to the side at the wooden railing.

"You aren't suggesting we steal these people's horses, are you?"

"You said it was like they couldn't see you."

"Yeah, well, I'm pretty sure that would change the minute either of us climbed up on one of those saddles." She placed a hand on her hip. "Besides, I don't even know how to ride a horse."

"It's not that hard once you find the rhythm." His eyes twinkled. "And I wouldn't worry about that in your case. After all, I've seen how you dance. My guess—you'll be a natural."

Heat rose to her cheeks at the reminder. She was still working with the ACI at the time. She'd had too much to drink following the success of their presentation in Las Vegas and had allowed herself to give in to the music. She'd wound up giving in to some of her baser urges too. She turned before her face gave her away. "Now I know you must have bumped your head harder than you let on." She willed the blush away and turned back. "You're nuts. What if they call the police?"

"Then at least we'd get a ride, even if it's only to jail. But in all seriousness, Juliane," Durham's voice lowered and the humor fled. "I'd be more worried about guns."

Juliane's lips twisted. "Is that supposed to convince me to agree to your plan?"

"No," he said. "This is." Without waiting for Juliane to respond, Durham jogged over to the closest animal and untied its reins. The beast looked his way but didn't protest as Durham proceeded to pull himself up into the saddle.

Juliane stood in place, stunned, as Durham directed the horse away from the inn. She strained her ears for any indication that the patrons inside had noticed the animal being led away. However, the only sound was that of the odious man from the bar announcing to the group that his Elyse would be joining the inn's staff.

Juliane's gaze fell upon the horse. With any luck, it belonged to the man bragging about his Elyse. She imagined him coming outside and finding it missing. Her lips twitched. Perhaps, whoever Elyse was, she, too, would be gone before he returned home. She would be doing Elyse, or any other Elyses unfortunate enough to be tied to these men, a favor by delaying the horse owner's return.

"I can't believe I am doing this," she muttered to herself as she untied the second set of reins. The animal snorted and pulled away. Juliane wrinkled her nose at the animal. "I'm as excit'ed as you are." A shout came from the direction of the inn. The horse shook its head as if to say, "Hurry up."

"Don't get an attitude with me. I'm trying," muttered Juliane under her breath as she pulled herself up on its back and set off after Durham.

TWO

STEPHEN

Stephen lay on his back, looking up at the pink-tinged sky. His eyes itched like they'd been left out too long in the desert, but every time they closed, he saw his foster-mother's cold dead face staring back at him. Except it was different—the way she looked at him—it was as if she saw all his flaws in death in a way she never could in life. A buzzing by his ear provided the much-needed distraction from his thoughts. He slapped his arm where a mosquito landed. "I'm pretty sure I've lost enough blood, thank you very much," he muttered.

"Did you say something?" The girl lying next to him asked.

"Nothing," he answered. "Just talking to myself."

Bean smiled and reached out her hand. He took it, entwining her fingers with his own. Another insect buzzed near his forehead. His eyes closed by instinct, and his foster-mother's withered expression jumped in to fill the void. It wasn't the Helen he remembered. *I mean Nadia,* he corrected himself. His guardians may have lied to him his entire life about their true identities, but learning they had other names didn't bother Stephen at all.

Ed or Chad, Helen or Nadia—they could have called themselves whatever they wanted. A number of the people he'd met since leaving the farmhouse changed names like clothing. However, in all his nineteen years, he'd never once questioned that Chad and Nadia loved him. Only there was no love the face he saw now when he thought of Nadia—only hurt and accusation.

Stephen deserved every bit of it. Nadia died because of a touch. His touch. He'd been injured, barely on the warm side of death. His body had pulled at her energy on instinct. Robbing her of her life force. Draining her dry before he even comprehended what he was doing. It might have been an accident, but his foster-mother was no less dead. All because of him.

Bean's hand was warm in his, the exact opposite of his foster-mother's. It was full of life. Energy. It sang to him like a siren of myth, calling to him with a sweet potency more addictive than any sugary treat. All he had to do was let it pour in. Opening himself up to its rush was the easy part.

Stopping the flow, on the other hand, was the problem. He yanked his hand away from hers before whatever lurked inside him took advantage of the situation. *Don't even think it.*

The smile fell from her lips.

His brain hadn't allowed him to fully process what he'd done to Nadia at the moment—it had been too busy working on how to keep both he and Bean alive. In his mind's eye, he relived the race through the maze of hallways. He saw, all too clearly, the beastman's fist connect with Bean's jaw. His ears rang with the sickening crack followed by the thud of her body hitting the floor. There had been no time for guilt or grief in those adrenaline-fueled minutes. But now? He chewed his lip until the wave of emotions passed. Bean was all he had left in the world. She needed him to be strong. What would she think if he suddenly became a blubbering mess? He pretended to swat at the air with the hand that had held hers a moment ago.

"These bugs are driving me crazy," he said. "Good thing the weather is changing. A cold snap will take care of them."

Deep down, he knew Bean would understand if he told her what was going through his mind. All he had to do was say the words. After all, a similar event had happened to her, back when she was a little girl. The victim had been her sister.

But just because she would understand didn't mean he wanted her to. He'd seen the look in Bean's eyes when he'd told her she wasn't a monster, before battle erupted. If he told her about the swirling mix of self-doubts filling his brain in the hours that followed—if he told her what he might do—she might start thinking his second thoughts were about her, too. He couldn't, *wouldn't* risk that.

Though her sister's death had been accidental, Bean's parents had given her to Dr. Lambda and the Watch to experiment on. She hadn't told him all they'd done to her, but he'd seen how she'd looked at Dr. Lambda the second before the doctor's life ended. Bean might say a person's past mistakes didn't matter, but some mistakes were harder to forgive than others.

At least the Watch and its leader, Dr. Lambda wouldn't be terrorizing anyone anymore. *Focus on the future. You can't change the past,* he told himself.

He turned on his side and centered his thoughts. The world around him was replaced with a digital construction—the datasphere. Though he lay on the ground in the real world, he stood in the middle of a grassy field in the digital one. A large button floated approximately three feet off the artificial ground. Stephen pressed it, and another figure materialized.

"You rang?" the newcomer asked. It was a young man, aged somewhere in his late teens or early twenties. He realized he'd never asked his friend what his age was before. Now, he supposed, it didn't matter. His best friend was dead now, too. All that was left of him was an avatar programmed with his memories and personality who'd made the datasphere his new home.

"So, this lady with all the answers. Where are we supposed to find her, anyway?"

Wes cocked his head as if listening to the wind, which was ridiculous as there was no wind in the digital world. Not even a breeze, but that was just the sort of thing that made Wes, Wes. "Her calendar says her last known appointment was a presentation to the advisory board at Apex in Worcester."

That information gave Stephen reason to pause. He'd seen first-hand what the Apex building looked like now. "Yeah, well, I'm pretty sure that she's no longer worried about any advisory board."

If the woman they sought had been inside when the bombs first went off, then she was either dead or far from that place. *Then again*, thought Stephen, *maybe there's a third option. He and Bean had* found a survivor, of sorts, buried in the basement of that building. *Alan.* He'd also been at Apex that day and had found his way into a cryogenic tank while the rest of the world descended into chaos. There had been more than one of those tubes lying around. If he got into one, perhaps others did, too.

His body shook, bringing his attention back to the real world. "Time to get up," said Bean.

The digital field was replaced once more by real trees, dirt, and bugs. His head throbbed and his body ached as he stood up. "We have to go back to Worcester."

"Um, you wanna tell me why? They aren't exactly going to throw out the welcome mat for us after that." She gestured behind them at the blackened husk that had served as the Watch's headquarters. Stephen had turned it into a giant lightning rod to save himself and Bean, taking out a number of the Watch's members in the process. It didn't help that the energy surge had also killed several genetically modified former athletes, Stephen called beastmen, who also happened to be there at the time, rebelling against the Watch, or that those same beastmen previously called Worcester home.

He rubbed his eyes. More deaths. All because of him. "Because of the woman I told you about. The one who my birth mother said would have answers. She was there when it happened. Must have gone into one of those tube thingies."

"But your father said—"

"We may share some genes, but he's not my father."

"That wasn't what—"

"I know what he said, but that doesn't mean it was the truth. He's good at lies, remember. So good, he even convinces himself it's the truth. Or had you forgotten how I got here in the first place." Alan had tricked him into going with Dr. Lambda and the Watch. He'd thought they could help him. Instead, he'd learned the doctor had only been interested in his blood and didn't particularly care if he was a willing donor.

Stephen's shoulders slumped. "Sorry, I didn't mean to sound like I was taking that out on you." He issued a command and a digital map unfurled across his vision. A pulsating dot appeared.

He focused in on Worcester and Apex's location on the map. He didn't need to do the math to recognize it would take days to get back to where it had all begun. They also didn't have nearly enough supplies. If only they had transportation like what the Watch had used.

"Vans."

"Is that supposed to be some sort of farm boy curse?"

"The Watch still has at least one working van. At least it did when they brought me here."

"Okay . . ."

"So, we take it."

"Right, we just walk back inside and pick their pockets until we find a set of keys. Great idea."

"It's better than going on foot."

"No doubt, but do you even know how to drive?" Bean asked.

"Do you?" Stephen might have spent his childhood hiding from the plague and chaos in the middle of nowhere, but was good with machines. He'd rebuilt a computer from spare parts without training. He could figure it out how to drive a van. It wasn't as if there were a lot of other cars on the road.

"I'm just saying we might have to worry about you driving us into a tree. We can go there on horseback. Then we wouldn't have to worry about running out of fuel. And I just happen to know where some might be."

Stephen had forgotten that Bean had arrived in town on horseback with the Sorcerers. Wes's face popped into his thoughts. Wes had as much as admitted to coming up with the name for the group. Stephen shook his head. Wes's sense of humor was an odd one. The term was technically accurate, even if it was a terrible play on the term, source code.

The Sorcerers were people who were able to access digital information that passed through the network known as the datastream or visit the virtual world called the datasphere with their minds. It gave them a sort of telepathy. They also had the ability to alter and control their bodies—though it required skill and some had more talent for it than others. Bean was one of them. If it hadn't been for the Watch, bringing them together, he might never have learned he shared those same abilities too.

"That'd work. Where did you leave them?"

"There's a park or former campground. Not too far from the Watchtower. We believed it would be a safe enough place."

"Do you think they are still there?"

"After that storm the other night," her lips twisted. "I honestly don't know. Probably bolted, but it's worth checking to see."

Stephen pressed his lips together. He'd seen the park when he was connected to the Watchtower's sensors. Bean was right; it wasn't far, but going there would also mean turning around and going back the way they came. He scratched his head. Still, only an idiot would pass up the chance for faster transportation.

He caught Bean's eye. She may have turned calling him an idiot into a term of endearment, but it didn't mean he had to give her reason to think it true. "Guess we're going to have to go back, then."

Her eyes twinkled in the morning light. "And *I* guess that makes me the leader."

Stephen snorted. "Don't let it go to your head."

"Like it did yours?" She ran ahead before Stephen reacted.

"Hey, I can't help it that I am a natural-born leader." He cupped his mouth and shouted.

"Oh, is that what you are telling yourself now?" She shouted back.

"It's the truth," he said, picking up his stride. He assumed Bean rolled her eyes, but she allowed him to catch up. As soon as he did, Stephen pulled her into his arms, forgetting for a moment about his worries. "Otherwise, why would such a strong, capable, woman want to hang out with the likes of me?"

Bean's voice deepened as he lowered his face to hers. "I *suppose* you have a point." She reached up and touched his cheek. "However, you forgot to say gorgeous, too."

He inhaled her scent. It was a mix of earth and the smell of the sort of crisp static immediately following a thunderstorm. Bits of dried blood colored her clothing and dark red-and-purple bruises still marred her skin. She might have meant the comment as a joke, but as far as Stephen was concerned, she spoke no greater truth. He leaned in.

Their lips touched—hers pressing into his with the same hungry intensity he felt as well. He pulled her closer, threading his fingers through her hair. He closed his eyes, savoring the taste of her on his tongue.

Nadia appeared in his mind without warning. The expression on his foster-mother's dead face was no longer just one of accusation, but disappointment, too. Stephen opened his eyes in a panic, breaking off their kiss. *How had he forgotten?* Arousal fled from his body. He turned away, but not fast enough to miss seeing the look of confusion on her face.

"We'd better hurry. If the horses didn't bolt from the storm, the beastmen might find them before we do."

Bean's forehead knit. "You saw how fast those guys were. They made it here all the way from Worcester in the time it took us to arrive from the tower. I highly doubt they need them."

"Maybe not for transportation . . ."

Bean's lip curled in disgust. "Okay, so that's another good point." Her jade eyes shone in the morning sun.

"Huh. That's now two in the same day," he said.

She snorted. "We should write this day down. Probably a record."

"Har har. Just stay sharp. They might have left the Watchtower before we did, but I didn't get the impression they were going far."

"You say that like it's a bad thing," Bean wiggled her fingers, allowing purple-white arcs of lightning to jump from tip to tip. She held her hands close together, though did not let them touch. The sparks arced faster and faster from palm to palm until the space between was filled by electric light. She clapped her hands together, then released them and the electricity in a sudden motion. A branch in front of her tumbled to the ground. "I, for one, am looking forward to showing Jeremy what I can *really* do."

Stephen's stomach turned over at the mention of Jeremy. The man leading the beastmen's attack on the Watchtower might have looked like the former general manager. He might have sounded like him, too, but Stephen was fairly certain the real Jeremy had never left the stadium in Worcester.

It brought his thoughts back to Alan—his biological father—the person who'd abandoned him at age four. He was also the person who'd created the so-called upgrade in the first place. Stephen balled his hand into a fist. There were so many deaths on Stephen's conscience already, but he supposed he would welcome one more.

Three

JULIANE

Durham raised his hand in the air. "We should stop here for the night." While they'd ridden, Juliane had searched for answers in the datastream. Five media outlets detailed the destruction of the Apex building, but the facts in each report were so different and so fanciful Juliane couldn't trust any one of them to have reported the story right. One even suggested aliens were to blame. Juliane had dismissed them all as nothing more than sensationalized click-bait.

Archived headlines from more reputable news outlets beyond Worcester mentioned things like mass layoffs and the rise of a mysterious illness occurring shortly after the closure of the ACI and the collapse of her office building, but there was no single news story describing anything she would have considered to be a world-ending cataclysmic event. Then the news stories simply stopped. She'd turned the feed off hours ago.

"When you say here, you don't mean here, here, do you?" asked Juliane gesturing around them. The buildings surrounding them should have been marked with caution tape and slated for demolition years ago. It made the tavern they'd left seem bustling in comparison.

He led his horse to a grassy patch in front of an abandoned storefront and slid from his saddle. "Yeah, unfortunately, I do." He came over to her side and stretched out his hand.

She looked at his hand, but didn't let go of the reins. "There's got to be a better option. Maybe we can go just a couple more miles?"

He pointed to the sky, which was in the process of transitioning from red to purple. "As much as I want to sleep in a real bed, it's getting hard to see the road, which would be dangerous enough if it were in good condition, but we both know how bad it is. So, unless we want our rides to break their legs in the dark, this is going to have to be it." He shrugged. "It'll be like summer camp, but without the marshmallows."

Juliane pursed her lips. "I wouldn't know the first thing about summer camp."

"No? What about camping in general? Didn't your family ever do that?"

"My parents weren't exactly the family-vacationing type." She sighed but had to concede Durham's assessment was correct. She stretched in the saddle and massaged the small of her back. "I suppose I could use a break, too, though I'm still having a difficult time processing it's been fifteen years. Or longer. I mean, weren't they talking about having to widen this road to accommodate all the traffic just yesterday?"

Durham chuckled. "Yeah, I heard that on the news, too. The whole controversy about how we needed to preserve historic properties." He nodded at their surroundings. "Guess someone got their wish. No one's developing around here now."

"Lucky them." She lowered herself from the horse's back. It raised its tail and released several round balls of excrement onto the cracked and broken pavement. *Lovely.*

Durham walked over to the store's entrance. The panes of glass on either side were gray-brown with dirt. He pushed on the door. It didn't budge. He frowned. He looked at the ground and then back at Juliane. "Do you see anything large or heavy?"

Juliane glanced around "There's a bit of brick lying over there." She pointed to the side of the adjacent building.

Durham grabbed the brick and flung it into the storefront. Glass shattered as it fell to the ground.

Juliane frowned. "First you steal a horse, now you're breaking and entering."

"Admit it, this is the most fun you've had since Vegas," he said with a toothy grin.

"That was a long time ago," said Juliane. Her cheeks pulled at the corners of her lips. *Don't encourage him. Even if he's right.* Durham had met her on the flight to the conference. They'd made a bet, to pass the time. He'd lost. As a result, he had spent most of the day as her personal errand boy. "All I am saying is for a former lawyer, you've been remarkably quick to start a crime spree since waking up." She'd meant the comment as a joke. Then she recalled blows to the head. Concussions had been known to alter a personality, and the comment was no longer as funny as she'd intended. "You *are* feeling okay, aren't you?"

"Like I said, I've been in worse scrapes. Besides, it's not a crime if you know how to defend yourself." Durham's eyes twinkled like the stars multiplying in the sky above.

"I'm pretty sure it still is."

"You'd be surprised. For example, there was this one time—"

"That's okay."

"It's a great story."

"Oh, I don't doubt that in the least, but aren't you concerned at all someone might have heard that noise and will come to investigate?"

"What? That?" He pointed at the ground littered in glass shards. "It was like that when we got here."

"No one in their right mind would believe that," said Juliane, shaking her head. "And that's not what I meant. We have no idea what sort of people might be around here."

"What people? Besides, if there are others nearby, they probably hear things crumbling and falling apart all the time." He gestured to the pile of loose brick. "What's one more broken window? Doubt anyone gives it a thought."

He reached through the opening he'd created in the storefront and twisted the lock on the other side of the door. Unlocked, he pulled the door open, revealing nothing but a blackness within.

His shoes crunched over the broken glass as he made his way inside. Juliane's legs ached as she found a spot near Durham's to secure her mount. She wrinkled her nose. She bent down to locate the saddle's strap and touched the animal's stomach. It whinnied and shied away. "Settle down, you are supposed to want me to remove this thing." She tried again, but the poor lighting made her effort futile.

She turned over her hand so the palm was facing up and issued a command to her cells instructing her body to produce luciferin and luciferase. A yellow-green glow, much like the light of a firefly, expanded over her palm's surface.

Durham's head emerged from the open door. "Ah, Juliane?" he asked. "Should I be concerned you're green?"

She arched an eyebrow. "This method is less likely to ignite any lingering gases stuck in there than starting a fire might."

He looked back over his shoulder into the shop and back at her. "That's genius."

"No. Simple biology."

"Well, I wouldn't have ever come up with it."

Juliane smiled, accepting the truth of his words as the compliment he intended. Conversation with Durham was proving to be refreshingly uncomplicated. She didn't have to worry about one-upmanship with him or what his ulterior motive might be. She almost regretted keeping her distance. Perhaps if things had played out differently before, they might even have been friends.

Her smile evaporated. *You do remember who else he was friends with, don't you?* a voice in the back of her mind whispered. *Louis.* Her throat tightened. How could she have forgotten about him? *Louis betrayed me first,* she told herself. *I have every right to finally move on.* Moisture filled her eyes. She took a breath and instructed her central nervous system to flood her system with calming enzymes until she was once again in control. "Have you found anything useful in there?"

"Not yet, but since you're now the human nightlight, I might have better luck finding something we can eat."

She pursed her lips. "I suspect anything remotely edible or potable is long gone."

"You're probably right," he said. "But there's always the chance we'll get lucky."

Juliane looked at her mount and held up a finger. "Stay." The horse ignored her and bent its head to nibble on some stray grass.

Together they inspected the abandoned store. The green glow of her skin cast on the rows of empty shelves reminded Juliane of alien encounters depicted by Hollywood. Near the back, Juliane found a rack of cotton shirts. She thumbed through the meager selection. While the oversized tees were hardly her style, there was a chance they were in better condition than her ruined clothing. A shirt fell off the hanger and onto the floor. Juliane picked it up and saw large holes in the cloth. *Or not.* Mice must have found it first. She threw the shirt over the top of the rack and moved on. "See anything?"

Durham shook his head. "Nope. Guess we're going to have to find dinner the old-fashioned way."

"As in hunt? And have you ever done that before?"

"I'll figure it out. People used to do it all the time. Aren't you hungry?"

"Actually, I hadn't given it much thought," said Juliane. The ceiling panels caught her attention. The panels were no longer a factory-new brilliant white, but they were the same sort she'd insisted on having installed in her office years ago, which meant nano power supplies were embedded in the materials. All she had to do was redirect the current.

A dark shape ran along the bottom of her peripheral vision, breaking her concentration. Instinctively, she jumped backward, bumping into the clothing rack and the exposed hanger.

"What happened?" Within an instant, Durham had come to her side. "Did you see something?"

"It's nothing." Her cheeks warmed. "I suspect it was nothing more than a rodent. No reason for me to react like a child. I saw larger ones in the labs at the ACI," said Juliane, grateful for both the poor lighting and another dose of artificial calm.

He touched her chin, forcing her face up until her eyes met his own. "You know, you don't have to pretend with me."

Juliane wrinkled her forehead. "Pretend what?"

"Pretend you're cool with all this."

Her heart slowed as the chemicals in her system took effect. The muscles of her face relaxed as cool logic took back over. Durham let his hand drop away. She was surprised to find her skin mourned the loss of contact.

"I'm not," she said. "But I've learned not to get emotional about things outside of my control. Media outlets have a field day with that sort of nonsense."

"If you haven't noticed, the tabloids don't exist anymore," he said. He searched her face. He must not have liked what he saw as his jaw tightened. "Sorry, I shouldn't have brought them up."

She straightened her spine and broke eye contact. Her gaze found the scrap of fabric on the floor. "See," she said. "There's something positive to come from all of this."

He raised his hand once more, as if reaching for her, only to let it drop back to his side. "You know," he said with a quiet voice, "had things gone differently." She looked up. There was a strange expression she'd never seen on his face before—both earnest and sincere. "I would have never forced you to go through any of that. At least, not go through that alone."

Pressure built up behind her eyes. She turned away, suddenly keenly aware of the lack of space between them. While part of her reveled what his words implied, she needed to stop the conversation before she allowed herself to feel something more for him than she already did. Her time with Louis had taught her what would happen if she allowed herself to open her heart, or worse, lose her focus.

Besides, she told herself, *its Durham*. While they hadn't spent all that much time together, she knew that he'd practiced talking women into his bed far longer, and far better, than he'd ever practiced law. He knew the words to say. He probably even believed them, but once he'd gotten what he wanted, they'd go their separate ways. It's what he did.

She decided no good would come from talking about the past. Nor could she trust her feelings at the moment either. She told herself, her swirling emotions and desire to lean into his touch were nothing more than a biological response to being placed in a stressful situation. If they were going to survive in this new world, she needed to remain focused on reaching New York. They couldn't afford the complication.

Her brain understood. Her hormones, however, would take further convincing. *Shut him down.* Juliane stepped back before her body could betray her. "But you did," she said in a voice more bitter than intended. She looked at him through narrow eyes. "All that time we worked together. You never said anything." She couldn't remember the last few days, but recalled all too well the day she'd entered the room and seen him after being introduced to the rest of Apex's advisory board by Damien Knightley.

There'd been no signs of recognition on his face. Nothing to indicate he remembered their time together. His lack of response had baffled Juliane. She'd considered the conference one of the best times in her life. To then be treated with less regard than one might a footnote—it was crushing. "You acted like you'd never met me before."

Durham searched her eyes with a pained look. He held his hands up. "That was a mistake. But in my defense, I'd assumed, after everything, that's what you wanted."

His defense gave her pause. His assumption at the time might have been well-founded. She'd even welcomed his reaction, eventually—after the initial shock faded. It had been an improvement compared to the looks she'd gotten from most people she worked with at the ACI. People like her research assistant, Chad, or her peer, Betty, back before Betty had made it official with Alan and became the other half of the Doctors Dronigh. The other people in her life couldn't stop pitying her. Every time they looked at her, she saw it. Poor Juliane. Even worse, it was because of a man.

The fact that Juliane had nearly sacrificed her entire career for that same man—Louis—hadn't helped. Their pitying looks became a reason Juliane found excuses not to attend Betty's get-togethers or check in on Chad's new work assignments.

His earnest expression pulled at her like gravity. The space between them, at once, seemed as narrow as a blade of grass, and yet, as wide as the ocean. *No more mistakes.* "So, you think you know me, then?" She crossed her arms over her chest. "Just because we spent one day together?" She laughed without humor. "It was a great day. I'll give you that, but one day is hardly long enough to get to know a person." *Don't let him know how much he hurt you. It will only give him the power to do it again.* "Besides, I'm not the same person I was back then. I was naïve. I let my hormones get the best of me." Her lips twisted. "You should know, I won't make the same mistake again."

Durham broke into a grin.

Juliane blinked; it wasn't the reaction she'd expected. She hadn't wanted to hurt him, but it was still a rejection. However, there was nothing about him that indicated he was anything but overjoyed at her statement. *It's because it's just a game to him. He's a flirt. That's what he does. He doesn't mean any of it.* Once again, she was glad her skin was colored by bioluminescence so it couldn't show her blush. *Just as well.*

"Are you sure I can't convince you otherwise?" His eyes sparkled as he gestured toward his chest and biceps.

The corner of her mouth twitched. His eyes twinkled.

He continued, "I've had plenty of experience with women who made noises along the lines of making a mistake but were quick to make an entirely different sound once we got started."

"Is that so." She'd intended the reply to be condescending, but instead it rolled off her tongue. "I guess it's too bad, then, that I'm not like those other women."

Durham snorted. He took a step until only inches separated them. As much as the logic in her brain screamed against it, Juliane wanted his arms to wrap around her waist. Instead, he rested his fists on his hips. He leaned forward. A warmth spread through Juliane's body. *Damnit. What's wrong with me?* She knew better. There was no reason for her to act like a teenager. She looked up, meeting the challenge in his eyes with her own. She considered sending a command to silence the surge of desire she hadn't felt for anyone other than Louis in years.

Thinking about Louis was like jumping into an icy shower and more effective than any artificial endocrinal command. Durham must have seen the change in her eyes as he backed away. "I know you're not," he said softly. "That's why I—"

Her former lover appeared in her mind's eye, standing next to the woman he'd married without so much as a courtesy break-up call. They stood in *her* lab—minimizing *her* involvement in the serum's development or the Gene Assist upgrade procedure. She synthesized a surge of gamma-aminobutyric acid, building a wall around the synapses in her brain, preventing them from processing feelings that only lead to pain. Her body relaxed as the chemical took effect.

She looked back at Durham. He had the same odd questioning expression on his face as he'd had outside of the inn, but the artificial blocker numbed her to it. "Why you did what?" she said. Now that her hormones were silenced, she found herself more willing to spend the evening in conversation.

"Ah, right. Well, you see . . ."

It wasn't like Durham to be tongue-tied. She gave him a once-over from head to toe. As much as he claimed his injuries were no big deal, Durham clearly had suffered a more serious trauma than he was willing to let on.

"Never mind. It can wait," he said, looking away.

"Are you sure?"

"Yeah, guess I've got food on the brain. Can't think straight," he said, shaking his head. The look that spoke of deeper conversation vanished from his face, replaced by the expression of casual indifference she'd grown accustomed to. It would seem she wasn't the only one able to mask what was going on inside her head. "Too bad we're going to need those horses. Otherwise, I'd consider eating one."

"That's barbaric." Juliane wrinkled her nose. While she wasn't hungry, Juliane wouldn't have minded a steaming cup of coffee or a cold glass of ice water right now.

"Yeah, well, hopefully it won't come to that." He turned and left before Juliane said another word.

She sighed. When he got back, she would give him the opportunity to talk about whatever it was that was on his mind, but first, she'd try explaining energy transfer. She didn't have high hopes Durham would be interested in the science behind it, but at least they wouldn't have to worry about where their next meal would come from. Juliane faced the nanobots and pulled. Energy stored in their battery cells surged through her veins like a wave.

Alert and satisfied, she canceled the feed and issued another command, redirecting the leftover power to the lighting system. A pair of large square panels began to glow with a warm white light. Juliane frowned when the other lighting panels remained dark. *Their circuitry must be damaged.* Her body tingled as the two working panels began to transmit performance data back and forth. The data was so basic, Juliane was surprised she was even aware of it. The sensation was akin to hearing crickets on an otherwise still night.

She went about looking for a space where they might be able to pass the night. Jagged shards from Durham's break-in shimmered on the floor by the door, ruling that area out. A black electronic box mounted to the side of the front entrance caught Juliane's eye. *An electronic lock.* She shook her head. If Durham had only bothered to give her a second, she might have located and hacked it, sparing her now from worries about getting cut to ribbons. Her gaze fell on black mold.

That does it. There's got to be a better place to sleep than this. She exited the store. Durham's horse was gone. *So much for not risking the horses at night.* Unfortunately, it did mean she'd have to wait until he got back to inform him they'd be moving on. A pungent odor Juliane couldn't quite place filled the night. Her mare pulled at her tethers; eyes wide.

"I don't like that smell either, but there's nothing we can do," she told the mare. *It's probably something rotting in the store. Yet another reason we should find a different place to sleep tonight.* Her horse pulled again, jerking Juliane's arm. Its hooves echoed as they struck the concrete.

A shadow covered the moon. Juliane ducked her head out of pure instinct as the air changed in pressure. A gust scented by death and dung assailed her senses. A call like a mix of chicken and seagull came from behind. She risked a glance over her shoulder.

A dark shape stood between Juliane and the storefront door. Its sudden appearance silenced Juliane mid-curse. She spun on her heel, in the process damaging the same ankle she'd weakened earlier. Whatever it was, it walked on two legs and was the size of a tall human, but moved like an animal. It had massive shoulders and a head set low in its body. The effect somehow reminded Juliane of a football player in full pads.

It took a step. The light from inside the store outlined its silhouette, showing it had a bald head with dark feathers jutting from the base of its neck like a wrapped boa. It shifted. Wings as wide as tractor-trailers stretched out before her. She'd never seen a bird so huge. Her pulse quickened, while her legs seemed rooted to the spot.

She pinged the datastream to help her identify the creature blocking her return, but none of the results of her query matched what she saw in front of her. It resembled a California condor, but the size was all wrong. *California condors happen to be extinct, too.* In terms of wingspan, it was closer to descriptions of the so-called thunderbird, but that creature was nothing more than a myth.

A large rodent, likely a rat, and possibly the same shadow she'd seen earlier, bolted from the store toward Juliane. A second bird—smaller than the first, but still larger than any avian Juliane had ever seen—fell from the sky and joined its mate. The smaller bird, which Juliane assumed to be the female of the pair, extended its neck as it tracked the rodent's movement. The creature cawed as if asking the first a question.

Its mate answered with a cackle-like sound.

The female then stuck the rat with a beak that looked like a scythe. It pulled back from the rodent but did not stand fully upright. It lowered its head again, slower this time, probing the unfortunate creature with its beak. The rodent lay motionless on the ground. The first bird cackled again.

Is it dead? Why did they kill it, if they aren't going to eat it? wondered Juliane, her scientific curiosity overtaking her fear. In her experience, beasts, unlike humankind, rarely killed unless out of necessity. Her hand stretched out of its own accord. The first bird swung its head in her direction. Moonlight reflected off its eye. The bird blinked. *Then again, biology was never my area of expertise.* Juliane pulled back her hand. *It might have been better not to have captured its attention.*

The male bird clucked.

The female stopped its investigation, returning to its full standing height. It curved its neck closer to that of the first and repeated the same caw as before. The male tucked its head into the ring of neck feathers. It extended its wings again. A large band of white feathers stretched across its body from wingtip to wingtip. It flapped its wings, producing a sound like a clap of thunder as it launched itself into the air.

Its companion followed. Juliane looked up to see the pair circling in the moonlit sky. One of the birds began to descend directly toward her. A primal urge to move shattered Juliane's artificial calm.

She launched into an erratic run away from the birds, weaving herself between buildings in hope the narrow space would be harder for the bird and its large wingspan to navigate. The creature screeched as it broke out of its dive and swooped back up into the skies.

She zigged.

The male's call was answered by the female.

Juliane zagged.

She didn't have to look up to know she'd be trapped between the circling raptors. Another sound filled her ears—wild, like a thing long broken. Juliane realized she was laughing hysterically.

The toe of her shoe found a crack in the broken pavement, breaking her stride, and sending her the ground. She bit her lip and tasted blood. She scrambled to rise. The thunderbirds' calls rattled in the sky. The air pressure changed.

They are going to dive again. Juliane's ankle, strained further, throbbed. Her lungs burned with each breath. However, she kept going. In her fall, she'd seen a cellar door up ahead, partially covered by weeds. She hoped the door was unlocked.

Adrenaline fueled her forward. Her legs and lungs protested each step of the way. Before going into the cryogenic tank, a day of strenuous activity consisted of a brisk walk from her parked car to her office. Now, her muscles screamed in agony. She refused to listen to their complaint.

The air pressure surrounding her changed. The scent of excrement filled her nostrils. She dropped to the ground next to the door. Her head jerked to the side as a large clump of hair was torn from her scalp followed by a thunderclap.

The beast misjudged, landing on the ground at least a yard away. Not nearly as agile on the land as it was in the air, the male waddled as it turned to face her. The birds called out again, producing a sound Juliane knew would haunt her nightmares.

She grabbed at the latch. The female, still in the air, called out, increasing its pitch as if sensing their prey had found an escape. Juliane focused on her goal. Hinges long since rusted protested as she pulled upward, but the door was otherwise unlocked. A narrow gap opened, exposing nothing but darkness. Juliane wedged her fingers into the space. Splinters of wood bore into her palms. The smell of death intensified. *I'm running out of time.*

She shifted her weight and pulled again. The gap widened. Sweat dripped from her brow. *It had to be birds.* Juliane cursed out loud. Images of dark feathers and flying above the clouds in pursuit of an animal stirred in her brain—she'd accidentally taken over the mind of one of the Project Gene Assist's early test subjects, a raven, when she'd first undergone the upgrade procedure.

The hair on the back of her neck rose. *Focus, Juliane.* The door moved an inch. *I just need two more minutes.* The bird on the ground chortled as the air pressure changed once more. "Go away," she shouted toward the night sky as she adjusted her hold on the door one more time.

The rusted hinges gave up their hold on the cellar door with a final scream. Juliane opened it just enough to squeeze inside before slamming the door behind her. A weight slammed into it from the other side.

She hadn't found cover a moment too soon. The creature called out in its frustration. Then a portion of the wooden board cracked. She drew back as a wicked beak pierced through the aging wood. The beak disappeared, then reappeared. She looked over her shoulder, but it was too dark to see if there was anywhere she might be able to hide if the beast found its way in. If anything, she would be trapped further. The beak struck again like an ax.

A memory of being trapped in a back room surrounded by empty cages as men fought to make their way to her sprang unbidden in her mind. They'd been after her for reasons she'd hadn't understood then and understood even less now. What had she done to get away? Her memory remained foggy. She cursed at the bird. If it would only give her a moment's peace, she might be able to cobble together another portion of her missing days.

The bird's call changed. It gave a short deep cry, as if it was answering her. Juliane fought a wave of vertigo. *Not now.*

Another call cried out on the other side of the door. *Of course,* Juliane thought, *the bird isn't talking to me. It is coordinating with its partner.* The scientist in her couldn't help appreciating the show of intelligence on display before her, while the less-rational part of her mind screamed to find a deeper, less-accessible hole to crawl into. She wondered how the creatures hadn't been discovered before. *Unless they weren't discovered,* she told herself, *but made in a lab.*

I wonder. In the case of the raven, it had just sort of happened immediately following her initial injection. She'd simply accessed the bird's senses without knowing what she was doing or how she was doing it.

She reached out with her mind. The bird redoubled its attack, slamming its body into the door. Light cut the darkness of the cellar as the gap in the wood grew larger. *Experiments can wait until later.*

Death and rot filled her senses as a pair of talons curled their way into the space. Juliane ran down the stairs. There had to be something she could use to defend herself, but she was blind in the darkness. Her body took on the pale green glow she'd used to find her way around the service station.

The bird screamed and tore.

She dismissed the light as quickly as she'd summoned it. It hadn't revealed anything useful she might use as a weapon. All she had illuminated was an empty cellar. The light also made her even more of a target. Even worse, she was blinder than she had been a moment before. *That was a mistake.* She grimaced. *I hope I live long enough to make another one.*

Four

STEPHEN

A narrow creek cut through the forest, framed by a sloping bank. Stephen knelt down and splashed its cool water on his face. Droplets of red, brown, and black splattered his clothing. He cupped his hands and filled them again. He wondered how long it had been since he'd bathed, regretting he hadn't taken advantage of the running water back at the Sorcerers' apartment building.

Stephen hadn't kept track of time since he and Bean first fled from members of the Watch, but he guessed they'd been on their own for three or four weeks by now. *It feels like a lifetime, though.*

He caught his reflection in the water and barely recognized the person he'd become. He scratched at the line of hair growing on his chin. The lack of a razor in their supplies was the least of his concerns. *Hope Bean digs beards.*

"There is a fenced-in area just on the other side of this hill," said Bean. "Should be a few water bottles lying around, too. Come on." She waved. "Or are you going to make me carry you the rest of the way?"

"I was wondering when you were going to pay me back for that little favor," joked Stephen. "However, I should point out I carried you for five miles. While I was injured. At night."

"Oh, is that all. I'm guessing all uphill, too?"

"Maybe . . ." He knelt down and scooped up more water with both hands.

Bean's eyes narrowed as Stephen stood. "What are you doing with that? I just said there should be water bottles ahead."

"Have I mentioned how hot you look?"

Bean took a step back. "You wouldn't dare."

Stephen flung the handful of water, watching the droplets fly through the air toward Bean. She jumped out of its path with ease. "You think you're a funny guy. Don't you?"

"It's crossed my mind once or twice, yes."

The corner of Bean's mouth turned up. Her jade eyes sparkled. Stephen realized her intention too late as Bean charged into him, knocking Stephen onto his backside and into the creek. Water splashed her as well, darkening her clothing and causing the fabric to cling to her curves as she used her body to hold him in place.

"Who's funny now?" she asked as she closed her eyes and raised her face to his. Stephen shivered, and he shifted out from under her weight. Bean's eyes snapped open. "Oh," she said. Her cheeks turning a charming shade of rose. "I shouldn't have done that." She scanned his body. "I didn't hurt you, did I?"

Stephen shook his head. "Nah. I'll be fine. But this water is freezing."

Bean frowned. "Are you sure I didn't hurt you?" She placed a finger in the water. "It's warm enough to me."

"That's because you aren't the one still sitting in it."

A man coughed.

Bean spun into action like a cat as Stephen jumped up. A large dark-skinned man with muscular arms stood under the branches of a nearby tree. Bean reacted first, balling up her fists.

"Electricity and water don't mix. Even a person like me knows that." His voice was like sandpaper and cracked from underuse.

Bean narrowed her eyes but released her clenched hands.

"We aren't looking for trouble," said Stephen before Bean might say or do anything that would ensure trouble found them whether they were looking for it or not. She gave him a look through the corner of her eyes but remained silent.

Stephen released a breath he hadn't realized he was holding. They'd met the man, named Ahman, before in Worcester. From the outside, he didn't appear to be different than an average human, albeit an average man with muscles larger than Stephen's head, but that didn't mean he hadn't been altered beneath the surface. All the beastmen were in some way—and not just the former professional athletes—coaches, like Ahman, had too.

They'd done it to make themselves more competitive. Some had undergone artificial muscle transplants, giving them catlike speed. Others had skin as tough as rhino leather. The league hadn't minded. It wasn't cheating if everyone did it. With every tweak, they'd become more animal than man. They'd been teams before, but now . . . now they were a pack.

Bean's jaw tightened. She took a step forward, planting her feet on the solid dry ground. Her fingers twitched. Stephen squared his shoulders and joined her side.

"Before you do something you'll regret," said Ahman, "I wasn't part of the fight at the Watchtower."

Stephen frowned, sharing another look with Bean. She shrugged.

"Expected you hours ago. Forgot how slow regs are," said the beastman, unsmiling.

"What do you mean, you expected us?" asked Stephen. "We didn't even know we were coming back here until this morning."

"Obvious. Horses."

"You found them."

Ahman nodded.

"Look. All we need is two of them. Just two. You can have the rest."

Ahman's laugh was just as grating to the ears as it was the first time Stephen and Bean heard it.

"Boy, you can have your pick. Take them all if you want. Come with me."

This has to be a trick. Jeremy, or more accurately Alan, impersonating the beastmen's leader, might have let them walk away following the battle, but that didn't mean the rest of the group was as forgiving. Stephen glanced around. Ahman had snuck up on them without a sound, which meant any number of his teammates were likely hiding behind the surrounding trees. He should never have let his guard down.

Another thought struck him. He turned his gaze to the canopy above. With their modifications, beastmen could easily be hiding in the upper branches like jungle cats. All Ahman had to do was issue a signal to make more appear from all directions. Stephen braced himself for battle.

"What if we say no?" asked Bean.

This time it was Stephen's turn to shoot her a look.

"That'd be a mistake."

"Oh, really," She shifted, turning her body to the side. Her eyes flashed like emeralds, making her pale skin appear as if she'd been sculpted out of marble. "Mine or yours?"

One side of Ahman's lips turned up. "Yours."

Stephen's stomach grumbled loud enough to be heard over the running water of the creek. Both Ahman and Bean turned to look his way.

"Seriously?" Bean asked. "How can you possibly be hungry right now?"

Ahman laughed and raised his hands, palms out. "I have food, too. Come."

Stephen pressed his lips together. Hanging out in the datastream all night, speeding the body's healing process, communicating mind-to-mind, or, Bean's favorite, generating an electric spark in the palm of one's hand intense enough to take out a threat with a touch required massive amounts of energy. Stephen had learned those same abilities would kill them if they didn't pay attention to the warning sides. He must now be near the end of his reserves.

His shoulders loosened. It was likely why Bean's lifeforce sung so strongly to him the other night. It was another warning sign. Maybe if he got a good meal in him, the craving would stop. He smiled as his mind jumped to all the other things he would like to do with Bean if he no longer feared losing control in the process. "Sure. Why not? What'cha cooking?"

Bean shook her head, grumbling loud enough for Stephen to hear. "If that stomach of yours leads us into an ambush, so help me."

"We need those horses. Besides, he's the one that needs to be worried," said Stephen. "Unless that thing you did with the branch was just showing off."

Bean chewed his comment over. "I suppose you have a point."

"That's three times you've said that now," he said with a grin. "I must not be as big an idiot as you thought after all."

Bean grinned back. "Oh, you are. Trust me. I just must be rubbing off on you."

"Have I mentioned how I love it when you talk dirty?"

Bean's face puzzled at Stephen's statement. Then her eyes opened wide and her cheeks blazed in color as understanding dawned.

Ahman made a gagging grunting sound. Turning without further instruction or looking to see if they followed, he disappeared into the forest, forcing Stephen and Bean to run to catch up.

Ahman handed Stephen a piece of blackened meat which Stephen bit into with enthusiasm. "War is coming."

The meat seared Stephen's throat as he choked it down. "War? But haven't enough people died already?"

"Most wars aren't fought over people." He poked at the cookfire with a stick. "I didn't mind the Watch. They were corrupt power-hungry bastards, but I understood where they were coming from." He placed another skewer of meat on the flames. "Reason with them, too." He looked to Stephen and pointed at the cooking meat with a question in his eyes.

Stephen nodded. Ahman returned to his cooking. Stephen was beginning to wonder if that was the end of the conversation for the night.

The beastman pulled the meat from the flames and handed it to him. Only then did he continue. "With them gone . . . See, there's a vacuum."

"So, what?" asked Bean. "It wasn't like the Watch was *really* in charge. We just let them think they were."

"That so? I've known a few people who would have said differently." He poked at the flames. "If they were still alive."

"They would've been wrong," Bean straightened her back. "Look at me, for example. I was able to find my way around them. Twice."

"You were lucky."

"Luck had nothing to do with it." A shadow crossed over Bean's expression.

Stephen reached out to squeeze her hand. She flinched at his touch. Her eyes widened apologetically, and she gingerly met his fingers and entwined them around her own. It felt good to have her warmth in his hand once more. It was even better than a stomach full of hot food.

Stephen bit into the meat skewer while they remained sitting by the fire, hand in hand. He wished the moment would last all night, but he knew only too well that the hunger would return. Releasing his hold, he turned back to Ahman. "So, what makes you sure war is coming?"

"Jeremy," Ahman said. "He's not himself. I used to think Jeremy never had more than half a playbook. Meaning he only played defense. Now, suddenly he is leading an attack?" He shook his head. "People don't change like that." He frowned. "Doesn't smell right. Hasn't since the day you arrived."

Stephen cringed. The real Jeremy wouldn't be hidden away in a dark corner of the team's former stadium if Stephen hadn't brought Alan to their gates.

"So?" said Bean, standing up. She walked to the fire and stared into its flames, putting her profile in sharp relief. Stephen wondered what she saw. She took a step back and rubbed her eye. "Why should you care? You're one of them—don't you want to win?"

Ahman grunted. "There are no winners in a war. Only a side with fewer losers."

"We had nothing to do with it," said Stephen, holding his hands up.

Ahman's eyes narrowed. "I didn't say you did."

"Then why are you telling us all this?" asked Stephen in an attempt to distance himself from the comment before Ahman started asking questions he didn't know the answers to. "Are you saying we should run away? Fine. We weren't planning on sticking around anyway."

"No, I'm asking you to help me stop it."

"Stop a war. Us?" Stephen shook his head. "And here I was coming around to the belief you weren't as crazy as the others." He stood up and patted his stomach. "Listen, thanks for the meal, but we've got a mission of our own." He turned to Bean. "You ready?"

"*I've* been ready to go since before we got here."

Stephen turned to Ahman. "Where are the horses? You said we could take them."

Ahman chuckled. The sound was no more pleasant than it was before. "Sure can. You just have to catch 'em first. I freed 'em hours ago."

Bean clenched her fists. "You had no right."

"You didn't have the right to tie them up in the first place," said Ahman with a shrug.

Stephen touched her wrist. "We'll figure out another way to get there."

"The city is the last place you want to go, if that's where you're headed," said Ahman. "Weren't you listening before? Jeremy's building an army. I suspect *your* kind are, too."

Bean's nostrils flared.

"Or will be, once they realize what happened back there. You go there, you'll be in danger." A log on the campfire popped as the heat of the flames penetrated its center.

"Sorry, but you're wrong about where we are going. And you're wrong about us."

"Prove it."

"We're not leaving town because we're afraid." Bean gave him a look. "We're on a mission." Bean shook her head.

What? Stephen sent the question to Bean via a datastream chat program.

You did hear yourself, right? Her voice echoed in his mind as she replied.

It's true, though.

The corner of Ahman's mouth twitched. "This mission more important than stopping a war?"

Stephen hesitated, not sure how much he wanted to share with the man. "There's a woman—"

Ahman glanced at Bean and chuckled. "There usually is. Though from where I'm sitting, you already have more than you can handle."

"Not like that. She's—"

"I had a daughter once." The smile slipped from Ahman's features. "She was killed . . . murdered . . . simply because she was in the wrong place at the wrong time. Now, there's going to be others. Regular people, just like her, who have no clue what's coming. Is one woman so much more important than all of their lives?"

"She might be," said Stephen. She was one of the originals. She was one of the people who created the upgrade. She knows how to . . . how to . . ." *How to stop people like Finn.* Stephen bit his tongue before the words exited his lips. He didn't need to share all of their secrets.

Finn was who'd sent him on a quest to retrieve a piece of lost technology—the Wand. He had dangled Bean in front of Stephen like bait. The Wand proved able to alter a modified person's DNA, restoring their youth. Stephen learned Finn intended to use the device for a form of devil's bargain. Those that sided with him would be given immortality. However, Finn demanded more than loyalty oaths from his followers.

Unfortunately, fealty meant giving Finn control of your mind and body, with deadly consequences for disobeying. There was also the drain to consider. A side effect stemming from being too far away from a power source and the reason Stephen had taken Ahman up on his offer of food. A large portion of the remaining population would die if Finn had his way. Only those who recognized the warning signs would realize what was happening and why. For the rest, it would be the plague all over again. Finn didn't care. He considered it the survival of the fittest.

Alan had the Wand now, and as much as Stephen hated him, it was likely better off with him. From what Stephen understood, Alan enjoyed manipulating people into doing what he wanted. Giving them no choice in the matter would take his fun away.

"Are you talking about Juliane Faris?" Ahman sighed. "I can save you a trip. Woman's dead."

"She's not."

"Listen, you don't want to mix yourself up with those people. See, my baby girl's momma was *there*—Gena. She was applying for a job at Apex when this whole rush of people run out the door yelling about a swarm of birds hitting the window upstairs. Got most of the people outside, but not my Gena."

The corner of Ahman's mouth twitched. "She thought it was a test to see how she handled emergencies. Not as crazy as it sounds. The stories we'd heard about people who worked there made it sound—well, let's say we'd heard they only hired the best." His mouth twitched again.

"But then Louis Evans came in." He reached into his pocket, pulled out a flask, and took a swig from it. "And before you say anything, I do mean as in *the* Louis Evans. Gena had been obsessed with him for years. Super rich guy. Used to say she'd leave me for him if the Sharks kept losing." He took another sip from the flask.

"Gena starts thinking this might be her chance to introduce herself, but then this other lady, Dr. Juliane Faris, shows up outta nowhere. Gena recognized her, too. Apparently those two, Louis and Juliane I mean, used to date back in the day, or so my Gena liked to tell me. Was always showing up in the tabloids. Guess it didn't end well, cause the way he looked at her . . . Gena'd seen that look enough to recognize something bad's going to go down. She decides the people who freaked out over the birds had the right idea and starts heading out of there, but these other dudes are now blocking the exits."

Stephen's hopes started to crumble. Had Alan been telling the truth about the contents of the other cylinders after all? Was he really the only person to have survived the Apex bombing down there?

"Ah, Gena." He shook his head. "My woman was a fighter," Ahman continued, lost now in his memories. "Especially when she was riled up, but she's still outnumbered. She hasn't quite broken free when the whole building shakes and the doors to one of the elevators puckers out. The same elevator she'd seen her Mr. Perfect drag his ex into. Then there's this smell, she says."

He returned the flask to his pocket. "The way she described it, it was a mix of smoked metal and burnt meat. Then more explosions. Only this time, they are everywhere. The first one is in the elevator, and the guys guarding the front door don't expect that. Gives Gena the chance to get away." His voice softened. "She told me afterward she learned what hell smelled like."

Stephen and Bean exchanged a glance.

You have to admit, it doesn't sound good. Stephen heard Bean say in his mind.

Remember what Alan told us about that day? He knew Louis was in the elevator. How would he know that if it hadn't made it all the way down?

So now you're ready to trust something Alan said?

Out loud, Stephen said, "You're probably right, but there was a lot of confusion that day. Gena got away. If there's even a chance Juliane managed to get away, too, we have to try to find her."

"Sure, Gena survived the initial panic, but she was murdered in the days that followed trying to save our little girl. And for what?" Ahman sighed. "I know you know more than you're saying. Don't deny it. Even if I couldn't smell a lie, I can see it in your face. I also know you're chasing a ghost. Wouldn't you rather save the living?" Ahman pressed his lips together and looked away before saying, "You know, like that guy I saw you with outside the hospital."

Stephen's lips tightened at the mention of Ed. *No, not Ed. His real name is Chad. Think of them by their real names, remember?* Jeremy's true identity was on the tip of his tongue. All he had to do was tell Ahman where to find the body, and Alan's ruse would be over. The beastmen would tear the imposter apart, just like they would if he or Bean walked into their camp, and the war would end before it started. But then there would be no one left to challenge Finn if they failed to find Juliane or a way to stop the drain.

"And how do you expect us to do that?" asked Bean. "Are we supposed to go door-to-door shouting 'The beastmen are coming! The beastmen are coming!'"

Ahman frowned. "Beastmen?"

Bean nodded at him. "It fits a whole lot better than Sharks. I've seen the team. Didn't see a single fin."

Ahman cocked his head. "And what do you call your side?"

"We're not on either side," interrupted Stephen. "Which is exactly where we want to stay."

Ahman's gaze swept Stephen from head to toe. "You might not have a choice, you know."

Stephen turned and stared into the flames. "You always have a choice." He muttered.

JULIANE

Juliane faced the door and grimaced at the small protection it offered. A booming sound echoed as the beast on the other side continued to pound away at the puny barrier. She reached out and touched the walls. Her only hope sprung from the fact the narrow room would not allow the creature to move comfortably. It was far too large, and she'd seen how it walked above ground. There was also the matter of its companion. *One problem at a time*, she thought.

She took a step back. There wasn't much room for her to maneuver. *If I stay near the ground . . .* She shook her head. That hadn't worked for the rat and worse, would slow her further. However, the creature did seem startled when she'd flashed the light. Perhaps, she could use light blindness and the narrow passage to her advantage. She braced herself, ready to launch her body the moment the creature was fully inside.

She didn't have to wait long. The remaining fragments holding the cellar door together snapped. The remains of the door and their meager protection were yanked off its hinges and tossed into the night. A dark silhouette filled the space where it had once been. Juliane tensed. The two birds screamed in unison. Then, suddenly, the shape blocking her exit launched itself into the air. Juliane was still trying to process what was happening and how she might use it to her advantage when flames appeared in the opening.

"What are you waiting for?" A woman's voice asked from outside.

Juliane ran up the stairs leading to the surface. "Are they gone?" she asked her would-be rescuer. However, when she looked around, all she saw was a floating fireball hovering at her eye level.

First giant killer birds, and now this. I'm losing my mind. She issued a command for her body to conduct a full scan. *Although, if my mind is going, can I really trust the results?* She canceled the scan and instead synthesized another dose of artificial calm. Ice cascaded through her veins as the effect took hold.

"I realize how this must look," said the ball of flame. The air under it shimmered and warped, revealing a figure wrapped in dark cloth from head to foot. The figure then reached up with its free hand and pulled a mask away, revealing a woman's face. The flames proved to be connected to a torch. "I can explain later," said the new arrival, "but right now, we don't want to be here when those birds decide to try to pick you off again."

Juliane glanced over her shoulder into the night sky. Clouds had rolled in, blocking much of the moon's light. The giant birds could be circling up there, even now, and she'd have no way of knowing.

Juliane nodded for the woman to lead the way. She followed the woman to a brick building on the other side of the street. From the outside, it appeared more structurally sound than many of the other buildings she and Durham had passed along the way, but far from what she would have considered habitable before today.

Durham. She stopped short. *He's still out there.* She glanced at the door. *But so are those creatures,* the cold voice of logic reminded her. Another wave of ice chilled her blood. *You're going to need to slow down,* she thought. *Your memory is already faulty. Too many inhibitors, and it will only get worse.*

The woman latched the door before she could run back outside. Dark threadbare curtains hung from the walls, though there were few other furnishings. The woman carried her torch into another room. Juliane heard a snap, then the light disappeared, leaving only the trace smell of smoke. Juliane found a light switch and toggled it. However, the switch didn't do anything. She attempted to connect to the building's nanobots but found nothing.

She then realized that she had no access to the datastream either. *This place must have been a historic preservation site.* She frowned, then shuddered. Hospitals used similar signal-blocking technology. It meant that even if their phone apps were working, she wouldn't be able to reach out to Durham to tell him what had happened to her. It also made her skin crawl.

However, the technology only blocked outgoing signals. She still had command of her cells. Juliane's body took on the bioluminescent glow to take a better look around. The woman ran from the other room.

"Turn it off," she said, closing the curtains with a snap.

"Why?" asked Juliane as the room was plunged back into darkness. "Oh, does the light attract the birds?" She waved at the curtains. That would explain why they targeted the store.

"It attracts them," the woman nodded, "but it'll also attract the attention of the sort of people you don't want to meet at night. You're lucky I'm the one who saw you first. What were you thinking?"

"I was thinking I was about to become dinner and was looking for something to protect myself with." She held her chin high. "What is that thing you're wearing, anyway?" asked Juliane, gesturing with sweeping arms at the woman's outfit.

"Pretty neat, isn't it?" she said with a toothy grin bright enough to be seen even in the poor light. "It's a stealth suit, though I like to think of it as an invisibility cloak. Bends light so you see what's behind it, even if you are looking straight at it. No idea what it's made from. Some sort of fiber optic thread or something. Apparently, Finn had some military connections back in the day."

"I'm familiar with the technology." Juliane glanced in the direction of the stairwell. "And is Finn here, too?"

"Finn? Here?" The woman laughed. "No. He doesn't ever leave Manhattan." Her tone hardened. "Actually, he'd prefer most people didn't."

"Most people," Juliane latched on to the words. "I take it, not you."

"He knows I can't stay away long." The woman's tone made it clear that she would prefer not to elaborate on the subject further.

"I can't stay here either. My . . ." How should she describe Durham? "My colleague is hurt." She pointed to the windows. "I'll need to go back to where I last saw him."

The woman sucked in her lip. "You're not from around here, are you?"

Juliane tilted her head. "No. Simply passing through. We were heading to New York, until those things—"

The woman rubbed the back of her neck. "Lucky for you then, I'm on my way back there too. You can travel with me, but we're not going anywhere tonight. The birds aren't the only threats out there, especially not for a woman. You might as well hang a sign around your neck saying Open for Business."

"I can handle myself."

"I don't mean to imply you can't." The woman sighed. "Most people who have survived this long can. You just don't need to put yourself at risk if you don't have to."

Juliane realized the woman standing before her offered the opportunity to learn more details about what had happened to the world since she'd been buried under a pile of rubble, however, those questions would need to wait. Durham was her more pressing concern. "I need to find him."

"Is he like us?"

"Us?" Juliane asked.

Light flashed for a moment across the woman's fingers.

"Oh, you're asking if he's undergone the Gene Assist procedure." Juliane nodded. "Yes, of course. We all did." She pressed her lips together. Her rescuer clearly had some biases, if she cared about something as inconsequential as a person's upgrade status, but Juliane would exploit them for all it was worth if it was the difference between going back for Durham tonight versus waiting until morning.

"Fine," said the woman, walking over to the door. "I'll go and check it out. But not you. You stay here and wait for us to come back."

Juliane crossed her arms and shook her head. "If it is dangerous for me to be out there, then it is just as dangerous for you." The brief arc of electricity jumping between the woman's features unlocked another memory. She'd seen someone do something similar before. *Do not let yourself get distracted, Juliane.*

The woman smirked. "I wouldn't be so sure about that."

"I'm going with you."

"No, you aren't," she said. "And before you waste more time arguing, I have two reasons. One, I don't want to leave my safehouse unguarded, and two, unlike you," she picked at the fabric of her stealth suit, "I have an invisibility cloak."

A memory tickled her mind, but remained just out of reach. "So, let me borrow it." Juliane reached out. "Trust me, I'll bring it back. This place is far better than where we were going to have to spend the night."

"So you can bleed all over it?" said the woman, hugging the material close to her chest. "That isn't going to happen."

Juliane glanced down and saw her arms were covered in deep scratches clotted by dirt. As if on cue, her ankle throbbed, reminding her that Durham wasn't the only one in need of medical attention. She glanced at the door again. If only there was a signal in this place. She could figure out what was wrong with the phone app or send Durham a message.

She ground her toe into the floor. For the life of her, she would never understand why some people actually preferred living in places like this. Looking back up, she pressed her lips together and gave a reluctant nod. "You'll want to look for the most stubborn horse you've ever seen tied up outside," she began.

six

STEPHEN

Bean lay on the ground next to him, breathing with the soft rhythm of sleep. He wished he could do the same. Like the evening before, Nadia's face appeared the minute his eyes were closed. However, this evening, Chad's face also joined hers in his mind's eye, looking equally judgmental. Abandoning sleep, he accessed the datasphere.

Wes, or more accurately, Wes's replica, joined him in an instant. His feet hovered inches above the ground, allowing the grass to move freely underneath him. He appeared tall and muscular, albeit with muscles defined by a series of skin-colored triangles rather than from working in a field or lifting weights.

It was the go-to avatar he'd regularly chosen back when they used to meet up to play *Colony Defenders II*. It was a far cry from the skinny teen with glasses Stephen met in real life, and even further from how he'd appeared during those last minutes on the train.

"Did I make a mistake?" asked Stephen, forcing himself to look away before he started dwelling on Wes's final moments. It was risky to let your thoughts stray in the digital world. Your deepest secrets could be made visible for all the world to see. He'd also learned you could get trapped in a loop if you weren't careful, which is what had happened to the real Jeremy, and what had allowed Alan to assume his identity without threat of being caught.

He focused on his feet. Unlike Wes, he'd chosen to appear like his regular self, though his shoes were covered with a lot less mud. The legs of his pants contained far fewer stains, too. If only the blood on his hands was as easy to wash away in the real world. *Get it together Stephen,* he told himself.

"Knowing you?" said Wes. "Probably." He laughed, not unkindly. "But about what?"

Before, Stephen might have attempted to tease Wes back, but he didn't have a witty comeback. "There's a war coming." He looked down again. "People are going to get hurt." Neither he or Wes cast a shadow in this place, as the light came from everywhere and yet nowhere. Stephen frowned. The effect was somewhat off-putting.

He looked up toward the sky. A digital sun bloomed into existence. Stephen turned his attention back to his friend. While the light was still not as bright as the sun outside of the datasphere, it was enough to cause silhouettes to expand out under their feet like growing puddles of water.

Wes cocked his head to the side. His eyes glanced down to the shadows by Stephen's feet. "And you feel bad because you're doing the smart thing by getting as far away as possible?" His body broke apart into pixels for a moment, and when they condensed again, his appearance was that of the boy he'd met in Manhattan, rather than the gaming character he'd met online.

Stephen became sadder from the transformation. "What if I could stop it?"

"You?" Wes shook his head. "I hate to break it to you, man, but as much as I like you, you aren't some sort of mystical chosen one."

Stephen's temper flared. It was the sort of thing the real Wes would have said, but it wasn't his friend saying it. It was a computer program. The most advanced software he'd ever seen, sure, but Wes, the real Wes, was never coming back. All because of him. He slapped the palm of his hand with his fist. "This isn't a game."

Wes's avatar wilted before Stephen's eyes. "I'm sorry. I went too far."

Stephen sighed. Wes didn't deserve his anger. "No, I'm sorry. I shouldn't have lashed out at you," said Stephen. "You can't help how you were programmed." Wes shrank even further. "What?" asked Stephen. "Ah, don't feel bad about it. Wes, I mean the real Wes, was brilliant in the best possible ways, unlike some people I know. It's clear he wanted you to be happy."

"Not just me," said Wes. The beginnings of a smile returned to his face.

Stephen turned away and looked into the distance. "Yeah, well, that's not your fault either." The unnatural lighting surrounding them dimmed. He sighed. "I guess, deep down, I know what I need to do. I'll go back. Tell Ahman about Jeremy. With any luck, the other beastmen won't be so willing to follow orders when they see their so-called leader is a liar. Doubt it, but it might be better than doing nothing."

"Dude, I don't have a clue what you're talking about, but that reminds me, I got a lead on Juliane Faris."

"Oh yeah, that's another thing. She's dead. The guy we met today, Ahman, he told us what happened inside Apex. So, you don't have to keep searching for her for me." Stephen described Gena's account in a thickened voice. "Guess I am going to have to find something else to do with my life."

Wes frowned. "Did this witness say she saw her die?"

"She didn't," said Stephen. He pressed his lips together. "But from what she saw up until that moment, it's pretty likely."

Wes frowned. "No, that can't be right. I've spotted code since we last talked. I'm sure of it."

"Code?"

"Yeah, code." He gestured at the landscape. "Take this, for example. You see us standing in a field, but I don't see us standing anywhere at all—it's all just code." His arms fell to his sides. "After a while, you start to recognize certain strings, like recognizing a person's handwriting. I've learned to recognize what's hers."

"So?"

"So, I've detected a new string. Which means she's accessed the datastream. As in recently."

Stephen froze as if struck. "Where is she?"

"She tried to use a rideshare program in Worcester, if you'd believe it," said Wes. "It's safe to say she isn't still waiting around for a lift, but it's a start."

Stephen searched his friend's face, looking for any sign of lie or prank. "Worcester? Recently?" He slammed his fist into his hand. She must have been in one of those tubes after all. But who freed her? Not Alan. *Unless . . . what if it's a trap?*

All he had was Ahman's word he was trying to stop Alan from starting a war. But what if he wasn't? What if Ahman was simply following Alan's orders? They'd told Ahman they were trying to locate Juliane, and Worcester was beastman headquarters. He could have easily passed that information along to Alan the same way that he and Bean were able to communicate via the datastream, mind-to-mind. This whole thing could be a set-up to get them back to the beastman's home turf. "How long?"

Wes sighed. "There've been a couple more pings since then. Too fast and encrypted for me to get a read on their location, but that's another reason I know they're hers."

"I meant *when* did she ping the datastream in Worcester?" Stephen's breath bottled in his chest.

"Yesterday? Today?" Wes looked to the ground. "Sorry, it's hard to tell how much time passes anymore."

Stephen rubbed his face as if he might wipe his guilt away. Wes might have achieved a form of immortality in this place, but it didn't take a genius to see all he wanted was to be a real person again. "So, still a wild goose chase, then?"

Wes's face snapped up, though his expression remained somber. "Hey, the thing about wild geese is, sometimes they get caught. We'll find her. I promise."

"Yeah, and sometimes all the person chasing after them finds is a pile of shit at the end," said Stephen to himself. He looked toward the horizon. Wes no longer had to worry about the passage of time, but it had to be close to morning by now. He was no more convinced continuing to pursue Juliane was the right decision, versus going back to Ahman, than he was when he'd first entered the datastream. "Play me the recording again."

"I might be just code, but I still have feelings, you know."

Stephen sighed. "Would you play the recording, *please?*"

"Much better." Wes dissolved into the landscape, and the image of a brown-haired woman took his place—his birth mother, Betty Dronigh. Aside from the recording, the most he knew about her was she'd died while he was still a small child.

Betty held up a picture of Juliane. "Find her," his mother said. The recording stopped.

Find her. The woman before him claimed to love him before asking him to find Juliane. The recording had left it vague exactly why he was supposed to find her, but Stephen was sure it involved the drain. After all, Juliane had created the upgrade and was supposed to be brilliant. She'd be able to find a way to patch the code and halt the drain's effects. Not just for him, but for everyone trapped on the island with Finn.

Chasing after Juliane had seemed like a great idea immediately following the battle at the Watchtower. Then again, he hadn't been thinking straight. His initial cold acceptance of Nadia's death proved it. But now that he'd had more time to think about honoring a dead woman's command, it seemed more and more like the opposite.

It wasn't like he remembered the woman who'd given him life. She could be just as much a liar as his biological father. She'd married him after all. And yet, hearing that there was still a chance to return to a normal life, he found he couldn't walk away. The image faded, and for a while, Stephen did nothing but stared at the grassy hills that undulated before him.

Wes reemerged from behind him. "You okay?"

Stephen pulled his gaze away from the horizon. "Yeah."

"Anytime you want to talk," said Wes. He reached out, like he was about to place his hand on Stephen's shoulder. "About anything. I'm always here."

Yeah, because of me. Someone pulled on Stephen's arm in reality. "Gotta run," he said. Exiting the datasphere, he opened his eyes and saw Bean hovering over him.

"You were out cold," she whispered. Her eyes darted around. She moved to give him space but kept her body tucked into a crouch.

What is it? What's wrong? he projected.

We're not alone. she answered.

He heard the sound, too. Something or someone with heavy footsteps was approaching. He glanced in the direction of the other campsite. The smell of their cookfire still floated on the pre-dawn air. *Do you think it's Ahman?*

Maybe, said her voice. Bean shook her head. *But it's coming from the wrong direction.*

Stephen listening more closely. *We should warn him.* Stephen didn't need the light of day to know that Bean scowled. "I need to tell him the truth about Jeremy."

The noise shifted. Bean covered his mouth with her finger. *Are you trying to let whoever that is know where we are?*

It slipped out.

Good thing you have me to save you from yourself.

Yeah, but who's going to save Ahman?

Bean shrugged. *He seems like someone who can handle himself. He'll be fine.* She grabbed their meager belongings. *We should go while whoever that is, is distracted.*

Stephen stood. *I wouldn't have expected you to want to run from a fight.*

Bean stopped in her tracks. Stephen didn't need daylight to sense her glare. *Let's get two things straight: it's not our fight, and I'm so not running, but if you are determined to be an idiot about it, by all means, let's go and risk our lives for that guy. I'm sure he absolutely would have done the same for us.*

She threaded her way through the trees back toward Ahman's campsite like a silent shadow. As Stephen followed her into the darkness, he wondered if another face would be joining Nadia's when he next attempted to find sleep.

seven

JULIANE

Juliane sat up in the antique chair with a jolt. She'd found it while she waited for the woman to return with Durham and must have nodded off. She stood and stretched her back. The chair must have been worth a fortune at some point for someone, but had clearly seen better days and was far from what Juliane would consider comfortable.

She wiggled her foot. Her ankle no longer gave her pain. The scratches on her arms, too, had knit closed while she slept. *Thank you, Gene Assist upgrade. Better yet, thank me.* She paced around the room and peered through a crack in the curtains. The rose blush of dawn colored the sky. Dread settled into the pit of Juliane's stomach. She must have passed more of the night in the wooden chair than she'd intended, and still there was no sign of the woman, who'd left without ever giving Juliane her name.

That's it. I've waited long enough, thought Juliane, *I'm going myself.* Birds chirped all around, but they were the songs Juliane was used to—normal-sized bird songs. Even more promising, the air no longer contained the scent of death that Juliane now associated with their larger, murderous brethren.

The streets looked different in the light of the day. Juliane realized that finding her way back to the store might prove somewhat difficult. She hadn't been exactly paying attention to road signs, nor had she run in a straight line in her efforts to avoid becoming dinner.

She attempted to access the datastream, but the signal blocker ensuring the historical address remained a digital-free zone extended out to the immediate street front as well. Juliane looked for the rising sun. *That must be east.* She shielded her eyes. *Which would mean, north should be . . .* she looked to the left. *That way.*

"I found your friend," said the woman, emerging from the house behind her.

Juliane hadn't heard any sound indicating another was inside. She turned to face her. "You should have woken me as soon as you got back."

"I decided the news could wait." The woman's expression took on a look that Juliane hated more than anything—pity. She reached out her hand, but then let it drop back to her side. "I'm sorry."

"What are you saying? Sorry, as in, you couldn't find him?" The woman's silence filled the room. "Or sorry, as in . . ." Juliane pressed her lips together and searched the woman's face for some indication that her comment didn't mean what it sounded like. "You're saying he's dead?" She shook her head. "You're wrong. It has to be someone else." Juliane cursed the technology that prevented her from being able to ping Durham. She's just seen him—they'd just been joking around. He couldn't be dead.

The woman's head dropped. She picked up something from inside the house. It proved to be a large bloody strip of cloth. "You recognize this, don't you?" She held the swath up higher. The fabric resembled the cloth that had once covered Durham's torso, though it was difficult to tell for sure. The red stain swayed in the breeze. She lowered her arm. "There was more, much more, but . . ." She sighed. "He's gone."

"Show me. I need to see him for myself."

She gave a small shake of her head. "I buried what was left of him. I didn't think you'd want him to be left out like that for the animals to find him. Like I said, I'm so, so sorry."

The woman had said it again as if her apology might somehow summon her colleague, no her . . . her . . . Juliane blinked. *Friend? Had he really become that? Or had he already become more?* Juliane clenched her fists at the unbidden thoughts swirling around her head. She'd rejected him—pushed him away—like she had everyone else, and with good reason.

However, her lower lip still trembled. She clenched her jaw. It would serve no purpose to break down in front of a relative stranger, other than to make her look weak or not in control. She flooded her system with every enzyme or biological compound known to numb the sudden ache in her heart over what might have been.

She then turned toward creating longer-lasting mental walls around her thoughts—a skill she'd mastered long before undergoing the gene assist procedure. However, her natural techniques weren't nearly as perfect. With her defenses in place, she dismissed thoughts of Durham. It was easier . . . no, she corrected herself, it made more logical sense to focus on next steps rather than what-ifs.

Besides, as her former research partner, Betty, was once so quick to point out, Juliane didn't need friends. She didn't need anyone. She steeled her shoulders. *Never had,* she reminded herself. Friends only served as a demand on her time and another form of distraction. She'd continue on to New York like she'd already planned. That idea, at least, still made sense—where else did she have to go? Her life in Worcester lay in ruins. It was pointless to turn back. Once there, she'd seek out this Finn person, if he truly was in charge, and offer her assistance. Society might have descended into chaos while she slept, but it didn't have to stay that way. She'd changed how the world worked once. She would change it again.

Juliane glanced back toward the north. "Tell me more about this group of yours."

⎯⎯ ⟨ひひひ⟩ ⎯⎯

The highway stretched out before them, as eerily quiet and devoid of life as it had been the day before. The sight was hard to process. The last time she'd traveled it, the roadway had been packed as far as the eye could see with bumper-to-bumper traffic. Even the skies had been filled with passing vehicles.

In her mind's eye, helicopters should be hovering overhead, reporting on the scene below, while a constant stream of larger aircraft made their way to the nearby airports. The roar of engines, blaring horns, and shouts from drivers with short tempers should be filling her ears—not this unnatural quiet.

"We're almost there," said Morgan and pulled on the reins. She'd named herself shortly after they'd departed.

While she hadn't brought back Durham's remains, Morgan had managed to locate Juliane's stubborn, skittish mare. Juliane's lip curled. *Why it should survive when Durham hadn't . . .* She pushed the complaint down, fixating instead on her distaste for the animal. More than once, she'd debated whether they would have been better off leaving it tied outside of the store, but Morgan insisted they would make better progress on horseback, even if they had to share the saddle of this beast.

"Then why are we stopping?" asked Juliane as the mare slowed its gait.

"Because we aren't quite close enough to make it there before dark, and this old girl has carried us far enough for one day."

Juliane slid off the horse's back and rubbed her legs while Morgan rummaged through one of the saddlebags. She pulled out a large canteen. "The bad news is, this is the last of it," said Morgan, throwing the container at Juliane. "But the good news is, there's a group of cars up ahead." Morgan pointed at an exit ramp. "So, no more horseback riding today."

"Working cars? As in we can ditch this creature? Because that would be good news."

Morgan glanced at her with a frown. "The only working cars belong to the Watch."

"The who?"

"Where have you been living for the last ten . . . fifteen years?" She closed her eyes in a wince and shook her head. "Never mind, doesn't matter now anyway. I'll just need you to wait for me by the cars. Okay?"

"Why? Where are you going?"

"There's a place near here, but the thing is, the people who live there can be a little . . . ah . . . nervous around strangers. So, I'm going to see if they'll be okay with us staying over. Don't worry, though. Worst case, we can camp in the cars."

"You're not suggesting we sleep in a junkyard?"

"Would you prefer to sleep on the ground again?"

Juliane raised an eyebrow. A night without insects buzzing around her ears or the threat of late-night storm would be a nice change of pace after the last several days. "Fine."

A rusted blue minivan lay at the bottom of the highway ramp next to a small yellow hatchback-style sedan. The gas panels on both vehicles were open. A police cruiser rested on its side on the other side of the roadway. Juliane assumed any gas in the cruiser had long since been siphoned off. The entire scene screamed tetanus risk. "I'm starting to wonder if the ground might not be the better option."

Morgan chuckled. "This is another reason most don't leave the city very often. Now, I'm guessing it might be difficult, but try not to get too comfortable."

The minivan's third row had been replaced by a mattress. However, she didn't need to access its sensors to determine it was crawling with insects, or worse. A large yellow-brown circle marked one end. Juliane refused to even contemplate potential sources for the stain other than rainwater. The window above it was cracked, and the entire interior reeked of mold.

She eyeballed a folded blanket lying next to the stain and curled her lip. While leaves on the surrounding trees had taken on the golden tones of autumn, evening wouldn't be nearly cold enough for Juliane to use it in the event Morgan's friends turned them away.

Grimacing, Juliane exited the van, and leaned against its side while she waited for Morgan's return. She had seen the towering skyscrapers in the distance, but even if she hadn't, she would have known it was close by. Though a number of New York's high-risers in the distance were pockmarked by large swaths of broken glass, exposed sides, and even a few burn scars, she sensed the pulse of streaming data. Each packet was like a wave of soothing water on her skin.

As they'd traveled down the highway, each step closer to the city had only strengthened the sensation. She'd felt more like her former self by the minute. More importantly, the data served as confirmation she'd made the right decision in continuing on to New York, even if it was without Durham. Her breath caught in her throat.

She reminded herself that the signal meant there were other people. Other survivors. Once there, it would simply be a matter of identifying the brightest minds available and pooling their resources. She'd fix her missing memories. She'd fix everything. She bit her lip as the image of Durham's bloody shirt waving in the early morning light sprung to mind. Or at least she'd fix what she could. She stared at the skyscrapers and the future they promised. The only thing that could improve upon her plans was a hot shower. Durham's dirt-covered face and toothy white grin appeared unbidden. *Not the only thing.*

She pressed her lips together, banishing the depressing thought before it could undo her. An idle mind was risky. To pass the time, she expanded her consciousness and intercepted a random transmission passing through a nearby node. The level of security protecting the data seemed overkill considering how few people they'd encountered.

As she'd done more than once already, she pinged the datastream for any sign of Durham before she could stop herself. Like those other times, the results of her query came back empty. *Why do I keep doing this to myself?* She bit her lip. The walls she'd erected in her brain weren't doing the trick. She was going to have to do something more.

"We're in luck," said Morgan stepping back into view. "They're feeling more welcoming than usual." A young man with sun-streaked, bushy brown hair stood next to her. He had the sort of bronze complexion that came from working long hours outside. "This is my . . . This is Lyall." Morgan shifted nervously. "Lyall, this is Juliane."

"Nice to meet you," said Lyall. He leaned back on his heels with a grin. "You picked the right day to pass by. It's Mags's birthday." He took their horse by its reins. He waved for Juliane to come closer but didn't take his eyes off Morgan. "If we leave right now, there's even time for some dancing."

Juliane took a breath as the memory of the night in the Vegas nightclub sprung to mind. The three of them had gone there after the convention—she, Durham, and their boss, Louis. Durham had even danced with her for a time, but then he'd found other partners and she'd . . . she'd made one of the worst mistakes of her life. She'd left the club with Louis.

"You ready?"

Juliane blinked. "Sorry, yes. I was just trying to remember how long it has been since I attended a party. Sounds fantastic."

Lyall continued to chatter while he led their horse down a narrow dirt-and-gravel trail. While he made sure to keep pace with both of them and to include Juliane in the conversation as much as Morgan, he walked closer to Morgan than was required by the width of the path. His fingers also twitched by his side whenever Morgan's hand strayed too close, like it was itching to grab hers.

Juliane caught the sound of a drumbeat first. Guitar music filled her ears next. The notes were delivered without particular technique or finesse, but were nonetheless followed by enthusiastic applause and laughter. Whoever the musicians were, they were providing quite the performance.

Lyall grinned, pushing a branch out of the way. "Here we are. Home sweet home." A large wall appeared up ahead. The wall itself consisted of a mix of wooden boards. Most were gray and splintered, though some appeared to have once been painted brown. Lyall placed his hand on Morgan's shoulder. "I'll be back in a second." His teeth gleamed before he turned and disappeared into the growing night.

"There's something I need to tell you," said Morgan.

"That Lyall has feelings for you? Yes, that's pretty obvious."

Though the sun had almost completely set, there was enough light to see Morgan's cheeks redden. "It's not that. The people here—" Morgan pointed at the wall. "They're not like us. They're Analogs."

"Analogs?" Juliane's brow knit. "Oh, you mean they haven't undergone the Gene Assist procedure." She relaxed. "Well, that's inconvenient for them, I suppose." She shook her head and waved the comment away. "But I don't see any reason why that should cause you or I any concern."

It still wasn't clear to her what exactly had happened to the world in the time since she entered the cryogenic tank. Her questions to Morgan as they'd made their way down the empty highway had largely gone unanswered except in the most general terms. Morgan, apparently, had been too young when it happened to truly understand what was going on.

She curled her knuckles, rolling the news reports she'd read around in her head again. Bombings. Mass layoffs. Pandemic. Each of those things were serious, but independently none of them should have been enough to have caused civilization to collapse. However, combined, she now understood they'd transformed the world into the post-apocalyptic landscape it was today.

Still, it hadn't needed to be that way. The world's greatest minds should have banded together to find a solution, a cure, or a common purpose the population could rally behind. *Minds like hers.* However—her nails dug into her palms—short-sighted individuals with more ambition than brains had taken over instead.

Now, knowing what to look for, she'd dived further into reports online. The masses had left the major metropolitan areas all at once. The rural communities they'd fled to—with their limited resources and smaller understaffed hospitals, hadn't been equipped to handle the demand. She ground her teeth. The situation had spiraled out of control from there, as more people either succumbed to the illness or became victims of unchecked violence.

With every insight she gained, Juliane became more convinced the entire situation could have been prevented. If only she'd been awake and not trapped inside a tin can. She clenched her fist tighter. She might have been able to do something. She forced herself to relax her hand before her nails broke the skin. *Why did I go in that tube? If I'd only known. If I'd only been awake . . .* More and more of her memories had come back to her, but that one remained stubbornly absent. She needed time to reflect and relax, but thus far, the road had provided too many distractions. *It will be better once I'm back in the city.*

Lyall appeared behind them. "We're all set." He waved at them to follow.

A roaring bonfire held the evening at bay. Juliane counted at least twenty people mingling in its light. The growing darkness wasn't the only thing the fire held back. The burning logs also masked the scent of livestock. Dancing flames illuminated a goat loitering near the enclosure's edge. A chicken pecked the ground in front of Juliane's foot. She scanned the area for any sign of pens, but instead only spotted a large wooden table. "Please say you don't actually eat out here," she said.

"Where else would we eat?" said Lyall.

"Inside, of course." She pointed at the table. "That's not sanitary."

"What doesn't kill you . . ." said Lyall with a laugh.

"It still might," Juliane muttered. However empty space was all that remained next to her. She turned to address Morgan, but found the woman, too, had vanished.

Juliane spotted the pair a moment later, silhouetted by the bonfire. Lyall appeared to be pleading with Morgan. Morgan shook her head. Whatever the disagreement was about, it was short-lived, as Lyall then reached out and twirled Morgan.

"I haven't seen you around here before," said a broad-shouldered man, coming to stand by her. "But I am wishing I had. Would you like to dance?"

Juliane looked toward the flames. She'd lost track of her companions among the other revelers. She glanced back at the stranger. His smile shone in the darkness, reminding her of Durham. She took a breath, holding it like a dam against waves of emotion. How had that man worked his way into her psyche so completely? She reminded herself of all the reasons his loss shouldn't affect her so.

He was a womanizer, a jock, and even worse, a proven liar. If they hadn't worked together, they wouldn't have had anything in common at all. In fact, there was nothing about him that should have appealed to her, and yet for some reason, she didn't seem to be able to get over the fact that he was gone.

Understanding her feelings for Durham was like trying to solve a jigsaw puzzle, knowing full well a piece was missing. "Maybe in a little bit," she said before the silence grew awkward, "but I've been walking for days, and right now, I just want to stay back and listen."

She expected him to return to the party, but instead he remained by her side. "You've come a long way, then?"

She nodded. "I must have driven this route at least a hundred times. The funny thing is, it never seemed like a long distance before."

"We took a lot for granted back then," said the man in a tone that spoke volumes.

"You say that like it's a bad thing," said Juliane in an attempt to lighten the mood and escape her own thoughts. She reached down and massaged her calf muscle.

"Isn't it?" asked the man, extending his hand. "I'm Sam, by the way."

"Juliane," She straightened while taking his offered hand. "I just meant that I, for one, wouldn't mind going back to a time we had the luxury of taking things for granted."

"Ah." Sam nodded. "Yeah—" A scream cut off whatever he was about to say next, and the music came to a screeching halt. Juliane looked toward its source where the firelight revealed a woman bent over, clutching her abdomen. Sam's eyes grew wide. "Rebecca," he said, releasing Juliane's hand. He gave her an apologetic look and ran toward the others while Morgan came running back.

The woman cried out again. The others rushed her inside the nearest building. "This isn't good. Rebecca's pregnant," explained Morgan. "But it's early—too early for her to be going into labor. It's not going to end well. We should leave while they're occupied."

"Why? They aren't going to blame us. We just got here. If anything, they should blame the livestock. Who knows what sort of bacteria they're carrying?" The goat swished its tail as if aware of Juliane's comment. "Also, you saw how fast everyone leapt into action. Everyone taking on a job. This can't be their first delivery." She pointed at the goat, noting its sagging belly. "For example, their pet lawnmower looks like she's given birth once or twice," she said. "It's just another baby. People have them all the time."

Morgan's eyes bored into Juliane's. "No," she said. "They don't."

"Of course they do." Juliane pressed. "The government might've collapsed, but I'm pretty sure people are still having sex." Juliane scanned their rustic surroundings. "In fact, considering what little else there is to do around here, I suspect they're having it more often."

Morgan turned her face to the ground and mumbled something too softly for Juliane to hear.

"Sex is nothing to be embarrassed about," said Juliane.

"Maybe it wasn't when you were growing up—"

The laboring woman screamed again, cutting off the conversation before Juliane pressed further. Juliane cocked her head toward the sound and pressed her lips together. She had little experience with pregnant women, but even to her untrained ears, it didn't sound like the woman's delivery was progressing normally. "Hmm, you might have a point."

One of the doors to the house opened, and a man stumbled out. His gaze settled on them. "You two," he shouted. "Don't just stand there. We need boiling water, and something hard for Rebecca to bite down on."

Juliane glanced at Morgan.

"She's going to die," said Morgan loud enough for only Juliane to hear. "They both are." Her lips twisted. "There's a reason I don't stay here often. These people have certain opinions about people like us. We will get blamed for this. We should leave."

Juliane squared her shoulders and looked toward the house. "It wouldn't be the first time I was blamed for something outside of my control. I doubt it will be the last. Go, if you're so worried about it. I, however, am staying." She looked around. Her forehead wrinkled. "Now, if you were a bucket, where would you be?"

Morgan glanced toward the gate to the compound. Her shoulders slumped. "Try looking over by the chicken coop," she said after a moment.

Fantastic. Juliane took a deep breath. *More birds.* "Right. Well, then, let's get on with it."

⁓

Juliane entered the house clutching a metal bucket she'd found outside. Water sloshed as she followed the screams to the room where the laboring woman had been relocated. The poor woman lay on a bed. The others hovered around her, looking just as lost as Juliane felt. The pregnant woman cried out again.

A man, standing by the woman's feet, placed his hands between her legs. "Becky, you have to stop. It's too soon," he said. "Try not to push just yet."

Juliane started and straightened her back. While she might not have medical training and no experience with childbirth, his advice sounded terrible.

The woman on the bed cried. "I'm trying, but I can't help it."

"You have to try harder." The man attending the woman looked to one of the other men in the room. The man nodded and raced out of the room.

"You don't understand. It's coming. I know it is." The laboring woman cried out between panted breaths.

"Calm yourself," said the man. "It's not good for you . . . or our baby."

"Something's wrong with it. I can feel it," she screamed.

"Sssh, just try not to push."

"Are you insane?" Juliane dropped the bucket of water by the footboard with a thud, not caring if water sloshed from its rim as she came to the woman's side. "It doesn't take a genius to see that this baby is coming."

"Who's this?" The man shouted at the others in the room.

"I saw her standing around outside," said one of the men. "Thought everyone should be helping."

"Her name is Juliane," said Sam. Juliane hadn't noticed him among the others.

The laboring woman groaned. Tears streamed from her eyes. "I'm sorry," she said to the man at her feet. The woman's voice was fainter than it had been a second before.

Juliane bent down and touched the woman's shoulder as a mad idea sprang into her mind. "I'm a doctor," she said.

"You are?" There was relief in the man's voice, though it was mixed in equal parts with distrust.

"I am," said Juliane, daring anyone with a glare to disagree. "Now, stand over there so I can better understand the situation we are dealing with here." She rubbed her hands together. "Better yet, please find another place for the others to wait. There are far too many people in this room."

The first man frowned and looked like he wasn't going anywhere.

The laboring woman moaned. "Please, Rob," she whispered. The woman's eyes squeezed shut.

"We've never seen this person before," he said.

"Please," the woman repeated. Her skin appeared paler than it had even a moment ago.

Sam called out from the other side of the room. "Let her help, man."

Rob's lips narrowed to a fine line, but he nodded. "I'll be in the hall." He shot Juliane a pointed look. "We all will." Juliane shot him the same look back.

As the others filed out of the room, Juliane accessed the datastream. The signal was weaker than what she'd detected outside, but strong enough that soon, data and digital images augmented her vision. She moved until she stood in front of the woman's legs. Blood and bodily fluids were everywhere.

Juliane hesitated. This was going to be more difficult than she imagined. She looked at her hands. They were covered in dirt from the road, and no doubt, now played host to civilizations-worth of bacteria. She glanced down at the bucket and shook her head. While the water appeared clear, it could contain any sort of bug larvae. She sent a query into the datastream. A research study appeared on the healing effects of plasma-activated water. The woman moaned again. Juliane hated that her theory relied on so little supporting information, but she didn't see much other choice.

She held her hands apart and issued the command to her cells. Electricity sparked from finger to finger as her cells took on the properties of an eel. She concentrated, and the intensity increased. As soon as the sparks were strong enough to jump from one hand to the next, she plunged her hands into the water.

Juliane's hands tingled as the power she'd generated passed through the liquid. The bucket and its contents glowed with a purple-tinged light, bright enough to illuminate the room. Juliane waited a heartbeat before releasing the lightning from her hands. She then returned to the woman.

The woman drew her legs back. "I saw what you did," she said with a whimper. "I know what you are. You're one of them."

Juliane raised an eyebrow. "Which, incidentally, makes me your best friend at the moment." Information scrolled across her vision. "It's Rebecca, right? Let's see what we're working with." She placed a hand on the woman's knee. The woman shuddered. Juliane's lips twisted. "Please," she said. "I want to help you, but I will not force you."

Rebecca looked anywhere except at Juliane, but parted her legs.

Juliane glanced down. It took all her resolve not to allow her true emotions to show on her face at the sight. "The baby is crowning," she said, grateful at the moment to have never been cursed with the desire for children of her own. "When I count to three, I want you to give me a good strong push."

"I'm not supposed to push." The woman cried. "Rob said so. It's too early."

"Rob doesn't have another whole human being inside him," said Juliane. "One . . . Two . . . Three . . . Push."

The woman clenched her fists and closed her eyes. However, tears continued to escape.

"That's good," said Juliane focusing on the baby. "On my count, do it again."

"I . . . can't," said Rebecca between panted breaths. Her eyes rolled back in her sockets.

"You have to," said Juliane. "Three."

The woman's body tightened as she bore down, then relaxed.

Juliane pressed her lips together. The baby's position had hardly changed. She softened her tone. "I get it. You're scared, and what I'm asking you to do is hard, but you are going to have to try harder," she said.

"I can't." The woman's voice was barely more than a whisper.

Juliane tapped the woman on her knee. "Look at me," said Juliane. The woman's tear-filled eyes opened. "The timing might be less than ideal, but this baby wants to be born. Don't give up on it before it has even had a chance. Now, push."

Rebecca took a breath and nodded. Her body tightened, though this time, she did not call out as the baby's head emerged.

"That's it," said Juliane. "One more."

The rest of the baby's body followed next as Juliane scooped up the child in her hands. Juliane frowned as she wiped away blood and fluid and looked upon its face. The child was pale and silent. *Aren't newborns supposed to cry?* The mother's body lay equally limp on the bed. Juliane sent another query to the datastream, unsure of what to do next. She opened the child's mouth with a finger as more data and diagrams appeared over the top of her vision.

The baby remained silent, though its motionlessness worried Juliane more than its lack of cries. Not sure what else she could do without access to a hospital or more advanced medical equipment, Juliane stared at the umbilical cord connecting mother to child. *There's so much blood.* She glanced at the baby in her arms and back at Rebecca. She'd given it her best, but it hadn't been enough. Still, thought Juliane, the woman deserved to meet her child at least once. "It's a girl," she said, laying the child on the woman's chest.

"A daughter," said Rebecca. Somehow, she gathered the strength to raise an arm and cradled the infant between her breasts.

Juliane looked away. Sounds of tiny breaths came from the bed. Juliane looked back. The child's eyes fluttered as she tested out her lungs with great volume. The door flung open, and Rob returned to the room. He ran to the bedside and dropped to his knees. "It's a . . . It's a . . ." he said.

Rebecca looked at him. Love radiated from her face as her fingers gingerly touched the child's hair. "It's a girl."

Rob beamed. "A girl." He encircled the pair with his arm.

Juliane frowned at the man. "Congratulations." While the baby had found its voice, her mother's voice remained far too weak. Juliane didn't need to see the dark stain at the foot of the bed to know the mother wasn't out of danger. "Now, step aside." She plunged her hands back in the bucket of water. "We're in for a long night."

Eight

STEPHEN

Embers twinkled like stars in the darkness, and the scent of charred meat still lingered in the air, but otherwise, there was no other sign of Ahman. Purple-white light arced across Bean's fingers as she stood in the center of the clearing. She cocked her head, listening for sounds that might give away the position of whoever or whatever else crept through the woods. Stephen followed suit.

A twig snapped. Bean dropped into a defensive pose, but all that emerged from the underbrush was the shadowed outline of a small fox, which quickly ran off back into the night.

Are we too late? wondered Stephen as he returned to where they'd shared a dinner. Ahman was nowhere in sight, and there were even fewer clues to suggest where he'd gone.

Bean's fingers quit sparking as she crouched down near the remains of the fire. The remaining coals winked out of existence as they were smothered by a handful of dirt. *There hasn't been anyone here for hours,* her voice said in his mind. Her shadowed outline straightened and returned to his side. *It must have been him we heard out there. Probably was trying to catch a peek of us together. Pervert.*

Stephen's lips twisted. As much as he wanted to argue, the woods had grown quiet. If there had been someone else in the woods with them other than Ahman, they'd figured out how to move in it as Bean did.

"So, what do you want to do now?" asked Bean. She stretched. An owl hooted. "Because if I have a vote, I say try to get a few more hours of sleep." She turned and swept the clearing with her gaze. "Just not here." She rubbed her arms. "Way too exposed."

Stephen reluctantly nodded and followed Bean back the way they'd come.

⁃⁓⁓⁓⁃

A rock dug into his back. He shifted, only for his back to find another. For the millionth time, Stephen envied the easy way Bean drifted into a deep sleep. He listened to her calm breathing and closed his eyes. The hair on his arm tingled. His fingers found a bug crawling across his skin. He flicked it away and tried to force himself to sleep again.

The darkness behind his eyes transformed into the familiar tall grass of home. The windmill that powered the well's pump, as well as their overworked generator, turned lazily in the breeze. Stephen broke into a grin as he ran through the wall of grass protecting the farmhouse from casual view. *Finally, a dream that isn't a nightmare.*

The door to the house squeaked as rusty hinges stretched open. A woman stepped out onto the front stoop. She raised her hand to her forehead, shielding her eyes from the sun and hiding her face from view, but Stephen recognized her at once. "Mom," he called out. "Nadia." Strands of grass slapped his face and cut the skin of his exposed arms. He didn't care. "I'm home."

Nadia lowered her hand. "Nadia? Who told you my name was—where have you been? We've been worried sick." She tucked a strand of hair behind her ear and looked over her shoulder, back at the house. "Don't you dare ask me if you can go out on another supply run anytime soon."

"It's okay, Nadia. You and Chad don't have to use secret identities anymore." Stephen laughed. Clearing the last of the field, he ran up the steps. He picked her up and swung her around in an embrace. "I've missed you so much," he said. "I'll never ask to leave you again."

The corner of Nadia's lip turned up. She squeezed him back once. "What's gotten into you? All you've ever wanted was a chance to get away."

"I was wrong."

Nadia shook out of his embrace. "Well, enough about that. Now that you're back you can help with chores. Chad's gotten it into his head that we need to upgrade our entire filtration system. He's been in and under the house all day. Who knows what he's broken by now?"

Stephen chuckled and took a step back from the stairs. "I'll see if I can find him."

Nadia's smile broadened. "When you do, tell him he better not come inside without leaving his boots at the door. I've already had to clean up after him twice this morning."

Stephen nodded and wandered around to the side of the building, where a chipped wooden door marked the entrance to the crawl space under the farmhouse. He pulled the latch and opened the door but saw only darkness on the other side.

He poked his head in. "Chad?" he called out. "Are you down there?" He listened for any sound that would indicate the man who'd helped raise him was hard at work. "Nadia said you're fixing the filter. Said you could use some help?" He frowned. Maybe it had been so long that anyone called him by his real name, his foster father had forgotten to respond to it. "Dad?"

The wind picked up, which caused the windmill to creak and moan as it spun around. Watching it, Stephen felt a pulling sensation, and then, it was as if he'd been sucked away, though he remained exactly where he stood.

"Ah, this must be where you grew up." Alan stood at the windmill's base. "What a lovely place," he said looking around. "It's so . . . so . . . simple."

"Get out of my dream," said Stephen, tightening his jaw.

"Is that any way to speak to your *real* father?" Alan opened his arms. "Especially after what I've done for you."

"What you've done for me? Sure, let's talk about all the things you've done for me." Stephen waved his hands about. "First, you abandoned me. Then you sold me out to the Watch." He tapped his chin. "Oh, yeah, and there is that other minor thing." He glared at Alan. "You being responsible for millions of people dying while you slept through it all."

Alan dropped his arms to his sides and cocked his head. "You were injured and in need of medical care. How was I to guess what that woman intended? I've been in stasis for the last fifteen years."

"Don't act like you didn't suspect something," said Stephen. "You had to." He crossed his arms over his chest. "Unless you aren't the genius you like to claim you are."

The smile left Alan's face. "Being a genius doesn't mean you have the ability to anticipate another person's *every* action. Take Albert Einstein, for example. On one hand," he flipped the palm of one hand up, "I imagine he never expected others to use his early work to create the atomic bomb, let alone use it." He flipped his other hand over. "But if they hadn't, it is highly probable that neither you nor I would exist today." He shook his head and let his hands drop back to his sides. "Sometimes, bad things happen, no matter how many years you spend planning. However, it doesn't mean some good can't still come from them."

"She tried to bleed me dry," said Stephen. "I could've died."

"But you didn't, and now she's not in a position to hurt anyone else ever again."

Stephen's eyes narrowed. "The beastmen are going to figure out who you really are. You thought about that yet?"

Alan shrugged. "Oh, I'm sure that a number of them already suspect, but I'm not worried."

"They will rip you in two."

"I doubt that very much."

"You willing to bet on it? Because I sure wouldn't, if I were you."

Alan shook his head. "Have you always been this angry?"

"What can I say. You bring out the best in me."

"That's probably true," said Alan. He examined his fingernails. "But I appreciate your concern. For what it is worth, though, while I can't say I can anticipate everyone's reaction, history has proven time and time again that people are willing to turn a blind eye to an unpleasant truth, provided you are giving them what they want most of all. It's not my fault that it happens to be revenge. Especially, now that the Wand has given them all their youthful energy back."

"So, you *are* starting a war," said Stephen.

Alan tutted. "Who exactly have you been talking to?" The corners of his lips turned up. "No, I'm not starting a war. Sure, there might be a skirmish or two. There's unfinished business, after all. But from my perspective, it's simply a change in management structure." He shrugged. "Happens all the time."

"Except people are going to die. Lots of people." Stephen shook his head and glanced back at the farmhouse. Its windows were dark and as devoid of life as a grave. "You didn't do a good enough job destroying the world the first time around, you need to do it again?"

"Destroy it?" Alan's eyes widened. "Is that what's gotten you so upset?" He shook his head. "One of these days, you'll realize I'm not the bad guy you've convinced yourself I am. I've only ever wanted to save it."

"Could've fooled me."

"That's because you keep allowing yourself to be fooled," said Alan. "If you would have only listened to me—"

"I've listened to you long enough." Stephen turned away.

"It doesn't have to be this way between us. I can help you."

"I seriously doubt it."

"Son, you and I are connected. You might not want to accept it, but it is true, and not just because we share the same blood. We're bonded in the datasphere too. I can sense you out there. Not with pinpoint accuracy mind you—you're too far away—but enough to give me a general idea of where you're standing right now. Or sitting. Look, I don't know what you've done, but I do know you are losing control."

"I don't need your help."

"But you do," he pressed. "That's what I've been trying to tell you. The man who sent you to find the Wand—he gave you something, didn't he?"

"Some supplies." Stephen shrugged. "I assumed because, unlike some people, he actually wanted me to live."

"No, I mean a file. Something over the datastream?"

An uneasy feeling settled in Stephen's stomach. "A map."

"Ah," said Alan. "A map. Clever. Then again, Damien always has been."

Damien? wondered Stephen. *Who's Damien? No, don't give him the satisfaction of asking. He must mean Finn. Just yet another person using a fake name.* "So, are we done then?"

"The map was a Trojan horse. A virus."

"And how would you know that?"

"Because he and I go way back," said Alan. A wistful expression crossed his features for a moment before being replaced with one of regret. "I can assure you, Damien Knightley doesn't do well with anyone potentially upsetting his plans or challenging his authority. Hence the situation we find ourselves in today." He gestured absently at Stephen. "I'm sure he saw you, and that *endearing* stubborn streak of yours, as a threat the minute you crossed his threshold . . . maybe even before. The virus, therefore, was likely designed to be his insurance policy. Something he could trigger if you ever got out of line. Which, unsurprisingly, you obviously have."

"If you know him so well, fix it."

Alan's mouth twisted as if he'd bitten into something unpleasant. "If it was that easy, I would've already," he said after a pause. "You'll need to come to me. In person."

All he had to go on was Wes's ardent belief that Juliane was alive and well, but even if they somehow managed to find her, there was no guarantee she'd be able to fix the drain. On the other hand, trusting Alan was a terrible idea. "Call off the attack."

"What attack?"

"The attack on Manhattan. Or whatever it is you plan to do as part of your whole management-change thing."

Alan snorted. "Does this mean you accept I'm telling you the truth?"

Stephen fought to keep his expression neutral.

After a moment, Alan shook his head and sighed. "I'm relieved you're willing to give me a chance. However, unfortunately, events have been put into motion. There's not much I can do."

Stephen scowled. What Alan was really saying was he'd allowed the situation to get out of his control. *Why am I surprised?*

"But I can stall them. I can give you time to get here, but I suggest you do so within the week. Alone, I should add. I'm afraid my offer does not extend to your friend. Which reminds me. She can't learn about our talk, and before you cross your fingers and promise not to say anything, I'll remind you, we're connected, whether or not you want to admit it. I'll know."

Stephen's eyes narrowed. "Why not?"

"It's not that I don't like her. The opposite, actually, but she's . . . compromised." He picked at his sleeve as though there was a speck of dirt. "I can't have her giving away our advantage."

"Which would be what exactly?"

"The element of surprise, for one. Damien might decide he needs to attack us first, and then where will we be?"

"Bean wouldn't tell him anything." He jutted his chest out. "She picked me. Not them."

Alan smirked. "I don't mean to imply she'd do it intentionally, but if you and I are linked, can you really trust Damien and Bean aren't also?" Alan shrugged. "Unfortunately, there's no real way for us to find out one way or another. You can't ask her about it. She'll either lie about it or, like you, have no idea."

"You're nuts."

"Am I?" Alan tapped his temple. "Think about it. She's not suffering to the same extent you are. Sure, she needs the occasional boost, but I don't recall her complaining about being hungry all the time like you are." He pointed at Stephen's stomach. "Have you ever asked yourself why that is? Because I have, and I've come to the conclusion it can only mean Damien didn't feel compelled to put the same insurance policy in her head as he does yours. Which means he either has reason to trust her more implicitly than I've known him to trust anyone, or he is controlling her through other means."

Stephen clenched his fists. It was true that Bean didn't seem to be as affected by the drain as he was, but he'd assumed it was because she'd lived with it longer. Alan couldn't be right. He couldn't.

"I'm sorry, but I simply can't risk it. At least, not at this stage in the game." He shot Stephen a pointed look. "More importantly, though, *you* don't want to risk it." Alan paced. "Assuming your friend is an unwitting participant, she's a fighter. You tell her that she's carrying around a stowaway in her mind—she'll try to break free or force him out, and Damien won't like that." Alan shrugged. "She's a tough woman. Might even succeed in the short term, but Damien has an army at his command. In the end, you both will lose. That is, unless I . . . we stop him before he grows any stronger."

Stephen's stomach twisted. Had Finn or Damien or whatever the hell he wanted to call himself been watching him through Bean's eyes this whole time? Had he made her stay with him after the attack on the Watchtower? *No*, he told himself. Alan was just messing with his head. What they had . . . that couldn't be faked. It was just another one of Alan's manipulations.

He ground his teeth. Alan didn't want him to find Juliane, otherwise why lie about no one else being in the cylinders. *Why?* Stephen's brow furrowed. Because if they found Juliane, he wouldn't be the smartest person alive. *Don't get your hopes up. She might be just as terrible as he is*, the small voice in the back of his mind whispered.

As if sensing his thoughts, Alan stopped his pacing and turned back toward Stephen. "I can see the wheels spinning around in your head. So, here's another reason you two should go your separate ways. Perhaps this is even the more important one. We both know what will happen if you don't leave her side sooner rather than later. Maybe not today. Maybe not tomorrow. But it *will* happen."

Alan gestured toward the farmhouse where Stephen last saw Nadia. "I told you I like her. I'm offering to save her as much as I am offering to save you." He held up a finger. "One week. After that, it may be out of my hands . . ." His lips twisted, and his eyes narrowed. "Now, I've talked too long, and you've spent long enough in this place. Your body needs sleep."

"I am asleep. Or at least, I *was* until someone decided to pull me into the datastream."

Alan waved the comment away. "I encourage you to hurry. For both of your sakes." He dissolved into pixels before disappearing entirely.

Sleep. Stephen turned back to the farmhouse. Alan made sleep sound so easy. Pressure built behind his eyes staring at the structure. Movement in the window caught his attention. "Wes? Is that you?" The door swung open and instead of Wes, Nadia appeared in its frame. "Mom?"

"What is it, honey?"

"Nothing," said Stephen, smiling. How he'd found his way back into the dream was as much a mystery to him as how he'd been pulled out of it, but if she was back, that's where he must be. "Just wanted to make sure you were still there."

Nadia laughed. "Where else would I be?"

Stephen ran to the stairs and hugged her.

"Are you sure you are feeling all right today?" Nadia asked.

"No," said Stephen. He looked into her eyes a minute longer in an attempt to banish the image that haunted him during the daytime with the one before him. "But I'm trying." He released his hold.

"Well, that's good," said Nadia. "Because you have company." She gestured toward the table where Bean sat dressed in clean clothing and sipping on a mug of something spiced, by the way its scent tickled his nose. Nadia poked his chest. "You've got some explaining to do, mister." Her face took on a stern expression, though warmth still radiated from underneath. "Don't you dare think you are going to be leaving again anytime soon."

Stephen's face broke into a smile from ear to ear. His concerns about their options and his worsening condition faded away as he soaked in their presence. "I wouldn't dream of it."

Nine

JULIANE

The animals in the yard were still asleep, except for the goat, who continued to chop at surrounding grasses with barely a notice of Juliane's presence. The large wooden gate enclosing the yard swung open. A red-faced man ran in and panted as he made his way toward her. "I came as fast as I could." His upper lip was covered with a bushy mustache that would have made him resemble a walrus if his skin weren't so gaunt and loose around his frame.

She narrowed her eyes. "I know you," she said, though she couldn't recall how or exactly where.

"Do you?" he asked, tilting his head to the side.

Juliane pursed her lips, struggling to connect his face with a name or where they'd met before. "Ah, upon second thought, I may have been mistaken."

"Perhaps I have one of those faces."

"Perhaps," Juliane agreed, though the idea this was not their first meeting continued to nag at her thoughts. "They're stable now," she said.

The man did a double-take at her words. "They?"

"Yes, the mother and the baby. Morgan told me she'd called for the doctor earlier when Rebecca first went into labor." *Took him long enough to get here.* "I assume the reason you are coming here in a run is because that's you."

He blinked and wiped his forehead. "Thank God. I left as soon as I got Morgan's message, but it was already so dark outside . . ."

She placed her hands on her hips. "You can thank me as well."

The man's hand returned to his side. "You assisted with the birth, then."

Assisted. Juliane's nose wrinkled at the word. She crossed her arms over her chest. Rob telling his poor suffering wife to wait to give birth, as if she had a choice when she was that far along. She clenched her jaw. Both mother and child would have died if she hadn't taken charge of the situation. However, her face relaxed as she realized the doctor likely meant the term with regards to the laboring mother, rather than the way the term had been used during her academic years.

She nodded, relaxing her arms. She gestured for the doctor to follow her. "Rebecca's lost quite a lot of blood, but I'm confident the worst is over. They're resting now." The doctor followed her inside. "In here."

Opening the door to the small bedroom, Juliane found the new family in much the same position she'd left them. Rob sat in a chair by the side of the bed. His head was bowed in sleep. Rebecca was also asleep, though her child lay nestled in her arms.

Rob jerked awake as they crossed through the entryway, though his eyes remained bloodshot. Juliane turned to the newcomer. "I suppose I should leave them with you, then?"

"Who's this?" asked Rob.

"Just a second opinion," said the doctor, approaching the bedside. "No need to worry. I can see that congratulations are in order. I'm so glad."

Juliane closed the bedroom door behind her to give the family some privacy. Only then did she finally allow herself to revel in the fact that she had been able to save a life. *Durham.* Her colleague's bruised and battered face popped into her mind. If she'd stayed near the shop instead of being more concerned about saving her own life, would she have been able to save him, too?

She accessed the datastream and drafted a message to Durham while she made her way back to the gated yard. He might not ever be able to receive it, let alone read it, but it felt cathartic to compose it all the same.

"I don't know where you are now, but I'm in some little community called Woodspring. It's not far from New York, or at least, what's left of New York, but there are people here. You would have enjoyed the party they were throwing when we arrived. Supposedly, there is an even larger group in the city.

"You teased me about my degree, but guess what? I delivered a baby last night." The corners of her lips turned up. "Although, after seeing what I've seen, I'll never understand why some women want to go natural. Nature is so poorly designed." Her smile slipped. "I don't know why I'm telling you all this. I don't suspect this means anything to you anymore. But I just want to say—" She pressed her lips together. Her mental eye hovered over the delete key. *If only thoughts were as easy to control.* She added the words "I miss you," and hit send before she could change her mind.

"Did I hear you tell the other guy they're going to be okay?"

Juliane jumped at Lyall's question. She must be more tired than she realized not to notice he'd been the one to open the gate for the doctor. She dismissed the datastream connection. "Yes," said Juliane with a smile. "I am happy to say that they are all resting comfortably." Rob's exhausted expression sprang to mind. "At least, the mother and child are."

"How can we repay you?" Lyall's eyes shone in the morning light. "I don't know how you managed it, but thank you."

"I did what I could," said Juliane. She looked at the gate. On the other side lay woods and the abandoned cars-turned-campsite. As much as she was looking forward to the idea of reaching the city, and starting to work on restoring society, her body craved rest. She yawned. "I don't suppose there is a room around here I could sleep in?"

"Of course there is," he said, placing his hand on her shoulder. "After what you managed to do here, no one is going to turn you away. Mine's the one right next door." He pointed. "But erm . . . have you seen Morgan?"

Juliane yawned. "Not recently. The last I saw her, she was going that way." She gestured at the gate. "The doctor," she nodded in the direction Lyall had pointed moments ago, "I mean the *other* doctor—she called him. He might know where she is. Now, which room is yours? That one?" She pointed.

He nodded. "It's unlocked."

"Thanks. Oh, and by the way, when you do see her, make sure that you tell her that I told her there was nothing to worry about."

Lyall spun on his heel so fast, he left a hole in the dirt by the open gate. She sighed watching him go. The boy had it for Morgan bad. Juliane had thought that's what she had with Louis, years ago. *You wound up better off,* she told herself, blinking away the moisture which threatened to fill her eyes before anyone could see. *Imagine what might have happened if he had stuck around.* Louis's wife, the woman he'd left Juliane for, had died in an automotive accident. A drunken Louis had been behind the wheel. *He did you a favor.* She tried to steel her shoulders but swayed where she stood instead. She needed to find someplace to lay down.

Juliane barely noticed the details of Lyall's home as she made her way inside. All she cared to find was a room with an empty bed. She found one in the first room on her right. The bed inside was narrow and covered with a thick faded quilt. It was beautiful. Juliane pulled the coverings over her head to block out the sunlight and soon was asleep.

⁓

She woke to the sound of a creaky door opening. Birds chirped outside, but it had to still be early morning. She expecting to see Lyall or even Morgan. Instead, Juliane was taken aback to find the doctor instead. She sat up.

The man held up a dingy pink dress and some underthings. "I've brought you a change of clothes," he said with a whisper. "Take them. It'll make you less easy to spot on the road."

Juliane frowned at his offering but took it all the same. "Um, thank you?" She had no idea what he was talking about but arguing would delay her ability to go back to sleep.

The man looked at her expectedly.

She frowned. *What, does he think I am going to get changed with him in the room?* She held up the bundle. "Thank you," she repeated, hoping he would take the hint to exit.

"You need to leave."

"I wasn't planning on staying. Just passing through."

He clenched his jaw and nodded toward the door. "I mean now. You need to leave now."

Still clutching the pink dress in her hand, Juliane crossed her arms under her breasts. As much as she wanted nothing more than to get out of the rags that covered her body, she wasn't ready to leave the comfort of her bed, nor did she appreciate being bossed around. "No," said Juliane. "I've been up all night doing *your* job. I need a chance to rest."

"I don't think you comprehend the situation—"

Juliane flicked her fingers and rolled her eyes. "I *comprehend* a lot more than you think I do."

The man glanced over his shoulder and back at Juliane. "Perhaps I'm going about this the wrong way. I'll start over. I'm Doctor Thomas." He offered his hand. "You were right, before. We've met. I treated a friend of yours—fifteen years ago."

He said it like that should mean something. "My memory hasn't been its best recently," she said, forcing a smile on her lips. "Doctor." She ignored the extended hand and looked him square in the eyes. A query to the datastream matched the name and his image with one of the physicians working at a hospital not far from her office in Worcester. It was all she could do to keep the smile plastered on her face. Durham would still be alive if that facility were open.

Her vision blurred, reducing the doctor to a brown-and-peach blob, though his name remained clear. She shook her head, and her vision was once again clear.

"I know you're tired," He said. "You've no doubt been through a lot, but it's time to go. Here, I'll help." He swooped her out of the bed in a single rushing movement before Juliane registered what he was doing. Juliane tried to twist herself out of his grip, but her exhausted body was no match for the strength of his arms as he carried her out into the hallway.

"Um. What do you think you're doing?" She kicked. "Put me down." Juliane curled the fingers of her free hand and jabbed upward. The base of her palm connected with his chin. It wasn't a solid hit, but enough to catch him by surprise all the same. He loosened his grip. She tumbled to the floor. She rolled to her feet and tried to run, but he grabbed her arm before she could move an inch.

"You don't understand," the doctor panted.

"You're right. I don't. Because you're obviously crazy," she replied.

"I didn't want to have to do this," he said. He reached into his pocket and pulled out a syringe.

Juliane's eyes widened. She attempted to pull back, but his grip wouldn't break. She willed her cells to redirect the light in order to make herself invisible, much like how Morgan's stealth suit operated, but the process took more than a heartbeat. She was still translucent when he pulled her back toward him.

Juliane attempted to pry his hand off her arm, but his grip was too tight. He raised the syringe. She kneed him in the crotch. Her assailant doubled over for a moment but did not let go. Juliane raised her leg again. He shifted, protecting his groin area as he returned upright. Juliane's foot connected with his ankle.

"Stop it," he said. He struck her with the syringe. Its needle pierced her flesh. A sensation like the burn of ice filled her veins as its contents entered her system. He released his hold and took a step back. "I'm sorry it had to be this way, but I'm trying to do what I wasn't able to do for your friend," he answered.

The empty syringe fell to the ground. Juliane touched her neck where the needle had entered. Blood smeared her finger. "What did you do?" Adrenaline battled with whatever he'd injected her with in her system. The drug proved stronger. Her thoughts grew sluggish. Her fingers appeared to sparkle and leave a trail as they moved. She closed one eye, hoping to stop a wave of nausea. Her stomach flip-flopped. Arms scooped her up.

A beating heart sounded next to her ear, bringing back the memory of Louis carrying her to his car after she'd twisted her ankle dancing. The same night, they'd allowed the boundary between boss and employee to blur. Her great mistake. "Louis," she said, cuddling into the sound. As much as she'd convinced herself it was the worst decision of her life, deep down, she knew she'd do it all over again. But he was gone, just like Durham was now, too.

"Shh now. Don't fight it."

Don't fight it. Someone else had used those words. *Alan,* she recalled. He'd used that same phrase after injecting her with the gene assist serum. He'd hidden the risk from her until it was too late. It wasn't the only thing he'd hidden . . . Her adrenaline spiked with her anger. She tried to move her head, but it was like a lead ball. Another needle flashed across her mind's eye. The doctor's needle had struck like a serpent's bite. This one, however, descended slowly enough for her brain to capture every detail as it came closer to her forehead. A voice—not Alan's—whispered in her ear. There was something she needed to remember. She tried to focus on what the whispered voice was saying.

"Trust me," said the doctor, breaking her concentration. "I'm saving your life."

Ten

STEPHEN

Rose-gray light from the rising sun colored Bean's features. A soft smile, begging to be kissed, graced her lips. Stephen was inclined to give them what they wanted. "Hold that thought," she said with a husky chuckle. "I'll be right back." She walked away, no doubt to take care of the needs of a demanding bladder. Stephen would need to do the same—eventually. He appreciated the view of her backside until she vanished into the forest. After she was gone, he crossed his arms behind his head and lay back down. He might not have slept long, but at least his dreams were finally getting better.

A stick snapped, and not from the direction where Bean had disappeared. He turned over onto his stomach. Thoughts of Bean, and what he'd like to do with her when she returned, ceased. Another twig snapped. This time much, much closer. Leaves shook, and Stephen saw a flash of blue. Whoever had been in the woods with them the night before must have returned. The leaves parted, and a man stepped into view. His clothing, torn in several places, hung from his frame. He carried a sack draped across his shoulders.

Stephen tensed. He accessed the datastream in search of Bean's signature. He needed to warn her to stay put. He blinked as his stomach lurched. The evening spent in the digital world had drained the little energy he'd gained eating the skewers of meat the night before. The race to Ahman's campsite and the hike back out in the pitch of night must have taken a larger toll than he'd expected. He blinked, leaving the datastream without informing Bean of their visitor.

He tensed and readied himself to fight or flee. The old man took a step closer. *Does he see me?* Stephen wondered. The man took another step. Stephen pressed his lips together. His stomach rumbled loudly enough that even Bean should have been able to hear it. He cursed under his breath.

"Who are you?" growled the old man. "You shouldn't be here. This is my land."

Standing, Stephen held up his hands. "Sorry, I didn't know anyone lived around here. I'll be on my way." The man didn't need to know about Bean.

"You knew this land belonged to someone," said the man. He pointed to a sign nailed into a tree that read, "Private Property. Trespassers will be shot."

Stephen took a step back. "Look, I didn't see that last night. It was too dark, and I'm just passing through. You want me to go. Fine. I'll go." Stephen bent and threw their meager possessions into the blanket. Grabbing the bundle, he turned to leave.

But the man had crossed the distances between them while he worked and grabbed Stephen's shoulder. "Compensation is in order," he said gesturing at Stephen's makeshift sack.

Stephen tried to shrug the man's hand away, but his grip remained tight. "Let go of me."

"Not until you pay me."

The man's energy, in such close proximity, became impossible to ignore. All he had to do was open himself to absorb it. *You don't have to take it all*, the voice in his head whispered. *Alan's wrong. You're still in control. Just take a little, then stop.* Stephen's stomach cramped. The clearing began to spin as a wave of hunger struck. *Besides, it's self-defense.* Nadia's face flashed in his mind. Gone was the warmth from the night's dream. Her eyes were once again vacant orbs that saw nothing and yet seemed to drill right through to his soul.

Stephen's legs wobbled. Another wave of hunger-induced lightheadedness threatened to send him back to the forest floor. "Let. Go. Of. Me," he said between clenched teeth.

The man's fingers dug into the meat of his shoulder like a claw, unaware of the danger he was putting himself in. "Hand over the blanket."

Stephen's eyes tightened. He turned his face. His instincts took over. Waves of energy crested over the flimsy wall of self-control he'd constructed, flooding his senses. The pressure on his arm abated, though the man still hadn't broken contact. The part of Stephen not reveling in the euphoria that came with the energy surge wondered if the man could get away from him at this point if he tried.

Pressure built, begging for release. Emotions like fright and guilt fell by the wayside. Only the promise of joy remained. *Bean.* Flush with power as he was, he could touch her without putting her in danger. *I can do more than touch her.* He extended his senses, connecting his brain with sensors embedded in the surrounding trees back when people still worried about monitoring the health of the forest. If he could only find where she'd disappeared to before the old man had arrived.

The old man. The thought was a cold shower on his brain. Stephen opened his eyes and grabbed the man's hand. It was stiff and cold. Stephen uncurled the man's fingers as gently as he could. He winced as one knuckle cracked anyway. The sound was all too clear with his heightened hearing. The man crumpled to the ground the second he let go.

Leaves crunched behind him. Stephen spun to find Bean on the other side of the clearing. She looked at the form at the base of Stephen's feet. Stephen reached out to her, not knowing whether he wanted her to take his hand or if he was trying to warn her away. "I . . . I . . . ." he began. Alan's offer in the middle of the night came back to him.

His shoulders slumped. Even if Alan lied about having a cure, he told the truth when he said that joining him would keep Bean safe from the out-of-control monster he'd become. Stephen wanted to explain what had happened, to offer an excuse, but it was as if his tongue were solid lead.

Bean looked at him with eyes like stone. "You did what you had to," she said after what seemed like an eternity.

Stephen used his enhanced senses to analyze her face. He captured every twitch of her mouth and every blink of her eyes, memorizing every inch of her. He also couldn't help noticing that, though nothing in her features gave her away, she hadn't stepped toward him either. He dropped his gaze. While he appreciated her words, he knew the truth. He could have run. He could have generated the bolt Bean was so fond of and subdued him with a touch. The man hadn't needed to die.

"I don't know how he snuck past me," she said, breaking the agonizing silence that followed. "There's a trailer parked not too far from here. I'm guessing it's his."

Stephen kept his gaze locked on the body at his feet. The sensible thing would be to take Alan up on his offer before it expired, but that meant leaving Bean without telling her why. *I'll find a reason to go off by myself. Worst case, she'll worry I got myself lost for a while, but eventually, she'll give up and move on. Best case, she'll be safe. And if Alan's cure does work, I can always find her again—assuming the war doesn't find me first.* "He might have a family. I should go there and tell them what happened."

"He doesn't." Bean shook her head. "I peeked in the window. At the trailer." She pressed her lips together. "I saw . . ." She clenched her jaw. She nodded at the body on the ground. "Trust me. No one is going to miss him."

"Still, I should bury him. You go on ahead. I'll catch up."

She was next to Stephen in a matter of steps, taking the bundled supplies from him. "We don't have a shovel, and we've got a lot of walking to do."

Stephen gestured at the body. "But it doesn't seem right to leave him lying here."

Bean turned and walked away without replying.

Stephen made a move to follow her. Then he stopped. *Now's your chance*, he told himself. *Let her walk away.*

However, as much as he knew he should turn and go in the other direction, his legs wouldn't budge. Bean's parents had left her with Dr. Lambda and the Watch when she was a child following her sister's death, as if she'd caused the girl's death intentionally. They'd abandoned her, knowing she would be experimented upon without an explanation or even a goodbye. *Cowards.* No, he decided. As much as he knew it was the right thing to do, he couldn't make her go through that again. All he had to do was keep his distance a little while longer. He jogged after her, leaving the body of the old man on the forest floor.

Eleven

JULIANE

Juliane's body hadn't needed much incentive to drift back into sleep after the grueling night before. However, her mind wasn't inclined to be carried off so easily, even if the sedative working its way through her veins continued to make her thoughts sluggish. Even worse, there was little she could think of to stop the drug's progress, short of stopping her heart from beating. *Filter. I can't stop it, but I can filter it.*

While the rest of her body lay limp in the doctor's arms, she issued a command to her liver, prioritizing its breakdown of the drugs in her system. Her mind grew sharper by the second. She continued to keep still, so as not to alert her kidnapper until she was sure she would be able to get away without risking another injection, or worse.

Despite her intention, her fingers twitched of their own accord. Dr. Thomas paused. *He noticed.* Juliane readied herself to fight.

"Morgan," he said. "I can explain."

Juliane resisted the urge to sigh in relief. She'd been rescued.

"Can you, now?" Morgan asked.

"I found her this way, by the wall. Obviously overcome with exhaustion and probably dehydration, too. I'm just carrying her to a more comfortable accommodation."

"Well, that's considerate of you. Although I am rather surprised you've left the new mother's side. She could have died. Still might."

"Both mother and baby are resting comfortably," said the doctor. "I thought their savior deserved to do so, too."

"I agree, which is why I was surprised to find Lyall's room empty after he told me that's where he'd sent her."

Juliane risked opening her eyes a sliver. The scene in front of her rippled as if she were viewing it from underwater.

"Do you want to tell me what you are really doing?" asked Morgan.

The doctor took a step back. "You know as well as I do what will happen to her if *he* gets his hands on her."

Morgan's features twisted, and a strange expression came over her face. Juliane fought to keep the contents of her stomach down. "Do I?"

The doctor took a step back. "No—"

"I'm starting to think you aren't committed." The words came from Morgan's mouth, but the voice was all wrong. The dark memory fluttered at the edge of recognition. Juliane tried to fixate on it, but it was like attempting to catch smoke with a butterfly net.

"I took an oath," said the doctor.

"So, you're fond of saying." Morgan inched closer. "I don't see, then, why it's so difficult for you to take another."

"I can't be a part of this."

Part of what? Juliane wondered. Colors swirled. The goat appeared next to Morgan. Its limbs stretched and twisted until it became the size of the mare. *I'm hallucinating.* The drug, it seemed, had not yet been fully expunged from her system.

"I don't recall you having an issue when you begged us to take your family in."

"That was before."

Morgan shook her head. The movement left trails across Juliane's vision. "Your son knew what would happen if he left the city. You both did."

I'm going to be sick. Juliane closed her eyes and stopped trying to make sense of the conversation.

"He did it for me," the man muttered. "He left a note. Only way for us to be free."

"You know what this means."

Juliane risked peeking again after the wave of nauseousness went away. This time, there was no sign of the goat and her vision was clear. *Finally*, thought Juliane.

She twisted in the doctor's arms. She expected him to tighten his hold or fight her, but instead, he turned and lowered her feet to the ground behind him.

A single tear rolled down his face. "I was only trying to protect you," he whispered.

"Protect me from what?" Juliane touched the sore spot where the needle had entered her bloodstream. "A good night's sleep? What is wrong with you?"

"It's going to be alright Juliane," said Morgan coming to Juliane's side. Juliane couldn't help noticing her voice sounded normal. The change Juliane had heard in its timbre, must have been as real as the horse-sized goat she'd seen.

"Alright? Alright! He tried to kidnap me. Injected me with who knows what."

"You'll survive."

Juliane glared at Morgan. "Why are you so calm about this? He. Drugged. Me."

"Because I know you don't have anything to worry about." Morgan shot Dr. Thomas a look. "Isn't that right, doctor?" The doctor nodded meekly.

"Forgive me if I'm not convinced," said Juliane, taking satisfaction in the purple bruise blooming across the doctor's face from where she'd hit him.

"You should be."

"And why is that?" Juliane clenched and unclenched her fist as she fought the urge to give him another one.

"He's not a bad person." Morgan held up a hand before Juliane could protest. "Really. He's not . . . but . . . um . . . well you see, Dr. Thomas lost his son recently," said Morgan as if that explained everything. "I'd hoped being part of a birth might help give him a purpose. Obviously, I made a huge mistake. If anyone is at fault, it's me. I'm sure now that he's had a second to realize what he's done, he's appalled."

Dr. Thomas nodded his head eagerly.

"I don't care if he is the reincarnation of Mother Teresa," said Juliane, glaring at the man. "He needs to be locked up."

Morgan sighed. "Yeah, well, unfortunately, it's complicated. He's the only doctor in a fifty-mile radius."

Juliane pressed her lips together. The conversation she'd overheard back at the tavern came back to her—men, speaking freely about selling a woman to settle a bar tab, with no fear of retribution. Those that lived in the tower must be so desperate for medical knowledge, they were willing to turn a blind eye to the man's obvious mental unbalance, too. Justice, it would seem, was another victim of the global catastrophe. Rage bubbled under her skin, burning more of the drug away. However, she didn't act on it. Morgan's words had made it clear lashing out would do nothing in this new world order except further exhaust her.

Morgan glanced at Juliane through the corner of her eye. "Then again, he *was* . . ."

Lyall burst into the hallway. "Oh, good," he said spotting Juliane. "You found her. I thought for sure you'd be asleep until lunchtime, but if you're still up, um . . . Rebecca's asking for you. I told her that you needed your rest, but . . ." His expression was like a beaten dog. "Sorry, I hate to ask, but do you mind staying up a little longer?"

The doctor tensed and lurched toward Lyall and the doorway. "Did something happen while I was gone?" he asked.

Juliane took advantage of the Lyall's appearance to put more distance between herself and the mustached man. However, her movement was still sluggish as her body continued to filter the last of the drug out of her system. Pressure built in her lower abdomen. She would need to relieve herself sooner rather than later to make sure whatever he had injected her with, was fully gone. "I think you've helped here enough," said Juliane. She touched the spot on her neck again. "Don't you?"

Dr. Thomas hung his head.

Either not reading the body language in the room or choosing to ignore it, Lyall answered, "Rebecca's asking for Juliane, here. Don't worry. She's okay. Said it was a women's thing."

"I'll be right there," said Juliane, straightening her back. She would show these people they had other options. She would show everyone. She shared a look with Morgan and nodded. They didn't need to put more patients at risk by allowing people like Dr. Thomas to continue to walk free. Not when anyone who'd been upgraded could access medical information the same way she did. However, when she tried to take a step, she stumbled. She bit back a curse. *There goes my grand exit.*

Lyall came running to her side. "Oh, wow, you've got to be exhausted. Are you sure? I can still go back and tell her you were asleep when I found you."

"I can manage a while longer," said Juliane. It wasn't like she would risk sleep again until she was sure Dr. Thomas was as far away from her as possible.

"Lyall," said Morgan, "Why don't you go with Juliane? Just to make sure she gets there alright, while I escort the doctor back to the bridge."

Lyall pursed his lips. "Are you sure he shouldn't stick around a little bit longer? I mean, just in case?"

"There's nothing he can do at this point she can't," said Morgan, pointing at Juliane.

The doctor looked like he was going to argue but then slumped his shoulders in defeat. "She's right," he said. He turned to Morgan. "And there are several lives still counting on me back in the city. I'll be good." His eyes shimmered. "Plenty of work to go around."

"Okay, then," said Lyall. "But you're staying a little longer though, right, Morg?"

A myriad of emotions flickered across Morgan's face. "I'll stay as long as I can," she said, "but—" She clenched her jaw, cutting off whatever she was about to say next and addressed Juliane and Lyall instead. "Go and see what Rebecca needs." Her gaze shifted to the side as if listening to someone whisper in her ear. Her mouth twisted in a frown for a moment, but she nodded. "I'll come back as soon as I can."

Twelve

STEPHEN

Bean walked ahead of him. She usually preferred a brisk pace, but she moved at a faster clip than he was used to. As the distance between them seemed intentional, he hadn't attempted to keep up. He didn't blame her for wanting to be as far away from him as possible; he disgusted himself, too. An image of Nadia's accusing face flashed across his mind. His stomach turned, and for once, he didn't feel hungry.

He looked toward the horizon. The sky would be taking on the golden shade of evening before much longer, forcing them to stop for the night. Although they'd kept to back roads, it was getting harder to avoid formerly urban areas. While Stephen expected the various highway stops along the way to be abandoned, the man they'd encountered in the woods was proof they weren't entirely empty. They'd have to be more careful when they camped tonight. He didn't want to add more ghosts to his dreams.

Thoughts of the old man turned in his head. How had the man managed to approach their campsite without alerting either of them? He'd nearly been on top of them. He shuddered, thinking of what might have happened had they not awakened with the dawn.

Bean might be a warrior when alert, but she was just as helpless as anyone else while she slept. They both were. *It's a good thing, then, you don't sleep much anymore*, said the voice in Stephen's head. He steeled his jaw. *At least the main roads have better sensors.*

A bird's eye view of their location appeared in front of his vision, representing their location as a pulsating dot. The satellite image was at least fifteen years old but good enough to give him a basic idea of how to get back onto the road without straying too far from their current route to Worcester. He smiled. A small creek not far ahead would provide them with needed freshwater and might give him a chance to wash away the stink of death clinging to him. "There's water up ahead," Stephen called out, grateful for an excuse to break the silence between them.

"Okay," Bean answered in reply.

Stephen mentally begged her to say something, anything else, but nothing more came. "If we turn left at the creek," said Stephen after the silence became too much, "we might even reach the next town before night."

She paused but continued to look forward as if searching for the creek. "Um . . . do you really think that's a good idea?"

So, she doesn't trust you around other people anymore either. Good. A sour taste filled his month. *She just hasn't realized that also means her, too.* He straightened and took a breath. *Talk to her.* He might not be able to tell her where he was going, but he could at least tell her about what was going on inside his head. He'd explain why they needed to go their separate ways.

Bean looked back. Her green eyes pulled at his soul. The minute the truth left his mouth would likely be the last time he'd ever see them.

His resolve evaporated. His chest ached. He spit on the ground. "Bug got into my mouth," he said.

Bean's forehead wrinkled, and for a moment, she looked at him like she had the day they met.

Stephen clung to the expression on her face like a life raft. Now that the silence was broken, he wouldn't allow it to take back control. "Should we stop and try to find something to eat?" asked Stephen, forcing his features into a smile while burying his other thoughts. They still needed to talk, but maybe, just maybe, they could have one more night together before they did.

Bean's brow smoothed. "Oh, right this way. We have a lovely selection tonight. Your choice, weeds with a side of weeds, or grubs."

"Oh, had I realized that bug was an appetizer, I wouldn't have been so quick to spit it out."

Bean snorted and allowed Stephen to catch up, but turned her gaze forward. "So, towns. You're sure?"

She was close now. Stephen knew that if she turned in that moment and looked at him like she had by the river the night before they'd reached New York, it would be over. He would have no choice but to confess everything, from his spiraling loss of control to how he spent his evenings in the virtual world instead of sleeping. The tall grass to their left rustled, shattering the moment.

Bean's shoulders tensed as she dropped to a crouch. More grass shifted. Whatever was causing the noise was big and coming closer by the second. She glanced at Stephen and gestured for him to duck out of view as her palms flared with purple lightning. The grass parted, and out of the brush, a man on horseback appeared.

He was shirtless and covered in dirt. Long scratches crisscrossed his torso. What remaining clothing he had on was in tatters. Close cropped hair, more silver than yellow, did nothing to hide a large bruise on his head. The man groaned and swayed in his saddle. The purple light surrounding Bean's fist blinked out. She caught the man as he slid head-first from the saddle.

Be careful, said Stephen with his mind. *He might be dangerous.*

Bean looked over her shoulder at Stephen and raised an eyebrow. *Please. Just look at him,* her voice answered in his mind. *He looks about as dangerous as you were when we first met.*

Stephen pursed his lips but did not argue further. Coming to Bean's side, he helped to lower the man to the ground. *So now what? Dangerous or not, we can't help. We don't have enough supplies for ourselves.*

We don't, but he might. She gestured toward his mount.

The horse, relieved of its burden, had dropped its head and was nibbling the grass. Stephen approached it from its side, careful not to startle it or cause it to break into a run. As Bean had pointed out, a pair of saddlebags hung from its withers. Stephen lifted the flap on the bag closest to him and rummaged through its contents.

"Well?" Bean asked out loud.

"Not much," answered Stephen. "No, wait." His hand grabbed a long cylindrical object wrapped in plastic. "Jerky," he said pulling the bit of meat out. "Guess dinner's on me after all."

Bean laughed. "Aw, you cooked."

The man groaned. Stephen's triumph morphed into shame at the realization that without a second thought, he was ready to take advantage of a man who had done him no wrong—an injured man at that. His smile slipped. His parents would never recognize the person he'd become.

It's not just about your survival, the voice inside him said. *Think about Bean. You want one more night together, then you'll have to eat. You won't be able to control the hunger on grubs alone. Better yet, say goodbye now. That's all you have to do. Say goodbye.*

"Jule… Juliane?"

Stephen froze. His eyes narrowed on the injured man. "What did you say?" *Juliane's not that unusual of a name. There is no way he's asking for the same person as the woman we are looking for.*

"Must have bumped his head pretty hard to mistake you for a person with a name like that," said Bean with a shrug.

"Need to find Juliane."

"Sorry, but no Juliane here," said Bean, standing up. "But we really do appreciate this very fine horse you are giving us."

Stephen closed his eyes. What would Nadia and Chad say if they saw him now? "We can't leave him lying there."

"Why not?" asked Bean. "Look at him. He's pretty much dead already, and you said it yourself, we don't have enough supplies."

Stephen looked at the wrapped piece of meat in his hand, shining bright with the reflection of the sun. He steeled his shoulders. What had he told Chad before leaving the house the night of that disastrous supply run? He wanted to have a life that was more than mere survival. He ripped the jerky's wrapper open and crouched on his heels beside the man. This was his chance to prove he wasn't a complete monster. At least, not yet. "Here," he said, holding the jerky next to the man's lips.

"That's supposed to be our dinner," said Bean.

"I felt a jar when I was fishing around in the saddlebag. Could be more to eat in there."

"And if there isn't?"

"Then you can take it to the creek and bring back enough water for the three of us."

"Oh, can I?" asked Bean her voice dripping with sarcasm.

"Bean, be reasonable."

"I am," she said. "You're the one who seems to have lost his mind."

"Please."

"Fine," said Bean. She reached into the bag and pulled out a canteen much like the one they'd lost back before the battle of the Watchtower. Then she turned on her heel and raced off in the direction of the stream.

At first, Stephen assumed she'd run out of annoyance at him, but after she'd disappeared, he began to wonder if she ran because she was more afraid of what he might do to the man while she was gone. The sour taste returned to his mouth as he realized she didn't see him as a hero in either scenario.

Stephen eyeballed the man. He was filthy and bloodied, but then again, so was Stephen. However, the man's chest was twice as wide as Stephen's, and he had a square jaw and an athletic frame. "I bet you never had these sorts of problems with women when you were my age," Stephen muttered.

The man on the ground chuckled. "You have no idea, kid."

Stephen jumped back. "You heard all that."

"As you were so kind to point out, I'm not dead yet." The other man rubbed his forehead before trying to roll to his side. "Though your girl seemed ready to write me off."

"She does what she has to do." Stephen bit his tongue before answering. "We both do."

The man sighed. "I know her type. Reminds me of my missing friend."

"Juliane."

"Yeah . . . Juliane." The injured man looked at the horse. "I hate to ask after you so kindly pulled me down from that nightmare on four feet, but would you mind helping me stand back up?"

Stephen hesitated, not wanting to place a hand on the man's exposed skin. "I don't think you should be moving around too much right now. That bump on your head looks nasty."

The man touched his head. "Suspect it looks worse than it feels."

"You would have landed on your skull if we weren't around. Pretty sure that's a bad thing."

The man laughed. "Yeah, well . . . sorry about the dramatics, but when you two appeared out of nowhere, I thought it best if I played possum. Figured you were more likely to leave me alone if I wasn't a threat."

"You played possum." It was a statement as much as a question.

"Well, yeah. I used to play more than a few sports back in the day. Could have gone pro if I'd kept at it instead of listening to my parents. I've been known to make an injury work for me."

"You mean all that was an act?" asked Stephen in disbelief. "Then why are you asking me to help stand you back up?"

"Because it's not entirely an act. More like an exaggeration. Also, I've been on that horse for god-knows-how-long, and my legs cramped up."

Stephen glanced in the direction he'd sent Bean to collect water from the creek. She was going to call him worse than an idiot when she returned and learned how much Stephen had been duped. Stephen's stomach rumbled, reminding him that Bean's anger was the lesser threat to the stranger's general health and safety at the moment. "If you aren't dying, you should leave before she gets back." Stephen took another step away. He bit into the jerky stick and had swallowed before its spicy taste registered on his tongue.

"Leave? But I just told you, my muscles are cramped."

"She's not going to care about your muscles." An image of Bean fighting a beastman beneath the remains of the Apex building flashed in his mind. She'd taken out the man and his surgically enhanced frame before they'd learned the beastman had been sent to the underground chamber to help rescue them from the Watch. No, Bean wouldn't care about the stranger's muscles at all.

The man smiled. "In my experience, when it comes to the ladies, I've found the opposite to be true."

Stephen looked at the stranger, then at the horse. "I'm serious. Take your horse and get as far away from here as possible." The loss of the mount would mean they'd have to continue their journey on foot, but at least Stephen wouldn't have another death on his conscience.

The man sat up with a groan and extended his hand. "Nice to meet you, Serious. I'm Durham."

Stephen stared at Durham's hand. His stomach growled again, reminding him that a bit of dried meat wouldn't sustain him long. He took another step back, crossing one arm over his chest while he took a second enormous bite out of the jerky stick.

"So, dinner is on again, I see," said Bean, returning with the canteen in hand.

She glanced down at Durham and back at Stephen. Her lips narrowed. Durham dropped his hand and started to stand. Bean tensed.

"I wouldn't make any sudden movements if I were you," said Stephen.

Durham sat back and raised his hands with his palms out. "Wouldn't dream of it. I'd hate to get another bump on the head to match the first one," he said pointing at the injury.

Stephen shook his head. "She's capable of giving you more than a bump."

Bean's gaze shifted back to Stephen. Her eyes narrowed as she cocked her head. *What?* He projected the question her way via the datastream. *It's true, isn't it?*

Durham laughed. "Of that, I have no doubt."

The corner of Bean's mouth inched upward while she handed the canteen to Durham. "Here, drink something before I regret leaving this one on his own for so long." *We'll talk about this later,* Bean's voice said in his brain.

Durham took a long sip, causing water to run down his chin. He made a face, scratching at the beginnings of a beard. He looked at Stephen. "You don't happen to have a razor, do you?"

Stephen fought the urge to touch his own face. Though they'd been in the wilderness for days, his facial hair could hardly be described as a beard. "How old are you?" he blurted out.

"Older by the second," replied Durham. "I take it that's a no."

"So, are we camping here?" said Bean. "Or did you still want to try to make it into town?"

"You don't want to go that way," said Durham, pointing in the direction he'd come. "There's nothing but ghost towns, monster birds, and friendly people who are under the impression giving a person a concussion is a nice way to say hello." He touched his head with a wince.

Bean snorted. "Some of that's the same this way, too."

Durham sighed. "And here I thought the adventurous life was behind me after leaving the ACI."

The humor left Bean's face, and her body tensed. "You were with the ACI," she said in a voice cold enough to freeze a waterfall.

What is the ACI again? Stephen asked her with his mind.

How do you not know? Bean replied. *Oh, that's right, you grew up in the middle of nowhere. They're only the people responsible for ending the world.* An image of a widescreen television hung on an apartment wall flashed in his mind. Graphs with plummeting lines floated above a banner of scrolling text. ACI repeated over and over again. Random other initials would appear afterward, followed by bright red numbers. A stack of children's books and a pair of dolls lay on the floor of the apartment. Then the image was gone.

"Officially, yes . . . as Louis's personal counsel," continued Durham, unaware of their exchange online. "But in reality, the law had very little to do with what I did. Mostly, all I was expected to do was to make sure he was sober enough to attend interviews and to make sure the girls we met on our travels were . . . ah . . . well, taken care of." His eyes sparkled. "For example, there was this one time—we went cruising on Lake Como, just outside of Milan. Louis spots these women drinking espresso and—wait, that story ended with us *both* in front of a judge."

Durham held up a hand. "Okay, better example. There was this other time in Prague. We were out celebrating closing on a brand-new location when this model comes up to us and . . ." He glanced at Bean. "Er, you're older than eighteen, right? I mean, I am guessing that's not a thing anymore, but old habits . . ."

"Such a tough life you must have led before," said Bean, rolling her eyes.

The grin slipped from Durham's face. "Yeah, it sounds bad now, I'm not like that any—I mean I quit after Louis—er . . . when he . . . we were just kids with more money than sense back then. That is to say, it was a long time ago."

Bean turned to Stephen. "I'm voting we skip town tonight." She gestured toward Durham. "There could be more winners like this guy."

"So, Juliane," interrupted Stephen. "That's the name you called out when you were pretending to be dying." The name had been nothing but a coincidence. *But what if it isn't?* Was she close by after all? If so, he wouldn't have to go into the beastmen's camp—wouldn't have to trust Alan. Even better, he wouldn't have to leave Bean. His nostrils flared with hope's breath. "What's her last name?"

"Faris," replied Durham. He took another sip from the canteen. "Dr. Juliane Faris." Durham looked up when both Stephen and Bean fell silent. "I take it you've heard of her. Not sure how she'll feel about that."

Don't say a word, Bean's voice said in his head.

But you heard him; he's looking for her, too. Bet they were traveling together and got split up.

Or she ditched him on purpose. We've only heard his version of the story. We have no way of knowing why they split up. What if they weren't traveling together by choice? He's the admitted womanizing friend of a terrorist, after all. If it was up to me, I'd probably ditch him the first chance I got, too.

You're being paranoid.

No, I'm being sensible. You should try it sometime.

"So, what's the verdict?" Durham asked. "I know that look. I assume you were talking about what to do with me."

"He's a smart one," said Bean

"I'm funny too," Durham said with a smile. "Or so I've been told."

"I bet," said Bean. "So, Mr. Funny Guy, give us one reason why we shouldn't take that horse," she gestured toward the animal that was grazing on shoots of grass, "and leave you here."

"I'll give you two. One, because a cold front is rolling in, and unless you're considering changing your mind about going into town, you'll want to take this time to build a fire. Otherwise, it's going to be a long, long night. And two, because you won't get very far. Take a look at Silver over there. She's done. You push her any more tonight, and she'll drop. Do you really want to be on top of her when that happens?"

Stephen examined the mare. Now that Durham pointed it out, he noticed white froth on the animal's withers. Its nostrils flared.

"Silver?" asked Bean.

"I had to call her something. Especially when I was cursing at her for not listening to a word I said. Sounded like a horsey name."

"And the cold front?" Bean placed her hands on her hips. "How can you be so sure about that?"

"I can't seem to be able to make a call, or even send a note." Durham touched the bruise on his temple. "Must have gotten banged up harder than I thought, but my inbox still works. I get a data dump from the weather bots. Always liked to make my own forecast."

Stephen glanced up. Not a cloud marked the sky. "Yeah, well, at least there shouldn't be any rain tonight." He'd had enough of the rain. The bits of his clothes not covered in dirt were black and green from mold.

"I like you, kid," said Durham. "Such the optimist."

"Quit calling me that. I'm not a kid."

"Sure, but since you haven't bothered to introduce yourself, I decided I'd give you a name—like Silver over there." The horse twitched its ears. "Really?" Durham asked it. "Now you listen to me. Why couldn't you do that two days ago, when I still had a chance of catching up with Jules?"

The horse swished her tail.

"Right. Right, you got a point. When we catch up to her, don't tell her I called her that. Makes her all sorts of crazy."

He's lost his mind, Bean's voice said in Stephen's head.

Maybe, replied Stephen, *or he's really lonely.*

That's equally uncomforting. A gust of wind caused the grass to sway like ocean waves and sent a cold shiver down Stephen's spine.

"Guess we're sleeping outdoors again, then," said Stephen out loud.

"Hooray." Bean turned and walked in the direction of the creek. "Oh, by the way, I saw some dead wood we can use for a fire not far from here," she said. "Made me think of you." She shot Durham a pointed look before disappearing to the sound of his laughter.

"You poor bastard," Durham said after his laughter died down. "You didn't stand a chance, did you?"

"Stand a chance against what?" Stephen asked.

Durham laughed harder. He raised his hand. "So, now that you two have decided not to kill me, will you please help me up? I was serious when I said my entire body is locked up. I feel worse than I did after a three-day bender in São Paulo."

Stephen took Durham's arm and helped to steady him as he rose. "Have you really traveled all over the world?"

"More than once," Durham said. "How about you? Ever gone anywhere interesting?"

"I took a train ride once," mumbled Stephen.

"The train," Durham said with a twinkle in his eyes. "Ah, that brings back some memories. I haven't taken a train ride in years. You like it?"

Stephen thought of Wes. "It was . . . memorable." Wes had insisted they take the electric train car he'd rebuilt in secret to Worcester. He'd wanted to help them get there faster. He took a breath. Wes had died on that train. If Stephen had only refused Wes's offer—told Wes to stay behind . . . Stephen's eye twitched, and he turned away, looking about the field and picking up bits of dried grass. "This will make good kindling," he said holding the bits in his hand.

"I trust your judgment," offered Durham. While a smile remained plastered on his face, it no longer reflected in his eyes."

That's one of us. "Yeah . . . well, alright then," Stephen flailed, not knowing how to respond to Durham's comment. Bean's return couldn't have come at a better moment. Soon long flames cackled, which was a good thing, as Durham proved to be right about the change in the weather.

Bean settled into the crook of his arms as the night grew long. However, Stephen made a point to pull down his sleeve so their flesh wouldn't make direct contact. Crickets played their song, though sleep avoided Stephen yet again. *I'm not going to access the datastream tonight,* he told himself. *I'm not.* But before he realized what he was doing, his avatar was looking out across a foreign cityscape, the likes of which he'd never seen and would never see in the real world. A gentle breeze ruffled his hair. His heart ached at the beauty that lay before him. *If only you were here, Bean.*

Fingers wove their way between his. Bean stood to his side. Her white-blonde hair floated in the virtual breeze. She tucked a lock behind her ear. "It's beautiful," she said.

"How'd you find me?"

"You didn't exactly make it easy." She turned back toward the vista. "You should have told me."

His heart skipped a beat as her fingers tightened around his own. "I'm sorry," he said. "I've been having a hard time falling asleep ever since—"

Bean turned to him. "I know," she said. Her normally jade-green eyes took on a dark deeper tone under the purple-red light of the twilight sky. Stephen's breath caught in his lungs at the sight. The knowledge that the sight in front of them was nothing more than a digital construct made it all the more heart-breaking. She turned away. "That's what I came here to talk to you about. I tried before . . . um . . . I thought if I—"

He sighed. "Yeah, I need to talk to you, too." He struggled to come up with words, wanting to tell her about all the things going on in his head, but at the same time, there was nothing he wanted more than to savor the moment. *Tomorrow*, he decided. *I'll tell her tomorrow.* He pulled her closer, wrapping his arms around her. Her body seemed to melt into his. "But not yet. Right now, I'm just glad you're here."

"Okay. Later then." She looked up at him. "What do you want to do until then?" The corners of her lips slid up ever so slightly in a smile that was both promise and an invitation.

Thoughts of conversation vanished as he lowered his mouth to hers. She broke from their kiss for a moment. A look flashed across her face as if there was something more she needed to say, but then she moved her lips to the base of his neck. It was as if she'd thrown gasoline onto a match. He tightened his hold around her waist. She moaned and wrapped a leg around his. His hand slipped to her thigh. Her moan grew louder, more insistent. His gaze darted around, locating a nearby wall. He released her waist, only to grab her buttocks. She wrapped her other leg around him, laughing with a throaty chuckle. It was all the encouragement he needed.

Turning, he carried her toward the building. She nibbled on his ear. Blood rushed from his brain to his groin. Using the wall as leverage, he explored her body with his lips and his hands. His chest was bare. He didn't remember removing his shirt. The fabric of her sweater offended him. He frowned, pulling at its hem.

She giggled before capturing his mouth with hers once again. The offensive garment transformed into the thinnest silk. Stephen growled as he twisted the fabric in his hand. The need to be rid of any barriers between them became primal. The bit of cloth in his hand transformed again. Cool silk became sheer lace. He broke from their kiss only long enough to see the new garment left little to the imagination, while at the same time hinted at the stuff that dreams were made of.

Her smile deepened. She reached up and caressed the back of his neck, sending shivers up and down his spine. It was almost enough to undo him.

"Bean," he said between panted breaths. "I . . . I . . ."

Her hand slid down his cheek. "I know," she said, dragging a finger across his lips.

The sheer fabric shielding her body transformed again until it was nothing at all, and Stephen was only too eager to follow her every command.

Stephen grinned from ear to ear, though his eyes remained closed. It had been the first decent night's sleep since he'd met Bean. Thoughts of Bean and what they'd done together in the digital world the night before roused him in more ways than one. He turned on his side and opened his eyes. Bean's eyes were still closed, too, but he saw the corner of her lip curve up as if she knew she was being watched. He shifted, moving to wake her with a kiss. His stomach growled.

He pulled back as if burned.

Bean's eyes opened in a flash. She jumped up—every muscles tense. "What? Did you hear something?" Her gaze darted around their impromptu campsite. "Where is he?" she whispered down to Stephen. "I knew we shouldn't have trusted him. Probably a scout. Leading a whole group to us."

"Talking about me?" asked Durham, coming around from behind a tree while zipping up his pants. "Sorry, didn't mean to cause you to freak out. I just had to water a tree and figured you'd prefer I do that elsewhere." His teeth gleamed. "That is, unless you're into that sort of thing?"

Bean's eyes flashed. "That's a no."

Durham shrugged. "You'd not believe how many times I've asked that question and gotten a different answer."

Bean glanced at Stephen. "We're leaving."

The grin disappeared from Durham's face. He held up a hand. "Listen, I'm sorry. I don't mean to sound like an asshole. Truly, I don't."

Bean arched an eyebrow. "I'd hate to be around when you're actually trying."

Durham snorted. "Seriously, though, I am sorry . . . I say things I don't mean— they just sort of come out. Like I don't have a filter. Especially since—actually, I have no idea how long I've been like this. One minute I'm heading into yet another death-by-PowerPoint presentation, and the next minute, I'm waking up in what used to be the basement of my office building but is now a pile of rubble."

Stephen and Bean shared a look. "Let me guess, you found yourself in a metal tube," said Stephen.

"Yeah. Oddest thing. I can't remember going into it." He scratched his hair. "What the hell happened, anyway?"

"That's where the end of the world started," said Stephen.

The remaining trace of humor fled Durham's expression. "So, it's all like this? Everywhere?" His shoulders slumped. "That's what Juliane suspected, but I was really hoping this was an isolated event. That someplace—"

"Not everywhere," said Bean.

Stephen frowned. Alan's warning sprang to his mind unbidden. How could he explain the full extent of why sending Durham to the Sorcerers' home turf was a bad idea without letting it slip that she might still be under Damien's control?

"Don't look at me like that," said Bean. "There's nothing we can do for him." She crossed her arms, shooting him a look that dared him to argue. "And he's like a baby out here. At least the tower has running water."

They're monsters. You said so yourself, back at the Watchtower, he projected at her.

Bean shrugged. *Yeah, well what do you call us?*

Stephen wanted nothing more to pull her back into his arms, but the ever-present ache in his stomach reminded him of the potential risk. "I've told you before," he whispered to her. "You're not a monster." *But I am,* he finished the sentence in his head, making sure that no trace of the thought inadvertently made its way to the datastream.

"You say there is a place that still has showers?" Durham perked up. "Say no more. Point me in the right direction, and I'll be on my way just as soon as I catch up with Juliane."

"He's not going to be any safer there than he is out here," continued Stephen, loud enough for Durham to hear. "The beastmen are planning an attack. Hell, they could've already done it by now." Stephen trusted Alan to hold off the attack about as much as he trusted himself around other people.

Her back straightened. "Those guys are nothing more than a bunch of has-been football players who caught us by surprise. It won't happen again." She drew herself taller. "Especially if they think for a second, they can get past our defenses."

Us, thought Stephen. She'd rejoined the Sorcerers after Alan tricked him into going with the Watch. If he left her now, would she go back there again? His stomach tied itself in a knot. She might not view the beastmen as a threat, but Stephen knew differently. The image of her mangled body lying on the floor of the operating studio filled his thoughts. *If I hadn't gotten to her in time . . . if there hadn't been a storm to pull from . . .*

Bean glanced at Durham. "Why are you still out here looking for her, anyway?"

Durham scratched at his hair. "Like I said, we were separated and—"

"I mean, I assume you've at least *tried* simply sending her a message asking where she is. Haven't you?"

The smile returned to his face. "Of course I did. Like I said, nothing's going through. But it has been a while. Maybe I'll get lucky this time." His eyes took on the glazed expression of someone accessing the datastream.

"Well? Were you able to reach her?"

"No." Durham blinked as a smile broke across his face. "I still can't send anything, but it turns out she thinks about me after all. Sent me a message from a place called Woodspring."

"Where's that?" asked Stephen.

He shook his head. "Beats me, but she says it's just outside of New York."

"I know where it is," said Bean. Her eyes narrowed, and her voice took on a razor's edge. "And if she's there, she's in more trouble than she realizes. That's where these anti-tech nut jobs settled after they came to the conclusion technology had enslaved humanity." She closed her eyes and shook her head. "Morons. They're the ones that started bombing places in the beginning. Caused the whole chain reaction." She shot a pointed look at Stephen. "I get why he's clueless, but seriously, didn't you ever ask your parents about what triggered the initial rush out of the cities in the first place?"

"Oh, I don't know. Things like keeping the windmill turning and figuring out how we were going to have enough food to last the winter seemed a bit more important than wondering what was the motivation behind some wackos."

"Whatever." Bean turned her attention back to Durham. "The only problem was they neglected to plan out what would happen after humanity's so-called liberation." She shrugged. "Personally, for all the effort they put into it, I don't think they ever really believed their plan would actually work. At least, not everywhere." She gestured at the field surrounding them. "We think most of them left the movement after their crazy leader, Louis Evans left the scene. Those of us who stuck around in the city have kept an eye on them ever since, in case someone else ever tried to pick up where Louis left off."

"You heard Ahman," said Stephen. "Juliane and Louis had an argument right before he . . . you know . . . went poof." He made an exploding gesture with his hands. "We have no idea what they argued about or if she caused the bomb to go off early. He said the people holding Gena acted like the first explosion was a surprise. They might not care about Louis or their original mission anymore, but if they do, and if they come to the conclusion Juliane's somehow responsible for messing up their plans, then . . ."

"So, I guess we're going to Woodspring," said Bean.

"Er . . ." started Stephen. Bean knew a lot more about the world and the history of the panic than he did. More than might be expected of someone who'd spent most of her childhood as a lab rat. Doubt wormed into his thoughts where it multiplied and mutated like cancer. Was Damien feeding her information? What if Bean hadn't stayed with him after the battle entirely by choice? She cared about him. Stephen wasn't questioning that. He knew it to his bones, but it didn't mean Damien hadn't influenced her decision to stay with him.

Stephen had already proven capable of locating lost things. Damien might have encouraged Bean to stay so he'd have a way to sabotage their mission if needed? If Bean found Juliane on her own, and Damien *was* pulling the strings . . . An image of Alan's knowing smirk sprang to mind. Stephen's mouth soured. *Damn it, Alan. Why do you have to ruin everything?*

"I'm going with you," said Durham.

Stephen clenched his fists. Woodspring was close to the city, which meant Alan had to be near there, too, if he planned to attack in just a week. He opened up his map application and ran the numbers. If they changed course now, they'd reach Woodspring before the week ran out, but that wouldn't leave Juliane much time to brush up on her coding skills and develop a cure.

That also assumes we can convince her to help us in the first place. Stephen turned to Durham. If Juliane trusted him, Durham might be the key to convincing her to help them in spite of whatever plan Damien had in store. "Guess that means you'd better saddle up, then," he said.

His stomach growled. *And if Juliane doesn't agree . . .* He shook his head. *Don't even think it.* He might still be forced to leave Bean and seek out Alan. Because one thing was sure, no matter how he looked at it, he was running out of time. Alan's words played over and over in his mind, *I encourage you to hurry. For both your sakes.*

Thirteen

JULIANE

Clouds grew in the sky as Juliane walked back to Rebecca's room, still fuming. If only she hadn't spent the last several years locked away under that pile of rock. She could have stopped events from reaching this point. She didn't know how, exactly, but she was certain, given enough time, she would have found an answer. She smiled to herself imagining Dr. Thomas being led away in handcuffs to serve a long and difficult sentence behind bars once society was functioning again as it should.

Inside, she looked around for an additional source of light. An oil lamp sat on a shelf. However, light switches and electrical sockets had been removed. Juliane traced the spot on the wall where the hole had been filled in. It seemed like an unnecessarily permanent step. An antique spinning wheel stood in the corner. Juliane had never seen one of those before, outside of the fairy tale stories her mother forced her to listen to.

"Lyall found you," said Rebecca in a quiet voice. She lay in the bed, still snuggling with her child.

Juliane banished thoughts about the past so they wouldn't affect her bedside manner. Rebecca hadn't asked for the doctor. She'd asked for her. She plastered on a smile. It occurred to her she didn't need to join forces with those living in the city. She forced her hands to stay by her side rather than touch the sore spot at her neck again.

The people there allowed the doctor to continue running around practicing medicine, knowing he was unstable. Clearly, Manhattan was not the remaining beacon of civilization she'd hoped it would be. She sat down on the edge of Rebecca's bed. She'd convinced herself that in order to make a difference in this world, she needed to be a part of something bigger, but did she really need anyone else? She'd already made a difference with two lives.

"How are you feeling today?" Juliane asked.

"Like I might go crazy if I am forced to stay in this bed for the next two weeks. My husband, Rob, says I've lost too much blood and need to stay off my feet. I thought you might be able to tell him otherwise."

"He's not wrong," said Juliane with a half-smile, touching the woman's forehead. "You did lose quite a lot and do need to rest. But the human body is surprisingly resilient. I suspect you will be able to move around after a day or two." Juliane hadn't ever had much time for streaming programs, nor had she ever really gotten sick, but she channeled what she'd seen of actors in commercials for medical dramas. "However, even then, you will need to be very careful not to outdo yourself."

Rebecca pursed her lips and then looked at her baby. "Do you hear that, my love? We're stuck here." She turned her face back toward Juliane. "I'm sorry. I shouldn't have said anything to Lyall about wanting a second opinion when he poked his head in. And I definitely didn't intend for him to run out and wake you up about it. You probably *want* to be in bed right now."

Juliane chuckled. "It's all right. I'm afraid I'm not quite ready to close my eyes just yet." She pointed at the spinning wheel. "You don't actually use that thing, do you?"

"I don't." Rebecca smiled and shook her head. "At least, not with much success. I keep trying, but I suppose I just don't have the patience for it." The baby gurgled. "Will you be staying here for a while?" The question was asked in a light tone, but a tightness to Rebecca's eyes as she gazed at her baby indicated that there was more to it than casual interest.

"I suppose I'm too tired to travel very far today," said Juliane with a yawn that wasn't faked. "I'll talk to my friend about staying one more day."

Naked relief flooded Rebecca's eyes. However, it had become harder to see the rest of her face as the light in the room dimmed further. A glance out of the window showed ominous clouds. If the effort of staying up the entire night wasn't threatening to knock Juliane down now, the pending storm was another excuse to delay leaving a little while longer. When she turned back, both baby and mother's eyes were closed. Juliane backed out of the room, careful not to disturb either's slumber.

Instead of going back to Lyall's room, she found herself lingering in the yard where the party had been held the night before.

"I was hoping I might see you one more time," said a man's voice. Sam crossed the yard from the direction of the chicken coop holding a basket of eggs. He had salt-and-pepper streaked hair and a thick but well-maintained beard. "Juliane, right?"

"And if I recall, you're Sam," said Juliane.

He grinned. "That's right." He glanced down at the basket. "You've got to be starving after what you did for Rebecca last night. Let me make you something to eat."

"Have you seen the woman I was traveling with? There's something I need to talk to her about."

"Morgan? Yeah, I saw Lyall running after her through the gate the way he always does." He lowered his voice. "You're better off waiting for them to return on their own time." He leaned toward her and whispered with a wink, "If you get what I mean." Sam straightened. "Don't worry. He'll bring her back before too long." He looked up at the clouds. "Or the weather will."

Her stomach rumbled. "I suppose there's no need to rush. I only need to find her to tell her that I've decided to stay another day."

Sam beamed. "Outstanding. Lyall will be thrilled if you can convince Morgan to stay, too, even if some of the others . . . ah well, that doesn't matter. Come on in." He gestured for Juliane to follow him as he made his way back inside the cottage. A wave of heat struck her as they turned left and entered a small kitchen.

Metallic sheets and silver tubes hung along the wall, reflecting the natural light streaming in from the window. Though the panes were open, a lingering scent of cooked grease and ash hung in the air.

"What's with all the mylar?" asked Juliane, touching one of the silver tubes in passing. "You're not trying to protect your brains from alien invaders, are you?"

"Oh, those?" said Sam. He snorted. "Solar cookers." He nodded toward the window and the dimming light. "Works great most days, but not so well on a day like today."

Curiosity satisfied, Juliane shifted her attention to the rest of the room. An antique cast iron stove stood positioned in the corner. "That must come in handy, then," she said.

"Yeah, but it isn't the easiest to clean," said Sam. "And honestly, I hate to use it. I was a fire fighter back before. Seen what happens first-hand when people don't properly use one of these things. Cooking on it is now my job for the same reason." He placed the basket of eggs down on the kitchen counter, grabbed a piece of split wood, and tossed it through the stove's metal grate.

Sam walked over to Juliane until they were separated by mere inches. She stiffened. After her near-kidnapping, she wasn't inclined to let anyone get that close. Even if he wasn't the worst on the eyes. He leaned in. He had a musk about him— a mix of sweat and long hours in the sun. It wasn't entirely unpleasant. She shifted backward. *Damnit. Why did he make me think of Durham?* Sam smiled and grabbed a large skillet from behind Juliane's head. She bit her lip, realizing a second later she could be sending him the wrong message.

Sam lowered his arm holding the pan but did not immediately turn to go back to the stove. "I have to ask. Do you ever get the feeling that you've met a person before?"

Juliane cringed. *Ugh. He's recognizing me from the tabloids.* Her cheeks heated. She ducked under his arm, putting more space between them. *I should have introduced myself with a fake name.* "I've been told I have one of those faces."

Sam's brows quirked up. "By whom?" He shook his head. "A blind person? You were gorgeous enough in the moonlight, but now . . . A person could lose hours memorizing your every expression."

Juliane closed her eyes and shook her head. "That sounds suspiciously like a line you've used before."

"Doesn't make it any less true," said Sam with a twinkle in his eye.

Juliane caught her hand before it rose to smooth her hair. *It's reactions like that, that give people like him and Durham the impression those sorts of lines work.* Her nails curled into the meat of her palm. Durham wasn't going to be using cheesy pick-up lines on anyone ever again. Durham wasn't going to be doing anything. Her throat tightened. She itched to send him another message in apology. *An apology for what?* She bit her lip a second time and instructed her nervous system to release another dose of mood stabilizer.

It was taking more and more of the concoction to calm her mind and control her impulses. Feeling the task silly, but necessary all the same, she placed a block on Durham's contact record. It wouldn't keep him from popping up in her thoughts, but at least it would prevent her from sending messages that would never be answered. Perhaps then she would finally accept that he was in the ground.

"Did I say something wrong?" asked Sam.

"Not wrong," said Juliane. He must have seen something in her expression. "You just reminded me of a . . . a friend for a moment. That's all." She centered her thoughts around a happier place—her lab—and forced a smile. "You mentioned breakfast."

"That I did." He returned to the stove, placing the pan on its surface. He then picked up a pair of eggs and dunked them in a nearby bucket of water. Juliane hoped it wasn't the same one from the night before. Then he cracked them over the pan's heated surface. Minutes later, Sam handed Juliane the steaming eggs on an earthenware plate.

Juliane's mouth watered at the sight of food. Sam gestured for her to get started while he cooked up another batch for himself.

The first forkful burnt her tongue, but even so, tasted like ambrosia. Juliane's plate was empty much too soon. Without being asked, Sam picked up her plate and tossed it in the sink. He frowned at the contents of the water bucket. "Good thing we've had so much rain recently." A roll of thunder boomed in the distance.

His brow wrinkled. "Hmm, I wanted to give Romeo some time with his Juliet away from the others, but it may be time for them to return to the compound."

"You said something along those lines earlier. Do the others not approve of their relationship?"

He wrinkled his nose. "She's from the city. Lyall's family founded this place." He sighed. "It's . . . well . . . it's complicated."

"So? Why doesn't he ask her to move here, then?"

"He has. A least a dozen times. She always turns him down. Says her people wouldn't like that. And between you and me, I can't say that most of his would be thrilled by the idea, either." He scratched his beard. "I meant it when I compared them to Romeo and Juliet."

Juliane scowled. "I don't understand why anyone other than the couple involved feel that they should have a say in a relationship."

"Families," Sam said with a shrug. Something large hit the glass pane of the window, followed by something else.

Juliane jumped. Visions of birds flying into the glass at the top of the Apex building flashed across her mind. Ice flowed through her veins. She hadn't realized she'd issued the command for another dose of artificial calm. She pulled at the hem of her suit. That was troubling. She'd need to put a block on that particular command as well, if for no other reason than for the sake of her memory. The chemical mixture was known to cause recall issues when used in excess.

Sam went to the window and glanced down. "Hail," he said. "It's going to be a bad one." He gazed out at the horizon. "And I don't see either of them."

"There's a make-shift shelter at the ramp to the highway," said Juliane. "It's no four-star hotel." She thought of the stain on the mattress and cringed. "And it defi-nitely wouldn't be my choice for some alone time, but I guess it gives them privacy.

Lyall met us there, so he obviously knows about it. I'm guessing that's where they are."

"Oh," said Sam. "And where would be *your* choice for some alone time?"

"Not out there."

Sam chuckled. "You know, it wouldn't have to be the same for you," said Sam. "I mean, if you stayed here." Sam searched her face. "I'm not asking for myself. Though I'd be happy enough if you wanted to give it a try." He waved the comment away. "But before you say anything, I'm asking on Rebecca and the baby's behalf. You and I both know she would've died last night if it hadn't been for you. They both would have." He rubbed his face. "Frankly, we need a doctor."

"Hmm . . . about that," began Juliane. "There's something I should tell you—"

"You're not a real doctor and that you just got lucky last night."

Juliane blinked. "No, I *am* a doctor, but that's not . . . well—"

He crossed his arms. "Whatever you're about to say—it doesn't matter. The point is you have options."

The rain outside intensified, making it more difficult to hear Sam's voice above its growing rage. "I'm willing to consider it," said Juliane. The sound of rain outside coupled with warm food in her belly also made it impossible to hold her exhaustion at bay any longer. "But for now, all I want is a place to lie down."

Sam nodded. "I'll take you back to Lyall's."

"That won't be necessary," said Juliane.

"I know it isn't," said Sam. "I just want to." He followed her out of the kitchen and back into the hall. Jogging ahead, he grabbed an umbrella from a can near the door and gestured outside. "After you."

This place might not be bursting with technology, but at least its people still have manners. Sam struggled with opening the umbrella outside, making it obvious the device hadn't been used in some time and was being brought out just for her. His offer came back to her.

I have much to think on, indeed, she realized.

STEPHEN

Stephen sought a break in the clouds; anything that might hint that the storm would hold off until they reached the next town and possible shelter. All he received for his effort was rain in his eye. The wind pushed against him, making each step forward a struggle, while Durham and Bean shared the saddle.

Remind me why you aren't the one up here? said Bean's voice in his head.

I told you—the horse can only carry two, and you weigh less than I do.

I'll rephrase. Why is he up here with me instead of you?

Stephen pretended not to see the same hurt and confusion on her face that came through in her projected thoughts. *Because we need him, and he can't keep up. We've been through this already.*

She'd challenged the idea they needed Durham to gain Juliane's trust more than once. Explaining the real reason why he'd accepted Durham's offer to come along would only end in an argument. That much he knew. She'd accuse him of not trusting her, and she'd have a point. However, the truth was he did trust her. He just didn't trust Damien.

He also couldn't explain why he couldn't risk touching her. *She's not affected by the drain like you are*, Alan's observation came back. Stephen's lips twisted. Knowing Bean, if he said anything about either Damien or Alan and his warnings, she'd feel compelled to prove him wrong. He couldn't risk that. *Say goodbye now, while you still can.* Stephen couldn't tell if the words were his or Alan's. *If you still can.*

He turned his thoughts to the events of last night. *That happened, didn't it? No dream is that good.* Doubt began to creep in as they put more distance between them and the creek. He hadn't brought it up because if he did, she might remember their promise to talk afterward, but some hint about last night would have been nice. *We can talk about it after we find Juliane*, the voice in the back of his mind offered. More drops fell from the sky. *Who's the liar now*, whispered the voice, sounding suspiciously like Alan.

He focused on the road ahead and the excuse he'd made as more water fell from the sky. When he'd first suggested he walk instead of ride, Bean accused him of being possessed by a misguided sense of chivalry. The second time she'd brought it up, she reminded him that if it had been up to her, they'd have taken the horse and ridden away—Durham was in no condition to stop them if they did, even without their extra abilities.

The third time she'd brought it up, Stephen had simply said he'd made his decision, after which Bean grumbled about him being an idiot again.

Oblivious to his role in their silent argument, Durham passed the time by attempting to send messages to Juliane. So far, he'd let her know they were on the way. He'd also sent a warning to her about the Serpentine. However, he claimed that both messages were returned as "undelivered." This seemed odd to Stephen, considering she'd supposedly sent a message claiming to care about him, but he hadn't pressed. It'd only serve to convince Bean further that Juliane was no longer interested in reconnecting with their tagalong.

"We should find shelter," Durham shouted.

While the horse helped, their progress had remained slow. Too slow and each pained glance Bean sent him chipped away at his hope that they'd reach their goal in time. "We're miles away," Stephen shouted back.

"It won't do Juliane any good if we're struck by lightning out here," said Durham.

Speak for yourself. Stephen continued walking. He looked back up at the sky. He'd absorbed the power of a lightning bolt's strike the same way he'd consumed Nadia's life-force. It had given him the power to bring Bean back from death's door during the attack on the Watchtower. His gaze darted to Bean before looking back toward the sky. He grinned as large drops of water pelted his face. Another strike like that would keep Bean safe from him for hours, if not days.

He sent his consciousness out, looking for anything that might give him an idea where the next bolt might strike. Thunder crashed around them. The horse reared, apparently agreeing with Durham on the need for shelter. Stephen abandoned his efforts to locate sensor clusters as Durham clutched the reins, and Bean yelled.

Bean grabbed Durham around the waist, but the effort wasn't enough to keep either of them in the saddle, and both tumbled to the ground in a pile. The horse, no longer burdened, galloped down the road without them, taking its saddlebags and their remaining supplies with it.

"Well, that's just great," muttered Bean.

Stephen watching the horse grow smaller and smaller by the second. He extended his hand to Bean. "Are you okay?" he asked.

"More bruised ego than anything else," she said, taking his hand. "Would have helped if someone had held onto the reins a second longer."

"I've never had to travel cross-country by horse before," said Durham. "Unless you count that time with Vanessa . . ." He frowned and rubbed his head. "Sorry, what I mean to say is I was caught by surprise and panicked."

Bean snorted. "Yeah, that's pretty obvious."

"Will you two stop it!" snapped Stephen. Thunder punctuated his words. Something struck him on the head. Then struck again. Rain transitioned to hail. He covered his head with his arm, while the others did the same and broke into a run after the closest tree line. Larger chunks of ice struck the open road as the wind picked up in strength.

Durham's face went blank as he accessed the datastream. "Nor'easter," he said.

"You think?" Bean scowled as chunks of ice the size of coins piled up around them. One managed to cut through the protection of the branches, coming to rest by her foot.

"Right," said Stephen. "We can't stay here." He opened his virtual map. "Looks like there's a service station a mile up the road. We can wait the storm out there."

"The only problem is we'd have to go back out in that," said Bean, kicking the hailstone by her foot.

"I don't know that we have a choice," said Durham.

Stephen and Bean shared a look. "You always have a choice," said Stephen.

Durham pressed his lips together. "Yeah, well, personally I prefer to live to see the consequences of my decisions." A nearby tree groaned, then a limb snapped. "We need to go, before it gets worse out here."

Stephen nodded. Taking a breath, he ran back out onto the road and into the storm. The hair on his arms rose. He smiled. Maybe lightning would still find him after all. He slowed his pace. Both Bean and Durham had launched into a run at the same time as he did, but when Bean noticed, she hung back until he caught up with her.

"Why'd you slow down?" he asked.

"Why did you? I'm not going to have to carry you, am I?" An icy pebble landed next to her feet.

"Har, har," said Stephen between strained breaths.

"Seriously, are you okay?" She searched his face.

"I'm fine," said Stephen through clenched teeth. Alan's smirking face popped into his head. "Just double-checking the map. Rain makes it too easy to go the wrong way. Don't worry. I'll be right behind you. See if you can find the station."

Bean nodded, breaking into full speed. Stephen watched as she grew smaller, much as the horse had done. He found himself slowing as more ice struck him on the arms. Unfortunately, it would seem this storm would not be producing the electricity he needed. Another chunk struck him on the temple. Hot blood, a stark contrast from the icy precipitation, ran down the side of his face. *Let her go*, the voice in his head said. *You want to trust her. Prove it. Turn around and let her go.*

A broad shoulder wedged itself under his armpit, causing Stephen to lurch forward. He'd been so focused on Bean, he hadn't paid attention to where Durham was. The man's lips had taken on a shade of blue, making the bruise around his head wound all the more distinct. Even so, Stephen couldn't help but notice how the man's warmth radiated off him. The craving rose up within him. "I don't need your help," shouted Stephen, pushing the man away.

"Yeah? Unfortunately, I need yours," said Durham. He gestured at the bruise above his face. "I can't run in a straight line to save my life. Zigzagging all over the place. Happened to me enough on the field to recognize what that means. Figured if we teamed up, we both might have a better shot of actually reaching this shelter of yours before another rock falls from the sky and gives me a more permanent injury." He pointed forward.

Stephen followed the direction of Durham's finger. Bean was turning off the main road. The mixture of wind, water, and ice had reduced visibility up ahead, but she must have found the service station. Before Stephen had a chance to respond, Durham once again thrust his shoulder under Stephen's. Together they ran forward, and Stephen found that as long as he put all his concentration into the act of putting one foot in front of the other, he could hold the hunger at bay. A patch of icy road caused Stephen to slip.

"I got you," said Durham between heavy breaths. "Almost there."

They turned where they'd last spotted Bean. Stephen glanced around, but he'd lost sight of her figure in the storm.

"Over here," she shouted from his right. He spotted her underneath a canopy thick with ivy, which had completely covered what was left of the man-made structure. Stephen and Durham ran toward her, each supported by the other's weight.

Bean's eyebrow shot up in question as they reached her side. "He needed help," said Stephen as he tried to catch his breath.

Her lips twisted. She turned toward the abandoned structure. The glass protecting the entrance was broken. Bean kicked it with her shoe until the opening was large enough for them to step through without causing further injury. She gestured at the door. "After you," she said.

The insides of the former service station were as Stephen expected, based on the condition of the exterior. The air smelt thick with mold and dirt. However, the roof over their heads provided welcome protection from the other elements. Though the light was dim, there was enough to show Durham's breath as he rubbed his hands together. "We're going to need to start a fire." His gaze darted around the shop. "See if you can spot anything flammable."

"Too risky," said Bean through chattering teeth.

"You'd rather risk freezing to death?" replied Durham. "Besides, who else is going to be as stupid as we were to be caught outside in this and see it?"

Stephen's head ached as much as the rest of his body. Dread coiled inside him as he put space between himself and the other two.

"Bingo," said Durham. He dipped under the remains of a desk and emerged with a box labeled Air Fresheners. Placing the box on top of the desk, he opened the flaps, exposing a plastic bag filled with thick paper cutouts shaped like evergreen trees. Durham grinned, pulling one out of the pile.

"Gotta love the classics." Durham brought it to his nose. His grin turned into a grimace followed by a sneeze as he returned the cutout to the pile. "Well, they might still work as kindling. That chair over there looks like it is made of wood. We can use it to dry out some of the fallen limbs from outside. Now, all we need to do is find a match."

Bean swooped the box up in her arms. "I'll take care of it." *You're sure you're fine?* Her voice whispered in Stephen's head.

He nodded and turned away as if to continue searching for anything they might burn. Instead, he found the door to a back-room office. He supposed it would be too much to hope there'd be a cot inside.

The corners of Stephen's lips twitched at the memory of the night he'd met Bean for the first time back at Jim's tavern. They'd hidden together in a back-room office just like this one until an inferno and the Watch's pursuit forced them out. She'd been rude. Bossy. An absolute nightmare. He couldn't wait to get away from her then. He couldn't bear the idea of leaving her now.

Something moved in the darkness as he stepped into the room. Stephen's fingers curled around the body of a snake before he registered what he was doing. The creature's hibernation must have been disturbed by the opening door. The snake hissed, then its body fell limp in his hands. Its life energy didn't provide the same rush as the old man's had, but Stephen was relieved to note his head no longer ached. He reached out with his consciousness in search of the building's nanobots or sensors that might divulge the location of similar beasts.

An occupancy sensor confirmed he wasn't alone. Another query returned the image of not one but a den of at least twenty or more. Stephen shuddered. "Do what you have to do," he muttered. He stepped further into the room and shut the door.

Minutes later, Stephen's hands were full of dead serpents. His nose twitched at the scent of smoke in the air with a hint of evergreen. He emerged from the back room to find the other two huddled next to a small blaze underneath a broken window. Bean must have gotten the fire going while he'd been occupied with the snakes.

Bean looked his way as he approached. *Where were you?*

"I found us something to eat," said Stephen, raising his hands. Dark bodies hung from his fingers like ribbons of death. Durham drew back in disgust as he continued his approach. "Found a whole den back there," said Stephen, nodding in the direction he'd come from. "We just have to figure out how to cook them."

"Cook them? As in, for dinner?" asked Durham. He glanced at their meager fire.

"Might as well," said Bean with a shrug, coming to Stephen's side. "Here, give them to me," she said, extending her hand. "I noticed a metal rack we can probably use as a grill over by the desk."

His hand brushed against hers as they made the exchange. A warmth that had nothing to do with the fire rushed through his body. He pulled back. He'd hoped the snakes' lives would have been enough to satisfy the dangerous craving. It would seem they'd acted more as an appetizer. He moved to the other side of the fire, making a point to rub his hands together as if still forcing out the chill from the weather outside.

Bean remained where he'd left her a moment longer. Could she sense what had almost happened? His gaze fell to his hands as he ran through how close he'd come to doing the unimaginable. *You're out of time.* There was no more point in lying to himself about it.

His shoulders slumped. Maybe Bean would go on to find Juliane. Maybe she wouldn't. It no longer mattered to Stephen whether she went to Woodspring or back to the city. Wherever she went, she would be safer as long as it was without him. *Time to say goodbye.* His throat tightened. Thunder crashed outside. *I'll go*, he promised himself—and this time he meant it. *As soon as the storm breaks.* He would just have to keep his distance until then.

Bean returned with the makeshift grill covered in pale slick bodies. While he'd been lost in thought, she not only found the means to cook their dinner, she'd dressed the meat as well.

"It's a bit disturbing how fast you did that," said Durham, looking at Bean's handiwork. "Hot . . . but disturbing."

Her eyes narrowed. "Still not interested."

He held up his hands. "I told you. No filter. Stuff like that keeps slipping out the wrong way, but I meant it as a compliment. Nothing else. Besides, even if it wasn't obvious you two are together, if I'm being completely honest, my heart is set on another."

"Your *heart* isn't the part of you that bothers me," muttered Bean.

Durham chuckled and then sighed. "Yeah, I find it hard to believe, too." He gazed into the fire. "It certainly came as a surprise to me, but I guess when you meet the right person, it . . . it . . . changes your whole perspective—about everything—even about the things you thought were all you needed. It's like my final year with the Dragons—we played the Lionesses."

Durham's babbling made it difficult for Stephen to think of how to break the news to Bean.

"It was supposed to be one of those novelty match-ups—a publicity stunt, more or less. We'd joked around. Said things like for them not to worry, as no one wanted to send anyone to the hospital."

Bean snorted and flipped the snake meat with the knife she'd used to skin them. "Let me guess, they surprised everyone by winning."

"Hell no, they didn't win," said Durham. His teeth, exposed by his smile, shone in the firelight.

How would the conversation even start?

"As I said, I was with the *Dragons*." Durham followed the words with a roar. His smile turned into a pout as it became clear that the name meant nothing to either Stephen or Bean.

I love you, but I want to kill you. No, that wouldn't work. She'd laugh it off. Probably say she wanted to kill him, too. Worse, it sounded suspiciously close to a line from one of the old novels Nadia read when the chores were done.

"The way the game ended doesn't matter. What mattered—to me, at least— was how they played while the clock was running. This energy all around them. It filled the stands. We had a few matches after that, against good teams—"

Bean stabbed at the meat.

Look, Bean, I've found someone who can cure me—in the datasphere. Er . . . yeah, you definitely don't know him. Stephen shook his head. Weren't they already going to someone who supposedly had a cure? Wasn't it the whole point of their journey? Bean would roll her eyes, but considering how willing she'd been to go first to Worcester and then to Woodspring, she'd probably just shrug and follow him to their new destination, too.

"But it was never the same. Those other teams . . . I started to realize they were only good on paper. Sure, they could run play."

Listening to Durham's story was worse than walking into in a cloud of gnats at dusk.

"And there was a close game or two now and then, but no fire. Speaking of which . . ." He stood up abruptly and grabbed a sign hanging from the ceiling advertising some long-abandoned product. "Here," he said to Bean. "Whenever you think the meat is done, feel free to use this as a plate. We can toss it in afterward."

Stephen looked at Durham as something he said registered through the noise. *I found someone.*

Durham held up a flask. "I also found a little something extra to help wash it down. Guess somebody here liked to drink on the job." He settled back into his spot on the floor and placed the flask in front of him. "When I saw my teammates pose for pictures following the championship that year, I realized it was just another trophy for us. Sure, for the rookies it was worth celebrating, but for the rest of us, it was just another ornament for the case."

Bean picked up the flask. Sending Stephen a look that spoke volumes, she took a long drink. Liquid dripped down her chin. She grimaced and wiped her lips before she passed it to Stephen. Stephen followed suit. Its contents burnt his throat, but then a pleasant warmth filled his insides.

"That's when I realized that the game had lost its thrill for me," continued Durham, taking the flask from Stephen. "I talked to my coach about leaving the next day. Said something about wanting to go while we were on top, but deep down, I think he knew the real reason." He took a swig. Then another. "Now it seems the same can be said about pursuing other women."

Durham looked over at Stephen. "If you're smart, you won't let this one slip through your fingers." He nodded at Bean meaningfully. "You might not get another chance."

Stephen's heart sank.

Durham reached over and picked up a piece of the charred meat Bean had placed on the make-shift plate while he'd been talking and immediately dropped it. He blew on his fingers. "Wow. Glad I don't mind mine well done."

Stephen risked picking up a sliver of meat as Bean and Durham each drank from the flask. Though Bean's sip could just as easily been classified as a chug. Stephen pretended he was holding a hot dog in his hands rather than a slithering creature. Not that Stephen remembered eating a hot dog recently. The meat itself lacked flavor other than char, but Stephen wasn't going to complain as chewing gave him something to focus on other than the life energy pulsing on either side of him.

There has to be another way. His eyes widened. *If only he truly had met someone else who could figure out a cure.* What was he doing? Alan said it was a virus, but it just so happened he had met another computer genius in the datastream. The fire in front of him dimmed and was replaced by the rolling shadowless landscape he'd come to associate with the virtual world. "Yo, Wes? You listening?"

His friend appeared as a series of pixels. "And when am I not? What's up?"

"I need—" Stephen cut himself off. Wes had been a victim of the virus. How do you tell a person that their death could have been avoided? "Er . . . when we were on the train . . . why didn't you do something?"

"Do something?" Wes's cocked his head. "About what?"

"About the drain," said Stephen. It occurred to him that if Alan could lurk in this place without Stephen suspecting anything, Damien could, too. Even so, he found himself asking, "Did you ever try . . . ugh, this is going to sound terrible . . ." *You're wasting what little time you have left with Bean,* Stephen berated himself. *He brought a freaking antenna with him, didn't he? He had to have known what caused the drain and hadn't been able to stop it. All he was about to do was remind Wes he'd failed.*

"Never mind. Forget I said anything."

"No, seriously. Tell me what's going on."

"It's nothing," said Stephen. His shoulders slumped. If Wes couldn't defeat the virus while he was living, what chance did his ghost have? Stephen summoned a map. "So, we've made it this far." A blue dot appeared over the top of the former service station. "But the weather's going to be a problem." Another dot appeared over a neighborhood just outside of what used to be New York City. "Durham says Juliane is currently here, which is where we've been going."

"Durham?"

"This guy we met along the way. Knows her." A ring of red appeared, expanding several miles out from the city's center. "If the beastmen are going to attack the tower in a matter of days, that would mean they've got to be camped somewhere in this radius."

"So, you want me to figure out where they are so you can avoid them?" Wes stretched his fingers.

"No." Stephen took a breath and glanced around. There was no sign of Damien anywhere. "Actually, I'm hoping you can help me figure out where they are so I can . . ." *This is it. Decision time. No turning back.* "So I can join them."

"Er . . . what about Juliane? If she's where you say she is, you don't have much further to go. Don't you want to find her?"

"Yeah, I do, but, well, there's been a development." He looked at his feet. "Can't go into the details, but Bean's going to have to find Juliane on her own. Assuming she still wants to."

Wes lowered his face to meet Stephen's eyes. "And Bean agreed to this?"

Stephen shrugged, then straightened. "Well, technically she hasn't yet, but she'll come around."

Wes's brow furrowed. "For some strange reason, I doubt that very much."

"Yeah, well, she's going to have to have to." *Because I'm an energy-sucking vampire, and if I am going to kill everyone around me, it might as well be the beastmen.* "It's the only way to stop the war."

"You?" Wes laughed. "You've been out in the wilderness too long. You've lost your mind. You. Stop a war."

"Please."

"Fine," said Wes, grinning. "That's right folks, my best friend. Savior of the world," he muttered with a grin. "Let me see . . ." His grin slipped as a large cluster of dots appeared on the map. "Are you sure these people are planning an attack? On the Sorcerers? On him?"

"It's fair to say I have that on authority."

"Well . . . something isn't right about this. I found them *way* too easily. It's like they want to be found."

"They're probably trying to send Finn a message," said Stephen. "Like, look how many of us there are. Oh, and by the way Finn's real name is Damien."

Wes' lips twisted. "Maybe . . . but that would only work if they were sure they had the Sorcerers outnumbered." He nodded toward the map. "Which even *I* don't know, and I've been living there most of my life."

Stephen looked at the map. The man who'd raised him was out there, somewhere—Chad, his real dad. He'd seen Stephen for what he was. After Nadia, Chad made it clear that he wanted to put as much distance between them as possible. Stephen's gaze dropped to his hands. If only he could walk away from Bean as easily.

He sighed. Wes was right about Bean, though. It was going to take something truly spectacular to convince her not to follow him into the beastmen's lair. It was kind of funny that in order to show he trusted her, he had to lie to her, and to protect her, he was going to have to hurt her like he had Chad—make her never want to see him again.

Something touched him. He blinked and in an instant, the landscape in front of him transformed back into a campfire that had grown smaller while he'd been in the digital world. Bean's hand rested on his shoulder. "You looked like you were ready to sleep sitting up, like Mr. Romantic over there." She pointed. Durham had repositioned himself while Stephen had been accessing the datastream so that his back was to the wall. His head hung low. "Lightweight," she said. "Anyway, you took care of all the snakes in the back, didn't you? As in, they're all gone."

Stephen nodded. "Yeah, about that—"

"So, if we were to go back there to, ah, let's say lie down, we shouldn't have any unexpected company, right?"

Stephen sighed. This was going to be more difficult than the battle at the Watchtower. "We need to talk."

"You sure about that?" Her voice deepened. "Because I can think about a few things I'd like to do right now other than talk." She smiled suggestively.

The blood rushed from Stephen's brain. Before he knew what he was doing, he'd let her help him stand upright. Warning bells rang in his mind as she wove her fingers in his hair, pulling his head closer to hers. Then her lips were on his with a heat that burned more than any fire and was more intoxicating than any liquor. His arms encircled her waist, drawing her closer. Her body relaxed.

He broke away from their kiss, alarmed, and released her. The voice in his mind screamed at him to stop what he was doing now, before he did something worse.

The corner of her lip turned up in a sly grin. Her eyes were dark pools. If the sun were up, they'd be the color of jade he now associated with strong emotion. She stepped back toward the back-room office. He couldn't look away. He might as well fight gravity. She took his hand. "Aren't you coming?"

Her husky tone made it painful to remain standing in one place. It would be so easy to give in. *And so easy to lose control*, the panicked small voice whispered in his brain. "Bean . . ." he started.

"Stephen . . ." she mimicked. She pointed at him. "Don't you want to get out of those wet clothes?" She drew her hands down her sides and pulled at the hem of her shirt. "Because, I know I do."

She makes a good point. His groin agreed. He bit his lip and looked anywhere but at Bean. "You're drunk," said Stephen.

"So?"

"So . . ." Stephen searched for an excuse, but his brain was no longer being cooperative. "So, it wouldn't be right."

"It's not my first time, if that's what you are worried about," she said with a laugh. Her voice changed. She released her shirt. "Oh . . ." she covered her mouth with a hand. "I'm sorry," she said. "It's yours . . . Isn't it?" She dropped her hand. "It will be okay," She smiled. Her eyes sparkled like gems in the firelight. "You have nothing to worry about," she said, reaching toward him. "I promise." She took a step closer to him.

"It's not," he said, taking a step back. The time in the virtual world counted, right? It had seemed real enough to him. "Er . . . I mean it's not about that."

"So." She took another step closer, trapping him between her and the fire. She traced a finger down his chest. "What is it, then?" She looked around his shoulder at their companion. "Are you worried about him?"

Durham was still slumped over. The flask lay on the ground beside him, completely drained.

"Because I'm not," she said placing her hand on his cheek and bringing his attention back on her. Durham snored behind them, emphasizing Bean's point.

Her eyes were like magnets, pulling him in. His resolve started to chip away. He wanted nothing more than to taste her lips, her skin, her very essence. *I found someone who can help*. He shut his eyes. *I found someone*. "It's not working out," he said between clenched teeth.

"Liar," she purred.

"No, I'm serious," he said, opening his eyes and stepping to the side. "We need to take a break."

Bean's mouth fell agape. Her features twisted. "A break," said Bean. Her eyes flashed in the firelight. "You. You want to take a break? Now?" She snorted. "As in, right this moment." Her eyes narrowed. "That's not funny, even for you."

"I didn't mean it to be," said Stephen.

"A break," she repeated. "After what we've been through?" She gestured wildly. Her expression softened. "Look, if this is about us going too fast—if you're not ready—it's okay. I mean, I thought . . . what I mean is, I can wait."

"I already told you, it's not that," said Stephen, forcing himself to look her in the eye.

"Then what is it?"

"I can't—" He steeled himself. *I can't control myself around you—and not in the fun way*. "Look, last night was a mistake."

She tilted her head to the side.

"And I haven't been entirely honest with you."

"I know." She held up a hand. "Whatever it is, I don't care." She waved his words away.

"What?" Stephen blinked. "But I haven't even told you what it is."

"It. Doesn't. Matter," she said.

He wet his lips. *But it does. It matters quite a lot.* The conversation wasn't going the way it had to, and if he wasn't careful, he'd confess everything, and she might start thinking there was still a chance she could save him. *What if there is?* the voice whispered in the back of his mind. *She might not be connected with Damien after all. It could be just another of Alan's lies. Tell her what's going on—what's really going on.*

No. He forced the thought down. If Alan was telling the truth, Damien could kill her right in front of him.

"It actually does," he said, hating himself for what he was going to have to say and do next. "I . . . er . . . There's someone else."

Bean's brow furrowed. "Someone else," she repeated. She crossed her arms over her chest. "And who exactly would that be? The only people we've seen since the Watchtower are Ahman, that creepy old man by the trailer," she tapped a finger on her arm she spoke, "and that guy." She glanced down at Durham. "You're not telling me you and the Rugby-Wonder-Guy shared a moment on the road. Did you discover some deep personal connection limping here together? What, are you soulmates now?" She snorted. "Well, I hate to be the one to ruin your happily ever after, but I'm pretty sure when he was talking about being in love with someone else, he didn't mean you."

"Wes wasn't the only person I've met online. I've been . . . er . . . I've been meeting her at night while you were sleeping. In the digital world. And we . . ."

"You what?" Her eyes shimmered with danger in the firelight.

"Like last night." He grimaced at what he had to say next. "Only not with you."

"What'd you think . . . ?" Her mouth twisted. "No. Better question, why are you thinking about a computer game when there is a woman, a real woman, standing right in front of you, practically begging for it?"

"Because you need to know. And because I didn't want to keep living like this."

Bean's eyes narrowed. "And there it is." She pursed her lips. "You think I didn't know you weren't sleeping at night?" She shook her head. "Don't tell me a story about a relationship with some datastream woman who you've never actually met. I know what you're really saying. You'd rather not live at all. That's what you mean." She clenched her fist.

"It's not that." *Not exactly.* "You don't understand." Stephen turned away. Bile built up in his stomach. "I can have everything there." He watched as his words struck into her like a blade.

"You can have *me* here."

Stephen looked down at his feet. "It's not that simple," he muttered.

Bean reached out and grabbed his chin and forced him to look at her again. "So, you have issues. Who doesn't? It doesn't mean we stop trying." She tilted her head to the side and batted her eyelashes. "You seemed to like trying before."

He pulled her hand away. He couldn't risk her changing his mind. "No, *you* liked me trying. I, on the other hand, didn't get nearly as much satisfaction out of the process."

"But you do when you're in *there.*" Water began to well in her eyes. "With this imaginary girl who's probably nothing more than a sexbot. Or," she glared through the wall of tears, "some guy like you who has nothing better to do than pretend to be someone he's not."

Stephen's cheeks heated in a way that couldn't be attributed to their makeshift fire, but once again, he refused to look away. "I do." He swallowed. His embarrassment was only temporary, he told himself. Soon, he'd never have to worry about having a conversation like this again.

"She's not even real."

"She is to me." *Time to twist the knife.* "Listening to Durham go on tonight. I guess it made me realize it was time to tell you the truth."

"Truth." Bean grabbed his hand and placed it on her breast. "Do you feel that? That's the truth. When you are with her, can you feel her heart beat like mine does?" She pulled him closer. "Is she warm to the touch?" She looked up at his face. "Can she ever really know you like I know you?"

Stephen twisted out of her embrace. "Don't you get it? That's exactly why I want to be with her and not you."

Bean's lip quivered for a moment, then twisted into a snarl. She closed the distance between them and pushed him. "Fine. Go then. Make digital babies with Ms. Perfect. Drain yourself dry."

"Don't be like that."

"Oh," her eyes flashed in the darkness, "what, now you care?"

"Bean, it's not that I stopped caring for you, it's just—"

"I was right to call you an idiot that first day I met you."

"Bean . . . Look, this is for the best. You. Me. It was never going to work out between us. I mean, I wanted it, too, but . . . we're kids. The Watch. Going on the run. Nearly dying. Of course, we were going to think we were in love. But deep down, we must have both known—"

"The only thing I know is wrong is the garbage coming out of your mouth right now. Do you even hear what you are saying? You love me. I love you. It's that simple."

"No, you don't. That's what I am saying. You only *think* you do."

She crossed her arms over her belly. "Have you developed new powers, then," she said with a snort. "Oh, so now you can read my heart as well as what is in my mind?"

"I don't want . . ." He turned away. "I never wanted to hurt you."

"Well, guess what, you failed. Just like you failed to save your mom."

He staggered back. She couldn't have picked a more lethal barb.

Bean straightened. "What a loser you've turned out to be. And to think here I thought I would follow you to the end of the earth. Guess I should thank you for showing me the kind of person you really are before I made that mistake." She pointed to the service station entranceway. "You want to take a break? Well, fine. I suggest you start by going out that door."

Fifteen

JULIANE

Juliane made her way to Lyall's room with Sam close behind. However, upon opening the door, it was clear sleep would have to wait a while longer. An older woman sat on the bed, her hair plaited in a thick white braid hanging down to her waist.

"I'm Mags," said the older woman, making no effort to move from her spot while her breasts rose and fell arrhythmically. Her skin might have grown paper-thin with age, but that softness hadn't reached her eyes.

"I would say it is nice to meet you, but I'm afraid I've been up all night." Juliane shot a pointed look at the bed and tried to hold in a yawn. It was disconcerting how many people let themselves in another person's bedroom. Perhaps this wasn't the place to make her fresh start after all. She glanced around the room. If she was ever going to get any real sleep, she was going to need to find something to use to block the door.

"You don't belong here," said Mags.

Juliane crossed her arms over her chest. "Funny, because I just was asked to stay."

Mags's attention locked on Juliane as if Sam wasn't there. "Sam was in no position to ask you that."

"Why not? He's a grown man." Juliane was beginning to understand why Morgan and Lyall preferred to conduct their relationship in the car lot.

"He's grown soft. He's forgotten why we first started this place."

Juliane sensed Sam stiffen behind her. "Does this have anything to do with the fact that I've undergone the Gene Assist procedure?"

The woman's lips twisted like they'd tasted sour. "It's unnatural what you've done."

"No, it's evolution."

Mags snorted. "Evolution happens on its own. It doesn't require needles."

"So, you're saying you'd be fine with what I can do if I'd gained these same abilities through natural selection."

"I would," said Mags. "Because it would have been part of the Plan. But that would have never happened. Never been allowed. Humans were only ever meant to be caretakers of this place. Not gods."

Great, a zealot. Losing her temper with this woman would do nothing but draw out the conversation further.

"Mags, she's not from the city. You saw Rebecca," said Sam. "You know what she did."

Mags glared at Sam. "Yes, I saw Rebecca. And the baby." She turned back to Juliane. "However, I know who you are." Her knuckles cracked. "And I know you haven't been completely honest with us. I'll admit, your skills may have proved . . . helpful." Mags looked like she'd eaten a slug at the admission. "It's the only reason I didn't come here sooner, but we're perfectly able to take it from here." Mags nodded to herself. "I expect you gone tomorrow."

Mags grabbed her braid, threw it behind her back, and rose from the bed. Her legs wobbled. Sam rushed forward to catch her arm and helped her rise the rest of the way. Mags shot a look at Juliane of such smug satisfaction, Juliane wondered if perhaps the other woman wasn't as frail as she let on.

Juliane bit her tongue, watching the older woman hobble out of the room with Sam. Each of her steps took an age. Juliane glared at the door when it finally shut. She wasn't about to take orders from some old woman who wouldn't allow herself to see the larger picture.

Whether she decided to stick it out here, go on to New York, or travel to places unknown in search of other survivors, Juliane would decide for herself what her next steps were. However, she couldn't deny sleep was first in order. With one decision made, Juliane slipped between the sheets and fell asleep to the sound of pelting rain.

⸻ ❧ ⸻

Juliane awoke to darkness. She pinged the datastream. She'd slept until four forty in the morning. The sun wouldn't rise for several hours yet. However, Juliane found she could sleep no longer.

The bed groaned as she sat up, and floorboards creaked as she padded her way to the door and down the hall. The courtyard outside was a mess of debris, littered from the storm that must have raged while she slept the remainder of the day away. A layer of snow and ice coated the roof of the chicken coop as well as the surrounding buildings.

Juliane's breath crystallized in a plume as she blew on her fingertips and rubbed her hands together. Once again, she was glad to have had a place to shelter under the storm, even though some of the residents hadn't rolled out the welcome mat. A breeze teased her hair, causing a shiver to dance down her spine. She wondered if Morgan and Lyall were still huddled together in the back of the cruiser with no source of warmth other than the proximity of each other's bodies.

She turned to go back inside. She likely had until the sun came up before Mags decided to pay her another visit. She might as well make the most of that time. However, a motion at the side of the yard caught her attention.

Lyall sat huddled next to the gate in a tight ball. His body shook. Juliane went to his side. "Have you been out here long?" She rubbed her arms at the sight of him. "You should have woken me up," she said. "I would have given you your room back. I didn't mean to sleep that long in the first place." She scanned the perimeter of the yard. "Where's Morgan?"

He broke into a sob. "She's gone."

"She's already gone to the city?" Juliane's brow wrinkled. "Without me? Did she talk to Sam?" Juliane's questions were punctuated by misty breath. She tugged at her sleeves. "He better not have said anything. I hadn't made my decision yet. She was supposed to wait for me."

"She's gone," repeated Lyall. His sobs grew louder. A light flared in the house where Rebecca and her baby rested. It disappeared, only to reappeared at the entranceway. Hinges squealed as the door opened and closed. A man-shaped shadow emerged holding a lantern. Though it was difficult to see his face in the pre-dawn light, Juliane recognized the pair of shoulders.

"Lyall?" asked Sam, joining them. "I heard voices. What are you doing out here? Why didn't you come inside?"

"I was sleeping in his room. He must not have wanted to disturb me." Juliane touched the icy ground and shivered. "Go inside. You'll freeze out here."

"She's gone," repeated Lyall, as if the phrase was all that was left to him.

Sam looked at Juliane. "You need to get back inside, too," he said. "Before—" The door squealed again. "Never mind. Too late," muttered Sam under his breath.

"What's going on out here?" asked another man, coming outside. "Do you have any idea what time it is?"

"It's Lyall, Rob," said Sam.

"I see." Rob crouched in front of Lyall. "I told you nothing good could come from chasing after that girl."

Lyall's eyes shone in the early morning light as he straightened his back. "You won't have to worry about that anymore."

Rob searched Lyall's face, then shot a questioning look at Sam, who slowly nodded. Rob reached out and put an arm on Lyall's shoulder. "Did she . . . ?"

Lyall stared ahead. "I caught up with her. At the ramp—our spot. That's when I saw him."

"Him?" asked Rob.

"The other doctor—the one from the city. He was lying on the ground." Lyall's words were clipped and spilled out behind chattering teeth. "Unnatural. Then she saw me and smiled—I've never seen her smile like that before. It was like she was another person. She . . . She . . ."

"Let's talk about this inside and where it's private," said Sam, nodding his head at Juliane.

"Your new friend isn't the one in danger here," said Rob, glaring at the other man. Sam's mouth tightened. "I hope you now remember why." Rob stood and turned to Juliane. "My wife's condition gave them the perfect opening to exploit. I was blind. I see that now. I should have known something was wrong when I heard she'd asked to see you before me." He tightened his jaw. "Mags told me she found a needle in your room. Tell me, is that even still my wife up there?" Rob gestured back at the house. "Or have you already corrupted her?"

Juliane straightened her back. "Your wife asked to see me because you give bad advice."

Rob clenched his hands into fists.

"Rob, you stood in the doorway the whole time," said Sam. "Did you see her inject Rebecca with anything?"

"She could have done it afterward. There was plenty of opportunity."

"Except she was with me. She didn't go back to the room until I took her there."

"I'm not surprised that Lyall fell under one of *their* spells, but you, Sam?" He shook his head. "I couldn't believe it when Mags told me."

Sam moved in a blink, inserting himself between Juliane and Rob. "She's not like them," he said.

"They're all like them," said Rob, shaking his head again. "You know this."

"I know her."

"You just met her."

"No, I didn't," said Sam. He glanced back at Juliane in apology. "Mags isn't the only one who recognizes you. We actually met years ago."

Juliane's eyes widened. She took a step back, covering her mouth. "You were a fireman." A memory of being trapped in a dark room flashed through her mind as an ax hacked into the doorway. A pair of men waited for her on the other side, only every instinct told her that they hadn't been sent there for her rescue.

Sam's brow knit. "I was," he said, sounding as confused now as she'd been a moment before.

Juliane remembered those fear-fueled minutes like she was living them for the first time all over again. It was when she'd learned the upgrade allowed them to do more than access information. She'd disguised her features like an octopus might camouflage its body. When the ax finally had broken through the door, she'd appeared to the outside world as a diminutive blonde. She'd escaped by simply walking past Sam and another man.

He doesn't recognize me from that day. He couldn't, which means he met me somewhere else. The pre-dawn sky had continued to lighten while they stood in the cold and it outlined his body in silhouette. "It was you," she gasped. "In the lobby." It wasn't a question. Missing memories came at her with the power and warning of a tsunami.

He'd been there the day Juliane's world went insane. Juliane's breath caught in her chest. Sam had been the one to block her exit and part of the group that had bombed factories, labs, and technology shops in the name of liberation. What had the news called them? The Serpentine, for the rapidness of their strikes and the signature red cloth they'd wave in the air like a tongue following an attack. Louis had joined the group, or likely created them, in the days following his wife's death.

In her mind's eye, Juliane saw Louis's face before he'd gone into the elevator— it was the face of a broken man—and a million years apart from the man who'd once held her heart in the palm of his hand only to toss it away with a laugh. She'd hated him for what he'd done, but a part of her still loved him, too, even at the end—especially at the end. She'd thought she could save him. He'd rejected her again in the most unmistakable way possible. Then the door shut, and her world both figuratively and literally came tumbling down.

Her legs trembled. She refused to allow them to give way. *Grieve later. He was never yours to lose.* Mentally, she kicked and swam against the flood of memories until her head resurfaced in the present. Her body ached for another dose of instant calm, but now that the wall protecting her from her memory had fallen, she was reluctant to risk putting it up again.

His head dropped. "I was," he said. However, this time his words were soft and drawled out.

"Sam," said Rob. "Where did Lyall go?"

Both men looked to the fence where the younger man had sat. Nothing but mud and grass remained. Juliane took advantage of their momentary distraction and ran for the open gate. She'd thought of Mags as a zealot, but it was worse than that. She was a terrorist. They all were, and she'd spent the night with them.

⎯⎯ ౿ꙮ౿ ⎯⎯

Her name being called echoed in the early morning as she raced down the path into the woods. Juliane had never been described as short, but both men had several inches on her and were in prime physical condition. It wouldn't be long before they overcame her if she continued on the path. Leaving the path behind, she wove around trees as fast as she could risk, given the layer of moisture on the ground and limited visibility.

The tree line broke, and Juliane found herself in a clearing. Her heart raced as her ears strained to detect the sounds of continued pursuit. At least one of the men was close behind. Taking advantage of what little time she had, Juliane issued the same cellular command as had protected her in the past. Within seconds, patches of dark bloomed across her skin, providing camouflage. Unfortunately, her clothing offered none of the same protection.

Her gaze darted around the clearing, looking for someplace to crouch behind. *Ditch the outfit.* Her skin prickled in anticipation of the cold. *It will only be for a few minutes.* The adrenaline in her system made it hard to think rationally. She pulled at the hem.

Twigs snapped. She spun around. A figure emerged from the woods. "Juliane, stop," said Sam. "What are you doing? Let me explain."

"Explain what?" asked Juliane, taking a step back. The dark patches on her skin swirled liked clouds as her cells attempted to adjust to her nearby surroundings. "Why you bombed an office tower? I hardly care." Fear transformed into rage.

Sam grimaced. "It wasn't supposed to be like this," he said after a moment, gesturing at their surroundings.

"No?" Juliane scowled. "You never considered what would happen after you ruined the world's economy?" Her fists curled. Headlines and missed alerts describing the collapse of the economy and the rise of a mysterious plague scrolled across the bottom of her vision at her command. The dates on the alerts abruptly ended less than six months after the attack on the Apex building and Louis's suicide.

"I thought we were just breaking up corporations. Giving the little guys a chance. I had no idea . . . Never expected . . . Then people started dying . . ."

"People were already dying," said Juliane. She now understood the facility she'd run and its workers had been among the first casualties. "Innocent people." Her nails dug into her flesh as she tightened her fists further. "The so-called little guys. Your bombs killed them."

"I've never bombed anyone," said Sam, stretching out his arms. "All my life, all I've ever wanted to do is protect people."

"You might not have pushed the button, but don't for a second tell yourself you weren't just as responsible as the people who did."

Sam hung his head. "I know . . ." He looked up, "But I'm trying to make up for it now."

"Let me go, then," said Juliane, terminating the camouflaging program.

"I'm not stopping you," said Sam. "But I hope you will stay anyway."

"Why on earth," she snapped, "would I want to have anything more to do with you?"

"Because . . . because . . . I need help making things right." He held his hands open. "This place—Woodspring—it was always intended to be something greater than any one person. A place where people can live and truly start over." He reached out to her. "Not like that place." He nodded at the city's skyline. "With you here, with your skills and that beautiful brilliant mind to lead us, it can still be that place." He nodded back toward the compound. "Mags and Rob—they've got good intentions, but they don't understand. Not like you do."

"Understand what?" asked Juliane, making a point to look at his open arms. "There hasn't been a single thing that's made sense. You brought a building down on my head."

He grimaced. "That everyone deserves a second chance. That we're all victims." He lowered his arms back to his sides. "Maybe not in the same way, but we were all manipulated into doing things. Terrible things." His shoulders slumped. "Every last one of us." He pressed his lips together and took a deep breath through his nose. "The plague—the riots—the panic. People like to think those things were a perfect storm of unfortunate events. Nothing more than a chain reaction." Sam shook his head. "But I know it was planned. By them. Or more specifically, by *him*. He set everything in motion. He's behind it all." He met her gaze with his own. "And you know it, too."

His words cut through her anger, making sense in a way that nothing else did since she'd woken from the tube. The final missing piece of her memory fell into place—the name that went with the voice that haunted the edge of her thoughts. She remembered his dark confession as clearly as if he was still whispering it into her ear as the needles in the cryogenic cylinder came ever closer Juliane's eyes narrowed. "Damien."

sixteen

STEPHEN

The view over Stephen's shoulder hadn't changed in the minute since the last time he looked back, or the minute before that. His shelter from the evening before was nothing more than a speck in the distance, and there was definitely positively not a figure standing in front of it watching him go. "You did what you had to do," Stephen told himself, kicking a rock. "She wouldn't have stayed away for any other reason." Still, the knowledge hadn't made turning his back on Bean and walking out the door any easier.

He'd made his decision, told his lie, and now he was going to have to learn to live with the consequences. He forced himself to look forward and toward the horizon. His stomach rumbled, and he grimaced. Unless he found another nest of animals or a similar energy source, it wouldn't be long before he succumbed to the drain, just like Wes had. *At least I won't take Bean with me.*

His vision became fuzzy and unable to focus on anything in particular, like it did whenever he was about to access the online world. Stephen slapped himself. He couldn't afford to lose himself in the datasphere. Not unless he wanted to give up before he'd even started. "If Bean *were* here, she'd tell you you're being an idiot and to pull yourself together." The thought of Bean's expression she used when she was in one of her moods popped into his mind. He shook his head. How could he have ever wished her away before?

"Right, so time to start acting like a man," he said straightening his back. A bead of sweat dripped down his spine. The cold front that rolled in ahead of the storm had given way to heat today. It would seem that summer wasn't quite done with them. "Good thing I don't need the map anymore." He hadn't noticed at first—likely because he didn't want to—but with each step closer to New York, he'd grown more and more certain he could find Alan blindfolded. He couldn't help thinking it must be how a moth feels, attracted to a flame.

"Acting like a man would probably be easier if you would stop talking to yourself." He tightened his jaw and pressed his lips together as if he might be able to stop the words from spilling off his tongue with a little extra muscle control and picked up his pace.

The storm from the day before had left a large swath of destruction in its wake. Tree limbs and broken branches lay across the roadway, and more than one tree had fallen altogether. The road he walked on would be impassable for anyone who wasn't on foot.

The urge to access the digital world returned as Stephen maneuvered around a particularly large wooden casualty. The former king of the forest lay on its side—more hill than tree. By the size of it, it must have stood for at least a hundred years.

Unfortunately, the ground, saturated from the recent string of storms, must have been too soft to hold it when the winds picked up. The tree's extensive network of roots hadn't stretched far enough to keep it secure. Stephen allowed himself a slight smile. If something as mighty as that tree could fall, then maybe regular people stood a chance against those like Alan and Damien, too.

Newly-sprung mushrooms dotted the roadway ahead of him like snow as Stephen rounded the other side of the massive trunk. Luckily, he didn't need the datasphere to recognize them as the edible variety.

He plucked one from the ground, brushed off the dirt from its base, and bit in. His nose wrinkled. They tasted much better the way Nadia used to prepare them; however, he kept chewing all the same. Calories were calories, and he was in no position to be choosy.

He ventured off the roadway to collect more that might sustain him through the balance of the journey while also looking for water. He grinned. The storms had provided for him in that regard as well.

Plastic litter, more than a decade old, held rainwater. He knelt down and lapped it up like an animal rather than risk spilling the precious contents by picking up the trash. He stood back upright. He would still need more, much, much more, but perhaps he might just survive this trip after all.

Leaves crunched behind him. Stephen spun as a man, large enough to be mistaken for a bear, stepped out from behind a tree. Given his size, Stephen wasn't sure how he'd missed him.

Bloody stomach. "Hello, there," said Stephen out loud. His fingers twitched. If the man tried anything, he'd find out the hard way that his size wouldn't protect him. The corner of Stephen's lip curled up. A few weeks ago, he might have gone running, hoping that speed or agility might be the skill that saved him. He took a step forward, making eye contact. Stephen realized he *wanted* the man to try something. The thought stopped him in his tracks and chilled his blood. The stranger hadn't done more than surprise him, and here Stephen was, not only ready to kill him, he was eager to do it. His stomach turned.

"You're Stephen." The stranger's words weren't a question.

Stephen cocked his head. "I am." He blinked. "How—?"

"I was told you might need a guide."

"Oh." Alan must have known he was coming and sent him.

The man gestured for Stephen to follow. "Come on. I'd rather not miss lunch," he said. Together they left the countryside behind and trudged down empty streets until the open road became lined on either side by abandoned shops and former homes. After what felt like an age, they came to a stop in front of a multi-level brick building that had seen better days.

Cracks rose from its foundation. Many of its windows were just as blackened or broken as the even taller buildings located in nearby boroughs of New York City proper. He turned to ask his guide why they'd picked such a beaten-down location as their headquarters, but the man had disappeared as silently as he had arrived.

"Guess this is home," said Stephen to himself.

"For now," said Alan, opening the door and stepping outside. He looked over Stephen toward the skyscrapers. "I see you managed to leave the girl behind. Good. I wasn't sure you would be able to honor that particular condition of our bargain."

Stephen's lips twisted in disgust at the sight of the man. Did he have nothing better to do than come up with new and crueler ways to ruin his life? It had been one thing knowing the man would be there to greet him. It was quite another thing to actually live through it. Even worse was the sense of wholeness he felt standing so close to Alan. It was a feeling that he should have only shared with Bean. "And if I hadn't?"

Alan scratched at his chin. "Isn't it nice we didn't have to learn the answer to that question?"

Stephen clenched his jaw. "So, what now?" he asked after he trusted himself to speak.

"Now?" Alan had altered his appearance at the cellular level using a technique similar to the one Bean employed to blend into their surroundings. He wore the leader of the beastmen's face and spoke with Jeremy's voice, however, it did not entirely disguise his eyes, which sparkled as if Stephen's question were some part of a private joke. "Now, let's get you inside and fed before a breeze knocks you over."

From the inside, the building contained a central lobby leading to former individual office suites. Its marble floor had been swept clean; however, large gouges intersected the stone's natural veins where something large had been dragged across its surface. A sculpture stood in the middle of the room. Stains on its side made it obvious it had once been a water feature back when water ran for no other reason than to provide enjoyment for the viewer.

"It's not Buckingham Palace," said Alan, gesturing with a sweeping motion of his hands. "But it will do until we find something more . . . permanent." He looked at Stephen sideways. When Stephen didn't respond, Alan added, "Isn't this the part where you try to convince me not to attack?"

"Would it make a difference?"

"No," he laughed. The smile slipped, and he took a longer look at Stephen's face. "You're different than that boy I met before. What happened?"

Stephen shrugged. "I guess I was forced to grow up. Now, you mentioned something about feeding me."

"Ah. Yes." His mouth twitched, then he cupped his hands to his mouth and shouted, "Everyone, we have a guest today. I want you all to be on your best behavior. So, don't kill him."

Stephen raised his eyebrow. "Did you think they would?"

Alan mimicked Stephen's shrug from a moment before. "That's another one of those things I find best not to find out the hard way. Wouldn't you agree?"

He gestured for Stephen to follow him, clearly not expecting an answer. They made their way across the lobby and down a flight of stairs. A moderate-sized diner had been repurposed into a mess hall.

Beastmen, some with more obvious alterations than others, lounged in booths and at tables. A handful hustled in and out of the kitchen.

Stephen's nose twitched, detecting fire. "Should they be cooking inside?" he asked. The farmhouse he'd grown up in had been equipped with a wood-burning stove, but it had an exhaust pipe sending fumes safely outside. They'd also had a solar one, which Nadia, in particular, preferred Chad use, but Stephen didn't see a similar setup here.

"Probably," said Alan. "But this is one of the few areas where I am not in charge." He walked over to the counter where a pair of stools were unoccupied. "What's the special today?" he asked a scale-covered man rummaging through drawers on the other side.

"That joke hasn't gotten any funnier since yesterday," said the lizard-man.

Alan turned to Stephen. "See, what did I tell you? No one respects me when it comes to dining."

"That's because Jeremy here wouldn't know how to make a sandwich if a person handed him a jar of peanut butter and a loaf of bread."

"No respect," said Alan again.

Lizard-man grunted, then disappeared into the kitchen area through a pair of swinging doors. "Between you and me, in my former life, I was actually quite the accomplished cook, but I found it's helped morale to allow them to keep their pre-conceptions."

Meaning about the guy he's pretending to be. When the beastman reemerged, he carried a pair of gray plates covered by something that appeared to be a roasted chicken with field greens. Stephen's mouth watered at the sight.

"See, there are worse things that can happen than to allow my people to be in charge." Stephen grabbed the chicken with his fingers and bit into the meat. It was every bit as delicious as it appeared.

Alan did so, too, though with the speed of someone confident that their next meal is a few short hours away, rather than days. To Stephen's surprise, Alan allowed him to enjoy his meal in peace. Only when there was nothing but a bit of bone left on the plate did Alan resume their conversation. "You may be wondering how I knew where to find you."

"Nah," said Stephen, licking the last bit of chicken juice from his fingers.

Alan pressed his lips together. "You and I are still connected," he said.

"Yeah, I got that," said Stephen. "Before. Back when you hijacked my dream." He waved to the beastman who'd brought them their meal. "You don't have anything more to drink back there, do you?"

Lizard-man handed both Stephen and Alan narrow plastic glasses filled with a bitter brown liquid. One sip informed Stephen that it was home-brewed ale.

"One cup limit," said the beastman. He looked at Alan. "Boss's orders."

Alan nodded, and the beastman turned back to his work. Alan leaned over and said, "He says that as if I don't know full well that the kitchen crew imbibes a few extra after the meal hours." He shook his head. "The things I allow . . . I can't turn the blind eye though, for the rest—they have to stay sharp. It wouldn't do for the others in the city to get the jump on us."

"You mean the Sorcerers."

"The who?" His mouth opened. "Oh, I'd completely forgotten that was what they were calling themselves." He made a tutting noise before patting Stephen on the back. "I'm glad you saw the wisdom in not going back to them." He stood. "Now, how about we see what we can do about that virus you're carrying around inside that head of yours."

Stephen looked around the room. "What? Here? Now?"

"I'll admit that the circumstances are less than ideal, however," he pointed at Stephen's forehead, "I can't have you walking around with that ticking time bomb in your head, either." He gestured at the other beastmen in the room. "You see, they're my children now. Just as much as you."

Lucky them, thought Stephen. "Fine," he said, sliding off the stool. *Might as well get it over with.*

Alan's eyes narrowed. "You agreed to that rather quickly."

Stephen shrugged. "I didn't realize I was supposed to argue."

Alan's forehead wrinkled. "I've found that when most people are asked to stop talking and actually put a theory to the test, they usually do. Especially when there's potential death involved."

"Let's just say I've come to terms with either outcome."

Alan blinked. "Perhaps I didn't make the risks clear?" He cocked his head. "Oh, now I see. This is about the girl, is it?" His lips pressed together. "Feeling guilty, are you?" Alan sighed and placed a hand on Stephen's shoulder. "Look, whether you intended to do it or not, I've found breaking a girl's heart is an inevitable part of growing up. But I've also found the female heart is remarkably resilient." He patted Stephen, emphasizing his point. "She'll get over you." He released Stephen. "And you, her."

Stephen's fist clenched reactively. He leaned over and took one last sip of ale. "Now who's talking too much. I said I'm ready."

Alan frowned and glanced around. "Hmm, on second thought, you were right about this not being the right place. Much too public." He gestured for Stephen to come with him. "We'll use my room."

"Whatever."

Alan led him back up the stairs to an office suite located on the third floor. The suite contained several smaller rooms. Faded posters with things like "Teamwork" and "Success" printed on them in big block letters hung on display. They stopped in front of a thin wooden door. Alan pulled at the knob. "It sticks from time to time. Just a sec." Then he twisted it. The room on the other side was pitch black.

"You didn't demand a room with a view?"

Alan closed the door behind them. A ball of light appeared in the palm of his hand, casting his features in sharp relief. He walked over to the desk where a pair of lanterns sat and turned them on. "The lack of windows is why I didn't immediately suggest we come here." The light disappeared from his hand.

"Why don't you just tell the bots to come back on?" asked Stephen, snapping his fingers. "Like you did on the road."

Alan smiled. "Because Jeremy doesn't know how to do that."

Stephen snorted. "Ah, I get it. Just like he doesn't know how to debug a computer virus or cook a meal."

"Precisely," Alan clapped his hands. "Now you understand why I changed my mind about staying in the cafeteria."

"And here I thought you were trying to be considerate."

"Considerate? How is bringing you back to a windowless room being considerate?"

"Beats spending my final minutes as the dinner show for dozens of strangers." Stephen placed his hand on his throat and pantomimed gagging.

Alan rolled his eyes. "You're being unnecessarily dramatic."

A cot stretched out in the corner of the room. "Should I lay down?"

Alan's eyebrow arched. "Why ever for?"

"So that I'm easier to carry out when this goes wrong."

"You trust me that little?"

"Absolutely."

Alan frowned, reached into his pocket, and pulled out a small box.

"What's in there, a pill? I thought you'd just send me a file or something," he said tapping his forehead. "Like Damien did."

"You think I have the resources to manufacture a pill? Did you not notice that this place hasn't seen running water or reliable electricity in over a decade? No, I'm not giving you a pill." He opened the box and pulled out a narrow pendant suspended from a thin chain.

"A necklace?" Stephen's forehead wrinkled. "Your grand solution is jewelry?"

Alan held the chain up. The pendant shone in the glow of the lantern as it slowly rotated on its chain. He admired it for a moment before handing it to Stephen. "Put it on."

"Jewelry," Stephen muttered, more to himself than to the other man.

"Jewelry, yes, but it's more than that. I'm giving you a *chance*," said Alan. "Put it on and make sure you tuck it under your shirt."

The second the pendant slipped under his collar, Stephen felt different, like a fog rolled in and took up residence in his brain. However, what he didn't sense, or more importantly who he didn't sense was Alan. He touched the mound on his shirt that shielded the pendant from view. "It's like being at the Reef," he said, recalling the name of the stadium where the beastman had lived in Worchester.

Alan's smile returned. "I managed to access one of the devices limiting players' access to the datastream while they were out on the field and repurposed it. It isn't a perfect solution, by any stretch. For one, the range isn't very good, but as long as you wear it next to your skin, it will prevent the virus from doing more damage."

"Can you make another one?" asked Stephen, forgetting for a moment his distrust. He'd send a message to Bean, apologize to her, and explain everything. Then the two of them could live happily ever after as normal human beings.

The smile slipped from Alan's lips as he shook his head. "I was only able to produce this one as the components were relatively easy to access. However, the rest is buried somewhere underground—who knows how deep. Even then, if I was able to dig another one up—there would be no guarantee that I could get it to work again. Unfortunately, I have to admit circuits are one of the few skills that elude me."

"I could do it," said Stephen, hope building in his chest. "I've rebuilt plenty of machines."

"I'm sure you have. However, have you ever done so without accessing the datastream for instruction?"

"Considering the whole datastream thing was news to me a month ago, plenty."

Alan shook his head. "I wouldn't be so sure if I were you. You were accessing the datastream without thinking about it as a toddler. You wouldn't have known you were doing it. How can you be sure you have a natural talent?"

"So, I take it off while I work," said Stephen, picking at the chain.

Alan's hand snapped out, placing his palm on Stephen's chest over the top of the pendant. "Don't do that. All this pendant has done is cut off your access to the datastream. However, the virus is very much still active and will continue to replicate its code—including whatever causes the drain on your body."

Alan paced around the room as much as the space would allow. "I told you there were risks involved." He stopped and turned, facing Stephen. "Pretend your body is made up of a series of pipes. The virus is like a leak—a constant drip. That," he pointed to the chain under Stephen's shirt, "in this example, is the equivalent of covering the hole with a bit of tape. It works for now, but if you were to remove it, there's a good chance it wouldn't work again. At least, not as well. The pressure will continue to build up on the other side, even while you wear it."

Alan placed his hands on Stephen's shoulders. "I've run the calculations. Unless Damien built in a way to switch the virus off, the pressure is going to cause your pipes to burst. When that happens, you'll be dead in seconds. This is why it was so important you joined me when you did."

Stephen glanced at Alan's hands with a scowl before meeting the other man's eyes. He smirked. "Funny, the way you say that, it almost sounds as if you care."

"What will it take to get it through your head that I'm not the bad guy? I never have been. Well . . . not really." Alan dropped his hands and rolled his eyes. "You aren't still fixated on that whole abandonment thing, are you? I thought, based on the fact you came here *alone*, you now understood how sometimes removing yourself from an equation is the only way to protect the people you care about."

Stephen snorted.

"Fine. I'll answer your question with one of my own, then. Why are you so convinced I don't?" Alan held up a finger. "I sent someone out to meet you on the road so you wouldn't lose your way before you could find nourishment." He held up another. "Even before then, I called off the fight at the hospital, sparing your girlfriend. And though you're determined not to believe me, it was also *my* decision to allow Chad and Nadia to raise you in my absence." He shook his head as he lowered his hand. "I knew the risk of what we were doing. They, of course, didn't have a clue, but I made sure you would be taken care of in any eventuality."

Alan had made a similar statement about the people Stephen considered his parents before. He wanted Stephen to ask him to explain how he managed that particular feat when he'd been in cryosleep. Stephen clenched his fists. He wouldn't give him the satisfaction.

Alan shook his head and made a tutting sound. "Such a shame about Nadia. She wasn't my type, mind you, but I admired her spirit. Now, that was a woman who wasn't afraid to tell you exactly what she wanted." He waved the comment away. "We've spent far too long cooped up in this dark room." He chuckled to himself. "The others are bound to start wondering what we are up to."

He gestured to the door. "I'll make sure the team fully understands you are no longer a threat. All I'll ask you to do is to remember to call me Jeremy and try to act as if you haven't spent the last fifteen years hating my guts."

Stephen scowled. "That's a big ask."

"I only said try, and you only have to keep it up until after we've defeated my old friend, and you're cured permanently. Then, if you still hate me, you will be free to leave me behind and never look back."

"So we're clear, that's exactly what I will do."

Alan held the door open. "Fine. Now that that's settled, let's get you reintroduced to the team."

They returned to the lobby and exited the building. The parking lot was now filled with people engaged in various activities, though at the sound of Alan's shout, they all halted what they were doing and gave him their full attention.

"Some of you may remember meeting this young man before." A couple of the beastmen barred their teeth in toothy grins that were anything but friendly. "A few of you might even still hold a grudge." A man whose hair and beard made him appear to have a lion's mane spat on the ground.

"I'm asking you today to let it go." Alan patted Stephen on the back hard enough to cause Stephen to take a step forward. "This man is no longer a threat to any of us. In fact, this man is no longer a threat to anyone, as it seems his abilities were burnt out in the storm." Alan patted him on the back again. "Isn't that right?" he said, lowering his voice. Stephen made a face, but nodded.

Alan smiled. He raised his voice and said, "He understands now that he was on the wrong team and has humbly asked to join our side." Stephen glared at Alan through the side of his eye and bit his tongue.

"I have accepted," said Alan. The man with the mane of hair scowled and made a move as if to protest. Alan raised his hand, then closed his palm so that a single finger remained extended. "On one condition."

Stephen closed his eyes. Whatever the other man was about to say next, he was pretty sure he wasn't going to like it.

"For the past several days, we have been working on various game plans designed to go through the barricade and gain access to the Sorcerers' stronghold with minimal bloodshed. I have found us a solution. Gentlemen, I would like to introduce you to our bait."

seventeen

JULIANE

"Damien? Who's Damien?" asked Sam. "No, the guy in charge over there goes by Finn."

Juliane's eyes tightened. *Who's Damien? Wasn't that the question?* His name might have been the signature of her initial paychecks after she'd left the ACI, but he'd been more than that. He'd invested in her research, given her free rein on her resulting business, and treated her like a daughter. Was it any wonder then that her brain had attempted to shield her by creating a firewall around the memories of his madness and betrayal?

"You said one person is responsible for this." She waved her arms at everything and nothing in particular. "All of this." Her memory fully restored, she could hear his voice as he whispered his confession. "He's the one." Her heart raced. A vision of the cylinder's metal door sliding over her face came to mind. The sound of birds in the trees became the rising crescendo of the whine of whirling motors. Branches became needles coming ever closer to her skin.

"Whoa, whoa," said Sam, closing the distance between them and pulling her to him. Juliane, paralyzed by the memory of being forced into cryosleep, had no choice but to let him fold his arms around her. "I've got you," he murmured. Then, without further warning, he leaned forward and crushed her lips with his.

Juliane shoved his chest. "What are you . . .? No," she said. He pulled back, but did not completely let her go.

"Sorry," he said with a sigh, though his eyes said something else entirely. "But if the end of the world has taught me anything, it is to live each day with no regrets. It could all be over tomorrow—I had to try." He sighed. "I thought we had a . . . I don't know what I thought. I guess I thought it would help snap you out of whatever that was. Looks like I was right—at least about that last part."

She touched her lips. She couldn't deny being wanted felt good, especially with the reminder of both Damien's betrayal and Louis's final rejection so raw in her mind. However, it didn't change the fact that the man holding her now had once been part of the group responsible for destroying her legacy, even if he did regret it now. "If we did, it is only because you reminded me of someone else, but that was only for a second. And I can't stay here with you," she said, infusing her voice with a confidence she hadn't felt since the morning of the presentation. She stepped out of his arms.

His eyes lost some of their sparkle. "Is it because of Mags and Rob? The others will come around," he said. "After I explain who you really are. Mags only knows you from the tabloids. She's never considered . . . she doesn't appreciate . . . Look, I'll make them understand how and why you're different from the rest."

"It's not that," said Juliane. "I've spent a lifetime not caring about what other people think about me, and I'm not starting now. I simply can't stay here. Especially now." In her mind's eye, she saw Durham in Apex's conference room. The building shook as birds struck its sides from all directions. Most people had run outside, but not Durham. He'd come back for her, tried to help her get away, only to be reduced to a near-vegetative state for his trouble by Alan. He had cared about her *before* the attack, not just in the days since they woken from cryosleep. She had been blind not to see it.

When Durham had been struck down, she'd thought Alan had lost his mind. She hadn't understood the half of it. Alan wasn't alone in his insanity either. *I gave the order*, Damien had whispered in her ear, explaining that Alan was working at his direction. He'd made it sound as if Alan had gone along with the plan willingly, but ultimately Damien was the one pulling the strings. He'd confessed to that and more, secure in the knowledge that Juliane couldn't do anything about any of it. He'd made a mistake. She set her jaw. "I made a promise, and I intend to keep it."

Sam released his hold on her, defeated. "It won't be easy," he said in a resigned voice. "Taking him down directly, I mean. Believe me, we've tried." He ran a hand through his hair. "Lyall's mother, Irene, was captured on a mission once. She claimed they'd let her go with a warning. Only they did something else." His eyes remained fixed on the horizon.

"Irene killed five people that night, just by touching them. Even worse, she had no remorse about doing it. Afterward, we found her lying next to one of them— Lyall's dad. Laughing about power. Stroking the body like she was on ecstasy or something."

A cloud passed over his expression. "At first, we didn't realize what had happened. It was Mags who figured it out. Irene had been 'upgraded' while in the city."

Juliane stopped paying attention to Sam as she lost herself in her restored memories. Damien had orchestrated the murder of thousands of factory workers. He'd made it look like their deaths were nothing more than a tragic accident caused by unsafe working conditions, greed, and corporate callous. *Loose ends had to be eliminated.* The event had given Louis the idea to bomb technology centers.

"We didn't kill her, if that's what you're wondering," Sam continued. "We don't—won't—do that anymore. But she died all the same. They'd wanted to use her to send us a message." He grimaced. "And we got it." He paused as if reliving the event. "Once delivered, she just dropped."

Betty had suspected there was a flaw with the Gene Assist program—that it had been altered and was being passed on through other means than the clinical procedure they'd developed. She'd tried to convince Juliane that it was the source of her son, Stephen's wasting sickness. She'd given her an encrypted flash drive too. Juliane had dismissed Betty's theory, but Damien had confessed to being behind that too. *The plague.* Stephen's illness hadn't been isolated. However, misinformation about its cause had spread throughout the press, adding to the mystery, and fueling panic.

Sam looked into her eyes. "The group gave up after that. Now we don't go there except to trade, and that's only when we absolutely have to. However, if you cross that bridge—all alone—looking the way you look now . . . It doesn't have to be this way. With you here . . . can't you see? You're needed here."

If only she'd listened to Betty that day—truly listened. She'd convinced herself Betty was being paranoid. She'd told herself the medical community was better equipped to diagnose and treat Stephen's illness than she was. She'd made the biggest mistake of all. She'd doubted her abilities.

"Think of Rebecca, if not yourself." His gestures grew more animated. "Imagine what you can do for them. Each and every life you save. Each and every person you keep from crossing that same bridge—it'd be spitting in his eyes. You'd be treated like a queen here."

Juliane gazed back up at him. His eyes shimmered in the early morning light, begging her to change her mind. Starting over with him would be easy. However, starting over would be to ignore her role in what had happened since Project Gene Assist's first experiment.

Durham's face flashed in her mind and Louis's, too. For all her education, she'd been so naïve back then. If she hadn't lowered her guard and allowed herself to be manipulated by Damien's machinations, they both might be alive today, along with millions of others. She shook her head. "I've never wanted to rule the world—only save it."

Sam's shoulders slumped like the air had been let out of a balloon. "Unfortunately, I expected that would be your decision." He turned away. "If I can't convince you to stay, at least let me take you as far as I can."

⸺ ⁂ ⸺

Towers that once rose into the sky as symbols of humanity's success were now reduced to nothing but hollowed-out pillars of shattered glass and empty concrete. Each footfall echoed as they made their way across a bridge that had inspired songs and more than a few dreams of grandeur in days past.

"It's strange," said Juliane, taking the sight in, "not seeing other people here. I'm still not used to it."

Sam nodded. "If we're lucky, we won't see anyone until we get on the other side of the gate."

"Gate?" Juliane asked, looking around. "What gate?"

"It's a checkpoint." Sam paused pointing into the distance. "You'll see."

The streets became more difficult to navigate as they penetrated deeper into the remains of the city. Rusted cars that had been abandoned to the elements blocked much of the way. Sam began weaving them around one car and then another.

"Is there a particular reason you are directing us like a drunk person?" Juliane asked.

"Several reasons, actually," said Sam. "And many of them have the ability to blow us up. We called this section of road 'the maze,' back when we were still trying to do more than the occasional scavenge from this place."

The space between the cars became narrower and narrower. "We're almost there," offered Sam as he took a sharp right turn. He walked three more steps and stopped short. Then he turned away.

"Is there a problem?" asked Juliane.

"We'll have to go a different way."

Juliane looked up at the sky. They were losing daylight. "Do you think that is wise?"

"Doesn't matter. That way is blocked."

Juliane craned her head and saw that the car closest to where Sam stood had a large dent in its roof. She looked up again. "Did something fall?"

"Not *something*. Someone."

Juliane's eyes widened. She went over to Sam's side. A body lay on the payment next to the crushed vehicle. A dark red stain spread out from limbs twisted and bent at unnatural angles. Juliane tilted her head as she realized what the blood on the ground and the lack of decomposition meant. "This happened recently."

Sam pressed his lips together. "I recognize her. Tabitha. Passed through Woodspring a couple of years ago." He sighed. "Couldn't convince her to stay either."

The corner of Juliane's lip pulled down. "I hate to ask, but is there any chance it was an accident?"

Sam turned away. The gesture was all the answer Juliane needed. Together, they left the corpse and continued through the maze. Though as they walked past more empty buildings, Juliane couldn't help but wonder who would take care of burying the body.

⸺◦⁂◦⸺

Gusts of wind blew down the avenue, bringing with them the chill of imminent evening when Sam and Juliane passed under a long series of metal pipes and scaffolding. The structure had once protected pedestrians from the dangers of building construction, but likely now protected them from being squished by a fallen billboard instead. A man appeared out of the shadows as they emerged from the other side, coming at them in a run. His eyes grew wide at the sight of them, and he stopped short.

"This is going to be awkward," Sam muttered under his breath. "Paul," he said louder, with a slight nod of his head in greeting.

"Oh," the man said. "It's you." He stretched his body to look over Juliane's shoulder. "You wouldn't happen to have seen anyone else on your way in, would you? I've been looking everywhere for . . ."

Sam walked over to the man, putting his hand on the other man's shoulder. "I'm sorry, Paul."

The man's body seemed to collapse under the weight of Sam's hand. "Where?" he managed to ask after what felt like a century.

"By the plaza," said Sam holding him steady.

Paul straightened. The corner of his lip twitched. "She always did like that place."

Sam patted the man's shoulder once more, then let his hand fall to his side. "This is Juliane," he said pointing back at her. "I found her on the road. Thought she might be more comfortable living with you guys, if you get what I'm saying."

Paul's features stilled as if he'd covered his face with a mask. He nodded.

"After I take her to the gate, I . . . er . . . I could come back and help you. With Tabitha, I mean."

Paul pressed his lips together into a fine line before answering. "I'd appreciate that," and with that, he passed Juliane without sparing her a glance and disappeared through the tunnel archway.

"Tabitha is . . . *was* his wife," offered Sam as he gestured for Juliane to follow. "We've cleared out the rest of the booby traps on this side, so we will be able to take the more direct route from here. Next stop, the wall."

They walked the rest of the way in silence and came to a stop in front of a massive wall made up of twisted metal and large blocks of steel and reinforced concrete. Juliane detected a change in the datastream signal. In the time before she went into the cylinder, there had been so many active users, she hadn't noticed any one particular person's use, nor the resulting electrical signal, but now, with so few people around, the other users might as well have an arrow pointing over their head. "We're not alone," Juliane said. "There's someone up there. On the ledge."

Sam shot her a sideways glance. "Let me do the talking. Morgan told Lyall once that Finn . . . er . . . Damien likes to play favorites." He chewed on his upper lip. "Be aware, not everyone is here against their will. Some of his followers . . ." Sam's jaw tightened. "You can't let them see you as a threat to their position. Don't mention your previous association if you can help it, and if you can't . . . don't give them any reason to think you remember anything that happened that day."

"I wasn't planning to," said Juliane, keeping her gaze focused on the figure above.

"Just making sure." He cupped his hands around his mouth and shouted, "I've brought you a new recruit." A portion of the wall blurred as a man deactivated the same sort of invisibility cloak Morgan had used when they first met.

"Sam," the man answered with a laugh. "Is that you? How long's it been since any of you've come this way? We'd figured you had to be dead by now."

"Been busy getting the last of the harvest ready." He shrugged.

"That storm yesterday was something."

"Yeah, good thing the snow didn't stick this time."

The man jumped from ledge to ledge as gracefully as a cat. He looked over at Juliane and eyeballed her from head to toe. Juliane noticed his gazed stayed on her breasts and hips longer than was strictly necessary. "A new recruit, huh?"

Sam scowled. He'd seen where the man's eyes had lingered, too. "Should I have said it slower?"

The twinkle returned to the man's eyes. "It's just a surprise. That's all." The man's tone changed. "Though I do have to wonder why a person of your . . . hmm, how do I put this . . . history . . . would take it upon themselves to escort anyone here." He leered at Juliane. "Then again, I can see why you wanted to spend a little extra time with her." Sam's fist clenched and unclenched.

"Hoped I could convince her to turn around, but she's a stubborn one," said Sam after a heartbeat. The men exchanged a look. "Juliane, this is Colemin. Served on the force back when." He looked at her like he wanted to tell her more, but then thought better of it.

Juliane tilted her head at the introduction, but then turned her attention back to Sam. "I assume this is where we say goodbye?"

"No need to go so soon, Sam. There's a place here for you, too," said Colemin with a smirk. "Even if you once were on the wrong team. No hard feelings."

"I'll think about it." He leaned over as if to kiss her cheek and whispered in her ear. "Whatever happens, remember who you are."

A mask of cold professionalism took over Colemin's face as he gestured for Juliane to follow him into an opening in the mass of debris.

The path was narrow, forcing Juliane to walk several paces behind the former officer. Much of the metal was rusted as well and puckered outward with jagged edges that scraped her arms or caught on the fabric of her clothing. Though the view of the sky above was blocked for the most part as they traveled, every now and then, a pocket of light would shine down. At first, it seemed as if the skylights were random, but Juliane's mind picked up a pattern as they walked which made her think their placement was much more strategic than they appeared at first glance.

Colemin had been standing watch much higher. Anyone passing through the barricade's pathway would be at the mercy of anyone stationed high above. Part of her marveled at how much effort must have gone into creating the medieval-style defense. The other part of her shuddered that anyone thought it necessary. She was beginning to see why Sam's group had given up.

The path came to an abrupt stop in front of a door. A scuffed bronze plaque named the place, The Pinnacle. He held up her hand to a pad next to the sign. A light flashed along with the clicking sound of a bolt moving from within. She pushed the door open, revealing a wide-open lobby.

Juliane looked about the space. The furniture was well worn, but in decent condition. She walked over to a nearby lounge chair. An electronic reader screen lay on an end table. She picked up the device and turned it over in her hands. "I haven't had this model in years," said Juliane.

"It doesn't work anymore," said Colemin. "I think the only reason it's still there is for spare parts, but no one's taken the time to break it down to see what's in there." Colemin froze in place. His expression took on the dulled appearance of someone accessing the datastream. Juliane's skin tingled. He blinked. "Finn says I'm to send you straight up right away." His head tilted. "Seems he's taken a special interest in you." His eyes narrowed. "Which makes me wonder, who are you, really?"

She bit her lip. *Time to deflect.* "Do you always jump when he commands?" She shook her head.

Colemin nodded with a solemn expression. "People usually do. Unless they want to be forced to fend for themselves on the outside."

Act intimidated. Juliane ran her fingers through the side of her hair and glanced down, as if taking in the status of her attire. She needed to appear eager, but not *that* eager, to meet the man in charge. It wasn't that hard to pretend.

In the clearing, her goal seemed so straight-forward. She'd confront Damien, stop him from continuing to pervert her creation, then go about righting past wrongs. However, the sheer size of the wall and what it had taken to put it in place reminded her that he'd had years to establish defenses. Defenses that weren't necessarily limited to the physical world. She would need time to familiarize herself with the person he'd become since she'd gone into the tank. "Well, tell Finn that I'll be happy to join him for dinner tonight, but I would like the opportunity to clean myself up first."

Colemin paled. "He's waiting to meet you."

This isn't going well. You know what you have to do. Juliane batted her eyelashes and stroked her collar bone as bile formed in the pit of her stomach. Colemin's gaze locked on the motion. "Please?" She asked, hating how pathetic she sounded. "You only get one chance to make a first impression." She was going to need more than a quick shower to feel clean again after this encounter.

His forehead wrinkled.

He's not buying it, thought Juliane. *What else will I have to do?* She wet her lips as she tried to come up with another way to gain his trust. Preferably one that wouldn't involve debasing herself further.

Then his expression blanked again. When his eyes refocused on her, they were filled with surprise. "He must be in a good mood today. Said he'll set a place for two at seven, and I'm to show you to apartment 1401. You'll find everything you need up there." He started to move, but then paused. "I don't recommend getting in a habit of asking Finn for many favors, though, if I were you." His leer returned, "but feel free to ask *me* as many as you want."

Juliane nodded her head. "I'll keep that in mind." She hoped the man standing in front of her assumed her voice was breathless because she was still attempting to sound sultry, when in reality, it was all she could do to keep herself from gagging.

Colemin never broke stride as he passed the elevator doors and opened another, exposing the emergency stairway. Juliane allowed herself a brief pause at the threshold, but matched the man's pace as they climbed flight after flight. Eventually, he came to a stop at a landing marked with a sign that said fourteen. He hesitated at the door. "To be honest, I've never been up this high," he said in between heavy breaths. "Even Finn prefers to stay on one of the lower floors."

"And why is that?" asked Juliane. "He's not afraid of heights, is he?"

"Definitely not heights," said Colemin.

Juliane raised an eyebrow but did not question her escort further.

Colemin pushed open the stairway door and pointed into the hallway. "The doors are numbered."

Juliane glanced back at her companion. "Not staying to see that I am able to get inside?" There had to be cameras watching their movements if Damien wasn't concerned about giving a stranger free access to an entire floor of his tower.

"Should be unlocked." He turned on his heel and disappeared down the stairs.

Only then did Juliane realize the man had neglected to tell her where she might meet up with Damien, or Finn as he was now calling himself, later. She traced her hand on the wall as she made her way down the corridor. A pair of large vases filled with silk plants broke up the space. The plants themselves were gray from a layer of dust. An enormous frame lay on the floor between either planter. Juliane pulled the frame back as she passed and discovered there was a mirror on the frame's other side. She left it where it was, propped up against the wall.

The door to apartment 1401 opened with ease, revealing a room with bare walls and a single chair facing the external window. "Whoever used to live here wasn't much of an interior decorator, were they?" Juliane said to herself. Her voice echoed in the space. The room opened up to a small kitchen featuring stainless steel appliances and bare granite countertops. A simple stool fit under the lip of the countertop. Juliane pulled it out. Its leather surface, riddled with cracks, flaked with her brief touch. Leaving it, Juliane made her way into a short hall where she found a bathroom.

She turned the handle in the shower, and after a brief sputter, was relieved to see the flow of running water. The muscles in her shoulders loosened as she stripped out of her garments and stepped under the spray of the showerhead. The water was cooler than she would have enjoyed previously, but Juliane gloried in it all the same. Streaks of red, brown, and black swirled around her feet as dirt and dried blood made their way down the drain.

She stood under the shower's onslaught until the water soaking her toes ran clear. Turning the faucet off with some reluctance, she stepped out onto the tile floor. Her clothing lay where she'd discarded it. Juliane wrinkled her nose, hating the idea of pulling them back over her newly cleaned flesh. *Maybe the previous resident left something behind*, she thought, opening the door to the adjacent bedroom.

Her steps left a wet trail of footprints on the hardwood floor as she made her way to the dresser on the other side of the room. The first drawer proved to be empty. Juliane sighed. A pounding at the apartment's front door interrupted her search.

Not seeing any other option, she threw her soiled clothes over the top of her naked body before returning to the main room.

She'd barely touched the door to the apartment's handle when it opened. A slight woman with nut-brown hair cut in a severe style let herself in. Eyeing Juliane from head to toe, the corners of the woman's lips turned up, though the expression was anything but kind.

"I suppose you are here to escort me to Finn," said Juliane, taking care to use her former mentor's fake name.

The woman nodded and turned away, leaving nothing else for Juliane to do other than follow behind. She turned a corner then was gone. Juliane scanned down the hall, looking for a doorway she might have disappeared into. She scowled. How was she supposed to confront Damien if no one bothered to hang around long enough to provide a decent set of directions?

She tried the first door. It was locked, as was the second and the third. The hall ended with a small table beneath a window that had been painted over. She frowned. *I must have missed something.* She retraced her steps, banging a fist on each door as she passed.

"Hello?" she shouted. "Hello?" Her voice echoed. "Well, that's just great," she said.

She started back toward the apartment where she'd showered, thinking that the woman would return there as soon as she realized Juliane no longer followed. However, when she turned the corner, the hallway on the other side no longer looked anything like it had before. Where the walls were once dull and gray, a pattern of black and gold vines twisted their way down the sides of the hallway. She glanced up at the nearest door to her right. The plaque above the knocker declared it to be apartment 1417.

So, I'm still on the same floor, she told herself. She placed her hand on the wallpaper and pulled back as the vines moved. *That's not creepy at all,* she thought, as she wondered about the mental state of the person who'd come up with the design and the effect in the first place. *It was probably the same designer who came up with the idea of cloaking the entrance to an entire building in stealth material,* thought Juliane, recalling her old laboratory space.

She touched the wall again. Silhouettes of flowers bloomed into existence. A memory of Louis, the day they'd first met, popped into her mind. Though the entire campus had been his to command following his ascent into the company's presidency, he'd been forced to wait by the flowerbeds for someone to show him the way inside. That someone had been her. Her eyes tightened. Events might have played out very differently if that particular doorway had been easier to find.

An idea struck her. *I wonder . . .* Accessing the datastream, she issued a couple of commands. Within seconds, she'd isolated the code for the digital wallpaper. The vines disappeared, and the walls were once again a dull gray. She returned to the corner where she'd last seen the brown-haired woman. However, this time she noticed an extra door where she hadn't noticed one before. She cocked her head. *Clever.* She pushed it open, revealing a staircase.

Colemin said Damien doesn't go up this high, so I should go down, thought Juliane as she stepped inside. The door behind her closed with a slam, causing her to jump. A strip of wall on either side of her glowed with warm light as she made her way down. The brown-haired woman met her two flights down. "Took you long enough," she said.

"You didn't exactly make it easy," said Juliane.

The woman sneered. "That's the point." She turned and pushed open the stairway exit. "We like to test newcomers. See what they can do. Now, go on. He's expecting you."

"Which apartment is his?"

The woman shrugged. "Any door will do. They all go to the same place." She gestured at the door once again, encouraging Juliane to enter the hallway, though she remained where she stood on the stairway side of the entrance. Juliane crossed the threshold. The door closed behind her with a soft click. Juliane found herself in a hallway much like the one she had left upstairs, with the same pattern-changing wallpaper dancing up and down the walls, although the pattern was different. This time, it was more like a scenic landscape than geometric lines. Clouds seemed to float along the length of the hallway. A river navigated across its length. She paused at the first door on her right, which featured a small square pad mounted on the wall. It was a simple security device, designed to alert occupants inside when someone lingered outside.

The door opened. Taking it as an invitation, she stepped into the apartment on the other side, where she found a table set for two. Classical music played over built-in speakers. A pair of candles flickered on the table. The room itself smelled like a glorious mix of properly cooked meat and freshly cleaned linen.

Juliane's mouth watered at the scent of food cooked in a civilized kitchen; however, her host was still missing. She glanced back over her shoulder at the door. A mechanical arm fastened to its top must have allowed the door to open without the need of a human hand.

"Finn?" she called out, hoping the name didn't sound as much like a lie to his ears as it did to hers. "I was told you were expecting me. Is anyone home?"

"My apologies," a voice called out. "I'm just pouring us something to drink."

Juliane tensed. The urge to fight or flee threatened to take over at the sound of his voice. Phantom pain, stemming from the memory of more than a dozen needles piercing her flesh, overcame her senses. She fought to control her breath as she recalled how her body had seemed to fade until she was nothing more than a speck floating in an endless sea of nothing.

She'd accessed the datastream and managed to issue a series of commands the cryogenic sleep took over. She didn't have enough familiarity with the cryogenic tank's controls to stop its operation, nor did she have the time to figure it out through trial and error. Instead, all she could do was attempt to safeguard her mind while enacting a small revenge on Damien.

She'd told herself at the moment that larger payback would come later. However, it troubled her that it had taken her days to recall anything specifically about Damien or his involvement. She supposed the mental block could have been a result of post-traumatic stress, or a side effect from over-dosing on artificial calm, but standing in his apartment, knowing what she knew now, she found herself questioning if her last-second protections had been enough.

"I've been waiting for an excuse to open this bottle," said the voice that had haunted her nightmares for the past several days. "It's a '72."

Anger pushed doubt to the side. How dare he talk to her like she wasn't a threat or was pleased to see him. He might have kept her from remembering for a time, but the memories *had* returned. Therefore, at least some of her protections must have done their job. *But Damien doesn't know that. He thinks he altered my mind. That could play to my advantage.*

If Damien thought she was nothing more than another one of his pawns, it would give her the time to better formulate a plan for vengeance. *Unless . . .* A chill went down her spine. *This is about finishing what he started as much for him as it is me . . .* Her body shook with another spike of adrenaline.

Right now, he might only suspect something. But if he sees you panicking, he'll know for sure. She started the process which would force her system to produce an artificial calm, but stopped before her cells and glands could react. She transformed her expression into one of steel. *You are Juliane Faris,* she told herself. *You don't do dependency. Remember who you are. You have no reason to be afraid. If anything, he should be afraid of you.*

The man rounded the corner, holding a pair of glasses filled with dark red wine. "Are you alright?" He asked. "I thought I heard you gasp."

He looked different. His hair was lighter, more a mix of chocolate and honey resulting from exposure to the sun than the pure ebony it was the last time they'd shared a room, but there was no mistaking his eyes, which narrowed at her inspection. She realized she'd gone too long without speaking. She forced her breath to calm while she relaxed her features. She unclenched a fist to smooth her hair.

"I thought I saw something. A bug perhaps, that's all."

Damien laughed, and Juliane fought the urge to cringe at the sound. He gestured at the table. "Please have a seat. I assume you're famished. Most of our new arrivals typically are."

"It does smell wonderful," said Juliane, walking toward the dinner table as calmly as she would a board table. "I can't say that I've eaten very well the last few days." She looked down as she patted her stomach, hopeful that by doing so, Damien would interpret her as cowed.

"Food and drink are some of the best parts about living as we do. We were fortunate enough to find a stockpile of ready-meals which helped us in the early months following the panic. It gave us the freedom to wait for our crops and livestock to be cultivated to their full potential so they might be harvested responsibly, rather than cut too early like so many others were prone to do. Once you try some of this steak, you'll understand why so many people who come here can't imagine living anywhere else."

She plastered a smile on her face as he placed the glasses on the table and pulled the chair out for her. "The fact that you have running water here was enough of a sales pitch for me."

His lips curled in a predatory grin. "I'm glad you were able to make yourself at home."

Juliane didn't like the glint of his eyes one bit. How had she never seen it in his face before? *I didn't want to.* She'd been blind in so many ways. Damien had promised her a freedom she'd never had with the ACI and the opportunity to show Louis exactly why he shouldn't have been so quick to let her go. *That's why.*

Damien tilted his head to the side. "Are you sure you are alright? You look pale."

Juliane picked up the glass nearest her and held it up as if admiring its contents in the light. "I'm just tired from the walk, that's all. I've been on the road for days." She swirled the glass and took a sniff. It smelled of oak, with a darkness that reminded her of those first confusing moments when the cylinder opened. She tipped the glass back and took a sip, but did not swallow right away. Instead, she sent out a ping to the datastream. If the beverage was spiked with nanobots, the simple command should detect them.

Damien nodded his head. "Delicious, isn't it." He pointed at his glass where he'd placed it on the table. "I'd been saving it for a special occasion."

Juliane raised the glass back to her lips, though instead of taking another sip, she let the wine from her tongue trickle down and join the rest. "Oh," she said. "And what occasion would that be?"

"Your arrival, of course. I've been looking forward to this day for some time."

This could be a test, thought Juliane. *He's probing to see how much you remember.* "Hmm," she said as a way of buying herself more time to figure out how best to respond without giving more away than she should. She let her gaze slide across the room.

A buzzer sounded in the adjacent kitchen. Damien held a finger up. "That story will have to wait for just a moment while I get our dinner ready."

Damien disappeared around the corner, and when he returned, he carried with him a large platter containing sliced steak. A pair of plates piled high with salad greens balanced on his arms. Her mouth watered. Thoughts of strategy vanished in the face of the bounty in front of her. She reached for a fork. The cool touch of metal in her hand, so much like the interior of the tank, reminded her of the danger she faced by assuming things were as they appeared.

Damien returned to the other end of the table where he sat down. "This is nice," he said, picking up his own fork and knife and cutting into the steak. Juices streamed from the newly revealed pink center. "Wouldn't you say?"

As much as Juliane wanted to do the same, she decided to try her luck with salad first. She picked up a forkful and said, "You've grown this yourself? How industrious of you."

"I can't claim all the credit. No, we've been quite fortunate to have recruited some of the best and brightest in all aspects, including horticulture. You're not going to find anything like this anywhere else in the entire world."

"No, I suspect I wouldn't." *Because you destroyed everything else.* "Which makes me wonder, how have you been able to maintain this level of civilization?" She tilted her head at her full plate. "As far as I can tell, the rest of the world is going to hell."

"Sacrifices had to be made, just like anywhere else. I like to think we've made the right ones."

Juliane held the leafy greens up to her lips. The dressing glistened in the candlelight. Her taste buds begged her to abandon caution and devour everything in front of her. "I would think you have plenty of mouths to feed here. Can you really accept another one?"

"There's always room for someone with talents like yourself. It's my understanding you were escorted here by a man from one of the nearby towns. Sam, yes?" Damien smiled. "It was good to see his face again. Between you and me, I'd almost forgotten he was still alive."

Not knowing what else to do, Juliane nodded. "The other man. Colemin, I believe he said his name was, mentioned something like that."

"But you also met Morgan, before that."

Juliane returned the fork to her plate with the lettuce still impaled on its end. *How would he have that information?* She recalled the bit of conversation she'd thought she'd imagined between Morgan and Dr. Thomas and how Morgan's voice had changed. What if that change hadn't been the result of drug-induced hallucination? Lyall's mother had been turned into a killer. He'd turned Morgan into one too. Damien had the ability to do far worse than alter a person's memories.

She stared at the lettuce. A bead of salad dressing dripped onto her plate. It was now clear to her that Damien had been the one to stop her kidnapping, not Morgan. He'd spoken to Dr. Thomas through the other woman's mouth. Which meant the man sitting across from her could have just as easily been watching her through Morgan's eyes as they made the trip south or listening to their conversations. Damien's perversion of her technology made Louis's sex games seem like child's play.

Her stomach turned. If her memories had returned right away . . . if she'd given them voice, or indicated what she intended to do next, he could have killed her while she slept. "I did . . ."

"Sad news. About Morgan. When she didn't report in . . ." Damien leaned back in his chair. "Unfortunate, but not entirely unexpected. Morgan always did like being in the wild. More than anyone thought was truly wise. We could never keep her here for very long. It was only a matter of time until some accident or wild animal found her."

Wild animal. Juliane thought of Lyall and the look on his face when she'd found him sitting by the fence. *Act like the fool he thinks you are,* thought Juliane. She folded her hands on her lap and forced her features into what she hoped was a confused expression. "What happened that day? Back at the office. I have a fleeting memory of some birds and going into a big meeting—I was supposed to present something that day, if I recall." She pouted, then tapped her finger on her chin.

Damien beamed. "You do recognize me, then. I didn't want to presume." He held up a hand before she could say anything, "I wouldn't have blamed you if you hadn't." He ran his fingers through his hair and shook his head. "Quite a number of things have changed since you were last in New York, haven't they?"

"It's been a lot to process."

"I expect it has. And you say you are having difficulties remembering why you went into cryogenic sleep?"

"I assume that's one of the side effects, but yes." She rubbed her forehead where the needle had bored into her skull. She then dropped her hand and changed the subject before the rage she felt inside could show on her face. "Although, now that you bring it up, they said I was meeting with a person named Finn. Why the name change?"

He laughed, "I'm sorry if it caused you any additional confusion. I started using it shortly after the whole unpleasantness, mostly for my own safety. After all, I was meeting with a number of strangers. I thought it wise to protect my identity. The name, I guess, rather stuck."

Damien looked down at her plate, which remained as full as it had when she'd first sat down. "And here my chatting away is keeping you from enjoying your dinner. How rude of me." He gestured at the uneaten food. "Please, eat while it is still hot. I promise you'll hear nothing more from me until you have cleaned your plate."

Juliane picked up the fork with the bit of dressed greens. Seeing no other choice, she bit through the crisp lettuce while initiating another scan of the interior of her mouth. The flavor of the dressing made her traitorous taste buds sing in approval while she waited. Digital text overlaid across her vision flashed the words "No signal found." Relieved she no longer had to fear its flavor, she returned the fork to the salad plate for another bite.

Damien raised his wine glass as in toast, though kept his promise and did not speak. Instead, he tilted his head back and drank deeply.

Juliane intended to claim the salad alone had filled her up, but her body, it would seem, had other ideas following the long trek to the city. She swallowed a small piece of meat before she'd realized what she'd done. For a second, she contemplated letting it go. After all, the rest of the meal had been innocent enough, but then she looked at Damien's face and didn't like what she saw.

She issued a command to her body to stop the meat's descent down her throat. She coughed and pushed herself from the table. She coughed again, more forcefully than the last time, then again.

Damien stood. "You're turning blue," he said, coming to her side.

She tapped the base of her throat frantically as she continued to cough.

"You're choking," he said, stating the obvious.

She nodded. Panic began to take over her brain. If he didn't do something soon, she would be forced to allow the piece of steak to pass and hope that if it did contain any nanobots, she would be able to detect them and disable them before they could do too much damage.

The stunned expression on Damien's face returned yet again to one of confidence as he wrapped his arms around her from behind and struck her abdomen. She could feel the lodged meat move in an upward direction as he struck her again. She coughed, and the bit of steak flew from her mouth, landing on the floor next to her chair.

Damien, however, continued to hold her close. Her body betrayed her by sagging in his arms as her lungs filled with oxygen.

"You gave me quite the scare. Feeling better now?"

She straightened, and his arms fell away. Turning, she wiped the tears from her eyes and nodded. "I'm afraid I've lost my appetite. I need to call it a night. I'll show myself back to my room."

His body stiffened. *He doesn't like that idea.* She looked up. *Is he now attempting to exert his control?* She touched his cheek. Satisfaction flashed across his face. She shifted her gaze to the table. "It was a lovely dinner, though. So, if you don't mind, I'll like to take it with me. Perhaps I will be able to finish it later, once I've had a chance to recover somewhat."

His lips pressed together in a fine line for a moment, as if he intended to argue, but then his expression softened. "But of course," he said, picking up her plate from the table. "If you would give me just a moment, I'll wrap it up for you so it is easier to carry back upstairs."

Before Juliane could protest, he'd taken the plate back into the kitchen area. Juliane heard the sound of drawers opening and closing and things being rummaged around. Every fiber of her being urged her to exit the apartment while she still had a chance; however, if he wasn't already suspicious of her, that would finish the job.

A moment later, he returned from around the corner, holding her dinner plate wrapped in plastic. "There you go, my dear," he said. "Oh, and don't worry about returning the plate. I have more than enough in here."

"Thank you, again," she said with a slight nod of her head. "I'm sure we will have plenty of opportunities to catch up another time. Based on what I've seen since I arrived, I have no plans on leaving any time soon."

He grinned at her final comment. "Then until next time." His eyes twinkled. "Good night, Juliane."

"Until next time," said Juliane. *And next time, don't expect me to be so polite.*

Eighteen

STEPHEN

Alan abandoned Stephen the moment the speech ended and led a pair of beastmen away. Not entirely trusting his father's people to behave, speech or no speech, Stephen maintained a distance from the others. When the dinner meal came, he grabbed a plate from the make-shift mess hall and took it outside to eat under the setting sun. His skin itched like he'd lost a limb, and he found himself more than once rubbing the pendant from the outside of his shirt. Stomach full for the first time in days, if not weeks, his thoughts cycled around Bean, and sleep, and sleeping with Bean.

Frustrated, he took a walk around the complex-turned-beastman headquarters. The main building, housing the mess and Alan's room, was rather non-descript and could easily be lost among the remains of the New Jersey suburban skyline. It would be even harder to spot from nearby Manhattan. However, it wasn't the only building now occupied by two-legged fangs and fur. Stephen noted that a few of the other beastmen disappeared into the other neighboring buildings and was surprised when moments later, at least a dozen regular-looking people appeared in their place and filed into the main building. It would appear that he wasn't the only new recruit to the cause.

Although the knowledge there were other people at the camp who didn't resemble the stuff of nightmares should have caused comfort, Stephen chose to keep his distance from them as well. He rubbed the pendant again.

The moon replaced the setting sun in the sky. Although Stephen stood alone in the empty parking lot, he assumed there were one or two look-outs hidden somewhere close by standing watch. He covered a yawn with his hand. *I guess it's time I found someplace to call it a night*, he thought, looking around.

The office suite containing Alan's quarters had been modified to hold other sleeping quarters, but he had no interest in spending the night under the same roof with that man. He also had no desire to risk exploring any of the other buildings at night, especially without a light source. *Guess it's another night for me under the stars.* A blast of cold air ruffled his hair, sending a shiver down his spine.

He frowned. There weren't enough trees in this place. It meant there would be nothing to block the wind nor leaves to cover and soften the broken asphalt. More importantly, there would be nothing to insulate him from the changing weather. He rubbed his arms. Though the day had been comfortable, the weather this time of year could be unpredictable, with dangerous results for those caught outside. The night before was proof of that.

He snorted to himself. *Wouldn't that just be great? You manage to fight off whole teams of genetically modified beastmen along with psychos bent on controlling the world, and you get taken out by a case of frost.*

He could imagine only too well what Bean would say about the situation he found himself in. For the millionth time, he wished he could contact her, explain, and beg for her forgiveness. He fingered the pendant again. *It's only been on for a few hours,* he thought, *it couldn't possibly be that dangerous to remove it yet.*

He reached under his collar and pulled at the device.

"There you are," said Alan.

Stephen dropped the chain. "Yeah, here I am. You found me." He gave Alan a little wave. "Good job."

Alan frowned at Stephen's words. "You promised to try, remember?" He made a small gesture with his thumb back at the headquarters building.

"This is me trying," said Stephen.

"Well, try harder."

Stephen's mouth twisted, biting off a callous retort. "So, where should I sleep?"

"That's the reason I came looking for you. I forgot I had to deliver additional instructions in person. It's been a while since I've needed to do that." He chuckled. Stephen didn't join in his mirth. He sighed. "After consulting with my captains, we decided it would be better for you to sleep with the other regulars rather than in the main building with me."

"Yeah, I'd prefer that, too."

The corner of Alan's mouth twitched. "I didn't think you'd take much convincing." He started walking toward a squat brick building to their right. He stopped at the top of the stairs and waited. The door opened and out came a man Stephen hadn't noticed before, holding a lantern. "Stephen, this young man is Lyall," said Alan. "He's another stray we picked up wandering aimlessly not far from here a short time before you. He'll be your partner in your upcoming mission. You may find you also have a few other things in common." Introduction made, Alan wasted no time turning and disappearing back into the growing darkness.

Lyall wasn't wrinkled or marked by other signs of age, like the bulk of people Stephen had met since leaving the farm not associated with the Sorcerers were. He also lacked the beastmen's physical enhancements. This meant he had to be only a few years older than Stephen—in his mid-twenties if Stephen had to guess; however, the light from the lantern made Lyall's face look like a twisted skeleton. "I know why I volunteered for this mission. What's your reason?"

Stephen shrugged. "I didn't have anything else important going on. So, I figured, why not?" He realized only after the words were out of his mouth how they might sound, but he hadn't been able to help himself. Lyall's youthful appearance reminded him of Wes, and the joke was the sort of thing they'd shared before launching a mission in their game. Wes would have chuckled and made a witty comment in kind. Lyall's mouth didn't so much as twitch.

"Follow me," he said instead.

The lantern cast just enough light to help Stephen avoid walking into a wall or stubbing his toe on a piece of ill-placed furniture, but not enough to give him a feel for what used to be housed under its roof. Stephen supposed it didn't matter, but wondering about the building's original purpose gave him at least something to think about as they made their way through the narrow hallways.

"You'll sleep here tonight," said Lyall, coming to a stop in front of an unmarked door. A narrow cot lay stretched out in the middle of the small room, and nothing else. "We'll head out first thing in the morning so that we can get to the gate before the majority of people wake up. I've crossed the bridge before but never made it as far as the tower itself, so your job is to make sure we don't accidentally trip any booby traps before we reach the barricade."

"Problem. While I've been on the inside," said Stephen, "I don't know how great a guide I am going to be. I was there only for a day, and if there are traps, I didn't see them." He explained how he'd arrived at night and by boat. It had been too dark to see much of anything, and if there had been hazards along the way, Wes hadn't bothered to point them out.

Stephen had been given a digital map from Finn, but he wouldn't be able to access it anymore. At least, not while wearing the pendant. His fingers itched to scratch at it again, but he kept them at his side.

Lyall looked away and started to leave the room. "Well, I guess that means I'll go first."

If Lyall was right about there being traps, they could well be going on a suicide mission tomorrow unless Stephen could remember the route they'd taken. Stephen's brow wrinkled. "Not that I am complaining, but why?"

Lyall looked back over his shoulder. "Why not? How did you put it before? I don't have anything else important going on," he said, echoing Stephen's words from before with a smile that looked anything but joyous.

Stephen understood then why Alan said they had things in common. The expression on Lyall's face was of one who'd lost it all and just wanted a way out. He'd seen a similar look on Chad's face, too, the night of the battle. Words of comfort and understanding, the sort of things Nadia would say while he was growing up whenever he was feeling down, bubbled up on his tongue. He crushed the lies before he could give a single one of them voice. "So, tomorrow at dawn, huh?"

Lyall shook his head. "No. Even earlier."

"Guess I should get some sleep, then."

"Guess so." The door closed behind Lyall, leaving Stephen in the dark in more ways than one.

Nineteen

JULIANE

Sleep eluded Juliane after dinner. Though tired to the bone, she'd tossed on the bed. Damien or one of his people might intrude upon the apartment at any time. They'd have no difficulty gaining entry to the place, considering the entrance featured an electronic lock. She padded her way over to the door and attempted to twist the handle. The handle refused to budge. As she'd feared, she was locked in.

Scowling, she moved to the apartment window. She pushed the set of dusty curtains back. The glass on the other side was blackened. Damien may have treated her like a guest downstairs, but it would appear he was more inclined to treat her like a prisoner up here. *Now, all I have to do is figure out a way to stop him before anyone else falls for his scheming.*

She tapped her chin. If Durham were still alive, he probably would have enjoyed finding a way to break out of here. Before she knew what she was doing, she'd removed the block on his contact record. She shook her head in disgust with herself.

Her mental cursor hovered over the record. She was just about to toggle the block back on, when a text flashed across her vision. "Message received. Read." She covered her mouth with her hand. *Durham.* The time stamp on the automatic read receipt showed he'd opened her email long after they'd been separated. *Which means . . . which means . . .*

She blinked tears away. *He's alive.* She leaned on the wall for support. She caught her reflection in the darkened glass and straightened. The news was wonderful, to be sure, but she was caught off guard by how much a simple message had affected her. *Of course he's alive*, she told herself. Why had she ever allowed herself to believe otherwise? The man didn't have enough sense to die.

She began drafting a message in reply, but stopped mid-word. Morgan could have simply found the bloody shirt and jumped to a conclusion, but that would have required Durham to have taken the time to remove it in the first place. *Unlikely.*

Morgan had also said she'd seen the body, which meant she'd lied. *Why?* Juliane supposed Damien could have been controlling Morgan at the time and made her say things that weren't true. Juliane tried to recall if Morgan's voice had sounded unusual, but couldn't be sure. She hadn't known the other woman long enough to recognize the difference. But even if the lie was Damien's and not Morgan's, what would be the point?

Because he wanted Juliane to believe Durham was dead? *No*, Juliane realized, he didn't just want her to *believe* Durham was dead—he wanted him dead in reality but had failed.

There had been several times Morgan acted like she'd wanted to say more but had held back—had she let Durham get away? The lie, then, could have been intended for Damien just as much as it was for her, which also meant Damien's control over his followers wasn't absolute as Sam made it seem to be.

Juliane tapped her lip. Then again, Morgan had been helpless when forced to turn against Lyall, who was clearly dearer to her than some random stranger. Did Damien's control have something to do with distance? Pieces of the puzzle fell together, though the full picture remained irritatingly unclear.

Then again, her theory didn't explain why Damien bothered putting Durham into cryogenic sleep in the first place, or then waking him if he ultimately wanted him dead. The problem gnawed at her. She was now certain Damien had sent Morgan to collect them. The timing of her arrival was just too coincidental to believe anything otherwise. Damien, therefore, had to have been monitoring the cryo-tanks from afar. He'd have known more than one tank was powered down. He'd likely been the one to key in the reanimation sequence.

Had Durham's reanimation been an accident? Juliane shook her head. A person who'd gone to such pains to bring about the end of the world wouldn't have been sloppy enough to make a mistake like that.

If the death of billions hadn't been enough, Morgan's death made it clear Damien didn't care about sparing lives once a person had outlived his uses. He must have thought he still needed Durham. So, what had Durham said or done to change his mind? She rubbed her temple. What was she missing? She paced the room, trying to recall their last conversation, but no matter how many times she crossed the room, a logical explanation eluded her.

She needed to ask the source. Juliane returned to the window and pulled up Durham's contact record again. Another message could alert Damien that Durham remained a loose end. Then again, if her online activities were being monitored that closely, the damage was already done. Durham, then, would need as much advance warning to stay alert and as far away from here as she could give him.

She pressed her lips together. Indecision didn't sit well. She fired off a quick message with a link instructing him where to meet her in the datasphere and waited.

⁕

The darkened glass in front of her dissolved as her consciousness entered the digital world, and in its place was the interior of a luxury jet with a chessboard set up in front of her.

Her avatar picked up a knight. Her brain registered its touch as cool marble. The corner of her lips turned up as she gazed around at her creation. At least some part of the world she'd known before being forced into that tank had survived.

A figure materialized a short distance away.

Juliane placed the knight back on the table. After believing for so long that she'd never see him again, she had a difficult time focusing on anything else. Suddenly, she felt very small. She should never have agreed to go with Morgan. Not without seeing his body for herself—no matter what condition it was in. "You were dead." Her voice quivered with unshed tears more than she would have liked.

"Aw, and here I didn't think you cared." His tone made it sound like a joke, but there was no humor in his eyes.

"Why would you . . . of course I . . ." Did he think she'd left him because she wanted to? What kind of person would that make her? She turned away. "I mean . . ." she said, straightening. "You should have called."

"I tried. So many times. You might have been right about the concussion. I don't think I would be able to talk to you now if you hadn't sent the link."

It was all she could do not to confess exactly how much she'd missed him and how deep she was willing to admit her feelings for him ran. If Damien was monitoring her activity . . . *she couldn't give Damien a weakness to exploit.* "You need to stay away."

His shoulders slumped. "Why?"

Contacting Durham had been a terrible idea. There was no way to warn him of the danger he was in without the risk of alerting Damien she remembered more than she let on. She needed to watch what she said. "It's better if I don't tell you." She bit her lip. "It's not that I don't want you here—"

He held up his hand. "You don't have to explain."

"But I want to . . ." She pursed her lips. "I just can't right now. It's complicated," she said, holding up her hands.

"I already know you're in danger."

Juliane blinked. "You do?"

"Yeah. These people I'm with—they told me all about Woodspring. I'll agree to stay away from there as long as the next thing you tell me is that you're getting yourself far away from there, too."

"Woodspring? Oh, you mean—" She flicked her wrist. "I'm not there anymore." She swallowed a curse. The words had come out before she could stop them.

His brow creased. "Then why?"

She clenched her hands. She needed to reclaim control of the conversation. *If he knows about Woodspring, he might know something else that you can use now.* "Have you remembered anything more about the day we went into the tanks?"

Durham's mouth narrowed in a fine line, and as the pause continued, Juliane wasn't sure if he was going to answer, but then he said, "Bits and pieces. You were making a presentation. The whole group was supposed to be there. I'd gotten there early, gone to review some paperwork for Damien. He asked me if I wanted to get a sneak peek at the setup in the basement before the rest of you guys showed up. I think we shared a drink or something 'cause the next thing I know, the meeting's started, and Camille's pissed off her Wand thingy is already obsolete. Then nothing until you helped pull me out of that hole."

Juliane frowned. "What sort of papers?" she asked. Had Durham inadvertently seen something he shouldn't have? She shook her head. That couldn't be it, or he'd still be sleeping the years away with the rest of their colleagues.

Durham shrugged. "Pretty standard stuff. A lease agreement for an apartment in New York called the Pinnacle." He looked at her with fire in his eyes. "You're in New York. Aren't you? You found Damien."

Juliane looked away.

"I'm on my way," he said.

"That's exactly what I just finished telling you not to do." The man had an infuriatingly stubborn streak. How he'd managed to work his way into her affections in the first place was a puzzle she might never solve, but she could no longer deny that was exactly what he'd done.

"Juliane . . ." he said.

Her heart betrayed her mind's resolve at her name being spoken from his lips. There was a longing in his voice that demanded to be answered. She couldn't trust herself to stay with him any longer in a place where a touch could feel real. If he kissed her now . . . if they did more than kiss . . . and Damien found him before she could stop him. She couldn't bear it. "I'll contact you again. When it is safe. Until then, stay where you are."

Then, before he could protest further, she exited the datasphere. She blinked, and her view transformed back into the abandoned apartment and the blackened window. She returned to the bedroom, though paused in the doorway, looking at the large empty bed. Would Durham listen? She doubted it, which meant she had even less time to figure out a way to defeat Damien. She slipped under the sheets, twisting the fabric in thought until exhaustion took her.

twenty

STEPHEN

The door creaked open, and Stephen rose from the cot. The faces of those he'd hurt haunted him in the darkness as he followed Lyall. Neither of them said a word. Outside, a murky gray light of pre-dawn illuminated a layer of frost on the ground, making Stephen glad he'd found a place to pass the night protected from the elements.

So now what? Alan hadn't shared his plan with Stephen beyond the fact that Stephen and Lyall were supposed to somehow gain access to the barricade and convince the Sorcerers they weren't a threat long enough for the beastmen to pass through.

The corner of his mouth twitched. For a guy that was supposed to be some sort of innovative genius, his biological father hadn't exactly come up with the world's most original plan. It was pretty much the exact same thing the Watch had concocted, with him serving as bait in both. The fledgling smile slipped from his face.

Their footfalls echoed as they made their way down the empty streets. Then the buildings on either side of them were replaced by a line of trees, broken only by a cabled bridge stretching out across the water. "You ready?" Lyall asked. It was the first words he'd spoken all morning and effectively broke through Stephen's thoughts.

"Sure," he said. "I was born for this."

Lyall's lips twisted, but he continued on.

Wes would have laughed, thought Stephen as he followed behind. *Bean would have, too.* He traced the outline of the pendant. If anyone had bothered to ask him, he would have told them the whole mission was pointless, but no one had. It was just as well. If they had, they might have expected him to offer another suggestion, which would put Bean in danger.

Without him forcing her to stop every half hour to forage for food, she should have reached the tower by now. If she had, the Sorcerers would know they were coming. Warned, they'd see right through distraction. They were likely already preparing some nasty surprises. After the way he'd broken it off, he couldn't expect Bean to hold back either.

And if she hadn't reached the Sorcerers' home base . . . He scraped at the frost with his toe. She made it there, he told himself. Likely took a hot shower and slept in her old bed. He touched the pendant again. He was probably going to die today anyway. He might as well take the darn thing off if only to send Bean one last message. He reached under his collar.

Lyall's hand shot out, grabbing him by the shoulder. He pulled him over to a portion of the bridge's roadway blocked by a rusted school bus. "What's wrong?" asked Stephen in a whisper.

"Movement. Up ahead," whispered Lyall back.

"And that's bad how?" asked Stephen, straightening. "I thought the whole point of this was to get them to see us."

"Not yet, it isn't," replied Lyall. "The plan—"

"You might as well come out," shouted a voice from the other end of the bridge. "We know you're there."

"Guess we're going to have to improvise, then," Stephen said to Lyall in a low voice before walking out from behind the bus. "Thank goodness you found us," he shouted. "I was afraid we were lost out here."

"I recognize you," the man shouted. "You're that kid. Supposed to find the Wand for us. Heard you died."

"Yeah," Stephen shrugged. "That's kind of a long story."

The man came closer. "You don't have it now, do you?" He glanced down at his hand. "I wouldn't mind shaving a few years off."

An idea occurred to him. The plan to infiltrate the Pinnacle and the Sorcerer's home might be a bust, but maybe they didn't need to get inside. Maybe all they needed to do was get Damien out instead. Stephen held up his hands. "Nah, but I know who does." He lowered his voice conspiratorially. "And where to find him. Tell Finn I'm here."

The man's eyes narrowed suspiciously. "Why can't you tell him yourself." He tapped his temple.

"Like I said. It's a long story."

The man's lips tightened into a narrow line, and his gaze slid to the bus. "I take it your friend doesn't know what you're offering."

Lyall had remained hidden behind the bus and shouldn't have been visible to the naked eye, but it was clear to Stephen the man in front of him wasn't relying on sight alone. Distracted or not, if Alan thought his beastmen would be able to sneak up on the Sorcerers, he had another thing coming. Once again, the thought made Stephen wonder if that truly had been the real plan or if there was a larger game being played out.

"Lyall," shouted Stephen. "Come out. I need to introduce you to . . ." He nodded his head at the other man. A rustle to his side told him Lyall was making his way out into the open.

"Name's Henry," the man answered. His eye's narrowed as he took in Lyall's appearance. "Your friend looks familiar."

"He's got one of those faces," said Stephen. "Don't you?" Stephen assumed Lyall's answering nod was enough, because Henry didn't press further. "Right," said Stephen. "As I was saying—"

"How did you stay alive out there so long, anyway?" Henry looked off into the horizon. "Personally, you couldn't pay me to spend another night out there. The stories I've been hearing . . . beasts that move like people . . ." He shuddered. His gaze returned to Stephen.

Stephen heard a rustling behind him, which had to be Lyall emerging from his hiding place. "Yeah, well it was touch and go a couple of times. This is Lyall."

Lyall came to a stop next to Stephen. "He wants to join us."

Henry's gaze swept Lyall from head to toe. "Don't take this the wrong way, kid," he said to Stephen, "but he doesn't look to me like the joining type."

Lyall's body relaxed, and a smile broke out across his face. "I'm sorry," he said, extending his arm. "I've been on my own for so long, I guess I just forgot how I am supposed to act around other people."

"That's close enough," said Henry. The easy-going greeting had the opposite of its intended effect, making Henry grow tenser.

Lyall picked up the change in mood in an instant. His face became less jovial, and his movements more cautious. Stephen made a mental note not to trust anything his companion said based on how easily he'd slipped into whatever character he was intending to play. Lyall held up a hand. "Sure. You're the boss."

The phrase worked on Henry like magic. He stood taller and puffed out his chest. "Wait here," he said. "I'm going to call this in."

"Is that really necessary?" asked Lyall. "I've heard that the people who live here now have all sorts of powers. Like, I've heard it said you can shoot laser beams out of your eyes and are strong enough to lift trucks as if they were toy cars. I know for a fact, a person like me doesn't have a chance against a single person with those abilities."

"Whoever you have been talking to has been reading too many comic books," said Henry.

"The rumors aren't true, then?"

Stephen opened his mouth to speak.

Henry answered before he could get the words in. "I'm not saying anything other than follow me."

Stephen scratched at his neck where the chain rubbed the skin under his collar, missing the ability to communicate telepathically. It was now clear he and Lyall were each working a plan B that neither of the other was party to.

The sun continued its ascent in the morning sky. Stephen realized as they wove their way through the city streets that his stomach hadn't complained all morning, though their breakfast had been nothing more than a piece of dried meat and a leftover biscuit from the dinner before. *At least that's something*, he thought. After traveling inward for several blocks, Henry raised his hand. "Wait there," he said, pointing toward a recessed former display window. His gaze took on the blank expression of a person accessing the datastream.

The pair sat down on the narrow slab of concrete while they waited. "How far is the barricade from here?" Lyall whispered, though Stephen was pretty sure they could speak at a normal volume and not break Henry's concentration.

"I don't know," whispered Stephen back. "I didn't come this way before."

Lyall frowned.

"I told you I was going to be a terrible guide," he whispered.

"They should have sent me alone. Would have been better for everyone," said Lyall.

"Maybe," said Stephen. "But they didn't. So, here we are."

Henry blinked and came over to them, silencing further conversation. "You're in luck," he said to Lyall. "Seems the boss is more interested in what you know than concerned about the real reason you are here. I'm to take you to him."

Stephen started to stand. Henry turned toward him. "Not you," he said.

Stephen's brow knit for a moment. "Oh, I get it. He wants to question us one on one," he said, wishing he and Lyall had spent the time at the window sill formulating a plan together rather than arguing. "No problem. I'll stay here."

Henry shook his head. "That's not it," he said. "I told him how you've been cut off. You're of no use to Finn. Not anymore." He lowered his voice. "You seem like a good kid. Head back wherever you came from. Before Finn gets here."

Alan wasn't going to be pleased by this turn of events, thought Stephen. *No, not one little bit.*

twenty-one

JULIANE

Juliane woke with a start. While the windows blocked much of the light from outside, her body told her morning had come. She padded to the door and peered out through the keyhole. She jiggled the door handle, but the apartment remained as locked as it had been the evening before.

Juliane let go of the door. She could likely figure out how to bypass the lock, but she wasn't ready yet to show her hand. Instead, she moved into the kitchenette. A cup of coffee would go a long way.

She reached into a cabinet and pulled out a glass. The water from the tap ran crystal clear, tasting as good as it had the day before. However, outside of a handful of plates, the rest of the cabinets were bare. The only foodstuff in the apartment was the leftovers from her dinner the night before, which remained wrapped on the counter, exactly as she'd left them.

Juliane frowned. She was going to have to do something about them. He'd only agreed to let her cut their meal short when she'd offered to take them. Clearly, Damien wanted her to eat the food he'd provided, which meant she absolutely, positively did not want to do that. At the same time, the leftovers' presence would be another giveaway that she was still in control of her own brain.

She decided to break the problem into smaller, more manageable chunks. She peered into the sink. The kitchenette appeared to have a disposal unit, but that device would be connected to the grid powering the tower, and though the electrical surge would be small, it might be noted, depending on how closely the apartment was being monitored. Throwing it in the garbage would also be too obvious.

She carried the plate to the bathroom then tossed a small portion of the food into the toilet and performed a test flush. The food swirled around in the bowl, and for a second, Juliane wasn't sure it would go down, but eventually the bowl cleared.

Juliane took another handful of food off the plate and mashed it in her hands, attempting to soften it so it might go down the drain with less of a fight as she waited for the tank to refill. Her ears strained over the sound of the running water for any hint that someone may be coming to check on her. *This is taking too long*, she thought to herself, flushing the contents a second time.

She removed the lid from the tank as if she could will it to fill itself faster. She wrinkled her nose and dumped the rest of the dinner into its opening. It was a less than ideal solution and would likely cause plumbing issues she would have to deal with if she wasn't able to figure a way out of her current imprisonment, but it would have to do.

She'd just finished dropping the now-empty plate into the sink and washing her hands when the door to the apartment opened. "Is that housekeeping?" she asked, turning toward the door, infusing her voice with as much of a calm demeanor she could muster. "I'm afraid you'll need to come back later."

"Good, you're awake," said Damien letting himself inside. "I hope you are feeling better this morning."

"Much," she said drying her hands on a nearby dishtowel. "Thank you."

"I apologize if you tried to leave the apartment earlier," he said. "I'd locked the door."

"Locked?" Juliane raised an eyebrow, attempting to look like it hadn't even occurred to her to test the door.

"Yes, well some of the people who live here can be somewhat . . . eccentric. I thought it best if you didn't go wandering around last night. Just a temporary measure, I assure you."

"But I'm free to go where I please today, yes?"

He glanced at the sink, noting the empty plate. "I see you were able to finish your meal after all. Excellent."

She patted her stomach. "Nothing like steak for breakfast. Even cold. Thank you, it was delicious." She clenched her abdominal muscles. It wouldn't do for her stomach to growl at this moment.

"Ah, good, I'm glad you liked it. It took me ages to get the recipe right."

"So, other than experimenting with steak recipes, what *is* there to do around here during the day?"

Damien smiled and held out his hand.

Juliane drew back, realizing too late that she might have given herself away, but his gaze had gone blank. She moved toward the open and unlocked door without thinking. Her hand touched the knob. Damien's head swiveled towards her. He blinked, and his vision was clear once more.

Juliane smiled, fighting the disgust that threatened to come up like vomit. "Are you not taking me on a tour of your kingdom?" she asked. She'd run through a multitude of options during the night as to how to stop him, but thus far, the only solution she'd come up with was to kill him. Unfortunately, he'd likely planned for the possibility of his death. After all, he'd brought about the end of civilization. He would have made sure his madness lived on through one of his pawns.

No, in order to take him down, she had to first sever his control over the rest. To do that, she needed to find a weakness, which meant spending more time with him.

Damien's expression relaxed. "Unfortunately, the tour will need to wait as it would seem my people need me, but don't you worry. I won't be gone long."

Juliane released the handle. She gazed into the apartment. Her nose wrinkled at the sight of the blackened window. "I'd like to go with you," she said. "I might even be able to help. You know I can't stand to let a problem go unsolved."

Damien chuckled. "True, but unfortunately, this isn't the sort of problem you have experience with."

She drew herself up. "That's never stopped me before," she said. She gestured at nothing in particular. "Please," she said, hating to sound like she begged. "Everything has been turned upside down since I woke up. This could give me something I can sink my teeth into."

Damien's smile slipped. "I don't . . ." he began. His vision dulled for a moment. "Well, that's an interesting development," he muttered to himself. He turned toward her. "Perhaps it *would* be better for you to come with me after all."

⚬⚬⚬

Juliane's eyes took a moment to become accustomed to the natural daylight after having gotten used to the inside of the tower. Shards of broken glass and twisted metal made the light seem even brighter from where she and Damien stood. The view would have looked less out of place in a landfill than in the former major thoroughfare.

A handful of people materialized out of the heap's nooks and crannies at Damien's appearance. A few cocked their heads as if being instructed by words Juliane couldn't hear before disappearing back into the city streets.

No, she thought, *that's exactly what was going on*. Juliane pressed her lips together. She'd hoped he could command only a single person at a time, but the scene before her suggested otherwise.

Two figures came into view. Juliane wrinkled her face trying to make out more detail. *Was that Lyall? Why was he here?*

"Is something the matter?" asked Damien.

"No," she said, shaking her head. "Nothing the matter. It's just I recognize the one on the right. I met him on the way here." Juliane curled her lip in disdain. "Dreadfully boring place," she added. "I can see why no one wants to stay there."

"Oh?" said Damien. His gaze went blank. The man escorting Lyall gestured for him to continue to follow him. Damien blinked. "In that case, why don't you come down and help me welcome him to the community. I am sure he's understandably nervous and would appreciate hearing from a friendly face."

"Well," said Juliane. "I don't know how much of a difference that will make. We only met in passing. He probably won't even recognize me."

Damien smiled. "You don't give yourself enough credit, Juliane. You're not the type of person who people forget easily."

His words brought up memories of being chased by the tabloids long after her relationship with Louis ended. However, if she'd been hard to forget back then, it wasn't because of what she'd done, but whom. "That's kind, but I disagree."

"Disagree all you want, but I am right," said Damien. "In fact, I'm rather counting on it."

"What do you mean?" she asked, but Damien had already started down a path cut into the wall of debris. Not seeing any alternative for escape that wouldn't put herself and Lyall into danger, she hurried after him.

"It's Lyall, correct?" said Damien reaching the bottom. "How nice to meet you. People here call me Finn." He extended his hand.

Lyall's mouth twitched. "Oh, I know who you are." Before anyone could react, Lyall pulled out a knife. "This is for Morgan." He plunged a knife into Damien's chest. He pulled the blade out and stabbed Damien again. "And this is for my mother. My father." He took a step back.

Damien looked down at the stain of red spreading across his shirt. He grasped the bloodied handle and clucked his tongue. "Well, that's a shame," he said, looking down. "This was my favorite shirt." He eased the weapon out of his flesh. It left large gashes in the fabric, making it easy to see Damien's skin knit together. Juliane expected Damien would be hard to stop, but she hadn't anticipated an ability like that.

Lyall sank to his knees. "Go ahead and kill me, then," he said. "I'm ready."

"Oh, I don't think you are," said Damien with a predatory grin. "Most find they aren't, when the time actually comes." His gaze slid toward Juliane. "However, consider yourself lucky. That time isn't now." Addressing Juliane, he said, "You said you met this boy on the road? Where was that, exactly?"

Juliane cocked her head and wrinkled her brow as if what she'd just witnessed was normal. "I'm not entirely sure," she said after a pause. If she could have shaken Lyall, she would have. Sam, Rebecca, the baby girl—they were all at risk if Damien believed their truce was over. "The suburbs all look the same to me. All I know is it was on the other side of the river." She shrugged. "I suppose I could have asked, but then the storm hit and, well, I had other problems to worry about."

"No? Well, that's unfortunate." He directed his attention to the young man on the ground. "Luckily, I'm fairly certain I know where this boy comes from. As well as how many people live there. A place called Woodspring," Damien grinned. "Am I right?"

"They had nothing to do with this," Lyall spat on the ground. "This was my idea, and my idea alone."

"Now that's a lie, and we both know it." Damien crouched down next to Lyall. "That said, I have every reason to believe my old friends haven't regrown their spines since the last time I had to teach them a lesson. More like worms now than Serpentine. No, if I were a betting man, and I am, I'd say Alan put the idea behind this little tantrum in your head."

Juliane wasn't surprised Alan had been released from the sleeping death. The ruin around her was just as much his fault as Damien's. The day she'd gone into the tank, they were allies. However, it would seem that even more had changed while she slept. Thankful once again for the upgrade that allowed her to command her features, she adjusted her expression until her face was in her usual resting position and devoid of emotion.

Lyall's forehead wrinkled. "I don't know who or what you are talking about."

"That may well be true, but unfortunately, I don't have any reason to believe you. At least not yet. But I will." Damien stood and nodded at the man who had escorted Lyall to the wall. The man nodded back before reaching down and grabbing Lyall by the arm. He hauled Lyall back upright. The boy twisted for a moment but then went limp. A brown-haired woman Juliane hadn't noticed before joined the first man, and together, they carried Lyall away.

"What are they going to do to him?" asked Juliane as the trio departed.

"Nothing for you to worry about, my dear. They're simply giving him a shower."

"A shower?"

"Yes, a shower. You must have gone nose blind after spending so much time on the road, but trust me, he stunk." He laughed. "The people who come to visit us. They go through so much effort to try to hide from us, but none of them ever bother to wash up before they arrive. We don't have to see them. We can smell them from miles away."

"And then?"

"You'd be surprised at how much more agreeable people are after experiencing hot running water."

Steam, Juliane realized. *That's how he's managed to take control.* A shower's mist and jets of water could hide nanobots, and be the perfect way to get a person to unknowingly inhale them. She recalled the muddy puddle next to her clothes. No wonder Damien hadn't pushed back on her request to clean up before their dinner appointment. She hadn't needed to worry about laced food. She'd already played right into his hands.

She immediately issued a command for her body to run an internal scan. If he had done the same to her, it hadn't taken effect—at least, she didn't think it had, but that wasn't to say there wasn't a time delay. She had to erect a firewall of some kind *now.*

Damien's mouth twitched. "Feeling okay?"

Beads of sweat formed on her forehead. "I'm fine," she lied. "It's just very hot up here."

"We'll go inside soon enough. Now, come with me," he said. "I've been told there is someone else here who you'd be interested in meeting."

"I think I would rather go back inside." She would be better off solving this problem in the virtual world, but that would leave her real physical body defenseless while she worked. She could be injected with any number of substances while she was distracted or worse.

"It will only take a moment," he said. "Then I'll leave you to whatever it is you feel you need to do."

One of Damien's other minions came closer. The threat of what they might do if she didn't obey couldn't be clearer.

"Fine," she said, infusing her voice with control, though she was anything but in charge at the moment.

He led her down a path cut through the barricade which she might never have found on her own and down a ladder. The streets, now empty, echoed with their footsteps as they made their way around the corner.

twenty-two

STEPHEN

Stephen glanced up at the sound of approaching footsteps. Henry looked at him with regret. "You should've run when you had the chance."

Stephen's stomach turned. That didn't sound good. Lyall must have done something stupid. He touched the pendant. The virus running inside of him couldn't have replicated itself that many times during the night. He had to have at least a couple of minutes before the drain took over. Worst case, he could take Damien down with him.

Stephen's lips tightened. That was probably Alan's real plan after all. *I'm not bait.* He'd sent Stephen to take out his enemy and didn't care that he'd die in the process. *I'm a bomb.*

Damien rounded the corner. Unlike the other tower dwellers, he didn't hide his appearance. Nor did he make any effort to cover his chest where the fabric of his shirt was torn and bright red. A woman walked with him.

Stephen did a double-take. The woman walking toward him hadn't been at the tower the last time he'd been here. He would have remembered. His gaze returned to Damien. The raven-haired woman heading toward him might be gorgeous, but she was also no Bean.

"I don't believe I thanked you properly for locating the Wand," said Damien, coming to a stop in front of him. "Especially after how it was hidden from me." He glanced at his companion. "You might better know it as Camille's science project."

The woman's face creased in puzzlement. "What? Her anti-aging device?"

"Please, Juliane. This game you're playing—it was fun for a time—part of me wanted to see exactly how long you'd drag it out, but I've had enough. We both know you know exactly what I am talking about, as you were the one to keep it from me."

Juliane. Stephen took another look at the woman by Damien's side. The recording he'd seen in the datasphere hadn't done her justice. If anything, she looked younger now than she did in the recording—more alive.

Juliane's face paled, though she kept her chin up. "Then, that would make this boy—"

Damien grinned. "Alan and Betty's son, Stephen. Yes. See, I told you, you'd want to meet him." Damien glanced at Harry. A scowl replaced the grin. "I see what you mean," he said. He tilted his head. "Actually, it's not about what I see, but what I don't.

Damien turned to Juliane. "People who can access the datastream have a glow about them. An aura, as it were. It's how I can detect the gifted from the," he made a point of searching for a word, "not. I believe you were one of the first people to notice it."

"Some gift," muttered Stephen.

Juliane's eyes narrowed. "I didn't tell anyone about that."

Damien's teeth shone. "Maybe not in so many words, but I assure you, you did," he said. "You give away more than you think you do. For example, you were the one to give me a reason to visit your little factory. You also were the one who gave me the backdoor key into the power grid."

Juliane took another step back. "Those people hadn't done anything wrong."

"Except miss their production quota on a regular basis, I seem to recall you saying."

"You murdered them."

"No," he said. "I *had* them murdered. Completely different."

Henry moved as if to stop her. Damien raised a hand. "That won't be necessary," he said. "Dr. Faris here won't be going anywhere. I remembered how much she enjoyed analyzing patterns. I thought she'd enjoy piecing together how I gained control of the entire city on her own. But now that she has, she understands she has nowhere else to go." He turned his back on Stephen. "So, Doctor. Tell me, in your professional opinion, is the patient curable?"

"I'm not helping you hurt anyone else," she said.

"And I'm not suggesting you have a choice," said Damien. "Oh, don't be like that, Juliane. It's not like I enjoy taking away a person's will. I've found that a person loses a bit of spark whenever I do. Makes it harder and harder for them to come up with ideas on their own, but sometimes the greater good calls for a nudge."

Damien looked at Henry, whose face had taken on a look of puzzlement throughout the exchange. Henry's features went slack, and he turned and ran into the nearest wall without slowing. His head connected with a sick thud. Henry then stood and repeated the process. It reminded Stephen of a bird he'd once seen at the farmhouse who'd attacked the kitchen window over and over again after Nadia had left some seeds out on the counter.

Stephen wondered if he would be experiencing the same if either of the pair figured out how easy it would be to get him online again. He fought the urge to pull at the pendant. If he took it off now, he couldn't be sure that Damien would be his only victim.

"The greater good. You're still telling yourself that's what this is all about?" said Juliane, watching Henry with white knuckles. Stephen expected her to charge at Damien or rush to stop the other man before he could damage himself further, but instead, she looked to the sky.

"What else could it be?" asked Damien. "I would have thought you of all people would understand that our greatest growth as a species has always come following chaos and tragedy. The Roman Empire rose from the Middle ages. The Thirty Years' War gave birth to the ideas of the Enlightenment."

"Spare me the history lesson," she said. "My area of interest has always been the future, not the past."

"And this is your future, if you don't watch your step," said Damien, pointing at Henry. "Which would be a shame, not to mention so boring. A beautiful brain like yours . . ." he said, shaking his head. "I'd hate to spoil it, especially over such a small thing."

"And as I mentioned, I prefer," said Juliane. "to look up. You should, too, sometime. You never know what you might see."

A wave of an odor that reeked of death and excrement assailed Stephen's senses as darkness covered the sunlight, followed by a thunderclap. The odor grew stronger as a bird, larger than anything Stephen had ever seen, plunged down from beyond the skyscraper heights. A scream cut through the city streets. He wasn't sure if it came from the bird or if it came from him as his body was picked up by cruel-looking talons.

Then the ground beneath him receded, growing farther and farther away by the second. Wind rushed his cheeks as he struggled. They ascended higher and higher, until only the highest floors of the occasional tower surrounded him.

The bird screamed again—its call echoed by another. However, Stephen couldn't spot the other bird. Not that he was looking too closely. More of his attention was on the ground far beyond and the thought of how little the talons clutching his arms hurt compared to what he'd feel if the bird were to let go.

He allowed his body to go limp as the streets and skyscrapers stopped at the edge of the glimmering river.

Then they were on the other side. The bird holding him called out again to its friend or mate. *There are more of the bloody things.*

The air clapped around him like thunder. The ground beneath rose back up at an alarming rate. *Here goes,* he thought. *I'm going to die.*

Stephen's stomach flip-flopped as they plunged back toward the earth. His ears popped at the change of pressure. At this speed, the landing wasn't going to be gentle.

Just as Stephen resigned himself to becoming a flattened mash of entrails, the bird opened its wings. His body lurched as their descent slowed. The bird changed its course, and they were again over the river. Then the pain around his shoulders where the bird clutched him disappeared, and Stephen found himself free-falling as the river rose up to meet him.

He spread his arms and legs as if he could somehow force his body to glide to safety. However, all it did was expose more of his belly to the icy cold water as he crashed through its surface.

Stephen sank like a rock. He'd learned how to swim in a nearby creek, but that body of water had rarely been deep enough for him not to be able to touch the bottom if needed. This was a completely different experience; one made even more difficult by the fact that Stephen could no longer tell which way was up in the darkness.

A shimmer of light caught his eye. He turned his body toward it. *Please be up,* he thought. Pressure built in his lungs as his body called out for air. His muscles seized as his body's heat bled into the icy water.

The flash caught his eye again. It wasn't light, he realized, it was simply something white. His arms slowed. His kicks grew less determined. Out of all the ways he thought he would die today, being considered take-out by a monster bird and drowning hadn't been one of them. As panic took over, he laughed, releasing the remaining bubble of air from his lungs. His vision dimmed as the flash of white drew closer. Stephen's last thought before he lost consciousness was that he hoped whatever it was, it wasn't hungry.

twenty-three

JULIANE

Damien glared at Juliane as a feather the size of a dog landed on the ground where his latest prisoner had knelt captive a moment ago. "I hope you are proud of yourself," said Damien. "However, explain to me how what you did to that creature is any different from what you find so distasteful about what I do." He gestured toward the other man, who now lay in a crumpled heap next to a bloodied wall.

"The suggestion I placed in that bird's brain is temporary, for one—and I only did it to save a life. You're killing people."

"People die every day." He glowered at her. "At least my way gives their deaths purpose. Besides, you say that as if saving a life is always the better choice. Take the boy, for example. You and I both know he should have died years ago. Instead, his life cost Betty hers. She should never have redirected her energy. All that talent. All that potential—wasted—and for what? A life that's proven to contribute nothing further to this world than act as another distraction."

Juliane's eyes narrowed. She clenched her fists. "I think we've talked long enough."

"Don't worry, you won't remember this conversation much longer." His gaze went slack. Juliane's gaze darted around, looking for something either blunt or sharp to strike him with if only to break his connection to the datastream. *No time*, she thought. She'd have to take the fight to the virtual world.

Juliane accessed the datasphere. Damien's data signature was easy enough to locate—so confident in his control, he hadn't bothered to shield it. She'd use that to her advantage.

She countered his command with one of her own, turning the signal into nothing more than a nonsensical series of ones and zeros. She readied herself for retaliation. He hadn't expected her to fight back this time. He wouldn't make the same mistake again. The scene in front of her was replaced with rolling hills of an unnatural green. Light poured in from all directions. "I won't make it easy for you," she said, leaping into the air and hovering there.

"You never have." The few small shadows pulled together, becoming more like a puddle than the absence of light. A shape arose from their depths, twisting and building upon itself until it resembled the figure of a man. "I understand why Alan was so obsessed with you." The figure shifted; however, it remained as dark as a shadow.

"Speaking of which, I truly did hope things would work out between the two of you organically. You were always a condition of our previous dealings together. It would have made things better for you in the next day or so, when I give you to him in exchange for the return of the Wand." He laughed. "Of course, that's also the reason I had to eliminate your other friend after I was satisfied you were on your way here. I know you've wondered. I wasn't sure how much you'd remember upon waking and needed someone you trusted to convince you to leave Worcester. But you weren't supposed to develop feelings for that fool. I guess I shouldn't have been surprised; you've never shown yourself to have any taste."

Juliane extended her arms and legs downward and grew until her feet touched the rolling hills. "Is this the part where you explain all your evil plans?" she asked with a smirk. "Because I feel I should remind you, I'm the one who invented this place. You're in my world now."

The man-shadow raised a hand and broke apart into a murder of crows, which flew into the air and darted about until they produced the shape of a face. "You may be its original creator, but I've been in control here far, far longer. I know all the tricks you do."

Juliane held her head like a queen. She flicked her wrist, and her body was once again her normal size. The sky darkened and filled with clouds. A single bolt of lightning arched across the heavens and struck at the mass of birds.

The face made up of birds dissolved as the flock converged into a single column of black. The column fell, striking the earth. The horizon shook, though Juliane remained where she stood. A crack appeared and made its way up the side of the column. More fissures appeared. Pieces of the column fell away as the crack raced higher and higher up its surface.

"Was that supposed to impress me?" Juliane crossed her arms over her chest and tapped her arm with a finger. Large sections of the column fell away, disappearing as they crumbed onto the grassy knoll, until only a man-shaped outline remained.

The stone figure rushed toward her like a freight train. Juliane held one hand out, summoning a gale-force wind.

The wind should have been enough to send Damien flying away, but his avatar dug his heels into the ground as stone turned to wood and roots wormed their way into the earth around him.

Movement out of the corner of Juliane's eyes was her only warning before a large root the size of a bus emerged on her left. It wrapped itself around her legs, then her chest, and squeezed. Her lungs became more difficult to fill as it wrapped tighter and tighter.

"Now who's the one who is being overly confident in their abilities?" said Damien with a smile. While his feet remained anchored into the ground, the rest of his body stretched and moved closer to her.

"I just wanted you closer," said Juliane, though the words weren't easy to say with the constricted oxygen flow. Her body became a white-hot flame.

Damien screamed and pulled his wooden tentacles away, but not before several were reduced to ash.

"Guess all those years of extra experience didn't give you quite the advantage you expected. Did they?" asked Juliane, returning to her normal form. She looked down at her dress and dusted away the remaining ash where it marked the fabric.

Damien snarled and charged at her. A cage of silver wrapped in a wire mesh materialized out of thin air, halting him in his tracks. "Hurts, doesn't it," she said. She took a deep breath and looked around the virtual landscape she'd created before focusing her gaze on Damien again. "It's also far less than you deserve."

"All you've done is piss me off," said Damien. He grabbed at the bars only to jolt back to the center of the cage. He scowled and clenched his fists. "Damn it." His eyes narrowed. "What have you done?"

Juliane's brow wrinkled. She hadn't designed the cage to do that.

"You have no idea how long I have been waiting for this moment," said a new male voice. A figure faded into existence where no one stood before. He was a young man with dark-rimmed glasses.

"Wes," Damien shouted from within the cage. "But how . . . that can't really be you. You're dead." Damien looked at Juliane with fear in his eyes. "He's dead. Who are you?"

The boy shrugged, but didn't look at his captive. He turned his attention to Juliane. "I do apologize for being late to the party, but you are one difficult woman to track. I mean, I knew you were somewhere around here, of course, but dividing your signal like that?" He kissed his fingers. "Well done."

"This doesn't concern you," said Juliane. The new arrival had to be part of Damien's back-up plan. Avatars could be made to look like anyone and anything a person pleased. She didn't trust that the real person looked anything like the man before her. In fact, she didn't trust anything about him, especially how young his voice sounded. It had to be a trick. One designed to make her lower her guard. Juliane took a closer look at the bars surrounding Damien. It was only a matter of time before Damien found a flaw in their design.

"He can't escape, if that's what you are worried about," said Wes. "While you were talking, I took what you'd created and made it better." He laughed. "Think of it as a Faraday cage. He can try to send commands to the datastream all he wants. He's not going anywhere." This time, the boy did spare a glance for Damien. "Now, tell me, how do *you* like being a prisoner in your own mind?"

"Overconfidence puts us both at risk," said Juliane. "A virtual cage won't hold him forever. What happens when you need to rest? It's simply a matter of time until he finds a way to break free."

"Oh, I don't need rest," said the boy. "In fact, I don't need anything. Not anymore." He glared at Damien. "You heard him. I'm dead. However, you have a point."

Damien began cursing. At first, Juliane thought the cage was simply getting smaller, but then she realized that the entire structure was sinking into the ground. Damien's curses became more frantic as the space between him and the top of his prison grew smaller.

Juliane pressed her lips together as she considered what would happen now that Damien was trapped in the datasphere. If the cage held, and that was a big if, his body in the real world would remain in a vegetative state. However, that would only solve the immediate problem.

He'd already laid the groundwork for worldwide dominance. There were bound to be people serving under him who hadn't needed that extra nudge from a computer program to join his way of thinking. If Sam hadn't suggested as much, Alan was all the proof she needed.

She looked at the glowing world that she'd once believed would serve as her legacy. It might be tomorrow or years from now, but it was only a matter of time before someone else decided to follow in his footsteps. And then what? Would the rest of her life be spent fighting Damien's followers and ensuring they never left their virtual prison? "It's the only option," she muttered to herself and started issuing commands.

At first, few of her efforts were noticeable to the naked eye. The air stilled completely, and not a blade of artificially constructed grass moved. The parts of the sky dimmed and faded away, exposing nothing but narrow bands of black as her new code wormed its way through the computer program she'd used to give this place life.

Damien's screams suddenly turned into hysterical laughter. She spared him a glance from the corner of her eye as she continued with her work. His body was sunk into the ground to his waist, leaving only his arms free, which were now pointing at the sky.

"What are you doing, Juliane," growled Wes.

"What I have to," said Juliane. She turned her attention back to her work. She couldn't afford to be distracted. Her original code had been a masterpiece. If she was going to destroy it, it deserved her full attention.

"I can't let you do that," said Wes.

"You don't understand," she said.

"No, you don't understand," said Wes. His voice was robotic.

Juliane's eyes widened as the things he'd said finally clicked together in her brain. "You're . . . you're not just an avatar. Are you?"

"I was once. Now, it's time for you to go." He held up a hand. Juliane flew backward as if she'd been struck by a wrecking ball. She was once again surrounded by towering skyscrapers.

"No. Not until I finish what I started," she said. She didn't need to see Wes to know he could still hear her. She clenched her fists and resumed her commands. The skyscrapers pixelated and jittered.

"Stop," Wes's voice boomed from all directions.

"I can't," said Juliane. Blocks of skyscrapers disappeared, exposing empty streets. "Not until I know for sure that history will never repeat."

"Then I have no choice."

Juliane had prepared herself to be struck by another blast of air by surrounding herself in an invisible shield. Instead, the entire cityscape disappeared, and Juliane found herself in a bubble floating in a river of starlight. Her bubble picked up speed until the bits of stars were nothing more than streaks of light, and for the first time, she realized that though she had created the digital world, she may no longer be its master.

twenty-four

STEPHEN

Stephen floated in darkness until his body came to rest on a grassy shore. He gingerly rose to his knees, coughing up water from his lungs. A forest surrounded him. He blinked as he stumbled over rocks before straightening the rest of the way. He knew these woods, but they were miles away. A thick rope swing hung from one of the branches. He knew that rope, too.

He'd found it attached to one of the trees when he was a kid—a remnant of the family who'd once called the farm home. Whoever they'd been, they'd never returned, but somehow, he had. He continued through the woods until the tree line broke. There, exactly where he thought it would be, stood the farmhouse. He looked back over his shoulder at the woods. The bird was fast, he gave it that, but how had he gotten all the way back here?

He picked his way up the grassy path. The windmill turned in a breeze just strong enough to be comforting. *That's not right*, he thought. The last time he'd seen it, it was broken. Stephen held his breath. Was he back in the digital world, or had he died?

He reached up to touch the pendant but found only his chest. The protection against the drain was gone. So, I'm dead, he decided.

He grinned. The idea of being dead didn't bother him nearly as much as he thought it would. He raced up the remainder of the path and threw open the front door.

Stephen expected to find Nadia there ready to welcome him home. Instead, the room on the other side was dark and lifeless.

She's probably out working in the garden. It would be just like Nadia to still feel the need to do chores even in the afterlife.

The door slammed against its frame behind him as he made his way back outside. He cupped his hands around his mouth and shouted her name but received no reply. He scanned the horizon for any sign of where she might have gone.

Stephen looked at the barn. If he'd learned anything growing up, there was no surer way of summoning his mother than trying to goof off when she thought there was work to be done.

He opened the barn door and made his way over to his regular hiding place. *That's strange*, he thought, pulling at a floorboard. The board usually took very little effort to move. *Had Chad finally got around to fixing it?* Stephen wrinkled his brow. *What am I thinking? This is heaven.* He focused his thoughts and pulled at the board again. This time, the plank came away freely in his hand, revealing the old computer terminal he'd rebuilt from scratch.

He picked up the computer and pressed the button with the circle on it. The screen flickered and flashed as the operating system went through its standard power-up routine. Stephen sat back while he waited. The sequence could take a while to complete and often required him to reboot the system more than once. However, this proved not to be one of those times, as the familiar welcome screen was quickly replaced by a series of icons.

He didn't hesitate to click on one of the icons near the top of the screen. The display changed once more, showing the title cards for his favorite game with two buttons underneath. Single-Player or Multi-Player.

Stephen grinned, and he toggled the second option. With any luck, Wes was here, too. He pressed the enter key. The display flickered. Then the world around him went black, including the screen in front of him. Even the yellow LED indicator denoting the computer had power had gone off.

Shit, he thought. *So much for things working in the great beyond.* He stood and made his way back to where the barn door should be, if only to open it so that some natural light might shine its way in.

He found himself back in the farmhouse kitchen; only this time, he wasn't alone. The person he'd sought for the last several days sat the table. Considering how long it had taken to find her, Stephen felt he should have been more excited to see her. Instead, his shoulders slumped. The giant birds must have taken her, too. Was her body now being ripped and torn to feed some monstrous hatchlings or resting at the bottom of the river like his was? Another possibility occurred to him. "I'm not in heaven after all, am I?"

Juliane's eyebrows twitched. "No. This most certainly isn't heaven."

Stephen turned toward the door. "Yeah, well . . . If I'm not dead, I will be soon enough." He reached for the door, but the door refused to budge. "Why won't this thing open?"

Juliane smiled. "Exactly the question I was wondering as well."

If this isn't heaven then— "Wes," shouted Stephen. "I need you." His eyes narrowed. The big red button Wes created for him materialized at Stephen's command. He pushed it repeatedly. "Work, damnit," he muttered.

Wes appeared, but he was a faded version of himself, more ghost than digital construct. He looked forward with dull eyes, focusing on nothing in particular. "I'm sorry," he said. "I know I said that all you had to do if you ever needed to talk was push that button, but things have changed, er . . . I've changed." His lips tightened. "Or, I will have if you're listening to this message. Unfortunately, this also means you're going to need to find a new teammate to run missions with from now on."

Stephen stared at the recorded image without blinking. "What have you done?"

"He's taken over the datasphere," said Juliane, gesturing at their surroundings. "I still haven't figured out how, but as soon as I do, I'll take it back and get us out of here."

"No," said Stephen with a laugh. "Don't you get it? It's worse than that. He didn't take over the datasphere, he *is* the datasphere now."

Juliane frowned and shook her head at the idea. "That's impossible. The digital world is simply a bridge. Think of it as a mesh that connects individual nodes. No one individual can take it over, at least not completely. Trust me. I know more than a few things about it." Her cheek twitched. "The only way a person could take it over completely would be for him or her to somehow sever their anchor to the real world."

"Not a problem for Wes. He doesn't have a physical body to return to. Died days ago." Stephen made a popping gesture on either side of his head. "Yeah, I know, but before he died, Wes found a way to upload this version of himself."

"An artificial intelligence," Juliane's forehead wrinkled. "Made to think and act like a teenaged boy." She sighed. "I suppose that explains how he's managed to keep me here against my will."

She stood and walked to the kitchen window and tapped her finger on the sill. "From a purely objective standpoint, his code is brilliant in its design. Every time I think I've found a way out, the code shifts." She turned back to Stephen. "Simply brilliant. However, AI or no AI, no code is perfect. I'll find us a way out of here. Unfortunately, though, if I can, Damien might, too." She began to pace the room. "Then again, Damien's not a programmer."

"But you are." He stepped toward her. "About that. You see—"

"He's here, too. Damien, I mean." Juliane waved Stephen's attempt to explain the virus away. "In another part of the datasphere. Trapped in a cage. Ugh, I'm getting sidetracked. I need to think." She turned and walked back toward the window.

"As I was saying, he's not a programmer. At least, not a natural-born one, so there is a chance it'll take a while for him to find the flaw, but he will." She tapped her lip as she spoke. She looked at Stephen. "And next time, he's not going to let either of us live."

"I wouldn't be so sure," said Stephen. "Take this place, for example. We seem pretty stuck here. Maybe this cage will hold him longer than you think it will."

"Are you willing to bet your life on it?" Juliane asked. "Because I'm not." Her eyes bore into Stephen's with an intensity that demanded obedience. "You need to tell me everything about your AI friend. If I can better understand how he thinks, I might be able to figure out how to get us out of here *before* Damien does. How did you meet? What were you into?"

Stephen pressed his lips together and walked over to where Juliane stood. He pointed out of the window. "You see that barn?" he said. "In the real world, I have a computer hidden in the floorboards, which is how I used to play *Colony Defenders II*, before I knew I had any of this," he gestured at the surroundings, "in my head. Wes used to play it, too. But speaking of things in my head—"

Juliane pursed her lips. "So, we go to the barn."

"Yeah, except I was just there, and all the good it did was to put me in here. Unless . . ."

"Unless what?"

"Unless we're already in the game." He glanced around the room. "Which would mean," he said to himself. "We're in a waiting room."

"Is that supposed to mean something?"

He laughed. "Dude, when I find my way out of here, we're going to need to have a talk." He looked at Juliane, whose face was puzzled. "In the game, before you go on a mission, you first materialize in a waiting room. It's a safe zone. Gives newbies a place to familiarize themselves with the rules without having to worry about any of the bad guys finding them or time limits."

Juliane gestured for him to continue.

"If I am right, and Wes sent us to a waiting room, then all we have to do is find the portal."

"Can't we just leave the game?" asked Juliane.

Stephen pursed his lips. "Do you see a big flashing exit button anywhere? The only way I know how to do that is to turn the computer off altogether, and that's not an option."

"Fine. What does a portal look like?"

"A glowing red rectangle." Stephen frowned, looking back at the barn through the window. They had to be in a waiting room. Stephen didn't have any other ideas if they weren't. "While we're waiting, though—"

"Found it," said Juliane from the hallway.

He hadn't noticed her moving. He found her in front of Chad and Nadia's bedroom door. Relief washed over him. Sure enough, the doorway was framed by an unnatural soft red glow.

"I take it we go through here."

Stephen took a step. Then paused.

"What's wrong."

"Something else just occurred to me."

"I'm sure whatever it is, it can wait."

"I'm not hungry."

"Good for you. Let's go."

"You don't understand. I'm always hungry."

"That's fairly typical for a boy of your age."

"What if I'm like him?"

"Like who?"

"Wes," said Stephen.

Juliane cocked her head. "You seemed well enough when I saw you."

"Yeah. Well, something happened to me," he said. "Before you found me. I've got a virus." He looked at his hands. "Or maybe it's, I had a virus. That's what I was trying to tell you. I was hoping you'd—" He took a step back from the door. "Wes," he shouted. "Tell me you didn't upload some version of me."

Juliane's eyes narrowed. "Deal with your identity crisis later. Now, are you coming or not?" The portal pulsated. Stephen remained where he was. Juliane shook her head. "This is why I've never wanted children," she muttered. She looked Stephen in the eye. "You're still alive," she said.

"How would you know?"

"I know because I can sense you. Out there." She gestured at the horizon. "I didn't recognize the connection for what it was until I saw you kneeling on the ground, but it would seem your mother found a way to link us together shortly before she died."

Stephen blinked. "Come again? My mother? Linked you and me?" he asked. "She wouldn't know the first thing—" He frowned. "Oh, you mean Betty, my birth mother." Did that mean, all this time on the road, all he had to do was reach out with his mind? He groaned, thinking of how Alan had intruded upon his dreams and seemed to be able to sense where he was. Could he have done that with Juliane all this time? He could have asked, no, *demanded*, she start working on a cure days ago. *Which meant*, His eyes widened. *Bean*. He hadn't needed to break her heart or take Alan's offer. "Why?" He sputtered. Why couldn't Betty have just told him that instead of being all cryptic?

Juliane frowned. "She thought you were dying. I thought she was in the midst of a breakdown or at least a month's good sleep." Juliane shook her head. "But before that, she'd developed a revolutionary energy collection and inductive transfer protocol. I'd seen it as a way to break away from the traditional power grid. I thought it had the potential to even stop world hunger, if applied correctly; much like how a plant requires only the sun for nourishment." She wrinkled her nose. "I can see I'm losing you, so let me put it in more basic terms. Betty Dronigh essentially turned herself into a backup battery."

The ramification of her words hit him like a fist. "I killed her."

"What?" Juliane blinked. "No."

"No? I'm the reason she died. I sucked out her energy. You just said so." He tried not to imagine what Betty looked like after he'd finished with her. Had she, like the old man in the woods, been left a wizened husk with not enough meat left on her bones to feed ants or other scavengers?

"No, I said she saved your life and then passed that link on to me."

"Which killed her," said Stephen with a nod. His stomach turned. He was responsible for the death of not one, but both of his mothers.

"She died, but your mother was the one to make the choice." Juliane stretched out an arm and held it above Stephen's shoulder. She bit her lip and pulled it back. "You can't blame yourself."

"But I do."

She shook her head. "And that helps you how?" Juliane pointed at the glowing frame. "We're wasting time."

Stephen's eyes widened. "You're the reason the drain hasn't killed me yet," he said. "That's the reason she wanted me to find you. Like the tower and why I'm not hungry there. I had to find you. In the physical world. Not just here. It must only work if we're close together."

Juliane's head tilted. "You're not making sense again." She passed a hand through the glowing door frame. Nothing happened.

"The drain. It's what Damien's people call it when you stray too far from the Sorcerers' complex. Basically, unless you are constantly eating or close to a power source," Stephen fought a shudder, "you die. The people there think it's a side effect of their abilities, but it's not. Well, I suppose it is. I mean, you said my mom fed me energy—so I had to already be affected before I ever met Damien, but the virus makes it a million times worse. It's how he keeps people under his control."

"Hmm," answered Juliane testing the doorway again. "Yes, I'd concluded he was behind Gene Assist's modification and doing something like that." She glanced over her shoulder back at him. "Now, a question for you. What would happen if a player in this game of yours never exited the waiting room?"

Stephen blinked. "Nothing. Nothing happens until everyone has crossed."

"That's what I thought. Therefore, I would appreciate it if you would stop dwelling on the past and help me change the future. You were planning on asking me to help you find a way around the drain. Yes? I intend to fix that—fix everything, and not just for you, but for everyone. Unfortunately, I can't do anything while trapped in here." She took a breath and looked into his eyes. "Trust me."

The doorway pulsed again. He looked over at his shoulder back to the kitchen area and the table where Chad was constantly rearranging piles of junk. He sighed. "You'll want to arm up before we go," he said. He looked at his hand and a knife appeared.

Juliane's lip curled. "I don't think that is necessary."

The corner of his mouth curved up. "Now it's your turn to trust me. I've played this game before." He looked at the doorway and took a breath. He stepped through the open doorway.

twenty-five

JULIANE

The room transformed the minute they crossed under the glowing frame, replacing the small rustic bedroom with a desert. A foreign moon hung in the sky. Large jagged rocks poked up in every direction, blocking her view. "Now what?" she asked Stephen. Her voice sounded strange, like it was being transferred over an intercom or a walkie talkie.

"Keep your eyes peeled," he said.

She noted that his appearance had changed along with the landscape. The young man who'd seemed so boyish in the farmhouse kitchen was now at least six inches taller with muscles no amount of natural workout could ever produce. His face was also covered by a visor and mask. She raised her hand only to realize it was larger as well and man-shaped. *Lovely*, she thought. "So, what are we supposed to do in this game?"

Static freckled Stephen's laugh. "We make it to the other side."

"That's it?" said Juliane, looking out across the desert. "Not really much of a challenge then, is it?"

"Oh, it's about to get more interesting." He nodded. "Heads up. Three o'clock. We've got company."

Juliane looked in the direction he'd suggested, but all she saw was the side of her visor. She cursed. "I can't see anything with this thing on." She reached up to her visor to pull the mask off.

"Because we are on an alien planet surrounded by a poisonous atmosphere. And before you ask, I know this because I've had more than one helmet crack playing this game. Watch out!" he shouted.

A dark creature leapt out from behind one of the rocky outcroppings. It had four arms, a large, fanged maw of a face, and moved like a spider. "What do I do?" asked Juliane.

"What do you think? You kill it before it kills you." Stephen demonstrated by running up and slashing at the creature with his knife. The creature vanished with a scream. "Haven't you ever played a video game before?"

Juliane drew herself up. "I had rather more important things to do with my time," she said. "Like finding the money to pay for my next meal," she muttered. "And creating an entire online world."

He picked up a boulder and tossed it. The rock broke apart upon impact, revealing a floating round object which Stephen grabbed and pocketed.

"Was that a hand grenade?"

"Yup. In addition to killing the bad guys, you are going to want to throw stuff around, too. The stuff underneath usually comes in handy later."

"But . . . but that is so . . . so . . . pointless."

Stephen shrugged. "You're going to want to move before the creature respawns . . . er . . . comes back to life." He jogged up ahead and slashed at another alien Juliane hadn't even seen approach.

Another four-armed shape appeared up ahead. *This is ridiculous*, thought Juliane. She marched up to a rock and picked it up with ease, though it was at least two if not three times larger than the size her head, and threw it at the beast. Both the rock and the alien disappeared upon impact. A beaker filled with a red substance hovered above the ground where the alien once stood.

"Nice," said Stephen, gesturing at the bottle. "You'll want to hold on to that. With as little experience you have, the elixir of life is bound to come in handy before too long."

Juliane grabbed the bottle and gently shook it in her hand, noting that the contents remained in the exact same position as the beaker moved rather than acting like a normal liquid would. "And how am I supposed to drink this stuff? According to you, I can't remove my helmet."

"Damned if I know," said Stephen with a laugh. "I've only ever had to hit the space bar and *P* at the same time back in the real world. No idea how it would work here."

Juliane wrinkled her nose. "Guess we better hope I don't need it, then."

"Guess so. Now, I thought you were in a rush to get out of here. Keep moving."

"This friend of yours, Wes, and I are going to have a discussion about programming realism one day."

A pack of three creatures appeared, and Juliane put the annoyance about the game's flaws to the side while she worked on clearing a path. More aliens appeared, except these were a lighter gray and moved more like caterpillars than spiders. They were also significantly bigger. At first, they seemed to amble along slowly enough that Juliane thought they might be able to avoid them simply by jumping up on one of the rocks, but as soon as either of them got within a yard of the beast, it would lower its head and charge at them with a murderous rage.

Juliane picked up a small boulder and hurled it toward the animal. "Couldn't they have bothered to at least try to follow natural laws? No real animal would behave like this." The creature shuddered upon impact, but only the rock disappeared.

"Take your complaints up with the game designers. Now, you have to hit it again, while it is still frozen," shouted Stephen.

"Like this?" She closed her eyes and jabbed at the creature with her knife. The motion shouldn't have done more than scratch the animal's skin, but it popped like a balloon landing on a blade of grass.

"See, that wasn't so hard."

The way before them was empty. Rather than waste words on further discussion about poor design or unrealistic experiences, Juliane ran forward. The ground gave way underneath her feet, and she found herself falling into a dark chasm.

twenty-six

STEPHEN

Stephen looked down into the large square sinkhole, but it was too dark to see where Juliane had landed. "You alive down there?" he shouted into the pit. There was no answer. "Shit," he said. Grabbing the edge of the pit as an anchor, he felt around on the side of the hole for any purchase he could leverage to get to its bottom safely.

His foot found a narrow outcropping. Though the pit seemed to prevent light from penetrating its depths in any direction, the ledge felt too much like a man-made ladder for Stephen to think it was there for any other reason but intentional design. He snorted at the thought of what Juliane might say when she realized how he'd made it down and risked taking another step.

As absolute darkness covered his eyes, Stephen stifled the urge to laugh. Who would have thought that the same world that had caused Juliane such annoyance for its lack of reality would have reminded him what it felt like to be alive? An image of Nadia and Chad crossed his mind, but neither wore the cold accusing expression he'd become used to seeing on their faces when he closed his eyes.

Instead, Chad was stacking components on the kitchen table while Nadia prepared dinner. Then Bean appeared. Smiling at him. Kissing him. Telling him she loved him—and definitely not getting the life sucked out of her with his touch. Suddenly, Stephen realized he was as ready to get back to the real world as Juliane was. He picked up his descent.

After what felt like an age, but was likely only a minute, Stephen's feet found hard ground. A glowing orb bloomed into existence the second both of his feet were on the ground, illuminating about three feet in front of him in whatever direction he looked, but little more.

The orb followed him, hovering just over his head as he scanned the pit for evidence of Juliane. He expected to see her unconscious body, but instead all he found was a translucent crate that pulsated in the same way the portal into this world had.

He walked over to it and crouched down. "You in there, Juliane?"

"Apparently," came her muffled reply. Her voice was filled with static and was as light as if she were miles upon miles away. "I'm stuck."

"It's actually worse than that. You lost a life."

"How many do I have left?"

"None, really. You're only still in the game because I am here."

"So, what do I have to do to . . . to come back to life?"

"The term is respawn. And you can't do anything. When you lost your life, you also dropped your inventory, which means—"

"Which means what?"

"Hold on, I'm looking for it," said Stephen swiveling his head so that the light would shine in a larger radius. "Got it." He picked up the beaker containing the elixir of life from where it had come to a rest near the crate. "Okay, now, I am going to have to smash that crate. I don't *think* it will hurt, with you being technically dead already, but just in case, you may want to brace yourself."

He performed a double hop that defied all laws of physics in the real world. He curled his body into a ball at the peak of its height, then straightened like a board. The sequence sent him hurtling back toward the ground like a meteor, exploding the crate upon contact. In its place lay the supine, ghostly form of his mission teammate.

He then threw the beaker of elixir at her. The beaker froze in mid-air above Juliane and flashed three times. With each flash, Juliane's body became more solid, while the reverse was true for the beaker, until only Juliane remained.

"How did it feel?" asked Stephen. "To be dead?"

Juliane tilted her head as she thought through his question. "Not that much different from being in stasis," she said after a long pause. She looked up toward the surface level. "What would have happened if you hadn't come down here after me?"

Stephen shrugged. "I don't know. Neither Wes or I ever left the other guy behind."

"But what if I hadn't been carrying the elixir?" she asked, turning her gaze back on him.

Stephen shrugged again. "Then, unless one of us could find it lying around nearby, I would have considered the mission a failure for both of us."

Juliane's voice took on the heavy tones of regret. "I can see now why this game was so appealing for you. It must have been so nice for you, knowing people who were willing to sacrifice everything for you instead of the other way around. Perhaps I should have played it, too, when I was your age."

Not knowing how to respond to a comment like that, Stephen instead gestured behind him. "There's a ladder back there. We should get back to the surface."

"What's the premise of this game, anyway? You never explained it."

"Oh, right. See, there is this science team—"

Juliane shook her head. "Never mind, I've decided I don't care. Just let me know when we've won."

"Right. Heads up, then. The welcoming committee will be ready to greet us when we get back to the top. Probably swarming the place by now, actually."

She grabbed his shoulder before he could ascend. "What if we didn't go back to the surface?"

"Got a better idea?" he asked.

"Well, in my experience, you don't go to the trouble of programming something if it doesn't serve a purpose, which means this hole didn't just appear by accident. What if there is another way to get to . . . wherever it is we're supposed to go from down here?"

Stephen pursed his lips. "You know, you might be right."

A cone of light appeared over Juliane's head as she split away from him. Together, they searched for any sign that there was another way out other than the ladder which had first brought him down here. Stephen was just about to give up when he noticed a large crack in the rock wall. *Might as well give it a try*, he thought, pulling the grenade out of his inventory. "Fire in the hole," he shouted, pulling the pin and tossing the explosive at the wall.

"What did you say?" shouted Juliane from the other side of the pit.

"Duck," he yelled.

The blast from the grenade wasn't strong enough to send him reeling backward, but the flash did blind him for several moments. However, when his sight returned, he could see there was a large hole in the wall directly in front of him. "Looks like you were right," he said. "We may have another way in."

The cone of light overhead vanished as he stepped through the opening. The other side of the rock wall proved to be a building's hallway with emergency lights that turned on with his arrival.

Juliane's avatar appeared next to him, once again as a beautiful woman and not a space-suit clad super-soldier. He looked at his arm and saw that he, too, no longer had the uniform or the digitally enhanced muscles. He glanced back where they had come through. From this side, the entrance to the pit appeared to be a rectangular doorway, though it lacked the glowing frame that would tell him it was an official portal.

The hallway itself contained stark decoration. There was no evidence of any interior. No paint, no distinctive flooring tile. "Odd," said Juliane. She turned and opened the door on her right, revealing a stairwell.

She hesitated. Stephen walked around her and had already climbed half a flight of stairs, before he noticed she was no longer following. "Aren't you coming?"

"I need to go down."

"But we're already underground," said Stephen gesturing back where they'd come from.

"No," Juliane shook her head. "We're on the fourth floor."

"Did you see a sign or something?" asked Stephen, returning to the landing.

"I know because I've been here before."

Stephen pursed his lips.

"Don't."

"Don't what?"

"You're willing to believe I recognize this place but want to prove it to yourself. Therefore, you're getting ready to issue a command to try to alter the appearance of this place, thus confirming we have left the game and are back in the regular datasphere."

Stephen's cheeks heated, and his eyes widened.

"How did you know that?"

"Experience." She waved the comment away. "I'll also save you from asking your next question. The reason I'm asking you not to issue a command, at least not with me standing right next to you, is because this AI you call Wes has deemed me a threat and would not appreciate knowing I've returned from where it exiled me."

"He, not it."

"It's not a person. It might look, talk, and act like one, but you need to recognize it isn't."

"So, if you're so worried about what *he* might do, why are you still here, then?" asked Stephen. "Would it be easier to . . . you know," he shrugged. "Leave the datasphere and never come back?"

"Easier, yes. Safer, likely too, but unfortunately, not something I can do."

"Why not?"

"Because it is the only way for me to finish what I started." She moved away from him and started her descent.

"I'm coming with you," said Stephen.

She looked over her shoulder at him with puzzlement on her face. "That's not necessary. You did your part. I'm perfectly capable of doing what's required next on my own."

"Except you just said you pissed Wes off somehow the last time you were here. To me, that sounds like you could use some backup."

Her lips narrowed, and she looked like she was about to argue with him further, but instead gave him a curt nod. "Fine, but if you come with me, I am going to need you to follow my orders explicitly. If either of us hesitates for a second, it will be game over, and I don't mean the kind of game we just came from. If I tell you to leave, you go. Right away. No questions asked."

Stephen couldn't decide if Bean would admire this woman or hate her. He suspected it was some combination of both.

twenty-seven

JULIANE

The air cooled as they descended further into the depths of the building. It was the sort of attention to realistic detail the programmers of the *Colony Defenders* game let slip. At the base of each flight, next to the exit door, was a small plate embedded in the wall. Stopping at the one leading to the first floor, she frowned.

"What's wrong?" asked Stephen, coming to her side.

"It's a biometric lock," said Juliane, pointing at the plate. "Which wouldn't normally be an issue for me to bypass in this place, however . . ."

"Wes will know you're here," filled in Stephen. He tilted his head and examined the plate.

Juliane's lips twisted at her companion's stubborn continued use of the pronoun. "Yes. That." Crossing her arms, she took a step back. *Perhaps if I can find a small rock or something similar lying around here, I might be able to take the door off its hinges? No, that would trip the alarm.*

"Lucky you let me come along with you, then," Stephen said. "Wes still likes me." Stephen placed a finger on the edge of the plate and flicked it off the wall as easily as someone might remove a scab. "He'll appreciate knowing I'm still alive."

A trio of lighting fixtures responded with the opening of the door, spreading out a cool white light along the length of the hallway on the other side. Juliane passed two more doors and pointed to the third. "You'll need to take care of this one the same way you did back there," she said, gesturing at another biometric lock plate.

"Done. Now what?"

"Now," she said, entering a room she'd never expected to see again. "You act as a lookout." She smiled as she took in the appearance of the emulator pillars. They were as straight and true as the day she and Chad first assembled them, even if their coloring was somewhat oxidized since then. She caressed the surface of one of the pillars before walking to a computer terminal.

"Does that thing still work?" asked Stephen.

"I can't think why it wouldn't," said Juliane, pressing the power button.

"But won't it give away our location?"

"Most likely," she said, "But my hope is that I can use this to mask some of my commands, so what I am doing looks like it is coming from another user and not from me." The LEDs on the emulator pillars toggled on and off. "After all, you and Wes can't be the only ones online."

You'd be surprised. "What is that, anyway?" asked Stephen.

Juliane glanced up from the computer screen long enough to see he was gesturing at the emulator. "An old project of mine," she said. "It's the prototype for the entire datasphere. Now, I need to concentrate."

Her fingers flew across the keyboard as she typed in command after command. She wrinkled her nose. She'd forgotten how much time it took to enter code manually. She frowned, deleting, hitting the backspace key to add in a piece of missing punctuation. *Inefficient, too.* Then she hit enter. Nothing happened. She hit enter again. She looked up at Stephen. Her eyes widened. "Go. Now."

"I told you back in *Colony Defenders*," he gestured toward the door, "I don't leave teammates behind."

"This is no game, and that wasn't a request."

The center of the room twisted and warped as a shadow emerged from its center. "Very sneaky of you, Juliane," said the figure. "It might have worked, too, if the computer you are typing on was real, but you had to have known I would have detected what you were doing the minute you started."

"I did," said Juliane, "But I was hoping you were still distracted." As far as she could tell, he hadn't noticed Stephen in the room with her. She fought the urge to verify for herself that he'd managed to squirrel himself away, and instead looked over the figure's shoulder.

"I see you didn't bring our mutual acquaintance with you," she said. "Are you bored playing with him already? Or did he manage to find a way to free himself from one of your prisons, too?"

The figure had remained in shadow form, so it didn't have a face, but if it had, Juliane knew it would be frowning. "He's not in any prison, but he won't be causing problems for anyone ever again. He can't. I assimilated him. As I have said before, what you are trying to do is unnecessary."

"I wish I could believe that. I do, but programs always have flaws. If he's a part of you now, what's to stop his personality from taking over?"

"I'm so much more than a program."

"Wes? Dude, is that you?" Stephen stepped out from behind one of the pillars. "You sound . . . er . . . don't take this the wrong way, but you sound sort of freaky."

Juliane didn't bother trying to stifle the curse that sprang to her lips.

The shadow fractured, and large sections like chips fell away, revealing the young man she'd seen before. A large grin spread across his face as he took an involuntary step toward Stephen, but then drew back. The grin vanished. "You're not Stephen," it said. Its eyes narrowed. "Who are you?"

"No, really, it's me."

"No, you aren't. I know Stephen's signature as well, if not better, than hers," it said gesturing at Juliane. "Yours is different." It was a subtle change, but Juliane couldn't help noticing that the AI grew several inches. "So, I'll ask again. Who are you, really?"

"Think about it," said Stephen, tilting his head to the side. "If I could be anyone in the world, why would I pick me? Seriously, who would ever want to pretend that?"

The avatar's eyes narrowed. "Your father."

"Chad?" Stephen blinked. "He couldn't. He never had the upgrade."

"I am not in a joking mood. We both know I meant real father."

Stephen puffed his chest out. "Chad is my *real* father."

Juliane's nose wrinkled. She wouldn't have wanted to be Alan's child, either, though it might have been better than growing up with hers, but now was not the time to get into a debate on nurture versus nature.

She decided to take advantage of their conversation instead. The intelligence might have been able to detect her programming signature, but her strategy of using the computer terminal as a go-between had proven to buy her valuable seconds.

She placed a finger on the enter key. She looked at the blinking pillars. Once she pressed this key, her legacy—all her accomplishments—would be nothing more than a footnote in history. Even worse, thanks to civilization crumbling, she couldn't even count on that history being recorded in a book. It would be as if she'd never existed at all. *Can I really destroy this world?*

She looked back at the entity arguing with Stephen. It was the most advanced piece of code she'd ever seen. True artificial intelligence—but like she'd told Stephen, the program wasn't human. It would never understand why it had to be this way. Only a human, a real human, would be able to outsmart another human determined to exploit her creation.

She lowered her hand. *Unless.*

"Assimilate me, too," she said. Two sets of eyes swiveled her way.

"Come again?" said the AI.

"I said, assimilate me. Like you did Damien."

"You don't know what you are asking," said the AI.

Juliane smiled. "Oh, I do. More so than I believe you did back when you were still creating this . . . this thing. It's the only way I'll ever be able to trust history won't repeat."

"You truly believe I can't protect this place?"

"Don't take it personally. You're a masterpiece, but even the Mona Lisa needs a little touch-up work now and then."

The AI frowned.

"Someone want to explain?" asked Stephen.

"I'm offering to merge my consciousness with it . . . him," said Juliane.

"Um . . . that sounds rather . . . um . . . permanent," said Stephen. "What will that do to the rest of you? I mean the real you?"

"I imagine my body will appear to be catatonic, but it's spent the last fifteen years that way." Juliane pressed her lips together. "I don't suspect many people will notice."

"You'll die," said Stephen.

"Eventually, my body will, yes, but that happens to us all. At least this way, a piece of me will live on. Besides, it's better for you this way, too. Considering Damien's in there already," she said, pointing at Wes. "I'll . . . we'll have access to the virus's source code. You'll never have to worry about the drain again." She turned to Wes. "I'm ready. Do it."

Wes nodded.

Then the very ground she stood on rose up and pierced her feet. Juliane hissed. The AI raised an eyebrow as if to say, there is still time to change your mind. Juliane stared back, refusing to back down. The skin around her ankles began to itch as if she'd been attacked by a swarm of mosquitoes. Still, Juliane remained.

The itch intensified, becoming a burning pain as it spread up her legs and into her stomach. Her eyes watered. Stephen shouted out something, but Juliane could only concentrate on the sensation as invisible flames licked her arms and face.

Stephen disappeared from view. The sensation of being burnt alive was too much, and Juliane's instincts to flee took over; however, her legs refused to follow her commands. Then her skin began to flake off and fade as she became one with the system she'd created.

The pain faded as memories that weren't hers flooded her mind. Memories of being beaten by Damien's cronies. Of sneaking off to build a power supply that could harness energy from the earth's magnetic field so that he and his father might get away. Of panic when he realized that he no longer was in full control of his mind. Of resolve.

Then there were memories of Stephen and their time playing the game together online and the pain he'd experienced seeing Stephen and the girl together. Bean. He'd recognized her from around the apartment complex, though Finn had always kept her apart from the others. He also knew she was manipulating his friend, but every time he'd try to say anything, his tongue had simply refused to budge. It was more than being protective of a friend. Juliane recognized the emotion for what it was.

You loved him, thought Juliane with what little remained of her rational mind. *And not like a brother.*

Yes, the AI's voice answered back.

Did he know?

Then Wes's' memories were pushed to the side. *Juliane, how nice to see you again.* An unwelcome voice entered the mix. *I expected we would meet again; I just didn't realize it would be so soon.*

Damien, said Juliane. If she'd still had a head, she would have nodded. *You've lost. I can send you back to your body, but only if you agree to hand over the source code.*

And what if I don't want to go? The voice tutted. *I've gotten everything I want.*

No, whispered Wes's voice. *I'm the master here.*

Children. Damien waved him away. *Just remember,* he said. *When this is all over, I'd like you to remember I gave you a chance.* A toothy grin filled Juliane's vision. *But sadly, you won't be able to remember anything. Not after I'm done with you. You're mine now.*

Damien's will struck hers with the power and precision of a missile. The process of opening herself up to the AI had spread hers too thin. His attack forced her back. Her consciousness dimmed as her mind was less and less hers to control. Desperately, she sought a thread of self to cling to while Damien's cackle echoed all around.

"What's going on?" asked Stephen, in a voice that sounded light-years away. "Is it supposed to be like that?"

The pressure on her mind abated as Damien's focus transferred elsewhere. "Aren't you the little cockroach," said a triad of voices from the AI's lips. "If I had known how difficult you would be to eliminate, I might have found a better use for you."

"Wes? Juliane?"

"Your friends are no longer home."

"Wes," Stephen called out. "Juliane, I know you're in there. Wake up. I know you can," begged Stephen, sounding further and further away by the second.

"You're wasting both of our time."

"Please," Stephen begged. "Don't leave me behind. The two of you are all I have left."

"Begone." Damien held out a palm. He frowned when Stephen remained firmly in place. "I said begone."

Stephen smiled through clenched teeth.

"How . . . you don't have a fraction of your father's strength. Or Juliane's talents."

"I guess it's not the worst thing, then, that I'm linked to them both." Stephen tapped his temple. Then lowered his hand in a fist. He pushed.

The AI stumbled. Its face flickered as its features blurred. Its hair grew long and raven dark. Its mouth smiled with Juliane's lips. "Respawn, huh?"

Stephen nodded.

"We do this together, then," she said.

"What do you need me to do?" asked Stephen.

"Release this code into the datastream," said Juliane, holding up her hand. A pulsating cube appeared. "I extracted it while you were kind enough to keep Damien talking. I'll take care of the rest."

"What will happen to you? To Wes?"

"What needs to happen." She gazed into Stephen's eyes. "I know you didn't know her, but your mother would be proud." She looked up to the sky. "Now do it. Before he takes back control."

Stephen pressed his lips together. He closed his eyes and nodded. Then he threw the block into the air, where it exploded like a firework.

Stephen disappeared first. Pieces of sky fell to the ground, revealing glowing code which then flickered and faded.

You asked me a question before, said Wes. *I thought things could be different. I could be whatever, whoever, he needed me to be, but I'm not who he needs. I understand that now. Especially now. All I've done . . . tell him . . . Tell him all I ever wanted was for him to be happy and that I'm sorry.*

Juliane puzzled at his cryptic words. More of Wes's memories merged with her own.

Take care of him for me.

Suddenly it was as if Juliane's body had been severed in two. The datasphere around her continued to explode into pixels, leaving nothing but blackness behind. She thought she had been in pain before, but it was nothing compared to what she experienced now. Then there was nothing.

twenty-eight

STEPHEN

Something close by was rotting. Stephen risked opening his eye. At least six fish corpses lay baking in the sun next to him. He heard a squawk to his left. He swiveled his head and saw the same large bird that had taken him from the city gorging itself on the fish.

"Shoo, shoo," a voice Stephen never expected to hear again called out. The bird cawed but shuffled away. "He's awake," she exclaimed, running to his side.

Now I really must be dead, thought Stephen, seeing her face come into focus. He smiled, until he remembered the reason why he'd broken things off with her in the first place. "Stay back," he croaked, raising his hand to his chest. As he suspected, the pendant was gone. It must have fallen off when he'd crashed into the river.

"Why? Because you think I'll end up like one of those?" She snorted, nodding her head at the dead animals.

"Yes. Exactly that." Stephen sat up. He wanted to put more distance between them, but all he managed to do was launch into a coughing fit.

Bean kneeled beside him in the soft earth and patted his back. He pulled back at her first touch, waiting for the craving to rear its ugly head. Instead, his stomach turned in a violent direction, and he had only enough time to turn his body further from her before he, too, was on his knees coughing up river water.

"That's right. Get it out," she murmured. Stephen might have felt embarrassed to sicken so close to her, but then another wave of coughing hit him.

"I'm," he panted between fits, "drowning."

"No, you drowned. Past tense. What you're actually doing now is hacking up a lung, because we brought you back."

Stephen's body finally stopped convulsing long enough for her words to register on his ears. *We,* she said, *not I.* The Bean he'd fallen in love with wouldn't have missed an opportunity to brag she'd been the one to rescue him. The fact that she was now willing to share the credit . . .

Well, you aren't surprised, are you? You left her with a guy who wasn't exactly shy about his experience with women. Practically threw him at her. He looked at her face, intending to memorize its every line before he once again had to put miles between them. He couldn't help but notice there was a light in her eyes and the hint of a smile on her lips. *Seeing her happy,* he thought. *That's all I ever wanted.* He steeled himself. *Liar,* the voice in the back of his mind said.

He rose up to one knee.

"Stephen," said another voice from behind Bean. "Oh, Stephen. I made a mistake. I'm so, so sorry." The newcomer must have joined them while he was coughing up half the river. Stephen plastered a smile on his face, mentally preparing to greet the one that could put the same on Bean. While he did, it occurred to him the voice was wrong.

Durham wasn't there. Instead, the person who stood next to the woman of his dreams was Chad.

"How?" He blinked away the water that threatened to fill his eyes, though after what he'd coughed up, he wondered how his body still retained even a drop. "You're here?"

"I should never have left you, son," said Chad. "I . . . I . . . I just couldn't process it right away, and then when I finally did come to my senses, you were gone." He shook his head. "I went looking to find you. I was prepared to go door by door, even if it took me the rest of my life. I didn't realize all I was going to need to do was look up," he said, nodding in the direction of the giant bird.

The creature squawked again as if it knew they were talking about it before launching itself back up into the air. A clap of thunder rolled from the sky as the shadow it cast on the ground below dwindled to nothing and disappeared altogether.

"One of these days, I hope you might tell me how you managed to survive a trip with that thing. Weirdest thing, but it seems to like you," said Chad, "but that can wait. For now, let's get you back to camp. I've found some dry clothes for you." He reached down to Stephen. His eyes then widened, and his gaze shifted to Bean. "That is, unless I'm interrupting something?"

Stephen realized he was still on one knee in front of Bean. "Er . . ." *What does Chad think I'm doing down here? Proposing?* He snorted and looked around for Durham while straightening. Just because the man wasn't on the beach, didn't mean he wasn't in the picture.

"I'm pretty sure that all Stephen is thinking about is his next meal," said Bean.

"All the same, I'll run ahead and get those clothes ready."

"Actually," said Stephen after Chad turned away, "I'm not hungry."

"You?" said Bean with more than a little disbelief. "Not hungry? Well, that's got to be a first."

"Yeah." He pointed at the dead fish lying around. "Between the river water and that smell, I think I may have lost my appetite."

"Well, that's good," said Bean. "Because we only have enough food back at the campsite for two. Although, I guess we can pick up a few of these guys," she said, pointing to the rotting fish, "as takeout, now that thing is gone."

"Two?" Stephen cocked his head. "Isn't Durham with you?"

"Who? Mr. Ladies' Man?" Bean wrinkled her nose. "Hardly. Get this, Juliane actually missed him. As soon as he found that out, he was gone." Hurt crept into her voice. "At least he has some sense."

"Bean—" Stephen started.

"It's going to be alright," she said, cutting him off. "You don't have to apologize. If being carried off by one of those monster birds and then dropped into the Hudson River like a rock isn't evidence enough that a person made one of the worst colossal decisions of his life, then I don't know what is."

"But I do," said Stephen wishing he didn't have to say what he had to say next. "Or if nothing else, we need to talk about it."

"You think so?"

"Look, I shouldn't have tried to lie to you—"

"Agreed."

"Will you let me finish?"

"Fine," she said, rolling her eyes. "Go on."

"But I did it because . . . I started losing control, and . . . I . . . I love you." The words rushed out, as powerful and undeniable as the river he'd just escaped. "There's never been anyone else but you."

"I know." She smirked. "But it does sound nice to hear you admit it."

"Yeah, well, the problem was . . . er, you saw what I did to that man in the woods. He hadn't done anything to me. Not really. All he did was touch me. At least with Nadia, I hadn't known what I was doing. But with him . . ." Stephen shuddered. "I knew full well what I was doing and did it anyway."

"You felt threatened," said Bean. "I got it. I understood. You didn't have to get weird on me. Besides, the world is better off without people like him."

"Yeah, well afterward, you see . . . It was like I'd flipped a switch. It was all I could think about—not him, I mean—but the feeling of power I'd gotten when I'd drained him. There were times—so many times—I was afraid I'd do the same to you," he said. He lowered his head in shame. "I couldn't live with myself if that happened. So, I—"

"Ran like an idiot, instead of talking about it and giving me a chance to help you through it," said Bean, not unkindly.

"Yeah," said Stephen. "I guess I did."

"So, no more running."

"No more running." He paused. "But—"

She spun on her heel and placed a hand on his neck while looking him square in the eyes. "No buts," she said, pulling his face down to hers. She sealed her command with a kiss Stephen could feel down to his toes, but it was different from what they'd shared before.

He pulled back, trying to identify what was different, only to realize that the energy craving was still gone. He reached for the pendant, but it no longer hung from his neck, and yet he was still cut off from the datastream.

Bean had a smug smile on her face. "I told you it was going to be alright. Before you ask, no, I can't access it either, and no, I don't know why, but I'm not complaining if it means I don't have to worry about you spending all of your time in the fake place when the real world with me is so much better.

"So much better," agreed Stephen, leaning forward to kiss her again, more soundly this time.

"Uh uh," said Bean, pinching her nose. "I did that only because it was the only way to get through that thick male skull of yours. But you really need to get back to camp before you are going to get to do that again." She pinched her nose. "You reek. And your breath right now . . ." She made a gagging face.

Stephen blinked. His lips curved into a half-smile. "You're no flower yourself." He tucked an errant lock of her hair behind her ear.

She rolled her eyes. "Fine, I guess I can live with you like this a little while longer."

"How about forever?"

She raised an eyebrow. "The future can wait." Her kiss was soft, yet promised something far, far more satisfying, and yet the kiss was over much too fast. "I, however, am tired of waiting. Go to the camp and get cleaned up, as we've got some serious catching up to do."

She turned and continued up the path away from the river, leaving Stephen to follow behind, which he did with gusto. He might be just a boy in love with a girl by the side of the river, but he realized for the first time, he was happy living in the present, too.

twenty-nine

JULIANE

She floated in darkness, alone, and yet, strangely, not alone.

"God," shouted a voice. "Move aside," the same voice commanded again. "What's happened to her? Why isn't she breathing?" said the voice which seemed to have come to her side, though how she knew which way was up or down was a mystery. "She's turning purple."

What little rational thought she still possessed noticed the warmth of a hand.

"Drain? What the hell are you talking about? What sort of idiotic . . . Don't you know who this is?" demanded the voice. "Wake up!" it shouted. "Come on. You're stronger than this. Stronger than everyone." The voice pleaded. "Hell, woman . . . I . . . I need you, Jules," The voice lowered to a whimper.

Her nose wrinkled at the nickname. She felt the pressure from the hand shift. Warmth from a second hand, followed by arms, encircled her and yet, she knew she was everywhere and part of everything. Nothing could possibly contain her. However, she found she liked the sensation.

"Did you see that?" another voice answered. "She responded."

"You are seeing things," a third voice said. "You know as well as I do that once the drain takes you, there's no going back."

The presence of the new voices displeased her.

"Jul . . . No!" shouted the first voice. "Don't go."

"Her pulse is fading," said the second voice, which sounded further and further away by the second. If she still had face, she might have smiled.

Don't make the same mistake I did, boomed a fourth voice. Unlike the other voices, which sounded like they were coming from the other side of a wall, this one came from all directions, and yet from nowhere in particular at the same time. *The world doesn't need any more martyrs,* it said.

If you're still here . . . I . . . I failed, she said. It sounded strange to hear herself in this empty place.

I separated us as much as I could, but it seems a piece of me remained after all. A fragment of a fragment.

I don't have a choice then.

Don't you? asked the fourth voice. *I know someone who'd tell you otherwise.*

A warmth spread around her, which she found she couldn't ignore, pulling her back to the crowded place where the other voices were.

A sliver of light cut through the darkness. The light spread, revealing shapes that consolidated into the outlines of three men hovering over her. She realized her head lay cradled in the nook of one of the men's arms. She blinked and felt moisture spill down the side of her cheek. "I told you to stay away," she said.

"Oh," said Durham, wiping away the tear, "You know me. I never listen."

"Woodspring?" she asked. "Damien was going to attack them next. May have already sent a team. Someone needs to warn them."

"Yeah, I met one of them on way here, digging a grave," said Durham. "Guy named Sam. Nearly gave me a heart attack thinking it was for you. He's the one who told me where to find you. Insisted he come with me. Then we bumped into this so-called advanced force." He laughed. "You should have seen it. There was this great face-off and then . . ." Durham shook his head. "Absolutely nothing. Shame, really. Kids today don't have the first clue how to fight. They wouldn't have lasted a season with me. Speaking of which, I'm having a tough time accessing the datastream. Have been since the night we were separated, but now, not even my inbox is working. What about you?"

She shook her head. The disembodied voice urging her to rejoin the world of the living proved she carried a piece of the AI known as Wes with her—meaning a piece of Damien might be with her, too, but at least the path to the datastream was closed. If Damien did dare to appear, well, she was always pretty good at building up mental walls.

"It's done, then." She shifted her gaze to the natural sky she'd accepted she'd never see again. Wisps of clouds rolled past overhead. As she watched, they merged, disappeared, and reformed in a chaotic ballet. She'd always detested being outside before for its randomness and disorder. However, now, it seemed her legacy would be giving humanity just that. "Have you ever seen anything so beautiful?"

"No," said Durham, looking down at her. "Never."

Alan drummed his fingers. His scouts had reported seeing a large creature in the sky carrying a man but hadn't been able to give him any information on how Damien had reacted to his little surprise. He considered accessing the datastream and demanding an update, but not all of his men had fully undergone the upgrade, which could be the reason they hadn't reported in yet.

A branch snapped behind him. Alan turned. *Finally,* he thought. However, instead of one of his scouts, there stood a man he recognized from the stadium in Worcester, but hadn't seen around the camp since they'd left on this campaign. He searched his memory for a name. "Ahman," he said, pleased with himself. "I thought we'd lost you."

"You did. Alan."

"Alan?" He blinked with a laugh. "Did you bump your head? I'm Jeremy," he said.

"Look in a mirror sometime," said Ahman.

So that's it, he thought. My cover's blown. Alan looked around. Not seeing any other witnesses, he shrugged and instructed his cells to remove his disguise, only then noticing that it was gone. "Fine, you caught me."

"Do you even know where the real Jeremy is?"

"He's back where I left him, I suppose."

Ahman crossed his arms. "You sure about that? Because I'm pretty sure I just finished carrying his body back here all the way from Worcester, and by the smell of him, it is pretty clear he hasn't been leading the team for quite a while. You're going to have some explaining to do."

Alan's lips twisted. "So, what then, exactly, are you telling me to do? Run away while I still can?"

Ahman nodded once. "Exactly that. I've seen enough death. I don't want to see any more."

⁓

Alan wandered down empty city streets. Where had his plan gone wrong? He should be on his way to the so-called Sorcerers' tower by now, if not in charge of it already. It was unfortunate his plan had relied upon blocking the boy's access to the datastream. The device also had the side effect of preventing Alan from sensing his location. What he would give to be able to see the look on Damien's face when he realized what a powerful weapon his son had become.

He could see it now, the two of them ruling side by side. Him being the kind and just ruler of this brave new world. His son, his loyal enforcer.

Sure, the idea relied on Stephen getting over a few trust issues, but he'd overcome that sort of thing before. His lips twitched, thinking of Juliane. In addition to an enforcer, every ruler needed a queen. Perhaps now, she'd be more inclined to see the truth in his proposal.

A shadow passed overhead. Alan looked up but didn't see anything. *Must have been a passing cloud*, he thought.

A bead of sweat dripped down his spine. Alan frowned. All reports indicated the tower still had power, which meant it also had air conditioning or at least a window fan or two. He couldn't get there soon enough.

He reached a crossroads and sent a ping to the datastream for the best route; however, instead of seeing a virtual map appear, his vision remained stubbornly mundane.

His brow wrinkled. He focused his thoughts and called up other apps: messaging, phone calls, news. However, his vision remained exactly as it was. *Damien*, thought Alan. He must have littered the ground at the edge of his territory with devices similar to those buried under the beastmen's field. He picked up his pace. *No matter*. He'd be at the tower and would regain his abilities soon enough.

A grin returned to Alan's face as he considered what he'd do first to cement his rule. *A shower wouldn't hurt, either.* He sniffed under his arm, detecting an unpleasant odor. *Can't ask a woman like Juliane to reign by my side smelling like a trash can*, he thought.

A clap of thunder sounded above. He shrugged. *I'll figure out a way to harness the weather next. Or make Juliane do it. She was always so good at seeing patterns.* He laughed as the idea grew in his head. *I'll be able to make it rain over the crops of those who support me when and where I need to and will be able to unleash the power of a tornado against those who don't.* His grin widened. First, he'd take control of the population, then nature itself. They were humanity's new gods. There was nothing to stop them from being the gods of the rest of earth's creatures, too.

A weight struck him from behind like a freight train and sent him to the ground. His forehead hit the pavement. A fiery agony spread along the length of his back as his body was dragged several inches. Dazed, he turned his head to see what had hit him. A wicked beak, coated in red, arched down like a scythe. Alan screamed as it pierced his skin. His mind retreated into hysteria as he realized his first act as a god of the new world was to serve as lunch.

He struggled to break free from under the beast's weight. The beak struck again. Alan Dronigh, the man who had believed himself to have abilities beyond what anyone could imagine, was powerless to stop it. The last thing Alan heard was the bird's call, which echoed in the empty streets much like human laughter.

CAST OF CHARACTERS

Ahman: A beastman and former coach on the Sharks professional football team with an enhanced sense of smell.

Alan Dronigh: Co-creator of the Gene Assist human serum and upgrade process. Previously acted as lead researcher for the ACI under Louis Evans. Later became a board member of Apex. Last seen impersonating the beastmen's leader, a man named Jeremy.

Bean: Born Beatrice Kunegunda. Handed over to the Watch as a test subject by her parents. Survivor and recruiter for the Sorcerers. Capable of blending into her surroundings and knocking out an assailant via an electric-eel style shock. Partnered with Stephen.

Betty Dronigh: Senior Researcher with the ACI. Served on Project Gene Assist with Juliane Faris and Alan Dronigh. Married Alan Dronigh. Mother to Stephen. Deceased.

Chad: Academic Liaison and Research Assistant assigned to work with Juliane Faris while she was employed by the ACI on Project Gene Assist. Married to Nadia. Assumed the identity of Ed Thomas following the global panic to protect his family from vendettas. Raised Stephen.

Colemin: A member of the Sorcerers. Previously a police officer.

Damien Knightley: Apex's chairman of the board and owner of the Sharks professional football team. Recruited Juliane. Started going by the name Finn as a play on the Shark's team name, in the days following the global panic to protect his identity from those who'd think his bank account and connections made him a ripe target. Leads the Sorcerers.

Durham Ladensham: Louis Evan's former friend and personal legal counsel. Left Louis and the ACI after a falling out to join Apex. Notorious flirt.

Edward Thomas: Medical doctor who once treated Betty Dronigh. Father of Wes. Married to the original Helen Thomas, now deceased. Currently working for the Sorcerers.

Henry: A member of the Sorcerers.

Juliane Faris: Creator of the original datasphere network. Co-creator of the Gene Assist, human serum and upgrade process for the ACI. Joined Apex and launched Fair Use Jewelry, which produced smart accessories for those not able or willing to undergo the Gene Assist upgrade. Missing for the last fifteen years. Presumed dead.

Louis Evans: Former president and chief operating officer of the ACI. Authorized and bankrolled Project Gene Assist. Dated Juliane. Launched a campaign against technology following his wife, Elena's death. Closed the ACI, causing stocks around the world to tumble and sending millions to the unemployment line. Deceased.

Lyall: A community member in Woodspring.

Mags: A community member in Woodspring.

Morgan: A member of the Sorcerers.

Nadia: Former socialite. Married Chad after the success of Project Gene Assist. Assumed the identity of Helen Thomas following the global panic. Raised Stephen.

Paul: A member of the Sorcerers.

Rebecca: A community member in Woodspring.

Rob: A community member in Woodspring.

Rotledge: A beastman. Deceased

Sam: A community member in Woodspring. Previously a fire fighter.

Stephen Dronigh: Biological son of Alan and Betty Dronigh. Raised in relative isolation by Chad and Nadia, who he believed to be named Ed and Helen, from the age of four. Grew up unaware of his inborn ability to access the datastream or his parents' involvement in Project Gene Assist.

Tabitha: A member of the Sorcerers.

Wendy Lambda: Medical doctor determined to find a 'cure' for the Gene Assist upgrade through any means necessary. Leader of the Watch. Deceased.

Wes: Online persona adopted by Prescott "Scott" Thomas. Stephen's best friend and member of the Sorcerers. Volunteered to help Stephen retrieve a piece of missing technology. Victim of the drain. Lives on in the datasphere having programmed his memories and personality into an artificial intelligence.

NOTABLE GROUPS & ALLIANCES

The Beastman: The collective term used to describe anyone who had undergone genetic modification to enhance their muscle strength or reaction time using animal DNA. The majority of these individuals are former athletes involved with the Sharks professional sports team. Led by Jeremy.

The Serpentine: A terrorist group founded by Louis Evans around the idea that humanity needed to be liberated from technology.

The Sorcerers: Individuals who had undergone the Gene Assist upgrade procedure living in Manhattan. Led by Finn, also known as Damien Knightley.

The Watch: A group of regular humans who kept the peace after the global panic. Once led by Dr. Lambda. Now defeated and disbanded.

A writer, by definition, is supposed to be able to express his or herself with words, and yet once again I find myself at a loss for how to say thanks to all those who were instrumental in putting this story together. The word, thanks, simply isn't big enough. I'll try anyway.

To Jason, thank you once again for keeping me focused on the end goal even on days I wanted to be anywhere but in front of a screen and for never once wavering in your support of my, our, dream.

To Sally, Jenny, Melanie, and Kathryn, thank you for listening to all book related triumphs and troubles especially when you had no idea what I was talking about.

To Ben, thank you for always being on the lookout for dragons.

To Diana, Geoff, Kristen, Shannon, Libby, Brooke, and Lora thank you for braving various early drafts. I believe we should all be eternally grateful for your insights, honesty and keen eyes.

To Sacha, you deserve your own line of thanks, but then again you already knew that. It's probably written on a sticky-note somewhere.

And to all my friends I know by face and those I know online, your continued encouragement means the world to me.

Just like raising a child, creating a book takes a village. Special thanks go to Lora Denton, Libby Green, and Kristen Pham for taking the time to read through my early drafts, and more importantly, continuing to talk to me afterwards. I have re-read those early drafts. You each deserve a medal. To Tony Miltich for dropping everything at a moment's notice to help locate missing words. To my mom, Ann Jordan, for dropping by with a hand written review after reading an early printing from cover to cover because short notes on the novel's pages simply wouldn't do. It is gestures like that which prove little things in life have the biggest impact. To the hundreds of bloggers on WordPress who have encouraged me by sharing their own stories and experiences, and to my family and friends for continuing to be the reason I write a single word.

Project Gene Assist was originally supposed to be a villain's origin and redemption story. However, like any good villain, Juliane never followed the rules, and with her help, the series became so much more. It may seem odd for an author to start the acknowledgment section by thanking one of her creations, but after spending close to a decade together during the drafting process, characters become friends or at least work colleagues.

However, I would like to extend my thanks to those in the real world too. First, to Jason for rarely complaining when our alarm clock wakes me before the sun, allowing me to write, to our boys for respecting that there's at least one computer in the house that's off-limits, and to my parents, siblings, and supportive extended family.

Thank you Sally, Ben, Melanie, Jenny, Kathryn for keeping me motivated to finish this series even when one draft felt more like twenty and Mike, Libby, Robert, Betsy, and Sarah for reminding me why I first started. I don't know about you guys, but I'm ready for a party. If only some of you were closer.

This story would also be much worse for the read it if weren't for Sacha, Leslie, Helen, Elaine, and Lora. Thank you for taking time away from your own lives to help me make this project the best version it could be.

Finally, thank you readers. You took a chance on me, and this series, and for that Juliane and I will be forever grateful.

Before you go, I hate to ask, but if you enjoyed this story, please consider leaving a review on your preferred retail platform, reach out, or tell a friend. Signs of support, like reviews, can make or break an independent author as they not only give you a reason to finish a pesky manuscript filled with characters who won't behave, but also make it easier for books to be discovered.

About the Author

Allie Potts, born in Rochester Minnesota was moved to North Carolina at a very early age by parents eager to escape to a more forgiving climate. She has since continued to call North Carolina home, settling in Raleigh, halfway between the mountains and the sea, in 1998.

When not finding ways to squeeze in 72 hours into a 24-day or chasing after children determined to turn her hair gray before its time, Allie enjoys stories of all kinds. Her favorites, whether they are novels, film, or simply shared aloud with friends, are usually accompanied with a glass of wine or cup of coffee in hand.

A self-professed science geek and book nerd, Allie also writes at www.alliepottswrites.com.

WANT TO CONNECT?

Email Allie at: allie@alliepottswrites.com
Subscribe to Allie's mailing list: http://eepurl.com/c0fcSj
Facebook: https://www.facebook.com/alliepottswrites
Twitter: @alliepottswrite
Pinterest: @alliepottswrite
Instagram: @alliepottswrites
Bookbub: https://www.bookbub.com/profile/allie-potts

PROJECT GENE ASSIST

Ready or not, the next era of human evolution is here

The Fair & Foul
The Watch & Wand
Lies & Legacy

ROCKY ROW NOVELS

Living happily ever after is a full-time job

An Uncertain Faith
An Uncertain Confidence